THE OXFORD LIBRARY OF
CLASSIC ENGLISH SHORT STORIES

VOLUME II

This second volume of short stories draws from work written during the period 1956–1975. Throughout those years foreign writers exerted an increasing influence on short fiction written in English. Represented in this selection are the leading US writers whose work continued to be read widely in the UK, and also a number of Commonwealth writers from such far-flung countries as Australia, Canada, India, New Zealand, South Africa, Nigeria, and the West Indies.

The stories were originally chosen for the English Association by T. S. Dorsch and Roger Sharrock.

D1608474

THE
OXFORD LIBRARY
OF
CLASSIC ENGLISH
SHORT STORIES

VOLUME II
1956–1975

GUILD PUBLISHING LONDON

This edition published 1989 by
Guild Publishing
by arrangement with Oxford University Press

C.N 6347

Set by CentraCet
Printed in Great Britain by
Richard Clay Ltd, Bungay, Suffolk

CONTENTS

NADINE GORDIMER
Charmed Lives

THERE were two men in the town, a deaf man and a drunkard.

The one was a watchmaker and the other a doctor, and they never met except when the watchmaker consulted the doctor about his stomach ulcer, or the doctor's watch needed cleaning, but they belonged together in the mind of twenty-year-old Kate Shand. Extraordinary to think in what unimaginable partnerships one may exist in the minds of others, with what faces one's own may be bracketed for ever, through some categorical connection, of which one will never know, in the memory of a third person. The association between the watchmaker and the doctor in Kate Shand's mind began when she and her brothers were children. For the Shand children there were two kinds of people. There were people their mother had a lot of time for, and people she had no time for. The definitions were not only expressive, but literal; the people she had a lot of time for she would allow to delay her endlessly, talking to them on street corners when she met them out shopping, visiting them when they were ill, stretching telephone conversations far beyond her normal brusque limits; the people she had no time for took up no more than the duration of a curt nod, or a half-sentence of dismissal should their names come up in conversation.

Both the watchmaker and the doctor were in Mrs. Shand's favoured category. The deaf watchmaker, Simon Datnow, was employed by Kate's father in his jeweller's shop. I've got a lot of time for Simon, Mrs. Shand would say consideredly, with a 'mind you', a sage reservation in her voice. That was because, on the whole, she did not care for relatives, and this man was, in fact, one of the procession of Lithuanian and Russian relatives whom Marcus Shand had 'brought out' to South Africa, before Kate was born, in the early twenties, and whom, ever after, he regarded with a surly indifference quite out of character with his gentle nature—a churlishness created by the conflict in him between family feeling for them, and a resentment against them for being the kind of people he would not have expected his wife to like. For though he winced under his wife's scorn of his relatives, there was a perverse pride in

him that he should have succeeded in marrying a wife who *would*
scorn them. They were used to sleeping, these foreigners (Mrs.
Shand said), on top of the stove. They did not bath more than once
a week. They ate disgusting food, salted fish and soup made of
beetroot. At that time the Shand kitchen still had a coal range; the
children pictured these strange aunts and cousins huddled together
on the sooty surface after the fire had been raked out in the evening,
greasy-fingered, like Esquimaux. It would not have surprised Kate,
William, and Dykie to hear that the aunts chewed their husbands'
boots to soften them.

For most of the immigrant relatives, for the women, certainly,
Mrs. Shand had no time at all. She would give them a moment or
two if she met them in the town (and in no time they had established
themselves there, the women getting busy and becoming the chief
breadwinners almost at once, dressmaking—they all sewed most
skilfully—or cooking in delicatessen shops, the men, slower to learn
English and to unlearn the ways of the old country, picking up odd
jobs in produce stores, or going from house to house, heavily dressed
in dark suits in the African heat, employed as official collectors for
charities connected with the synagogue or the Jewish Burial Society)
but Mrs Shand never visited them in their homes unless there was
the ceremony of an occasion such as a wedding or funeral to demand
her presence. Even then she sat stiffly, her plain clothes conspicuous
among their elaborately festive or sorrowful garb, enquiring politely
about the health and ages, to date, of their children, and refusing,
with great courtesy and a careful aversion of her eyes from the
proffered plate, their traditional refreshments. The only person with
whom Mrs. Shand attempted conversation at these gatherings was
the deaf watchmaker, Simon Datnow.

Simon Datnow was not actually a blood relation of Marcus
Shand, but merely the brother of one of Mr. Shand's sisters'
husbands. The husband was dead and Simon had 'come out with
his sister-in-law as a kind of substitute protector. Perhaps it was
because there was no blood-tie to rein his resentment with guilt
that, if Mrs. Shand liked Simon most, Mr. Shand liked him least of
the immigrant relations. It seemed to annoy Marcus Shand that,
after the first year, the deaf watchmaker really owed him nothing;
had, unlike the others, nothing in particular for which to be grateful
to him. Simon Datnow had paid back the passage money which
Mr. Shand had advanced, and he was a skilled watchmaker whose

equal Mr. Shand could not have hoped to find in South Africa. Kate always remembered the watchmaker as she used to see him from the door, whenever she entered her father's shop, sitting in his little three-sided glass cage with the inscription, in gold leaf, WATCH REPAIR DEPARTMENT, showing like a banner across his bent head. As Kate grew up, the gold leaf began to peel, and behind the faint loop of the first P, you could see his left ear more and more clearly. In that ear, from time to time, a new hearing-aid, flesh-coloured, black or pearly, would appear, but usually, when he was working, he did not wear one. He would put it on only when you approached to speak to him, and in the moment before you did speak, the moment when the device dropped into contact with his ear, you would see him wince as the roar of the world, from which he had been sealed off like a man dropped in a diving-bell to the floor of the ocean, burst in upon him.

A curved bite had been sawn out of the work-table at which he sat, and the edge of the wood had long since been worn smooth by the rub of his body as he leaned forward over his work, and it seemed to Kate that he fitted into the table as the table fitted into its glass walls. Before him were tiny, shallow receptacles and metal work-platforms a few inches square, on which the delicate tweezers and probe-like instruments with which he worked stalked like timid, long-legged insects among specks of red jewel and minute wheels, and springs that looked like a baby's hair you had run through thumb-and-fingernail. Tiny glass bells protected the innards of watches on which he was not working. She felt she dared not breathe too near the exposed ones, lest they took off on the current and sailed into some crack in the scored and worn table-top. Yet the instruments that worried at them delicately, that picked them up and dipped them into a dewdrop of oil or spirit, and finally fitted them together, were controlled by a pair of blunt, curled hands with broken nails like plates of horn embedded in, rather than growing from, chapped fingers. The skin of these hands was permanently tarnished from contact with oil and metal, and in winter, was swollen and fissured with dreadful chilblains. The WATCH REPAIR DEPARTMENT was in the draughtiest corner of the shop, and it was then that the watchmaker, blue-nosed and pale above his grey muffler, reminded Kate of one of those zoo animals which, denied the lair of its natural habitat, shudders out the cold months in a corner of its cage.

In the summer the watchmaker worked in his shirt-sleeves, with shiny expanding armbands to pull the cuffs up out of the way, and a constant trickle of sweat making his short, greying hair spring out slowly into curl from its confinement of pomade. Summer and winter, most days he looked up only when Marcus Shand came stumping over to shove at him a watch for diagnosis, bellowing 'Loses twenty-five minutes in twenty-four hours' or 'Oiling and cleaning. See if it's in working order.' 'What?' the deaf man would say in his sibilant, half-audible voice, frowning vacantly and fumbling for his 'machine'—as he always called his hearing-aid—while he held back from the force of his employer in nervous distaste. Shand would shout in impatient repetition, so that half of what he said would not be heard by the watchmaker, and the other half would thunder in upon him as his aid was switched on. The force of this half-sentence would strike the watchmaker like a blow, so that for a moment he was bewildered and unable to understand anything. Then Shand would become more impatient than ever, and shout twice as loud. Because of this communication at cross purposes, Marcus Shand tended to phrase everything he had to say to his watchmaker as shortly as possible, and to dispense with all graces of politeness, and so almost all that came to Simon Datnow of the outside world for eight hours a day was an assault of surly questions and demands.

Because his watchmaker and relation by marriage was sensitive to the tick of a watch but not an undertone of the human voice, Marcus Shand got into the habit of abusing Simon Datnow in mumbled asides, before his very face. It was a great comfort to Shand to be able to abuse someone with impunity. Yet although it was true that he was able to say abusive things without being heard, it was, of course, not possible for these not to show on his face while he said them, and so it was that Simon Datnow felt the revilement more cuttingly than if it had come to him in words, and a wall of thick, inarticulate hostility, far more impenetrable than that of deafness, came to exist between the two men.

It infuriated Mrs. Shand that the only person whom her husband should have the courage to abuse should be someone only half of this world, and, as a result, too uncertain of his ground to take a stand upon it. She herself had tried, and, in fact, went on trying all her life, to get her husband to stand up to *her*. But no; the only person before whom Marcus would dare raise the timid flag of his spirit was a man who couldn't trust himself to interpret the challenge clearly. Mrs. Shand retaliated by championing Simon Datnow. Datnow, she gave her children to understand, was a natural gentleman, a kind of freak incidence among the immigrant relations. His drudgery became an ideal of conscientious service; his enforced remoteness from the world, an ideal of contemplation. The bewildered, impotent rage that showed in his eyes—the repressed daze of savagery in the eyes of the bull who cannot see where the darts have lodged in the nerves of his shoulders—before the rudeness of her husband which he could not hear, she interpreted as the self-control of a superior being. The meek aspect which his deafness imposed upon him as he went about the town during his lunch hour, seemed to her the quality that should inherit the earth. Even the stomach ulcer from which he suffered as a result of the tension of his work and the fragmentary intensity of his communication with the world, came, through their mother, to be associated in the minds of the Shand children with a quality of exceptional sensitivity.

When Kate was small she would sometimes stand for a long time with her face close to the glass cage, smiling respectfully at the watchmaker when he smiled his low, saliva-gleaming smile back at her, and nodding her interest when he held up some part of a watch, a piece of metal confetti, for her to see. At the approach of her father she would go still; taking cover from the crude and puzzling aspect of him which showed when he spoke to Simon Datnow. This gruff man with the thick strings of vein rising against his collar had nothing to do with the father who would put his cheek to hers and ask, humbly, for a kiss.

One day, a week before Christmas in the year when Kate was nine years old, she was hanging about her father's shop. In the burning midsummer December of South Africa, the gold-mining town was seedily festive with borax snow in the shop windows, red and blue lights strung round the Town-hall, and the beery voices of miners in sports blazers slapping each other on the back outside the bars. The jeweller's shop was very busy. Kate ran errands for her father and the young Afrikaans sales-girl, and drank lukewarm lemon squash in the room behind the shop where cardboard boxes and straw and sheets of tissue-paper for packing were kept, and the mice were so impudent that anything edible disappeared while you turned your back.

At this time of year, the watchmaker was constantly interrupted at his work by requests to fit gleaming new watch-straps to customers' watches, or to make minor adjustments to necklaces that were too long, or to mend silver bracelets with faulty catches. In order to get his watch repairing done, he came to work early in the morning, before the shop was open, and stayed behind long after it was closed. And all day, while the bustle of customers and the rustle of parcels and the ring of the cash register filled the shop around him, he was bent over his table, trying to do several things at once, often under the harassing, impatient eye of Marcus Shand or the sales girl. His lunch sandwiches remained uneaten. Once, a mouse from the back room ventured into the shop to gnaw at them. His morning and afternoon tea turned pale and scummy in the cup. On the crowded table before him, the tiny viscera of his watches got mislaid beneath the metal straps, the necklaces, the bracelets. He looked like a worried mouse himself, grey-backed, rustling furtively over his jumble of work.

On this particular day, he was so busy that the face of the little girl, who had wandered over to watch him through the glass, did not penetrate his concentration. She watched him a minute or two, nevertheless. He fitted a tiny spring into the intricacy of a watch's belly; over it went a wheel; into some pin-sized holes, three chips of ruby. Then he put out his long tweezers to peck from its spirit-bath something that proved not to be there; he felt about with the tweezers, looked in another dish; at last, lifted his eyebrow so that the jeweller's loop in his left eye-socket fell out into his hand. He stood up from his stool and looked carefully and methodically under every glass bell, in every dish. He rummaged systematically through the cardboard box-lid where he kept the filings, little twirls of yellow and silver metal like punctuation marks, from the watchstraps, the necklaces, the bracelets. He paused a moment, as if deliberating where he should look next. And then, the light of a solution, a calm relief relaxed his face. Slowly, he stood back, creaking his stool away behind him over the cement floor. Then he grasped his work table firmly, palm up under its top, and brought it over, crashing and slithering all its conglomeration of contents on top of himself.

He stood there with his hands hanging at his sides, amid the wreckage. His eyes glittered and his mouth clenched, so that the skin, in which the growing beard showed like fine blue shot, was white above and below his stiffened lips. He was breathing so loudly that it could be heard right across the sudden silence of the shop full of people.

Before the shock of that silence broke, Kate ran. Her running broke the silence; she heard, as she pulled the heavy back door of the shop closed behind her, babble and movement spill out. She went trembling across the dirty yard which the shop shared with several others contiguous with it, and sat on a rotting packing-case against the wall of the lavatory. It was dank there, with the solitude of dank places. She stayed a long time, playing with some old letterheads, puffy with rain.

When she went back into the shop again, there was a cheerful delegation from a mine, in the part of the shop known as the jewellery department, choosing a canteen of cutlery for presentation to a retiring official. Behind the WATCH REPAIR DEPARTMENT, the watchmaker was putting the last of his tiny containers back at the angle at which it had always stood; only the glass bells were missing, and they must have been swept away by Albert, the African cleaner. The face of the watchmaker, behind the gold-leaf letters, was pale and calm.

Presently, he looked up and beckoned to her across the shop, and, hesitantly, she went to him. He gave her one of the three-cornered buns filled with poppyseed which he had brought for his tea, and that he knew she loved. Holding it between finger and thumb, she took the bun to the back room and hid it in a corner, for the mice.

Mrs. Shand had even more time for the doctor that she had for the watchmaker. When Kate, or William, or Dykie were ill, and Mrs. Shand was expecting Dr. Connor on his morning round of calls, she would have a plate of fresh scones baked ready for tea from before ten o'clock. And if he happened to come earlier, while the Shand house was still in the uproar of cleaning which not even consideration for the patient was allowed to interrupt, Amos and Fat Katie, the servants, and their shining vacuum-cleaner and buzzing floor-polisher were banished at his approach, trailing the cords of their machines behind them. Mrs. Shand would stand smiling, with her hands on her hips, while the doctor did his examination of the patient. Even if she had been voicing the gravest misgivings about the nature of the child's malady to her sister or mother over the telephone ten minutes before, Mrs. Shand always seemed to be transformed into a mood of level-headed confidence the moment the doctor appeared. Her attitude became jocular and skittish: 'Show doctor the old tum-tum, darling—really, Dykie, must you wear these pyjamas? Why *do* they take fancies to the most unsuitable things, sometimes? Children, oh children . . .!'

Then, the moment the examination was completed, Mrs. Shand and the doctor would disappear into the living-room, talking in an intimate undertone, and the child, fevered with self-importance and the desire to know if the pain really might be appendicitis, would lie cross and rigid, straining to separate the murmuring voices into words. If the other children were at home, they would hang about the passage outside the living-room, and now and then the door would open suddenly and their mother's face would appear, requesting more hot water, or another jug of milk. There would be a glimpse of the living-room, blue with cigarette smoke, fragrant with tea, the doctor sitting in the big armchair—and then the door would shut firmly again. When Dr. Connor rose to leave, Mrs. Shand would accompany him all the way down the garden path and then stand talking over the gate, or at the window of his car.

She would come slowly back up the path to the house after he had driven off, holding carefully in her hand the prescription he had written. Slowly through the house and into the bedroom where her child lay. The child seemed almost a surprise to her. . . . 'Well, there you are, darling,' she would say, absently. 'No school for you for a few days. Now I must go down to the chemist and get this made up. And you're to stay in your bed and not jump about, do you hear? Dr. Connor says——' Then she would go to the telephone and speak to her mother and her sister again. 'Well, he's been. That's what I like about him, when you need him, he's there at once. And, of course, it's just as I thought, a real chill on the stomach, that's all, and he recognised it at once. Good old Robert Eldridge, I'd trust him with my life, any day, in spite of his faults.'

Their mother always talked about Dr. Connor by the two imposing Christian names which she had seen on his degree diplomas at his consulting-rooms, Robert Eldridge. For years, Kate thought of this form of address vaguely as some sort of description; it was like speaking of The Major, or The General Manager, or The Editor. The 'faults' in spite of which Mrs. Shand, and, indeed, half the town, trusted Robert Eldridge were, of course, his drunkenness. He was not merely addicted to drink, he was dejectedly chained to it, as the great sheepish dog whom he resembled might be chained to a kennel. He did not drink at parties, or with friends, but in no company but his own, in solitary, irregular and frequent bouts; sometimes every week, sometimes at intervals of several months, sometimes every day for a month. Once he was sober for more than a year; once he was scarcely sober at all for a year. Unless he had had a particularly long bout and was in very bad shape indeed, he did not drink at home, but drove out into the veld with his African garden boy and a case of raw South African brandy—the cheapest brand; he did not care what he drank. There he would stay for two or three days. The brandy ensured oblivion, and the African, who asked no questions and offered neither protest nor sympathy nor arguments for reformation, ensured survival. For the odd thing was that this wretched man, who crept away to drink himself not into euphoria but into stupor and delirium, shamefully, like a sick animal following the instinct to hide its sickness from the sight of others of its kind, wanted to survive. The desire was so strong in him that it seemed to protect him from harm; he drove his car when he was drunk and did not kill himself, and he operated on his patients when he was drunk and did not kill them. So it was that he came to bear, for the people of the town, the legend of a charmed life, and they were not afraid to entrust themselves to him.

He lived alone with his old mother in a large, neglected house which had the stunned, withdrawn atmosphere of walls, furniture, possessions which have absorbed the unhappy stare of silent inmates. Here, in the living-room with the empty vases, he had sat in morose penitence with his unreproachful mother. Here, in the consulting-room where he examined his patients beneath a pale photograph of his first wife in a Suzanne Lenglen tennis outfit (his wives had come and gone without any sympathy from anyone), he had, in desperate times, concealed brandy in bottles bearing the labels of medicaments. And here, in the hall, where years of dust had turned the black shaggy curls of a mounted wildebeest head into a powdered wig, he had lain at the foot of the stairs whole nights, unable to get up to his room. The house was silent, yet spoke of all this. Kate, when she was thirteen, heard it. She was going to Dr. Connor's house every day at the time, to have a course of penicillin injections for an outbreak of adolescent boils. She was filled with a bewildering self-disgust because of the boils (her body was punishing her, or being punished; she was guilty, that she knew, though she did not know of what) and there was something in this house of Dr. Connor that recognised, instantly, found common cause with, self-disgust. The wildebeest head, the vases, the pale dead girl in the bandeau claimed kinship with her. You are not alone, they said; there is a whole side of life along with which your feelings belong. The claim filled her with dismay and a sense of struggle against some knowledge being forced upon her that she did not want. For the first time, the bony, prematurely white head of Dr. Connor, bent over his big, clean hands as they snapped the top off an ampoule and plunged into it the needle of a syringe, did not seem to her the image of succour and skill and reassurance that it had been all those other times, the times of measles, of tonsillectomy, of the broken arm. He was a mouth-breather, with a loose, wet, kindly lower lip; but today there was no comfort in that audible intake and outlet of breath. Today the uninhabited blue eyes—she had not noticed before that there was no one there—filled her with an indignant, frightened questioning. Where was he gone, and why did everyone go on pretending he was still there? Why, why, why? He had been someone to revere; someone for whom her mother had had a lot of time, 'in spite of'. Yet why must there always be excuses for grown-ups? Why couldn't they be strong, beautiful, happy? Lying down on the white-covered couch and baring her behind for the needle, she felt her young heart fill with cold cruelty toward the mild-voiced, broken man bending over her.

As Kate Shand grew up, she went less and less often into her father's shop. She was away from the town, of course; first at a boarding-school, then at a university. When she did come home, it was always with something of a shock that she saw the shop exactly as it had always been, the watchmaker still at his work in the booth behind the gold-leaf lettering. At seventeen, eighteen, she felt the world revolving with her; how could it be that *these* remained static, were found as you had left them, like the castle where the princess pricked her finger and put everything to sleep for a hundred years? She smiled at the watchmaker across the shop, but she did not cross to speak to him, as if to do so would be to fill with substance again the shadow of the little girl who used to stand there, on the other side of the lettering, watching. The little girl who had seen, one hot Christmas time, the work-table turn over shuddering to the ground, as if some beast that slept beneath industry and submissiveness stirred in impotent protest.

Once the childish ills were behind her (the Shand children had run through the whole alphabet of them, from croup to whooping cough, under Dr. Connor) Kate did not need a doctor again for many years, but her mother often did, and, home from the university one vacation, Kate was irritated to hear that Mrs. Shand had 'just been over to see Robert Eldridge'. 'Good God, mother, why can't you go to a *doctor*?' 'That's all right. I'd rather have him than any of these fancy young men.' Dr. Connor still drove in the car that people gave way to as if it were a sacred cow wandering about the streets, was still accepted, without comment, back under the photograph in the consulting-room in the old house after his periodical disappearances.

In books, worms turned, drunkards ended violently in the gutter, the world moved; in the small town, Kate felt, everything held back tolerantly to the pace of—well, for example, those two men for whom her mother had such a lot of time, two men who apprehended the world from a remove, the one looking through glass into an aquarium where silent, mouthing fish swam up to him incomprehensibly and swam away, the other through the glassiness of his own eyes, through which he saw even his own hands as if he had escaped from them, going on mechanically stitching flesh and feeling pulses.

When Kate graduated and her mother, with her usual capability, announced that she had used her influence with the school board (there were people on it who had a lot of time for *her*) and that a post awaited Kate in a local school, all the reasons the girl gave why she would not, could not, ever live in the town again were the logical, rational ones which children have always used in the process of severing themselves from their parents. But, oddly, for Kate, even as she argued them, pleaded them, they were not true. She was not thinking about the greater academic opportunities, the wider social choice, the cultural stimulation of the city to which she would go; and even if she had dropped the clichés and bluntly substituted for them more money, more men, more pleasure, she would have been no nearer the real reason why she had to go. This reason—and it was a kind of panic in her—had taken shape for her, slowly, out of all her childhood, in the persons of those two men whom she had known, really, so slightly—the deaf man and the drunkard. Why them? Two harmless and handicapped people who, as her mother often said, had never done a scrap of harm; whom, as a child, Kate had automatically respected because they belonged to the people for whom her mother had a lot of time.

And yet, at twenty, it was because of *them* that Kate knew she could not come back to live in the town. They belonged together in her mind, and from them, from the shards of their images there, she must turn away, to live.

VIOLA MEYNELL
The Size of a Pocket Handkerchief

IF Hale had learnt it from anyone else—if a third person had come to him and said: Have you heard Simpson has bought that bit of land? he would have said: That's a lie—or if it isn't he's the dirtiest scoundrel unhung. But Simpson had himself told him: 'By the by, I've bought that field of Shorts',' hoping no doubt to make it sound the most natural thing in the world; and what with the surprise and the unlikelihood of face-to-face abuse between two friends, there had been a few moments' time-lag before Hale's reaction got under way. Those moments had lost him his chance. He had only uttered an ominous: 'So that's what you've done is it?' when they were interrupted. Fortune had favoured Simpson—an additional injustice, and he must be thanking his lucky stars. Or—yes, there was no doubt of it, Simpson had chosen a moment when interruption was secure. But let him wait.

It riled Hale beyond words that Simpson probably thought that he, Hale, having said those few words, would now let it go at that, would let them stand for all the resentment which the situation was worth. The thought of Simpson congratulating himself on the ease with which the thing had been carried off gave Hale no respite from planning just how he would be undeceived. Perhaps he thought that injuries sometimes merely fade away. Well, he would quickly be hearing some home-truths, deadly to any false hopes on the subject. And the facts, when they would be recapitulated to Simpson that evening, would need no doctoring; they were completely damning.

'In the first place you wouldn't be here at all, would you, but for me. Directly I heard of a good holding coming up for sale I wrote and told you, didn't I, because I remembered our talks when we were prisoners together. I knew it was the thing for you, and I was as keen on your getting it as you were yourself, wasn't I?'

He'd say yes to that.

'And in these three years I've smoothed out a few things for you, or done my best to. And I thought we were on a decent footing as between neighbours and friends.'

He might mumble: Well, aren't we?

'Then a few weeks ago I said in your hearing that that bit of land between yours and mine was coming into the market and it would suit me well enough and I intended to buy it. And you've gone behind my back and bought it. I've come across some unscrupulous customers in my time, but this is as nasty a bit of work as I've met with.'

Simpson wouldn't answer that because he couldn't; it was the exact truth.

But that evening, by another stroke of ill-luck, Hale had the exasperation of still being unable to speak his mind. He saw Simpson at the Club and waited for an opportunity when they should not be overheard or disturbed. The Club was full; the two men were always at some distance. When the company thinned a little and there was likely to be more chance of a private exchange, their eyes met across the room for a moment which gave time to develop the grim purposeful look of the one man and the unmistakably hangdog look of the other. Hale was held in conversation; when he freed himself Simpson was gone.

Hale pushed his way angrily to the door and opened it in the hope that Simpson had but just sneaked out. Closing the door behind him to shut in the noise of the club-room, he listened in the darkness for the sound of retreating footsteps, but all was quiet. Like someone just missing a train it was essential he should catch, he stood there so baffled that it seemed some miraculous happening must defeat the logic of Simpson's escape.

He thought of following him to his house, but would not care to say what he had to say in front of his wife. He turned on his heel and went back into the club-room.

Galling as the delay was, it yet served to allow of mature consideration of the form of the indictment. Protests made in a hurry can leave out telling points. And a man may commit a treacherous act and just because the right words of accusation are not found, may think his infamy is not fully realized, and may even become only half-convinced of it himself. Hale did not waste the time of waiting; he got on to more familiar terms with the injury done him, and would have more to say than he would have had in the first place.

'Perhaps you think I'm the only one to know you for what you are—that I'm sore because I lost it, but that no one else is taking any notice. All right, take Chadwick, a man you like to stand well

with. I saw you and him talking and having a drink just as usual,
and I daresay you're feeling set up because his manner didn't show
a bit of difference. Nor it might—to you. Now I'll tell you what he
said to me. He said "It's an eye-opener." He said "What a low-
down thing to go and do." That's in case you think it's just me
kicking up a fuss.'

He'd probably say, Well, I didn't think you'd mind all that much
(which would be a lie) and anyway it's done now.

Whether by good luck or good management Simpson's move-
ments were untraceable the next day. Certainly good luck played
its part, for on Hale going to Simpson's yard at a time when he
would normally have found him feeding his calves, only the fact
that Simpson had received an emergency summons from his wife
prevented his being found. Good management, on the other hand,
was not absent. To avoid Hale consistently, considering that they
lived so much along the same lines, would not have been a
reasonable ambition; but Simpson could induce circumstances
favourable to a postponement. He should have driven past Hale's
farm on his way home that afternoon; on many a day Hale was
about when he did so, and he stopped and they chatted. But today,
uneasily aware that Hale might be on the look-out for him, he
remembered an errand he had some time to perform, and chose to
do it today, thus taking another way home—while Hale was
actually waiting.

Simpson was not a man who had gone into hiding, but while not
making avoidance of Hale his main object, if he could reasonably
apply himself to do a job that took him out of Hale's way he did so.

Hale could hardly believe that twenty-four hours after hearing of
Simpson's act he should still not have spoken his mind. His
indignation boiled up in him. The offence should have been
stigmatized from the very start. But as things were, he could at least
rehearse his interview with Simpson, and if he could not deliver his
oration he could at any rate add to it.

'It's not such a wonderful bit of land, there's only nine acres of it,
but that's not the question. You not only heard from me that I was
going to buy it, but you heard me say that I wanted it for some
grass. You trod on me and on my needs. I wonder where you'd
stop. I don't see why you don't pinch the corn out of my barn, or
the money out of my pocket if it comes to that.'

He'd say that he too wanted the field, that it's handy for him too, and what about him wanting some grass.

'So you might need some, but I happened to be in on this first, and you knew nothing of it but what I told you. And when I told you I was going to buy you didn't say a word, you only crept off on the sly.'

He might say Why did you tell me?

'I told you because I didn't know you had it in you to do what you did. I told you as one man talks to another he believes is a decent fellow.'

The next morning Hale had unfortunately to be away taking calves to market, but whatever he did his mind ran on the talk with Simpson which the afternoon would bring about.

'The last thing I would remember in an ordinary way is the help I've tried to be to you since your wife was ill. But how you've behaved serves to put me in mind of it. I suppose that in an ordinary neighbourly manner I've done your work for you twenty times since poor Mrs. Simpson started having her fits—I couldn't do any other. I took her to hospital when you weren't there. God knows it isn't my idea to bring up a thing like that, I only mean I thought we were neighbours one to another.'

He'd probably say You know I was grateful to you. He'd say Until I did this I never acted in an unneighbourly manner. There wasn't much someone like me could do for you because trouble doesn't seem to come your way. Still when you had that bad go of pneumonia twelve months ago last January I did some of your jobs for you and was glad to.

'That's my point. We were neighbours and friends. That's what makes this a damned low-down way to behave.'

So Hale was well-primed for the talk. He had an infallible scheme for trapping Simpson this afternoon. As regular as clockwork Simpson went to his bank at two-thirty on Friday afternoons. On his road home Simpson in his car would meet Hale in his. Hale would stop him and say his piece at last.

'You're no doubt very pleased with yourself for pulling this thing off, but you know it won't do you much good. I met Short this morning. He said when you turned up to buy the field he concluded I was off it—and you let him think so, or else he'd never have dreamed of selling to you. You'll find it doesn't pay in the long run to get that kind of reputation.'

He might say Yes, Short would rather sell it to you than to me—
and why? Because you've made a success of things and that always
goes down well. You're in with more people than I am because
you've got more time and more money. To him that hath . . . that's
the kind of thing.

'There's an excuse for everything nowadays. But if you think you
can make excuses for what you've done you won't deceive anyone
except yourself.'

But Simpson was to achieve yet one more lucky escape before the
actual encounter took place.

Hale drove slowly along the road at the time when Simpson's car
was nearing on its way from the town. They could not avoid
passing, and soon they were aware of each other's approach. Both
realized that the show-down was now inevitable.

Simpson put on his brake; but the charabanc immediately behind
him could not overtake him until he and Hale had passed each
other; they therefore passed. It would still be the natural thing for
himself and Hale to draw up at the roadside. On the other hand
acceptance of the charabanc incident as a reason for continuing on
their way would also be normal, especially if the two occupants had
nothing particular to say to each other. Either course was open.
When Hale looked back it was to see that Simpson had driven on.

As if Hale's pursuit of his quarry were closing in and narrowing
down, it assuredly seemed that this, the most fortuitous of his
escapes, must be the last—and so it proved.

By now one thing was certain: the occasion was not going to find
Hale unprepared.

'I'm not grasping, that I know of. You can ask who you like. If
this bit of ground had been put up to auction and it had fallen to
you, I wouldn't have had anything to say except good luck to you.
I've got a use for it certainly, but it's all in the fortunes of war, and
if I'd lost it fairly and squarely that would have been all right by
me. What I don't like is what no man likes—and that's a stab in
the back.'

He'd say If it had been put up to auction a fat chance I'd have
had if you'd wanted it. As for your having a use for it, I daresay you
have, but for me it'll make just that difference of being able to milk
a cow or two to help my business along. That's what I need,
something to help me along. I've not been one of you lucky ones,
and it's not for want of hard work. I lost my pigs the year before

last, didn't I, and this year my bit of barley has failed. My home's in a muddle with my wife in and out of hospital, and I have to pay someone to come and do her work. I've had a good deal against me. What I want is to get properly on my feet, and once I'd done that I could carry on.

'I don't doubt all that. So could I improve my business if I played a shabby trick or two. So could any man, you're not the only one. It's just a matter of what you're willing to do. And what you'll do once you'll do again. It doesn't make for good feeling, does it, if you're ready to knock anyone down and stand on them to make yourself taller.'

Up till now Hale had mostly calculated to catch Simpson in the ordinary coming and going of every day, to fall in with him in the same circumstances as those in which they were used to meet and speak. Thwarted in that, he now set out to pin him down on his home-ground.

He walked out into the pearly dawn of the March morning, along field-paths well known to his feet, cutting corners, scrambling through a hedge; he was a born time-saver. Not that he was a quick walker—perhaps because his eyes had plenty to do; for at the end of a walk like this he had an exact knowledge of the condition of every bit of cultivated ground, hedge, ditch or wild life, as far as the eye could see; also perhaps because he was built on the heavy side. (But in some emergency, such as a driven heifer to be headed-off from escape down a side-track, or a sheep to be pounced on for examination, the slow heavy walk could be turned in an instant into a run of amazing agility.)

At length he reached the fence bordering Simpson's holding, and there he stood and waited. He was not used to seeing Simpson at this hour of the morning, but Hale knew that his assignment in his yard for the first jobs of the day was as inflexible as that of a soldier on parade.

Hale stood with his legs slightly apart, as if his stoutness made them be so; the firm wide planting of his feet always made whatever ground, pavement or floor he stood on seem to belong to him.

He had not been there for five minutes when he saw Simpson. He was emerging from the paddock into his yard, a bucket in either hand. He did not see Hale until he heard his name called sharply.

'Simpson!'

He started, stared, put down the buckets and commenced the

slow approach from which there was no escape. He had some way to come, across the width of the yard and the corner of an untidy orchard in which the hens were pecking at their early feed. If this meeting had been a sporting contest Hale was certainly in the position of the player who had won the toss, for while he stood immovable at the fence Simpson had to cover the distance under his eye.

Hale had time to observe his man from head to toe. There was no mistaking the general demeanour of that figure as it approached—it was an incongruous mixture of sheepishness and defiance.

Simpson was a lanky type. He gave the impression that all the tasks he did were more irksome on account of his having to stoop further to them than another man would; his loose-limbed figure was not typical of his calling. Hale realized, as he watched him, that he was a man rarely to be seen without his sporting a sign of some minor physical disability (changing according to the season as if by the vagaries of some fashion), which decorated him with a bit of bandage or a finger-stall or a scab or a scar. Today's demonstration of distress was a square inch of plaster affixed to the side of his neck but standing out a half-inch from it, while he carried his head a bit stiffly. Shaving, it seemed, took place later in the day, or perhaps he sometimes gave it a miss. His clothes were the rough and grubby ones of anyone doing the like kind of chores, except for the almost indefinable difference of their non-country origin and of their having received their first layer of shabbiness in town-wear. (When Simpson spoke, too, his voice had a remotely cockney sound not otherwise to be heard for many a mile around.)

The fact that he had to make his approach while Hale was held at the fence could not do otherwise than make him seem like an accused person coming up for judgement; and every step he took had the subtle reluctance of someone drawing near to punishment. He had no cover. Offenders being apt to carry off their misdeeds, a grown man does not often have to cut so sorry a figure before his friend, and an attempt at jauntiness on Simpson's part carried no conviction. One would not have wished to be in his shoes. Hale may have had to wait for his feast, but it was served to him on a gold plate now.

'Well I daresay I know what you're here for,' Simpson said, coming to a standstill, and perhaps having a blustering hope that

there was an advantage in taking the initiative. 'You want to have
a word with me about me buying that bit of ground.'

'Wa—al, that's the kind of idea,' said Hale in the drawling voice
he sometimes used, with unconscious artistry, at the start of a
subject which was going to work up to high words.

'All right. I suppose I did know when I did it that you'd cut up
rough, but I've got something to say for myself all the same.'

'You would have. And you'd need to.'

Simpson had a defeated look for a moment, which imparted an
unlikely dignity to him. But he rallied to his own defence.

'Can't you take the luck of the draw? I mean to say——'

'I wouldn't say much if I was you. You'll only get deeper in.'

Having checked him again, Hale saw him painfully at a loss, and
surprisingly now felt no pleasure on that account. It seemed too
easy.

'What you can't do,' said Simpson, 'you can't put yourself in my
place. I've had some bad luck. I——'

'Hold on a minute,' drawled Hale. 'Who says I can't put myself
in your place?' He was temporizing. 'But you can't turn black into
white, you know.'

This was a favourite oft-repeated axiom, but he found himself
saying it now automatically, without the usual relish. He was not
comfortable. He felt unaccountably small. He had become less
conscious of himself than of the lanky man in front of him, complete
with warts, scabs, cotton-woolled neck, shifty eye and spluttering
mouth so ready for its job of self-defence. Somehow that figure had
stolen the morning. The importance had shifted away from himself
and lay with Simpson standing there, the perfect illustration to his
own hard-luck story.

'If you want to try and make me pass the sale over to you I don't
see what right——'

But Hale drowned the rest with the weighty emphasis which he
made use of for silencing people.

'I wasn't aware of that being my intention——'

But what *was* his intention? He no longer felt sure. It wasn't what
it had been. He knew he had a lot of things to say, but they seemed
remote and unreal now. But his voice took on the soft persuasive
tone he used when things were going his way.

'What's there in that bit of field to make a lot of fuss about anyway?' he said. 'It's only the size of a pocket handkerchief. Still I daresay you can make some use of it. How's the wife?'

'She's on the mend.'

'Present my compliments to her,' said Hale in the formal stilted voice he used for society manners. 'As to that bit of ground, put it down to clover if I were you,' he told Simpson, for he always liked to give advice. They chatted about the day's weather and parted, Simpson returning to his chores, and Hale sauntering back through the delicious morning of spring.

WILLIAM SANSOM
Cat up a Tree

A WILD, glassy morning—all winds and glitter . . . the sun glared low between the chimneys, through black winter branches, blinding you at a slant, dazzling white and bright straight in the eyes—it made a splintering dance of everything, it made for squints and sniggering. . . .

Winds swept from nowhere, scooping up leaves and hustling them round the corner, knocking little dogs sideways, snatching and flapping at your trouser-legs. Cold nipped at noses and pinched ears red . . . it sang with cold in the keen bright light. Under a white sky the walls, roads, people, trees shone brightly coloured, red, green, blue, grey colours, as in a folk-tale, as if everything were made of coloured glass. Behind white cloud the sun hung and fiercely glowed, a monstrous incandescent mantle. A gentleman crossing the road moved like a puppet, parts of him glittering—one feared that by his own tread he might smash to smithereens his polished boots on the brittle macadam. . . .

Gentleman? He was no gentleman, he was a fireman. A jerky, puppety fireman, in blue trousers piped red, black jogging topboots, and in his braces and white sleeves. He carried a broom. He looked like a puppet because he was then crossing the road in the light— he walked so slowly against the hustling and swirling of the leaves, the dust, the winds, the shattering light.

Hindle Rice, alias Pudden Rice, number sefenty-too-fife, going then through the big red door into the Appliance Room, white-tiled like a scrubbed lavatory for motor-cars, where big top-heavy engines stood and waited, where now Pudden Rice would sweep together over the tiled floor a few small piles of dust, leaving these neat pyramids for the officers to see as they passed in their peaked caps, while in the shelter of such evidence of work proceeding Pudden Rice would for the rest of the morning lean on his broom and think or chat or smile to the good-mornings, or break-for-tea, or perhaps if he felt brave drop the precious broom altogether and abandon his alibi to collect and break up twigs for firewood at home.

Rice soon dropped the broom. Out in front of the station the

black wintry twigs cracked and snapped in his hands. That sunlight
caught his eyes, so he could see nothing in front but bright light, as
of a halo; and to each side things moved too quickly and glittered
like glass. A cat went dashing past, its fur ruffled forward by a
following gust of wind. Up the street two navvies were hitting at a
metal spike with steel hammers—the blows came ringing on the
wind like sharp bells distorted. An old woman in black scurried by
with her veil blown fast into her teeth: she mouthed as this tickled
under her nose, grimacing at Pudden Rice with her head tilted
queerly to one side. Yet in a little garden opposite a girl sat reading,
sheltered by a bush in a warm pocket of sunlight! A paper bag
sailed like a wingless pouter suddenly out from some trees and on
over her head—then disappeared abruptly over the top of a bush.
The girl waved at its shadow, as if it might have been a fly, and
remained throughout reading unconcerned.

Rice smiled to see the girl sitting so quietly. Then he saw a pile
of leaves on the pavement in front form suddenly into a single file,
trickle round in a wide circle, then run for the shelter of a tree-
trunk.

A window above banged open and a voice piped: 'Rice! Rice!'

Pudden dashed for his broom and then carrying it walked slowly
to the stairs. He climbed the stone steps, circling with them the
black-barred well down which hung long grey hose lengths and
ropes, and muttered to these shiplike hangings: 'Now what's the
matter? Now what's up? I swept the tiles, didn't I? I done my job?'

He had reached the landing and was about to turn in through the
green swing doors—when the whole station leapt alive with
sound, sudden as a thunderclap, high-pitched and vibrating for
ever, flashing off the tiles, reverberating round the brass
BRNNNNNNNNG—the deafening alarm bell gripped in its electric
circuit and ringing on and on for ever. . . .

Rice flung down his broom and dived through the swing doors.
Across the room and into a passage—to a sudden end where two
brass rails stood flanking a steel pole. Now the clatter of footsteps
everywhere, and the alarm bell still jangling, Rice stamped his foot
on a brass doorknob, a spring trap-door shot open upwards—and
there was the hole! He jumped over it and gripping the smooth steel
pole disappeared flying down. A rubber mat at the bottom, and all
around suddenly the Appliance Room's white tiles again, with the
engine of the Pump already roaring, men scrambling into boots,

and more coming sailing down the pole, on that light-headed morning like a rain of heavy angels. But angels with funny faces— Nobby redhaired and pointed like a fox, Graetz with his comic round moon-face sprouting high up like a sunflower, Sailor with no neck and like John Bull washed white by a bad liver, Curly with his bright bald head, fairhaired Teetgen like a fresh blank Apollo with black teeth. These all came sliding down and scrambled for the Pump, Rice among them. He jumped up on to one of the high side seats and started to pull up his leggings. The automatic door flew open and the Pump clanged out into the sunshine, as into a fog of white crystal, so that as they turned and roared off down the street light struck up from each brass fitting and from the axes and silver buttons—and somehow the heaviness was washed away.

Perched high up on the side, Pudden struggled into his coat. It flapped and blew out its short tails. He was just able to see the girl in the garden smile—and then his helmet fell down over his eyes. One legging flapped loose. The engine tore along, accelerating faster and faster, until it seemed to Pudden high up above the windshields that perhaps they had left the ground and were scudding through the air itself. The officer in front clanged the clapper of the brass bell as fast as a hand could move. Up England's Lane they tore, down Downshire Hill, through the Crescent, up Flask Walk, down Well Walk, sweeping along the middle of the wide roads like an angry brass beetle, roaring up the narrow streets and scattering dogs and cats and barrows and once an old lady carrying even in November a lilac parasol.

That morning the weather had made poets of the people. It sometimes happens—an angular trick of the sun, a warmness of a wind, something stirs an exultation in the most unexpected hearts. Not in the hearts of all the people ever, but sometimes in those ready to be stirred, and sometimes also in dull hearts of which this would never have been imagined, but these people too receive a sudden jerk, a prod in the spirit, a desire for more than they usually want. Memories arise of things that have never been, tolerance arrives. They laugh—but perhaps that is only because they are nervous at the odd look of things. A trick of the weather has transformed the street, the hour, life. Perhaps this trick is a more powerful agent than the liver or even the libido. Perhaps one day it will be agreed that finally the most critical words of all are 'good morning'.

The passers-by smiled, one waved his hat, and a middle-aged
butcher brandished a chop at them. Pudden still struggled with his
uniform—how it eluded him! The belt and axe caught in the hooks
behind him, his round helmet kept falling over an eye, an ear—and
once his foot missed its support on the running-board and he nearly
fell off the machine. He gripped the brass rail just in time. Yet,
awkwardly as these things tugged at him—the wind, the clothes,
the belt—he began to grin: 'What an odd engine—how peculiar
that on most days it seems so heavy, so oiled and dully heavy with
its iron extinguishers, its massive suction pipes, its hard wood
ladders—yet today . . . all I can see about it is light, and how high
it seems, how topheavy, and most striking of all are the brass rails
and the red leather cushions! It's as upright as a queen's coach!
And here we are—Nobby, Graetz, Teetgen, Sailor and me and the
officer—all sitting and standing high up on top, like exuberant Boy
Scouts, or tin soldiers, or travellers packed up on top of an old-
fashioned coach! Ridiculous!'

But it was really so. The engine was built higher than cars are
built usually, and brass rails armed the erect leather seats, vestiges
of the horse days, a tradition to be surrendered unwillingly.

The bare trees skidded past. Rows of front doors approached and
receded, innumerable windows winked and flashed in the fierce
glare. The skyline of roofs and chimneys stood out black, giantly as
against a milk-white sunset. Far off there appeared a church spire,
it grew into a pointed little church, into a large grey church, and
then this too was gone, veering off to the left. At last Pudden got
himself straight. He then stood up and faced the wind, one leg
crouched up by the ladders. This made him feel a dashing fellow.
Phlegmatic usually, this pose in the wind and this clinging to a
precarious rail excited him, never failing to rouse in him old postures
of bravado learnt from early adventure books. Then, in the sharp
sunlight, with the little houses flashing by, he thought suddenly:
'Good Lord—we're going to a fire! Perhaps to a real fire! It may
possibly be a false alarm pulled by a boy or a drunk or someone.
(He saw a sheet of figures—over 1,000 False Alarms Malicious last
year—one of them fatal—a fireman was killed, crushed against the
garage door in the rush for somebody's funny joke.) But . . . perhaps
it really is a fire, this one time, by chance the real thing? Asphyxia,
boiling, frying—I saw a fireman frizzled up in burning oil till he
was like a little black monkey, a charred little monkey wearing a

helmet several sizes too big for him. And when Sailor tripped in the molten rubber—his arm. Andy's neck after that sulphuric acid job. . . .'

Rice looked down at the two shining round helmets primping up in front of him. He laughed, and felt the corners of his mouth split and all the teeth catch in the wind, he laughed and seemed inside to shine with laughter; how could frying and falling walls happen on this kind of a glass morning? Hot smoke in this pure air? Such things happen to a rosy-cheeked crew of bright tin soldiers? The wind echoed in his ears like a sea-breeze, thrumming past as regular as telegraph wires, and still the sun shot pinpoints off the brass and glared whitely from the chimney-tops ahead. Suddenly Pudden began to hum a march, a high-pitched jigging march for dwarfs stomping off to the forest and the anvils—as joyfully repetitive as train music. . . .

They skidded round a corner and braked to a stop. They were in a cul-de-sac made up of small white houses with painted doors. Trees growing behind showed above the roofs, an effect peculiar in a large city. These looked like country cottages, and the windows were in each case so cramped up and warped that the houses seemed to be no more than a pack of doors and windows clustered together, balancing for breath. A few trained bushes stood in tubs like sentinel birds before the black and pink and primrose doors. And there on the pavement corner stood the fire alarm post, singular and red, as bright a red as when the snow is on the ground.

They leapt off the machine, the officer ran up to the alarm and then stood by it, looking right and left, uncertain, while the broken glass twinkled beneath his polished boots. Rice thought: 'Bright as the day Teetgen went to the paint factory fire and came away with his boots varnished, bright for days!'

The officer peered into the alarm—it had certainly been pulled. But no one was there to direct him. He looked up at the windows, then behind him—searching with his eyes anxiously for smoke. 'That's the crazy people they are,' thought Rice, 'pulling the bell and then running away expecting us to find the job by magic. That's them.'

A small boy appeared from behind one of the bird-bushes. The officer frowned and strode heavily towards him in his big boots.

'Well, son—and who pulled it?' He looked like a giant wooden soldier towering above the suddenly real boy. Blue coat splashed with red, silver buttons and axe, round red face as neat as a doll's, shining black leggings stiff-legged.

Ignoring the question, the boy said: 'Is there a fire, mister?'

'How long have you been here?' the officer asked, his voice sharpening with suspicion—then turned his head so that his face shone brightly in the sunlight. He yelled over his shoulder to the firemen peering about: 'One of you—scout round the corner!'

Attracted by the sound of bells and brakes and the stamping of boots, there had by then collected a small crowd of onlookers. Half of these were boys, carrying rifles and swords, or driving small pedal cars. One wore on his head a top hat peaked with half a brim only, painted blue and labelled *La France*. Two painters in white overalls looked sadly at the fire engine. A tall man with a thin face clouded with red veins asked if he could lend a hand. A smartly dressed woman dragging a trolley laden with shopping smiled and smiled, as though she was the mother of all and 'she knew'. A man in a blue uniform winked at Teetgen, because *he* knew too—he knew it was just another bloody exercise, mate. Three Jewish exiles passed hurriedly, twisting their necks round to keep the uniforms in sight, frightened, round-eyed as owls.

By then Graetz, a tall white sunflower with his round face drooping off his long neck—Graetz was standing isolated in a circle of boys and saying aloud for their benefit: 'It's a false alarm—and from now on we've got our eye on this post. Got a policeman on it, we have, so in future . . .'

When suddenly in a garden wall between two houses a door burst open and a fat woman in a broad white apron came bustling out. She ran towards the Pump with her arms outstretched, as though the Pump might at any moment recede and vanish. She began shouting as soon as she appeared: 'Don't go! Don't go! Oh, I'm so glad you came! Milly's up a tree.' Then paused for breath as the officer went up to her. 'It's round the back, round the back,' she panted, 'and I pulled the alarm, you see. They told me it was right—you see, she's been up there since last night. She mews so.'

The officer said, 'How do we get through?' And at the same time shouted back to the men, 'Cat up a tree. Bring the ladders.'

Teetgen and Nobby jumped up to the front of the ladders on top of the Pump. Graetz and Rice began to pull at the bottom. The straps uncoiled and then the long ladder came sliding out. Once again Rice felt like a puppet, a wooden soldier clockworked with the others into an excited, prearranged game. The sunlight seemed to blow by in bright gusts. Now everybody was laughing—except one of the lugubrious painters, who began to grumble loudly about the bleeding waste of petrol and men's time. But the other onlookers found it great sport, and in the laughing dazzling light began to shout: 'Pretty Pussy!' and 'Mind it don't bite you now! and 'See you keep her nightdress down!'—this last from the thin man with the bad veins.

Pulling at the ladder Nobby said: 'Last week an old girl called us for a parrot up a tree. But we wouldn't go. Cat-up-a-tree's legal, parrots isn't.'

Now the fat woman in the apron bolted back through the garden door with the officer following. The four men carrying the ladder squeezed through at the double. Rice at the rear end nearly jammed himself between the brick wall and the heavy wooden ladder, catching his fingers in the extension pawl, nearly coming a cropper and laughing again. Then they were in the garden—apple-trees and young beech saplings, a black winter tracing of branches everywhere against the glowing white cloud beyond. The sun glared through this filigree, striping the litter of dry leaves, striping the air itself with opaque lightshafts.

'There she is, lads,' shouted the doll officer, pointing upwards. The other dolls doubled up with the ladder working like clockwork, raising their knees in a jocular movement as they ran.

Above them, isolated at the very top of a tall sapling, crouched on the tapering end of this thin shoot so that it bent over under the weight like a burdened spring—sat a huge dazed cat.

In a book of children's stories this cat would have seemed improbable and amusing. Its position was as improbable as that of a blue pig flying. It looked like a heavy young puma borne by what appeared to be a tall and most resilient twig. In real life a branch so thin would have snapped. Yet here this was—happening on a bright November morning, a real morning though rather lightheaded. In children's books too there are pictured with vivid meaning certain fantasies of the weather—lowering black storms, huge golden suns, winds that bend all the trees into weeping willows, skies of electric blue with stars dusted on them like tinsel, moons encircled by magical haloes. These appear highly artificial, drawn from the inspiration of a dreamland: but they are true. These skies and suns and winds happen quite frequently. So that on that morning what appeared to be unreal was real, apparently richened by association, but originally rich in its entity that had created the fairy association. Thus this was a witches' morning, a morning of little devils and hats popping off, of flurry and fluster and sudden shrill laughter.

Teetgen put his weight on the foot of the ladder and the others ran up underneath so that the ladder rose with them until at last it was upright. It was thicker by far and heavier than the sapling— but as its head crashed into the tapering sprout branches they supported it easily. They swayed precariously, then sprang back into position, while the cat, refusing to be disturbed by these alien perplexities, looked away scornfully—or, as animals often do, pretended to look away, keeping an ear cocked sharply towards the new varnished ladder-head now extending towards it.

The officer began to climb at the run, stamping on the ladder as firemen are taught to stamp, to punish the ladder and thus to control it. More than ever he appeared to be playing a game with this deliberate kicking of his boots. Pudden and the others held the ladder firm at the bottom. They were thinking: 'What if he breaks his neck? A man for a cat? What a life . . .' Through the rungs of the ladder a line of gaily coloured underclothes flapped and danced their strange truncated dances. The fat woman stood a little way off, chequered by sunlight, her hands clasped, talking all the time. Some birds started singing, and in the middle of the city a cock crowed.

The officer pranced to the top and picked off the cat by the scruff of its neck. He stuck it on his shoulder and climbed down. The crowd now jammed in the doorway cheered and whistled. They all wanted to stroke the cat. So did Pudden. But as the officer reached the bottom rung the cat jumped from his shoulder to the ground. It was a black cat, fully grown, with white whiskers and paws. As it collected itself on the ground, several of the firemen stretched down their free hands to stroke it, somehow to congratulate it also upon its narrow escape.

However, the cat never even looked at them. With deliberation it stiffened its legs, so that it seemed to stand on its toes, flung up its tail straight as a poker—and walked disdainfully away from the firemen, leaving only the bright adieu beneath its tail.

By the time they had reached the station again, the cloud had thickened. Beneath this new low blanket the winds had died and the air had grown dull.

Pudden jumped off the machine and looked across to the girl in the garden, ready to smile and perhaps shout across to her what they had done. But she had gone indoors.

As they backed the Pump into the Appliance Room an officer walked through and said that no coal had been delivered—it would be a cold day inside, no fire in the mess-room, an empty grate littered with cigarette ends as after some night before. Nobby said: 'Firemen! And not even a bleeding fire we can call our own.'

The white tiles looked dull, clean, solid and efficient. This was again an engine-room for engines, smelling of petrol, decked with ladders and drums of oil. The fire engines again assumed their weight—their massive tyres appeared again hard and heavy to touch, slugging and relentless, heavily set in duplicate on thick oiled axles. The ladders and hooks and ropes and hose all appeared dull and intractable, bruising to the fingers.

Pudden Rice looked over at Teetgen taking off his jacket, at the braces and the soiled striped shirt emerging, at the man peeled of the doll. 'Well,' he thought, and for a moment hesitated standing there, thinking he was thinking. Suddenly he looked up, in surprise—there seemed nothing to think about—and walked slowly over into the boothole, where under the bare electric light he took up the blacking brush and looked round, without success, for something to polish.

ANGUS WILSON
Ten Minutes to Twelve

PALE shafts of winter sunshine lit up Lord Peacehaven's great
walnut desk as he began to write; before he had ended, the gentle
melancholy of twilight had driven the more acute sadness of the
sunshine from the room. On the desk stood an old-fashioned brass
lamp with a smoke-grimy, dark green silk shade. He snapped on
the lamp switch irritably. He was a vast, heavy man—too heavy it
seemed even for the substantial leather chair in which he sat. His
head was square and his neck bulged thickly over his stiff collar.
His cheeks, which should surely have been an apoplectic purple,
were pale from a life confined indoors. Across their flabby pallor,
however, ran little purple and blue veins that recalled his former
unhealthy flush. His grey moustache was neatly clipped, but the
thick white hair that fringed his shining bald head was perhaps a
shade too long. Hairs, too, projected from the nostrils of his fleshy,
pitted nose. His green-brown eyes had a melancholy, anxious look,
but as he wrote they gleamed both with anger and with bitter
amusement. He muttered continuously the words he was writing.
The emotions his face expressed seemed unsuitable to such an old
and compact looking man. Yet his pepper and salt rough tweed suit
was neat and cared for, his brown brogue shoes were brightly
polished. Now and again water collected at the corners of his eyelids
and he wiped it away with a large Paisley silk handkerchief.

MEMORANDUM TO THE BOARD OF DIRECTORS OF HENRY BIGGS AND
SON, he wrote at the top of his folio sheet of paper. And then after a
pause, when he chuckled slightly—FROM THEIR CHAIRMAN. Then at
the side of the paper he wrote in even larger letters TEN MINUTES
TO TWELVE.

The following, he wrote on, are the *only* conditions on which I am
prepared to continue to serve as Chairman. N.B. When I say the
only conditions, the merest simpleton (supposing there to be any
such on the Board and there most certainly are) may understand
what I mean and will not, I trust, waste my time by sending me
alternative conditions or any damn fool nonsense which I will not

under any conditions entertain. (This means that they will go into the waste-paper basket with all the other bumph that idiotic fools continue to bother me with.)

1. I am to have *sole* direction of Henry Biggs—the organisation which I *built up from nothing* in days before it was thought necessary for a pack of self-styled experts and interlopers to poke their noses into all sorts of business that does not concern them.

2. The direction of Henry Biggs is here intended to include any and every 'associated' or subsidiary firm whatsoever and wheresoever. (Subsidiary it should be clear to any fool means subordinate and the 'associated' firms only associated themselves because they were incapable of running their own businesses and knew that they would make greater profits if they *were* subordinated to *me*.)

3. The organisation will revert to its original name of Henry Biggs and cease to be called Henry Biggs and Son. The incorporation of 'and Son' has only led to the interference of a lot of petty officials and jacks in office who have their own interest in mind and not that of the firm. Indeed it is probable that the whole 're-organisation' of the last years was engineered solely for that purpose and *not* as was stated in the interests of my son Walter. In any case the Son has being in and through the Father. This is an IMMUT-ABLE MORAL LAW and nothing to do with re-organisation for efficiency, being in line with the contemporary market, the wishes of foreign customers, satisfactory labour relations or any other canting claptrap.

4. Those who do not like the conditions *must quit*. I cannot undertake to run an organisation where burkers, shirkers and the rest of it are undermining confidence behind my back. I haven't time for such pettiness and if I had I shouldn't choose to use it that way.

5. *In any case* the following gentlemen will leave the organisation forthwith—Messrs Powlett, Rutherford, Greenacre, Barton (T. C.) and (R. L.), Timperley and Garstang. They are well aware that I have done everything possible to work with them and that only their own obstinacy has prevented it.

6. THERE MUST BE UNITY.

7. The Annual dividend will be declared on my sole responsibility. I will, of course, consult the accounting branch, but it must be clearly understood that they are *an advisory body not an executive power*.

8. The wage structure of the organisation will be decided by me

and by me alone. I should like to place it on record that I have the highest opinion of Trade Unions and have worked excellently with them *when they have remembered that they are a British Institution.* I do not propose to deal with foreigners or with those who ape their ways. (No names, no pack-drill.)

9. Henry Biggs always dealt in perfect harmony with customers abroad within and without the Empire while I was in sole charge. Our customers respected us because we dealt with them in good faith and *stood no nonsense.* This practice *must be reverted to.* (They were perfectly satisfied with the tune we played until we started all this business of asking them whether they wanted to hear something else. From now on we shall play 'Rule Britannia' and they will like it.) If anybody doesn't understand what this means, it can be quite simply stated in a few words: Foreign branches and the Foreign Orders branch will stem as they should from the parent tree—that is to say MYSELF.

10. The watchword of the firm will henceforth be ACTION and plenty of it. The Orders for the day will be ACTION STATIONS. Henry Biggs is a living organism and organisms must be active (Keep your bowels open is an old and true saying). Shilly shallying, red tape, passing the buck and other practices of that sort will cease.

Staff Managers will concern themselves with what concerns them, i.e. canteen arrangements, sanitary conditions and the like. Sales Managers will concern themselves with *getting sales orders. The Board will meet for action.* Everything else must be left to THE MAN AT THE TOP.

These are the *only* conditions on which I will continue to act as Chairman. *An immediate Affirmative is absolutely necessary.* Look at the top of this memorandum and you will see TEN MINUTES TO TWELVE. That means the SANDS OF TIME ARE RUNNING OUT. (Any fool knows what 'wait and see' led to with that dangerous old woman Asquith.)

The old man read the memorandum through slowly, smiled to himself and signed neatly but with a concluding flourish: Peace-haven. He then shook a small Benares ware handbell. The door opened and a sadly smiling woman of thirty-five or so appeared. 'I want you to see that this letter goes immediately, Miss Amherst,' Lord Peacehaven said. He folded it, placed it in a long envelope, addressed the envelope 'The Board of Directors. Henry Biggs' and handed it to the woman. 'Certainly, Lord Peacehaven,' she said. The old man looked suddenly tired and a little puzzled. 'And, and,' he hesitated in his speech, 'I think I should like my breakfast.'

Nurse Carver's high heels clicked along the parquet flooring of the upstairs landing. The panelling of the walls, the broad light oak staircase and the wooden railing always reminded her of a man-of-war in olden times. When she reached the large panelled lounge hall the whole family were assembled there, cocktail glasses in their hands, awaiting the summons to dinner.

Walter Biggs was standing, legs apart, warming his bottom before the red brick open log fire. His wife Diana was crouched on the long low tapestried fireside seat. They both looked up at the sound of Nurse Carver's high heels.

Walter's lined red face showed petulance at the interruption. He knocked his pipe noisily against the fireside wall and said sharply, 'Yes, nurse?'

Diana turned her swan neck towards him and frowned at his tone. She got up from the low seat, letting her lemon scarf drape around her waist and the crooks of her arms.

Old Lady Peacehaven, too, was stirred by the note in her son's voice. She sat forward on the sofa, hurriedly, slopping a little of her drink on her dove grey evening dress. Mopping it up with a little handkerchief, she said, 'How is he this evening, Carvie?' Her voice was cracked and flat; the vowels more faintly common than Cockney.

'Ready for bed, I think, Lady Peacehaven,' Nurse Carver answered, 'when he's had his supper. He seemed a little agitated earlier this afternoon, but he's done his bit of writing and that's worked it off. I shall give him a sedative though at bedtime.'

'Then I won't come up to say good-night,' the old lady decided, 'it will only unsettle him.'

Her younger son Roland's thin face twitched for a moment. He was seldom at home and he found so much there that made him want to snigger. He ran his hand over his face and through his greying fair hair, hoping that his mother had not noticed his flickering smile.

'This is the paper Lord Peacehaven wrote,' Nurse Carver announced, holding out the long envelope.

'Yes, yes,' Walter said irritably, 'I imagine you can dispose of it though.'

Nurse Carver's sad, sweet, somewhat genteel smile threatened for a moment to freeze, but she was accomplished at thawing. 'Dr. Murdoch has asked for all Lord Peacehaven's writings to be kept, Mr. Biggs,' she said, 'he wants to show them to the new specialist he's bringing down next month.'

'Oh, yes, Walter, I forgot to tell you. We're keeping all Henry's writings now.' Lady Peacehaven announced it as though it were a new school rule about exercise books. Her plump body and heavy, old grey face looked more than ever 'comfortable' as she spoke and she stroked the grey silk of her dress complacently, but she looked for a second anxiously to Nurse Carver for support.

'Good Heavens,' Walter said, 'what on earth for?' He raised his eyebrows and his red forehead wrinkled up into the scurfy patches where his ginger hair was straggly and thinning. 'Murdoch's had father's case for years. He knows everything about him. There's no possible point in fussing now unless he's trying to use the old man as a guinea pig.'

Diana fussed again with her lemon scarf. Their daughter Patience looked up for a moment from *Anna Karenina* and stared at her father as though he had sneezed over her. Their son Geoff went on reading the evening paper, but he scowled over its pages.

'I'm sure Dr. Murdoch would only do what's best for your father, wouldn't he, Carvie?' Lady Peacehaven said.

Before Nurse Carver could answer, Roland Biggs had turned towards his brother and said contemptuously, 'You love to throw around words like "guinea pig", Walter, don't you? You've no knowledge of any branch of medicine any more than of any other science. At bottom you're as frightened as any primitive savage, but a bit of bluster helps to warm the cockles of your heart.'

Walter laughed to reduce the level of his brother's words to schoolboy ragging. 'A bio-chemist naturally understands every aspect of mental disease, I suppose,' he said, and when his brother gave no answer, his laughter ceased and he added aggressively, 'Well, isn't that what you're trying to claim?' Roland hesitated for a moment whether to accept the challenge, then he said wearily, 'No, no, Walter, only that a competent, modern business man knows nothing about anything.'

'Now, Roland,' his sister-in-law said, 'you're being absurd. Lots of business men are very intelligent even if Walter isn't.'

'Oh dear,' Lady Peacehaven cried, 'if I'd spoken to Henry like that . . .' She turned to Nurse Carver, 'You'll join us to see the New Year in, won't you, Carvie?'

Now Nurse Carver allowed herself the pleasure of a genuine smile, 'Unless you think I should be with the Finns and Sicilians. What do *you* think, Mr. Biggs?' she asked Walter. He hesitated at her remark for a second before he smiled in return, but the teasing relation between them was an old one and therefore acceptable to him.

'You're reprieved from the kitchen New Year, Miss Carver,' Roland said. He hoped to emphasise the fact that Walter appeared to take charge in their mother's house—or could one still say, their father's?

Diana gave her famous little mocking chuckle. 'You're frightfully good for Walter, Carvie,' she cried. 'That was enchanting.'

Her son Geoff turned his growl on her now rather than on the newspaper. 'Why is it enchanting to attack Daddy?' he asked. A lock of black hair fell over his glasses, but the recession at the temples pointed to his father's balding pate. 'Well,' he continued quickly to prevent a remonstrance from his sister, 'if I shouldn't say that, why is it enchanting to avoid a kitchen celebration? I should have thought it was just as clever . . .'

'I don't understand,' Patience finally pulled herself out of Levin's harvesting and announcd it, 'I don't understand why there has to be a kitchen New Year. Couldn't they join us?'

'Oh, my dear,' her grandmother said quickly, 'they have their own ways—all sorts of foreign customs.'

'I shouldn't have thought Finnish ways could be much like Sicilian ones,' the girl insisted.

'You heard what your grandmother said, Patience,' Walter was stern, 'she knows best about it.'

'I can't imagine anybody could know more about foreign servants than we do at Four Mile Farm.'

'How true, how sadly true,' Diana smiled across at her daughter. 'You've only had Finns and Sicilians, dear mother-in-law'—Lady Peacehaven laughed dutifully as she always did when Diana addressed her so—'we have had Portuguese, Germans, Norwegians, Swiss, Belgians and—shall we ever forget her?—a Lapp as well.'

'The Lapp,' said Walter, 'was jolly pretty.'

Girolamo came to announce dinner and the company rose. Diana and Lady Peacehaven led the way in intimate laughter about the comic vagaries of foreign domestics.

Nurse Carver stood for a moment, looking at the great Tudory lounge hall with her sad-sweet smile. Then she sniffed, laid Lord Peacehaven's memorandum on the refectory table and made her clicketing way up the broad oak staircase.

After dinner they watched television for a short while. Patience read on in *Anna Karenina*.

'She gets such a lot of television at home,' Diana said in apology to her mother-in-law.

'You speak as though I was ten, Mother, instead of nearly seventeen,' Patience said.

'I'm afraid my set isn't as good as yours.' Lady Peacehaven had strange notions of appeasement.

'I don't think it's a question of sets, Mother,' Walter declared, 'it's more the programmes. They're designed for a mass audience and you naturally tend to get the lowest common multiple. On the whole, that is,' he added judicially. He was essentially balanced in his outlook.

'Ah,' Roland cried delightfully, 'I see we have a new class now. There used to be those who had the tele and those who were above it. Now we have those who have the tele and are still above it. Good, Walter, good.' Patience looked up at him from her corner for a moment with interest. 'I suppose,' he went on and his tone was now as judicial as his brother's, 'that like anything else it must be used discriminatingly.' She returned to her book.

'Fisher the new history man organised some discussion groups last term,' Geoff told them. 'I said I thought television was one of the chief reasons why everything was so dead to-day. I mean it puts everybody on a level and nobody does anything about anything because they're all so used to just sitting and watching.'

'They have such a lot of discussions at school nowadays, Mother,' Diana said. Patience looked up once more in the hope that her mother might have spoken sarcastically, but she returned to her book disappointed.

Lady Peacehaven, however, was suddenly more than disappointed. Her fat, fallen cheeks flushed pink. She got up and turned off the television.

There was an astonished silence for a moment, then Roland said, 'So you think everything's dead to-day, do you Geoff? Have you

any conception of the progress that's being made in the world?' He
turned on Walter. 'It ought to be made a capital crime,' he cried,
'to give people a non-scientific education these days.'

Geoff blushed red, but he glowered at his uncle and answered, 'I
don't think scientific progress . . .'

But Walter had had enough. 'Why don't we play contract,
Mother?' he asked. 'Geoff's even better at that than he is on the
soapbox.'

The card game left Roland to pace about the room. Finally he
stopped before his niece. 'Can you be persuaded for a moment to
come out of your wallow in romantic adulteries and use your brain
for a bit?' he asked. She looked up in surprise. 'Come on. Play a
game of chess.' He sounded so like a disgruntled small boy that she
burst into laughter and accepted his offer.

After some time Lady Peacehaven began to lose interest in the
game of bridge. Despite Walter's pursed lips and Geoff's frown, she
made desultory conversation. Diana tried to answer politely without
increasing the men's annoyance.

'Nineteen fifty-five has been a very good year on the whole, hasn't
it, Walter?' the old lady said, 'considering, that is, how years can be
these days.' After a pause, she added, 'Of course, we've got a
sensible government and that makes a difference.' Then to their
horror, she said, 'I wish so much I could tell Henry that we've got
a proper Conservative majority now. But then he never knew that
we had those dreadful Socialists, thank God.' She sighed.

Walter seemed to feel that a comment was preferable to the
charged silence. 'I can't think what on earth need Murdoch has
fussing about father's papers like that,' he said testily.

Lady Peacehaven was quite sharp. 'Henry's been very restless
lately,' she said; 'sometimes Carvie's found him as much as she
could manage. I'm only glad Dr. Murdoch is keeping an eye on
things. You don't want your father to have to go away again,
Walter, I suppose.'

Walter mumbled in reply, but once or twice again he returned to
the charge during the game. 'I wish Murdoch wouldn't interfere in
the old man's affairs,' he said. He seemed to feel that the doctor's
interest was impertinent and indecent rather than medical.

'Things seem better in Russia from what I can read,' Lady
Peacehaven said. 'Of course, they're up one day and down the
next.'

'I've ceased to read the papers,' Diana seemed gently to rebuke her mother-in-law, 'they're so sensational.' Lady Peacehaven smiled a little patronisingly at her daughter-in-law. 'Oh, I think one ought always to keep abreast of the times, but then I suppose when you've been at the centre of things as I was in Henry's day. . . . The Geddeses made things hum,' she added, but no one seemed to care. 'Of course these wage claims are a bit disturbing,' she told them, 'but on the whole everyone seems very happy.'

Their lack of response to public affairs came home to her at last. 'When do you go to Switzerland, Diana?' she asked.

'At the end of next week,' Diana replied. 'We shall just get a fortnight before Geoff's term begins. This mild weather isn't very promising though.'

'Saint Moritz used to be so much the place,' Lady Peacehaven said, 'but I never took you children. Henry was very much against people going abroad in winter, although, of course, he was very good when I had that attack of pneumonia in 1928. He took me all the way to Monte Carlo himself and travelled back the next day. The Blue Train it used to be.'

'No Switzerland next year,' Diana announced, glancing at Patience, 'unless Geoff goes with some party. Patience and I will stay at the flat. It's high time she had a winter of London social life.'

'Next winter,' Patience's voice came from the corner of the room, 'I shall be busy working for Oxford entrance.'

'This is a game which demands concentration,' her uncle said, 'a thing that no humanist ever has.' He frowned at his niece in mock sternness.

'Oh heavens,' Diana cried, 'don't give her any more high sounding names. She's blue stocking enough as it is. Neither of the children have *any* sense of humour.'

Geoff said, 'If Granny can attend to the game, I should think you could, Mummy.'

Walter said, 'Now Geoff!'

While he was dummy, Walter got up and fussed around the room. Finally, he picked up Lord Peacehaven's memorandum. 'You've no objection to my opening this, have you, Mother?' he asked, and before she could answer he had done so. Soon he began mumbling the words of the Memorandum to himself and now nobody's attention was really on the games.

Roland, on occasions, of course saw Lord Peacehaven, but the old man seldom recognised his son for who he was and, when he did, more often than not he remained obstinately silent. Only in his memoranda, Roland was given to understand, did he retain a kind of lucidity. Diana never saw her father-in-law, on a plea, purely evasive and generally accepted as such, that it would only upset him. In fact, she disliked the idea of someone closely related who did not know of her existence. To the young people their grandfather was an alluring mystery. Only Lady Peacehaven remained detached. In her daily contact with her husband she lived as really in the past as he did and this existence was not wholly pleasure. But for all of them the memorandum was secretly an intriguing affair.

'The old man seems to have slipped back,' Walter said crossly. 'The last time he knew me properly, I'm pretty sure I got it over to him that the firm had been part of the Development Trust for years.' He prided himself on his capacity to reach his father's comprehending powers where no one else could.

'Poor old Timperley died last month,' he said, 'he was invaluable to the firm in his day.'

'Of course, the incredible thing is,' he said, 'that, allowing for the extravagance of a lot of this, the old man *did* run the firm almost as autocratically as he writes here. He could, of course, in those days, but even before I joined him, things were getting into a ghastly mess. People just wouldn't stand for it. I well remember how we lost three or four very big South American customers in the crisis of '31 just because of the old man's attitudes.'

'Labour relations!' he exclaimed. 'I'd like to see some of the men's faces to-day if they read this.' And he began suddenly to read the memorandum aloud from the beginning.

'Really, darling, I don't think this is quite the place . . .' Diana began. But Roland turned on her angrily, 'I think I have as much right as Walter to hear what my father has to say. Jacob had the blessing, you know, not Esau.'

'I didn't mean you,' Diana cried, but Lady Peacehaven's voice put an end to the discussion.

'I'm sure,' she said quietly, 'that there is no reason for anyone not to hear what Henry has written. The children are old enough,' she looked in turn to Patience and Geoff, 'to appreciate that what their grandfather writes doesn't come from his real self. He's sick in mind. But we're not ashamed of his illness. It's a misfortune not a disgrace.' She smiled at Diana to show her that no one attributed her attitude to ill intention, only to ignorance.

Both Lady Peacehaven's sons seemed a little discomforted by her words; it almost appeared that Walter would not continue his reading. However their mother said, 'Go on, Walter, we're waiting,' and he felt obliged to continue. As he read Lady Peacehaven sat very quietly with her hands folded as she did when anyone insisted on hearing a 'talk' on the wireless.

When he had finished, Walter said, 'I don't know. Nobody seems to realise the scope and the complication of business to-day. In father's day they could bludgeon their way through things. Now-adays it's like a sensitive precision instrument—the least faulty handling in one department and the effects may be felt right through the whole Trust. And the nation depends on it for survival,' he added, in what should surely have been a proud manner, but came out in the same grumbling, whining voice as the rest.

Roland smiled; he could not believe in anything depending upon his brother. 'What I find so distressing,' he said, and his tone was genuinely sad, 'is the awful note of anxiety and fear that runs right through that document. And I don't believe it's just because father's not in his right mind. I think that's what he must have always felt, with all his courage and individualism and high handedness. Of course,' he went on, 'their certainty was so limited. In fact it wasn't there. There was only a bottomless pit beneath their strength of will. I wonder how he would have managed in a world like ours where we pretty well know the answers—technical and scientific. It probably wouldn't have been any good, he would never have had the patience to wait for results, and that's the essential.'

Diana handed her glass to her husband for a refill and began to rearrange her shawl preparatory to changing the subject, but she was too late, for Geoff burst out in a loud, excited voice:

'I think it's frightfully good what grandfather says. It's perfectly true we *do* want action. I mean a lot of us at school think that. And that about making things alive instead of flat and dull and having good reasons for doing nothing. I hate all those good reasons. I don't believe he's mad at all.'

Patience sprang up from her chair. 'Don't you? I do. I think it's appalling to write like that—ordering people about and demanding power for oneself and never stopping to think properly. I hope I should always fight bullying like that whenever I met it. It's no better than Russia.'

'Why shouldn't people be ordered about?' Geoff shouted, 'if they get in the way and don't pull their weight. What's the good of being in charge if you don't give orders? Anyway it's not like Russia. You didn't listen properly. The whole point is that the firm's *English*. Grandfather said so.'

'I know,' Patience said. Her eyes were large with anger. 'That's what's so shameful. Oh, I'm sorry, Granny, but it's made me feel so ashamed.'

'I should hope so,' Walter said sternly, 'what an exhibition from both of you. You should *both* apologise to your grandmother.'

'At least,' said Roland, 'it's brought the younger generation to life.'

Diana looked horrified. 'If it takes the words of someone who isn't . . .' She stopped and put her hand on her mother-in-law's arm. 'I'm sorry,' she said.

'That's all right,' Lady Peacehaven declared, 'perhaps it wasn't a very good thing to read poor Henry's letter really. But I don't know. He always liked to raise an argument.' She took up the pack of cards and began shuffling them. 'Your grandfather had great drive, you know,' she said to the young people, 'and he worked so hard. He liked to do it all himself. He was very good to people when they fitted in with his ways. But I think Roland's right. He *was* always very anxious. He seemed to want to reassure himself that things were as he wanted them—no matter how well everything went. And he never relaxed or took a holiday. I used to go with you children,' she spoke now to Walter and Roland, 'to Angmering or Budleigh Salterton, but if he came down for a day that was as much as he could manage. One year, it must have been when you were still at St. Stephens, Roland, some parents of a boy there, I think it must have been those Capels, suggested that we should to to Thorpeness, but we never did.' She paused, realising her digression. 'Your father used to ring up though, every evening. I don't think he felt convinced that I knew how to look after you. He *couldn't* let people do things their way. It was just the same when you grew up, it wasn't that he wasn't fond of you both, but he was shy and he couldn't believe you could manage on your own. Of course, it got worse, as time went on. I ought to have seen it really. I *did* make him go for a holiday. We went to Le Touquet and stayed at the

Westminster. It was very comfortable although some people said we should have stayed at the Hermitage. But Henry only stayed three days. He started so many law suits then. He *knew* that right was on his side. And so it often was, but not always. He got so angry sometimes that I could hardly recognise him, and moody too. His face seemed different. Like someone changing in a dream. One minute it's them and the next minute it's someone else. I think the first time I really realised how ill he was came about through that. It was New Year's Eve 1935.' She stopped and then said, 'Perhaps I shouldn't tell it now, but there's no sense in superstition. Henry was sent out into the garden before midnight. You know—the darkest man must come in with something green. Although Henry was already turning very grey. But when he came in again, I didn't recognise him for the moment. It seemed as though someone else had been substituted for him when he was outside. And soon after that he had that terrible scene at the "office".' She put down the cards. 'Well, this isn't at all a cheerful sort of talk for a party evening,' she said.

'No, indeed,' Roland cried. He disliked personal revelations. 'Anyhow, now it is *really* ten minutes to twelve. Where's Miss Carver?'

A moment later Nurse Carver came down the stairs. 'He's fast asleep,' she said, 'so I thought I might join the merrymakers before I go off to bed myself.' She gazed at rather sombre faces. 'Well now, Geoff,' she cried, 'I don't know whether I ought still to call you that. You're so much the man. The darkest man present too. You'll have to go outside to bring the New Year luck in.'

Geoff jumped to his feet. 'All right,' he said, 'I'll bring in 1956. You'll see. I'll make it a year of adventure and action.'

Walter was about to stop him, but Lady Peacehaven said, 'Don't be silly, Walter. Of course he can go.'

There was silence when Geoff had left them. 'He's the spit image of Lord Peacehaven, isn't he?' Nurse Carver cried, 'perhaps *he'll* grow up to be quite a great man.'

Diana shuddered. Patience came behind her mother and put her arms round her neck. She kissed her cheek.

Nurse Carver looked at the downcast features of the family with consternation. 'Only a taste of champagne for me,' she said to Walter in the brightest voice she could muster.

RHYS DAVIES
Afternoon of a Faun

No one took any notice of the ordinary, strong-legged mountain boy as he stood in truant-looking calculation on a street corner that golden October afternoon. The day-shift miners were clattering their way home; a few women scuttled, concentratedly as crabs, in and out of the shops; in the gothic-arched porch of Lloyds Bank the minister of the prosperous Baptist chapel stood brandishing an unnecessary umbrella in debate under the long, doubtful nose of the Congregational minister, whose sermons were much bleaker than his rival's. Even the constable stepping out from the police station, which had eight cells for violent men, did not rest his pink-lidded eyes on the meditating boy. The afternoon remained entirely the property of grown-ups.

A few minutes earlier, Mr. Vaughan, the headmaster, had walked into his classroom in the grey school up behind the main street. After beckoning to him from behind the big globe atlas, which had just been wheeled in for a geography lesson, Mr. Vaughan had whispered, 'You have to go home at once, Aled; your mother has sent for you. . . .' The old duffer, in that unreliable way of his, had smiled, hesitated, attempted to pat the pupil's ducking-away head; then, giving the globe—skittishly it seemed—a spin in its sickle, he had stalked off to his own quarters. Had he come with good news which, in his punishing way, he decided finally to withhold? A back-row boy had made a whinnying neigh, and Aled's own departure was accompanied by a chorused groan from the others of Standard 4: they thought he was summoned out for the usual. In those days, corporal punishment was rife in the schools, and Mr. Vaughan's only authority lay in a resined willow cane, though his incessant use of this had about as much real body as a garrulous woman's tongue. All the boys of Standard 4 despised him, unerringly divining his lack of true moral stature, unforgiving him for not being masterful as a bloody oath.

Humming like a bee with a ripe peach in its vicinity, Aled had swooped down the hill from the stone jail and come to a bouncing halt in the main street. It was a full hour before the school would close for the day, and the liberation made time prodigal. A yellow sun wallowed high above the mountains. He half guessed why he had been called from school. His father, who lately had become more bad-tempered, was due to go to Plas Mawr, the hospital and rest home for sick miners, away in another valley, and the horse-drawn ambulance van must have arrived that afternoon; no doubt his mother had gone in it too, to see his father installed. He was only needed to look after the house until she returned by train. It wasn't necessary, he decided, to hurry home just for that. Willie Dowlais' mother, who lived next door, would be keeping an eye on the house meanwhile.

But what was there to do? He gazed dreamily at the Baptist preacher, and, in the syle of a pigeon-fronted old gentleman of well-behaved disposition, he took an imitative strut down the main street, hands clasped behind him, a leisurely eye cocking into shop windows. Suddenly, he halted again and, neck stretched out, advanced closer to a window of Morgan's General Emporium, stared into it intently, and loped a rapid step backwards. The afternoon lost all its festival tints.

Morgan's hotch-potch window display included a bulky black perambulator, and in this sat, among silken cushions, a most successful-looking wax baby. Cosy as a cauliflower among leaves, its face bulged out from a price-ticketed bonnet of green ribbons. A snowy diaper, also priced, dangled from a triumphantly lifted hand. Other articles relevant to worship of this enthroned pest lay scattered below its carriage—garish toys, shoes of knitted blue wool, a little pot painted with garlands of roses, and embroidered bibs to catch dribbles from that smirking and overfed mouth.

Nose puckered, he continued to stare at the omen in mesmerized suspicion. *That* was why Mr. Vaughan had twitched into a smile and attempted to pat his head! About a month ago, while she was ladling baked custard on to his plate, his mother had confided in him that he might expect either a sister or a brother soon. Although withholding comment at the time, he had not been favourable at all. The sovereignty of his reign, now in its eleventh year, had never been disputed before.

'I'm sure it's a sister you'd prefer,' his mother had added, in that deciding-for-you manner of grown-ups, and looking at him as if it was only for his comfort that this act was being done. 'She'll be company for you. . . . But, of course, they *might* send you a brother instead. They handle so many that often they get careless and stupid.'

They, they—who were these mysterious, two-faced *theys?* He didn't believe in them, they were invented by treacherous grown-ups who wanted to hide their own mistakes. He had stared angrily at the photo of his grandfather above the chiffonier, and asked, 'Why don't *they* go on strike for shorter hours or more money, like the miners do?' It was his sole pronouncement at the time.

'That's enough, Aled!' his mother had said, escaping into another of the despotisms of grown-ups. 'You're a spoilt boy. Eat your custard.'

Since then, the news had been too outlandish to preoccupy him. He turned from the grinning wax horror at last, hesitated, and stood frowning on the gutter kerb. Further brooding weighed him down. The thought of Ossie Ellis had arrived logically, and, also logically, his stomach sank lower.

Ossie, often seen obediently pushing a battered old pram— usually it contained two babies—through the streets, was the derision of his fellow pupils of Standard 4. He was seldom in the position to enjoy a cowboy Saturday in the mountains because he was obliged to stay at home to look after his brothers and sister, all unjustly younger than himself. One Saturday, when called for at his home to go on a pre-arranged spree, he had put his head round the door and said, depressingly, 'Can't come, Aled. I'm the old nanny goat again today; four to mind and feed, and one of them's going to get measles, I think.' Shirt sleeves rolled up, Ossie wore a girl's stained pinafore, and a smelly noise came out of the ramshackle house. His mother was a befeathered tartar, his father a drunkard, but Ossie, always solemn behind steel-rimmed spectacles, never took umbrage when taunted by Standard 4 with his kowtowing to domestic tyranny.

'Do a bunk from home some day,' Aled advised, on another thwarted occasion. 'Run away and get lost all night—that will teach them.'

Ossie had blinked owlishly, and said, 'No, it won't. But I'll never get married, Al.'

'Nor me,' Aled had said, without just cause then.

He looked up. The pink-lidded eyes of the policeman, who was patrolling the main street in the usual suspicious manner of his kind, rested assessingly on him now. Without further delay, Aled turned on his heel, walked with laborious meekness up the street, and vanished into a quiet turning. But he hurried down the rough-stoned, deserted alleyway which lay in a homewards direction, leading to the bridge that he crossed twice a day, to and from school. He looked back over his shoulder furtively. It was as though the golden day had darkened into night and avenging footsteps plodded behind him, like the feet of pursuit in a nasty dream.

Forebodings of drastically curtailed pleasures, of assaults to dignity, bereft his sandalled hooves of their usual nimble leap as he climbed the gritty steps which led to the old iron footbridge. On the top step he paused to gaze up at the bluish green mountains encircling the valley. It was a look of farewell. He was a great lover, even in winter, of the coarse highways and byways in the mountains; he knew their secrecies as shrewdly as the rams and ewes inhabiting those antique places. A baby's perambulator could never reach them.

Ahead, on the shivering middle span of the old bridge, tramped a last day-shift miner. The rickety Victorian structure linked, with three long, nervously zigzagged spans, two hillside communities. It was a short cut for pedestrians, and it crossed the big, sprawling colliery yard. In winter storms uneasy people avoided it. Two pit shafts, aerial wheels whirling, towered a quarter mile up the narrowing valley. Downwards, lay a long view of swirls of mountain flank retreating from the valley in flowing waves ungrimed as a sea.

He began to increase his step, after a last backwards glance. The miner ahead had stopped to peer over the bridge railing—the colliery yard ended just there with a steep 'tip', down which rubble, slag and useless coal-dust from the pits was thrown every day—and Aled, when he reached him, stopped to peer down too, looking through an opening in the trellised ironwork.

What he saw below made him grip the railings. The afternoon flowered.

'His back got broken,' the old miner said, noticing the boy standing beside him. 'There's been a fall of roof down in Number 2 pit today. They had to stun him to put him out of his misery.' His voice was casual, and his hands hung from the dirtily ragged sleeves of his pit jacket like crumpled shapes of old black paper. For a miner, he looked frail and ghostly.

Aled drew away for a moment and, astounded, asked, 'They are going to throw him on the tip?'

'No. The wagon will be shunted back after they've emptied the stuff from the others. He was called Victor in Number 2.' The miner, his face anonymous in its mask of negroid dust, looked at the boy again. The whites of his eyes shone glossy as candlewax. 'Dan Owen's boy, aren't you?' he asked. 'How's your dad getting on?'

'He's going to Plas Mawr,' Aled replied, inattentive, a foot jerking in excited impatience. Why didn't the man go?

'Oh, aye. A good place for them.'

The miner tramped off unconcerned. The middle span quaked under his studded boots. Expert as a squirrel, Aled scrambled up the railing and sat on the shaky ledge. Now he could view unimpeded the train of four small-size wagons below. It had run on a narrow gauge track from the pit shafts and stood drawn up to the tip's edge. But no labourer was in attendance. A horse lay in the end wagon. The boy sat rigid. All the wealth of the Indies might have been below in the monotonous yard.

If only because of its size, a collapsed horse is an arresting spectacle, and this one—he was of the cob breed suited to the pits— had been dumped into a wagon much too mean for his awkward proportions. From the chained body a foreleg was thrust up stiffly into the air. The long neck, a sorrel gush under the dishevelled, grit-dulled mane, hung inert over the wagon's end. But the staid profile of the head could be seen, its eye open in a dull, purposeless fixity. Gaunt teeth showed yellow under lips drawn back as if in a snarl, and from the mouth dripped—yes!—an icicle of purplish fluid. Victor looked an old horse. Had he been stunned on that bone inset so strongly down the long, desolate face?

No one crossed the bridge now, no one was visible in the whole yard. All the smashed horse was his. He stared down calculatingly, wanting to retain the exclusiveness of this treat, jealously store this gala exhibit. An item from an elementary school lesson of the past returned to him; *The horse is a quadruped, a beast of burden, and a friend to man,* and he felt a brief compassion. Everybody spoke well of horses. He remembered seeing a couple of young ones trotting in fastidious energy, tossing their bright manes, as they were led up the valley for their life down in the pits. Horses dragged the small wagons of coal from the facings to the bottom of the pit shafts, and he had heard that when they were brought up for retirement, or to be sent to the knackers, they could no longer see clearly in daylight: they would stand bewildered at the pit-head, neighing in chagrin, lost from their warm, dim-lit stables deep under the earth. . . .

He jerked up his head, glanced swiftly at the sky, swivelled round on the ledge, made a clean jump, and galloped over the bridge. Willie Dowlais' camera! The light would be good for a long time yet, but the horse might be removed at any moment. With snapshots of this treasure in his possession he would be a prince among the other boys.

Anxiety began as he leapt the far steps and it occurred to him that Mrs. Dowlais the Parrot might not be at home or, alternatively, would be unwilling to lend Willie's camera.

Springing up the path on the slope, above which the piled streets and terraces began, he heard Angharad Watkins singing as she pegged washing on a rope in the tilted, flower-cushioned garden of her old cottage, which stood isolated on the slope. She called to him when he stampeded past her gate, but he only waved an impatient hand; they were old friends and he owed money in her amateur shop. Above, the length of Noddfa Terrace was abolished in a flash.

On the corner of Salem Street, swarthy old Barney Window Panes shouted his customary, 'Hey, boy, know anyone with a broken window?' Barney was also called The Wandering Jew, because with a load of glass pieces strapped to his bowed, homeless-looking back, he tramped over the mountains, never using trains even after sunset, and no one knew where he lived. He gave pennies to boys for information of people's broken windows. Although Aled knew of a couple, he dashed past heedlessly, rounding the corner into the empty roadway of Salem Street in champion galloping style.

His shouted name brought him to an abrupt halt. The call home! He had forgotten about it. He stood poised in the road, glaring sidewise towards the open door of his home, a leg still lifted. 'There you are at last!' Aunt Sarah's voice cried, further. 'Come here, Aled. You've taken a long time!'

Why was *she* there? She stood just inside the doorway with Willie Dowlais' mother. He lowered his leg and, cautiously, approached them. 'What do you want?' he demanded, his voice rising to a shout—'I've got to go back to school. . . . For the geography!'

Mrs. Dowlais the Parrot—as, usually, she was called—gave Aunt

Sarah a bunch of the chrysanthemums which grew in her back garden and waddled past him silently to her own door: he watched her go in despair. Aunt Sarah never failed in reducing him to a surly feeling of guilt. She lived across the bridge, in the fashionable part, and always looked as though she had been awarded medals all her life. The owner of five terrace houses, and an influential member of the Baptist chapel, she sang solo in the chapel's famous annual performance of Handel's *Messiah*, heaving herself out of her seat on the specially erected platform, when her items came, and growing twice her size as she gave vent. Even now, statuesque, she stood as if expecting applause that she was there.

His kingdom came toppling down. He had forgotten about her, too, and anguish became more acute as he realized she would have been called across the valley for such a ceremonious event as the arrival of a baby. The usurper *had* arrived!

'Come in, Aled,' Aunt Sarah said, her voice different. He edged a step or two inside the doorway, avoiding her hand and throwing a glance of extreme anxiety in the tip's direction. 'Your father asked for you,' she said. 'He has left us.'

'Gone to Plas Mawr?' He still breathed heavily, but half in relief now. He did not proceed further into the house. A peculiar silence, such as comes after an important departure of a person, lurked about the interior.

'No.' Aunt Sarah's pince-nez glimmered down on him. 'He died this afternoon, Aled.' She added, in comforting afterthought, 'You wouldn't have arrived here in time, in any case.'

'Died?' The word dropped down his throat like a swallowed sweet. He stared at her. 'Why?'

'Why?' The familiar, other tone returned. 'He had a relapse. . . . A haemorrhage.' She used the word importantly and, noticing his uncomprehending stare, added, 'His lungs, my boy. The silicosis.'

Silicosis. It was a word he knew well. The blight word of the valley. Some men of the pits stayed at home with the disease for years, living on the compensation money paid by the colliery owners; others went to Plas Mawr for cure or not. Men got it from breathing the gritty dust of the pits. Now and again, in streets or shops, he had heard gossiping women relate, 'The test says he's got it hundred per cent.' Or it would be the gamble of eighty per cent; or a more cheerful fifty. Even men who were cured never went down the pits again, and always there were others, younger, coming up the valley to take their places.

'Your mother is upstairs with him.' Aunt Sarah said, returning to her grown-up oblivion. She bunched the neighbour's chrysanthemums and began to mount the staircase. Her voluminous grey skirt swished majestically.

'Shall I come up?' he mumbled, stretching his neck as he advanced. He wanted a cup of water.

'No; wait,' she replied, not turning. 'I'll call you when we're ready.'

He stood baulked before the staircase, gazing up. The sense of frustration became more desperate. That unfamiliar silence came down the stairs like an exhalation; it made his scalp contract. Yet he could hear the gentle press of feet shifting across the floor above. Then he heard his mother's voice—it sounded both swollen and hollow—saying, 'Give me the sponge, Sarah.' He made a headlong plunge to the open front door.

A new agony, as he banged on the neighbour's door, was the sudden thought that there would be no roll of negatives in the camera, though he knew Willie had bought one on Saturday. Mrs. Dowlais the Parrot was ages in answering the bang. 'Yes, Aled?' she said, bending a puce ear closer, as if she hadn't heard his immediate babbling request. 'Your mother wants something?'

'Willie's camera——' he panted.

'Willie's camera!' Her eyes widened in astonishment. Within the house, her aged parrot gave a squawk that sounded mocking.

His feet strutted on the doorstep like a dancer's. But he sensed that she was willing to grant any request because of what had happened next door. 'I've got to take photos of a horse on the tip, before it's taken away!' he shouted. 'For school! We're having lessons about horses. Willie said I could borrow his camera. . . . The CAMERA!'

His crescendo yell did not upset her. A comfortable woman, very esteemed in the valley, she waddled and sighed her way into her sympathetically darkened house, its blinds down. She rummaged there for an unbearably long time. A whine came from him when he snatched the camera from her hand. Running, he examined the indicator of the black, ten-shilling box, saw that only three negatives had been used, and streaked round Salem Street corner. The Wandering Jew was still there, sunk in reverie, waiting for informing boys to come from school. In the sky the delicate mountain-blue of early October had darkened a shade.

He had scrambled down to the yard by a workmen's path on the slope and, chest bursting in foreboding of this last frustration, arrived at the exact place below the bridge. But the horse was gone. The three wagons of waste stuff remained. But, again, no labourer was visible. He could have gone in pursuit of the shunted wagon; the man in charge would have understood this special flouting of the *Trespassers will be Prosecuted* notices posted at the yard's main entrances. He did not move. All desire to photograph the horse left him.

A fanfare of approaching yells made him start into attention, and, immediately, he dashed to the shadows under the bridge. The boys were out of school. They stampeded over the spans in whooping droves. Leaning against a trembling stanchion, he listened to their cries as though hearing them for the first time, and with no wish for their confederacy now. The last feet pattered away into the distance. Still, passive and exhausted, he lingered in the hiding place, looking at a heap of mildew-green tree trunks maturing for use down in the pits. He knew, now, that he would never brag to the boys about the horse, never even mention it. He could hear them—'Hark at Al! . . . You saw a dead horse, eh? Shoved into a little wagon on top of the tip! Purple stuff dropping from his mouth, eh? Sure he didn't have billiard balls for teeth, too?'

The yard stretched unfamiliarly silent and deserted. Had he really seen a horse? Had a man with an unknown, dustily black face spoken to him on the bridge, and asked a question about his father? It seemed a long time ago, though yellow sunlight still splashed on the tenacious clumps of seeded thistles and thorn bushes growing from this grit-thick waste ground. He looked about him vaguely. It no longer seemed unusual that he had not seen a labourer. This closed territory, where he trespassed, was not the same yard which he viewed daily from the footbridge. It was his first visit to below.

When he came from the hiding place he stood irresolutely on the tip's crest. The sun, veering towards a mountain, had become a deeper gold; a seagull visitant winged through a shaft of thickening light, returning down the quiet valley to its coastal haunts. People were gathering into their houses. He took a few slow steps home-wards, stopped, and moodily kicked a piece of slag down the tip.

Forgetful of prosecution, he stood looking everywhere but in the direction of his home. A rope of lazily flapping coloured garments caught his eye—Angharad's washing, hung above a spread of dahlias, chrysanthemums and Michaelmas daisies. He hesitated, remembering his debt, then slowly crossed the yard and scrambled up a slope to the path beside which her old, silverstone cottage stood alone, the only one remaining from the valley's remote rural days.

Angharad's grandmother had left the house as a legacy to her, together with its litter of pigs and a cow. After the funeral, about a year ago, she instantly got rid of the pigs and cow and almost as instantly married Emlyn Watkins, a sailor conveniently home on leave from the Royal Navy. But Aled could never think of her as a woman shut-up properly by a wedding: she didn't have that style.

A chewing woman customer, chronically married-looking and with a ponderous goitre, came out of the cottage. To companion herself during Emlyn's long absences—she had no children to bother her, so far—Angharad had opened a shop in her front parlour, the stock consisting mainly of confectionery, cheap remedies for sicknesses, household oddments, and cigarettes for workmen dashing in off the colliery yard. Credit was allowed some children, who were selected emotionally and not according to social prestige. He owed her for three lots of stopjaw toffee, a bag of marbles, and two cartons of chalk crayons.

A dramatic soprano shriek greeted him as he walked into the odorous parlour. 'Aled!' Angharad cried, 'I've only just heard about it from Mrs. Price the Goitre!' And, full-based, down she collapsed to a chair behind the big table, which was heaped with open boxes of sweets, satchels and bottles of stuff for toothache, bellyache and headache, culinary herbs, pencils and cotton reels, cards of hairpins, illustrated packets of flower seeds, and the kitchen scales of burnished brass on which she usually gave very good measure to favoured children. 'Another good man gone!' she wailed. 'It's wicked.' She might have been bewailing loss at sea of her own husband.

A chair, for gossiping, stood on the customer's side of her well-spread table. Aled sat on its edge, eyeing a newly-opened box of Turkish Delight. The rose and yellow chunks, elegantly perfumed and pearl-dusted, were always beyond his means. He felt he was there under false pretences. Why had he come?

'They're upstairs with him,' he mumbled, waiting for her outburst to subside, but also relieved by it.

'I'd close all the damned pits!' she went on, shrilly. 'Or make people dig for their own dirty coal!' Momentarily the origin of all sorrow, she yet managed to remain lavish as a lot of lambs gambolling on a hillock. A tight heliotrope frock, stamped with a design of pineapples and pale shells, held her body in precarious bondage.

He dreaded that she would ask him what he wanted—the room, after all, was a shop. Simmering down in her abuse of the pits, she peeped at him out of the corner of her blue eyes. At random, he said, 'My mother made a lemon jelly this morning—she said it would set in time for his tea. Dad liked lemon jelly. . . .' He lapsed into pondering. Because of all that was going on upstairs, he thought, no one would prepare a meal now, and the jelly would remain forgotten in the cool place under the kitchen sink.

Angharad's woe entirely ceased. She dabbed at her fresh-coloured face with a man's large handkerchief, and invited, 'Take a piece of Turkish Delight.' When, slowly, he shook his head, she urged, 'Aled, I'll let you off your account. You don't owe me anything!' She jabbed a tiny gift fork into a yellow chunk and, smiling, held it out.

'My Aunt Sarah is there,' he said, taking the honey-soft chunk. He heard the hiss of the goose-grey bombazine skirt going upstairs.

'*She's* got a good voice in the *Messiah*.' Angharad wagged her head. 'Too loud and showy for my taste, though.' She pushed a piece of Turkish Delight into her own mouth, which, shaped like a clover-leaf, was surprisingly small.

He sat back. The scented luxuriance melted in his mouth. 'She's always criticizing me,' he remarked.

'A rose one this time?' Angharad held out another chunk, dismissing Aunt Sarah. A drop of juice, like a golden ooze from fruit, came from the corner of her mouth, and for a moment, staring, he remembered the horse. 'It's what they eat in harems in the East,' she said, and she, too, eating a rose piece, seemed to purr in understanding of women reclining lazy in satin bloomers on a marble floor. 'But these are made in Bristol,' she said.

'Have you been in a harem?' he asked, exact.

'No, certainly not! And neither has Emlyn, though his ship's been to the East.' Angharad remained amiably regal as her ancient name.

No one came in to buy: everybody, by that time, was gathered about the routine teapot and a plate of bread and butter. Angharad, after giving him another peeping glance, placed the lacefrilled box of Turkish Delight in a position convenient to both of them, and took a letter from a fat cookery book lying on the table. 'From Emlyn!' she whispered, confidentially. 'I'll read it to you. . . . Help yourself,' she said, pointing.

It was a long letter, and she read it in leisurely gratification, a hand reaching occasionally for Turkish Delight. Emlyn seemed to be exceedingly fond of her and interrupted anecdotes of life in ship and port to reiterate, like the last line in a ballad's verses, '*Angharad, girl—roll on, Christmas leave! You'll have to shut shop then!*' Once or twice, she paused to omit something, shaking her head and peeping at her guest.

Interest in Emlyn's ramblings dwindled from him. He watched her hand playing with beads distributed about her freckled throat, where it went into her sleepy-looking chest. Vaguely he thought of something tucked-in and warm, and, for some reason, he remembered the speckled thrush's egg which he and Willie Dowlais had taken from a nest last spring: the startling private warmth of the nest, as he put his hand in it, returned to him.

She folded the letter at last and gave a heave, murmuring, 'Home by Christmas! My big Santa Claus. . . .' She started, looked at Aled guiltily, craned her neck, and squealed, 'My God, we've eaten the whole boxful! Seven shillings' worth, at cost price! No wonder Emlyn always asks me what I've done with my profits.'

Aled said, rapidly. 'I've got a loan of this camera. I thought I'd take photos of you, to . . . to send to Emlyn.' He glanced at the window. 'We'll have to be quick.'

She jumped up with alacrity, crying, 'Oh, yes, yes! But let me get my new hat and fur.'

Willie Dowlais would need appeasing for this unsanctioned use— far less understandable than for the eccentric treasure of a dead horse—of his roll of negatives. They hurried into the garden. He took nine shots of her, among the explosive dahlias, lolling chrysanthemums and dried washing; for some he, the expert in charge, commanded her to remove the cygnet-winged hat of Edwardian dimensions which was balanced on a head which always he had trusted. She posed with proud docility. The cherry-red sun leaned on a mountain top. He guessed the prints would be dim.

'Sailor though he is, Emlyn will break down and cry, when he sees me among my dahlias and washing!' Angharad, after stretching a hand to feel if a pale blue nightdress had thoroughly dried, began to pluck the freshest dahlias and chrysanthemums. 'But serve him right for joining the Navy!' She turned, quickly. 'All the same, Aled, don't go down the pits when you grow up! Join the Navy. It's healthier.'

He wound the completed roll, and said, 'There was a dead horse on the tip this afternoon. I was going to take photos of it. But it had disappeared. . . .' His voice loitered and his eyes wandered in the tip's direction.

Angharad paused, turned to look at him again, then only remarked, 'Well, better a live woman inside that box than a dead horse, don't you think?'

Her face was serious, but, within the clear eyes, smiled. She began to walk towards him, flowers—milky purple, golden, sorrel-red, russet, deep claret—in the crook of her arm. As, vaguely, he stood watching her approach, the apparition came again. But, now, the defeated neck, the dead eye, the snarling yellow teeth, the mouth from which thick liquid dropped, were like glimpses recalled from a long-ago dream . . . Angharad had come close to him; he did not look up to her face. Her right hand pressed his head into her, under the breast. He seemed to smell a mingle of earthily prosperous flowers, sweets and herbs, and warm flesh. She had to pull his head away by the hair.

'Aled,' she said. 'I've kept you too long. You must go home now. You'll be needed.'

'Yes,' he agreed, waking.

'Take these flowers with you?' she suggested.

He shook his head, definitely. 'No; I can't carry flowers through the streets.'

'What!' But she smiled at once, and, walking down the garden with him, only said, 'Men!'

'Bring them up to the house tonight?' he invited, adding, without dubiousness. 'My mother is going to have a baby.'

'Aren't you lucky!' Angharad said, unsurprised. 'When my time comes, you'll be able to advise me how to bring them up.' At the garden gate, she promised, 'I'll come up tonight with the flowers.'

'You can have the prints on Saturday,' he shouted from the slope, waving the camera.

The sun was slipping out of sight. Grey dusk already smudged the valley's far reaches. Soon, the air would stir under the crescent moon's rise, with the evening star sparkling in clear attendance. He hurried, without anxiety.

DAL STIVENS
The Pepper-Tree

My father often spoke about the pepper-tree when we were kids, and it was clear it meant a lot to him. It stood for something—like the Rolls-Royce he was always going to buy. It wasn't what he said about the pepper-tree—my father had no great gift for words—but how he said it that counted. When he spoke of the pepper-tree at Tullama where he had been brought up you saw it clearly; a monster of a tree with long shawls of olive-green leaves in a big generous country-town backyard. 'A decent backyard—none of your city pocket-handkerchief lots,' my father said. There were berries on the tree that turned from green to pink with wax-like covers which you could unpick and get the sticky smell of them all over your fingers. In this spanking tree there was always, too, a noisy traffic of sparrows and starlings fluttering and hopping from branch to branch.

When we lived at Newtown, Sydney, I used to look for pepper-trees when my father took me for a walk on Sunday afternoons. 'Look, there's a pepper-tree,' I'd say to him when I saw one with its herring-bone leaves.

'By golly, boy, that's only a little runt of a tree,' my old man would say. 'They don't do so well in the city. Too much smoke, by golly. You ought to see them out west where I come from.'

My father was a tall, thin man with melancholy brown eyes and the soul of a poet. It was the poet in him that wanted to own a Rolls-Royce one day.

'First our own house and then some day, when my ship comes home, I'll buy a Rolls-Royce,' he'd say.

Some of his friends thought my old man was a little crazy to have such an ambition.

'What would you do with one of those flash cars, Peter?' they'd tease him. 'Go and live among the swells?'

My father would stroke his long brown moustache, which had only a few bits of white in it, and try to explain, but he couldn't make them understand. He couldn't even get his ideas across to my mother. Only now do I think I understand what a Rolls-Royce meant to him.

'I don't want to swank it, as you put it, Emily,' he'd say to my mother. 'No, by golly. I want to own a Rolls-Royce because it is the most perfect piece of machinery made in this world. Why, a Rolls-Royce——'

And then he'd stop and you could feel him groping for the right words to describe what he felt, and then go on blunderingly with the caress of a lover in his voice, talking about how beautiful the engine was. . . .

'What would a garage mechanic do with a Rolls-Royce, I ask you!' my mother would say. 'I'd feel silly sitting up in it.'

At such times my mother would give the wood stove in the kitchen a good shove with the poker, or swish her broom vigorously. My mother was a small plump woman with brown hair which she wore drawn tight back from her forehead.

Like the pepper-tree, the Rolls-Royce symbolized something for my father. He had been born in Tullama in the mallee. His father was a bricklayer and wanted his son to follow him. But my father had had his mind set on becoming an engineer. When he was eighteen he had left Tullama and come to the city and got himself apprenticed to a mechanical engineer. He went to technical classes in the evening. After two years his eyes had given out on him.

'If I had had some money things might have been different, by golly,' my father told me once. 'I could have gone to the university and learnt things properly. I could have become a civil engineer. I didn't give my eyes a fair go—I went to classes five nights a week and studied after I came home.'

After his eyes went, my father had to take unskilled jobs but always near machinery. 'I like tinkering but I had no proper schooling,' he said once.

He knew a lot and in spite of his eyes he could only have learnt most of it from books. He knew all about rocks and how they were formed. He could talk for hours, if you got him started, about fossils and the story of evolution. My mother didn't like to hear him talking about such things because she thought such talk was irreligious. Looking back now I'd say that in spite of his lack of orthodox schooling my father was a learned man. He taught me more than all the teachers I ever had at high school. He was a keen naturalist, too.

Just before the depression came when we were living at Newtown, my father had paid one hundred pounds off the house. He was forty-seven years old then. I was twelve.

'By golly, we'll own the house before we know where we are,' he said.

'Will we?' said my mother. 'At a pound a week we have twelve years to go—unless we win Tatts.'

'You never know what may turn up,' said my old man cheerfully.

'I have a good idea what with people losing their jobs every day.'

'I haven't lost mine,' my father said, 'and what's more, if I do, I have a way of making some money.'

'I suppose it's another of your inventions, Peter? What is it this time, I ask you?'

'Never you mind,' said my father. But he said it gently.

One of my mother's complaints was that my father was always losing money on the things he tried to invent. Another was that he was always filling the backyard up with junk.

'What can you do with these pocket-handkerchief lots?' my father would ay. 'Now, when I was a nipper at Tullama we had a decent backyard—why it was immense—it was as big——'

He'd stop there not being able to get the right word.

Auction sales, according to my mother, were one of my father's weaknesses. He could never resist anything if it looked cheap, even if he had no use for it, she'd say. Soon after my old man had told my mother he had something in mind to make some money, he went away early one Sunday morning. He came back about lunch-time in a motor lorry. On the back of the Ford was a two-stroke kerosene engine. I came running out.

'I've bought it, Joe, by golly,' he told me.

He had, too. Both engine and lorry.

'Dirt cheap. Forty quid the lot,' he said. 'Ten quid down, boy, and ten bob a week.'

My mother cut up when she heard.

'Wasting money when it could have gone into the house, Peter.'

'This'll pay the house off in no time, by golly,' my father said. 'And buy a lot of other things, too.'

I knew by the way he looked up and over my mother's head he was thinking of the Rolls-Royce which to him was like a fine poem or a great symphony of Beethoven.

All that day he was very excited, walking round the engine,

standing back to admire it, and then peering closely at it. He started
it running and stopped it continually all the afternoon. Every night
when he came home from the garage during the next week, he'd go
first thing and look at the engine. He had some plan in his mind
but wouldn't say what it was at first.

'Wait and see, Joe,' he'd said. 'You'll see all right.'

He didn't let me into his secret for over a week, although I knew
he was bursting to tell someone. In the end, he drew me aside
mysteriously in the kitchen one night, when my mother was in the
bedroom, and whispered, 'It's an invention for cleaning out underground wells, boy.'

'For cleaning out wells?'

'Underground wells.'

He listened to hear if my mother was coming back.

'I'm rigging a light out there tonight, boy,' he whispered. 'Come
out later and I'll show you.'

My father's idea, he explained later, was to clean underground
wells in country towns by suction. You pushed a stiff brush on the
end of the pipe down the sides and along the bottom of underground
wells. The pipe sucked up the silt and you didn't lose much water
from the well.

'Every country town has half a dozen underground wells, boy,'
he said. 'The banks and one or two of the wealthier blokes in the
town. Just like it was in Tullama. There's money in it because you
can clean the well out without losing too much water. It's a gold-
mine.'

It sounded good to me.

'When do you start?' I asked.

'Soon, by golly,' he said. 'The job at the garage won't spin out
much longer.'

He was right about that, but until the day she died my mother
always had a sneaking idea that the old man had helped to give
himself the sack. It was early in 1930 when the old man set out in
the lorry, heading out west.

'You've got to go to the low-rainfall districts,' he said.

'like Tullama?' I said.

'Yes, like Tullama, by golly.'

I started thinking of the pepper-tree then.

'Will you go to Tullama and see the pepper-tree?'

My father stroked his long straggling moustache. Into his eyes came that look like when he was thinking or talking about the Rolls. He didn't answer me for a bit.

'By golly, yes, boy, if I go there.'

Soon after this he started off. Every week brought a letter from him. He did well too. He was heading almost due west from Sydney and I followed the towns he spoke of in my school atlas. It took him nearly a day on a well, so in the larger towns he might stay over a week, in the smaller a day or a day and a half.

After he had been away for two months he still had a good few wells to go before he reached Tullama. You could see that he was heading that way.

'Him and that silly pepper-tree!' said my mother, but she didn't say it angrily. My father was sending her as much money as he used to bring home when he worked at the garage.

But in spite of what my mother said about the pepper-tree, she became a bit keen as my father got only two weeks off Tullama. She made a small pin-flag for me to stick on the map. About this time a change came in the old man's letters home. At first they had been elated, but now they were quieter. He didn't boast so much about the money he was making, or say anything about the Rolls. Perhaps excitement was making him quieter as he got nearer to the pepper-tree, I thought.

'I know what it is,' my mother said. 'He's not getting his proper meals. He's too old to be gallivanting off on his own. I bet he's not cooking proper meals for himself. And without a decent bed to sleep in—only the back of that lorry.'

I thought the day would never come, but soon enough my dad had only one town to do before he would reach Tullama. His letters usually arrived on a Tuesday—he wrote home on the Sundays—but round this time I watched for the mail every day and was late for school three mornings running. When a letter did come I grabbed it from the postman's hand and hurried inside with it, reading the post-mark on the run. It was from Tullama.

'All right, all right, don't rush me, Joe,' my mother said. 'You and your pepper-tree.'

I read over her elbow. There was only one page. There was nothing about the pepper-tree. Dad was well and making money, but he was thinking of returning soon. Only a few lines.

I couldn't understand it.

On the next Tuesday there was no letter. Nor on the Wednesday.

On the Thursday my father came home. He turned up at breakfast-time. He gave us a surprise walking in like that. He said that he had sold the truck and engine and come home by train. He looked tired and shamefaced and somehow a lot older. I saw a lot more white in his moustache.

'The engine was no good,' he said. 'It kept breaking down. It cost me nearly all I earned and it was hungry on petrol. I had to sell it to pay back what I borrowed and get my fare home.'

'Oh, Peter,' my mother said, putting her arms round him. 'You poor darling. I knew something was wrong.'

'Mother reckoned it was the food,' I said. 'She reckoned you weren't getting your proper meals.'

'I'll make you a cup of tea, Peter,' my mother said, bustling over to the stove and pushing another piece of wood into it. 'Then I'll get you some breakfast.'

'By golly, that sounds a bit of all right,' my father said then. This was the first time since he had walked in that he had sounded like his old self.

My mother hurried about the kitchen and my father talked a bit more. 'I thought I was going to do well at first,' he said. 'But the engine was too old. It was always spare parts. It ate up all I earned.'

He talked on about the trip. I had got over my surprise at seeing him walk in and now wanted to know all about the pepper-tree.

'Did you see the pepper-tree, dad?'

'Yes, I saw it all right.'

I stood directly in front of him as he sat at the table, but he was not looking at me but at something far away. He didn't answer for what seemed a long time.

'It was a little runt of a tree, boy—and a little backyard.'

He wouldn't say any more than that and he never spoke of the pepper-tree—or the Rolls—again.

H. E. BATES
Great Uncle Crow

ONCE in the summer-time, when the water-lilies were in bloom and
the wheat was new in ear, his grandfather took him on a long walk
up the river, to see his Uncle Crow. He had heard so much of Uncle
Crow, so much that was wonderful and to be marvelled at, and for
such a long time, that he knew him to be, even before that, the most
remarkable fisherman in the world.

'Masterpiece of a man, your Uncle Crow,' his grandfather said.
'He could git a clothes-line any day and tie a brick on it and a
mossel of cake and go out and catch a pike as long as your arm.'

When he asked what kind of cake his grandfather seemed irritated
and said it was just like a boy to ask questions of that sort.

'Any kind o' cake,' he said. 'Plum cake. Does it matter? Caraway
cake. Christmas cake if you like. Anything. I shouldn't wonder if he
could catch a pretty fair pike with a cold baked tater.'

'Only a pike?'

'Times,' his grandfather said, 'I've seen him sittin' on the bank
on a sweltering hot day like a furnace, when nobody was gettin' a
bite not even off a blood-sucker. And there your Uncle Crow'd be
a-pullin' 'em out by the dozen, like a man shellin' harvest beans.'

'And how does he come to be my Uncle Crow?' he said, 'if my
mother hasn't got a brother? Nor my father.'

'Well,' his grandfather said, 'he's really your mother's own
cousin, if everybody had their rights. But all on us call him Uncle
Crow.'

'And where does he live?'

'You'll see,' his grandfather said. 'All by hisself. In a little titty
bit of a house by the river.'

The little titty bit of a house, when he first saw it, surprised him
very much. It was not at all unlike a black tarred boat that had
either slipped down a slope and stuck there on its way to launching
or one that had been washed up and left there in a flood. The roof
of brown tiles had a warp in it and the sides were mostly built, he
thought, of tarred beer-barrels.

The two windows with their tiny panes were about as large as chessboards and Uncle Crow had nailed underneath each of them a sill of sheet tin that was still a brilliant blue, each with the words 'Backache Pills' in white lettering on it, upside down.

On all sides of the house grew tall feathered reeds. They enveloped it like gigantic whispering corn. Some distance beyond the great reeds the river went past in a broad slow arc, on magnificent kingly currents, full of long white islands of water-lilies, as big as china breakfast cups, shining and yellow-hearted in the sun.

He thought, on the whole, that that place, the river with the water-lilies, the little titty bit of a house, and the great forest of reeds talking between soft brown beards, was the nicest he had ever seen.

'Anybody about?' his grandfather called. 'Crow!—anybody at home?'

The door of the house was partly open, but at first there was no answer. His grandfather pushed open the door still farther with his foot. The reeds whispered down by the river and were answered, in the house, by a sound like the creak of bed springs.'

'Who is't?'

'It's me, Crow,' his grandfather called. 'Lukey. Brought the boy over to have a look at you.'

A big gangling red-faced man with rusty hair came to the door. His trousers were black and very tight. His eyes were a smeary vivid blue, the same colour as the stripes of his shirt, and his trousers were kept up by a leather belt with brass escutcheons on it, like those on horses' harness.

'Thought very like you'd be out a-pikin',' his grandfather said.

'Too hot. How's Lukey boy? Ain't seed y'lately, Lukey boy.'

His lips were thick and very pink and wet, like cow's lips. He made a wonderful erupting jolly sound somewhat between a belch and a laugh.

'Comin' in it a minute?'

In the one room of the house was an iron bed with an old red check horse-rug spread over it and a stone copper in one corner and a bare wooden table with dirty plates and cups and a tin kettle on it. Two osier baskets and a scythe stood in another corner.

Uncle Crow stretched himself full length on the bed as if he was very tired. He put his knees in the air. His belly was tight as a bladder of lard in his black trousers, which were mossy green on the knees and seat.

'How's the fishin'?' his grandfather said. 'I bin tellin' the boy——'

Uncle Crow belched deeply. From where the sun struck full on the tarred wall of the house there was a hot whiff of baking tar. But when Uncle Crow belched there was a smell like the smell of yeast in the air.

'It ain't been all that much of a summer yit,' Uncle Crow said. 'Ain't had the rain.'

'Not like that summer you catched the big 'un down at Archer's Mill. I recollect you a-tellin' on me——'

'Too hot and dry by half,' Uncle Crow said. 'Gits in your gullet like chaff.'

'You recollect that summer?' his grandfather said. 'Nobody else a-fetching on 'em out only you——'

'Have a drop o' neck-oil,' Uncle Crow said.

The boy wondered what neck-oil was and presently, to his surprise, Uncle Crow and his grandfather were drinking it. It came out of a dark-green bottle and it was a clear bright amber, like cold tea, in the two glasses.

'The medder were yeller with 'em,' Uncle Crow said. 'Yeller as a guinea.'

He smacked his lips with a marvellously juicy, fruity sound. The boy's grandfather gazed at the neck-oil and said he thought it would be a corker if it was kept a year or two, but Uncle Crow said:

'Trouble is, Lukey boy, it's a terrible job to keep it. You start tastin' on it to see if it'll keep and then you taste on it again and you go on tastin' on it until they ain't a drop left as'll keep.'

Uncle Crow laughed so much that the bed springs cackled underneath his bouncing trousers.

'Why is it called neck-oil?' the boy said.

'Boy,' Uncle Crow said, 'when you git older, when you git growed-up, you know what'll happen to your gullet?'

'No.'

'It'll git sort o' rusted up inside. Like a old gutter pipe. So's you can't swaller very easy. Rusty as old Harry it'll git. You know that, boy?'

'No.'

'Well, it will. I'm tellin' on y'. And you know what y' got to do then?'

'No.'

'Every now and then you gotta git a drop o' neck-oil down it. So's to ease it. A drop o' neck-oil every once in a while—that's what you gotta do to keep the rust out.'

The boy was still contemplating the curious prospect of his neck rusting up inside in later years when Uncle Crow said: 'Boy, you got outside and jis' round the corner you'll see a bucket. You bring handful o' cresses out on it. I'll bet you're hungry, ain't you?'

'A little bit.'

He found the watercresses in the bucket, cool in the shadow of the little house, and when he got back inside with them Uncle Crow said:

'Now you put the cresses on that there plate there and then put your nose inside that there basin and see what's inside. What is't, eh?'

'Eggs.'

'Ought to be fourteen on 'em. Four-apiece and two over. What sort are they, boy?'

'Moor-hens'.'

'You got a knowin' boy here, Lukey,' Uncle Crow said. He dropped the scaly red lid of one eye like an old cockerel going to sleep. He took another drop of neck-oil and gave another fruity, juicy laugh as he heaved his body from the bed. 'A very knowin' boy.'

Presently he was carving slices of thick brown bread with a great horn-handled shut-knife and pasting each slice with summery golden butter. Now and then he took another drink of neck-oil and once he said:

'You get the salt pot, boy, and empty a bit out on that there saucer, so's we can all dip in.'

Uncle Crow slapped the last slice of bread on to the buttered pile and then said:

'Boy, you take that there jug there and go a step or two up the path and dip yourself a drop o' spring water. You'll see it. It comes out of a little bit of a wall, jist by a doddle-willer.'

When the boy got back with the jug of spring water Uncle Crow was opening another bottle of neck-oil and his grandfather was saying: 'God a-mussy man, goo steady. You'll have me agoin' one way and another——'

'Man alive,' Uncle Crow said, 'and what's wrong with that?'

Then the watercress, the salt, the moor-hens' eggs, the spring water, and the neck-oil were all ready. The moor-hens' eggs were hard-boiled. Uncle Crow lay on the bed and cracked them with his teeth, just like big brown nuts, and said he thought the watercress was just about as nice and tender as a young lady.

'I'm sorry we ain't got the gold plate out though. I had it out a-Sunday.' He closed his old cockerel-lidded eye again and licked his tongue backwards and forwards across his lips and dipped another peeled egg in salt. 'You know what I had for my dinner a-Sunday, boy?'

'No.'

'A pussy-cat on a gold plate. Roasted with broad-beans and new taters. Did you ever heerd talk of anybody eatin' a roasted pussy-cat, boy?'

'Yes.'

'You did.'

'Yes,' he said, 'that's a hare.'

'You got a very knowin' boy here, Lukey,' Uncle Crow said. 'A very knowin' boy.'

Then he screwed up a big dark-green bouquet of watercress and dipped it in salt until it was entirely frosted and then crammed it in one neat wholesale bite into his soft pink mouth.

'But not on a gold plate?' he said.

He had to admit that.

'No, not on a gold plate,' he said.

All that time he thought the fresh watercress, the moor-hens' eggs, the brown bread-and-butter, and the spring water were the most delicious, wonderful things he had ever eaten in the world. He felt that only one thing was missing. It was that whenever his grandfather spoke of fishing Uncle Crow simply took another draught of neck-oil.

'When are you goin' to take us fishing?' he said.

'You et up that there egg,' Uncle Crow said. 'That's the last one. You et that there egg up and I'll tell you what.'

'What about gooin' as far as that big deep hole where the chub lay?' grandfather said. 'Up by the back-brook——'

'I'll tell you what, boy,' Uncle Crow said, 'you git your grand-father to bring you over September time, of a morning, afore the steam's off the winders. Mushroomin' time. You come over and we'll have a bit o' bacon and mushroom for breakfast and then set into the pike. You see, boy, it ain't the pikin' season now. It's too hot. Too bright. It's too bright of afternoon, and they ain't a-bitin'.'

He took a long rich swig of neck-oil.

'Ain't that it, Lukey? That's the time, ain't it, mushroom time?'

'Thass it,' his grandfather said.

'Tot out,' Uncle Crow said. 'Drink up. My throat's jist easin' orf a bit.'

He gave another wonderful belching laugh and told the boy to be sure to finish up the last of the watercress and the bread-and-butter. The little room was rich with the smell of neck-oil, and the tarry sun-baked odour of the beer-barrels that formed its walls. And through the door came, always, the sound of reeds talking in their beards, and the scent of summer meadows drifting in from beyond the great curl of the river with its kingly currents and its islands of full blown lilies, white and yellow in the sun.

'I see the wheat's in ear,' his grandfather said. 'Ain't that the time for tench, when the wheat's in ear?'

'Mushroom time,' Uncle Crow said. 'That's the time. You git mushroom time here, and I'll fetch you a tench out as big as a cricket bat.'

He fixed the boy with an eye of wonderful, watery, glassy blue and licked his lips with a lazy tongue, and said:

'You know what colour a tench is, boy?'

'Yes,' he said.

'What colour?'

'The colour of the neck-oil.'

'Lukey,' Uncle Crow said, 'you got a very knowin' boy here. A very knowin' boy.'

After that, when there were no more cresses or moor-hens' eggs, or bread-and-butter to eat, and his grandfather said he'd get hung if he touched another drop of neck-oil, he and his grandfather walked home across the meadows.

'What work does Uncle Crow do?' he said.

'Uncle Crow? Work?—well, he ain't—Uncle Crow? Well, he works, but he ain't what you'd call a reg'lar worker——'

All the way home he could hear the reeds talking in their beards. He could see the water-lilies that reminded him so much of the gold and white inside the moor-hens' eggs. He could hear the happy sound of Uncle Crow laughing and sucking at the neck-oil, and crunching the fresh salty cresses into his mouth in the tarry little room.

He felt happy, too, and the sun was a gold plate in the sky.

MORLEY CALLAGHAN
The Runaway

In the lumber-yard by the lake there was an old brick building two storeys high and all around the foundations were heaped great piles of soft sawdust, softer than the thick moss in the woods. There were many of these golden mounds of dust covering that part of the yard right down to the blue lake. That afternoon all the fellows followed Michael up the ladder to the roof of the old building and they sat with their legs hanging over the edge looking out at the whitecaps on the water. Michael was younger than some of them but he was much bigger, his legs were long, his huge hands dangled awkwardly at his sides and his thick black hair curled up all over his head. 'I'll stump you all to jump down,' he said suddenly, and without thinking about it, he shoved himself off the roof and fell on the sawdust where he lay rolling around and laughing.

'You're all stumped,' he shouted, 'You're all yellow,' he said, coaxing them to follow him. Still laughing, he watched them looking down from the roof, white-faced and hesitant, and then one by one they jumped and got up grinning with relief.

In the hot afternoon sunlight they all lay on the sawdust pile telling jokes till at last one of the fellows said, 'Come on up on the old roof again and jump down.' There wasn't much enthusiasm among them, but they all went up to the roof again and began to jump off in a determined, desperate way till only Michael was left and the others were all down below grinning up at him and calling, 'Come on, Mike. What's the matter with you?' Michael longed to jump down there and be with them, but he remained on the edge of the roof, wetting his lips, with a silly grin on his face, wondering why it had not seemed such a long drop the first time. For a while they thought he was only kidding them, then they saw him clenching his fists. He was trying to count to ten and then jump, and when that failed, he tried to take a long breath and close his eyes.

In a while the fellows began to jeer at him; they were tired of waiting and it was getting on to dinner-time. 'Come on, you're yellow, do you think we're going to sit here all night?' they began to shout, and when he did not move they began to get up and walk away, still jeering. 'Who did this in the first place? What's the matter with you guys?' he shouted.

But for a long time he remained on the edge of the roof, starring unhappily and steadily at the ground. He remained all alone for nearly an hour while the sun like a great orange ball getting bigger and bigger rolled slowly over the gray line beyond the lake. His clothes were wet from nervous sweating. At last he closed his eyes, slipped off the roof, fell heavily on the pile of sawdust and lay there a long time. There were no sounds in the yard, the workmen had gone home. As he lay there he wondered why he had been unable to move; and then he got up slowly and walked home feeling deeply ashamed and wanting to avoid everybody.

He was so late for dinner that his stepmother said to him sarcastically, 'You're big enough by this time surely to be able to get home in time for dinner. But if you won't come home, you'd better try staying in tonight.' She was a well-built woman with a fair, soft skin and a little touch of gray in her hair and an eternally patient smile on her face. She was speaking now with a restrained, passionless severity, but Michael, with his dark face gloomy and sullen, hardly heard her; he was still seeing the row of grinning faces down below on the sawdust pile and hearing them jeer at him.

As he ate his cold dinner he was rolling his brown eyes fiercely and sometimes shaking his big black head. His father, who was sitting in the armchair by the window, a huge man with his hair nearly all gone so that his smooth wide forehead rose in a beautiful shining dome, kept looking at him steadily. When Michael had finished eating and had gone out to the veranda, his father followed, sat down beside him, lit his pipe and said gently, 'What's bothering you, son?'

'Nothing, Dad. There's nothing bothering me,' Michael said, but he kept on staring out at the gray dust drifting off the road.

His father kept coaxing and whispering in a voice that was amazingly soft for such a big man. As he talked, his long fingers played with the heavy gold watch fob on his vest. He was talking about nothing in particular and yet by the tone of his voice he was expressing a marvellous deep friendliness that somehow seemed to become a part of the twilight and then of the darkness. And Michael began to like the sound of his father's voice, and soon he blurted out, 'I guess by this time all the guys around here are saying I'm yellow. I'd like to be a thousand miles away.' He told how he could

not force himself to jump off the roof the second time. But his father
lay back in the armchair laughing in that hearty, rolling, easy way
that Michael loved to hear; years ago when Michael had been
younger and he was walking along the paths in the evening, he used
to try and laugh like his father only his voice was not deep enough
and he would grin sheepishly and look up at the trees overhanging
the paths as if someone hiding up there had heard him. 'You'll be
all right with the bunch, son,' his father was saying, 'I'm betting
you'll lick any boy in town that says you're yellow.'

But there was the sound of the screen door opening, and
Michael's stepmother said in her mild, firm way, 'If I've rebuked
the boy, Henry, as I think he ought to be rebuked, I don't know
why you should be humouring him.'

'You surely don't object to me talking to Michael.'

'I simply want you to be reasonable, Henry.'

In his grave, unhurried way Mr Lount got up and followed his
wife into the house and soon Michael could hear them arguing; he
could hear his father's firm, patient voice floating clearly out to the
street; then his stepmother's voice, mild at first, rising, becoming
hysterical till at last she cried out wildly, 'You're setting the boy
against me. You don't want him to think of me as his mother. The
two of you are against me. I know your nature.'

As he looked up and down the street fearfully, Michael began to
make prayers that no one would pass by who would think, 'Mr.
And Mrs. Lount are quarrelling again.' Alert, he listened for faint
sounds on the cinder path, but he heard only the frogs croaking
under the bridge opposite Stevenson's place and the far-away cry of
a freight train passing behind the hills. 'Why did Dad have to get
married? It used to be swell on the farm,' he thought, remembering
how he and his father had gone fishing down at the glen. And then
while he listened to the sound of her voice, he kept thinking that his
stepmother was a fine woman, only she always made him uneasy
because she wanted him to like her, and then when she found out
that he couldn't think of her as his mother, she had grown resentful.
'I like her and I like my father. I don't know why they quarrel.
They're really such fine people. Maybe it's because Dad shouldn't
have sold the farm and moved here. There's nothing for him to do.'
Unable to get interested in the town life, his father loafed all day
down at the hotel or in Bailey's flour-and-feed store but he was such
a fine-looking, dignified, reticent man that the loafers would not

accept him as a crony. Inside the house now, Mrs. Lount was crying quietly and saying, 'Henry, we'll kill each other. We seem to bring out all the very worst qualities in each other. I do all I can and yet you both make me feel like an intruder.'

'It's just your imagination, Martha. Now stop worrying.'

'I'm an unhappy woman. But I try to be patient. I try so hard, don't I, Henry?'

'You're very patient, dear, but you shouldn't be so suspicious of everyone and everybody, don't you see?' Mr. Lount was saying in the soothing voice of a man trying to pacify an angry and hysterical wife.

Then Michael heard footsteps on the cinder path, and then he saw two long shadows flung across the road: two women were approaching, and one was a tall, slender girl. When Michael saw this girl, Helen Murray, he tried to duck behind the veranda post, for he had always wanted her for his girl. He had gone to school with her. At night-time he used to lie awake planning remarkable feats that would so impress her she would never want to be far away from him. Now the girl's mother was calling, 'Hello there, Michael,' in a very jolly voice.

'Hello, Mrs. Murray,' he said glumly, for he was sure his father's or his mother's voice would rise again.

'Come on and walk home with us, Michael,' Helen called. Her voice sounded so soft and her face in the dusk light seemed so round, white and mysteriously far away that Michael began to ache with eagerness. Yet he said hurriedly, 'I can't. I can't tonight,' speaking almost rudely as if he believed they only wanted to tease him.

As they went on along the path and he watched them, he was really longing for that one bright moment when Helen would pass under the high corner light, though he was thinking with bitterness that he could already hear them talking, hear Mrs. Murray saying, 'He's a peculiar boy, but it's not to be wondered at since his father and mother don't get along at all,' and the words were floating up to the verandas of all the houses: inside one of the houses someone had stopped playing a piano, maybe to hear one of the fellows who had been in the lumber-yard that afternoon laughing and telling that young Lount was scared to jump off the roof.

Still watching the corner, Michael suddenly felt that the twisting and pulling in the life in the house was twisting and choking him.

'I'll get out of here, I'll go away,' and he began to think of going to the city. He began to long for freedom in strange places where everything was new and fresh and mysterious. His heart began to beat heavily at the thought of this freedom. In the city he had an Uncle Joe who sailed the lake-boats in the summer months and in the winter went all over the south from one race-track to another following the horses. 'I ought to go down to the city tonight and get a job,' he thought: but he did not move; he was still waiting for Helen Murray to pass under the light.

For most of the next day, too, Michael kept to himself. He was up-town once on a message, and he felt like running on the way home. With long sweeping strides he ran steadily on the paths past the shipyard, the church, the railway tracks, his face serious with determination.

But in the late afternoon when he was sitting on the veranda reading, Sammy Schwartz and Ike Hershfield came around to see him. 'Hello Mike, what's new with you?' they said, sitting on the steps very seriously.

'Hello, Sammy, hello, Ike. What's new with you?'

They began to talk to Michael about the coloured family that had moved into the old roughcast shack down by the tracks. 'The big coon kid thinks he's tough,' Sammy said. 'He offered to beat up any of us so we said he wouldn't have a snowball's chance with you.'

'What did the nigger say?'

'He said he'd pop you one right on the nose if you came over his way.'

'Come on, guys. Let's go over there,' Michael said. 'I'll tear his guts out for you.'

They went out to the street, fell in step very solemnly, and walked over to the field by the tracks without saying a word. When they were about fifty paces away from the shack, Sammy said, 'Wait here. I'll go get the coon,' and he ran on to the unpainted door of the whitewashed house calling, 'Oh, Art, oh, Art, come on out.' A big coloured boy with closely cropped hair came out and put his hand up, shading his eyes from the sun. Then he went back into the house and came out again with a big straw hat on his head. He was in his bare feet. The way he came walking across the field with Sammy was always easy to remember because he hung back a little, talking rapidly, shrugging his shoulders and rolling the whites of his eyes. When he came close to Michael he grinned nervously, flashing his teeth, and said, 'What's the matter with you white boys? I don't want to do no fighting.' He looked scared.

'Come on. Get ready. I'm going to do a nice job on you,' Michael said.

The coloured boy took off his big straw hat and with great care laid it on the ground while all the time he was looking mournfully across the field and at his house, hoping maybe that somebody would come out. Then they started to fight, and Michael knocked him down four times, but he, himself, got a black eye and a cut lip. The coloured boy had been so brave and he seemed so alone, licked and lying on the ground, that they sat down around him praising him, making friends with him and gradually finding out that he was a good ball player, a left-handed pitcher who specialized in a curve ball, and they agreed they could use him, maybe, on the town team.

Lying there in the field, flat on his back, Michael liked it so much that he almost did not want to go away. Art, the coloured boy, was telling how he had always wanted to be a jockey but had got too big; he had a brother who could make the weight. So Michael began to boast about his Uncle Joe who went around to all the tracks in the winter making and losing money at places like Saratoga, Blue Bonnets and Tia Juana. It was a fine, friendly, eager discussion about far-away places.

It was nearly dinner-time when Michael got home; he went in the house sucking his cut lip and hoping his mother would not notice his black eye. But he heard no movement in the house. In the kitchen he saw his stepmother kneeling down in the middle of the floor with her hands clasped and her lips moving.

'What's the matter, Mother?' he asked.

'I'm praying,' she said.

'What for?'

'For your father. Get down and pray with me.'

'I don't want to pray, Mother.'

'You've got to,' she said.

'My lip's all cut. It's bleeding, I can't do it,' he said.

Late afternoon sunshine coming through the kitchen window shone on his stepmother's graying hair, on her soft smooth skin and on the gentle, patient expression that was on her face. At that moment Michael thought that she was desperately uneasy and terribly alone, and he felt sorry for her even while he was rushing out of the back door.

He saw his father walking toward the woodshed, walking slow and upright with his hands held straight at his sides and with the same afternoon sunlight shining so brightly on the high dome of his forehead. He went right into the woodshed without looking back. Michael sat down on the steps and waited. He was afraid to follow. Maybe it was because of the way his father was walking with his head held up and his hands straight at his sides. Michael began to make a small desperate prayer that his father should suddenly appear at the woodshed door.

Time dragged slowly. A few doors away Mrs. McCutcheon was feeding her hens who were clucking as she called them. 'I can't sit here till it gets dark,' Michael was thinking, but he was afraid to go into the woodshed and afraid to think of what he feared.

So he waited till he could not keep a picture of the interior of the shed out of his thoughts, a picture that included his father walking in with his hands as though strapped at his sides and his head stiff, like a man they were going to hang.

'What's he doing in there, what's he doing?' Michael said out loud, and he jumped up and rushed to the shed and flung the door wide.

His father was sitting on a pile of wood with his head on his hands and a kind of beaten look on his face. Still scared, Michael called out, 'Dad, Dad,' and then he felt such relief he sank down on the pile of wood beside his father and looked up at him.

'What's the matter with you, son?'

'Nothing. I guess I just wondered where you were.'

'What are you upset about?'

'I've been running. I feel all right.'

So they sat there quietly till it seemed time to go into the house. No one said anything. No one noticed Michael's black eye or his cut lip.

Even after they had eaten Michael could not get rid of the fear within him, a fear of something impending. In a way he felt that he ought to do something at once, but he seemed unable to move; it was like sitting on the edge of the roof yesterday, afraid to make the jump. So he went back of the house and sat on the stoop and for a long time looked at the shed till he grew even more uneasy. He heard the angry drilling of a woodpecker and the quiet rippling of the little water flowing under the street bridge and flowing on down over the rocks into the glen. Heavy clouds were sweeping up from the horizon.

He knew now that he wanted to run away, that he could not stay there any longer, only he couldn't make up his mind to go. Within him was that same breathless feeling he had had when he sat on the roof staring down, trying to move. Now he walked around to the front of the house and kept going along the path as far as Helen Murray's house. After going around to the back door, he stood for a long time staring at the lighted window, hoping to see Helen's shadow or her body moving against the light. He was breathing deeply and smelling the rich heavy odours from the flower garden. With his head thrust forward he whistled softly.

'Is that you, Michael?' Helen called from the door.

'Come on out, Helen.'

'What do you want?'

'Come on for a walk, will you?'

'For a moment she hesitated at the door, then she came toward him, floating in her white organdie party dress over the grass toward him. She was saying, 'I'm dressed to go out. I can't go with you. I'm going down to the dance hall.'

'Who with?'

'Charlie Delaney.'

'Oh, all right,' he said. 'I just thought you might be doing nothing.' As he walked away he called back to her, 'So long, Helen.'

It was then, on the way back to the house, that he felt he had to go away at once. 'I've got to go. I'll die here. I'll write to Dad from the city.'

No one paid any attention to him when he returned to the house. His father and stepmother were sitting quietly in the living-room reading the paper. In his own room he took a little wooden box from the bottom drawer of his dresser and emptied it of twenty dollars and seventy cents, all that he had saved. He listened solemnly for sounds in the house, then he stuffed a clean shirt into his pocket, a comb, and a toothbrush.

Outside he hurried along with his great swinging strides, going past the corner house, on past the long fence and the bridge and the church, and the shipyard, and past the last of the town lights to the highway. He was walking stubbornly with his face looking solemn and dogged. Then he saw the moonlight shining on the hay stacked in the fields, and when he smelled the oats and the richer smell of sweet clover he suddenly felt alive and free. Headlights from cars kept sweeping by and already he was imagining he could see the haze of bright light hanging over the city. His heart began to thump with eagerness. He put out his hand for a lift, feeling full of hope. He looked across the fields at the dark humps, cows standing motionless in the night. Soon someone would stop and pick him up. They would take him among a million new faces, rumbling sounds, and strange smells. He got more excited. His Uncle Joe might get him a job on the boats for the rest of the summer; maybe, too, he might be able to move around with him in the winter. Over and over he kept thinking of places with beautiful names, places like Tia Juana, Woodbine, Saratoga and Blue Bonnets.

NORAH LOFTS
Forty Years On

JOHN BULLYER and I met for the first time in 1956 when we were both in our early sixties, but it is true to say that he did more to shape my life than any other person, and is largely responsible for the diffidence which has, I know, been a handicap to me, though I am told that I conceal it very well.

John Bullyer came into my life when my Uncle George, who lived close by us, married, rather late in life, a most delightful woman who thus became my Aunt Carrie and quite my favourite relative. In those days wholesale indulgence of the young had not yet come into full fashion, and a pretty aunt always free with caresses, sweets, words of praise and excuses for misdoings was something of a rarity and greatly to be treasured. For me she had but one drawback; she was also aunt to John Bullyer, the son of her sister who lived in Gloucestershire. She invariably referred to him as 'Little-John-my-other-nephew' all in one word, and she referred to him far too often.

Later in my life I could see her motive; she came to us as a stranger; my mother was a relative by marriage, a near neighbour and a potential friend; we children were common ground, a safe topic for those early, difficult conversations over the teacups.

From Aunt Carrie's point of view it was fortunate, from mine, disastrous, that John Bullyer and I were of comparable age, practically twins, in fact, having been born within four days of one another. Probably hundreds of comparisons were made before I became aware of them. The first that I remember with any clarity was made soon after I began school where I had lain on the floor and wailed that I wanted to go home. Shortly after that my mother reported in a voice that was to become all too familiar, that Little-John-Aunt-Carrie's-other-nephew had started school on the same day and taken to it like a duck to water.

And so it went on. Incredible boy, he knew his nine-times table, while I was still hopelessly bogged in the fours; he was dealing expertly with fractions what time I wrestled unsuccessfully with tens and units. I began to dread Aunt Carrie's erstwhile most welcome visits. She was still just as pretty and gay, still as sweet-smelling, still ready to take part in any childish game, to be enthusiastic about any pursuit, certain to produce chocolate or sixpence from her reticule; but as soon as she had gone, Mother was sure to say the dread words:

'Aunt Carrie was telling me that John Bullyer . . .'

The comparisons were, without exception, to my detriment. The wretched boy never set foot upon a football field without scoring a goal; never took bat in hand without making some notable number of runs. I was hopeless at games; at football I fell in the mud, and caught a cold which became bronchial; at cricket I made ducks, dropped easy catches and was afflicted with nose-bleeding. I became so conscious of my inferiority that even when I overheard my parents speak of John Bullyer as 'The Child Wonder' I never even suspected the irony; I took it literally and believed that they regarded him with the same awe and envy as I did.

To me it seemed sinister that Mother always passed on, with pitiable pride, any small achievement of mine. Once, at my prep. school, I had a story in the magazine and Mother was momentarily jubilant.

'I must have another copy of that,' she said, 'so that Aunt Carrie can send it for John Bullyer's mother to see.' What a boomerang that proved! By return of post came the news that John had won a scholarship.

To anyone now on the bright side of forty it will seem strange that we boys never met, but in those days Gloucestershire was as far removed, in travelling time, from Suffolk, as New York is today, and my father was a man who preferred his own bed to any other. Aunt Carrie kept saying, 'Really, you boys should know one another, I'm sure you'd be such friends,' and once or twice she tried to arrange that John should stay with her in the holidays. Mercifully for me something always prevented him from doing so.

I did have, however, one horribly narrow escape. An elderly couple, distant relatives of my father's, were celebrating their Golden Wedding. They lived in London, reasonably accessible, and they issued such a pressing, sentimentally-worded invitation that even Father was bound to accept. As soon as he had done so Aunt Carrie came over in a state of high excitement. Wasn't the world a small place, the Bullyer family and Father's old relatives had once been near neighbours and all three Bullyers had been bidden to the feast.

I saw my mother look at me, not, I admit, with any lessening of affection, but with a strange, anxious appraisement. When Aunt Carrie had gone Mother said to me:

'You sit there huddled over a book until your back is bent like a bow. Go out and get some air.' I stood up, obediently, and she added, 'Oh, I wish the sun would shine; you look so much better with a little tan.' I realised from that that she and I visualised John Bullyer in the same way, tall, big for his age, straight as a ram-rod, with a handsome brown face and hair like the man pictured on Father's bottle of hair tonic.

Walking made no perceptible difference to my posture and the sun remained disobliging, so Mother, like the practical believer in self-help that she was, tried another tack:

'You'll need a new suit at Easter anyway, you might as well have it now. *And* I'm going to find a different barber. I *cannot* believe that that piece of hair would stick up like that if it were properly cut.'

It was plain to me that I was repulsive to look at as well as being a clown at games and a booby at arithmetic.

On the evening before we were to make our early morning start for London, Mother came into my room and made me try on the new suit. I could see, by the expression on her face, that it worked no miracle. Nor, alas, had the new barber. But Mother did not take defeat easily; looks weren't everything, my manners, at least, should pass muster! So while I glumly divested myself of the wasted suit, she gave me a few final instructions. I kept saying, 'Yes, Mother' and 'No, Mother', and 'I'll remember, Mother', and gritted my teeth together until my jaws ached.

'Have you anything in your mouth *now*?' she demanded.

'No, Mother.'

'Well, hurry into bed and get a good night's sleep.' (Everything looks better in the morning!) She kissed me, fondly, but at the same time she stroked down the obstinate tuft of hair. I felt exactly like a very ugly dog of low pedigree which some doting owner has entered for a show!

I did not sleep well; I had, in fact, the worst night I had ever known. Although I had ceased gritting my teeth my jaws still ached. The pain spread up into my head, back into my ears, down into my throat. With the covers over me I broke into a hot sweat, when I pushed them off deadly chills shook me. In addition to my physical woes I had mental agonies, including that first sad loss of simple faith; I had prayed, as never before, that something might occur to prevent this meeting. The smallest excuse would have served; Father was already regretting his acceptance, he would have seized gladly at any chance to retract it.

I saw the dawn that morning, watched my window grow grey, heard the first bird chorus. After several centuries had dragged by I heard the strident alarm go off in my parents' room and thankfully rose from my bed of torment. I felt little, if any, better when I was on my feet. I washed more thoroughly than usual, hopefully plunging the whole of my stuffy-feeling head into the cold water; then I dressed and, in honour of the occasion, went to the looking glass to arrange my tie. For a moment, I swear, I thought that nervousness had affected my eyesight; the face that looked back at me was a dreadful caricature of my own, only just recognisable. My ears, ordinarily so prominent, were hidden by the bulge of my jaws and I seemed to have no neck.

Horrified I reeled into my parents' room; Mother was settling a beribboned corset-cover over her bosom and Father was gloomily stropping his razor.

'Do *you* think I look funny this morning?' I blurted.

They both turned. Mother screamed. Father said:

'I wouldn't say *funny*. You look damned peculiar.'

It was mumps. It left me very open-minded about prayer.

Aunt Carrie thought it a great pity that John and I could not go to the same public school; I was spared that by the intransigence of our respective fathers. Harrow, in its charity, accepted my unpromising self; John took his talents to Winchester.

Time went on; so did the comparisons. By word of mouth during the holidays, by phrases that leaped out of letters during term time, I was kept up to date with John's prowess and progress. Thus goaded I began at last to look round for something that I *could* do, something at which I could excel. When I found it I worked with a savage intensity, minding nothing else; let this be mine, John Bullyer could have all the rest.

I was, however, still a Grub Street hack, counting it a good week in which I made five pounds, when John attained some glittering appointment in India. That ability to master the nine-times table had proved no flash-in-the-pan; he had developed into some kind of financial wizard and was now being 'lent' to the Maharajah of a native state whose exchequer was in a deplorable tangle. There was a paragraph in the daily papers about it.

Aunt Carrie took the cutting to show to my mother. I was glad later that she had that pleasure, for that was her last visit, her last report. She was dead before her other nephew reached his destination. The line which had for so many years vibrated between Gloucestershire and Suffolk was lifeless and dumb.

Three or four times during the next forty years I saw mention of John Bullyer in the press. His was not the kind of career to attract much publicity but those rare paragraphs charted a steady success which culminated in a knighthood when he retired in 1956. On that occasion there was a half column about him; it said that his last job, the handling of some currency crisis in a young South American Republic, had forestalled a revolution. When asked, in an interview, what he intended to do with his leisure, Sir John replied, 'I hope to take up golf; I have never had time to take it seriously.' I pictured him again, lean and tanned, with a head of well kept grey hair, getting his handicap down in record time. I was sorry that Aunt Carrie could not cut out that half column, sorry too that there was no photograph; I could have looked at it almost unflinching, I thought. I was, by that time, not unsuccessful in my own line.

Late that year, in November, I was in my club, sipping a glass of sherry before dinner. A rather deprecating cough at my elbow made me look round. I saw a short stout man, a round dumpling of a man, glitteringly bald, with a little snub nose that looked too small to support the framework of his heavy glasses. They were of that peculiarly thick kind which reduce the eyes to pin-points. Diffidently, with more than a suggestion of a stammer, he spoke my name and I somewhat grudgingly admitted my identity. Since I attained some measure of fame I have on occasion been accosted by strangers and no matter how flatteringly they speak I am always horribly embarrassed.

'You d-don't know m-me,' said the little man. 'My name's John B-Bullyer. We once sh-shared an aunt, C-Caroline Lacey.'

I leaped up and shook hands, expressing my pleasure at meeting him at last, and then we settled down to drink sherry together. His stammer, like my shyness, soon wore off.

'I used to hear so *much* about you,' he said with a grin. 'Then I learned that you were a member here and I could not resist asking someone to point you out to me. Though, if you'd looked the least bit as I always imagined I don't think I'd have d-dared to approach you. You see . . . I grew up with the idea that you were at least eight feet tall, tremendously handsome and more talented than da Vinci.' His grin broadened—and I knew why! 'Really,' he said, 'the letters Aunt Carrie used to write about you and the way my mother used to read them out. You were the b-bug-bear of my life.'

'They were nothing,' I said, 'to the letters *your* mother used to write about *you*. I was told every time you got a sum right. I always thought of you as nine feet high, better looking than Robert Taylor and more versatile than Churchill. So they played the game both ways, did they?'

We laughed.

'But it was worse for me,' he said. 'I've always been undersized, and I always had these.' He touched his glasses. 'And there were you, tall and handsome, with *such* nice manners. And so clever too. I had to do something; and all I could ever do was sums, and jolly well kill myself at games in an effort to be popular. I might almost say,' he said, with something like resentment, 'that because of you I've been doing sums all my life!'

'Substitute spinning yarns for doing sums and you have exactly my story,' I said.

We looked at one another. Then it probably dawned on us both that the place in which we sat is not the haunt of men who have been failures in life, and that, boys being what they are, an occasional prod in the rear is no such bad thing. Together we lifted our glasses, and though neither of us spoke, I know that we drank to the memory of Aunt Carrie.

BILL NAUGHTON
Late Night on Watling Street

IT was after midnight when I drew my lorry on to the parking ground in front of 'Lew's' caff. I switched off the engine and lights, got out of the cab, knew it would be safe without locking it up, and stretched my limbs and looked up at the sky. It was all starry. The air had a nice fresh rinsed taste to it. I walked round the wagon and kicked my tyres, testing the ropes round my load, and with that nice week-end feeling you get on a Friday night, I went inside.

It was nearly empty. I went up to the counter. Ethel, Lew's young wife, was making a fresh pot of tea, and Lew was watching her. I heard him say: 'Make it any stronger an' you'll hatta serve it with knives and forks.'

'I can't stand the sight of weak tea,' said Ethel.

'You can get it a good colour without putting all that much in,' said Lew.

'It's not colour a man wants,' said Ethel, 'it's body.' She winked at me. 'Eh, Bolton?'

Lew hadn't seen me listening, and he tried to laugh it off. I didn't take much notice of him. I never do. He's turned fifty, has a thin face with red cheeks and sandy hair. He always wears a big jersey with a polo collar, a check cap, and sandals, and he always has a fag in his mouth. Box? You could blow him over. But during the war, with all the shortage of food and fags, he suddenly found himself important, like most little shopkeepers and café owners and he started giving orders, and took to wearing this boxer's rig-out. I hate fakes and show-offs, and Lew's one. But maybe he's not a bad bloke at heart, for they say he's good for a touch if you're short of cash. But I can never forget that he used to put soda in his tea urn, and I blame that for the guts' ache I used to get. That was before he married Ethel.

I said nothing to Ethel except to give her my usual warm nod and wink, and then I ordered a large tea, and asked could I have some egg and chips.

'Yes,' said Lew. 'She's got the chip pan all ready.'

'I'll bring your tea over,' said Ethel.

I knew he was getting at her over something. And I'd a good idea what it was—a driver called Jackson. Ethel wouldn't shut shop until he'd been. I said nothing because I reckoned I was lucky to get my egg and chips. Practically the only spot in the British Isles you could get them on a Friday night at that hour. I walked across to the big table where Taff and Ned were sitting, and sat at one end.

'I see old Babyface is out on the scout again,' said Taff.

'That dirty little bleeder,' said Ned. 'I've known many a speed cop in my day, but never one like him, an' his mate. The way they creep up on your tail and hang there.'

'He's done that man Jackson three times,' said Taff.

'Once more,' said Ned, 'an' his licence will go for a walk for six months.'

Ethel brought my tea. She came up behind me and put it on the table. I saw her brown arm and strong woman's fingers. I like a healthy woman. Especially when she's just on thirty. A woman's best age. I could have made her for myself until Jackson came on the scene. Our feeling had been warming up nicely in looks. But at forty-two you don't compete with a bloke of twenty-eight. But if she had known it, I was better than I'd ever been in my life. Outside a lorry drew on to the parking ground and the engine revved up and then shut off. Taff said, 'That'll be Jackson.' I could see Lew looking a bit tense.

'It's not Jackson,' said Ethel. She smiled at me, and went back to the counter. The door opened and in came Walter, a driver from St. Helens, and behind him his trailer-mate, Willie.

Walter, a short little stiff chap, carrying his lunch basket, and Willie, one of these artistic lads you see around these days, with a silk scarf round his neck. He always followed Walter like a faithful poodle. Walter let out a shout and when he came up to Lew he got up on his toes and began boxing. This just suited Lew who began throwing in what he thought were snappy lefts. Old Walter could have let him have one and knocked him out for good. But he always liked to gee old Lew up a bit. He went up and kissed Ethel on the cheek. Those cherry blokes, I thought, can get away with murder.

'Love me as much as ever, love?' said Walter to Ethel.

'You know me, Walter,' said Ethel.

'That's why I'm asking,' said Walter.

Old Lew said, 'Lay off mate, in front of the husband.'

'You can always rely on a chap as does it under your nose, Lew,' said Walter.

It was a lively little entrance and it brightened the place up.

Taff called out, 'Did you see old Babyface on your way down?'

'Did we see him, Willie!' said Walter. 'Ethel, double eggs and chips for my mate. I'm treating him.' Walter came over to the table and cocked his leg across a chair. 'We were just coming down the Long Hill there, we had the stick out, doing a nice forty-five, and old Willie here crooning away, when he suddenly broke off like he'd been shot. "What's up, Willie?" I says. "Sum'dy on our tail," says Willie. I revved up and put the old stick in and got into gear. I looked through the mirror. Not a thing in sight. I watched closely, not a thing. And I think the lad must be seeing something. I get the old speed down to a bit of a crawl, and still nothing in sight. "Are you sure, Willie?" I says. "I am that an' all," says Willie here. Well, I'm crawling along and still can't see nothing and I comes to thinking that old Willie's psychic bump has let him down. So I tells him to lean out of the cab at his side while I give a chancy swerve and switch off my own lights for better seeing. Right enough it was that damn great mardarse, Babyface. Him and his mate had been stuck on our tail.'

'What happened then?' said Ned.

'They knew they'd been rumbled,' said Walter. 'So the next thing they drew ahead and went into a side road. And there they're stuck this minute, waiting for the next poor sod that comes down.'

Ethel came across with my egg and chips. A minute later she was back with Willie's.

'Ee, were you expectin' me, Ethel?' said Willie, all smiles.

'Not *you*,' said Lew, looking at the door.

I was wiping my plate clean with bread when a lorry came belting off the road on to the parking ground outside. It hammered along and stopped with a loud brake squeal right at the door. Nobody looked up.

'That's Jackson now,' said Willie.

'And a good job his anchors are all right,' said Taff, 'or else——'

'Curse the bloody man,' said Lew. 'He'll drive up to the blasted counter one of these fine days.' He turned what he must have thought was a tough face to the door. We all gave a look that way. It was Jackson all right. Lew quickly dropped his stare and started wiping a table.

'Has he got the rats in him!' said Ned.

'He's not in the best of moods surely,' said Taff.

Jackson came striding up slowly. He had a dark chin, pale face, black hair. As he was passing our table he saw Willie still eating his egg and chips. The sight of the plate seemed to stop him dead. His face went even darker. Willie looked dead nervous. Walter picked up the sauce bottle.

'Here y'are,' Willie boy,' he said in a loud easy-going way, 'have a shake of the old bottle.'

Willie smiled at Walter. Jackson went to the next table, an empty one. When Lew saw that Walter had got one over Jackson, he seemed to take heart. He went up to the table.

'What is it?' he said.

'What's what?' said Jackson, looking for Ethel.

'Have you ordered?' said Lew.

'Ordered?' said Jackson. 'I'm not getting measured for a suit. Small tea.'

'That's all?' said Lew.

'That an' a bit of peace,' said Jackson.

'You're supposed to bring your own,' said Lew, walking away.

When he went up to the counter I could see he said something to Ethel, and I heard her say: 'There's times when your funny stuff just isn't funny, Lew. I'll serve him.'

'You're welcome,' said Lew.

He looked hurt. She took his arm and smiled at him. He smiled back.

'Sorry,' said Ethel.

'We've had eighteen hours of it,' said Lew, looking at the clock. 'Another half-hour and we're through. What about a tune?'

Ethel takes the tea across to Jackson. He gives one tight grip over her wrist.

'You want your egg an' chips, don't you, Jack?' she says.

Jackson shakes his head. Lew dropped his coin into the juke-box, and the next thing you can hear a woman singing something about 'Waltzing with her darling'. It's called *The Tennessee Waltz*. Jackson kissed Ethel's arm. Then Ethel moved slowly away from his table, looking like a woman with a dream on her mind.

As it happens, old Lew is just moving away from the juke-box, and this music and woman's voice is filling the place, and Ethel comes up facing Lew with that faraway walk, and the next thing

Lew has got hold of her and is dancing her gently around to a slow foxtrot or something.

Although I don't like him I had to admit to myself that he handled it nicely. And he danced nicely too, with a nice skilful movement. They all began calling out, 'Life in the old dog yet', and 'Go on', but there was no doubt they all liked to see the dance. All except Jackson. His face went dead poisonous. He kept himself sitting there for a time and then he got to his feet. He went across to the juke-box, half turned his back on it, and gave it a back-heeler. It was a dead sharp kick, and the next thing there was a groan and the tune died away in the middle of the woman singing something about 'remembering the night'.

I looked up and saw old Lew's face. One second it had that look that comes over a chap's face when he's enjoying a dance. The next it had the look of a child that's had its dummy snatched out of its mouth in the middle of a good suck. Ethel gave Jackson a sharp sort of look and went behind the counter. Willie looked towards Lew, his big eyes soft and wide open with sympathy. Lew stood there in a daze for a couple of ticks, then he went across to Jackson.

'You did that,' he said.

'What about it?' said Jackson.

'You'd no right,' said Lew. 'Didn't you see us dancin'?'

'I saw you,' said Jackson.

'I won't bloody stand for it,' said Lew.

'What'll you do?' said Jackson.

'I'll show you what I'll do,' said Lew. Then he weakened. 'I mean, we were doin' no harm.'

'I told you I wanted some peace,' said Jackson. 'I've had enough din in my ears for the last five hours.'

'But you'd no right,' said Lew. He went across to the juke-box and shook it. You could hear the record whirring round but missing the needle or something. He came hurrying back to Jackson. 'You had no right to do what you did,' he said, talking legal like. 'I'd put my money in that box.'

Jackson leant back in his chair. 'Why didn't you say it was the money was troubling you?' he said. He put his hand in his pocket and drew out a fistful of silver and copper. 'Here y'are,' he said, holding out his hand. 'You can take it outa that.'

Lew being a money-mean sort of bloke, couldn't help being caught off guard. The sight of money carelessly handled seems to make some people so that they can't think for a minute. He just stared at Jackson and at the money and didn't know what to do. Then Ethel came walking up behind Lew. She went round him in a gentle way, until she was facing Jackson, and before he knew what was happening she brought up her hand with a swift smack under his. The money went right up in the air and flew all over the place.

'And you,' she said, 'can take it out of that!'

Then she turned to Lew like a mother who has gone out into the street to help her lad who is being challenged by a bigger lad. 'Come on, Lew,' she said and led him back to the counter. We drivers said nothing. After all, Jackson himself was a driver. Jackson didn't know where to look or what to do. Then another lorry stopped outside.

The door opened with a quick jerk and in came Clive. A real spiv kid, the clothes, the walk, the lot, even to the old rub of the hands, as though he's going to sell you something. He comes whistling along.

'What you all bleedin' talkin' at once for?' he says, everything being dead silent. 'Large tea, Ethel, two of toast and drip. Don't be tight with the jelly—m'back's bad.'

Clive eyes everybody.

'Howzit goin', Bolton?' he says to me.

'Not bad,' I says.

Suddenly he makes a dive for something on the floor.

'Coo, I'm in bleedin' luck,' he says, picking up half a crown. I beckon with my thumb to where Jackson is sitting. Clive catches on. He goes across and puts it on the table in front of Jackson.

'I wouldn't rob you, Jackson,' he says. 'You might need it. I see old Babyface did you again—back up the road there on the Long Hill.'

As soon as Clive said that, the atmosphere changed.

'Bloody hard luck, Jackson,' said Ned.

'I hope they don't scrub your licence,' said Taff.

I gave him a look. He didn't seem to have Babyface on his mind. A lot had happened to him since that.

'He must have nailed you just after he left us,' said Walter. He took out his fags, handed them round, hesitated, then held the packet out to Jackson. Jackson thought it over for a moment, and then took one. The matey feeling came up then, the feeling of all being drivers and the law always after you.

Clive leant over the table and looked at Jackson: 'I was stuck in a lay-by up the road, mate, with a floozie, when you came whamming past. You was goin' like the clappers of hell. *Whoof* . . . "Wot's that?" she says. She went dead cold on me.'

Ethel came up with Clive's tea and toast and drip.

'You was goin' at a hell of a lick, Jackson,' went on Clive. 'What was on your bleedin' mind?'

Ethel was leaning over the table. I saw Jackson give her a long and hungry look. Ethel looked at him. She picked up his cup. 'Piece of my apple pie?' she said. He nodded. Then he looked at Clive. 'What did you say?' he said.

'Let it pass,' said Clive, his eyes following Ethel. He didn't miss much.

The atmosphere had come on matey, and even Lew came up and hung around.

'I wouldn't like to say what I'd do to a cop like that,' said Taff.

'Babyface?' said Lew. 'Got his job to do, ain't he? That's what he's paid for—bookin' you! Well, ain't it?'

'He ain't paid bleedin' bonus on the job,' said Ned. 'He don't have to creep on your tail. None of the others do it.'

'It's legal, ain't it?' said Lew. 'You keep to the law too, then nob'dy can touch you.'

They went on yapping about the law then, about loads, log sheets, brakes, licences, and all the rest of it, with old Lew sticking his motty in at every chance.

Then Walter said: 'Has it ever struck you, Lew, what a dangerous caper it is—tailing a lorry?'

I saw Jackson suddenly take an interest.

Clive said: 'Suppose you didn't know this geezer was on your tail! Say you was doin' a nice fifty-five, when you spotted something just ahead of you?'

'Yeh,' said Ned, 'an' down on the bleedin' anchors.'

'Pull up with a jerk,' said Clive, 'and where's Babyface?'

'Over the bloody top,' said Taff.

'No, he ain't,' said Ned, 'he's *under* the back. You get out an' run around the back, and there's the bleedin' bogeymen an' their car, practically buried under the back axle. "Wot wuz you a-doin' of?" said Babyface. So you says, "Testin' my bleedin' brakes for efficiency. Why, officah, you've scratched your radiator—not to mention bashin' in your National 'Ealth dentures!"'

'Come on, Ned,' said Taff rising, 'you'd talk all night.'

'It's about time you was all off,' said Lew. 'We want to get to bed.'

Ethel came over with Jackson's tea and apple pie. 'You go off, Lew,' she said. She looked at Jackson as she put the piece of pie in front of him, but he was staring down at the table. He didn't seem to notice the pie, or, come to that, Ethel herself.

'Can I trust you to lock up properly if I go off?' said Lew to Ethel.

'I'll help her,' said Walter.

'Then I think I'll go off to bed,' said Lew.

'That's right,' said Clive, 'let your bleedin' brains cool down. "Keep to the law." Never heard such bull in all my life.'

'Come on, Taff,' said Ned.

They went off.

'I think I'll go,' said Lew.

'All right,' said Walter, 'go, but stop natterin' about it.'

'Don't be long, Ethel,' said Lew. 'Turf 'em out.'

'It's too late to hurry,' said Ethel.

'Goodnight, Lew,' said Willie.

'Goodnight, Willie lad,' said Lew.

When Lew had gone off, Clive turned to me: 'Fancy a game of darts, Lofthouse?'

They either call me by the town I come from or its best-known footballer.

'I'm getting down for ten minutes,' I said.

'I'll give you a game, Bermondsey,' said Walter.

They went off, up beside the counter for their darts game. I put my cap on the table and rested my forehead on it, and shut out all the light with my arms. Even if you don't sleep the eyes and head get rested. You need some relief when you've been driving a ten-tonner through the night. Ethel must have come up and sat at Jackson's table, because after a bit I could hear their voices.

'What made you blow your top?' he said.

'I won't stand by and see a young chap taking the micky out of an older one,' she said. 'I don't like you being that way, Jacky.'

'Before I forget,' said Jackson. 'I've something here for you. Hope they're not too squashed. I had to keep 'em out of sight.'

There was a bit of rustling and then Ethel whispered: 'Roses! how lovely, Jacky! Well, I never expected roses!'

Even with my head down I could smell roses.

Ethel must have given him a hand squeeze. He went on: 'Come off with me tonight. I'll wait for you outside in my tub. We'll drive off together. Don't worry about clothes—look, see, I've enough money in that book to buy you all the clothes you want.'

Post Office savings book. But I knew how he felt. The thought of having a woman in the warm cab there beside you, as you drive through the night, is the most tempting thought a driver can get. At least, that I can get. It's so cosy in the cab of your own lorry, with the faint warm smell of diesel oil, but it gets lonely. If only you had a woman beside you. For part of the time anyway.

Ethel went on about Lew. 'When I first came in that door,' I heard her say, 'I wasn't much to look at. I'd had things rough, I can tell you that, Jacky. And Lew is the first man I've ever met who has treated me with respect. He never tried anything on. And that's what I liked about him.'

'Am I trying anything on?' said Jackson. 'I'm asking you to come off with me.'

'And the day we got back after the marriage,' went on Ethel, 'he already had a new sign up outside. It said, "*Lew's and Ethel's*".'

'Come off it,' said Jackson. 'He made the ropiest cup of tea between here and Gretna Green. The place was fallin' apart, an' so was he. You've pulled it all together. You're straight with him.'

'Another thing Lew gave me,' said Ethel, 'was security.'

Jackson seemed to fly off the handle at that. 'Security? What the hell are you talking about? I come bashing down Watling Street tonight—never a bloody stop except to snatch your roses. One thought on my mind—will I see you? How do you think that rat Babyface caught me again?—and you talk to me about security.'

'Sorry, Jacky,' said Ethel. 'What happens if they take your licence?'

'No licence, no job,' said Jackson. 'But we'll see about that. They won't get me working under a roof that easily.'

Just then the juke-box let go *The Tennessee Waltz* again. I looked up with a start, as though I'd been asleep. Willie was standing beside it. He called across to Walter. 'That's not the record I picked, Walter.' It was just then I looked towards Jackson. He looked real poisonous. He got up and walked slowly towards Willie at the juke-box.

'Jacky!' whispered Ethel. He took no notice.

Walter had spotted him. He left the darts game and hurried casually across to Willie beside the juke-box. Willie had seen Jackson, and he looked white.

'Enjoy yourself, lad,' said Walter. Then he turned and faced Jackson. I got up and walked across. Same as they used to say, Lancashire helps Lancashire. Walter was only a bantam; Jackson was on the big side and tough.

'Move over, Scouse,' said Jackson.

'What d'you want?' said Walter.

'I'm going to stop that bloody thing,' said Jackson.

'I don't think you are,' said Walter. His eyes never left Jackson as he handed the darts to Willie. I could see what Walter had in mind. He'd grab Jackson's coat lapels in a tick and pull him down and tup him with his head. And Jackson wouldn't be able to see for blood. I could almost hear the crack of Jackson's nose in my ears, even before it happened.

Ethel slipped round.

'What's up?' she said.

'Willie's paid to hear a tune,' said Walter, 'and he's goin' to hear one.'

'Yeh, but it might not be the one he's paid for,' said Jackson.

Jackson had a savage look on his face. But Walter was determined, and on the aware.

'Don't make any trouble,' said Ethel. 'Please go, and let me lock up.'

Jackson turned and looked at her. Walter was ready to make his grab, I stepped in.

'Come on, Walt,' I said.

'Not till the bloody tune's up,' he said.

So we all stood there for half a minute until the woman on the record stopped singing.

'You can all go now,' said Ethel.

'Ee, but we haven't paid yet, Ethel,' said Willie.

'Ee, lad, so you haven't,' said Ethel, taking him off a bit.

That seemed to break up the tension.

'What about the old darts?' said Clive.

Walter took the darts off Willie.

'Is it me?' he said.

'Yip,' said Clive. 'You want seventy-nine for game. Not be a minute, Ethel.'

Walter toed the line. He threw a nineteen, then a twenty, and a double-top with the last dart.

'Who'd 'ave bleedin' thought it!' said Clive, putting down his darts.

We all paid and walked to the door. 'Have you a minute, Bolton?' said Jackson. I nodded. He slipped back and had a last word with Ethel. Maybe a hug. I went up beside Walter.

'I was right there behind you, Walter,' I said, 'but I reckoned you didn't need me.'

Walter took off his cap and patted his head: 'I had this ready for him,' he said.

I went across to my tub. Then Jackson came up.

'I was going to ask you,' he said; 'you ain't got an old driving mirror, have you?'

As soon as he said it I remembered I had one in my tool-box. And it struck me that he must have seen it when I once lent him a spanner. He took out his fags and handed me one. Then he shone the torch in my tool-box. I got the driving mirror out. It was one that had been wrenched away when I drew too close to a wagon at the sidings one day. The metal arm had been ripped from the bracket.

'That do you?' I said.

'It might,' he said.

I didn't ask him what he wanted it for. If he wants me to know, I reckoned, he'll tell me.

'You've been done for speeding?' he said.

'More'n once,' I said.

'The cop who charges you has got to have a witness—that so?' he said.

'His mate,' I said, 'that's all.'

'There's got to be two of 'em in court?' he said.

'If you plead "not guilty" an' make a case of it,' I said. 'But how many drivers do? You know damn well you're guilty.'

'But they've *both* got to be there,' he said. 'Haven't they?'

'Look here, Jackson,' I said, 'if you're goin' on about Babyface doin' you tonight, forget it. You——'

'Look here,' cut in Jackson, 'if you want to question his witness and his witness fails to appear, or either one of them fails to appear——'

'Then it's "failure to produce witnesses",' I said, 'and you get "Case Dismissed".'

'That's what I wanted to know,' said Jackson.

'But I'll tell you one thing you're sufferin' from, Jackson,' I said, 'that's a bad dose of *copitis.*'

'You said it,' he said. 'I could murder the bleedin' lot of 'em.'

'It won't get you nowhere,' I said. 'We've all had it some time or other. Anyway, they won't take your licence just for speedin'.'

'It's not speedin'. He's doin' me for dangerous drivin',' said Jackson.

'That's a bit more serious,' I said.

'An' not only that,' said Jackson.

'What else?' I said.

'I'd a fiver folded up in my licence when I handed it over,' he said.

'A fiver! You must be crazy,' I said. 'It should be a quid. An' you get the licence back with a caution an' no quid. What's wrong with that? I'd sooner give a cop a quid than a magistrate a fiver.'

'I'd sooner cut their bleedin' throats,' said Jackson, 'the lot of 'em. Babyface is trying to make out I wanted to bribe him.'

'I suppose you said you kept it in your licence for safety?' I said.

Jackson nodded.

'Then,' I said, 'it's your word against his.'

'Against his and his mate's, and I know whose they'll take,' he said. Then he picked up the mirror and had a good look at it. 'We'll see,' he said. 'They ain't heard the charge yet. There's another three weeks to go. Anything could happen in that time.' He waved the mirror and went off.

It was a fortnight later, about two o'clock in the morning, a pitch black night, and I was belting along Watling Street, hoping I might make 'Lew's' in time, have a bite to eat and get a look at Ethel. She'd begun to get into my thoughts a lot. I was going at a fair lick, because you can see better on a dark night, since your headlights carve out the road for you, and you don't get those dicey shadows the moon makes. I had my eye watching out for Babyface, for I knew I was on his beat.

Suddenly, ahead down the road, I saw a lorry's headlights flashing on and off, giving me the danger signal. I flashed back, braked, and watched the road behind me and the road ahead. You can't be too careful on a trunk road at night. I once knew a young driver called Sam who got out to mend his tail light on the road. It was the last ever seen of him. Another wagon was belting down the road behind him. The driver, a Geordie, not seeing any light, came hammering along. It was too late to do anything about it when he saw the lorry. He went clean into the back of it as Sam was fixing his tail light.

I drew up in a safe clear spot. In the beam of my headlight I could see a lorry skew-whiff across the road. There was a black car that had crashed into the back of it and with such force that it seemed to be buried under the chassis. I lit a fag. As I was getting out a driver came running up to me.

'Leave your headlights on, Bolton,' he called. 'They need all the light they can get.'

'That you, Ned?' I said. 'What's happened?'

'A right bleeding smash up,' said Ned. He whispered. 'It's old Jackson. Police car run into the back of him. They're trying to get the bodies out.'

We walked down together to the smash up. The police and ambulance men were on the job. They were trying to jack up the back axle of the lorry so that they could get the car out. The police car hooter was going all the time. The blue plate on the back of the car with the word 'POLICE' on it was intact, but that was about all that was. Nobody would ever drive that car again. As for the two blokes inside, well, one glimpse was enough.

'Babyface?' I said to Ned.

'It was,' said Ned. 'Poor old sod. His mate, too.' He gave me a knowing look, but said no more.

I heard someone talking in a husky voice and I turned and saw Jackson. He was talking to a young patrol cop who was making notes in his book.

'Well, I'll tell you all I know,' said Jackson. 'I'm coming along at a fair crack. No use wrapping it up, I had my toe down, because I wanted to get to the caff down the road before they close. I usually have egg and chips about this time. But I was keeping my eyes open and the road was dead clear in front and behind me—so far as I could see. I could have sworn to it. And I was just coming along there, when on the bend here, dead in front of me, I saw what looked like a body curled in the roadway.'

'A body?' said the cop. 'Where is it now?'

'I looked after,' said Jackson. 'See—under there.'

He pointed under his lorry. We all looked.

'That old overcoat?' said the cop.

'I can see what it is *now*,' said Jackson. 'But catch it in your headlights an' it looks different.'

The cop nodded.

'I've known many an old geezer get drunk and go to sleep in the middle of the road,' went on Jackson. 'Anyway, I slammed on my brakes at once. Then I got the shock of my life. *Something hit me from behind.* I couldn't think what had happened. It wasn't a tap, it was a real bash. Even with my brakes on it knocked me across the road.'

The patrol cop looked sympathetic.

'What did you do then?' he asked.

'It took me a minute or two to come round,' said Jackson. 'The shock and one thing and another. Then I got out of the cab and walked round to the back. It's dark, see, and for a bit I couldn't make out what had happened. I could hear this horn blowing away in my ears, but I didn't know where it was coming from, not at first. Then suddenly I began to make it out. I looked inside the car and saw 'em. It was a shock, mate, I can tell you that. How are they? Will they be all right?'

'Take it easy,' said the cop. 'We're doing all we can.'

Jackson wiped his face with his hand. 'Is it all right if I walk down the road and get myself a cup of tea?' he asked. 'I feel all out.'

The cop said: 'Just a minute, I'll see.' He went up to a police sergeant and one of the ambulance men. Jackson turned and winked at me, then he went on wiping his forehead. The patrol cop came back and said, 'So long as you are not too far away.'

Jackson said, 'I'll be in the caff.'

'Better let me have your licence,' said the cop.

'I'll get it out of my coat pocket,' said Jackson, 'in the cab.' He turned to me. 'You'll give me a lift down the road, Lofty?'

The cop warmed up: 'Come on,' he said, 'let's get the road clear, or we'll be having another smash up. Tell the other drivers not to line up along there.'

Jackson got into my cab. I drove round by his lorry and down the road to Lew's. He was thinking about something and he said nothing as we went down the road, and I didn't feel like talking either. When I drew up to a halt outside Lew's he turned to me and digging his hand inside his coat he carefully pulled something out.

''Ere you are, mate,' he said.

I looked. In his hand was the driving mirror I had lent him. The glass was broken.

'It came in handy,' he said.

I didn't say anything. He looked like a man at peace with himself.

'I had it planted down below the floorboards,' he said.

'Oh, aye?' I said.

I wasn't as surprised as I made it sound.

'It was there waiting for Babyface,' he said. 'I knew whenever he crept on my tail, even if he had all his lights out, I'd spot him down in that mirror. Half an hour ago I caught him creeping up behind me. Right, I thought to myself, I'll draw you on, Charlie. I stuck in the booster gear and put my toe down. They fell for it and crept right up behind me. I was coming down Long Hill and I knew the exact spot he'd overtake me, just near the bend at the bottom. So as we were drawing near to it I got every ounce I could out of the old tub. We were fair cracking along, I can tell you. *Right mate*, I thought, *you're trying to do me, but I'm going to do you instead.* So, I steeled myself for the shock, then I slammed both feet down at once and swung on the handbrake at the same time.'

Jackson scratched his nose.

'I've got some lovely anchors on the old wagon. They drew me up like that. They'd have had to be bloody good drivers to stop that quick. They didn't have a chance. They crashed right clean in the back.'

I felt I needed a bit of fresh air after that lot, so I got out of the cab. Jackson got out at the other side and walked round to me.

'First thing I did, when I stopped,' he said, 'was to take that old mirror out and put the floorboard back straight. Breaking that mirror brought 'em bad luck all right. Then I took that old topcoat that I had specially for the job and planted it on the road under the lorry. It's not mine.'

He followed me round as I kicked at my tyres, and tested my loading ropes.

'Well, here's your mirror, mate,' he said.

I could hardly bear to look at it, let alone take hold of it.

'If you don't want it, I can soon lose it for you,' said Jackson. He was back in a minute. 'Take a bloody good detective to find it now,' he said.

'Jackson,' I said, 'what's the idea telling me all this?'

He smiled softly at me and then he said, 'A bloke don't want to

walk round with a basinful of that on his mind. I know I'm safe
with an old driver. Come on, let's see if Ethel has the egg and chips
ready.'

I followed him. At the door he turned and said to me, 'Nothing I
like better than getting one across the law. Y'know what it means
for my dangerous drivin' charge?—*Case dismissed.*'

I went in after him. There were half a dozen drivers in. Walter
and Willie, young Clive, a driver and his mate from Glasgow, and
an old driver from Hull. They all gave nods and waves to me. But
as for Jackson, not a word was spoken. Not a sign was made. You
felt everything going dead quiet. Lew was wiping the tables and
kept right away from where Jackson sat. Ethel was behind the
counter and she never gave him so much as a glance. She looked
across to me and waved her hand. Jackson looked at her but she
didn't seem to see him. I knew then the word had gone round. It
doesn't take long. He might have got one across the law, but he
hadn't got one across Watling Street. Nobody would split, but
already, North and South, they were putting the poison in for him.
Within a week he'd be lucky to get a civil cup of tea anywhere along
the A.5. And I could see by the look on Jackson's face, he knew one
thing at least—no matter what the police found or didn't find—
he'd never get anywhere with Ethel now. And his driving days on
Watling Street were over. And, looking across to the counter, where
Ethel was working with her sleeves rolled up, I couldn't help
thinking to myself, *Bolton, this is where you might move in.*

PETER USTINOV
The Man in the Moon

JOHN KERMIDGE walked down the street in Highgate to the letter-box, a bulky package in his hand. He felt as though he had been plunged backwards into another, more ample century, when the legs of men were still in constant use as a means of propulsion, not just as members groping for brake and accelerator. He smiled at the sky as though greeting a half forgotten friend. There was a trace of troubled conscience in his smile. He had kept the sky waiting for so long. Usually, when he looked up, he saw nothing but the perpetual night of his laboratory.

Since he was a scientist, it would have been inhuman if he had not in some measure surrendered to tradition and been a little absent-minded. Not in his work, but in relatively unimportant matters. When he wrote, he did so with vast application, and the meaning of his words could only be fathomed by a few dozen endowed creatures in various universities; but often, as now, having filled pages with mysterious logic, he forgot to stick any stamps to the envelope. The letter was addressed to Switzerland, to a Doctor Nussli, in Zurich. Considering that Dr. Nussli was perhaps John's best friend, it was strange, if typical, that the name on the envelope was spelled with a single *s*.

'Where did you go?' asked his wife anxiously when he returned.

'I posted that letter to Hans.'

'Couldn't it have waited until the morning?'

Although the weather was cold, John mopped his brow with his handkerchief. 'No,' he said.

'The last mail's gone anyway,' Veronica grumbled.

It was curious that John should feel irritated in his hour of triumph, but he allowed himself a moment of harshness.

'No,' he repeated, unnecessarily loud.

There was a pause, with thunder in the air.

For quite a few months, Veronica and John had seen very little of each other. Veronica had permitted herself quite a few questions during this time; John had failed to gratify her with even a single answer.

'I thought you mind like to see the children before they went to bed,' she said.

He grunted and asked, 'Where's Bill?'

'Bill? I don't know. Sir Humphrey called.'

'Sir Humphrey?' John started angrily. 'What the hell did he want?'

'He didn't say, but he was unusually nice to me.'

'That's a bad sign.'

'Seemed very elated.'

'Elated?' John kicked a chair.

'What's the matter with you?' Veronica almost shouted.

The doorbell rang.

'That'll be the champagne,' John said, going into the entrance hall.

'Champagne?'

It wasn't the champagne. It was Bill Hensey, John's assistant, a bearded fellow in an old sports jacket, with a dead pipe permanently in his mouth. He seized John by the arm, didn't even acknowledge Veronica, and started speaking agitatedly in a soft voice. Veronica wished she'd married a bank clerk, a man with simple problems and a little courtesy. She heard nothing of the conversation apart from an occasional reference to Sir Humphrey, but she saw Bill's baleful blue eyes darting hither and thither with excitement.

She was a pleasant girl without much temperament, the ideal wife for John, if there was such a thing. She didn't wish to attract attention to herself, since she knew that both men were engaged in important work and that they were under some strain which it was her unhappy duty to understand without being inquisitive. Just then, however, the children burst into the room, engaged in a running fight over the cactus-covered plains of the frontier badlands. Dick, dressed as a sheriff over his pyjamas, opened murderous fire with a cap pistol from behind an armchair, while Timothy plunged into cover behind the radiogram, his eyes shining evilly through the slits of his bandit's mask.

John exploded. 'Get out of here,' he yelled.

It was only natural for Veronica to leap to her children's defence. 'They're only playing,' she cried. 'God Almighty, what's the matter with you?'

'Can't you see we're working?' answered John, covering up his guilt in testiness.

But Veronica was roused, and launched into a big scene. While the children slunk out unhappily, she released all her resentment in a flood of tears and invective. She had been packing for this blasted trip to Washington. Did he think she wanted to go to Washington? She'd much rather stay at home. Why didn't he go alone? And if he went, why didn't he stay? What thanks did she get? To her the unglamorous lot: the paying of bills, the checking of accounts, the necessary bedtime stories which taxed the imagination. Why didn't he marry Bill?

She was interrupted by the doorbell. The champagne, no doubt.

It wasn't the champagne. It was Sir Humphrey Utteridge, accompanied by an affected youth in a bowler hat.

'Kermidge, allow me to congratulate you,' Sir Humphrey said in a voice that was quivering with emotion.

John and Bill exchanged a quick, anxious look.

'Thank you, Sir Humphrey,' John answered, with some impatience.

'This event will mark the beginning of a new era, not only in the annals of recorded history, but in the indelible odyssey of the British Commonwealth of Nations.'

This was the fine, rolling language for launching a ship, but nobody wants a ship launched in his living-room.

'Old ass,' thought John, but said, 'It's very good of you to say so.'

'D'you remember me, Kermidge?' asked the affected youth, leaning heavily on his umbrella. 'Oliver de Vouvenay. We were at Charterhouse together.'

'Good gracious. No wonder John didn't remember him, he hadn't changed a bit. John's hair was turning white, but this immaculate, pink creature looked exactly as he had at school. If he was now successful it was a triumph of conformity. He was successful.

After John had grudgingly shaken hands, Oliver de Vouvenay announced that he hadn't done badly, since he was now the Principal Private Secretary of the Prime Minister, the Right Honourable Arthur Backworth, and hoped to stand in the next election.

'Not as a Socialist,' said John.

Oliver de Vouvenay laughed uproariously and expressed his conviction that the joke was a good one.

Before there was time for more banter, the doorbell rang again.

'That'll be——' Sir Humphrey began, but John interrupted him. 'I ordered some champagne,' he said. 'I'll go.'

John opened the door and found himself face to face with a detective. The man didn't say he was a detective, but it was obvious. His disguise would only have deceived another detective. 'This is it, sir,' called the detective to a waiting Rolls-Royce.

The door of the limousine opened slowly, and an elderly man of some distinction struggled cautiously on to the pavement.

John felt the colour draining from his face. He recognised the man as the Right Honourable Arthur Backworth, Prime Minister of Great Britain and Northern Ireland.

'May I come in?' said the Prime Minister, with a vote-catching smile.

Here was a wonderful, perverse moment to say no, but John said yes.

Veronica, amazed, and with an intense feeling of shame at having even mentioned such trivialities as accounts and packing, watched her humble surburban boudoir gradually filling with celebrities who had only graced it previously as guests on the television screen.

'You will probably wonder why I am here,' crooned Mr. Backworth.

Once again John was seized with a desire to say no, but to the Prime Minister the question was a rhetorical one, and he continued in august and measured tones.

'When Sir Humphrey informed me early today of the success of your experiment, I immediately called a Cabinet meeting, which ended not half an hour ago. It goes without saying that what you have achieved is perhaps the most glorious, the most decisive step forward in the history of science—nay, of the human race. What recognition a mere government may accord you will be yours, rest assured.'

'It would have been impossible without Bill here——' John said.

'Yes, yes, both of you, both of you,' the Prime Minister went on with some impatience. He was used to the interruptions of politicians, but the interruptions of laymen were an impertinence. 'Now, it must be obvious to you,' he continued, 'that what you have accomplished is of such magnitude that it cannot fail to affect the policy of nations, and,' he added, with a trace of exalted mischief, 'of this nation in particular. After all, the Russians will, at any moment, be able to land a dog on the moon; the Americans have, I am told, a mouse in readiness; but we, without fanfares of magniloquence, have by-passed these intermediary stages and are ready to land a man, or men. You may not realise what this means.'

John smiled and said modestly, 'I am very fortunate, sir, that it should have fallen to me to head the team which managed, perhaps more by luck than by virtue, to achieve this success. I am, of course, looking forward immensely to my visit to Washington, and to the possibility of breaking this news to our American friends.' John was slightly annoyed with himself for adopting this formal tone, but in talking to Prime Ministers one apparently didn't talk, one made a speech.

Mr. Backworth looked at John curiously, and smiled. 'I want you to come to dinner on Thursday at Number 10,' he said.

'I can't, I'll be in Washington.'

'No, you won't.'

'What?'

The Prime Minister nodded at Sir Humphrey, who cleared his throat and spoke. 'It has been decided by the Cabinet—and I was present at the meeting—to send Gwatkin-Pollock to Washington in your place. We need you here.'

'But Gwatkin-Pollock knows not the first thing about interplanetary travel!' John cried.

'Then he will give nothing away,' said the Prime Minister, pleasantly.

'This is outrageous. I want to go!'

'You can't,' replied the Prime Minister.

'Can't!' echoed John, and then fell back on the conventional reaction of the perplexed democrat. 'This is a free country.'

'Yes,' growled the Prime Minister, in his heroic style, 'and we must keep it free.'

His remark didn't mean much, but any student of politics will recognise the fact that it is more important to make the right noise than to talk sense.

The Prime Minister smiled, relaxing the unexpected tension. 'Do you really think that we have sunk so low as to reward you by curbing your liberties?' he asked.

John felt childish. 'I was looking forward to Washington,' he said.

'You scientists take such a long view of events that it needs simple souls like ourselves to open your eyes to the obvious on occasion. Of course you are flushed with pride of achievement. Of course you wish to announce your world-shattering discovery to your colleagues. That is only human. But alas! Your colleagues may be near to you in spirit, but they also carry passports, they also speak their various languages and boast their various prejudices. There can be no pure relationship between you and, say, a Russian scientist because you both have divergent responsibilities, however warm and cordial your contact in your laboratories or over a cup of coffee. Now, you harbour a tremendous, a dangerous secret. Have you the experience to keep it, all by yourself, without help from us? Will not the strain on you be utterly inhuman, however loyal your intentions? These are questions to which we must find answers within the next few weeks.'

'How do you intend to go about it?' asked John, too surprised to be really angry.

'By keeping your mind occupied,' said the Prime Minister, earnestly. 'Thursday is the day after tomorrow. I wish you to dine with me and with General Sir Godfrey Toplett, Chief of the General Staff.'

'We will have absolutely nothing in common,' said John.

'Before dinner, perhaps not. After dinner, I believe you will,' replied the Prime Minister coolly.

'I presume that I may go on seeing which friends I please?' asked John, his voice charged with irony.

The Prime Minister ignored the irony and said, 'Up to a point.'

John looked at Oliver de Vouvenay, who smiled fatuously.

Bill rose from his seat. He hadn't said anything, but was visibly dismayed. 'If you'll excuse me . . .' he began.

'Don't be alarmed if you should feel yourself followed,' said the Prime Minister. 'You will be.'

Gwatkin-Pollock was a man of science often selected by the British Government for official missions, since he had a quality of aloof and calculating majesty which those seated with him round a conference table never failed to find disturbing. He always seemed to be hiding something. He also had a habit of suddenly, unreasonably laughing at a comic situation of a day, a week, a year ago, usually while a serious statement was being read by someone else. His enigmatic quality was completed by his utter silence when it was his turn to make a statement.

It so happened that at the very moment Gwatkin-Pollock was seated with American scientists at a top-level conference in Washington, John was puffing one of the Prime Minister's better cigars and rather losing his critical sense in its lullaby of fumes. The dark plans of the British Government were working well for the time being on both fronts. A brilliant American scientist, who spoke for some reason with a thick German accent, was just expounding a remarkable plan for projecting a whole battalion of white mice into space, when Gwatkin-Pollock, remembering a humorous event from his youth, laughed loudly. The American delegation looked at each other with consternation and asked themselves whether the President had been wise to let the British into these top-secret conferences.

In London, meanwhile, General Toplett, a soldier with a face like a whiskered walnut, was busy producing some large photographs from his portfolio.

'You see,' he said to John and to the Prime Minister, 'it's quite clear that whatever nation is the first to land even light forces on Crater K here—I've marked it in red—will control all the lateral valleys on this side of the moon's face. My plan, therefore, is to land light air-borne forces as near the perimeter of the crater as possible, and to advance from there in four columns until we reach this green line here.'

This was too much for John, who leaped to his feet. 'It's revolting!' he cried. 'I didn't evolve a man-carrying moon rocket in order to see it subjected to the kind of thought which has made such a mess of our planet! I don't want dim soldiers and soiled politicians to pollute my moon!'

'Steady there, steady,' snarled the General, holding the photograph of the crater in the air as though it were a hand-grenade.

The Prime Minister laughed. 'Don't you think, Kermidge,' he said quietly, 'that there is a pleasant irony in this turn of events? Don't misunderstand me; the Americans are, and always will be, our allies. That goes without saying. But in a way, we do have a . . . friendly score to settle, don't you think?'

'In the world of science there is always an element of quite innocuous rivalry——' John said, as reasonably as he could.

'I wasn't referring to the world of science,' the Prime Minister interrupted. 'I was referring to history. Kermidge, we are taxing our ingenuity to the limit to keep over fifty million people fully employed and well fed on this tiny island. Naturally our rules are stringent, our taxation inhuman, and naturally we tend to appear to other nations as somewhat avaricious in our methods and as almost ludicrously inflexible in our regulations. Can this give us pleasure? We, who gave the world so much?'

'We took quite a lot, too,' said John.

'I must ask you to listen to me without interruption,' replied the Prime Minister with a trace of irritation. He had to put up with this kind of thing from the opposition all the year round. There was on reason, he felt, why he should put up with contradiction in his own dining-room, in his own cigar smoke. 'The Americans are a most generous people,' he continued, 'but they can afford to be. A man with one hundred pounds in the bank giving a penny to a beggar is making the same financial sacrifice as a man with one million pounds in the bank giving four pounds, three shillings, and four pence to a beggar.' These statistics were so glib that they obviously formed a staple argument of the Prime Minister's.

'The widow's mite,' said John.

The Prime Minister gave him a withering look, which dissolved rapidly into a winning smile. Politics taught a man self-control as no other profession.

'Call it what you will, the facts are clear. We need space. We need to expand, not only in order to survive, but in order to conserve our national character, our even temper, our serenity.'

'Even Hitler thought of better reasons than that,' John heard himself saying.

The Prime Minister was unruffled.

'Would we ever attack our neighbours to achieve this end? Never. But'—and he leaned forward, searchingly—'once there is space, who knows? We've never shied at adventure. And think of it— rolling acres on the moon, or on other planets. Untold mineral wealth. Kermidge, we are in the shoes of Columbus, with the added proof of the unknown continent's existence. Look out of the window. You will see it. And we have the ship to get us there.'

'You want to paint the moon red,' murmured John. 'You want a moon worthy of Kipling, on which the sun never sets.'

'Rather well put,' said the General, now that the conversation had taken an understandable turn.

'Exactly—and why not?' cried the Prime Minister. 'Nothing in history is final. History is like the sea, constantly changing, a patchwork of phases, a mosaic of impermanent achievements. We were an occupied people once. The Saxons, the Danes, and the Romans had their will of us. Then we rose, with the determination of underdogs, and conquered the greatest empire the world has ever known. Times changed, and with them the conception of Empire. Whether we like it or not, we now live in an Era of Liberality, in which every tinpot republic has its own voice in the United Nations. We, in our great wisdom and experience, must sit silently by while Guatemala lays claim to British Honduras. This kind of thing taxes our dignity to the uttermost, but need it last? Must we accept the defeat of Burgoyne as final? We say we lose every battle but the last. Has the last battle been fought?' He dropped his voice from a rhetorical level into the intimacy of sincerity. 'Please understand me, I do not advocate war, least of all war with America. That would be unthinkable and stupid. In any event, we would lose it. However, I, for one, do not accept Burgoyne's defeat as the end of a story.'

'Burgoyne was a fool,' said the General gratuitously.

'Let us reach the moon first. This would not only give us the space we need, it would also give us the enormous moral ascendancy necessary to resume the leadership of the free world. There can be no doubt whatever that Russia is working rapidly towards the results you have so brilliantly attained. She is, as it were, breathing down our neck. Sharing our information with the Americans would only waste valuable weeks at this juncture, and by the time we had put our mutual scheme into operation the Americans would be taking all the credit. They are too flushed with their own technological efficiency to admit that anyone can achieve anything without stealing their plans. Kermidge, we have made our gesture. We have sent them Gwatkin-Pollock. Let us do the rest ourselves.'

There was a pause.

John began speaking slowly, trying hard to control his voice, which was quivering. 'I hold no brief for American scientists, or for Russian scientists, or for British scientists for that matter. I have friends and enemies in all camps, since to the true men of science there are no frontiers, only advances; there are no nations, only humanity. This may sound subversive to you, but it is true, and I will explain, as temperately as I can, why it is true, what has made it true. You, sir, talked of Columbus. In his day, men for all their culture, fine painting, architecture, humanism, the rest, were still relatively savage. Life was cheap. Death was the penalty for a slight misdemeanour, slavery the penalty for an accident of birth. And why? Because there was space to conquer, horizons full of promise. Conquest was the order of the day. The avid fingers of Britain, France, Spain, and Portugal stretched into the unknown. Then, abruptly, all was found, all was unravelled. Germany and Italy attempted to put the clock back, and behaved as everyone had once behaved, and were deemed criminal for no other reason than that they were out of date and that their internal persecutions were carried against men of culture, and white men at that, instead of against their colonial subjects. They were condemned by mankind, and rightly so, because they were hungry for glory at a time when other nations were licking their chops, sated by a meal which had lasted for centuries. And why did we all become civilised, so abruptly? Because, sir, there was nothing left to conquer, nothing left to seize without a threat of general war; there was no space left.' John mopped his brow briefly and continued. 'Now what has happened? We have become conscious of space again. Cheated of horizons down on earth, we have looked upwards, and found horizons there. What will that do to us? It will put us back to pre-Columbian days. It will be the signal for military conquest, for religious wars. There will be crusades for a Catholic moon, a Protestant moon, a Muslim moon, a Jewish moon. If there are inhabitants up there, we will persecute them mercilessly before we begin to realize their value. You can't feel any affection for a creature you have never seen before, especially if it seems ugly by our standards. The United Nations will lose all control, because its enemy is the smell of space in the nostrils of the military. Life will become cheap again, and so will glory. We will put the clock back to the days of darkness, and our growing pains in the stratosphere will be at least as painful as those we suffered here on earth. I want no part of it.'

The Prime Minister looked at him with genuine affection and offered him another cigar, which he accepted automatically, with a shaking hand.

'You are looking at the world with the eyes of a historian,' said the Prime Minister, 'but the world is not run by historians. It is a luxury we cannot afford. We can't study events from such a comfortable distance, nor can we allow ourselves to be embittered so easily by the unfortunate parallels and repetitions of history. As a historian, you are no doubt right, since you look back so far in order to look forward, but as a politician you are wrong, you are wrong as a patriot.'

'I have no ambitions as a patriot,' John answered. 'I want to be a man the world is proud of.'

'You are young,' said the Prime Minister, lighting a match for John. 'Incidentally, the Archbishop of Canterbury has expressed an urgent desire to meet you.'

'I knew it,' cried John, 'a Church of England moon!'

When he returned home, John sat up all night writing a letter. Veronica, as she lay sleepless, heard the febrile stutter of the typewriter and an occasional angry outburst. The cabin trunks still stood half-filled in the bedroom, a measure of how disappointed John and Veronica were at not going to Washington and of their uncertainty about the future.

John didn't go to bed that night, but left the house at six-thirty to post his letter. He noticed a detective loitering on the opposite pavement, but ignored him.

There was practically no conversation between Veronica and John all day, and even the children modified their games. It was as though disaster had struck the family.

After lunch, they suffered the surprise visit of a grave Sir Humphrey, accompanied by Oliver de Vouvenay at his most petulant, and a rosy-faced inspector from Scotland Yard called Peddick.

'What may I offer you?' asked John, investing his question with sarcasm. He seemed incapable of saying anything without sarcasm these days.

'Nothing. Nothing at all,' answered Sir Humphrey.

'Perhaps we could sit down?' said de Vouvenay.

'I see nothing to prevent you,' said John.

There was a brief, awkward silence.

'Well?'

In silence, Oliver de Vouvenay opened his briefcase and produced the letter which John had posted that morning. It was open.

'What are you doing with that?' John asked hotly.

'Perhaps I should take over, sir?' It was Inspector Peddick speaking. 'Did you write this?'

'What business is it of yours?'

'It's addressed to Switzerland, sir.'

'I can explain that. It is addressed to Switzerland because I intended it to arrive in Switzerland.'

'I gather, sir, that it contains information of a highly secret nature.'

'It contains information which emanated from my brain and which I do not consider secret. And in any case, for how long has it been the practice, in this free country, for the police to intercept private letters?'

'We have authority, sir, under the Official Secrets Act.'

'Could you tell me what you find particularly secret about the information contained in this letter?'

The Inspector smiled. 'That's hardly my province, sir. It doesn't make much sense to me, but I've been told it's secret from higher-up, and I acted accordingly.'

'But you've read it?'

'Oh, I skimmed through part of it, yes, sir, in the course of duty.'

John broke a vase and shouted a profanity.

Sir Humphrey raised a restraining hand. 'You must realise, John, that you must be in some measure subject to government policy. You can't go on being a rebel all your grown life. What you have accomplished is far too important for us all for you to attempt to destroy it by what you imagine to be scientific integrity. John, I implore you to regard yourself as the caretaker of a secret, and not to do anything in your moment of imminent triumph which will bring you into disrepute.'

'I am not the caretaker of a secret,' thundered John, 'I am the inventor of a public utility!'

'You wrote a letter to Switzerland, to a Professor Nussli. Professor Nussli has been to Moscow recently,' said de Vouvenay, smoothly.

'So what?' snapped John. 'I've been to Trinidad, that doesn't mean I sing calypsos all day. What god-awful idiots you all are. Just because a man is inquisitive, just because he wants to find out, you think automatically that he's tarnished by whatever he went to investigate.'

'I didn't insinuate that at all.'

'Why did you mention it then? What do people mean when they

say the word "Moscow" out of the blue? How naïve do you think I am? I've known Nussli for nearly forty years—in other words, all my life. I was brought up in Switzerland when I was young because I had asthma. I went to school with Hans. We were firm friends. He's a brilliant man now as he was a brilliant boy then, and he knows probably more about my particular field than any other man alive today. He's a thoroughly enlightened, liberal chap.'

'I'm very gratified to hear it,' said de Vouvenay.

'*You're* gratified to hear it?' shouted John, losing his temper. 'And who the hell d'you think you are? I very much regret leaving my Swiss school, where I worked and had fun, to come back here for the sole privilege of watching your nasty little career developing from the selfrighteous goody-goody with the only unbroken voice in school which could do justice to the soprano solos in the *Messiah* to the pompous prig who has the impertinence to ventilate opinions about which he knows nothing, nothing, nothing! Get out of here.'

De Vouvenay rose, flushed with anger, his yellow hair falling over one eye. 'Your letter will be confiscated for the time being,' he said, 'and perhaps, in time, you will learn to behave yourself sufficiently for us to be able to entrust you with Herr Nussli's answers.'

John was aghast. 'D'you mean——'

Sir Humphrey looked at him steadily and openly. 'I will apologise for Mr. de Vouvenay,' he said, 'since Mr. de Vouvenay evidently hasn't the resources to apologise himself.'

'Letters to me——'

'Yes, John. I deplore the practice of opening other people's mail. Especially do I deplore it when it is perpetrated by a government. But, as an Englishman, and as one who recognised your great talent early in your life, I must say that I realise the necessity for such an emergency measure at this time. We must not only protect our secret from any enemy, but we must protect you from yourself. I don't know what you have been writing to Professor Nussli during these past months, but the one answer in our possession suggests that he has a detailed and even a brilliant insight into our methods. What is especially disturbing is his apparent knowledge of our fuel——'

'Our fuel, fiddlesticks. It was his fuel as much as mine. How do you think two friends work when they are fired by the same ambition? They share their information, selflessly, for the common good.'

'In the mail? Neither of these letters was so much as registered.'

'Surely the mail is more discreet than the telephone, and it's certainly less expensive. I never for one moment believed that my letters would be opened. Had I known that, I would have found other methods of communication.'

'Such as?' asked de Vouvenay.

'Pigeons,' spat John.

When the visitors had left, John chided himself for not having hit de Vouvenay. He had actually been forced to defend himself from a position which was as strong as any position could be in a country with democratic traditions. His correspondence had been confiscated, and yet somehow he didn't feel that he had been able to bring it home to his tormentors how unethical their conduct had been. He had certainly become very angry, but his anger had somehow been dissipated by his sheer amazement that such things were possible in this day and age, in the twentieth century. The twentieth century? The threshold of the second fifteenth century more likely: the age of discovery, of casual death and roughshod life.

He made a quick decision. Lifting the telephone, he called British European Airways and booked a flight on the plane to Zurich. With two hours to kill, he paced the room reconstructing the scene with his three visitors and his dinner with the Prime Minister, his mood settling into one of cold and righteous indignation as he thought of all the choice phrases he would have used had he had the presence of mind.

Then, with forty minutes to go, he put his passport in his pocket, decided not to say goodbye to his wife, since explanations would only dilute his fury, and left the house, quietly closing the front door. The taxi arrived at London Airport with some minutes to spare, and John went into the departure hall. The young ladies were very polite and directed him into Immigration. Here, a colourless gentleman looked at his passport for a small eternity, seeming to read mysterious meanings into old visas. Eventually the colourless gentleman looked up, not at John, but past him.

A voice in John's ear said, 'I'm sorry, Mr. Kermidge.'

It was Inspector Peddick.

Veronica worried about John for the next three weeks. Although he was not ill, he showed no inclination to rise, and began to grow a beard out of sheer indolence. He never spoke except to say on one

occasion, 'I'm a patriot, my dear. I'm staying in bed to make it easy
for the police. In these hard days of intensive burglary and juvenile
delinquency, it would be unfair to put too much pressure on the
Yard by moving around.'

Sir Humphrey came to the house once or twice, but John just
stared at the ceiling, refusing to say a word. Preparations were
being made to launch John's rocket, and Sir Humphrey, a kind of
devoted man at heart, sought to cheer up Veronica by telling her
that a peerage was in the air. 'Even if John bridles at being Lord
Kermidge, he'd surely wish to see you Lady Kermidge.'

'I don't care so long as he eats.'

One night, some twenty-five days after John's attempt to fly to
Zurich, the Press the world over noticed mysterious and intensive
diplomatic activity.

It was remarked by vigilant American journalists that the Secretary of State left a public dinner at Cincinnati in order to fly to
Washington. A few minutes later, the President of the United States
interrupted a fishing holiday and left for Washington by helicopter.
The faces of these two dignitaries were exceptionally grave.

Newspapermen in Moscow observed that a meeting of the
Supreme Soviet had been called at only an hour's notice and that
grim-faced deputies were disrupting the traffic as they poured into
the Kremlin. Areas were cordoned off, and the police were uncom-
municative. In Paris, a crisis was stopped in midstream as a rumour
spread, making the rising spiral of the cost of living seem frivolous
indeed.

The Right Honourable Arthur Backworth left Chequers at four
in the morning for Number 10 Downing Street. Observers caught a
glimpse of his ashen face in the dark bowels of his Rolls-Royce.

The wires from America reported not only the unexpected
presence of the President and the Secretary of State in the federal
capital, but also of an unusual number of generals and admirals, all
of them sullen and thunderous. Businessmen attempting transatlan-
tic calls found that there were endless delays. Tempers were frayed
the world over.

One of the last to know the reason why was John, who was fast
asleep when Veronica and Bill burst into his room with all the
morning papers. He glanced at the headline of the first paper and
began to laugh, slowly at first, then hysterically, until the tears
poured from his eyes in a stream, coursing through his young beard,

staining his pyjama top. For a full quarter of an hour he laughed, weeping, moaning, gripping his sides, tearing the sheets with a delight which overlapped into anguish, panting like a dying man, and dragging Bill and Veronica with him in his lunatic joy. Suddenly the laughter stopped, and John, Bill, and Veronica looked at each other without energy, without emotion.

John, breathing deeply, took up the newspaper and read the headline again.

It said, in banner type, SWISS REACH THE MOON.

GEORGE LAMMING
A Wedding in Spring

LONDON was their first lesson in cities. The solitude and hugeness
of the place had joined their lives more closely than ever; but it was
the force of similar childhoods which now threatened to separate
them: three men and a woman, island people from the Caribbean,
who waited in separate rooms of the same basement, sharing the
nervousness of the night.

The wedding was only a day away.

Snooker thought he could hear the sweat spilling out of his pores.
Talking to himself, old-woman-like in trouble, he started: 'Is
downright, absolute stupid to make me harness myself in dis
mornin' costume.... I ain't no Prince Philip or ever want to
be....'

A pause drew his attention to the morning suit he had rented.
The top hat sat on its crown, almost imitating itself. It provoked
Snooker. He watched it, swore at it, then stooped as though he was
going to sit on it.

'Now what you think you doin'?'

Snooker was alerted. He heard the closing creak of the door and
the blurred chuckle of Knickerbocker's voice redeeming the status
of the top hat.

Snooker was silent. He watched Knickerbocker hold the top hat
out like some extraordinary fruit in his hand.

'Is what Beresford think it is at all?' he said, turning his back on
the suit to face Knickerbocker. 'My body, not to mention my face,
ain't shape for dis kind o' get-up.'

'Even de beggar can be king,' said Knickerbocker, 'an' dis is de
kind o' headpiece kings does wear.' He cuddled the top hat to his
chest. 'An' tomorrow,' he added, lifting his head towards Snooker,
'I goin' to play king.'

'You goin' to play jackass,' Snooker said sharply.

'So what?' Knickerbocker smiled. 'Christ did ride on one.'

'Is ride these clothes goin' ride you tomorrow,' said Snooker,
''cause you ain't got no practice in wearin' them.'

'You goin' see who ride what,' said Knickerbocker, 'I sittin' in de

back o' dat limousine jus' so, watch me, Snooker.' He was determined to prove his passion for formal dress. He had lowered his
body on to the chair, fitting the top hat on his head at precisely the
angle his imagination had shaped. He crossed his legs, and plucked
at the imaginary seams of his morning trousers. The chair leaned
with him while he felt the air for the leather rest which would hold
his hand.

Snooker refused to look. But Knickerbocker had already entered
the fantasy which the wedding would make real. His head was loud
with bells and his eyes turned wild round the crowd, hilarious with
praise, as they acknowledged his white gloved welcome. Even the
police had removed their helmets in homage to the splendour which
he had brought to a drab and enfeebled London. He was teaching
the English their own tune. So he didn't hear Snooker's warning
until the leather rest refused his hand and the crowd vanished into
the shadows which filled the room. The chair had collapsed like a
pack of cards under Knickerbocker's body. He looked like a cripple
on his back.

Now he was afraid, and he really frightened Snooker too, the way
he probed his hands with fearful certainty under and across his
thighs. His guess was right. There was a split the size of a sword
running down the leg and through the crutch of the only pair of
trousers he owned.

'You break up my bes' chair,' Snooker said sadly, carrying the
top hat like wet crockery across the room. It had fallen into the
sink.

The crisis had begun. Knickerbocker crouched on all fours, his
buttocks cocked at the mirror, to measure the damage he had done.
The basement was still: Knickerbocker considering his black expo-
sure while Snooker collected the wreckage in both hands, wondering
how he could fit his chair together again. They didn't speak, but
they could hear, behind the door, a quiet tumble of furniture, and
after an interval of silence, the sullen ticking of the clock in Flo's
room.

She was alone, twisting her hair into knotty plaits that rose like
spikes out of her skull. She did not only disapprove of her brother's
wedding but she also thought it a conspiracy against all they had
learnt. Preoccupied and disdainful, she saw the Vaseline melt and
slip like frying lard over her hands. The last plait done, she stuck
the comb like a plough into the low shrub of hair at the back of her

neck. She scrubbed her ears with her thumb; stretched the under lid of each eye to tell her health; and finally gave her bottom a belligerent slap with both hands. She was in a fighting mood.

'As if he ain't done born poor,' she said, caught in that whispering self-talk which filled the basement night. 'Borrowin' an' hockin' every piece o' possession to make a fool o' himself, an' worse still dat he should go sell Snooker his bicycle to rent mornin' suit an' limousine. Gran Gran. . . . Gawd res' her in de grave, would go wild if she know what Beresford doin' . . . an' for what . . . for who he bringin' his own downfall.'

It was probably too late to make Beresford change his mind: what with all those West Indians he had asked to drop in after the ceremony for a drink: the Jamaican with the macaw face who arrived by chance every Sunday at supper time, and Caruso, the calypsonian, who made his living by turning every rumour into a song that could scandalise your name for life. She was afraid of Caruso, with his malicious tongue, and his sly, secretive, slanderous manner. Moreover, Caruso never travelled without his gang: Slip Disk, Toodles and Square Dick; then there were Lice-Preserver, Gunner, Crim, Clarke Gable Number Two, and the young Sir Winston. They were all from 'back home', idle, godless, and greedy. Then she reflected that they were not really idle. They worked with Beresford in the same tyre factory.

'But idle or no idle,' she frowned, 'I ain't want Beresford marry no white woman. If there goin' be any disgrace, let me disgrace him first.'

She was plotting against the wedding. She wanted to bribe Snooker and Knickerbocker into a sudden disagreement with her brother. Knickerbocker's disapproval would have been particularly damaging since it was he who had introduced the English girl to Beresford. And there was something else about Knickerbocker that Flo knew.

The door opened on Snooker who was waiting in the passage for Knickerbocker. Flo watched him in the dark and counted three before leaning her hand on his head. Her anger had given way to a superb display of weakness: a woman outraged, defenceless, and innocent of words which could tell her feeling.

'Snooker.'

'What happen now?'

'I want all you two speak to Beresford,' she said. Her voice was a whimper appropriate with grief.

'Let the man make his own bed,' said Snooker, 'is he got to lie down in it.'

'But is this Englan' turn his head an' make him lose his senses.' Flo crouched lower, tightening her hand against Snooker's neck.

'He keep his head all right,' said Snooker, 'but is the way he hearken what his mother say, like he walkin' in infancy all life long.'

'Ma wasn't ever goin' encourage him in trouble like this,' Flo said.

'Is too late to change anything,' said Snooker, 'except these kiss-me-tail mornin' clothes. Is like playin' ju-ju warrior with all that silk cravat an' fish-shape' frock they call a coat. I ain't wearin' it.'

'Forget 'bout that,' said Flo, 'is the whole thing we got to stop complete.'

Knickerbocker was slipping through the shadows, silent and massive as a wall which now rose behind Flo. The light made a white mask over his face. Flo seemed to feel her failure, sudden and complete. Knickerbocker had brought a different kind of trouble. He was fingering the safety-pins which closed the gap in his trousers. He trusted Flo's opinion in these details. He stooped forward and turned to let her judge whether he had done a good job.

'Move your tail out of my face,' she shouted, 'what the hell you take me for?'

Knickerbocker looked hurt. He raised his body to full height, bringing his hands shamefully over the safety-pins. He couldn't understand Flo's fury: the angry and unwarranted rebuke, the petulant slam of the door in his face. And Snooker wouldn't talk. They stood in the dark like dogs shut out.

Beresford was waiting in the end room. He looked tipsy and a little vacant under the light; but he had heard Flo's voice echoing down the passage, and he knew the others were near. It was his wish that they should join him for a drink. He watched the bottle making splinters with the light, sugar brown and green, over the three glasses and a cup. The label had lost its lettering; so he turned to the broken envelope on his stomach and went on talking to himself.

All night that voice had made dialogue with itself about his bride. His mood was reflective, nostalgic. He needed comfort, and he turned to read his mother's letter again.

*   *   *

. . . concernin the lady in question you must choose like i would have you in respect to caracter an so forth. i excuse and forgive your long silence since courtship i know takes time. pay my wellmeanin and prayerful respects to the lady in question. give flo my love and my remembrance to snooker and knick. . . .

The light was swimming under his eyes; the words seemed to harden and slip off the page. He thought of Flo and wished she would try to share his mother's approval.

. . . if the weddin come to pass, see that you dress proper, i mean real proper, like the folks in that land would have you. hope you keepin the bike in good condition. . . .

The page had fallen from his hand in a moment of distraction. He was beginning to regret that he had sold the bicycle to Snooker. But his mood didn't last. He heard a knock on the door and saw Knickerbocker's head emerge through the light.

'Help yuhself, Knick.'

Beresford squeezed the letter into his pocket while he watched Knickerbocker close in on the table.

'I go take one,' Knickerbocker said, 'just one.'

'Get a next glass if the cup don't suit you.'

'Any vessel will do,' Knickerbocker said.

Knickerbocker poured rum like water as though his arm could not understand the size of a drink. They touched cup and glass, making twisted faces when the rum started its course down their throats.

'Where Snooker?'

'Puttin' up the bike,' Knickerbocker said. 'But Flo in a rage.'

'She'll come round all right,' said Beresford. 'Is just that she in two minds, one for me an' one 'gainst the wedding.'

'You fix up for the limousine?'

'Flo self do it this mornin',' said Beresford, 'they comin' for half pas' four.'

'Who goin' partner me if Flo don't come to the church?'

'Flo goin' go all right,' said Beresford.

'But you never can know with Flo.'

Beresford looked doubtful, but he had to postpone his misgivings. Knickerbocker poured more rum to avoid further talk, and

Beresford held out his glass. They understood the pause. Now they were quiet, rehearsing the day that was so near. The room in half light and liquor was preparing them for melancholy: two men of similar tastes temporarily spared the intrusion of female company. They were a club whose rules were part of their instinct.

'Snooker ask me to swap places wid him,' Knickerbocker said.

'He don't want to be my best man?' Beresford asked.

'He ain't feel friendly with the morning suit,' Knickerbocker said.

'But what is proper is proper.'

'Is what I say too,' Knickerbocker agreed. 'If you doin' a thing, you mus' do it as the done thing is doed.'

Beresford considered this change. He was open to any suggestion.

'Snooker or you, it ain't make no difference,' he said.

'Then I goin' course wid you to de altar,' Knickerbocker said.

Was it the rum or the intimacy of their talk which had dulled their senses? They hadn't heard the door open and they couldn't guess how long Flo had been standing there, rigid as wire, with hands akimbo, and her head, bull shaped, feeding on some scheme that would undo their plans.

'Get yuhself a glass, Flo,' Beresford offered.

'Not me, Berry, thanks all the same.'

'What you put your face in mournin' like that for?' Knickerbocker said. He was trying to relieve the tension with his banter. 'Those whom God join together . . .'

'What you callin' God in this for?' Flo charged. 'It ain't God join my brother wid any hawk-nose English woman. Is his stupid excitement.'

'There ain't nothin' wrong wid the chick,' Knickerbocker parried.

'Chick, my eye!' Flo was advancing towards them. 'He let a little piece o' left-over white tail put him in heat.'

'Flo!'

Beresford's glass had fallen to the floor. He was standing, erect, wilful, his hands nervous and eager for action. Knickerbocker thought he would hit her.

'Don't you threaten me wid any look you lookin',' Flo challenged him. 'Knickerbocker, here, know what I sayin' is true. Look him good in his face an' ask him why he ain't marry her.'

'Take it easy, Flo, take it easy,' Knickerbocker cautioned. 'Beresford marryin' 'cause he don't want to roam wild like a bush beast in this London jungle.'

'An' she, you know where she been roamin' all this time?' Flo answered. Knickerbocker fumbled for the cup.

'Is jus' what Seven Foot Walker tell you back in Port-o'-Spain,' Beresford threw in.

Whatever the English girl's past, Beresford felt he had to defend his woman's honour. His hands were now steady as stone watching Flo wince as she waited to hear him through.

'That man take you for a long ride, Flo, an' then he drop you like a latch key that won't fit no more. You been in mournin' ever since that mornin' he turn tail an' lef' you waitin'. An' is why you set yuh scorpion tongue on my English woman.'

'Me an' Seven Foot Walker . . .'

'Yes, you an' Seven Foot Walker!'

'Take it easy,' Knickerbocker begged them. 'Take it easy . . .'

'I goin' to tell you, Berry, I goin' to tell you . . .'

'Take it easy,' Knickerbocker pleaded, 'take it easy . . .'

Flo was equipped for this kind of war. Her eyes were points of flame and her tongue was tight and her memory like an ally demanding vengeance was ready with malice. She was going to murder them with her knowledge of what had happened between Knickerbocker and the English girl. Time, place, and circumstance: they were weapons which now loitered in her memory waiting for release. She was bursting with passion and spite. Knickerbocker felt his loyalty waver. He was worried. But Flo's words never came. The door opened and Snooker walked in casual as a bird, making music on his old guitar. He was humming: 'Nobody knows the trouble I've seen.' And his indifference was like a reprieve.

'The limousine man outside to see you,' he said. 'Somebody got to make some kind o' down payment.'

The crisis had been postponed.

London had never seen anything like it before. The spring was decisive, a hard, clear sky and the huge sun naked as a skull eating through the shadows of the afternoon. High up on the balcony of a fifth-floor flat an elderly man with a distressful paunch was feeding birdseed to a flock of pigeons. He hated foreigners and noise, but the day had done something to his temper. He was feeling fine. The pigeons soon flew away, cruising in circles above the enormous crowd which kept watch outside the church; then closed their ranks and settled one by one over the familiar steeple.

The weather was right; but the crowd, irreverent and forgetful in their fun, had misjudged the meaning of the day. The legend of English reticence was stone-cold dead. An old-age pensioner with no teeth at all couldn't stop laughing to the chorus, a thousand times chuckled: 'Cor bli'me, look at my lads.' He would say, "Ere comes a next in 'is tails, smashers the lot o' them,' and then: 'Cor bli'me, look at my lads.' A contingent of Cypriots on their way to the Colonial Office had folded their banners to pause for a moment that turned to hours outside the church. The Irish were irrepressible with welcome. Someone burst a balloon, and two small boys, swift and effortless as a breeze, opened their fists and watched the firecrackers join in the gradual hysteria of the day.

Snooker wished the crowd away; yet he was beyond anger. Sullen and reluctant as he seemed he had remained loyal to Beresford's wish. His mind alternated between worrying and wondering why the order of events had changed. It was half an hour since he had arrived with the bride. Her parents had refused at the last moment to have anything to do with the wedding, and Snooker accepted to take her father's place. He saw himself transferred from one role to another; but the second seemed more urgent. It was the intimacy of their childhood, his and Beresford's, which had coaxed him into wearing the morning suit. He had to make sure that the bride would keep her promise. But Beresford had not arrived; nor Knicker-bocker, nor Flo.

Snooker remembered fragments of the argument in the basement room the night before; and he tried to avoid any thought of Flo. He looked round the church and the boys from 'back home' looked at him and he knew they, too, were puzzled. They were all there: Caruso, Slip Disk, Lice-Preserver, and an incredibly fat woman whom they called Tiny. Behind him, two rows away, he could hear Toodles and Square Dick rehearsing in whispers what they had witnessed outside. There had been some altercation at the door when the verger asked Caruso to surrender his guitar. Tiny and Slip Disk had gone ahead, and the verger was about to show his firmness when he noticed Lice-Preserver who was wearing full evening dress and a sword. The verger suddenly changed his mind and indicated a pew, staring in terror at the sword that hung like a frozen tail down Lice-Preserver's side. Snooker closed his eyes and tried to pray.

But trouble was brewing outside. The West Indians had refused to share in this impromptu picnic. They had journeyed from Brixton and Camden Town, the whole borough of Paddington and the Holloway Road, to keep faith with the boys from 'back home'. One of the Irishmen had a momentary lapse into prejudice and said something shocking about the missing bridegroom. The West Indians bristled and waited for an argument. But a dog intervened, an energetic, white poodle which kicked its hind legs up and shook its ears in frenzy at them. The poodle frisked and howled as though the air and the organ music had turned its head. Another firecracker went off, and the Irishman tried to sing his way out of a fight. But the West Indians were showing signs of a different agitation. They had become curious, attentive. They narrowed the circle to whisper their secret.

'Ain't it his sister standin' over yonder?'

They were slow to believe their own recognition.

'Is Flo, all right,' a voice answered, 'but she not dress for the wedding.'

'Seems she not goin',' a man said as though he wanted to disbelieve his suspicion.

'An' they wus so close,' the other added, 'close, close, she an' that brother.'

Flo was nervous. She stood away from the crowd, half hearing the rumour of her brother's delay. She tried to avoid the faces she knew, wondering what Beresford had decided to do. Half an hour before she left the house she had cancelled the limousine and hidden his morning suit. Now she regretted her action. She didn't want the wedding to take place, but she couldn't bear the thought of humiliating her brother before this crowd. The spectacle of the crowd was like a rebuke to her own stubbornness.

She was retreating further away. Would Beresford find the morning suit? And the limousine? He had set his heart on arriving with Knickerbocker in the limousine. She knew how fixed he was in his convictions, like his grandfather whose wedding could not proceed; had, indeed, to be postponed because he would not repeat the words: *All my worldly goods I thee endow.* He had sworn never to part with his cow. He had a thing about his cow, like Beresford and the morning suit. Puzzled, indecisive, Flo looked round at the faces, eager as they for some sign of an arrival; but it seemed she had lost her memory of the London streets.

* * *

The basement rooms were nearly half a mile from the nearest tube station; and the bus strike was on. Beresford looked defeated. He had found the morning suit, but there was no way of arranging for another limousine. Each second followed like a whole season of waiting. The two men stood in front of the house, hailing cabs, pleading for lifts.

'Is to get there,' Beresford said, 'is to get there 'fore my girl leave the church.'

'I goin' deal wid Flo,' Knickerbocker swore. 'Tomorrow or a year from tomorrow I goin' deal wid Flo.'

'How long you think they will wait?'

Beresford had dashed forward again, hailing an empty cab. The driver saw them, slowed down, and suddenly changed his mind. Knickerbocker swore again. Then: a moment of revelation.

'Tell you what,' Knickerbocker said. He looked as though he had surprised himself.

'What, what!' Beresford insisted.

'Wait here,' Knickerbocker said, rushing back to the basement room. 'I don't give a goddam. We goin' make it.'

The crowd waited outside the church, but they looked a little bored. A clock struck the half-hour. The vicar came out to the steps and looked up at the sky. The man in the fifth-floor flat was eating pork sausages and drinking tea. The pigeons were dozing. The sun leaned away and the trees sprang shadows through the early evening.

Someone said: 'It's getting on.'

It seemed that the entire crowd had agreed on an interval of silence. It was then the woman with the frisky white poodle held her breast and gasped. She had seen them: Beresford and Knickerbocker. They were arriving. It was an odd and unpredictable appearance. Head down, his shoulders arched and harnessed in the morning coat, Knickerbocker was frantically pedalling Snooker's bicycle towards the crowd. Beresford sat on the bar, clutching both top hats to his stomach. The silk cravats sailed like flags round their necks. The crowd tried to find their reaction. At first: astonishment. Later: a state of utter incomprehension.

They made a gap through which the bicycle free-wheeled towards the church. And suddenly there was applause, loud and spontaneous as thunder. The Irishman burst into song. The whole rhythm of the day had changed. A firecracker dripped flames over the church steeple and the pigeons dispersed. But crisis was always near. Knickerbocker was trying to dismount when one tail of the coat got stuck between the spokes. The other tail dangled like a bone on a string, and the impatient white poodle charged upon them. She was barking and snapping at Knickerbocker's coat tails. Beresford fell from the bar on to his knees, and the poodle caught the end of his silk cravat. It turned to threads between her teeth.

The crowd could not determine their response. They were hysterical, sympathetic. One tail of Knickerbocker's coat had been taken. He was aiming a kick at the poodle; and immediately the crowd took sides. They didn't want harm to come to the animal. The poodle stiffened her tail and stood still. She was enjoying this exercise until she saw the woman moving in behind her. There was murder in the woman's eyes. The poodle lost heart. But the top hats were her last temptation. Stiff with fright, she leapt to one side seizing them between her teeth like loaves. And she was off. The small boys shouted: 'Come back, Satire, come back!' But the poodle hadn't got very far. Her stub of tail had been safely caught between Flo's hand. The poodle was howling for release. Flo lifted the animal by the collar and shook its head like a box of bones.

Knickerbocker was clawing his rump for the missing tail of the morning coat. Beresford hung his head, swinging the silk cravat like a kitchen rag down his side. Neither could move. Flo's rage had paralysed their speech. She had captured the top hats, and it was clear that the wedding had now lost its importance for her. It was a trifle compared with her brother's disgrace.

The vicar had come out to the steps, and all the boys from 'back home' stood round him: Toodles, Caruso, and Square Dick, Slip Disk, Clarke Gable Number Two, and the young Sir Winston. Lice-Preserver was carrying the sword in his right hand. But the poodle had disappeared.

Flo stood behind her brother, dripping with tears as she fixed the top hat on his head. Neither spoke. They were too weak to resist her. She was leading them up the steps into the church. The vicar went scarlet.

'Which is the man?' he shouted. But Flo was indifferent to his fury.

'It don't matter,' she said. 'You ju' go marry my brother.'

And she walked between Knickerbocker and her brother with the vicar and the congregation of boys from 'back home' following like a funeral procession to the altar.

Outside, the crowd were quiet. In a far corner of sunlight and leaves, the poodle sat under a tree licking her paws, while the fat man from the fifth-floor flat kept repeating like an idiot to himself: 'But how, how, how extraordinary!'

JOHN WAIN
A Message from the Pig-man

HE was never called Ekky now, because he was getting to be a real boy, nearly six, with grey flannel trousers that had a separate belt, and weren't kept up by elastic, and his name was Eric. But this was just one of those changes brought about naturally, by time, not a disturbing alteration; he understood that. His mother hadn't meant that kind of change when she had promised, 'Nothing will be changed.' It was all going to go on as before, except that Dad wouldn't be there, and Donald would be there instead. He knew Donald, of course, and felt all right about his being in the house, though it seemed, when he lay in bed and thought about it, mad and pointless that Donald's coming should mean that Dad had to go. Why should it mean that? The house was quite big. He hadn't any brothers and sisters, and if he *had* had any he wouldn't have minded sharing his bedroom, even with a baby that wanted a lot of looking after, so long as it left the spare room free for Dad to sleep in. If he did that, they wouldn't have a spare room, it was true, but then, the spare room was nearly always empty; the last time anybody had used the spare room was *years* ago, when he had been much smaller—last winter, in fact. And, even then, the visitor, the lady with the funny teeth who laughed as she breathed in, instead of as she breathed out like everyone else, had only stayed two or three nights. *Why* did grown-ups do everything in such a mad, silly way? They often told him not to be silly, but they were silly themselves in a useless way, not laughing or singing or anything, just being silly and sad.

It was so hard to read the signs; that was another thing. When they did give you something to go on, it was impossible to know how to take it. Dad had bought him a train, just a few weeks ago, and taught him how to fit the lines together. That ought to have meant that he would stay; what sensible person would buy a train, and fit it all up ready to run, even as a present for another person—*and then leave?* Donald had been quite good about the train, Eric had to admit that; he had bought a bridge for it and a lot of rolling-stock. At first he had got the wrong kind of rolling-stock, with wheels too close together to fit on to the rails; but instead of playing the usual grown-ups' trick of pulling a face and then not doing anything about it, he had gone back to the shop, straight away that same afternoon, and got the right kind. Perhaps that meant *he* was going to leave. But that didn't seem likely. Not the way Mum held on to him all the time, even holding him round the middle as if he needed keeping in one piece.

All the same, he was not Ekky now, he was Eric, and he was sensible and grown-up. Probably it was his own fault that everything seemed strange. He was not living up to his grey flannel trousers—perhaps that was it; being afraid of too many things, not asking questions that would probably turn out to have quite simple answers.

The Pig-man, for instance. He had let the Pig-man worry him far too much. None of the grown-ups acted as if the Pig-man was anything to be afraid of. He probably just *looked* funny, that was all. If, instead of avoiding him so carefully, he went outside one evening and looked at him, took a good long, unafraid look, leaving the back door open behind him so that he could dart in to the safety and warmth of the house . . . no! It was better, after all, not to see the Pig-man; not till he was bigger, anyway; nearly six was quite big but it wasn't really *very* big. . . .

And yet it was one of those puzzling things. No one ever told him to be careful not to let the Pig-man get hold of him, or warned him in any way; so the Pig-man *must* be harmless, because when it came to anything that *could* hurt you, like the traffic on the main road, people were always ramming it into you that you must look both ways, and all that stuff. And yet when it came to the Pig-man, no one ever mentioned him; he seemed beneath the notice of grown-ups. His mother would say, now and then, 'Let me see, it's to-day the Pig-man comes, isn't it?' or, 'Oh dear, the Pig-man will be coming round soon, and I haven't put anything out.' If she talked like this, Eric's spine would tingle and go cold; he would keep very still and wait, because quite often her next words would be, 'Eric, just take these peelings', or whatever it was, 'out to the bucket, dear, will you?' The bucket was about fifty yards away from the back door; it was shared by the peple in the two next-door houses. None of *them* was afraid of the Pig-man, either. What was their attitude, he wondered? Were they sorry for him, having to eat damp old stuff out of a bucket—tea-leaves and eggshells and that sort of thing? Perhaps he cooked it when he got home, and made it a bit nicer. Certainly, it didn't look too nice when you lifted the lid of the bucket and saw it all lying there. It sometimes smelt, too. Was the Pig-man very poor? Was he sorry for himself, or did he feel all right about being like that? *Like what?* What did the Pig-man look like? He would have little eyes, and a snout with a flat end; but would he have trotters, or hands and feet like a person's?

Lying on his back, Eric worked soberly at the problem. The Pig-man's bucket had a handle; so he must carry it in the ordinary way, in his hand—unless, of course he walked on all fours and carried it in his mouth. But that wasn't very likely, because if he walked on all fours, what difference would there be between him and an ordinary pig? To be called the Pig-man, rather than the Man-pig, surely implied that he was upright, and dressed. Could he talk? Probably, in a kind of grunting way, or else how would he tell the people what kind of food he wanted them to put in his bucket? *Why hadn't he asked Dad about the Pig-man?* That had been his mistake; Dad would have told him exactly all about it. But he had gone. Eric fell asleep, and in his sleep he saw Dad and the Pig-man going in a train together; he called, but they did not hear him and the train carried them away. 'Dad!' he shouted desperately after it. 'Don't bring the Pig-man when you come back! Don't bring the Pig-man!' Then his mother was in the room, kissing him and smelling nice; she felt soft, and the softness ducked him into sleep, this time without dreams; but the next day his questions returned.

Still, there was school in the morning, and going down to the swings in the afternoon, and altogether a lot of different things to crowd out the figure of the Pig-man and the questions connected with it. And he was never further from worrying about it all than that moment, a few evenings later, when it suddenly came to a crisis.

Eric had been allowed, 'just for once', to bring his train into the dining-room after tea, because there was a fire there that made it nicer than the room where he usually played. It was warm and bright, and the carpet in front of the fireplace was smooth and firm, exactly right for laying out the rails on. Donald had come home and was sitting—in Dad's chair, but never mind—reading the paper and smoking. Mum was in the kitchen, clattering gently about, and both doors were open so that she and Donald could call out remarks to each other. Only a short passage lay between. It was just the part of the day Eric liked best, and bed-time was comfortably far off. He fitted the sections of rail together, glancing in anticipation at the engine as it stood proudly waiting to haul the carriages round and round, tremendously fast.

Then his mother called, 'Eric! Do be a sweet, good boy, and take this stuff out to the Pig-man. My hands are covered with cake mixture. I'll let you scrape out the basin when you come in.'

For a moment he kept quite still, hoping he hadn't really heard her say it, that it was just a voice inside his head. But Donald looked over at him and said, 'Go along, old man. You don't mind, do you?'

Eric said, 'But tonight's when the Pig-man *comes*.'

Surely, *surely* they weren't asking him to go out, in the deep twilight, just at the time when there was the greatest danger of actually *meeting* the Pig-man.

'All the better,' said Donald, turning back to his paper.

Why was it better? Did they *want* him to meet the Pig-man?

Slowly, wondering why his feet and legs didn't refuse to move, Eric went through into the kitchen. 'There it is,' his mother said, pointing to a brown-paper carrier full of potato-peelings and scraps.

He took it up and opened the back door. If he was quick, and darted along to the bucket *at once*, he would be able to lift the lid, throw the stuff in quickly, and be back in the house in about the time it took to count ten.

One—two—three—four—five—six. He stopped. The bucket wasn't there.

It had gone. Eric peered round, but the light, though faint, was not as faint as *that*. He could see that the bucket had gone.

The Pig-man had already been.

Seven—eight—nine—ten, his steps were joyous and light. Back in the house, where it was warm and bright and his train was waiting.

'The Pig-man's gone, Mum. The bucket's not there.'

She frowned, hands deep in the pudding-basin. 'Oh, yes, I do believe I heard him. But it was only a moment ago. Yes, it was just before I called you, darling. It must have been that that made me think of it.'

'Yes?' he said politely, putting down the carrier.

'So if you nip along, dear, you can easily catch him up. And I *do* want that stuff out of the way.'

'Catch him up?' he asked, standing still in the doorway.

'Yes, dear, *catch him up*,' she answered rather sharply (the Efficient Young Mother knows when to be Firm). 'He can't possibly be more than a very short way down the road.'

Before she had finished Eric was outside the door and running. This was a technique he knew. It was the same as getting into icy cold water. If it was the end, if the Pig-man seized him by the hand and dragged him off to his hut, well, so much the worse. Swinging the paper carrier in his hand, he ran fast through the dusk.

The back view of the Pig-man was much as he had expected it to be. A slow, rather lurching gait, hunched shoulders, an old hat crushed down on his head (to hide his ears?) and the pail in his hand. Plod, plod, as if he were tired. Perhaps this was just a ruse, though, probably he could pounce quickly enough when his wicked little eyes saw a nice tasty little boy or something . . . did the Pig-man eat birds? Or cats?

Eric stopped. He opened his mouth to call to the Pig-man, but the first time he tried, nothing came out except a small rasping squeak. His heart was banging like fireworks going off. He could hardly hear anything.

'Mr. Pig-man!' he called, and this time the words came out clear and rather high.

The jogging old figure stopped, turned, and looked at him. Eric could not see properly from where he stood. But he *had* to see. Everything, even his fear, sank and drowned in the raging tide of his curiosity. He moved forward. With each step he saw more clearly. The Pig-man was just an ordinary old man.

'Hello, sonny. Got some stuff there for the old grunters?'

Eric nodded, mutely, and held out his offering. What old grunters? What did he mean?

The Pig-man put down his bucket. He had ordinary hands, ordinary arms. He took the lid off. Eric held out the paper carrier, and the Pig-man's hand actually touched his own for a second. A flood of gratitude rose up inside him. The Pig-man tipped the scraps into the bucket and handed the carrier back.

'Thanks, sonny,' he said.

'Who's it for?' Eric asked, with another rush of articulateness. His voice seemed to have a life of its own.

The Pig-man straightened up, puzzled. Then he laughed, in a gurgling sort of way, but not like a pig at all.

'Arh Aarh Harh Harh,' the Pig-man went. 'Not for me, if that's whatcher mean, arh harh.'

He put the lid back on the bucket. 'It's for the old grunters,' he said. 'The old porkers. Just what they likes. Only not fruit skins. I leaves a note, sometimes, about what not to put in. Never fruit skins. It gives 'em the belly-ache.'

He was called the Pig-man because he had some pigs that he looked after.

'Thank you,' said Eric. 'Good-night.' He ran back towards the house, hearing the Pig-man, the ordinary old man, the ordinary usual normal old man, say in his just ordinary old man's voice, 'Good-night, sonny.'

So that was how you did it. You just went straight ahead, not worrying about this or that. Like getting into cold water. You just *did* it.

He slowed down as he got to the gate. For instance, if there was a question that you wanted to know the answer to, and you had always just felt you couldn't ask, the thing to do was to ask it. Just straight out, like going up to the Pig-man. Difficult things, troubles, questions, you just treated them like the Pig-man.

So that was it!

The warm light shone through the crack of the door. He opened it and went in. His mother was standing at the table, her hands still working the cake mixture about. She would let him scrape out the basin, and the spoon—he would ask for the spoon, too. But not straight away. There was a more important thing first.

He put the paper carrier down and went up to her. 'Mum,' he said. 'Why can't Dad be with us even if Donald *is* here? I mean, why can't he live with us as well as Donald?'

His mother turned and went to the sink. She put the tap on and held her hands under it.

'Darling,' she called.

'Yes?' came Donald's voice.

'D'you know what he's just said?'

'What?'

'He's just asked . . .' She turned the tap off and dried her hands, not looking at Eric. 'He wants to know why we can't have Jack to live with us.'

There was a silence, then Donald said, quietly, so that his voice only just reached Eric's ears, 'That's a hard one.'

'You can scrape out the basin,' his mother said to Eric. She lifted him up and kissed him. Then she rubbed her cheek along his, leaving a wet smear. 'Poor little Ekky,' she said in a funny voice.

She put him down and he began to scrape out the pudding-basin, certain at least of one thing, that grown-ups were mad and silly and he hated them all, all, *all*.

L. P. HARTLEY

A High Dive

THE circus-manager was worried. Attendances had been falling off and such people as did come—children they were, mostly—sat about listlessly, munching sweets or sucking ices, sometimes talking to each other without so much as glancing at the show. Only the young or little girls, who came to see the ponies, betrayed any real interest. The clowns' jokes fell flat, for they were the kind of jokes that used to raise a laugh before 1939, after which critical date people's sense of humour seemed to have changed, along with many other things about them. The circus-manager had heard the word 'corny' flung about and didn't like it. What did they want? Something that was, in his opinion, sillier and more pointless than the old jokes; not a bull's-eye on the target of humour, but an outer or even a near-miss—something that brought in the element of futility and that could be laughed at as well as with: an unintentional joke against the joker. The clowns were quick enough with their patter but it just didn't go down: there was too much sense in their nonsense for an up-to-date audience, too much articulateness. They would do better to talk gibberish, perhaps. Now they must change their style, and find out what really did make people laugh, if people could be made to; but he, the manager, was over fifty and never good himself at making jokes, even the old-fashioned kind. What was this word that everyone was using—'sophisticated'? The audiences were too sophisticated, even the children were: they seemed to have seen or heard all this before, even when they were too young to have seen and heard it.

'What shall we do?' he asked his wife. They were standing under the Big Top, which had just been put up, and wondering how many of the empty seats would still be empty when they gave their first performance. 'We shall have to do something, or it's a bad look-out.'

'I don't see what we can do about the comic side,' she said. 'It may come right by itself. Fashions change, all sorts of old things have returned to favour, like old-time dances. But there's something we could do.'

'What's that?'

'Put on an act that's dangerous, really dangerous. Audiences are never bored by that. I know you don't like it, and no more do I, but when we had the Wall of Death——'

Her husband's big chest-muscles twitched under his thin shirt.

'You know what happened then.'

'Yes, but it wasn't our fault, we were in the clear.'

He shook his head.

'Those things upset everyone. I know the public came after it happened—they came in shoals, they came to see the place where someone had been killed. But our people got the needle and didn't give a good performance for I don't know how long. If you're proposing another Wall of Death I wouldn't stand for it—besides, where will you find a man to do it?—especially with a lion on his bike, which is the great attraction.'

'But other turns are dangerous too, as well as dangerous-looking. It's *being* dangerous that is the draw.'

'Then what do you suggest?'

Before she had time to answer a man came up to them.

'I hope I don't butt in,' he said, 'but there's a man outside who wants to speak to you.'

'What about?'

'I think he's looking for a job.'

'Bring him in,' said the manager.

The man appeared, led by his escort, who then went away. He was a tall, sandy-haired fellow with tawny leonine eyes and a straggling moustache. It wasn't easy to tell his age—he might have been about thirty-five. He pulled off his old brown corduroy cap and waited.

'I hear you want to take a job with us,' the manager said, while his wife tried to size up the newcomer. 'We're pretty full up, you know. We don't take on strangers as a rule. Have you any references?'

'No, sir.'

'Then I'm afraid we can't help you. But just for form's sake, what can you do?'

As if measuring its height the man cast up his eyes to the point where one of the two poles of the Big Top was embedded in the canvas.

'I can dive sixty feet into a tank eight foot long by four foot wide by four foot deep.'

The manager stared at him.

'Can you now?' he said. 'If so, you're the very man we want. Are you prepared to let us see you do it?'

'Yes,' the man said.

'And would you do it with petrol burning on the water?'

'Yes.'

'But have we got a tank?' the manager's wife asked.

'There's the old Mermaid's tank. It's just the thing. Get somebody to fetch it.'

While the tank was being brought the stranger looked about him.

'Thinking better of it?' said the manager.

'No, sir,' the man replied. 'I was thinking I should want some bathing-trunks.'

'We can soon fix you up with those,' the manager said. 'I'll show you where to change.'

Leaving the stranger somewhere out of sight, he came back to his wife.

'Do you think we ought to let him do it?' she asked.

'Well, it's his funeral. You wanted us to have a dangerous act, and now we've got it.'

'Yes, I know, but——' The rest was drowned by the rattle of the trolley bringing in the tank—a hollow, double cube like a sarcophagus. Mermaids in low relief sported on its leaden flanks. Grunting and muttering to each other the men slid it into position, a few feet from the pole. Then a length of hosepipe was fastened to a faucet, and soon they heard the sound of water swishing and gurgling in the tank.

'He's a long time changing,' said the manager's wife.

'Perhaps he's looking for a place to hide his money,' laughed her husband, and added, 'I think we'll give the petrol a miss.'

At length the man emerged from behind a screen, and slowly walked towards them. How tall he was, lanky and muscular. The hair on his body stuck out as if it had been combed. Hands on hips he stood beside them, his skin pimpled by goose-flesh. A fit of yawning overtook him.

'How do I get up?' he asked.

The manager was surprised, and pointed to the ladder. 'Unless you'd rather climb up, or be hauled up! You'll find a platform just below the top, to give you a foot-hold.'

He had started to go up the chromium-plated ladder when the manager's wife called after him: 'Are you still sure you want to do it?'

'Quite sure, madam.'

He was too tall to stand upright on the platform, the awning brushed his head. Crouching and swaying forty feet above them he swung his arms as though to test the air's resistance. Then he pitched forward into space, unseen by the manager's wife who looked the other way until she heard a splash and saw a thin sheet of bright water shooting up.

The man was standing breast-high in the tank. He swung himself over the edge and crossed the ring towards them, his body dripping, his wet feet caked with sawdust, his tawny eyes a little bloodshot.

'Bravo!' said the manager, taking his shiny hand. 'It's a first-rate act, that, and will put money in our pockets. What do you want for it, fifteen quid a week?'

The man shook his head. The water trickled from his matted hair on to his shoulders, oozed from his borrowed bathing-suit and made runnels down his sinewy thighs. A fine figure of a man: the women would like him.

'Well, twenty then.'

Still the man shook his head.

'Let's make it twenty-five. That's the most we give anyone.'

Except for the slow shaking of his head the man might not have heard. The circus-manager and his wife exchanged a rapid glance.

'Look here,' he said. 'Taking into account the draw your act is likely to be, we're going to make you a special offer—thirty pounds a week. All right?'

Had the man understood? He put his finger in his mouth and went on shaking his head slowly, more to himself than at them, and seemingly unconscious of the bargain that was being held out to him. When he still didn't answer, the knot of tension broke, and the manager said, in his ordinary, brisk voice.

'Then I'm afraid we can't do business. But just as a matter of interest, tell us why you turned down our excellent offer.'

The man drew a long breath and breaking his long silence said, 'It's the first time I done it and I didn't like it.'

With that he turned on his heel and straddling his long legs walked off unsteadily in the direction of the dressing-room.

The circus-manager and his wife stared at each other.

'It was the first time he'd done it,' she muttered. 'The first time.' Not knowing what to say to him, whether to praise, blame, scold or sympathize, they waited for him to come back, but he didn't come.

'I'll go and see if he's all right,' the circus-manager said. But in two minutes he was back again. 'He's not there,' he said. 'He must have slipped out the other way, the crack-brained fellow!'

L. E. JONES
The Bishop's Aunt

A PICTURE of peace and happiness. That is how most of us who are inclined to think in simple terms would have described the appearance of the compact and ancient town of P. Had we been gazing at it, on a May day in the year 1946, from the café terrace across the river. The warm brown roofs hung in folds, as if a massive rug had been thrown across the descending ridge; at the top of the town rose the castle and the thin flêche of the little cathedral (for P. was an old Catholic see), round which the swifts swooped and shrilled; between the river and the town a row of chestnut trees, still in full bloom, drew, with their continuous shadows, a bold, dark line. The May sunshine, bright and beneficent, lay over all.

But in the town itself was neither peace nor happiness. For P. was in Eastern Europe; the Red Army was occupying the country, and tragedy had come to this quiet little place.

Two days earlier a Russian soldier, sitting unarmed in a café on the small cobbled square, had been assassinated, stabbed in the back by an assailant who had escaped. Even today the edges of a thin, paper-like crust of dried blood and dust lifted and fell in the breeze below the iron chair in which the dead soldier had been sitting. The general of the Division occupying the district had immediately arrested twenty of the leading citizens, including the Catholic Bishop and the Mayor, and had issued a proclamation announcing that, unless the assassin surrendered, or was given up, within forty-eight hours, the twenty hostages would be shot. That period had expired at eleven o'clock on this lovely May morning. At half-past eleven the Bishop and the Mayor were brought, under guard, from the Castle to the small Gothic Town-hall. Here, in the Mayor's parlour, sat the General, with a list of the hostages upon the table before him. There was nothing typical of Russian generals—if photographs can be trusted—in his appearance. His face could have been that of a thoughtful, energetic and efficient senior officer in any Western army; it was strong, but not hard; and he had the air, uncommon in generals, of being capable of listening as well as of speaking. All the same, he could shut his mouth tightly indeed. At the moment his expression was stern, but his grey eyes were not happy.

The two prisoners who now stood before him, the Bishop and the Mayor, had nothing, so far as appearances go, in common. The Bishop, who was in cassock and skull-cap, was a slight wisp of a man in his fifties, with a touch of the peasant about him; his thin face was unremarkable except for the candour, the trustfulness of his wide-open blue eyes. He stood there very much at his ease; even if born a peasant, he moved, stood and spoke like a bishop. The Mayor, on the contrary, was a great bull of a man with angry eyes. His stiff black hair was *en brosse* over a creased forehead; he had a habit of jerking back his head and moving his heavy shoulders under his loose alpaca jacket, that came from his habitual impatience with stupid people—among whom he placed the Bishop. For the Mayor was an aggressive infidel.

When the guards had finished with all those noisy stampings and time-markings, ending with the thump, as they grounded arms, which punctuates military justice everywhere, the General spoke:

'Well, gentlemen, I am sorry it has come to this. The time is up: you have not given up your man: you know the consequences.'

'Naturally we have not given anybody up,' said the Bishop, with a touch of indignation in his rather flat voice. 'Firstly because we do not betray one another and secondly because we don't know who he is.'

'I know who he is,' said the Mayor.

'Oh you do, do you?' said the General, but before he could say more the Bishop had turned on the Mayor, red in the face.

'In that case, Mr. Mayor, you should have persuaded him to give himself up.'

'I beg your pardon?' The Mayor swung round, genuinely surprised.

'Murder,' said the Bishop, 'is always a sin, and a deadly one.' The Mayor turned to the General, putting, for the Bishop's benefit, a weary note into his voice.

'There he goes again, General.' He turned once more to the Bishop. 'As I have wasted far too much of the public's time on telling you and them, Bishop, you always get things mixed up. Murder is a sin: all right. But killing a lance-corporal in the General's army is not murder. It's an act of war. You yourself used to appoint days of prayer for Victory——'

'But the war is over,' interrupted the Bishop. 'We capitulated. And the man was unarmed—stabbed to death, while drinking coffee. It was a cowardly, as well as a wicked murder.'

'Cowardly!' The Mayor began to shout. 'My dear Bishop, I should like to know if *you* would have the guts to allow twenty of your fellow-citizens, including my worshipful self, to be executed, rather than let the General here get away with this futile game of hostages? The man's a hero!'

The Bishop smiled. 'I agree that I might never have had the nerve to let *you* be shot, my son. The thought of your almost certain fate in the next world would be too much for me. But when your man assassinated that poor fellow in the café——'

The General cut him short.

'You can save your sympathy for the "poor" fellow, Bishop. His C.O. tells me he was suspected of Trotskyism, and is better dead. And of course the Mayor is right. If you are going to have a Resistance movement, there can be no rules. But my business, gentlemen, is to suppress the Resistance movement——'

'Which remains unsuppressed,' said the Mayor. 'Our man has beaten you.'

'Don't be too sure, Mr. Mayor,' said the General. 'For one hero, as you call him, there will be fifty others who will think twice before sending a Bishop to paradise and a Mayor to—where did you hint that the Mayor may by before six o'clock, Bishop?'

'I never claimed Paradise, General,' said the Bishop hastily. 'I shall be fortunate if, by Divine Grace, it proves to be Purgatory.'

'I'm in Purgatory now, General,' said the Mayor. 'It's this sentry of yours—I can't abide garlic—could he stand a little farther off?'

'But of course,' said the General, with a glance at the N.C.O. in charge of the guard. There was a bark; a rattle; some more stamping, and the sentry retreated two paces.

'Thank you,' said the Mayor.

'Don't mention it,' said the General. 'No, Mr. Mayor,' he continued, 'I cannot admit that my system of hostages has failed. At the same time I agree that in this particular case things might have gone better. Perhaps I arrested the wrong people. In a town like this there are bound to be individuals whom public opinion would like to see shot.'

'Our Mayor,' said the Bishop, 'is enormously—and from my point of view I must add deplorably—popular.'

'Our Bishop,' said the Mayor, 'muddle-headed though he is, is universally beloved.'

'Were some of the other hostages thought to be expendable, perhaps?' asked the General.

'They are all most highly respected,' said the Bishop.

'It may have been a mistake to include the Inspector of Taxes,' said the Mayor.

'I see,' said the General. 'Do you think that if I released the Inspector of Taxes your man would surrender to save the rest?'

'Not a hope,' said the Mayor. 'Actually he raised the point with me last night.'

The General, for a second or so, looked more startled than a general should.

'Are you telling me,' he replied, 'that you have been in touch with this man since your arrest?'

The Mayor spoke soothingly. 'Our Resistance is not an amateur movement, General. As I was saying, he did mention the Inspector of Taxes. It's one grain of comfort to him in his heroic unhappiness.'

'Aha. So he is unhappy?'

'Undoubtedly,' said the Mayor. 'But then he's a very sensitive type. For most of us these shootings of yours have become just a thing that happens. If I may say, you make them too common, General.'

'It is interesting that you should say that,' said the General, 'because it is exactly what I have been thinking myself. An announcement that so many notables have been executed at dawn in a prison-yard—it has become rather *vieux-jeu*. Our capacity for being horrified is strangely limited, don't you agree, Bishop?'

'Alas, it is only too true,' said the Bishop. 'Compassion, the most divine of virtues, is also by far the most fatiguing. It is perhaps the supreme horror of atrocities—that in the end they cease to excite horror.'

'Then it looks,' said the General, 'as if you may both feel at any rate an intellectual sympathy with my decision—a decision which I have come to since it appeared pretty certain that the murderer was not going to be given up. It seemed to me that I must do something more horrifying, more spectacular, better calculated to impress than a mere routine execution. So I am going to make you an offer, Bishop. I shall not insist upon it, if you refuse: but if you will volunteer to be publicly crucified in the market-place tomorrow, I will let the other nineteen go free, including your admirable Mayor.'

'Never!' shouted the Mayor, on whose great neck two veins were swelling.

'Silence, sir!' rapped out the General, 'I am speaking.' He turned to the Bishop. 'I think a crucifixion should make a decided impression. The mere announcement of it might cause your man to surrender at the eleventh hour. What do you say?'

'Never!' yelled the Mayor once more. 'It's an outrageous suggestion. It shall never be allowed. Never!'

'I am speaking to the Bishop, Mr. Mayor,' the General shouted back. 'He can allow it, or he can refuse it. Well, Bishop?'

'What time, tomorrow?' inquired the Bishop.

The General looked a little puzzled. 'Whenever I order it, of course. But what has the time got to do with it?'

'It has a great deal to do with it,' said the Bishop. 'How could I possibly face the sublime honour of crucifixion without due preparation? I must make my Confession, I must get shaved and bathed. I must choose the proper vestments in which to approach the Cross; above all, I must have time for prayer and meditation. I cannot be rushed. This is not a small thing you offer me, General. And you must let me go home tonight—under guard, of course.'

'That will be quite in order, Bishop,' said the General. 'You may go home now, under guard, and the crucifixion will be at noon tomorrow.'

'Then I accept your offer,' said the Bishop.

The Mayor, who had been listening to the Bishop's words with his mouth as wide open as his eyes, again broke in.

'It can't be allowed! It's too utterly horrible!'

The Bishop looked shocked.

'Hush, my son. That is not the way to speak of a crucifixion.'

'Of course it's horrible,' said the General, 'but I thought we were agreed that, from my point of view, a little more horror is indicated. And *I* am the one who allows things in this town, Mr. Mayor.'

'There is just one question, General,' said the Bishop, 'that I should like to ask. Why don't you crucify the Mayor, instead of me?'

'A very good idea,' said the Mayor, turning eagerly towards the General. 'Why don't you?'

'Common sense, I suppose,' said the General. 'If one is compelled, unhappily, to destroy, one destroys the most dangerous man first.'

The Mayor actually laughed.

'Dangerous? Our good Bishop is the most harmless person alive. Why, he even wanted our brave Resistance fighter to give himself up to you.'

'That,' said the General, 'is the reason why he is so formidable compared to you, with your rather crude belief in violence. We can always beat you at that game—provided, that is, that the Bishop's fifth column is not permitted to corrupt us.'

The Bishop's face suddenly shone.

'Is it your meaning, General, that you chose me and not the Mayor for this great honour because of the Faith I hold?'

'It could be put like that, I suppose,' said the General.

'Then God be praised for His great goodness!' exclaimed the Bishop, radiant. 'I shall, after all, die for the Faith.' He held out a hand to the Mayor. 'Congratulate me, my son.'

The Mayor took his hand.

'You're a hero, Bishop.'

The Bishop laughed. 'Who's muddle-headed now?' he said. He turned to the General. 'What can we do, General, with a man so uninstructed that he confuses martyrs with heroes?'

The General looked puzzled.

'Is he so far wrong? I agree a hero need not be a martyr, but surely a martyr is a hero?'

'I see that I must pray for your brains too,' said the Bishop. 'If all goes well, I hope by tomorrow night to be in a position to do something substantial for both of you. Till then, good-bye, gentlemen, and once again my thanks, General.'

'Don't mention it,' said the General.

The General rose from his seat; the corporal of the guard barked out another order; there was stamping and banging and turning about, and the Bishop with his escort reached the door. The General called out to him:

'Won't you take my car, Bishop?'

'No, thank you,' said the Bishop, 'I shall enjoy the walk.' And he went out tranquilly, but with care to keep in step with his guards, up the narrow cobbled street to his home in the cathedral square.

The General turned to the Mayor. 'I expect you will wish to be the first to tell the good news to your friends, Mr. Mayor.'

'Send your own man,' said the Mayor. 'I haven't the courage to break it to them.'

It was past noon, an hour when the people went home to their dinners, and nobody noticed the Mayor as he walked, heavily and with his chin on his chest, to his house a few doors away from the Town-hall. But in less than half an hour the people were out in the streets again, for a military car equipped with a loud-speaker was going at a foot's pace through the town, blaring out the news that the hostages had been released, all but the Bishop who, at his own free choice, would, unless the assassin was delivered up, be crucified at noon tomorrow in the market-square. Upon which there arose a murmuring and a buzz of talk which kept the town pigeons restless and uneasy for an hour or more.

At five o'clock that same afternoon a little old lady, all in black and carrying a shopping-bag with no bulge in it, slipped out of a postern door in the Cathedral and crossed the little square to the Bishop's house. The square was almost deserted, since the people still thought the Bishop to be a prisoner in the Castle, and it was before the great doors of the inner keep that they had gathered to cheer him. The old lady's eyes were red, but her mouth was firm and her chin in the air. She paused for a moment on the doorstep, and stared at the familiar, nail-studded door as if it had turned suddenly into something strange and hostile; then, visibly pulling herself together, she twisted the heavy iron stirrup-handle and went into the house. Inside she paused again; again made an effort, and opened the door of the Bishop's study. In it sat the Bishop, reading, in his easy chair. On a hard chair by the empty grate sat a Russian soldier. The little old lady appeared thunderstruck.

'Joseph! What on earth are you doing here? I thought you were dead.'

'I am reading the fifteenth chapter of the Gospel according to St. Mark, Aunt.'

'But why haven't you been shot? Here I've been wasting half the day in church, praying for your soul and weeping my old eyes out, and all for nothing! Beside, I've only brought home enough food for one supper. Have you seen to the kitchen fire? And have you been reprieved? What's that man doing here? Don't you stand up for a lady?'

The soldier, who understood nothing but Russian, remained seated.

'He's a sentry,' said the Bishop. 'He's guarding me. But haven't they told you the news?'

'I tell you, I've been in the Cathedral since ten this morning. Are you really reprieved, dear Joseph?'

'Better than that, far better,' said the Bishop.

'Has he given himself up?'

The Bishop shook his head. 'No. But I—your nephew, dear Aunt—am to win a martyr's crown. I can still hardly believe it.'

'You a martyr? Don't be foolish, Joseph. You're a good man, but we don't have martyrs in our family. What have they been doing to you? Would you like a drop of cognac?'

'I know it sounds impossible,' said the Bishop, 'and nobody knows better than I do how unworthy I am. But God in His great goodness has willed it. Tomorrow I am to share the fate of my Blessed Lord. And only because of my Faith—the General made that perfectly clear.'

'Hush, Joseph—you mustn't talk like that—what's come over you?' She moved quickly to his side, full of concern. 'Have they been hitting you over the head? If so, you must not on any account have cognac.'

The Bishop took her hand.

'Please listen, dear Aunt,' he said. 'It's the General's decision but God must have put it into his head. The other hostages are to be released, but I, because of my Faith—although unworthy—am to be publicly crucified in the market-place tomorrow at noon.'

'Crucified?' said his aunt, drawing away her hand. 'Don't be blasphemous, Joseph, how can *you* be crucified?' Suddenly her hands flew to her temples. 'Mother of God! You don't mean that those devils, these filthy heathen Communists, are going to dare to——'

'No, no,' said the Bishop, 'nothing of the sort. I freely chose it. There was no compulsion at all. The General could not have been fairer. Either we were all shot together, or I was to be crucified alone. He left it entirely to me.'

His aunt's face took on a look of blank incredulity.

'And you chose the—the *cross*, Joseph?'

'But of course,' said the Bishop.

'Then I'm ashamed of you,' said his aunt bitterly. 'I wouldn't have believed it of you? You were always a bit of a simpleton—but to walk into that trap! and you a Bishop! You'll go back to the General this minute, and tell him that you've changed your mind. Really, Joseph, there are times when one would take you for a small boy. Martyr indeed!'

It was the Bishop's turn to look blank.

'I don't understand. A trap? What do you mean by "walking into a trap"?'

'Oh, you noodle,' said his aunt. 'Can't you see their wicked thoughts? How could they better belittle and make a mock of our Blessed Saviour than by crucifying a little man like you, Joseph? What will your Master's Sacrifice and Passion mean to your people after they have watched *you* being tortured on a cross? Who do you suppose is going to have their prayers and adoration for the next hundred years—our Blessed Lord, or their own little St. Joseph, Bishop and Martyr? Aren't you always complaining that your flock seem to think more of our local saints than of the Christ? And who's going to be their favourite saint, do you imagine—when they've seen you, their own dear Bishop, martyred before their eyes?'

'Perhaps they won't come to the—er—market-place,' said the Bishop. 'They may not want to see me—it will be painful, of course.'

'Not come? Of course they'll come. It will be the day of their lives. No, my poor Joseph, you've been made a fool of, and the sooner you put things right the better.'

For thirty years the Bishop, although he did not know it, had been ruled by his aunt, and he had lost the capacity, through long disuse, of thinking her mistaken. He looked very downcast indeed.

'This is—this is rather a shock to me,' he said. 'I confess I had not looked at it from that point of view. It's all very difficult. I suppose, in a way, it does seem rather presumptuous——'

'It's downright blasphemy.'

'But since it was to save the lives of so many good men——'

His aunt snorted. 'The Inspector of Taxes, for instance?'

'Our Saviour died for him,' said the Bishop.

'All the less reason why you should. You've been altogether above yourself, Joseph.'

The Bishop sighed heartily. 'It's a terrible responsibility to go back now and ask for those men to be shot. Think of their families, Aunt.'

'I've been praying for their families for the last forty-eight hours—when I wasn't housekeeping. And it's not your responsibility, it's the General's. Besides, better a thousand men shot than let the Cross be mocked.'

The Bishop sighed again.

'You're a good woman, Aunt. And I'm afraid you are right. I didn't think, or worse, I was thinking of myself.'

'You were dazzled, Joseph. That's the plain truth of it.'

'Yes,' said the Bishop, 'I'm afraid I was dazzled. And now, oh dear, the thing must be undone. How shall I ever explain it to the Mayor?'

'Explain it?' said his aunt. 'Have you no sense, Joseph? Of course you can't explain it. Are you going to tell that atheist and his friends that the glory and holiness of our dear Lord's Crucifixion are not safe in the keeping of your own flock? That you can't trust Christians to know the difference between the Cross of Christ and the murder of a hostage? You know you are not.'

'No, I suppose not,' said the Bishop. 'No, I shall say nothing. They must just think me a coward.'

'Then they'll think wrong,' said his aunt. 'It won't be the first time. And now be off with you. You'd better go by the back lane, and avoid the crowds.'

'On the contrary, there is something I have got to say to the crowds. I'm afraid it will be bitter news to some of them.'

'Then I shall come with you,' said his aunt.

'Don't you trust me?'

'I don't trust crowds,' said his aunt.

'I am their Bishop. What are you afraid of?'

'Mightn't they,' said his aunt, '—oh, dear God, now it's my turn to be blasphemous—mightn't they cry: Crucify him! Crucify him!'

'Nonsense,' said the Bishop. But she was not far wrong.

The Bishop, who knew a word or two of Russian, spoke to the sentry on the chair, and explained that he wished to be taken back to the Town-hall. The rest of the guard tramped in from the kitchen, but the Corporal made difficulties. The news had spread that the Bishop was now in his own house, and there was a big crowd gathering in the Cathedral Square, he said, in a highly excitable state. Women in tears, men crying: 'Long live our Bishop.' He had only six men; if a rescue were attempted, he would have to fire on the crowd.

The Bishop's aunt tried to explain to him that by 'Long live our Bishop' they did not mean that they wished their Bishop to live longer than noon tomorrow, and that an attempt at rescue was the last thing to be feared. She did not add that she herself was more afraid of an attempt on his life, but she did point out to the Corporal that the back lane, which avoided the Square altogether, would probably be deserted.

'I've only six men,' said the Corporal doubtfully.

'Only five,' said the Bishop. 'One of them must go to the General to tell him I wish to see him immediately in the Town-hall.'

'But I,' said his aunt, 'will be worth another six men at the least.'

'I must speak to the people first,' said the Bishop.

'Then you must speak from a window,' said the aunt. 'We will then slip out by the back door.'

The Bishop went to the formal parlour at the front of the house, a soldier on one side of him, his aunt on the other, and stood at an open window. A great roar went up from the crowd, and the town pigeons rose as one bird from the roofs. The Bishop put up his hand for silence. All sounds died away, for the Bishop's authority, always great, had become absolute by reason of his proclaimed martyrdom.

The Bishop's voice, when he spoke, was high and clear.

'My people,' he said, 'I have sad news for you. You have been told that, by my own free choice, I was to have been crucified tomorrow. Well, I have changed my mind. There will be no crucifixion. Together with my fellow-hostages, I shall be shot instead.'

He held up two fingers in sign of benediction and withdrew from the window.

For a few seconds the crowd was dumb. Then it began to murmur; the murmur turned to a growl; a man shouted something, and was answered by a roar; in no time the frightening 'rhubarb, rhubarb' noise of stage tradition filled the little square.

Inside the Bishop's house, the Corporal was hustling his captive out into the back lane which, as the aunt had guessed, was entirely deserted. Down it the little party marched briskly to the Town-hall. Only the Bishop's aunt failed to keep step; she trotted.

In the Mayor's parlour they had not long to wait. As the General strode in, spurs jingling, with a tight mouth, the noise of distant booing came through the open window.

'Shut that window, Corporal,' snapped the General. He turned to the Bishop as he took his seat.

'So a prisoner, Bishop, sends a peremptory summons to his captor? This is something new. Who is this lady?'

'Allow me to present to you my aunt, General,' said the Bishop.

The General made the slightest inclination of his head.

'I wish I could bid you welcome, madam. But this is highly irregular—may I ask to what I owe this honour?'

'Can't you hear them howling?' said the aunt. 'My nephew needed an escort.'

'He had my guards,' said the General.

'They would have eaten up your guards. But they still respect a woman—in this country,' said the aunt.

The General turned to the Bishop.

'What has happened to your people, Bishop? A little while ago they were cheering for you like——'

He was interrupted by a clatter of feet outside, the bursting open of the parlour door, and the bull-like rush of the Mayor, head down, angry, pushing a soldier out of his path. He ignored the General altogether.

'What the devil's the meaning of this, Bishop?' The town's completely out of hand. There's a rumour going round that you've ratted—absurd, of course, but you'll have to come and speak to them yourself, at once.'

The General used his parade voice.

'Mr. Mayor, you forget yourself. *I* happen to be present.'

The Mayor took a pull at himself.

'I'm sorry, General. I apologise, but there's no time to be lost. You haven't a loud-speaker ready, have you?'

'I have already spoken to them,' said the Bishop.

'The devil you have! Then why the—what have you been telling them?'

'I told them that I had changed my mind. There will be no crucifixion tomorrow,' said the Bishop.

The Mayor stared at him. He had an air of never having seen the Bishop before. His eyes, for an instant, were full of curiosity. Then his great face flushed red.

'You—you bloody coward!' he cried.

'A lady present, Mr. Mayor,' said the General. 'This is news to me, Bishop.'

'Yes,' said the Bishop. 'I asked for this meeting in order to tell you.'

'You little rat,' said the Mayor.

'And you wish the previous arrangement to stand?' said the General. 'Mr. Mayor here and the other hostages are to be shot?'

'I'm afraid that follows,' said the Bishop. 'And me, of course.'

'Shooting hurts less, eh?' said the Mayor.

'Silence, sir,' said the General to the Mayor. 'You have no right yet to assume anything. Perhaps, Bishop, as you have put me to a good deal of trouble in arranging for your crucifixion, you will tell me your reasons for this sudden change of plan?'

'Careful, Joseph,' said the Bishop's aunt.

'I'm sorry. I have no reason to give,' said the Bishop.

'Aha!' said the Mayor.

'No explanation at all?' said the General. 'There's the people to be considered as well, you know, not to speak of your fellow-hostages and their families.'

'No explanation at all,' said the Bishop.

'So we draw our own conclusions,' said the Mayor.

The General looked grave. 'We draw our own conclusions,' he said.

The Mayor swung round to face the General.

'Then let me tell you, General, that there will be a crucifixion tomorrow. Your arrangements can stand.'

'I fail to understand,' said the General.

'You will crucify *me*,' said the Mayor. 'Better tell the people now, I think. It may quieten them.'

The Bishop, for the first time in the affair, lost his serenity. He all but shouted.

'No, no, no, General. You can't do that! It was to me you gave the chance, not to him.' He turned to the Mayor, speaking gently once more. 'You are a brave man, all the same.'

'Pray don't excite yourself, Bishop,' said the General. 'I have no intention of crucifying the Mayor. I don't believe in torture—if I did, I should have tortured him long ago. Doesn't he know all the names I am looking for? Not that he would have disclosed them.'

'Thank you, General. I wish I was as sure of that. But look here, you were quite ready to torture the Bishop. If him, why not me? It's so unfair on the other hostages. If you were ready to let them be ransomed by a crucifixion, what difference can it make whose crucifixion it is?'

'It makes the whole difference,' said the General. 'The Bishop represents a Faith which is one of the major obstacles, in this benighted country, to the spread of our own enlightened doctrines. I had hoped, by publicly crucifying him, to cheapen one of the central mysteries of the Faith. Your case is quite different. Like me, you are an atheist. To crucify instead of shooting you would be mere pointless savagery.'

The Mayor rubbed the back of his great head. 'You're an artful one, I must say, General. I should never have thought of it myself. So the failure of that wretched man's nerve has cheated you of your little game. It's almost funny in a way.'

'I don't think the Bishop's nerve failed him,' said the General. 'I believe he saw through my little game, as you call it. Am I right, Bishop?'

The Bishop shook his head, mournfully.

'No, General, to my shame, I did not see through you. I have always been a bit simple. Fortunately my aunt here did see through you.'

The General turned to the aunt with an ironical inclination of the head.

'You did, madam? I congratulate you.'

'It was sticking out a mile,' said the aunt. 'I certainly can't congratulate *you*, General. And you, Mr. Mayor, will now kindly apologise for your disgraceful abuse of my nephew. He may be a simpleton—but he's certainly a hero.'

'I agree with you, madam,' said the General. 'It takes a brave man to choose crucifixion, but it takes a braver one still to send you, Mr. Mayor, and eighteen others to the firing squad, knowing that he will be branded for ever as a coward for doing so.'

The Mayor nodded.

'And perhaps you realise now,' continued the General, 'why I am so much opposed to the Bishop's Faith. It has qualities which, I am very much afraid, are almost invincible.'

The Mayor held out his hand to the Bishop.

'Bishop, I apologise. Forgive me.'

'You had every excuse, my son,' said the Bishop. 'There is nothing to forgive.'

'And you, Joseph,' said his aunt, 'must not let your head be turned. Brave as you have been, you are not in the same street for courage as the mayor.'

'Right again, madam,' said the General.

'What nonsense is this?' said the Mayor.

'It's quite simple,' said the aunt. 'My nephew, crucified or not, dies with a sure and certain hope of his reward in Heaven. You, Mr. Mayor, are prepared to undergo the same sufferings with no hope at all. If there's to be a prize for sheer courage, you win hands down.'

'We must all agree there,' said the General.

'There can be no question,' said the Bishop.

'And it's a thousand pities, if you ask me,' said the aunt, still addressing the Mayor, 'that you should have to suffer eternal torment.'

'My dear aunt!' said the Bishop, 'God's mercy is infinite.'

'That may be, but He knows the Mayor,' said the aunt.

The General held up his hand.

'If I may interrupt these interesting conjectures, I would like to say that, if the Bishop—or perhaps I should say his lady aunt—has beaten me, you Mr. Mayor are also of an invincible type. What can I do against men who, without hope or faith, will face torture? Luckily such men are rare. If I get rid of you and the Bishop, I think I can afford to let the other hostages go free. I admit I did not realise at first what a valuable catch I had made. Would dawn tomorrow suit you, gentlemen?'

'Perfectly,' said the Bishop.

'Whenever you like,' said the Mayor.

'Don't be absurd, General,' said the Bishop's aunt. 'You have just admitted that the Mayor is invincible, and that such men are rare. But if you shoot him, you will be making them common. There's nothing like example to make men brave. For every one invincible you shoot, you will make fifty more invincibles. Heroism is catching. The dear God knows it's not for me to save you from weakening yourself, but I never could hold my tongue when I see stupidity, and to shoot the Mayor would be grossly stupid.'

The General looked hard at her. He blinked once or twice.

'Upon my word,' he said, 'you're a very intelligent person, madam. I wish I had you on my staff. I am greatly obliged to you. You have saved me from a blunder. Mr. Mayor, you are free.'

'I would rather your released the Bishop,' said the Mayor.

'I'm sorry,' said the General, 'but the Bishop's case is, as I told you, different. He is the product of a Faith. By shooting him I shall neither weaken nor strengthen this Faith. Besides, I must shoot somebody.'

'May I open the window, General?' said the aunt. Without waiting for his permission she crossed the room and opened it. Once more the sounds of booing were heard. She closed the window and resumed her position. 'Did you hear that?' she said. 'They are out for the Bishop's blood. Are you going to oblige them?'

'I shall of course explain to them that, so far from being the coward they think, the Bishop is a hero.'

'You can't make sense of that without giving away your own little plot, and how he beat you.'

'How *you* beat him, dear Aunt,' said the Bishop.

'Is that story going to be good for your prestige?' said the aunt. 'The attempt to crucify a Bishop which failed? Will Moscow think it funny?'

The General stroked his chin.

'They might not. You may be right. It would be difficult to explain to a mob, in any case. No, I'm sorry, Bishop, but I'm afraid it's not practical to explain. You must be content, as you were just now, with your own conscience being clear.'

The Bishop nodded.

'Then, General,' said his aunt, 'you will be shooting at dawn tomorrow the one man the people will be willing to see shot—the cowardly Bishop who ratted. As I said, I ought not to want to save you from yourself, but the pointlessness of it! It's so downright silly.'

For the first time the General looked savage.

'I know who I should *like* to shoot—madam!'

'Nobody but Joseph here would care a hoot if you did,' said the aunt.

'I imagine you are not popular,' said the General. 'People who are always in the right seldom are.' He made a gesture of annoyance. 'Very well, you can go, Bishop.'

'Into that howling mob?' said the aunt, 'with the stain of cowardice on him? You will stay here, Joseph, while I go and explain to the people.'

'Explain what?' said the Bishop.

'That the crucifixion was planned by the General as an insult to our Faith, and that you—that we saw through it. Goodbye, General. Good-night, Mr. Mayor.'

The General was a man of resource.

'Wait a moment, madam,' he said; 'I will save you any further trouble. I propose to send out my loud-speaker to inform the crowd that the crucifixion had been already cancelled, not by the Bishop, but by myself, and that the hostages have been released since it has come to light that the murdered man was the aggressor in a brawl.'

'And our man killed him in self-defence?' said the Mayor.

'Exactly,' said the General.

'A dreadful lie, General,' said the Bishop. 'I have misjudged you, I fear. I thought you were at least a man of truth.'

'And whose fault is it that I am not, I should like to know? Who has driven me into a corner from which only a falsehood can extricate me? There she stands, gentlemen—and she a Bishop's aunt!'

'There's another thing,' said the Mayor. 'Your announcement does not clear the Bishop. Unfortunately he himself told his people that he had changed his mind.'

'His aunt will clear him, you'll see,' said the General.

The Bishop shook his head.

'What I have said, I have said. My people may think me a coward; they will never believe I could tell an untruth.'

'My dear Joseph,' said his aunt, 'I shall merely tell them that you were acting under my orders. I shall take the full responsibility.'

The Bishop smiled at her.

'You'll never convince them of that,' he said.

'I shan't have to convince anybody,' said his aunt. 'They've known it for thirty years.'

Twenty minutes later the military car with the loud-speaker was again patrolling the streets, blaring out the General's announcement. And while the crowds were cheering for the release of the hostages, a little old lady in black, with her chin in the air, was passing from group to group, button-holing the most talkative of the citizens. Within the hour a crowd was in the Cathedral Square, cheering for the Bishop. The swifts continued to swoop and shrill round the Cathedral spire, and had you been seated on the café terrace across the river, you would have thought the old town, now bathed in the yellow evening light, the very picture of peace and happiness. And this time you would have been right.

MARY LAVIN
The Great Wave

THE Bishop was sitting in the stern of the boat. He was in his robes, with his black overcoat thrown across his shoulders for warmth, and over his arm he carried his vestments, turned inside out to protect them from the salt spray. The reason he was already robed was because the distance across to the island was only a few miles, and the island priest was spared the embarrassment of a long delay in his small damp sacristy.

The islanders had a visit from their Bishop only every four years at most, when he crossed over, as now, for the Confirmation ceremony, and so to have His Grace arrive thus in his robes was only their due share: a proper prolongation of episcopal pomp. In his alb and amice he would easily be picked out by the small knot of islanders who would gather on the pier the moment the boat was sighted on the tops of the waves. Yes: it was right and proper for all that the Bishop be thus attired. His Grace approved. The Bishop had a reason of his own too, as it happened, but it was a small reason, and he was hardly aware of it anywhere but in his heart.

Now, as he sat in the boat, he wrapped his white skirts tighter around him, and looked to see that the cope and chasuble were well doubled over, so that the coloured silks would not be exposed when they got away from the lee of the land and the waves broke on the sides of the currach. The cope above all must not be tarnished. That was why he stubbornly carried it across his arm: the beautiful cope that came all the way from Stansstad, in Switzerland, and was so overworked with gilt thread that it shone like cloth of gold. The orphreys, depicting the birth and childhood of Christ, displayed the most elaborate work that His Grace had ever seen come from the paramentenwerkstätte, and yet he was far from unfamiliar with the work of the Sisters there, in St. Klara. Ever since he attained the bishopric he had commissioned many beautiful vestments and altar cloths for use throughout the diocese. He had once, at their instigation, broken a journey to Rome to visit them. And when he was there, he asked those brilliant women to explain to him the marvel, not of their skill, but of his discernment of it, telling them of his birth and early life as a simple boy, on this island towards which he was now faced.

'Mind out!' he said, sharply, as one of the men from the mainland who was pushing them out with the end of an oar threw the oar into the boat, scattering the air with drops of water from its glossy blade. 'Could nothing be done about this?' he asked, seeing water under the bottom boards of the boat. It was only a small sup, but it rippled up and down with a little tide of its own, in time with the tide outside that was already carrying them swiftly out into the bay.

'Tch, tch, tch,' said the Bishop, for some of this water had saturated the hem of the alb, and he set about tucking it under him upon the seat. And then, to make doubly sure of it, he opened the knot of his cincture and re-tied it as tight about his middle as if it were long ago and he was tying up a sack of spuds at the neck. 'Tch, tch,' he repeated, but no one was unduly bothered by his ejaculations because of his soft and mild eyes, and, didn't they know him? They knew that in his complicated, episcopal life he had to contend with a lot, and it was known that he hated to give his old housekeeper undue thumping with her flat iron. But there was a thing would need to be kept dry—the crozier!

'You'd want to keep that yoke there from getting wet though, Your Grace,' said one of the men, indicating the crozier that had fallen on the boards. For all that they mightn't heed his little old-womanish ways, they had a proper sense of what was fitting for an episcopal appearance.

'I could hold the crozier perhaps,' said Father Kane, the Bishop's secretary, who was farther up the boat. 'I still think it would be more suitable for the children to be brought over to you on the mainland, than for you to be traipsing over here like this, and in those foreign vestments at that!'

He is thinking of the price that was paid for them, thought the Bishop, and not of their beauty or their workmanship. And yet, he reflected, Father Kane was supposed to be a highly-educated man, who would have gone on for a profession if he hadn't gone for the priesthood, and who would not have had to depend on the seminary to put the only bit of gloss on him he'd ever get—Like me—he thought! And he looked down at his beautiful vestments again. A marvel, no less, he thought, savouring again the miracle of his power to appreciate such things.

'It isn't as if *they*'ll appreciate them over there,' said Father Kane, with sudden venom, looking towards the island, a thin line of green on the horizon.

'Ah, you can never say that for certain,' said the Bishop mildly, even indifferently. 'Take me, how did I come to appreciate such things?'

But he saw the answer in the secretary's hard eyes. He thinks it was parish funds that paid for my knowledge, and diocesan funds for putting it into practice! And maybe he's right! The Bishop smiled to himself. Who knows anything at all about how we're shaped, or where we're led, or how in the end we are ever brought to our rightful haven?

'How long more till we get there?' he asked, because the island was no longer a vague green mass. Its familiar shapes were coming into focus; the great high promontory throwing its purple shade over the shallow fields by the shore, the sparse white cottages, the cheap cement pier, constantly in need of repairs. And, higher up, on a ledge of the promontory itself there was the plain cement church, its spire only standing out against the sky, bleak as a crane's neck and head.

To think the full height of the promontory was four times the height of the steeple.

The Bishop gave a great shudder. One of the rowers was talking to him.

'Sure, Your Grace ought to know all about this bay. Ah, but I suppose you forget them days altogether now!'

'Not quite, not quite,' said the Bishop, quickly. He slipped his hand inside his robes and rubbed his stomach that had begun already to roll after only a few minutes of the swell.

When he was a little lad, over there on the island, he used to think he'd run away, some day, and join the crew of one of the French fishing trawlers that were always moving backwards and forwards on the rim of the sky. He used to go to a quiet place in the shade of the Point, and settling into a crevice in the rocks, out of reach of the wind, he'd spend the day long staring at the horizon; now in the direction of Liverpool, now in the direction of the Norwegian fjords.

Yet, although he he knew the trawlers went from one great port to another, and up even as far as Iceland, he did not really associate them with the sea. He never thought of them as at the mercy of it in the way the little currachs were that had made his mother a widow,

and that were jottled by every wave. The trawlers used to seem out
of reach of the waves, away out on the black rim of the horizon.

He had in those days a penny jotter in which he put down the
day and hour a trawler passed, waiting precisely to mark it down
until it passed level with the pier. He put down also other facts
about it which he deduced from the small vague outline discernible
at that distance. And he smiled to remember the sense of satisfaction
and achievement he used to get from that old jotter, which his
childish imagination allowed him to believe was a full and exhaus-
tive report. He never thought of the long nights and the early
dawns, the hours when he was in the schoolroom, or the many times
he was kept in the cottage by his mother, who didn't hold with his
hobby.

'Ah son, aren't you all I've got! Why wouldn't I fret about you?'
she'd say to him, when he chafed under the yoke of her care.

That was the worst of being an only child, and the child of a sea
widow into the bargain. God be good to her! He used to have to
sneak off to his cranny in the rocks when he got her gone to the
shop of a morning, or up to the chapel of an afternoon to say her
beads. She was in sore dread of his even looking out to sea, it
seemed! And as for going out in a currach! Hadn't she every
currach-crew on the island warned against taking him out?

'Your mammy would be against me, son,' they'd say, when he'd
plead with them, one after another on the shore, and they getting
ready to shove their boats down the shingle and float them out on
the tide.

'How will I ever get out to the trawlers if I'm not let out in the
currachs?' he used to think. That was when he was a little fellow, of
course, because when he got a bit older he stopped pestering them,
and didn't go down near the shore at all when they were pulling
out. They'd got sharp with him by then.

'We can't take any babbies out with us—a storm might come up.
What would a babby like you do then?' And he couldn't blame
them for their attitude because by this time he knew they could
often have found a use for him out in the boats when there was a
heavy catch.

'You'll never make a man of him hiding him in your petticoats,'
they'd say to his mother, when they'd see him with her in the shop.
And there was a special edge on the remark, because men were
scarce, as could be seen anywhere on the island by the way the

black frieze jackets of the men made only small patches in the big
knots of women, with their flaming red petticoats.

His mother had a ready answer for them.

'And why are they scarce?' she'd cry.

'Ah, don't be bitter, Mary.'

'Well, leave me alone then. Won't he be time enough taking his
life in his hands when there's more to be got for a netful of ling than
there is this year!'

For the shop was always full of dried ling. When you thought to
lean on the counter, it was on a long board of ling you leant. When
you went to sit down on a box or a barrel it was on top of a bit of
dried ling you'd be sitting. And right by the door, a greyhound
bitch had dragged down a bit of ling from a hook on the wall and
was chewing at it, not furtively, but to the unconcern of all, growling
when it found it tough to chew, and attacking it with her back teeth
and her head to one side, as she'd chew an old rind of hoof parings
in the forge. The juice of it, and her own saliva mixed, was trickling
out of her mouth on to the floor.

'There'll be a good price for the first mackerel,' said poor Maurya
Keely, their near neighbour, whose husband was ailing, and whose
son Seoineen was away in a seminary on the mainland studying to
be a priest. 'The seed herring will be coming in any day now.'

'You'll have to let Jimeen out on that day if it looks to be a good
catch,' she said, turning to his mother. 'We're having our currach
tarred, so's to be all ready against the day.'

Everyone had sympathy with Maurya, knowing her man was
nearly done, and that she was in great dread that he wouldn't be fit
to go out and get their share of the new season's catch, and she
counting on the money to pay for Seoineen's last year in the
seminary. Seoineen wasn't only her pride, but the pride of the whole
island as well, for, with the scarcity of men folk, the island hadn't
given a priest to the diocese in a decade.

'And how is Seoineen? When is he coming home at all?' another
woman asked, as they crowded around Maurya. 'He'll soon be
facing into the straight,' they said, meaning his ordination, and
thinking, as they used the expression, of the way, when Seoineen
was a young fellow, he used to be the wildest lad on the island,
always winning the ass-race on the shore, the first to be seen flashing
into sight around the Point, and he coming up the straight, keeping
the lead easily to finish at the pier-head.

'He'll be home for a last leave before the end,' said his mother, and everyone understood the apprehension she tried to keep out of her voice, but which steals into the heart of every priest's mother thinking of the staying power a man needs to reach that end. 'I'm expecting him the week after next,' she said, then suddenly her joy in the thought of having him in the home again took place over everything else.

'Ah, let's hope the mackerel will be in before then!' said several of the women at the one time, meaning there would be a jingle in everyone's pocket then, for Seoineen would have to call to every single cottage on the island, and every single cottage would want to have plenty of lemonade and shop-biscuits too, to put down before him.

Jimeen listened to this with interest and pleased anticipation. Seoineen always took him around with him, and he got a share in all that was set down for the seminarian.

But that very evening Seoineen stepped on to the pier. There was an epidemic in the college and the seminarists that were in their last year like him were let home a whole week before their time.

'Sure, it's not for what I get to eat that I come home, Mother!' he cried, when Maurya began bewailing having no feasting for him. 'If there's anything astray with the life I've chosen it's not shortage of grub! And anyway we won't have long to wait.' He went to the door and glanced up at the sky. 'The seed will be swimming inward tomorrow on the first tide!'

'Oh God forbid!' said Maurya. 'We don't want it that soon either, son, for our currach was only tarred this day!' and her face was torn with two worries now instead of one.

Jimeen had seen the twinkle in Seoineen's eye, and he thought he was only letting-on to know about such things, for how would he have any such knowledge at all, and he away at schools and colleges the best part of his life.

The seed was in on the first tide, though, the next day.

'Oh, they have curious ways of knowing things that you'd never expect them to know,' said Jimeen's own mother. It was taken all over the island to be a kind of prophecy.

'Ah, he was only letting-on, Mother,' said Jimeen, but he got a knock of her elbow over the ear.

'It's time you had more respect for him, son,' she said, as he ran out the door for the shore.

Already most of the island boats were pulling hard out into the bay. And the others were being pushed out as fast as they could be dragged down the shingle.

But the Keely boat was still upscutted in the dune grass under the promontory, and the tar wetly gleaming on it. The other women were clustered around Maurya, giving her consolation.

'Ah sure, maybe it's God's will,' she said. 'Wasn't himself doubled up with pain in the early hours, and it's in a heavy sleep he is this minute—I wouldn't wake him up whether or no!—He didn't get much sleep last night. It was late when he got to his bed. Him and Seoineen stayed up talking by the fire. Seoineen was explaining to him all about the ordination, about the fasting they have to do beforehand, and the holy oils and the chrism and the laying-on of hands. It beat all to hear him! The creatureen, he didn't get much sleep himself either, but he's young and able, thank God. But I'll have to be going back now to call him for Mass.'

'You'll find you won't need to call Seoineen,' said one of the women. 'Hasn't him, and the like of him, got God's voice in their hearts all day and they ever and always listening to it. He'll wake of himself, you'll see. He'll need no calling!'

And sure enough, as they were speaking, who came running down the shingle but Seoineen.

'My father's not gone out without me, is he?' he cried, not seeing his own boat, or any sign of it on the shore, a cloud coming over his face that was all smiles and laughter when he was running down to them. He began to scan the bay that was blackened with boats by this time.

'He's not then,' said Maurya. 'He's above in his bed still, but leave him be, Seoineen—leave him be—' she nodded her head back towards the shade of the promontory. 'He tarred the boat yesterday, not knowing the seed 'ud be in so soon, and it would scald the heart out of him to be here and not able to take it out. But as I was saying to these good people it's maybe God's will the way it's happened, because he's not fit to go out this day!'

'That's true for you, Mother,' said Seoineen, quietly. 'The poor man is nearly beat, I'm fearing.' But the next minute he threw back his head and looked around the shore. 'Maybe I'd get an oar in one of the other boats. There's surely a scarcity of men these days?'

'Is it you?' cried his mother, because it mortally offended her notion of the dignity due to him that he'd be seen with his coat off maybe—in his shirt sleeves maybe—red in the face maybe along with that and—God forbid—sweat maybe breaking out of him!

'To hear you, Mother, anyone would think I was a priest already. I wish you could get a look into the seminary and you'd see there's a big difference made there between the two sides of the fence!' It was clear from the light in his eyes as they swept the sea at that moment that it would take more than a suit of black clothes to stop him from having a bit of fun with an oar. He gave a sudden big laugh, but it fell away as sudden when he saw that all the boats had pulled out from the shore and he was alone with the women on the sand.

Then his face hardened.

'Tell me, Mother,' he cried. 'Is it the boat or my father that's the unfittest? For if it's only the boat then I'll make it fit! It would be going against God's plenitude to stay idle with the sea teeming like that—Look at it!'

For even from where they stood when the waves wheeled inward they could see the silver herring seed glistening in the curving wheels of water, and when those slow wheels broke on the shore they left behind them a spate of seed sticking to everything, even to people's shoes.

'And for that matter, wasn't Christ Himself a fisherman! Come, Mother—tell me the truth! Is the tar still wet or is it not?'

Maurya looked at him for a minute. She was no match for arguing with him in matters of theology, but she knew all about tarring a currach. 'Wasn't it only done yesterday, son?' she said. 'How could it be dry today?'

'We'll soon know that,' said Seoineen, and he ran over to the currach. Looking after him they saw him lay the palm of his hand flat on the upturned bottom of the boat, and then they heard him give a shout of exultation.

'It's not dry surely?' someone exclaimed, and you could tell by the faces that all were remembering the way he prophesied about the catch. Had the tar dried at the touch of his hands maybe?

But Seoineen was dragging the currach down the shingle.

'Why wouldn't it be dry?' he cried. 'Wasn't it a fine dry night. I remember going to the door after talking to my father into the small hours, and the sky was a mass of stars, and there was a fine, sharp wind blowing that you'd be in dread it would dry up the sea itself! Stand back there, Mother,' he cried, for her face was beseeching something of him, and he didn't want to be looking at it. But without looking he knew what it was trying to say. 'Isn't it towards my ordination the money is going? Isn't that argument enough for you?'

He had the boat nearly down to the water's edge. 'No, keep back there, young Jimeen,' he said. 'I'm able to manage it on my own, but let you get the nets and put them in and then be ready to skip in before I push out, because I'll need someone to help haul in the nets.'

'Is it Jimeen?' said one of the women, and she laughed, and then all the women laughed. 'Sure, he's more precious again nor you!' they said.

But they turned to his mother all the same.

'If you're ever going to let him go out at all, this is your one chance, surely? Isn't it like as if it was into the Hands of God Himself you were putting him, woman?'

'Will you let me, Ma?' It was the biggest moment in his life. He couldn't look at her for fear of a refusal.

'Come on, didn't you hear her saying yes—what are you waiting for?' cried Seoineen, giving him a push, and the next minute he was in the currach, and Seoineen had given it a great shove and he running out into the water in his fine shoes and all. He vaulted in across the keel. 'I'm destroyed already at the very start!' he cried, laughing down at his feet and trouser legs, and that itself seemed part of the sport for him. 'I'll take them off,' he cried, kicking the shoes off him, and pulling off his socks, till he was in his bare white feet. 'Give me the oars,' he cried, but as he grippd them he laughed again, and loosed his fingers for a minute, as one after the other he rubbed his hands on a bit of sacking on the seat beside him. For, like the marks left by the trawler men on the white bollard at the pier, the two bleached oars were marked with the track of his hands, palms, and fingers, in pitch black tar.

'The tar was wet!'

'And what of it?' cried Seoineen. 'Isn't it easy to give it another lick of a brush?'

But he wasn't looking at Jimeen and he saying it, his eyes were lepping along the tops of the waves to see if they were pulling near the other currachs.

The other currachs were far out in the bay already: the sea was running strong. For all that, there was a strange still look about the

water, unbroken by any spray. Jimeen sat still, exulting in his luck.
The waves did not slap against the sides of the currach like he'd
have thought they would do, and they didn't even break into spray
where the oars split their surface. Instead, they seemed to go
lolloping under the currach and lollop up against the far side, till it
might have been on great glass rollers they were slipping along.

'God! Isn't it good to be out on the water!' cried Seoineen, and
he stood up in the currach, nearly toppling them over in his
exuberance, drawing in deep breaths, first with his nose, and then
as if he were drinking it with his mouth, and his eyes at the same
time taking big draughts of the coast-line that was getting farther
and farther away. 'Ah, this is the life: this is the real life,' he cried
again, but they had to look to the oars and look to the nets, then,
for a while, and for a while they couldn't look up at sea or sky.

When Jimeen looked up at last, the shore was only a narrow line
of green.

'There's a bit of a change, I think,' said Seoineen, and it was
true.

The waves were no longer round and soft, like the little cnoceens
in the fields back of the shore, but they had small sharp points on
them now, like the rocks around the Point, that would rip the
bottom out of a boat with one tip, the way a tip of a knife would slit
the belly of a fish.

That was a venomous comparison though and for all their
appearance, when they hit against the flank of the boat, it was only
the waves themselves that broke and patterned the water with
splotches of spray.

It was while he was looking down at these white splotches that
Jimeen saw the fish.

'Oh look, Seoineen, look!' he cried, because never had he seen the
like.

They were not swimming free, or separate, like you'd think they'd
be, but a great mass of them together, till you'd think it was at the
floor of the sea you were looking, only it nearer and shallower.

There must have been a million fish; a million, million, Jimeen
reckoned wildly, and they pressed as close as the pebbles on the
shore. And they might well have been motionless and only seeming
to move like on a windy day you'd think the grass on the top of the
promontory was running free like the waves, with the way it rippled
and ran along a little with each breeze.

'Holy God, such a sight!' cried Seoineen. 'Look at them!'

But Jimeen was puzzled.

'How will we get them into the net?' he asked, because it didn't seem that there was any place for the net to slip down between them, but that it must lie on the top of that solid mass of fish, like on a floor.

'The nets: begod, I nearly forgot what we came out here for!' cried Seoineen, and at the same time they became aware of the activity of the other boats, which had drawn near without their knowing. He yelled at Jimeen. 'Catch hold of the nets there, you lazy good-for-nothing. What did I bring you with me for if it wasn't to put you to some use!' and he himself caught at a length of the brown mesh, thrown in the bottom of the boat, and began to haul it up with one hand, and with the other to feed it out over the side.

Jimeen, too, began to pull and haul, so that for a few minutes there was only a sound of the net swishing over the wood, and every now and then a bit of a curse, under his breath, from Seoineen as one of the cork floats caught in the thole pins.

At first it shocked Jimeen to hear Seoineen curse, but he reflected that Seoineen wasn't ordained yet, and that, even if he were, it must be a hard thing for a man to go against his nature.

'Come on, get it over the side, damn you,' cried Seoineen again, as Jimeen had slowed up a bit owing to thinking about the cursing. 'It isn't one net-full but thirty could be filled this day! Sure you could fill the boat in fistfuls,' he cried, suddenly leaning down over the side, delving his bare hand into the water. With a shout, he brought up his hand with two fish, held one against the other in the same grip, so that they were as rigid as if they were dead. 'They're overlaying each other a foot deep,' he cried, and then he opened his fist and freed them. Immediately they writhed apart to either side of his hand in two bright arcs and then fell, both of them, into the bottom of the boat. But next moment they writhed into the air again, and flashed over the side of the currach.

'Ah begorras, you'll get less elbow-room there than here, my boys,' cried Seoineen, and he roared laughing, as he and Jimeen leant over the side, and saw that sure enough, the two mackerel were floundering for a place in the glut of fishes.

But a shout in one of the other currachs made them look up.

It was the same story all over the bay. The currachs were tossing tipsily in the water with the antics of the crews, that were standing up and shouting and feeding the nets ravenously over the sides. In some of the boats that had got away early, they were still more ravenously hauling them up, strained and swollen with the biggest catch they had ever held.

There was not time for Seoineen or Jimeen to look around either, for just then the keel of their own currach began to dip into the water.

'Look out! Pull it up—! Catch a better grip than that, damn you. Do you want to be pulled into the sea. Pull, damn you, pull!' cried Seoineen.

Now every other word that broke from his throat was a curse, or what you'd call a curse if you heard them from another man, or in another place, but in this place, from this man, hearing them issue wild and free, Jimeen understood that they were a kind of psalm. They rang out over the sea in a kind of praise to God for all his plenitude.

'Up! Pull hard—up, now, up!' he cried, and he was pulling at his end like a madman.

Jimeen pulled too, till he thought his heart would crack, and then suddenly the big white belly of the loaded net came in sight over the water.

Jimeen gave a groan, though, when he saw it.

'Is it dead they are?' he cried, and there was anguish in his voice.

Up to this, the only live fish he had ever seen were the few fish tangled in the roomy nets, let down by the old men over the end of the pier, and *they* were always full of life, needling back and forth insanely in the spacious mesh till he used to swallow hard, and press his lips close together fearing one of them would dart down his gullet, and he'd have it ever after needling this way and that inside him! But there was no stir at all in the great white mass that had been hauled up now in the nets.

'Is it dead they are?' he cried again.

'Aahh, why would they be dead? It's suffocating they are, even below in the water, with the welter of them is in it,' cried Seoineen.

He dragged the net over the side where it emptied and spilled itself into the bottom of the boat. They came alive then all right! Flipping and floundering, and some of them flashing back into the sea. But it was only a few on the top that got away, the rest were kept down by the very weight and mass of them that was in it. And when, after a minute, Seoineen had freed the end of the net, he flailed them right and left till most of them fell back flat. Then, suddenly, he straightened up and swiped a hand across his face to clear it of the sweat that was pouring out of him.

'Ah sure, what harm if an odd one leps for it,' he cried. 'We'll deaden them under another netful! Throw out your end,' he cried.

As Jimeen rose up to his full height to throw the net wide out, there was a sudden terrible sound in the sky over him, and the next minute a bolt of thunder went volleying overhead, and with it, in the same instant it seemed, the sky was knifed from end to end with a lightning flash.

Were they blinded by the flash? or had it suddenly gone as black as night over the whole sea?

'Oh God's Cross!' cried Seoineen. 'What is coming? Why didn't someone give us a shout? Where are the others? Can you see them? Hoy there! Marteen! Seumas? Can you hear——?'

For they could see nothing. And it was as if they were all alone in the whole world. Then, suddenly, they made out Marteen's currach near to them, so near that, but for Seoineen flinging himself forward and grabbing the oars, the two currachs would have knocked together. Yet no sooner had they been saved from knocking together than they suddenly seemed so far sundered again they could hardly hear each other when they called out.

'What's happening, in Christ's name?' bawled Seoineen, but he had to put up his hands to trumpet his voice, for the waves were now so steep and high that even one was enough to blot out the sight of Marteen. Angry white spume dashed in their faces.

'It's maybe the end of the world,' said Jimeen, terror-stricken.

'Shut up and let me hear Marteen!' said Seoineen, for Marteen was bawling at them again.

'Let go the nets,' Marteen was bawling—'let go the nets or they'll drag you out of the boat.'

Under them then they could feel the big pull of the net that was filled up again in an instant with its dead weight of suffocating fish.

'Let it go, I tell you,' bawled Marteen.

'Did you hear? He's telling us to let it go,' piped Jimeen in terror, and he tried to free his own fingers of the brown mesh that had closed right tight upon them with the increasing weight. 'I can't let go,' he cried, looking to Seoineen, but he shrank back from the strange wild look in Seoineen's eyes. 'Take care would you do anything of the kind!'

'It's cutting off my fingers!' he screamed.

Seoineen glared at him

'A pity about them!' he cried, but when he darted a look at them, and saw them swelling and reddening, he cursed. 'Here—wait till I take it from you,' he cried, and he went to free his own right hand, but first he laced the laden fingers of his left hand into the mesh above the right hand, and even then, the blood spurted out in the air when he finally dragged it free of the mesh.

For a minute Seoineen shoved his bleeding fingers into his mouth and sucked them, then he reached out and caught the net below where Jimeen gripped it. As the weight slackened, the pain of the searing strings lessened, but next minute as the pull below got stronger, the pain tore into Jimeen's flesh again.

'Let go now, if you like, now I have a bit of a hold of it anyway— now I'm taking the weight of it off you,' said Seoineen.

Jimeen tried to drag free.

'I can't,' he screamed in terror, '—the strings are eating into my bones!'

Seoineen altered his balance and took more weight off the net at that place.

'Now!'

'I can't! I can't!' screamed Jimeen.

From far over the waves the voice of Marteen came to them again, faint, unreal, like the voices you'd hear in a shell if you held it to your ear.

'Cut free—cut free,' it cried, 'or else you'll be destroyed altogether.'

'Have they cut free themselves? That's what I'd like to know!' cried Seoineen.

'Oh, do as he says, Seoineen. Do as he says,' screamed Jimeen.

And then, as he saw a bit of ragged net, and then another and another rush past like the briery patches of foam on the water that was now almost level with the rowlocks, he knew that they had indeed all done what Marteen said; cut free.

'For the love of God, Seoineen,' he cried.

Seoineen hesitated for another instant. Then suddenly made up his mind and, reaching along the seat, he felt without looking for the knife that was kept there for slashing dogfish.

'Here goes,' he cried, and with one true cut of the knife he freed Jimeen's hands the two together at the same time, but, letting the

knife drop into the water, he reached out wildly to catch the ends of
the net before they slid into it, or shed any of their precious freight.

Not a single silver fish was lost.

'What a fool I'd be,' he gasped, 'to let go. They think because of
the collar I haven't a man's strength about me any more. Then I'll
show them. I'll not let go this net, not if it pull me down to hell.'
And he gave another wild laugh. 'And you along with me!' he cried.
'Murder?' he asked then, as if he had picked up the word from a
voice in the wind. 'Is it murder? Ah sure, I often think it's all one to
God what a man's sin is, as long as it's sin at all. Isn't sin poison—
any sin at all, even the smallest drop of it? Isn't it death to the soul
that it touches at any time? Ah then! I'll not let go!' And even when,
just then, the whole sea seemed littered with tattered threads of net,
he still held tight to his hold. 'Is that the way? They've all let go!
Well then, I'll show them one man will not be so easy beat! Can
you hear me?' he cried, because it was hard to hear him with the
crazy noise of the wind and the waves.

'Oh cut free, Seoineen,' Jimeen implored, although he remembered the knife was gone now to the bottom of the sea, and although
the terrible swollen fingers were beyond help in the mangling ropes
of the net.

'Cut free is it? Faith now! I'll show them all,' cried Seoineen.
'We'll be the only boat'll bring back a catch this night, and the sea
seething with fish.' He gave a laugh. 'Sure that was the only thing
that was spoiling my pleasure in the plenty! thinking that when the
boats got back the whole island would be fuller of fish than the sea
itself, and it all of no more value than if it was washed of its own
accord on to the dirty counters of the shop! Sure it wouldn't be
worth a farthing a barrel! But it will be a different story now, I'm
thinking. Oh, but I'll have the laugh on them with their hollow
boats, and their nets cut to flitters! I'll show them a man is a man,
no matter what vows he takes, or what way he's called to deny his
manhood! I'll show them! Where are they, anyway? Can you—see
them—at all?' he cried, but he had begun to gasp worse than the
fishes in the bottom of the boat. 'Can you—see them—at all? Damn
you, don't sit there like that! Stand up—there—and tell me—can—
you—see—them!'

It wasn't the others Jimeen saw though, when he raised his eyes
from the torn hands in the meshes. All he saw was a great wall, a
great green wall of water. No currachs anywhere. It was as if the

whole sea had been stood up on its edge, like a plate on a dresser. And down that wall of water there slid a multitude of dead fish.

And then, down the same terrible wall, sliding like the dead fish, came an oar; a solitary oar. And a moment afterwards, but inside the glass wall, imprisoned, like under a glass dome, he saw—oh God!—a face, looking out at him, staring out at him through a foot of clear green water. And he saw it was the face of Marteen. For a minute the eyes of the dead man stared into his eyes.

With a scream he threw himself against Seoineen, and clung to him tight as iron.

How many years ago was that? The Bishop opened his eyes. They were so near the shore he could pick out the people by name that stood on the pier-head. His stomach had stopped rolling. It was mostly psychological; that feeling of nausea. But he knew it would come back in an instant if he looked leftward from the shore, leftwards and upwards, where, over the little cement pier and over the crane-bill steeple of the church, the promontory that they called the Point rose up black with its own shadow.

For it was on that promontory—four times the height of the steeple—they had found themselves, he and Seoineen, in the white dawn of the day after the Wave, lying in a litter of dead fish, with the netful of fish like an anchor sunk into the green grass.

When he came to himself in that terrible dawn, and felt the slippy bellies of the fish all about him, he thought he was still in the boat, lying in the bottom among the mackerel, but when he opened his eyes and saw a darkness as of night, over his head, he thought it was still the darkness of the storm and he closed them again in terror.

Just before he closed them, though, he thought he saw a star, and he ventured to open them again, and then he saw that the dark sky over him was a sky of skin, stretched taut over timber laths, and the star was only a glint of light—and the blue light of day at that—coming through a split in the bottom of the currach. For the currach was on top of him!—Not he in the bottom of it.

Why then was he not falling down and down and down through the green waters? His hands rushed out to feel around him. But even then, the most miraculous thing he thought to grasp was a fistful of sand, the most miraculous thing he thought to have to believe was that they were cast up safe upon the shore.

Under his hands though, that groped through the fishes, he came, not on sand, but on grass, and not upon the coarse dune grass that grew back from the shore at the foot of the Point. It was soft, sweet little grass, that was like the grass he saw once when Seoineen and he had climbed up the face of the Point, and stood up there, in the sun, looking down at all below, the sea and the pier, and the shore and the fields, and the thatch of their own houses, and on a level with them, the grey spire of the chapel itself!

It was, when opening his eyes wide at last, he saw, out from him a bit, the black grey tip of that same chapel-spire that he knew where he was.

Throwing the fish to left and right he struggled to get to his feet.

It was a miracle! And it must have been granted because Seoineen was in the boat. He remembered how he prophesied the seed would be on the tide, and in his mind he pictured their currach being lifted up in the air and flown, like a bird, to this grassy point.

But where was Seoineen?

'Oh Seoineen, Seoineen!' he cried, when he saw him standing on the edge of the Point looking downward, like they looked, that day, on all below. 'Oh Seoineen, was it a miracle?' he cried, and he didn't wait for an answer, but he began to shout and jump in the air.

'Quit, will you!' said Seoineen, and for a minute he thought it must be modesty on Seoineen's part, it being through him the miracle was granted, and then he thought it must be the pain in his hands that was at him, not letting him enjoy the miracle, because he had his two hands pressed under his armpits.

Then suddenly he remembered the face of Marteen he had seen under the wall of water, and his eyes flew out over the sea that was as flat and even now, as the field of grass under their feet. Was Marteen's currach lost? And what of the others?'

Craning over the edge of the promontory he tried to see what currachs were back in their places, under the little wall, dividing the sand from the dune, turned upside down and leaning a little to one side, so you could crawl under them if you were caught in a sudden shower.

There were no currachs under the wall: none at all.

There were no currachs on the sea.

Once, when he was still wearing a red petticoat like a girsha, there had been a terrible storm and half a score of currachs were lost. He remembered the night with all the women on the island down on the shore with storm lamps, swinging them and calling out over the noise of the waves. And the next day they were still there, only kneeling on the pier, praying and keening.

'Why aren't they praying and keening?' he cried then, for he knew at last the other currachs, all but theirs, were lost.

'God help them,' said Seoineen, 'at least they were spared that.'

And he pointed to where, stuck in the latticed shutters on the side of the steeple, there were bits of seaweed, and—yes—a bit of the brown mesh of a net.

'God help you,' he said then, 'how can your child's mind take in what a grown man's mind can hardly hold—but you'll have to know some time—we're all alone—the two of us—on the whole island. All that was spared by that wall of water——'

'All that was on the sea, you mean?' he cried.

'And on the land too,' said Seoineen.

'Not my mother——?' he whimpered.

'Yes, and my poor mother,' said Seoineen. 'My poor mother that tried to stop us from going out with the rest.'

But it was a grief too great to grasp, and yet, yet even in face of it, Jimeen's mind was enslaved to the thought of their miraculous salvation.

'Was it a miracle, Seoineen?' he whispered. 'Was it a miracle we were spared?'

But Seoineen closed his eyes, and pushed his crossed arms deeper under his arm-pits. The grimace of pain he made was—even without words—a rebuke to Jimeen's exaltation. Then he opened his eyes again.

'It was my greed that was the cause of all,' he said, and there was such a terrible sorrow in his face that Jimeen, only then, began to cry. 'It has cost me my two living hands,' said Seoineen, and there was a terrible anguish in his voice.

'But it saved your life, Seoineen,' he cried, wanting to comfort him.

Never did he forget the face Seoineen turned to him.

'For what?' he asked. 'For what?'

And there was, in his voice, such despair, that Jimeen knew it wasn't a question but an answer; so he said no more for a few minutes. Then he raised his voice again, timidly.

'You saved my life too, Seoineen.'

Seoineen turned dully and looked at him.

'For what?'

But as he uttered them, those same words took on a change, and a change came over his face, too, and when he repeated them, the change was violent.

'For what?' he demanded. 'For what?'

Just then, on the flat sea below, Jimeen saw the boats, coming across from the mainland, not currachs like they had on the island, but boats of wood made inland, in Athlone, and brought down on lorries.

'Look at the boats,' he called out, four, five, six, any amount of them; they came rowing for the island.

Less than an hour later Seoineen was on his way to the hospital on the mainland, where he was to spend long months before he saw the island again. Jimeen was taken across a few hours later, but when he went it was to be for good. He was going to an aunt, far in from the sea, of whom he had never heard tell till that day.

Nor was he to see Seoineen again, in all the years that followed. On the three occasions that he was over on the island, he had not seen him. He had made enquiries, but all he could ever get out of people was that he was a bit odd.

'And why wouldn't he be?' they added.

But although he never came down to the pier to greet the Bishop like the rest of the islanders, it was said he used to slip into the church after it had filled up and he'd think he was unnoticed. And afterwards, although he never once would go down to the pier to see the boat off, he never went back into his little house until it was gone clear across to the other side of the bay. From some part of the island it was certain he'd be the last to take leave of the sight.

It had been the same on each visit the Bishop made, and it would be the same on this one.

When he would be leaving the island, there would be the same solicitous entreaties with him to put on his overcoat. Certainly he was always colder going back in the late day. But he'd never give in to do more than throw it over his shoulders, from which it would soon slip down on to the seat behind him.

'You'd do right to put it on like they told you,' said the secretary, buttoning up his own thick coat.

But there was no use trying to make him do a thing he was set against. He was a man had deep reasons for the least of his actions.

MORLEY CALLAGHAN
Last Spring They Came Over

ALFRED BOWLES came to Canada from England and got a job on a Toronto paper. He was a young fellow with clear, blue eyes and heavy pimples on the lower part of his face, the son of a Baptist minister whose family was too large for his salary. He got thirty dollars a week on the paper and said it was surprisingly good screw to start. For five a week he got an attic room in a brick house painted brown on Mutual Street. He ate his meals in a quick-lunch near the office. He bought a cane and a light-gray fedora.

He wasn't a good reporter but was inoffensive and obliging. After he had been working two weeks the fellows took it for granted he would be fired in a little while and were nice to him, liking the way the most trifling occurrences surprised him. He was happy to carry his cane on his arm and wear the fedora at a jaunty angle, quite the reporter. He liked to explain that he was doing well. He wrote home about it.

When they put him doing night police he felt important, phoning the fire department, hospitals, and police stations, trying to be efficient. He was getting along all right. It was disappointing when after a week the assistant city editor, Mr. H. J. Brownson, warned him to phone his home if anything important happened, and he would have another man cover it. But Bowles got to like hearing the weary, irritable voice of the assistant city editor called from his bed at three o'clock in the morning. He liked to politely call Mr. Brownson as often and as late as possible, thinking it a bit of good fun.

Alfred wrote long letters to his brother and to his father, the Baptist minister, using a typewriter, carefully tapping the keys, occasionally laughing to himself. In a month's time he had written six letters describing the long city room, the fat belly of the city editor, and the bad words the night editor used when speaking of the Orangemen.

The night editor took a fancy to him because of the astounding puerility of his political opinions. Alfred was always willing to talk pompously of the British Empire policing the world and about all

Catholics being aliens, and the future of Ireland and Canada resting with the Orangemen. He flung his arms wide and talked in the hoarse voice of a bad actor, but no one would have thought of taking him seriously. He was merely having a dandy time. The night editor liked him because he was such a nice boy.

Then Alfred's brother came out from the Old Country, and got a job on the same paper. Some of the men started talking about cheap cockney labourers crowding the good guys out of the jobs, but Harry Bowles was frankly glad to get the thirty a week. It never occurred to him that he had a funny idea of good money. With his first pay he bought a derby hat, a pair of spats, and a cane, but even though his face was clear and had a good colour he never looked as nice as his younger brother because his heavy nose curved up at the end. The landlady on Mutual Street moved a double bed into Alfred's room and Harry slept with his brother.

The days passed with many good times together. At first it was awkward that Alfred should be working at night and his brother in the day-time, but Harry was pleased to come down to the office every night at eleven and they went down the street to the hotel that didn't bother about Prohibition. They drank a few glasses of good beer. It became a kind of rite that had to be performed carefully. Harry would put his left foot and Alfred his right foot on the rail and leaning an elbow on the bar they would slowly survey the zigzag line of frothing glasses the length of the long bar. Men jostled them for a place at the foot-rail.

And Alfred said: 'Well, a bit of luck.'

Harry grinned and raising his glass said: 'Righto.'

'It's the stuff that heals.'

'Down she goes.'

'It helps the night along.'

'Fill them up again.'

'Toodleoo.'

Then they would walk out of the crowded bar-room, vaguely pleased with themselves. Walking slowly and erectly along the street they talked with assurance, a mutual respect for each other's opinion making it merely an exchange of information. They talked of the Englishman in Canada, comparing his lot with that of the Englishman in South Africa and India. They had never travelled but to ask what they knew of strange lands would have made one feel uncomfortable; it was better to take it for granted that the Bowles boys knew all about the ends of the earth and had judged them carefully, for in their eyes was the light of far-away places. Once in a while, after walking a block or two, one of the brothers would say he would damn well like to see India and the other would say it would be simply topping.

After work and on Sundays they took a look at the places they had heard about in the city. One Sunday they got up in good time and took the boat to Niagara. Their father had written asking if they had seen the Falls and would they send some souvenirs. That day they had as nice a time as a man would want to have. Standing near the pipe-rail a little way from the hotel that overlooks the Falls they watched the water-line just before the drop, smooth as a long strip of bevelled glass, and Harry compared it favourably with a cataract in the Himalayas and a giant waterfall in Africa, just above the Congo. They took a car along the gorge and getting off near the whirlpool, picked out a little hollow near a big rock at the top of the embankment where the grass was lush and green. They stretched themselves out with hats tilted over their eyes for sunshades. The river whirled below. They talked about the funny ways of Mr. Brownson and his short fat legs and about the crazy women who fainted at the lifted hand of the faith healer who was in the city for the week. They liked the distant rumble of the Falls. They agreed to try and save a lot of money and go west to the Pacific in a year's time. They never mentioned trying to get a raise in pay.

Afterwards they each wrote home about the trip, sending the souvenirs.

Neither one was doing well on the paper. Harry wasn't much good because he hated writing the plain copy and it was hard for him to be strictly accurate. He liked telling a good tale but it never occurred to him that he was deliberately lying. He imagined a thing and straightway felt it to be true. But it never occurred to Alfred to depart from the truth. He was accurate but lazy, never knowing when he was really working. He was taken off night police and for two weeks helped a man do courts at the City Hall. He got to know the boys at the press gallery, who smiled at his naïve sincerity and thought him a decent chap, without making up their minds about him. Every noon-hour Harry came to the press gallery and the brothers, sitting at typewriters, wrote long letters all about the country and the people, anything interesting, and after exchanging letters, tilted back in their swivel chairs, laughing out loud. Heaven only knows who got the letters in the long run. Neither one when in the press gallery seemed to write anything for the paper.

Some of the men tried kidding Alfred, teasing him about women, asking if he found the girls in this country to his liking; but he seemed to enjoy it more than they did. Seriously he explained that he had never met a girl in this country, but they looked very nice. Once Alfred and Bun Brophy, a red-headed fellow with a sharp tongue who did City Hall for the paper, were alone in the gallery. Brophy had in his hands a big picture of five girls in masquerade costumes. Without explaining that he loved one of the girls Brophy asked Bowles which of the lot was the prettiest.

'You want me to settle that,' said Alfred, grinning and waving his pipe. He very deliberately selected a demure little girl with a shy smile.

Brophy was disappointed. 'Don't you think this one is pretty?'— a colourful, bold-looking girl.

'Well, she's all right in her way, but she's too vivacious. I'll take this one. I like them kittenish,' Alfred said.

Brophy wanted to start an argument but Alfred said it was neither here nor there. He really didn't like women.

'You mean to say you never step out?' Brophy said.

'I've never seemed to mix with them,' he said, adding that the whole business didn't matter because he liked boys much better.

The men in the press room heard about it and some suggested nasty things to Alfred. It was hard to tease him when he wouldn't be serious. Sometimes they asked if he took Harry out walking in the evenings. Brophy called them the heavy lovers. The brothers didn't mind because they thought the fellows were having a little fun.

In the fall Harry was fired. The editor in a nice note said that he was satisfied Mr. H. W. Bowles could not adapt himself to their methods. But everybody wondered why he hadn't been fired sooner. He was no good on the paper.

The brothers smiled, shrugged their shoulders and went on living together. Alfred still had his job. Every noon-hour in the City Hall press room they were together, writing letters.

Time passed and the weather got cold. Alfred's heavy coat came from the Old Country and he gave his vest and a thin sweater to Harry, who had only a light spring coat. As the weather got colder

Harry buttoned his coat higher up on his throat and even though he looked cold he was neat as a pin with his derby and cane.

Then Alfred lost his job. The editor, disgusted, called him a fool. For the first time since coming over last spring he felt hurt, something inside him was hurt and he told his brother about it, wanting to know why people acted in such a way. He said he had been doing night police. On the way over to No. 1 station very late Thursday night he had met two men from other papers. They told him about a big fire earlier in the evening just about the time when Alfred was accustomed to going to the hotel to have a drink with his brother. They were willing to give all the details and Alfred thankfully shook hands with them and hurried back to the office to write the story. Next morning the assistant city editor phoned Alfred and asked how it was the morning papers missed the story. Alfred tried to explain but Mr. Brownson said he was a damn fool for not phoning the police and making sure instead of trying to make the paper look like a pack of fools printing a fake story. The fellows who had kidded him said that too. Alfred kept asking his brother why the fellows had to do it. He seemed to be losing a good feeling for people.

Still the brothers appeared at noontime in the press room. They didn't write so many letters. They were agreeable, cheerful, on good terms with everybody. Bun Brophy every day asked how they were doing and they felt at home there. Harry would stand for a while watching the checker game always in progress, knowing that if he stood staring intently at the black and red squares, watching every deliberate move, he would be asked to sit in when it was necessary that one of the players make the rounds in the hall. Once Brophy gave Harry his place and walked over to the window where Alfred stood watching the fleet of automobiles arranged in a square in the courtyard. The police wagon with a load of drunks was backing toward the cells.

'Say, Alfie, I often wonder how you guys manage,' he said.

'Oh, first rate.'

'Well, you ought to be in a bad way by now.'

'Oh no, we have solved the problem' said Alfred in a grand way, grinning, as if talking about the British Empire.

He was eager to tell how they did it. There was a store in their block where a package of tobacco could be got for five cents; they did their own cooking and were able to live on five dollars a week.

'What about coming over and having tea with us sometimes?'
Alfred said. He was decidedly on his uppers but he asked Brophy to
visit them and have tea.

Brophy, abashed, suggested the three of them go over to the café
and have a little toast. Harry talked volubly on the way over and
while having coffee. He was really a better talker than his brother.
They sat in an arm-chair lunch, gripped the handles of their thick
mugs, and talked about religion. The brothers were sons of a Baptist
minister but never thought of going to church. It seemed that
Brophy had travelled a lot during war-time and afterwards in Asia
Minor and India. He was telling about a great golden temple of the
Sikhs at Amritsar and Harry listened carefully, asking many
questions. Then they talked about newspapers until Harry started
talking about the East, slowly feeling his way. All of a sudden he
told about standing on a height of land near Amritsar, looking down
at a temple. It couldn't have been so but he would have it that
Brophy and he had seen the same temple and he described the
country in the words Brophy had used. When he talked that way
you actually believed that he had seen the temple.

Alfred liked listening to his brother but he said finally: 'Religion
is a funny business. I tell you it's a funny business.' And for the
time being no one would have thought of talking seriously about
religion. Alfred had a casual way of making a cherished belief or
opinion seem unimportant, a way of dismissing even the bright
yarns of his brother.

After that afternoon in the café Brophy never saw Harry. Alfred
came often to the City Hall but never mentioned his brother.
Someone said maybe Harry had a job but Alfred laughed and said
no such luck in this country, explaining casually that Harry had a
bit of a cold and was resting up. In the passing days Alfred came
only once in a while to the City Hall, writing his letter without
enthusiasm.

The press men would have tried to help the brothers if they had
heard Harry was sick. They were entirely ignorant of the matter.
On a Friday afternoon at three-thirty Alfred came into the gallery
and, smiling apologetically, told Brophy that his brother was dead;
the funeral was to be in three-quarters of an hour; would he mind
coming? It was pneumonia, he added. Brophy, looking hard at
Alfred, put on his hat and coat and they went out.

It was a poor funeral. The hearse went on before along the way to the Anglican cemetery that overlooks the ravine. One old cab followed behind. There had been a heavy fall of snow in the morning, and the slush on the pavement was thick. Alfred and Brophy sat in the old cab, silent. Alfred was leaning forward, his chin resting on his hands, the cane acting as a support, and the heavy pimples stood out on the lower part of his white face. Brophy was uncomfortable and chilly but he mopped his shining forehead with a big handkerchief. The window was open and the air was cold and damp.

Alfred politely asked how Mrs. Brophy was doing. Then he asked about Mr. Brownson.

'Oh, he's fine,' Brophy said. He wanted to close the window but it would have been necessary to move Alfred so he sat huddled in the corner, shivering.

Alfred asked suddenly if funerals didn't leave a bad taste in the mouth and Brophy, surprised, started talking absently about that golden temple of the Sikhs in India. Alfred appeared interested until they got to the cemetery. He said suddenly he would have to take a look at the temple one fine day.

They buried Harry Bowles in a grave in the paupers' section on a slippery slope of the hill. The earth was hard and chunky and it thumped down on the coffin case. It snowed a little near the end.

On the way along the narrow, slippery foot-path up the hill Alfred thanked Brophy for being thoughtful enough to come to the funeral. There was little to say. They shook hands and went different ways.

After a day or two Alfred again appeared in the press room. He watched the checker game, congratulated the winner and then wrote home. The men were sympathetic and said it was too bad about his brother. And he smiled cheerfully and said they were good fellows. In a little while he seemed to have convinced them that nothing important had really happened.

His last cent must have gone to the undertaker, for he was particular about paying bills, but he seemed to get along all right. Occasionally he did a little work for the paper, a story from a night assignment when the editor thought the staff was being overworked.

One afternoon at two-thirty in the press gallery Brophy saw the last of Alfred, who was sucking his pipe, his feet up on a desk, wanting to be amused. Brophy asked if anything had turned up. In a playful, resigned tone, his eye on the big clock, Alfred said he had until three to join the Air Force. They wouldn't take him, he said, unless he let them know by three.

Brophy said, 'How will you like that?'

'I don't fancy it.'

'But you're going though.'

'Well, I'm not sure. Something else may come along.' It was a quarter to three and he was sitting there waiting for a job to turn up before three.

No one saw him after that, but he didn't join the Air Force. Someone in the gallery said that wherever he went he probably wrote home as soon as he got there.

DAVID OWOYELE
The Will of Allah

THERE had been a clear moon. Now the night was dark. Dogo
glanced up at the night sky. He saw that scudding black clouds had
obscured the moon. He cleared his throat. 'Rain tonight,' he
observed to his companion. Sule, his companion, did not reply
immediately. He was a tall powerfully-built man. His face, as well
as his companion's, was a stupid mask of ignorance. He lived by
thieving as did Dogo, and just now he walked with an unaccustomed
limp. 'It is wrong to say that,' Sule said after a while, fingering the
long, curved sheath-knife he always wore on his upper left arm
when, in his own words, he was 'on duty'. A similar cruel-looking
object adorned the arm of his comrade. 'How can you be sure?'
'Sure?' said Dogo, annoyance and impatience in his voice. Dogo is
the local word for tall. This man was thick-set, short and squat,
anything but tall. He pointed one hand up at the scurrying clouds.
'You only want to look up there. A lot of rain has fallen in my life:
those up there are rain clouds.'

They walked on in silence for a while. The dull red lights of the
big town glowed in crooked lines behind them. Few people were
abroad, for it was already past midnight. About half a mile ahead
of them the native town, their destination, sprawled in the night.
Not a single electric light bulb glowed on its crooked streets. This
regrettable fact suited the books of the two men perfectly. 'You are
not Allah,' said Sule at last. 'You may not assert.'

Sule was a hardened criminal. Crime was his livelihood, he had
told the judge this during his last trial that had earned him a short
stretch in jail. 'Society must be protected from characters like you,'
he could still hear the stern judge intoning in the hushed court-
room. Sule had stood in the dock, erect, unashamed, unimpressed;
he'd heard it all before. 'You and your type constitute a threat to
life and property and this court will always see to it that you get
your just deserts, according to the law.' The judge had then fixed
him with a stern gaze, which Sule coolly returned: he had stared
into too many so-called stern judges' eyes to be easily intimidated.
Besides, he feared nothing and no one except Allah. The judge

thrust his legal chin forward. 'Do you never pause to consider that the road of crime leads only to frustration, punishment, and suffering? You look fit enough for anything. Why don't you try your hand at earning an honest living for a change?' Sule had shrugged his broad shoulders. 'I earn my living the only way I know,' he said. 'The only way I've chosen.' The judge had sat back, dismayed. Then he leaned forward to try again. 'Is it beyond you to see anything wrong in thieving, burglary, crime?' Again Sule had shrugged. 'The way I earn my living I find quite satisfactory.' 'Satisfactory!' exclaimed the judge, and a wave of whispering swept over the court. The judge stopped this with a rap of his gavel. 'Do you find it satisfactory to break the law?' 'I've no choice,' said Sule. 'The law is a nuisance. It keeps getting in one's way.' 'Constant arrest and imprisonment—do you find it satisfactory to be a jail-bird?' queried the judge, frowning most severely. 'Every calling has its hazards,' replied Sule philosophically. The judge mopped his face. 'Well, my man, you cannot break the law. You can only attempt to break it. And you will only end up by getting broken.' Sule nodded. 'We have a saying like that,' he remarked conversationally. 'He who attempts to shake a stump only shakes himself.' He glanced up at the frowning judge. 'Something like a thick stump—the law, eh?' The judge had given him three months. Sule had shrugged. 'The will of Allah be done. . . .'

A darting tongue of lightning lit up the overcast night sky for a second. Sule glanced up. 'Sure, it looks like rain. But you do not say: It will rain. You are only a mortal. You only say: If it is the will of Allah, it will rain.' Sule was a deeply religious man, according to his lights. His religion forbade being dogmatic or prophetic about the future, about anything. His fear of Allah was quite genuine. It was his firm conviction that Allah left the question of a means of livelihood for each man to decide for himself. Allah, he was sure, gives some people more than they need so that others with too little could help themselves to some of it. It could certainly not be the intention of Allah that some stomachs remain empty while others are overstuffed.

Dogo snorted. He had served prison sentences in all the major towns in the country. Prison had become for him a home from home. Like his companion in crime, he feared no man; but unlike him, he had no religion other than self-preservation. 'You and your religion,' he said in derision. 'A lot of good it has done you.' Sule did not reply. Dogo knew from experience that Sule was touchy about his religion, and the first intimation he would get that Sule had lost his temper would be a blow on the head. The two men never pretended that their partnership had anything to do with love or friendship or any other luxurious idea; they operated together when their prison sentences allowed because they found it convenient. In a partnership that each believed was for his own special benefit, there could be no fancy code of conduct.

'Did you see the woman tonight?' Dogo asked, changing the subject, not because he was afraid of Sule's displeasure, but because his grasshopper mind had switched to something else. 'Uh-huh,' grunted Sule. 'Well?' said Dogo, when he did not go on. 'Bastard!' said Sule without any passion. 'Who? Me?' said Dogo thinly. 'We were talking about the woman,' replied Sule.

They got to a small stream. Sule stopped, washed his arms and legs, his clean-shaven head. Dogo squatted on the bank, sharpening his sheath-knife on a stone. 'Where do you think you are going?' 'To yonder village,' said Sule, rinsing out his mouth. 'Didn't know you had a sweetheart there,' said Dogo. 'I'm not going to any woman,' said Sule.

'I am going to collect stray odds and ends—if it is the will of Allah.' 'To steal, you mean?' suggested Dogo. 'Yes,' conceded Sule. He straightened himself, pointed a brawny arm at Dogo: 'You are a burglar too . . . and a bastard besides.'

Dogo, calmly testing the edge of the knife on his arm, nodded. 'Is that part of your religion, washing in midnight streams?' Sule didn't reply until he had climbed on to the further bank, 'Wash when you find a stream; for when you cross another is entirely in the hands of Allah.' He limped off, Dogo following him. 'Why did you call her a bastard?' Dogo asked. 'Because she is one.' 'Why?' 'She told me she sold the coat and the black bag for only fifteen shillings.' He glanced down and sideways at his companion. 'I suppose you got on to her before I did and told her what to say?' 'I've not laid eyes on her for a week,' protested Dogo. 'The coat is fairly old. Fifteen shillings sounds all right to me. I think she has done very well indeed.' 'No doubt,' said Sule. He didn't believe Dogo. 'I'd think the same way if I'd already shared part of the proceeds with her. . . .'

Dogo said nothing. Sule was always suspicious of him, and he returned the compliment willingly. Sometimes their suspicion of each other was groundless, other times not. Dogo shrugged. 'I don't know what you are talking about.' 'No. I don't suppose you would,' said Sule drily. 'All I'm interested in is my share,' went on Dogo. 'Your second share, you mean,' said Sule. 'You'll both get your share—you cheating son without a father, as well as that howling devil of a woman.' He paused before he added, 'She stabbed me in the thigh—the bitch.' Dogo chuckled softly to himself. 'I've been wondering about that limp of yours. Put a knife in your thigh, did she? Odd, isn't it?' Sule glanced at him sharply. 'What's odd about it?' 'You getting stabbed just for asking her to hand over the money.' 'Ask her? I didn't ask her. No earthly use asking anything of characters like that.' 'Oh?' said Dogo. 'I'd always thought all you had to do was ask. True, the coat wasn't yours. But you asked her to sell it. She's an old "fence" and ought to know that you are entitled to the money.' 'Only a fool would be content with fifteen shillings for a coat and a bag,' said Sule. 'And you are not a fool, eh?' chuckled Dogo. 'What did you do about it?' 'Beat the living daylight out of her?' rasped Sule. 'And quite right too,' commented Dogo. 'Only snag is you seem to have got more than you gave her.' He chuckled again. 'A throbbing wound is no joke,' said Sule testily. 'And who's joking? I've been stabbed in my time, too. You can't go around at night wearing a knife and not expect to get stabbed once in a while. We should regard such things as an occupational hazard.' 'Sure,' grunted Sule. 'But that can't cure a wound.' 'No, but the hospital can,' said Dogo. 'I know. But in the hospital they ask questions before they cure you.'

They were entering the village. In front of them the broad path diverged into a series of tracks that twined away between the houses. Sule paused, briefly, took one of the paths. They walked along on silent feet, just having a look around. Not a light showed in any of the crowded mud houses. Every little hole of a window was shut or plugged, presumably against the threatening storm. A peal of languid thunder rumbled over from the east. Except for a group of goats and sheep, which rose startled at their approach, the two had the village paths to themselves. Every once in a while Sule would stop by a likely house; the two would take a careful look around; he'd look inquiringly down at his companion, who would shake his head, and they would move on.

They had been walking around for about a quarter of an hour when a brilliant flash of lightning almost burned out their eyeballs. That decided them. 'We'd better hurry,' whispered Dogo. 'The storm's almost here.' Sule said nothing. A dilapidated-looking house stood a few yards away. They walked up to it. They were not put off by its appearance. Experience had taught them that what a house looked like was no indication of what it contained. Some stinking hovels had yielded rich hauls. Dogo nodded at Sule. 'You stay outside and try to keep awake,' said Sule. He nodded at a closed window. 'You might stand near that.'

Dogo moved off to his post. Sule got busy on the crude wooden door. Even Dogo's practised ear did not detect any untoward sound, and from where he stood he couldn't tell when Sule gained entry into the house. He remained at his post for what seemed ages—it was actually a matter of minutes. Presently he saw the window at his side open slowly. He froze against the wall. But it was Sule's muscular hands that came through the window, holding out to him a biggish gourd. Dogo took the gourd and was surprised at its weight. His pulse quickened. People around her trusted gourds like this more than banks. 'The stream,' whispered Sule through the open window. Dogo understood. Hoisting the gourd on to his head, he made off at a fast trot for the stream. Sule would find his way out of the house and follow him.

He set the gourd down carefully by the stream, took off its carved lid. If this contained anything of value, he thought, he and Sule did not have to share it equally. Besides how did he know Sule had not helped himself to a little of its contents before passing it out through the window? He thrust his right hand into the gourd and the next instant he felt a vicious stab on his wrist. A sharp exclamation escaped from him as he jerked his arm out. He peered at his wrist closely then slowly and steadily he began to curse. He damned to hell and glory everything under the sun in the two languages he knew. He sat on the ground, holding his wrist, cursing softly. He heard Sule approaching and stopped. He put the lid back on the gourd and waited. 'Any trouble?' he asked when the other got to him. 'No trouble,' said Sule. Together they stooped over the gourd. Dogo had to hold his right wrist in his left hand, but he did it so Sule wouldn't notice. 'Have you opened it?' Sule asked. 'Who? Me? Oh, no!' said Dogo. Sule did not believe him and he knew it. 'What can be so heavy?' Dogo asked curiously. 'We'll see,' said Sule.

He took off the lid, thrust his hand into the gaping mouth of the gourd, and felt a sharp stab on his wrist. He whipped his hand out of the gourd. He stood up. Dogo too stood up, and for the first time

Sule noticed Dogo's wrist held in the other hand. They were silent for a long time, glaring at each other. 'As you always insisted, we should go fifty-fifty in everything,' said Dogo casually. Quietly, almost inaudibly, Sule started speaking. He called Dogo every name known to obscenity. Dogo for his part was holding up his end quite well. They stopped when they had run out of names. 'I am going home,' Dogo announced. 'Wait!' said Sule. With his uninjured hand, he rummaged in his pocket, brought out a box of matches. With difficulty he struck one, held the flame over the gourd, peered in. He threw the match away. 'It is not necessary,' he said. 'Why not?' Dogo demanded. 'That in there is an angry cobra,' said Sule. The leaden feeling was creeping up his arm fast. The pain was tremendous. He sat down. 'I still don't see why I can't go home,' said Dogo. 'Have you never heard the saying that what the cobra bites dies at the foot of the cobra? The poison is that good: just perfect for sons of swine like you. You'll never make it home. Better sit down and die here.' Dogo didn't agree, but the throbbing pain forced him to sit down.

They were silent for several minutes while the lightning played around them. Finally Dogo said, 'Funny that your last haul should be a snake-charmer's gourd.' 'I think it's funnier still that it should contain a cobra, don't you?' said Sule. . . . He groaned. 'I reckon funnier things will happen before the night is done,' said Dogo. 'Uh!' he winced with pain. 'A couple of harmless deaths, for instance,' suggested Sule. 'Might as well kill the bloody snake,' said Dogo. He attempted to rise and pick up a stone from the stream; he couldn't. 'Ah, well,' he said, lying on his back. 'It doesn't matter anyway.'

The rain came pattering down. 'But why die in the rain?' he demanded angrily. 'Might help to die soaking wet if you are going straight to hell from here,' said Sule. Teeth clenched, he dragged himself to the gourd, his knife in his good hand. Closing his eyes, he thrust knife and hand into the gourd, drove vicious thrusts into the reptile's writhing body, breathing heavily all the while. When he crawled back to lie down a few minutes later the breath came whistling out of his nostrils; his arm was riddled with fang-marks; but the reptile was dead. 'That's one snake that has been charmed for the last time,' said Sule. Dogo said nothing.

Several minutes passed in silence. The poison had them securely in its fatal grip, especially Sule, who couldn't suppress a few groans.

It was only a matter of seconds now. 'Pity you have to end up this way,' mumbled Dogo, his senses dulling. 'By and large, it hasn't been too bad—you thieving scoundrel!' 'I'm soaked in tears on account of you,' drawled Sule, unutterably weary. 'This seems the end of the good old road. But you ought to have known it had to end sometime, you rotten bastard!' He heaved a deep sigh. 'I shan't have to go up to the hospital in the morning after all,' he mumbled, touching the wound in his thigh with a trembling hand. 'Ah,' he breathed in resignation, 'the will of Allah be done.' The rain came pattering down.

R. PRAWER JHABVALA
The Interview

I AM always very careful of my appearance, so you could not say
that I spent much more time than usual over myself that morning.
It is true, I trimmed and oiled my moustache, but then I often do
that; I always like it to look very neat, like Raj Kapoor's, the film
star's. But I knew my sister-in-law and my wife were watching me.
My sister-in-law was smiling, and she had one hand on her hip; my
wife only looked anxious. I knew she was anxious. All night she had
been whispering to me. She had whispered, 'Get this job and take
me away to live somewhere alone, only you and I and our children.'
I had answered, 'Yes,' because I wanted to go to sleep. I don't
know where and why she has taken this notion that we should go
and live alone.

When I had finished combing my hair, I sat on the floor and my
sister-in-law brought me my food on a tray. It may sound strange
that my sister-in-law should serve me, and not my wife, but it is so
in our house. It used to be my mother who brought me my food,
even after I was married; she would never allow my wife to do this
for me, though my wife wanted to very much. Then, when my
mother got so old, my sister-in-law began to serve me. I know that
my wife feels deeply hurt by this, but she doesn't dare to say
anything. My mother doesn't notice many things any more, otherwise she certainly would not allow my sister-in-law to bring me my
food; she has always been very jealous of this privilege herself,
though she never cared who served my brother. Now she has
become so old that she can hardly see anything, and most of the
time she sits in the corner by the family trunks and folds and strokes
her pieces of cloth. For years now she has been collecting pieces of
cloth. Some of them are very old and dirty, but she doesn't care,
she loves them all equally. Nobody is allowed to touch them. Once
there was a great quarrel, because my wife had taken one of them
to make a dress for our child. My mother shouted at her—it was
terrible to hear her: but then, she has never liked my wife—and my
wife was very much afraid and cried and tried to excuse herself. I
hit her across the face, not very hard and not because I wanted to,

but only to satisfy my mother. The old woman kept quiet then and
went back to folding and stroking her pieces of cloth.

All the time I was eating, I could feel my sister-in-law looking at
me and smiling. It made me uncomfortable. I thought she might be
smiling because she knew I wouldn't get the job for which I had to
go and be interviewed. I also knew I wouldn't get it, but I didn't
like her to smile like that. It was as if she were saying, 'You see, you
will always have to be dependent on us.' It is clearly my brother's
duty to keep me and my family until I can get work and contribute
my own earnings to the family household. There is no need for her
to smile about it. But it is true that I am more dependent on her
now than on anyone else. Since my mother has got so old, my sister-
in-law has become more and more the most important person in the
house, so that she even keeps the keys and the household stores. At
first I didn't like this. As long as my mother managed the household,
I was sure of getting many extra tit-bits. But now I find that my
sister-in-law is also very kind to me—much more kind than she is
to her husband. It is not for him that she saves the tit-bits, nor for
her children, but for me; and when she gives them to me, she never
says anything and I never say anything, but she smiles and then I
feel confused and rather embarrassed. My wife has noticed what
she does for me.

I have found that women are usually kind to me. I think they
realize that I am a rather sensitive person and that therefore I must
be treated very gently. My mother has always treated me very
gently. I am her youngest child, and I am fifteen years younger
than my brother who is next to me (she did have several children in
between us, but they all died). Right from the time when I was a
tiny baby, she understood that I needed greater care and tenderness
than other children. She always made me sleep close beside her in
the night, and in the day I usually sat with her and my grandmother
and my widowed aunt, who were also very fond of me. When I got
bigger, my father sometimes wanted to take me to help in his stall
(he had a little grocer's stall, where he sold lentils and rice and
cheap cigarettes and coloured drinks in bottles) but my mother and
grandmother and aunt never liked to let me go. Once he did take
me with him, and he made me pour some lentils out of paper bags
into a tin. I rather liked pouring the lentils—they made such a nice
noise as they landed in the tin—but suddenly my mother came and
was very angry with my father for making me do this work. She

took me home at once, and when she told my grandmother and aunt what had happened, they stroked me and kissed me and then they gave me a hot fritter to eat. The fact is, right from childhood I have been a person who needs a lot of peace and rest, and my food too has to be rather more delicate than that of other people. I have often tried to explain this to my wife, but as she is not very intelligent, she doesn't seem to understand.

Now my wife was watching me while I ate. She was squatting on the floor, washing our youngest baby; the baby's head was in her lap, and all one could see of it was the back of its legs and its naked bottom. My wife did not watch me as openly as my sister-in-law did; only from time to time she raised her eyes to me, I could feel it, and they were very worried and troubled. She too was thinking about the job for which I was going to be interviewed, but she was anxious that I should get it. 'We will go and live somewhere alone,' she had said. Why did she say it? When she knows that it is not possible and never will be.

And even if it were possible, I would not like it. I can't live away from my mother; and I don't think I would like to live away from my sister-in-law. I often look at her and it makes me happy. Even though she is not young any more she is still beautiful. She is tall, with big hips and big breasts and eyes that flash; she often gets angry, and when she is angry, she is the most beautiful of all. Then her eyes are like fire and she shows all her teeth which are very strong and white, and her head is proud with the black hair flying loose. My wife is not beautiful at all. I was very disappointed in her when they first married me to her. Now I have got used to her and I even like her, because she is so good and quiet and never troubles me at all. I don't think anybody else in our house likes her. My sister-in-law always calls her 'that beauty', but she does not mean it; and she makes her do all the most difficult household tasks, and often she shouts at her and even beats her. This is not right; my wife has never done anything to her—on the contrary, she always treats her with respect. But I cannot interfere in their quarrels.

Then I was ready to go, though I didn't want to go. I knew only too well what would happen at the interview. My mother blessed me, and my sister-in-law looked at me over her shoulder and her great eyes flashed with laughter. I didn't look at my wife, who still sat squatting on the floor, but I knew she was pleading with me to get the job like she had pleaded in the night. As I walked down the stairs, the daughter of the carpenter, who lives in one of the rooms on the lower floor, came out of her door and she walked up the stairs as I walked down, and she passed very close beside me, with her eyes lowered but her arm just touching my sleeve. She always waits for me to come out and then she passes me on the stairs. We have never spoken together. She is a very young girl, her breasts are only just forming; her blouse has short sleeves and her arms are beautiful, long and slender. I think soon she is to be married, I have heard my sister-in-law say so. My sister-in-law laughed when she told me, she said, 'It is high time' and then she said something coarse. Perhaps she has noticed that the girl waits for me to pass on the stairs.

No, I did not want to go to the interview. I had been to so many during the last few months, and always the same things happened. I know I have to work, in order to earn money and give it to my mother or my sister-in-law for the household, but there is no pleasure for me in the work. Last time I had work it was in an insurance office and all day they made me sit at a desk and write figures. What pleasure could there be for me in that? I am a very thoughtful person, and I like always to sit and think my own thoughts; but while I thought my own thoughts in the office, I sometimes made mistakes over the figures and then my superiors were very angry with me. I was always afraid of their anger, and I begged their forgiveness and admitted that I was much at fault. When they forgave me, I was no longer afraid and I continued doing my work and thinking my thoughts. But the last time they would not forgive me again, though I begged and begged and cried what a faulty, bad man I was and what good men they were, and how they were my mother and my father and how I looked only to them for my life and the lives of my children. But when they still said I must go, I saw that the work there was really finished and I stopped crying. I went into the washroom and combed my hair and folded my soap in my towel, and then I took my money from the accountant without a word and I left the office with my eyes lowered. But I was no longer afraid, because what is finished is finished, and my brother still had work and probably one day I would get another job.

Ever since then my brother has been trying to get me into government service. He himself is a clerk in government service and enjoys many advantages: every five years he gets an increase of ten rupees in his salary and he has ten days sick-leave in the year and when he retires he will get a pension. It would be good for me also to have such a job; but it is difficult to get, because first there is an interview at which important people sit at a desk and ask many questions. I am afraid of them, and I cannot understand properly what they are saying, so I answer what I think they want me to answer. But it seems that my answers are not after all the right ones, because up till now they have not given me a job.

On my way to this interview, I thought how much nicer it would be to go to the cinema instead. If I had had ten annas, perhaps I would have gone; it was just time for the morning show. The young clerks and the students would be collecting in a queue outside the cinema now. They would be standing and not talking much, holding their ten annas and waiting for the box-office to open. I enjoy these morning shows, perhaps because the people who come to them are all young men like myself, all silent and rather sad. I am often sad; it would even be right to say that I am sad most of the time. But when the film begins, I am happy. I love to see the beautiful women, dressed in golden clothes with heavy ear-rings and neck-laces and bracelets covering their arms, and their handsome lovers who are all the things I would like to be. And when they sing their love-songs, so full of deep feelings, the tears sometimes come into my eyes; but not because I am sad, no, on the contrary, because I am so happy. After the film is over, I never go home straight away, but I walk around the streets and think about how wonderful life could be.

When I arrived at the place where the interview was, I had to walk down many corridors and ask directions from many peons before I could find the right room. The peons were all rude to me, because they knew what I had come for. They lounged on benches outside the offices, and when I asked them, they looked me up and down before answering, and sometimes they made jokes about me with one another. I was very polite to them, for even though they were only peons, they had uniforms and jobs and belonged here, and they knew the right way whereas I did not. At last I came to the room where I had to wait. Many others were already sitting there, on chairs which were drawn up all round the room against the wall. No one was talking. I also sat on a chair, and after a while an official came in with a list and he asked if anyone else had come. I got up and he asked my name, and then he looked down the list and made a tick with a pencil. He said to me very sternly, 'Why are you late?' I begged pardon and told him the bus in which I had come had had an accident. He said, 'When you are called for interview, you have to be here exactly on time, otherwise your name is crossed off the list.' I begged pardon again and asked him very humbly please not to cross me off this time. I knew that all the others were listening, though none of them looked at us. He was very stern with me and even scornful, but in the end he said, 'Wait here, and when your name is called, you must go in at once.'

I did not count the number of people waiting in the room, but there were many. Perhaps there was one job free, perhaps two or three. I knew that all the others were very worried and anxious to get the job, so I became worried and anxious too. The walls of the room were painted green halfway up and white above that and were quite bare. There was a fan turning from the ceiling, but it was not turning fast enough to give much breeze. Behind the big door the interview was going on; one by one we would all be called in behind this closed door.

I began to worry desperately. It always happens like this. When I come to an interview, I don't want the job at all, but when I see all the others waiting and worrying, I want it terribly. Yet at the same time I know that I don't want it. It would only be the same thing over again: writing figures and making mistakes and then being afraid when they found out. And there would be a superior officer to whom I would have to be very deferential, and every time I saw him or heard his voice I would begin to be afraid that he had found out something against me. For weeks and months I would sit and write figures, getting wearier of it and wearier, so that more and more I would be thinking my own thoughts. Then the mistakes would come, and my superior officer would be angry and I afraid.

My brother never makes mistakes. For years he has been sitting in the same office, writing figures and being deferential to his superior officer; he concentrates very hard on his work, and so he doesn't make mistakes. But all the same he is afraid; that is why he concentrates so hard—because he is afraid that he will make a mistake and they will be angry with him and take away his job. He is afraid of this all the time. And he is right: what would become of us all if he also lost his job? It is not the same with me. I think I am afraid to lose my job only because that is a thing of which one is expected to be afraid. When I have actually lost it, I am really relieved. But I am very different from my brother; even in appearance I am very different. It is true, he is fifteen years older than I am, but even when he was my age, he never looked like I do. My appearance has always attracted others, and up to the time I was married, my mother used to stroke my hair and my face and say many tender things to me. Once, when I was walking on my way to school through the bazaar, a man called to me, very softly, and when I came he gave me a ripe mango, and then he took me into a dark passage which led to a disused mosque, and he touched me under my clothes and he said, 'You are so nice, so nice.' He was very kind to me. I love wearing fine clothes, very thin white muslin kurtas which have been freshly washed and starched and are embroidered at the shoulders. Sometimes I also use scent, a fine khas smell; my hair-oil also smells of khas. Some years ago, when the carpenter's daughter was still a small child and did not yet wait for me on the stairs, there was a girl living in the tailor's shop opposite our house and she used to follow me when I went out. But it is my brother who is married to a beautiful wife, and my wife is not beautiful at all. He is not happy with his wife; when she talks to him, she talks in a hard scornful way; and it is not for him that she saves the best food, but for me, even though I have not brought money home for many months.

The big closed door opened and the man who had been in there for interview came out. We all looked at him, but he walked out in a great hurry, with a preoccupied expression on his face; probably he was going over in his mind all that had been said at the interview. I could feel the anxiety in the other men getting stronger, so mine got stronger too. The official with the list came and we all looked at him. He read out another name and the man whose name was called jumped up from his chair; he did not notice that his dhoti had got caught on a nail in the chair and he wondered why he could not go farther. When he realized what had happened, he tried to disentangle himself, but his fingers shook so much that he could not get the dhoti off the nail. The official watched him and said, 'Hurry, now, do you think the gentlemen will wait for you for as long as you please?' Then the man also dropped the umbrella he was carrying and now he was trying both to disentangle the dhoti and to pick up the umbrella. When he could not get the dhoti loose, he became so desperate that he tore at the cloth and ripped it free.

It was a pity to see the dhoti torn because it was a new one, which he was probably wearing for the first time and had put on specially for the interview. He clasped his umbrella to his chest and walked in a great hurry to the interviewing room, with his dhoti hanging about his legs and his face swollen with embarrassment and confusion.

We all sat and waited. The fan, which seemed to be a very old one, made a creaking noise. One man kept cracking his finger-joints—*tik*, we heard, *tik* (it made my own finger-joints long to be cracked too). All the rest of us kept very still. From time to time the official with the list came in, he walked round the room very slowly, tapping his list, and then we all looked down at our feet and the man who had been cracking his finger-joints stopped doing it. A faint and muffled sound of voices came from behind the closed door. Sometimes a voice was raised, but even then I could not make out what was being said, though I strained very hard.

The last time I had an interview, it was very unpleasant for me. One of the people who was interviewing took a dislike to me and shouted at me very loudly. He was a large fat man and he wore an English suit; his teeth were quite yellow, and when he became angry and shouted, he showed them all, and even though I was very upset, I couldn't help looking at them and wondering how they had become so yellow. I don't know why he was angry. He shouted: 'Good God, man, can't you understand what's said to you?' It was true, I could not understand, but I had been trying so hard to answer well. What more did he expect of me? Probably there was something in my appearance which he did not like. It happens that way sometimes—they take a dislike to you and then of course there is nothing you can do.

When I thought of the man with the yellow teeth, I became more anxious than ever. I need great calm in my life. Whenever anything worries me too much, I have to cast the thoughts of it off immediately, otherwise there is a danger that I may become very ill. All my limbs were itching so that it was difficult for me to sit still, and I could feel blood rushing into my brain. It was this room that was doing me so much harm: all the other men waiting, anxious and silent, and the noise from the fan and the official with the list walking round, tapping his list or striking it against his thigh, and the big closed door behind which the interview was going on. I felt great need to get up and go away. I didn't *want* the job. I wasn't even thinking about it any more—I was thinking only about how to avoid having to sit here and wait.

Now the door opened again and the man with the torn new dhoti came out. He was biting his lip and scratching the back of his neck, and he too walked straight out without looking at us at all. The big door was left slightly open for a moment, and I could see a man's arm in a white shirt-sleeve and part of the back of his head. His shirt was very white and of good material, and his ears stood away from his head so that one could see how his spectacles fitted into the back of his ears. I realized at once that this man would be my enemy and that he would make things very difficult for me and perhaps even shout at me. Then I knew it was no use for me to stay there. The official with the list came back and great panic seized me that he would read out my name. I got up quickly, murmuring, 'Please excuse me—bathroom,' and went out. The official with the list called after me, 'Hey mister, where are you going?' so I lowered my head and walked faster. I would have started to run, but that might have caused suspicion, so I just walked as fast as I could, down the long corridors and right out of the building. There at last I was able to stop and take a deep breath, and I felt much better.

I stood still for only a little while, then I moved on though not in any particular direction. There were many clerks and peons moving around in the street, hurrying from one office building to another and carrying files and papers. Everyone seemed to have something to do. I was glad when I had moved out of this block and on to the open space where people like myself, who had nothing to do, sat under the trees or in any other patch of shade they could find. But I couldn't sit there; it was too close to the office blocks, and any moment someone might come and say to me, 'Why did you go away?' So I walked farther. I was feeling quite light-hearted; it was such a relief for me not to have to be interviewed.

I came to a row of eating-stalls, and I sat down on a wooden bench outside one of them, which was called the Paris Hotel, and asked for tea. I felt badly in need of tea, and since I intended to walk part of the way home, I was in a position to pay for it. There were two Sikhs sitting at the end of my bench, who were eating with great appetite, dipping their hands very rapidly into brass bowls. In between eating they exchanged remarks with the proprietor of the Paris Hotel, who sat high up inside his stall, stirring in a big

brass pot in which he was cooking the day's food. He was chewing
a betel leaf, and from time to time he spat out the red betel juice far
over the cooking-pot and on to the ground between the wooden
benches and tables.

I sat quietly at my end of the bench and drank my tea. The food
smelt very good, and it made me realize that I was hungry. I
decided that if I walked all the way home, I could afford a little
cake (I am very fond of sweet things). The cake was not new but it
had a beautiful piece of bright-green peel inside it. On reaching
home I would lie down at once to sleep and not wake up again till
tomorrow morning. That way no one would be able to ask me any
questions. I would not look at my wife at all, so I would be able to
avoid her eyes. I would not look at my sister-in-law either; but she
would be smiling, that I knew already—leaning against the wall
with her hand on her hip, looking at me and smiling. She would
know that I had run away, but she would not say anything.

Let her know! What does it matter? It is true I have no job and
no immediate prospect of getting one. It is true that I am dependent
on my brother. Everybody knows that. There is no shame in it:
there are many people without jobs. And she has been so kind to
me up till now, there is no reason why she should not continue to
be kind to me. Though I know she is not by nature a kind woman,
she speaks mostly with a very harsh tongue and her actions also are
harsh. Only to me she has been kind.

The Sikhs at the end of the bench had finished eating. They
licked their fingers and belched deeply, the way one does after a
good meal. They started to laugh and joke with the proprietor. I sat
quiet and alone at my end of the bench. Of course they did not
laugh and joke with me. They knew that I was superior to them, for
whereas they worked with their hands, I am a lettered man who
does not have to sweat for a living but sits on a chair in an office
and writes figures and can speak in English. My brother is very
proud of his superiority, and he has great contempt for carpenters
and mechanics and such people who work with their hands. I am
also proud of being a lettered man, but when I listened to the Sikhs
laughing and joking, the thought came to me that perhaps their life
was happier than mine. It was a thought that had come to me
before. There is the carpenter who lives downstairs in our house,
the one whose daughter waits for me on the stairs, and though he is
poor, there is always great eating in his house and many people

come and I hear them laughing and singing and even dancing. The carpenter is a big strong man and he always looks happy, never anxious and sick with worry the way my brother does. He doesn't wear shoes and clean white clothes like my brother and I do, nor does he speak any English, but all the same he is happy. Even though his work is inferior, I don't think he gets as weary of it as I do of mine, and he has no superior officer to make him afraid.

Then I thought again about my sister-in-law and I thought that if I were kind to her, she would continue to be kind to me. I became quite excited when I thought of being kind to her. I would know then how her big breasts felt under the blouse, how warm they were and how soft. And I would know about the inside of her mouth with the big strong teeth. Her tongue and palate are very pink, like the pink satin blouse she wears on festive occasions, and I had often wondered whether they felt as soft as the blouse too. Her eyes would be shut and perhaps there would be tears on the lashes; and she would be making warm animal sounds and her big body too would be warm like an animal's. I became very excited when I thought of it; but when the excitement had passed, I was sad. Because then I thought of my wife, who is thin and not beautiful and there is no excitement in her body. But she does whatever I want and always tries to please me. I remembered her whispering to me in the night, 'Take me away, let us go and live somewhere alone, only you and I and our children.' That can never be, and so always she will have to be unhappy.

I was very sad when I thought of her being unhappy; because it is not only she who is unhappy but I also and many others. Everywhere there is unhappiness. I thought of the man whose new dhoti had been torn and who would now have to go home and sew it carefully so that the tear would not be seen. I thought of all the other men sitting and waiting to be interviewed, all but one or two of whom would not get the job for which they had come to be interviewed, and so again they would have to go to another interview and another and another, to sit and wait and be anxious. And my brother who has a job, but is frightened that he will lose it; and my mother so old that she can only sit on the floor and stroke her pieces of cloth; and my sister-in-law who does not care for her husband; and the carpenter's daughter who is to be married and perhaps she also will not be happy. Yet life could be so different. When I go to the cinema and hear the beautiful songs they sing, I know how different it could be; and also sometimes when I sit alone and think my thoughts, then I have a feeling that everything could be so beautiful. But now my tea was finished and also my cake, and I wished I had not bought them, because it was a long way to walk home and I was tired.

MAURICE SHADBOLT
The People Before

MY father took on that farm not long after he came back from the
first war. It was pretty well the last farm up the river. Behind our
farm, and up the river, there was all kind of wild country. Scrub
and jagged black stumps on the hills, bush in gullies where fire
hadn't reached; hills and more hills, deep valleys with caves and
twisting rivers, and mountains white with winter in the distance.
We had the last piece of really flat land up the river. It wasn't the
first farm my father'd taken on—and it certainly wasn't to be the
last—but it was the most remote. He always said that was why he'd
got the place for a song. This puzzled me as a child. For I'd heard,
of course, of having to sing for your supper. I wondered what words,
to what tune, he was obliged to sing for the farm; and where, and
why? Had he travelled up the river, singing a strange song,
charming his way into possession of the land? It always perplexed
me.

And it perplexed me because there wasn't much room for singing
in my father's life. I can't remember ever having heard him sing.
There was room for plodding his paddocks in all weathers, milking
cows and sending cream down river to the dairy factory, and cursing
the bloody government; there was room in his life for all these things
and more, but not for singing.

In time, of course, I understood that he only meant he'd bought
the place cheaply. Cheaply meant for a song. I couldn't, even then,
quite make the connexion. It remained for a long while one of those
adult mysteries. And it was no use puzzling over it, no use asking
my father for a more coherent explanation.

'Don't be difficult,' he'd say. 'Don't ask so many damn questions.
Life's difficult enough, boy, without all your damn questions.'

He didn't mean to be unkind; it was just his way. His life was
committed to winning order from wilderness. Questions were a
disorderly intrusion, like gorse or weed springing up on good
pasture. The best way was to hack them down, grub out the roots,

before they could spread. And in the same way as he checked incipient anarchy on his land he hoped, perhaps, to check it in his son.

By that time I was old enough to understand a good many of the things that were to be understood. One of them, for example, was that we weren't the first people on that particular stretch of land. Thirty or forty years before, when white men first came into our part of the country, it was mostly forest. Those first people fired the forest, right back into the hills, and ran sheep. The sheep grazed not only the flat, but the hills which rose sharply behind our farm; the hills which, in our time, had become stubbly with manuka and fern. The flatland had been pretty much scrub too, the day my father first saw it; and the original people who had been gone twenty years—they'd given up, or been ruined by the land; we never quite knew the story. The farmhouse stood derelict among the returning wilderness.

Well, my father saw right away that the land—the flat land— was a reasonable proposition for a dairy farm. There was a new launch service down to the nearest dairy factory, in the township ten miles away; only in the event of flood, or a launch breakdown, would he have to dispose of his cream by carrying it on a sledge across country, three miles, to the nearest road.

So he moved in, cleared the scrub, sowed new grass, and brought in cows. Strictly speaking, the hills at the back of the farm were his too, but he had no use for them. They made good shelter from the westerlies. Otherwise he never gave the hills a thought, since he had all the land he could safely manage; he roamed across them after wild pig, and that was about all. There were bones up there, scattered skeletons of lost sheep, in and about the scrub and burnt stumps.

Everything went well; he had the place almost paid off by the time of the depression. 'I never looked back, those years,' he said long afterwards. It was characteristic of him not to look back. He was not interested in who had the farm before him. He had never troubled to inquire. So far as he was concerned, history only began the day he first set foot on the land. It was his, by sweat and legal title: that was all that mattered. That was all that could matter.

He had two boys; I was the eldest son. 'You and Jim will take this place over one day,' he often told me. 'You'll run it when I get tired.'

But he didn't look like getting tired. He wasn't a big man, but he was wiry and thin with a lean face and cool blue eyes; he was one of those people who can't keep still. When neighbours called he couldn't ever keep comfortable in a chair, just sitting and sipping tea, but had to start walking them round the farm—or at least the male neighbours—pointing out things here and there. Usually work he'd done, improvements he'd made: the new milking-shed, the new water-pump on the river. He didn't strut or boast, though; he just pointed them out quietly, these jobs well done. He wanted others to share his satisfaction. There was talk of electricity coming through to the farm, the telephone; a road up the river was scheduled. It would all put the value of the property up. The risk he'd taken on the remote and abandoned land seemed justified in every way.

He didn't ever look like getting tired. It was as if he'd been wound up years before, like something clockwork, and set going: first fighting in the war, then fighting with the land; now most of the fighting was done, he sometimes found it quite an effort to keep busy. He never took a holiday. There was talk of taking a holiday, one winter when the cows dried off; talk of us all going down to the sea, and leaving a neighbour to look after the place. But I don't think he could have trusted anyone to look after his land, not even for a week or two in winter when the cows were dried off. Perhaps, when Jim and I were grown, it would be different. But not until. He always found some reason for us not to get away. Like our schooling.

'I don't want to interfere with their schooling,' he said once. 'They only get it once in their lives. And they might as well get it while they can. I didn't get much. And, by God, I regret it now. I don't know much, and I might have got along all right, but I might have got along a damn sight better if I'd had more schooling. And I'm not going to interfere with theirs by carting them off for a holiday in the middle of the year.'

Yet even then I wondered if he meant a word of it, if he really wasn't just saying that for something to say. He was wrangling at the time with my mother, who held opinions on a dwindling number of subjects. She never surrendered any of these opinions, exactly; she just kept them more and more to herself until, presumably, they lapsed quietly and died. As she herself, much later, was to lapse quietly from life, without much complaint.

For if he'd really been concerned about our schooling, he might have been more concerned about the way we fell asleep in afternoon classes. Not that we were the only ones. Others started getting pretty ragged in the afternoons too. A lot of us had been up helping our fathers since early in the morning. Jim and I were up at half-past four most mornings to help with the milking and working the separators. My father increased his herd year after year, right up to the depression. After school we rode home just in time for the evening milking. And by the time we finished it was getting dark; in winter it was dark by the time we were half-way through the herd.

I sometimes worried about Jim looking worn in the evenings, and I often chased him off inside before milking was finished. I thought Jim needed looking after; he wasn't anywhere near as big as me. I'd hear him scamper off to the house, and then I'd set about stripping the cows he had left. Father sometimes complained.

'You'll make that brother of yours a softy,' he said. 'The boy's got to learn what work means.'

'Jim's all right,' I answered. 'He's not a softy. He's just not very big. That's all.'

He detested softies, even the accomplices of softies. My mother, in a way, was such an accomplice. She'd never been keen about first me, then Jim, helping with work on the farm. But my father said he couldn't afford to hire a man to help with the herd. And he certainly couldn't manage by himself, without Jim and me.

'Besides,' he said, 'my Dad and me used to milk two hundred cows'—sometimes, when he became heated, the number rose to three hundred—'when I was eight years old. And thin as a rake too, I was. Eight years old and thin as a rake. It didn't do me no harm. You boys don't know what work is, let me tell you.'

So there all argument finished. My mother kept one more opinion to herself.

And I suppose that, when I chased Jim off inside, I was only taking my mother's side in the argument, and was only another accomplice of softies. Anyway, it would give me a good feeling afterwards—despite anything my father would have to say—when we tramped back to the house, through the night smelling of frost or rain, to find Jim sitting up at the table beside my mother while she ladled out soup under the warm yellow lamplight. He looked as if he belonged there, beside her; and she always looked, at those times, a little triumphant. Her look seemed to say that one child of hers, at least, was going to be saved from the muck of the cowshed.

And I suppose that was the beginning of how Jim became his mother's boy.

I remained my father's. I wouldn't have exchanged him for another father. I liked seeing him with people, a man among men. This happened on winter Saturdays when we rode to the township for the football. We usually left Jim behind to look after my mother. We tethered our horses near the football field and went off to join the crowd. Football was one of the few things which interested my father outside the farm. He'd been a fine rugby forward in his day and people respected what he had to say about the game. He could out-argue most people; probably out-fight them too, if it ever came to that. He often talked about the fights he'd had when young. For he'd done a bit of boxing too, only he couldn't spare the time from his father's farm to train properly. He knocked me down once, with his bare fists, in the cowshed; and I was careful never to let it happen again. I just kept my head down for days afterwards, so that he wouldn't see the bruises on my face or the swelling round my eye.

At the football he barracked with the best of them in the thick of the crowd. Sometimes he called out when the rest of the crowd was silent and tense; he could be very sarcastic about poor players, softies who were afraid to tackle properly.

After the game he often called in, on the way home, to have a few beers with friends in the township's sly-grog shop—we didn't have a proper pub in the township—while I looked after the horses outside. Usually he'd find time, while he gossiped with friends, to bring me out a glass of lemonade. At times it could be very cold out there, holding the horses while the winter wind swept round, but it would be nice to know that I was remembered. When he finished we rode home together for a late milking. He would grow talkative, as we cantered towards dark, and even give me the impression he was glad of my company. He told me about the time he was young, what the world looked like when he was my age. His father was a sharemilker, travelling from place to place; that is, he owned no land of his own and did other people's work.

'So I made up my mind, boy,' he told me as we rode along together, 'I made up my mind I'd never be like that. I'd bend my head to no man. And you know what the secret of that is, boy? Land. Land of your own. You're independent, boy. You can say no to the world. That's if you got your own little kingdom. I reckon it was what kept me alive, down there on the beach at Gallipoli, knowing I'd have some land I could call my own.' This final declaration seemed to dismay him for some reason or other, perhaps because he feared he'd given too much of himself away. So he added half-apologetically, 'I had to think of something, you know, while all that shooting was going on. They say it's best to fix your mind on something if you don't want to be afraid. That's what I fixed my mind on, anyhow. Maybe it did keep me alive.'

In late winter or spring we sometimes arrived back, on Saturdays, to see the last trembling light of sunset fade from the hills and land. We'd canter along a straight stretch, coast up a rise, rein in the horses, and there it was—his green kingdom, his tight tamed acres beneath the hills and beside the river, a thick spread of fenced grass from the dark fringe of hill-scrub down to the ragged willows above the water. And at the centre was his castle, the farmhouse, with the sheds scattered round, and the pine trees.

Reining in on that rise, I knew, gave him a good feeling. It would also be the time when he remembered all the jobs he'd neglected, all the work he should have done instead of going to the football. His conscience would keep him busy all day Sunday.

At times he wondered—it was a conversation out loud with himself—why he didn't sell up and buy another place. There were, after all, more comfortable farms, in more convenient locations nearer towns or cities. 'I've built this place up from nothing,' he said. 'I've made it pay, and pay well. I've made this land worth something. I could sell out for a packet. Why don't I?'

He never really—in my presence anyway—offered himself a convincing explanation. Why didn't he? He'd hardly have said he loved the land: loved, in any case, would have been an extravagance. Part of whatever it was, I suppose, was the knowledge that he'd built where someone else had failed; part was that he'd given too much of himself there, to be really free anywhere else. It wouldn't be the same, walking on to another successful farm, a going concern, everything in order. No, this place—this land from the river back up to the hills—was his. In a sense it had only ever been his. That was why he felt so secure.

If Sunday was often the day when he worked hardest, it was also the best day for Jim and me, our free day. After morning milking, and breakfast, we did more or less what we liked. In summer we

swam down under the river-willows; we also had a canoe tied there
and sometimes we paddled up-river, under great limestone bluffs
shaggy with toi toi, into country which grew wilder and wilder.
There were huge bearded caves in the bush above the water which
we explored from time to time. There were also big eels to be fished
from the pools of the river.

As he grew older Jim turned more into himself, and became still
quieter. You could never guess exactly what he was thinking. It
wasn't that he didn't enjoy life; he just had his own way of enjoying
it. He didn't like being with his father, as I did; I don't even know
that he always enjoyed being with me. He just tagged along with
me: we were, after all, brothers. When I was old enough, my father
presented me with a .22 rifle; Jim never showed great enthusiasm
for shooting. He came along with me, all right, but he never seemed
interested in the rabbits or wild goat I shot, or just missed. He
wandered around the hills, way behind me, entertaining himself
and collecting things. He gathered leaves, and tried to identify the
plants from which the leaves came. He also collected stones, those
of some interesting shape or texture; he had a big collection of
stones. He tramped along, in his slow, quiet way, poking into
everything, adding to his collections. He wasn't too slow and quiet
at school, though; he was faster than most of us with an answer. He
borrowed books from the teacher, and took them home. So in time
he became even smarter with his answers. I grew to accept his
difference from most people. It didn't disturb me particularly: on
the farm he was still quiet, small Jim. He was never too busy with
his books to come along with me on Sundays.

There was a night when Jim was going through some new stones
he'd gathered. Usually, in the house, my father didn't take much
notice of Jim, his reading, or his hobbies. He'd fought a losing battle
for Jim, through the years, and now accepted his defeat. Jim still
helped us with the herd, night and morning, but in the house he
was ignored. But this night my father went across to the table and
picked up a couple of new stones. They were greenish, both the
same triangular shape.

'Where'd you get these?' he asked.

Jim thought for a moment; he seemed pleased by the interest
taken in him. 'One was back in the hills,' he said. 'The other was in
a cave up the river. I just picked them up.'

'You mean you didn't find them together?'

'No,' Jim said.

'Funny,' my father said. 'They look like greenstone. I seen some greenstone once. A joker found it, picked it up in the bush. Jade, it is; same thing. This joker sold it in the city for a packet. Maori stuff. Some people'll buy anything.'

We all crossed to the table and looked down at the greenish stones. Jim's eyes were bright with excitement.

'You mean these used to belong to the Maoris?' he said. 'These stones?'

'Must have,' my father said. 'Greenstone doesn't come natural round here. You look it up in your books and you'll see. Comes from way down south, near the mountains and glaciers. Had to come up here all the way by canoe. They used to fight about greenstone, once.' He paused and looked at the stones again. 'Yes,' he added. 'I reckon that's greenstone, all right. You never know, might be some money in that stuff.'

Money was a very important subject in our house at that time. It was in a lot of households, since that time was the depression. In the cities they were marching in the streets and breaking shop windows. Here on the farm it wasn't anywhere near so dramatic. The grass looked much the same as it had always looked; so did the hills and river. All that had happened, really, was that the farm had lost its value. Prices had fallen; my father sometimes wondered if it was worth while sending cream to the factory. Some of the people on poorer land, down the river, had walked off their properties. Everything was tighter. We had to do without new clothes, and there wasn't much variety in our eating. We ran a bigger garden, and my father went out more frequently shooting wild pig for meat. He had nothing but contempt for the noisy people in the city, the idlers and wasters who preferred to go shouting in the streets rather than fetch a square meal for their families, as he did with his rifle. He thought they, in some way, were to blame for the failure of things. Even so, he became gripped by the idea that he might have failed himself, somehow; he tried to talk himself out of this idea—in my presence—but without much success. Now he had the land solid beneath his feet, owned it entirely, it wasn't much help at all. If it wasn't for our garden and the wild pig, we might starve. The land didn't bring him any money; he might even have to leave it. He had failed, perhaps much as the land's former owners had failed;

why? He might have answered the question for himself satisfactorily, while he grubbed away at the scrub encroaching on our pasture; but I doubt it.

'Yes,' he said. 'Might be some money in that stuff.'

But Jim didn't seem to hear, or understand. His eyes were still bright. 'That means there must have been Maoris here in the old days,' he said.

'I suppose there must have,' my father agreed. He didn't seem much interested. Maoris were Maoris. There weren't many around our part of the river; they were mostly down towards the coast. (Shortly after this, Jim did some research and told me the reason why. It turned out that the land about our part of the river had been confiscated from them after the Maori wars.) 'They were most places, weren't they?' he added.

'Yes,' Jim said. 'But I mean they must have been here. On our place.'

'Well, yes. They could of been. Like I said, they were most places.' It didn't seem to register as particularly important. He picked up the greenstones again. 'We ought to find out about this,' he continued. 'There might be a bit of money in it.'

Later Jim took the stones to school and had them identified as Maori adzes. My father said once again that perhaps there was money in them. But the thing was, where to find a buyer? It mightn't be as easy as it used to be. So somehow it was all forgotten. Jim kept the adzes.

Jim and I did try to find again that cave in which he had picked up an adze. We found a lot of caves, but none of them seemed the right one. Anyway we didn't pick up another adze. We did wander down one long dripping cave, striking matches, and in the dark tripped on something. I struck another match and saw some brownish-looking bones. 'A sheep,' I said. 'It must have come in here and got lost.'

Jim was silent; I wondered why. Then I saw he wasn't looking at the bones, but at a human skull propped on a ledge of the cave. It just sat there sightless, shadows dancing in its sockets.

We got out of that cave quickly. We didn't even talk about it when we reached home. On the whole I preferred going out with my .22 after rabbits.

2

It was near the end of the depression. But we didn't know that then, of course. It might have been just the beginning, for all we knew. My father didn't have as much interest in finishing jobs as he used to have. He tired easily. He'd given his best to the land, and yet his best still wasn't good enough. There wasn't much sense in anything, and his dash was done. He kept going out of habit.

I'd been pulled out of school to help with the farm. Jim still more or less went to school. I say more or less because he went irregularly. This was because of sickness. Once he was away in hospital two months. And of course it cost money; my father said we were to blame, we who allowed Jim to become soft and sickly. But the doctor thought otherwise; he thought Jim had been worked hard enough already. And when Jim returned to the farm he no longer helped with the herd. And this was why I had to leave school: if he couldn't have both of us working with him part-time, my father wanted one full-time. Jim was entirely surrendered at last, to the house and his books, to school and my mother. I didn't mind working on the farm all day, with my father; it was, after all, what I'd always wanted. All the same, I would have been happier if he had been: his doubts about himself, more and more frequently expressed, disturbed me. It wasn't like my father at all. He was convinced now he'd done the wrong thing, somewhere. He went back through the years, levering each year up like a stone, to see what lay beneath; he never seemed to find anything. It was worst of all in winter, when the land looked bleak, the hills were grey with low cloud, and the rain swirled out of the sky. All life vanished from his face and I knew he detested everything: the land which had promised him independence was now only a muddy snare; he was bogged here, between hills and river, and couldn't escape. He had no pride left in him for the place. If he could have got a price for the farm he would have gone. But there was no longer any question of a price. He could walk off if he liked. Only the bush would claim it back.

It was my mother who told us there were people coming. She had taken the telephone message while we were out of the house, and Jim was at school.

'Who are they?' my father said.

'I couldn't understand very well. It was a bad connexion. I think they said they were the people who were here before.'

'The people who were here before? What the hell do they want here?' His eyes became suspicious under his frown.

'I think they said they just wanted to have a look around.'

'What the hell do they want here?' my father repeated, baffled. 'Nothing for them to see. This farm's not like it was when they were here. Everything's different. I've made a lot of changes. They wouldn't know the place. What do they want to come back for?'

'Well,' my mother sighed, 'I'm sure I don't know.'

'Perhaps they want to buy it,' he said abruptly; the words seemed simultaneous with his thought, and he stiffened with astonishment. 'By God, yes. They might want to buy the place back again. I hadn't thought of that. Wouldn't that be a joke? I'd sell, all right— for just about as much as I paid for the place. I tell you, I'd let it go for a song, for a bloody song. They're welcome.'

'But where would we go?' she said, alarmed.

'Somewhere,' he said. 'Somewhere new. Anywhere.'

'But there's nowhere,' she protested. 'Nowhere any better. You know that.'

'And there's nowhere any worse,' he answered. 'I'd start again somewhere. Make a better go of things.'

'You're too old to start again,' my mother observed softly.

There was a silence. And in the silence I knew that what my mother said was true. We all knew it was true.

'So we just stay here,' he said. 'And rot. Is that it?' But he really wished to change the subject. 'When are these people coming?'

'Tomorrow, I think. They're staying the night down in the township. Then they're coming up by launch.'

'They didn't say why they were interested in the place?'

'No. And they certainly didn't say they wanted to buy it. You might as well get that straight now. They said they just wanted a look around.'

'I don't get it. I just don't get it. If I walked off this place I wouldn't ever want to see it again.'

'Perhaps they're different,' my mother said. 'Perhaps they've got happy memories of this place.'

'Perhaps they have. God knows.'

* * *

It was early summer, with warm lengthening days. That sunny Saturday morning I loitered about the house with Jim, waiting for the people to arrive. Eventually, as the sun climbed higher in the sky, I grew impatient and went across the paddocks to help my father. We were working together when we heard the sound of the launch coming up the river.

'That's them,' he said briefly. He dropped his slasher for a moment, and spat on his hands. Then he took up the slasher again and chopped into a new patch of unruly gorse.

I was perplexed. 'Well,' I said, 'aren't you going down to meet them?'

'I'll see them soon enough. Don't worry.' He seemed to be conducting an argument with himself as he hacked into the gorse. 'I'm in no hurry. No, I'm in no hurry to see them.'

I just kept silent beside him.

'Who are they, anyway?' he went on. 'What do they want to come traipsing round my property for? They've got a bloody cheek.'

The sound of the launch grew. It was probably travelling round the last bend in the river now, past the swamp of raupo, and banks prickly with flax and toi toi. They were almost at the farm. Still chopping jerkily, my father tried to conceal his unease.

'What do they want?' he asked for the last time. 'By God, if they've come to gloat, they've got another think coming. I've made something decent out of this place, and I don't care who knows it.'

He had tried everything in his mind and it was no use: he was empty of explanation. Now we could see the launch white on the gleaming river. It was coasting up to the bank. We could also see people clustered on board.

'Looks like a few of them,' I observed. If I could have done so without upsetting my father, I would have run down to meet the launch, eager with curiosity. But I kept my distance until he finished arguing with himself.

'Well,' he said, as if he'd never suggested otherwise, 'we'd better go down to meet them, now they're here.' He dug his slasher into the earth and began to stalk off down to the river. I followed him. His quick strides soon took him well ahead of me; I had to run to keep up.

Then we had our surprise. My father's step faltered; I blundered up alongside him. We saw the people climbing off the launch. And we saw who they were, at last. My father stopped perfectly still and silent. They were Maoris. We were still a hundred yards or more away, but there was no mistaking their clothing and colour. They were Maoris, all right.

'There's something wrong somewhere,' he said at last. 'It doesn't make sense. No Maori ever owned this place. I'd have known. Who the hell do they think they are, coming here?'

I couldn't answer him. He strode on down to the river. There were young men, and two old women with black headscarves. And last of all there was something the young men carried. As we drew nearer we saw it was an old man in a rough litter. The whole party of them fussed over making the old man comfortable. The old women, particularly; they had tattoos on their chins and wore shark-tooth necklaces. They straightened the old man's blankets and fixed the pillow behind his head. He had a sunken, withered face and he didn't look so much sick, as tired. His eyes were only half-open as everyone fussed around. It looked as if it were a great effort to keep them that much open. His hair was mostly grey, and his dry flesh sagged in thin folds about his ancient neck. I reckoned that he must have been near enough to a hundred years old. The young men talked quickly among themselves as they saw my father approaching. One came forward, apparently as spokesman. He looked about the oldest of them, perhaps thirty. He had a fat, shiny face.

'Here,' said my father. 'What's all this about?' I knew his opinion of Maoris: they were lazy, drank too much, and caused trouble. They just rode on the backs of the men on the land, like the loafers in the cities. He always said we were lucky there were so few in our district. 'What do you people think you're doing here?' he demanded.

'We rang up yesterday,' the spokesman said. 'We told your missus we might be coming today.'

'I don't know about that. She said someone else was coming. The people who were here before.'

'Well,' said the young man, smiling. 'We were the people before.'

'I don't get you. You trying to tell me you owned this place?'

'That's right. We owned all the land round this end of the river. Our tribe.'

'That must have been a hell of a long time ago.'

'Yes,' agreed the stranger. 'A long time.' He was pleasantly spoken and patient. His round face, which I could imagine looking jolly, was very solemn just then.

I looked around and saw my mother and Jim coming slowly down from the house.

'I still don't get it,' my father said. 'What do you want?'

'We just want to go across your land, if that's all right. Look, we better introduce ourselves. My name's Tom Taikaka. And this is——'

My father was lost in a confusion of introductions. But he still didn't shake anyone's hand. He just stood his ground, aloof and faintly hostile. Finally there was the old man. He looked as though he had gone to sleep again.

'You see he's old,' Tom explained. 'And has not so long to live. He is the last great man of our tribe, the oldest. He wishes to see again where he was born. The land over which his father was chief. He wishes to see this before his spirit departs for Rerengawairua.'

By this time my mother and Jim had joined us. They were as confused as we were.

'You mean you've come just to——' my father began.

'We've come a long way,' Tom said. 'Nearly a hundred miles, from up the coast. That's where we live now.'

'All this way. Just so——'

'Yes,' Tom said. 'That's right.'

'Well,' said my father. 'What do you know? What do you know about that?' Baffled, he looked at me, at my mother, and even finally at Jim. None of us had anything to say.

'I hope we're not troubling you,' Tom said politely. 'We don't want to be any trouble. We just want to go across your land, if that's all right. We got our own tucker and everything.'

We saw this was true. The two old women had large flax kits of food.

'No liquor?' my father said suspiciously. 'I don't want any drinking round my place.'

'No,' Tom replied. His face was still patient. 'No liquor. We don't plan on any drinking.'

The other young men shyly agreed in the background. It was not, they seemed to say, an occasion for drinking.

'Well,' said my father stiffly, 'I suppose it's all right. Where are you going to take him?' He nodded towards the old sleeping man.

'Just across your land. And up to the old *pa*.'

'I didn't know there used to be any *pa* round here.'

'Well,' said Tom. 'It used to be up there.' He pointed out the largest hill behind our farm, one that stood well apart and above the others. We called it Craggy Hill, because of limestone outcrops. Its flanks and summit were patchy with tall scrub. We seldom went near it, except perhaps when out shooting; then we circled its steep slopes rather than climbed it. 'You'd see the terraces,' Tom said, 'if it wasn't for the scrub. It's all hidden now.'

Now my father looked strangely at Tom. 'Hey,' he said, 'you sure you aren't having me on? How come you know that hill straight off? You ever been here before?'

'No,' Tom said. His face shone as he sweated with the effort of trying to explain everything. 'I never been here before. I never been in this part of the country before.'

'Then how do you know that's the hill, eh?'

'Because,' Tom said simply, 'the old men told me. They described it so well I could find the place blindfold. All the stories of our tribe are connected with that hill. That's where we lived, up there, for hundreds of years.'

'Well, I'll be damned. What do you know about that?' My father blinked, and looked up at the hill again. 'Just up there, eh? And for hundreds of years.'

'That's right.'

'And I never knew. Well, I'll be damned.'

'There's lots of stories about that hill,' Tom said. 'And a lot of battles fought round here. Over your place.'

'Right over my land?'

'That's right. Up and down here, along the river.'

My father was so astonished he forgot to be aloof. He was trying to fit everything into his mind at once—the hill where they'd lived hundreds of years, the battles fought across his land—and it was too much.

'The war canoes would come up here,' Tom went on. 'I reckon they'd drag them up somewhere here'—he indicated the grassy bank on which we were standing—'in the night, and go on up to attack the *pa* before sunrise. That's if we hadn't sprung a trap for them down here. There'd be a lot of blood soaked into this soil.' He kicked at the earth beneath our feet. 'We had to fight a long while to keep this land here, a lot of battles. Until there was a day when it was no use fighting any more. That was when we left.'

We knew, without him having to say it, what he meant. He meant the day when the European took the land. So we all stood quietly for a moment. Then my mother spoke.

'You'd better come up to the house,' she said. 'I'll make you all a cup of tea.'

A cup of tea was her solution to most problems.

We went up to the house slowly. The young men followed behind, carrying the litter. They put the old man in the shade of a tree, outside the house. Since it seemed the best thing to do, we all sat around him; there wouldn't have been room for everyone in our small kitchen anyway. We waited for my mother to bring out the tea.

The the old man woke. He seemed to shiver, his eyes opened wide, and he said something in Maori. 'He wonders where he is.' Tom explained. He turned back to the old man and spoke in Maori.

He gestured, he pointed. Then the old man knew. We all saw it the moment the old man knew. It was as if we were all willing him towards that moment of knowledge. He quivered and tried to lift himself weakly; the old women rushed forward to help him. His eyes had a faint glitter as he looked up to the place we called Craggy Hill. He did not see us, the house, or anything else. Some more Maori words escaped him in a long, sighing rush. '*Te Wahiokoahoki*,' he said.

'It is the name,' Tom said, repeating it. 'The name of the place.'

The old man lay back against the women, but his eyes were still bright and trembling. They seemed to have a life independent of his wrinkled flesh. Then the lids came down, and they were gone again. We could all relax.

'*Te Wahiokoahoki*,' Tom said. 'It means the place of happy return. It got the name when we returned there after our victories against other tribes.'

My father nodded. 'Well, I'll be damned,' he said. 'That place there. And I never knew.' He appeared quite affable now.

My mother brought out tea. The hot cups passed from hand to hand, steaming and sweet.

'But not so happy now, eh?' Tom said. 'Not for us.'

'No. I don't suppose so.'

Tom nodded towards the old man. 'I reckon he was just about the last child born up there. Before we had to leave. Soon there'll be nobody left who lived there. That's why they wanted young men to come back. So we'd remember too.'

Jim went into the house and soon returned. I saw he carried the greenstone adzes he'd found. He approached Tom shyly.

'I think these are really yours,' he said, the words an effort.

Tom turned the adzes over in his hand. Jim had polished them until they were a vivid green. 'Where'd you get these, eh?' he asked.

Jim explained how and where he'd found them. 'I think they're really yours,' he repeated.

There was a brief silence. Jim stood with his eyes downcast, his treasure surrendered. My father watched anxiously; he plainly thought Jim a fool.

'You see,' Jim added apologetically, 'I didn't think they really belonged to anyone. That's why I kept them.'

'Well,' Tom said, embarrassed. 'That's real nice of you. Real nice of you, son. But you better keep them, eh? They're yours now. You find, you keep. We got no claims here any more. This is your father's land now.'

Then it was my father who seemed embarrassed. 'Leave me out of this,' he said sharply. 'You two settle it between you. It's none of my business.'

'I think you better keep them all the same,' Tom said to Jim.

Jim was glad to keep the greenstone, yet a little hurt by rejection of his gift. He received the adzes back silently.

'I tell you what,' Tom went on cheerfully, 'you ever find another one, you send it to me, eh? Like a present. But you keep those two.'

'All right,' Jim answered, clutching the adzes. He seemed much happier. 'I promise if I find any more, I'll send them to you.'

'Fair enough,' Tom smiled, his face jolly. Yet I could see that he too really wanted the greenstone.

After a while they got up to leave. They made the old man comfortable again and lifted him. 'We'll see you again tomorrow,' Tom said. 'The launch will be back to pick us up.'

'Tomorrow?' my father said. It hadn't occurred to him that they might be staying overnight on his land.

'We'll make ourselves a bit of a camp up there tonight,' Tom said, pointing to Craggy Hill. 'We ought to be comfortable up there. Like home, eh?' The jest fell mildly from his lips.

'Well, I suppose that's all right.' My father didn't know quite what to say. 'Nothing you want?'

'No,' Tom said. 'We got all we want, thanks. We'll be all right. We got ourselves. That's the important thing, eh?'

We watched them move away, the women followed by the young men with the litter. Tom went last, Jim trotting along beside him. They seemed, since the business of the greenstone, to have made friends quickly. Tom appeared to be telling Jim a story.

I thought for a moment that my father might call Jim back. But he didn't. He let him go.

The old women now, I noticed, carried green foliage. They beat it about them as they walked across our paddocks and up towards Craggy Hill; they were chanting or singing, and their wailing sound came back to us. Their figures grew smaller with distance. Soon they were clear of the paddocks and beginning to climb.

My father thumbed back his hat and rubbed a handkerchief across his brow. 'Well, I'll be damned,' he said.

We sat together on the porch that evening, as we often did in summer after milking and our meal. Yet that evening was very different from any other. The sun had set, and in the dusk we saw faint smoke rising from their campfire on Craggy Hill, the place of happy return. Sometimes I thought I heard the wailing sound of the women again, but I couldn't quite be sure.

What were they doing up there, what did they hope to find? We both wondered and puzzled, yet didn't speak to each other.

Jim had returned long before, with stories. It seemed he had learned, one way and another, just about all there was to be learned about the tribe that had once lived on Craggy Hill. At the dinner table he told the stories breathlessly. My father affected to be not much interested; and so, my father's son, did I. Yet we listened, all the same.

'Then there was the first musket,' Jim said. 'The first musket in this part of the country. Someone bought it from a trader down south and carried it back to the *pa*. Another tribe, one of their old enemies, came seeking *uta—uta* means revenge—for something that had been done to them the year before. And when they started climbing up the hill they were knocked off one by one, with the musket. They'd never seen anything like it before. So the chief of the tribe on Craggy Hill made a sign of peace and called up his enemies. It wasn't a fair fight, he said, only one tribe with a musket. So he'd let his enemies have the musket for a while. They would have turns with the musket, each tribe. He taught the other tribe how to fire and point the musket. Then they separated and started the battle again. And the next man to be killed by the musket was the chief's eldest son. That was the old man's uncle—the old man who was here today.'

'Well, I don't know,' said my father. 'Sounds bloody queer to me. That's no way to fight a battle.'

'That's the way they fought,' Jim maintained.

So we left Jim, still telling stories to my mother, and went out on the porch.

The evening thickened. Soon the smoke of the campfire was lost. The hills grew dark against the pale sky. And at last my father, looking up at the largest hill of all, spoke softly . . .

'I suppose a man's a fool,' he said. 'I should never have let that land go. Shouldn't ever have let it go back to scrub. I could of run a few sheep up there. But I just let it go. Perhaps I'll burn it off one day, run a few sheep. Sheep might pay better too, the way things are now.'

But it wasn't, somehow, quite what I expected him to say. I suppose he was just trying to make sense of things in his own fashion.

3

They came down off Craggy Hill the next day. The launch had been waiting for them in the river some time.

When we saw the cluster of tiny figures, moving at a fair pace down the hills, we sensed there was something wrong. Then, as they drew nearer, approaching us across the paddocks, we saw what was wrong. There was no litter, no old man. They all walked freely, separately. They were no longer burdened.

Astonished, my father strode up to Tom. 'Where is he?' he demanded.

'We left him back up there,' Tom said. He smiled sadly and I had a queer feeling that I knew exactly what he would say.

'Left him up there?'

'He died last night, or this morning. When we went to wake him he was cold. So we left him up there. That's where he wanted to be.'

'You can't do that,' my father protested. 'You can't just leave a dead man like that. Leave him anywhere. And, besides, it's my land you're leaving him on.'

'Yes,' Tom said. 'Your land.'

'Don't you understand? You can't just leave dead people around. Not like that.'

'But we didn't just leave him around. We didn't just leave him anywhere. We made him all safe and comfortable. He's all right. You needn't worry.'

'Christ, man,' my father said. 'Don't you see?'

But he might have been asking a blind man to see. Tom just smiled patiently and said not to worry. Also he said they'd better be catching the launch. They had a long way to go home, a tiring journey ahead.

And as he walked off, my father still arguing beside him, the old women clashed their dry greenery, wailing, and their shark-tooth necklaces danced under their heaving throats.

In a little while the launch went noisily off down the river. My father stood on the bank, still yelling after them. When he returned to the house, his voice was hoarse.

He had a police party out, a health officer too. They scoured the hills, and most of the caves they could find. They discovered no trace of a burial, nor did they find anything in the caves. At one stage someone foolishly suggested we might have imagined it all. So my father produced the launchman and people from the township as witness to the fact that an old Maori, dying, had actually been brought to our farm.

That convinced them. But it didn't take them anywhere near finding the body. They traced the remnants of the tribe, living up the coast, and found that indeed an old man of the tribe was missing. No one denied that there had been a visit to our farm. But they maintained that they knew nothing about a body. The old man, they said, had just wandered off into the bush; they hadn't found him again.

He might, they added, even still be alive. Just to be on the safe side, in case there was any truth in their story, the police put the old man on the missing persons register, for all the good that might have done.

But we knew. We knew every night we looked up at the hills that he was there, somewhere.

So he was still alive, in a way. Certainly it was a long time before he let us alone.

And by then my father had lost all taste for the farm. It seemed the land itself had heaped some final indignity upon him, made a fool of him. He never talked again, anyway, about running sheep on the hills.

When butter prices rose and land values improved, a year or two afterwards, he had no hesitation in selling out. We shifted into another part of the country entirely, for a year or two, and then into another. Finally we found ourselves milking a small herd for town supply, not far from the city. We're still on that farm, though there's talk of the place being purchased soon for a city sub-division. We think we might sell, but we'll face the issue when it arises.

Now and then Jim comes to see us, smart in a city suit, a lecturer at the university. My father always found it difficult to talk to Jim, and very often now he goes off to bed and leaves us to it. One thing I must say about Jim: he has no objection to helping with the milking. He insists that he enjoys it; perhaps he does. It's all flat-land round our present farm, with one farm much like another, green grass and square farmhouses and pine shelter belts, and it's not exactly the place to sit out on a summer evening and watch shadows gathering on the hills. Because there aren't hills within sight; or shadows either, for that matter. It's all very tame and quiet, apart from cars speeding on the highway.

I get on reasonably well with Jim. We read much the same books, have much the same opinions on a great many subjects. The city hadn't made a great deal of difference to him. We're both married, with young families. We also have something else in common: we were both in the war, fighting in the desert. One evening after milking, when we stood smoking and yarning in the cool, I remembered something and decided I might put a question to Jim.

'You know,' I began, 'they say it's best, when you're under fire in the war, to fix your mind on something remote. So you won't be afraid. I remember Dad telling me that. I used to try. But it never seemed any good. I couldn't think of anything. I was still as scared as hell.'

'I was too. Who wasn't?'

'But, I mean, did you ever think of anything?'

'Funny thing,' he said. 'Now I come to think of it, I did. I thought of the old place—you know, the old place by the river. Where,' he added, and his face puckered into a grin, 'where they buried that old Maori. And where I found those greenstones. I've still got them at home, you know, up on the mantelpiece. I seem to remember trying to give them away once, to those Maoris. Now I'm glad I didn't. It's my only souvenir from there, the only thing that makes that place still live for me.' He paused. 'Well, anyway, that's what I thought about. That old place of ours.'

I had a sharp pain. I felt the dismay of a long-distance runner who, coasting confidently to victory, imagining himself well ahead of the field, finds himself overtaken and the tape snapped at the very moment he leans forward to breast it. For one black moment it seemed I had been robbed of something which was rightfully mine.

I don't think I'll ever forgive him.

MAY C. JENKINS
I Can Play 'Schools'

I WAS writing to my mother, one sunny afternoon in the school holidays, while my daughter Marian sat on the grass, just outside the french window. She was playing 'Schools' with her dolls. Annoyed because they were 'not attending', she was scolding them, making expressive gestures with her hands, as her teacher might have done; it was interesting to watch her.

What would I write about Marian? It was never easy to find something new to say, and I did not want to use the same phrases as last week and—probably—the week before. Mother was in Canada, eager for news of home; she would scan the lines for news of Marian, for whom she had an anxious love.

Studying the child now, as if for inspiration, I thought for the thousandth time how lovely she was, with dark curls framing her small pointed face, dark serious eyes—too serious, perhaps, for a seven-year-old—and full, sensitive lips. Deep, loving pride in her stirred in me. She was such a dear, intelligent girl. But I felt disappointment too, for I had dreamed of a different child. I had seen a golden girl, golden voiced, moving with confidence through the world.

'Anne, you're being very stupid,' my husband had said, when, in the months before she was born, I drew this picture for him. 'You don't even know that you'll have a girl—and, supposing you do, you can't order one to a pattern like that. You're just heading for trouble.'

He was right, of course; the baby was a girl, but not as I had imagined her. I still thought wistfully, sometimes, of the child that might have been, and never would be, now. For my husband had been killed in a car crash, shortly before Marian was born. I did not have him now, to share my days, to comfort me.

Sometimes my friends spoke of re-marriage. But I had loved Tom very much, so much that our days together, alight with love, were still too close to me. Then there was Marian. Step-parents—in fiction and fact—were apt to cause disharmony, that might have deep, far-reaching consequences. She had to come first.

This afternoon her game did not satisfy her. Without being told, I knew what was wrong; she wanted Christabel. This was her favourite doll, left that morning in the attic. The game was tasteless without her, Marian decided, and rose, shaking the grass off her blue cotton dress.

Turning, she saw the amusement in my eyes; her own lit up with rare and lovely laughter. 'I know it's silly,' they seemed to say, 'but I can't help it, I must have her.' She went off; the garden seemed cold with her absence, the dolls forgotten. She is my love, my lamb, my darling, after all, I thought; we understand each other, words are unnecessary; how many parents can say that? and, my spirits lighter, I bent again over the desk.

'As you know, Marian is at home just now. It is wonderful to have her. I wish the holidays were longer——'

A shadow passed in front of the french window, dulling the sunny garden. For a moment, foolishly, I expected to see Marian. But it was a long way up to the attic; besides once there, she would probably become interested in something else. I looked up. It was the little girl from next door. She was tossing an orange into the air and catching it again. 'You'd think this was *her* garden!' I said inwardly. 'No shyness there!'

Her family had come only two short weeks before, but already it seemed a long time to me. I had not yet 'called on' the mother—in our small town it is still considered friendly to visit new neighbours—but I could not count the number of times that her daughter had appeared in the garden saying,

'Please may I play with your little girl today?'

She was perhaps a year or two older than Marian. Slim and fair-skinned, her hair was like ripe corn in sunlight, her eyes a sparkling, vivid blue. As if this were not enough, she had a voice as clear and careless as a mountain stream. I suppressed that ever-recurring envious ache.

'I've come again,' she announced.

'Is that so?' I was amused, in spite of annoyance.

(When would I get back to my letter? Mother would be looking for it, would worry if it did not come. That was the worst of agreeing to send mail at a certain time.)

'I saw your little girl in the garden. I can play "Schools" too, I love it.'

'How often have I told you——'

'But she plays all by herself, all the time. She'll be lonely.'

'Marian likes to play by herself.' It was true, I reflected sadly. She shrank from children in the neighbourhood, thinking she could not play their games properly; feared their laughter, thinking it was at her expense; did not understand their jolly, slangy conversations.

'Still, she must be lonely,' the other child said shrewdly. She was, but knew no way to avoid it; all the avenues which she had tried had led her further away, if anything, from that carefree, shouting world. 'I am too. I haven't got brothers or sisters. And I don't know anyone here yet.'

Well, you won't be long before you do, I thought grimly, wishing that Marian had one quarter of the self-confidence which this child scattered so blithely to the four winds. In the face of her stubborn persistence I almost gave way. But what was the use? It had been tried so often before. The result was always the same. Marian would come home as soon as she could, her drooping shoulders expressing a despair that went to my heart.

With me, she was quite different. We played together contentedly, or went for walks. It was always a pleasure to go for a walk with Marian. She loved to see small, delightful things; a new bud, a wild rose, or thistledown floating like magic through the air, would bring a dreamy softness to her eyes, a lightness to her feet. Released, enchanted, she would run over springy grass, among kindly trees; it was her unassailable world. What was that poem, left by an unknown writer in an air-raid shelter, during the war? 'Beauty has ramparts nothing can destroy.' Marian had already discovered that.

I pulled myself together. 'It's no use, dear.' All the irritation had left me; I felt only gentleness. 'It's very good of you to say you'll play with Marian. It's good of all the children to come. But the thing is—you just don't know what it means. You get tired of her and then she thinks you don't like her—she doesn't understand. For a child like her you need so much patience.'

Evidently at a loss, she stared at me. 'Why? What's wrong with her?'

'Didn't you know?' Of course, she had been next door for a very short time. But I had assumed that she knew, that someone would have told her. I had thought, as we are apt to do, that my private tragedy was large and important to others, too.

'No. What is it?'

'She is deaf and dumb.'

After a minute she said, 'Does she speak on her fingers?'

'A bit . . . and in other ways as well . . . she goes away to a school.' Suddenly I was immensely tired. 'So you see why you can't play with her, child.'

'Don't call me Child, my name's Freda,' she said impudently. Then she moved from the window. 'Give this to Marian, I brought it for her.' She handed me the orange and was gone, walking with a lazy grace down the path, her yellow pigtails swinging.

I thought, it never does to open your heart to a child. Try it and she slaps your face. 'Give her the orange,' Freda had said, salving her conscience; she did not want to play with Marian, now. Well, what had I expected? I had tried to discourage her, hadn't I?'

Turning, I saw Marian. How long had she been there? How much had she understood? Her eyes were following Freda—for a moment, surprised, I thought she was sorry to see the gate open and close. But I decided I had been mistaken. She never wanted to play with other children.

Then, speaking rapidly 'on her fingers' as Freda had put it, Marian said,

'Mother, would you rather have her than me?'

Deeply shocked, I put my arms round her. She had sensed my desire for a child without her handicap . . . she had been bitterly hurt. . . . Did that account, partly, for her great unhappiness, her sense of inadequacy, in the world of other children? Oh, my darling, my best-loved—and this time I did not add, after all. It came to me at last how much my love meant to her—so much more than it would have meant to Freda, who was so well-equipped to look after herself. I pressed my lips on the shining dark hair, and finally and forever my foolish longings died.

When I released her, she looked at me intently for a minute. Then, seemingly satisfied, she ran outside with Christabel. I finished my letter—cheerfully, in spite of the chaos of my thoughts—and went upstairs, to prepare for the afternoon shopping.

When I came down, half-an-hour later, Freda was in the garden with Marian. She had brought her own dolls over; the 'class' seemed larger and brighter, and had a comfortable air. Marian, the Headmistress, sat in her 'office'; Freda, as Assistant Teacher, pretended to consult her, and made notes in a little book. She looked up, carelessly, when she saw me.

'I said I could play "Schools",' she remarked.

JOHN UPDIKE
Should Wizard Hit Mommy?

In the evenings and for Saturday naps like today's, Jack told his daughter Jo a story out of his head. This custom, begun when she was two, was itself now nearly two years old, and his head felt empty. Each new story was a slight variation of a basic tale: a small creature, usually named Roger (Roger Fish, Roger Squirrel, Roger Chipmunk), had some problem and went with it to the wise old owl. The owl told him to go to the wizard, and the wizard performed a magic spell that solved the problem, demanding in payment a number of pennies greater than the number Roger Creature had but in the same breath directing the animal to a place where the extra pennies could be found. Then Roger was so happy he played many games with other creatures, and went home to his mother just in time to hear the train whistle that brought his daddy home from Boston. Jack described their supper, and the story was over. Working his way through this scheme was especially fatiguing on Saturday, because Jo never fell asleep in naps any more, and knowing this made the rite seem futile.

The little girl (not so little any more; the bumps her feet made under the covers were halfway down the bed, their big double bed that they let her be in for naps and when she was sick) had at last arranged herself, and from the way her fat face deep in the pillow shone in the sunlight sifting through the drawn shades, it did not seem fantastic that something magic would occur, and she would take her nap like an infant of two. Her brother, Bobby, was two, and already asleep with his bottle. Jack asked, 'Who shall the story be about today?'

'Roger . . .' Joe squeezed her eyes shut and smiled to be thinking she was thinking. Her eyes opened, her mother's blue. 'Skunk,' she said firmly.

A new animal; they must talk about skunks at nursery school. Having a fresh hero momentarily stirred Jack to creative enthusiasm. 'All right,' he said. 'Once upon a time, in the deep dark woods, there was a tiny little creature name of Roger Skunk. And he smelled very bad——'

'Yes,' Jo said.

'He smelled so bad none of the other little woodland creatures would play with him.' Jo looked at him solemnly; she hadn't foreseen this. 'Whenever he would go out to play,' Jack continued with zest, remembering certain humiliations of his own childhood, 'all of the other tiny animals would cry, "Uh-oh, here comes Roger Stinky Skunk," and they would run away, and Roger Skunk would stand there all alone, and two little round tears would fall from his eyes.' The corners of Jo's mouth drooped down and her lower lip bent forward as he traced with a forefinger along the side of her nose the course of one of Roger Skunk's tears.

'Won't he see the owl?' she asked in a high and faintly roughened voice.

Sitting on the bed beside her, Jack felt the covers tug as her legs switched tensely. He was pleased with this moment—he was telling her something true, something she must know—and had no wish to hurry on. But downstairs a chair scraped, and he realized he must get down to help Clare paint the living-room woodwork.

'Well, he walked along very sadly and came to a very big tree, and in the tiptop of the tree was an enormous wise old owl.'

'Good.'

'"Mr. Owl," Roger Skunk said, "all the other little animals run away from me because I smell so bad." "So you do," the owl said. "Very, very bad." "What can I do?" Roger Skunk said, and he cried very hard.'

'The wizard, the wizard,' Jo shouted, and sat right up, and a Little Golden Book spilled from the bed.

'Now, Jo. Daddy's telling the story. Do you want to tell Daddy the story?'

'No. You me.'

'Then lie down and be sleepy.'

Her head relapsed onto the pillow and she said, 'Out of your head.'

'Well. The owl thought and thought. At last he said, "Why don't you go see the wizard?"'

'Daddy?'

'What?'

'Are magic spells *real*?' This was a new phase, just this last month, a reality phase. When he told her spiders eat bugs, she turned to her mother and asked, 'Do they *really*?' and when Clare told her

God was in the sky and all around them, she turned to her father and insisted, with a sly yet eager smile, 'Is He *really*?'

'They're real in stories,' Jack answered curtly. She had made him miss a beat in the narrative. 'The owl said, "Go through the dark woods, under the apple trees, into the swamp, over the crick——" '

'What's a crick?'

'A little river. "Over the crick, and there will be the wizard's house." And that's the way Roger Skunk went, and pretty soon he came to a little white house, and he rapped on the door.' Jack rapped on the window sill, and under the covers Jo's tall figure clenched in an infantile thrill. 'And then a tiny little old man came out, with a long white beard and a pointed blue hat, and said, "Eh? Whatzis? Whatcher want? You smell awful." ' The wizard's voice was one of Jack's own favorite effects; he did it by scrunching up his face and somehow whining through his eyes, which felt for the interval rheumy. He felt being an old man suited him.

' "I know it," Roger Skunk said, "and all the little animals run away from me. The enormous wise owl said you could help me." '

' "Eh? Well, maybe. Come on in. Don't git too close." Now, inside, Jo, there were all these magic things, all jumbled together in a big dusty heap, because the wizard did not have any cleaning lady.'

'Why?'

'Why? Because he was a wizard, and a very old man.'

'Will he die?'

'No. Wizards don't die. Well, he rummaged around and found an old stick called a magic wand and asked Roger Skunk what he wanted to smell like. Roger thought and thought and said, "Roses." '

'Yes. Good,' Jo said smugly.

Jack fixed her with a trancelike gaze and chanted in the wizard's elderly irritable voice:

> ' "Abracadabry, hocus-poo,
> Roger Skunk, how do you do,
> Roses, boses, pull an ear,
> Roger Skunk, you never fear:
> *Bingo!*" '

He paused as a rapt expression widened out from his daughter's nostrils, forcing her eyebrows up and her lower lip down in a wide noiseless grin, an expression in which Jack was startled to recognise his wife feigning pleasure at cocktail parties. 'And all of a sudden,' he whispered, 'the whole inside of the wizard's house was full of the smell of—*roses!* "Roses!" Roger Fish cried. And the wizard said, very cranky, "That'll be seven pennies."'

'Daddy.'

'What?'

'Roger *Skunk*. You said Roger Fish.'

'Yes. Skunk.'

'You said Roger *Fish*. Wasn't that silly?'

'Very silly of your stupid old daddy. Where was I? Well, you know about the pennies.'

'Say it.'

'O.K. Roger Skunk said, "But all I have is four pennies," and he began to cry.' Jo made the crying face again, but this time without a trace of sincerity. This annoyed Jack. Downstairs some more furniture rumbled. Clare shouldn't move heavy things; she was six months pregnant. It would be their third.

'So the wizard said, "Oh, very well. Go to the end of the lane and turn around three times and look down the magic well and there you will find three pennies. Hurry up." So Roger Skunk went to the end of the lane and turned around three times and there in the magic well were *three pennies!* So he took them back to the wizard and was very happy and ran out into the woods and all the other little animals gathered around him because he smelled so good. And they played tag, baseball, football, basketball, lacrosse, hockey, soccer, and pick-up-sticks.'

'What's pick-up-sticks?'

'It's a game you play with sticks.'

'Like the wizard's magic wand?'

'Kind of. And they played games and laughed all afternoon and then it began to get dark and they all ran home to their mommies.'

Jo was starting to fuss with her hands and look out of the window, at the crack of day that showed under the shade. She thought the story was all over. Jack didn't like women when they took anything for granted; he liked them apprehensive, hanging on his words. 'Now, Jo, are you listening?'

'Yes.'

'Because this is very interesting. Roger Skunk's mommy said, "What's that awful smell?"'

'Wha-at?'

'And Roger Skunk said, "It's me, Mommy. I smell like roses."
And she said, "Who made you smell like that?" And he said, "The
wizard," and she said, "Well, of all the nerve. You come with me
and we're going right back to that very awful wizard."'

Jo sat up, her hands dabbling in the air with genuine fright. 'But
Daddy, then he said about the other little animals run *away*!' Her
hands skittered off, into the underbrush.

'All right. He said, "But Mommy, all the other little animals run
away," and she said, "I don't care. You smelled the way a little
skunk should have and I'm going to take you right back to that
wizard," and she took an umbrella and went back with Roger
Skunk and hit that wizard right over the head.'

'No,' Jo said, and put her hand out to touch his lips, yet even in
her agitation did not quite dare to stop the source of truth.
Inspiration came to her. 'Then the wizard hit *her* on the head and
did not change that little skunk back.'

'No,' he said. 'The wizard said "O.K." and Roger Skunk did not
smell of roses any more. He smelled very bad again.'

'But the other little amum—*oh!*—amum——'

'Joanne. It's Daddy's story. Shall Daddy not tell you any more
stories?' Her broad face looked at him through sifted light,
astounded. 'This is what happened, then. Roger Skunk and his
mommy went home and they heard *Woo-oo, woooo-oo* and it was the
choo-choo train bringing Daddy Skunk home from Boston. And
they had lima beans, pork chops, celery, liver, mashed potatoes,
and Pie-Oh-My for dessert. And when Roger Skunk was in bed
Mommy Skunk came up and hugged him and said he smelled like
her little baby skunk again and she loved him very much. And
that's the end of the story.'

'But Daddy.'

'What?'

'Then did the other little ani-mals run away?'

'No, because eventually they got used to the way he was and did
not mind it at all.'

'What's evenshiladee?'

'In a little while.'

'That was a stupid mommy.'

'It was *not*,' he said with rare emphasis, and believed, from her
expression, that she realized he was defending his own mother to

her, or something as odd. 'Now I want you to put your big heavy head in the pillow and have a good long nap.' He adjusted the shade so not even a crack of day showed, and tiptoed to the door, in the pretense that she was already asleep. But when he turned, she was crouching on top of the covers and staring at him. 'Hey. Get under the covers and fall faaast asleep. Bobby's asleep.'

She stood up and bounced gingerly on the springs. 'Daddy.'

'What?'

'Tomorrow, I want you to tell me the story that that wizard took that magic wand and hit that mommy'—her plump arms chopped fiercely—'right over the head.'

'No. That's not the story. The point is that the little skunk loved his mommy more than he loved aaalll the other little animals and she knew what was right.'

'No. Tomorrow you say he hit that mommy. Do it.' She kicked her legs up and sat down on the bed with a great heave and complaint of springs as she had done hundreds of times before, except that this time she did not laugh. 'Say it, Daddy.'

'Well, we'll see. Now at least have a rest. Stay on the bed. You're a good girl.'

He closed the door and went downstairs. Clare had spread the newspapers and opened the paint can and, wearing an old shirt of his on top of her maternity smock, was stroking the chair rail with a dipped brush. Above him footsteps vibrated and he called, '*Joanne.* Shall I come up there and spank you?' The footsteps hesitated.

'That was a long story,' Clare said.

'The poor kid,' he answered, and with utter weariness watched his wife labor. The woodwork, a cage of moldings and rails and baseboards all around them, was half old tan and half new ivory and he felt caught in an ugly middle position, and though he as well felt his wife's presence in the cage with him, he did not want to speak with her, work with her, touch her, anything.

FRANK SARGESON
A Hen and Some Eggs

I THINK that one time when my mother set a hen on some eggs was about the most anxious time I've ever experienced in my life.

The hen was a big black Orpington, and mother set her inside a coop in the warmest corner of our yard. My brother and I went out one night and held a candle, and mother put the hen in the coop and gave her thirteen eggs to hatch out. And the next morning we ran out and looked inside the coop, and it was wonderful to see the hen looking bigger than ever as she sat on the thirteen eggs.

But besides being wonderful to see the hen sitting on the eggs, it was a worry to see that she had one egg showing. And it was the same way each time we looked. It wouldn't have been so bad if we could have been sure that it was the same egg each time, because mother had put the thirteenth egg in just to see if thirteen was an unlucky number, and if it hadn't hatched out it wouldn't have mattered much. But we couldn't be sure, and we'd go to school thinking that if our hen was silly enough to let each one of the thirteen eggs get cold in turn, then we wouldn't have any of the eggs hatch out at all.

Then an even worse worry was trying to get the hen to eat. We'd put her food just by the hole in the coop but she'd take no notice. And after we'd got tired of waiting to see her come out and eat and had gone away and left her, sometimes the food would disappear, but as often as not it wouldn't. And when it did disappear we could never be sure that it wasn't the sparrows that had taken it. So each time we looked inside the coop we thought our hen was getting thinner and thinner, and if there happened to be two eggs showing instead of one we were sure that it was so, and we said that after all our trouble there probably wouldn't be one egg that'd hatch out after all. And we thought that our hen might be even silly enough to let herself starve to death.

Then one Saturday morning when it was nearly time for the eggs to hatch out, something terrible happened. My brother and I were chopping kindling wood in the yard and suddenly my brother said,

Look! And there was the hen walking up and down inside the wire-netting part of the coop, something which we had never seen her doing before.

We thought she must be hungry, so as fast as we could we took her some wheat. But the hen didn't seem to be hungry, and instead of eating the wheat she started cackling, and if we stayed near her she'd run up and down inside the wire-netting instead of just walking. Well, we went and told mother, and mother told us to leave the hen alone and she'd go back to the eggs. So we stood in the yard and watched, and the hen went on walking up and down, so we went and told mother again. And mother looked at the clock and said, Give her five minutes from now and see what happens.

Well, the hen went on walking up and down, and we could hardly bear it. It was awful to think of the thirteen eggs getting colder and colder. Anyhow mother made us wait another five minutes, then she came out and we tried to shoo the hen back into the coop. But it was no good, the hen went on like a mad thing, and mother said we'd just have to leave her alone and trust to luck. We all went inside to look at the clock and we reckoned that the hen must have been off the nest for at least twenty minutes, and we said that the eggs couldn't help being stone cold by that time.

Then when we came outside again we saw the most astonishing thing happen. The hen suddenly left off cackling and walking up and down. She stood there without moving just as if she was trying to remember something, then she ran for the hole in the coop and disappeared inside.

Well, it was ourselves who went on like mad things then. But after a few minutes we started talking in whispers, and we chopped our kindling wood round the front of the house so as not to disturb the hen, and we'd keep coming back into the yard to creep towards the coop and look in from a distance, and it was more wonderful than ever to see the hen sitting there, even though she had the one egg showing as usual.

And a few days later twelve of the eggs hatched out, but the thirteenth egg was no good. To this day I've wondered whether it was the same one that was always showing, and whether that was the one that was no good. My brother said that the hen knew it was no good and didn't bother to keep it warm. He may have been right. Children are rather like hens. They know things that men and women don't know but when they grow up they forget them.

ELIZABETH TAYLOR
A Dedicated Man

In the dark, raftered dining-room, Silcox counted the coned napkins and, walking among the tables, lifted the lids of the mustard pots and shook salt level in the cellars.

At the beginning of their partnership as waiter and waitress, Edith had liked to make mitres or fleurs-de-lis or water-lilies of the napkins, and Silcox, who thought this great vulgarity, waited until after he had made his proposal and been accepted before he put a stop to it. She had listened meekly. 'Edwardian vulgarity,' he had told her. Taking a roll of bread from the centre of the petalled linen, he whipped the napkin straight, then turned it deftly into a dunce's cap.

Edith always came down a little after Silcox. He left the bedroom in plenty of time for her to change into her black dress and white apron. His proposal had not included marriage or any other intimacy and, although they lay every night side by side in twin beds, they were always decorous in their behaviour, fanatically prim, and he had never so much as seen her take a brush to her hair, as he himself might have said. However, there was no one to say it to, and to the world they were Mr. and Mrs. Silcox, a plain, respectable couple. Both were ambitious, both had been bent on leaving the hotel where they first met—a glorified boarding-house, Silcox called it. Both, being snobbish, were galled at having to wait on noisy, sunburnt people who wore freakish and indecent holiday clothes and could not pronounce *crêpes de volaille*, let alone understand what it meant.

By the time Silcox heard of the vacancy at the Royal George, he had become desperate beyond measure, irritated at every turn by the vulgarities of seaside life. The Royal George was mercifully as inland as anywhere in England can be. The thought of the Home Counties soothed him. He visualized the landscape embowered in flowering trees.

In his interview with the manageress he had been favourably impressed by the tone of the hotel. The Thames flowed by beyond the geranium-bordered lawns; there would be star occasions all summer—the Fourth of June, Henley, Ascot. The dining-room, though it was small, had velvet-cushioned banquettes and wine-lists in padded leather covers. The ashtrays advertised nothing and the flowers had not come out of the garden.

'My wife,' he said repeatedly during the interview. He had been unable to bring her, from consideration to their employer. The manageress respected him for this and for very much else. She could imagine him in tails, and he seemed to wear the grey suit as if it were a regrettable informality he had been unable to escape. He was stately, eyes like a statue's, mouth like a carp's. His deference would have that touch of condescension which would make customers angle for his good will. Those to whom he finally unbent, with a remark about the weather or the compliments of the season, would return again and again, bringing friends to whom they could display their status. 'Maurice always looks after me,' they would say.

Returning to the pandemonium—the tripperish hotel, the glaring sky—he made his proposal to Edith. 'Married couple', the advertisement had stipulated and was a necessary condition, he now understood, for only one bedroom was available. 'It has twin bedsteads, I ascertained,' he said.

Marriage, he explained, could not be considered, as he was married already. Where the person in question (as he spoke of his wife) was at present, he said he did not know. She had been put behind him.

Until that day, he had never spoken to Edith of his personal affairs, although they had worked together for a year. She was reserved herself and embarrassed by this unexpected lapse, though by the proposal itself she felt deeply honoured. It set the seal of his approval of her work.

'I think I am right in saying that it is what matters most to both of us,' he observed, and she nodded. She spoke very little and never smiled.

The manageress of the Royal George, when Edith went for her separate interview, wondered if she were not too grim. At forty-five, her hair was a streaked grey and clipped short like a man's at the back. She had no make-up and there were deep lines about her mouth which had come from the expression of disapproval she so often wore. On the other hand, she was obviously dependable and efficient, would never slop soup or wear dirty cuffs or take crafty nips of gin in the still room whenever there was a lull. Her predecessor had done these things and been flighty, too.

So Edith and Silcox were engaged. Sternly and without embarrassment they planned arrangements for bedroom privacy. These were simply a matter of one staying in the bathroom while the other dressed or undressed in the bedroom. Edith was first to get into bed and would then turn out the light. Silcox was meanwhile sitting on a laundry basket in his dressing-gown, glancing at his watch until it was time to return. He would get into bed in the dark. He never wished her goodnight and hardly admitted to himself that she was there.

Now a week had gone by and the arrangements had worked so smoothly that he was a little surprised this evening that on the stroke of seven o'clock she did not appear. Having checked his tables, he studied the list of bookings and was pleased to note the name of one of his *bêtes-noires*. This would put a spur to his pride and lift the evening out of the ordinary ruck. Pleasant people were not the same challenge.

Upstairs, Edith was having to hurry, something she rarely deigned to do. She was even a little excited as she darted about the room, looking for clean cuffs and apron, fresh dress preservers, and some pewter-coloured stockings, and she kept pausing to glance at a photograph on the chest of drawers. It was postcard size and in a worn leather frame and was of an adolescent boy wearing a school blazer.

When she had gone back to the bedroom after breakfast she saw the photograph for the first time. Silcox had placed it there without a word. She ignored it for a while and then became nervous that one of the maids might question her about it, and it was this reason she gave Silcox for having asked him who it was.

'Our son,' he said.

He deemed it expedient, he added, that he should be a family man. The fact would increase their air of dependability and give them background and reality and solid worth. The boy was at a public school, he went on, and did not divulge to his friends the nature of his parents' profession. Silcox, Edith realized with respect, was so snobbish that he looked down upon himself.

'How old is he?' she asked in an abrupt tone.

'He is seventeen and working for the Advanced Level.'

Edith did not know what this was and wondered how she could manage to support the fantasy.

'We shall say nothing ourselves,' said Silcox, 'as we are not in the habit of discussing our private affairs. But he is there if wanted.'

'What shall we . . . what is his name?'

'Julian,' Silcox said and his voice sounded rich and musical.

Edith looked with some wonder at the face in the photograph. It was a very ordinary face and she could imagine the maids conjecturing at length as to whom he took after.

'Who is he really?' she asked.

'A young relative,' said Silcox.

In Edith's new life there were one or two difficulties—one was trying to remember not to fidget with the wedding ring as if she were not used to wearing it, and another was being obliged to call Silcox 'Maurice'. This she thought unseemly, like all familiarities, and to be constant in it required continual vigilance. He, being her superior, had called her Edith from the start.

Sleeping beside him at night worried her less. The routine of privacy was established and sleep itself was negative and came immediately to both of them after long hours of being on their feet. They might have felt more sense of intimacy sitting beside one another in deckchairs in broad daylight, for then there would be the pitfalls of conversation. (How far to encroach? How much interest to show that could be shown without appearing inquisitive?)

Edith was one of those women who seem to know from childhood that the attraction of men is no part of their equipment, and from then on to have supported nature in what it had done for them, by exaggerating the gruffness and the gracelessness and becoming after a time sexless. She strode heavily in shoes a size too large, her off-duty coat and skirt were as sensible as some old Nannie's walking-out attire. She was not much interested in people, although she did her duty towards them and wrote each week to her married sister in Australia: and was generous to her at Christmas. Her letters, clearly written as they were, were still practically unreadable—so full of facts and times: where she took the bus to on her day off and the whole route described, where this road forked and that branched off and what p.m. she entered this or that café to progress from the grapefruit to the trifle of the table d'hôte (five and sixpence). Very poor service usually, she wrote—odd knives and forks left on the table while she drank her coffee, for no one took any pride nowadays.

Edith had no relations other than her sister; her world was peopled with hotel staff and customers. With the staff she was distant and sometimes grim if they were careless in their work, and with her customers she was distant and respectful. She hardly responded to them, although there were a very few—usually gay young men or courtly and jovial elderly ones—to whom she behaved protectively, as Nannie-ish as she looked when she wore her outdoor clothes.

The other person in her life—Silcox—was simply to her the Establishment. She had never worked with anyone she respected more—in her mind, he was always a waiter and she always thought of him dressed as a waiter. On his day off, he seemed lowered by wearing the clothes of an ordinary man. Having to turn her eyes away from him when she glimpsed him in a dressing-gown was really no worse. They were not man and woman in one another's eyes, and hardly even human beings.

No difficulties they were beset with in their early days at the Royal George could spoil the pleasures of their work. The serenity of the dining-room, the elaborate food which made demands upon them (to turn something over in flaming brandy in a chafing-dish crowned Silcox's evening), the superiority of the clientele and the glacial table linen. They had suffered horrors from common people and this escape to elegance was precious to them both. The hazards that threatened were not connected with their work, over which both had mastery from the beginning, but with their private lives. It was agonizing to Edith to realize that now they were expected to spend their free time together. On the first day off they took a bus to another hotel along the river and there had luncheon. Silcox modelled his behaviour on that of his own most difficult customers, and seemed to be retaliating by doing so. He was very lordly and full of knowledge and criticism. Edith, who was used to shopping ladies' luncheons in cafés, became nervous and alarmed. When she next wrote to her sister, she left this expedition altogether out of the letter and described instead some of the menus she had served at the Royal George, with prices. Nowadays, there was, for the first time in her life, an enormous amount that had to be left out of the letters.

She was dreading their next free day and was relieved when

Silcox suggested that they should make a habit of taking the train to London together and there separating. If they came back on the same train in the evening, no suspicions would be roused.

In London, she enjoyed wandering round the department stores, looking without surprise or envy at all the frivolous extravagancies. She made notes of prices, thinking that her sister would be interested to compare them with those in Melbourne, and she could spend a whole day over choosing a pair of gloves, going from shop to shop, studying the quality. One day, she intended to visit the Zoo.

Silcox said that he liked to look in the jewellers' windows. In the afternoons, he went to a News Cinema. Going home in the train, he read a newspaper and she looked at the backs of houses and little gardens, and later, fields or woods, staring as if hypnotized.

One morning, when she had returned to their bedroom after breakfast, he surprised her by following her there. This was the time of day when he took a turn about the garden or strolled along by the river.

When he had shut the door, he said quietly, 'I'm afraid I must ask you something. I think it would be better if you were less tidy in here. It struck me this morning that by putting everything away out of sight, you will give rise to suspicion.'

Once, he had been a floor waiter in an hotel and knew, from taking breakfast in to so many married people, what their bedrooms usually looked like. His experience with his own wife he did not refer to.

'I overheard Carrie saying what a tidy pair we were and she had never met anyone like it, not a pin in sight when she came into this room, she said.'

'I respect your intentions,' he said grandly, 'but the last thing to serve our purpose is to appear in any way out of the ordinary. If you could have one or two things lying about—your hairbrush, perhaps—well, I leave it to you—just a pot of something or other on the dressing-table. A wife would never hide everything away in the drawers. Carrie's right, as it is there isn't even a pin to be seen. Nothing to show it's anyone's room at all, except for the photograph.'

Edith blushed and pressed her lips tightly together. She turned away and made no reply. Although she knew that it had been difficult for him to make the suggestion, and sensible and necessary as she saw it to be, she was angry with him. She wondered why his words had so humiliated her, and could find no reason. He had reproved her before about her work—the water-lily napkins, for instance—but he had never angered her.

She waited for him to leave her and then she removed from the drawer a large, harsh-bristled brush, a boxful of studs and safety pins and a pot of Vaseline which she used in cold weather when her lips were chapped. In the early evening, when she came up to change, she found Silcox's brushes beside hers, a shoe-horn dangled from the side of the mirror and his dressing-gown had been taken from his clothes' cupboard and was hanging at the back of the door.

She felt very strange about it all and when she went downstairs she tried to direct all her thoughts towards her work.

'He couldn't be anyone else's,' said Carrie Hurt, the maid, looking at the photograph. She had the impertinence to take it up and go over to the window with it, to see it better.

'He is thought to take more after his father's side,' Edith said, tempted to allow the conversation to continue, then wondering why this should be.

'I expect it's his father's side that says it,' Carrie replied. 'Oh, I can see you. The way his hair grows on his forehead. His father's got quite a widow's peak.'

Edith found herself looking over Carrie's shoulder, as if she had never seen the photograph before.

'As a matter of fact, he is a little like my sister's eldest boy,' she conceded. 'His cousin,' she added, feeling wonder at the words.

'Well, you must be proud of him. Such an open face.' Carrie said, replacing the photograph in its right position and passing a duster over the glass.

'Yes,' said Edith. 'He's a good boy.'

She left Carrie and went downstairs and walked in the garden until it was time to go on duty. She went up and down the gravel paths and along by the river, but she could not overcome the excitement which lately disturbed her so, the sensation of shameful pleasure.

By the river's edge, she came upon Silcox, who had taken up fishing in his spare time—a useful excuse for avoiding Edith's company. He stood on the bank, watching the line where it entered the water, and hardly turned his head as Edith approached him.

'Where does he—where does Julian go to in the holidays?' she asked.

'He goes to relatives,' Silcox answered.

She knew that she was interrupting him and that she must move on. As she did, he heard her murmuring anxiously, 'I do so hope they're kind.'

He turned his head quickly and looked after her, but she had gone mooning back across the lawn. The expression of astonishment stayed on his face for a long time after that, and when she took up her position in the dining-room before lunch, he looked at her with concern, but she was her usual forbidding and efficient self again.

'Don't we ever go to see him?' she asked a few days later. 'Won't they think us strange not going?'

'What we do in our free time is no concern of theirs,' he said.

'I only thought they'd think it strange.'

He isn't real, none of it's true, she now constantly reminded herself, for sometimes her feelings of guilt about that abandoned boy grew too acute.

Sometimes, on Sunday outings from school, boys were brought by their parents to have lunch at the hotel, and Edith found herself fussing over them, giving them huge helpings, discussing their appetites with their parents.

'They're all the same at that age,' she would say. 'I know.'

It was so unlike her to chat with the customers and quite against Silcox's code. When he commented disdainfully upon her unusual behaviour, she seemed scarcely to listen to his words. The next Sunday, serving a double portion of ice cream to a boy, she looked across at his mother and smiled. 'I've got a son myself, madam,' she said. 'I know.'

Silcox, having overheard this, was too enraged to settle down to his fishing that afternoon. He looked for Edith and found her in the bedroom writing a letter to her sister.

'It was a mistake—this about the boy,' he said, taking up the photograph and glaring at it. 'You have not the right touch in such matters. You carry the deception to excess. You go too far.'

'Too far?' she said brightly, but busy writing.

'Our position is established. I think the little flourishes I thought up had their result.'

'But they were all *your* little flourishes,' she said, looking up at him. 'You didn't let *me* think of any, did you?'

He stared back at her and soon her eyes flickered, and she returned to her writing.

'There won't be any more,' he said. 'From me, or from you. Or any more discussion of our affairs, do you understand? Carrie in here every morning gossiping, you chatting to customers, telling them such a pack of lies—as if it were all true, and as if they could possibly be interested. You know as well as I do how unprofessional it is. I should never have credited it of you. Even when we were at that dreadful place at Paignton, you conducted yourself with more dignity.'

'I don't see the harm,' she said mildly.

'And I don't see the necessity. It's courting danger for one thing—to get so involved. We'll keep our affairs to ourselves or else we'll find trouble ahead.'

'What time does the post go?'

Without reading her letter through, she pushed it into an envelope. Goodness knows what she has written, he thought. A mercy her sister was far away in Australia.

The photograph—the subject of their contention—he pushed aside, as if he would have liked to be rid of it.

'You don't seem to be paying much attention,' he said. 'I only warn you that you'd better. Unless you hope to make laughing stocks of both of us.'

Before she addressed the envelope, she looked gravely at him for a moment, thinking that perhaps the worst thing that could happen to him, the thing he had always dreaded most, was to be laughed at, to lose his dignity. I used to be the same, she thought, taking up her pen.

'Yes, I made a mistake,' he said. 'I admit it freely. But we shall stand by it, since it's made. We can hardly kill the boy off, now we've got him.'

She jerked round and looked at him, her face even paler than usual, then seemed to gather her wits again and bent her head. Writing rather slowly and unsteadily, she finished addressing the envelope.

'I hope I shan't have further cause for complaint,' he said— rather as if he were her employer, as in fact he always felt himself to be. The last word duly spoken, he left her, but was frowning as he went downstairs. She was behaving oddly, something was not quite right about her and he was apprehensive.

Edith was smiling while she tidied herself before slipping out to the pillar box. 'That's the first tiff we've ever had,' she thought. 'In all our married life.'

'I find *her* all right,' Carrie Hurt said to the still-room maid. 'Not stand-offish, really, when you get to know her.'

'It's him I can't abide.'

'I'm sorry for her. The way he treats her.'

'And can't you tell he's got a temper? You get that feeling, don't you, that for two pins he'd boil over?'

'Yes,' I'm sorry for her. When he's not there, she likes to talk. And dotes on that boy of theirs.'

'Funny life it must be, not hardly ever seeing him.'

'She's going to soon, so she was telling me, when it's his birthday. She was showing me the sweater she was knitting for him. She's a lovely knitter.'

Silcox found Edith sitting in a secluded place at the back of the hotel where the staff were allowed to take the air. It was a cobbled courtyard, full of empty beer-crates and strings of tea-towels hung to dry. Pigeons walked up and down the outhouse roofs and the kitchen cat sat at Edith's feet watching them. Edith was knitting a white, cable-stitch sweater and she had a towel across her lap to keep the wool clean.

'I have just overheard that Carrie Hurt and the still-room girl discussing you,' Silcox said, when he had looked round to make sure that there was no one to overhear him. 'What is this nonsense about going to see the boy, or did my ears deceive me?'

'They think we're unnatural. I felt so ashamed about it that I said I'd be going on his birthday.'

'And when is *that*, pray?'

'Next month, the eighteenth. I'll have the sweater done by then.'

She picked up the knitting pattern, studied it frowning.

'Oh, it is, is it? You've got it all cut and dried. But his birthday happens to be in March.'

'You can't choose everything,' she said. She was going on with her knitting and smiling.

'I forbid you to say any more about the boy.'

'You can't, you see. People ask me how he's getting on.'

'I wish I hadn't started the damn fool business.'

'I don't. I'm so glad you did.'

'You'll land us in gaol, do you realize that? And what is this you're knitting?' He knew, from the conversation he had overheard.

'A sweater for him, for Julian.'

'Do you know what?' he said, leaning towards her and almost spitting the words at her, one after the other, 'I think you're going out of your mind. You'll have to go away from here. Maybe we'd both better go, and it will be the parting of the ways.'

'I don't see any cause for that,' said Edith. 'I've never been so happy.'

But her happiness was nearly at an end: even before she could finish knitting the sweater, the spell had been broken.

A letter came from her sister, Hilda, in Melbourne. She wrote much less frequently than Edith, and usually only when she had something to boast about—this time it was one of the boys having won a tennis tournament.

'She has always patronized me,' Edith thought. 'I have never harped on in that way about Julian. I don't see why I should have hidden his light under a bushel all these years.'

She sat down at once and wrote a long letter about his different successes. Whatever Hilda's sons may have done, Julian seemed to find it easy to do better. 'We are sending him for a holiday on the Continent as a reward for passing his exams,' she finished up. She was tired of silence and modesty. Those qualities had never brought her any joy, none of the wonderful exhilaration and sense of richness she had now. Her attitude towards life had been too drab and undemanding; she could plainly see this.

She took her letter to the village and posted it. She imagined her sister looking piqued—not puzzled—when she read it.

Silcox was in the bedroom when she returned. A drawer slid quickly shut and he was suddenly busy winding his watch. 'Well, I suppose it's time to put my hand to the wheel,' he said in a voice less cold than it had been of late, as he went out.

Edith was suspicious of this voice, which was too genial, she thought, and she looked round to see if anything of hers had been tampered with. She was especially anxious about her knitting, which was so precious to her; but it was still neatly rolled up and hanging in a clean laundry-bag in her cupboard.

She opened the drawer which Silcox had so smartly closed and found a letter lying on top of a pile of black woollen socks. A photograph was half out of the envelope. Though he had thrust it out of sight when she came into the room, she realized that he had been perfectly easy in his mind about leaving it where it was, for it would be contrary to his opinion of her that she would pry or probe. 'He knows nothing about me,' she thought, taking the photograph to the window so that she could see it better.

She was alarmed at the way her heart began to leap and hammer, and she pressed her hand to her breast and whispered, 'Hush' to its loud beating. 'Hush, hush,' she implored it, and sat down on her bed to wait for the giddiness to pass.

When she was steadier, she looked again at the two faces in the photograph. There was no doubt that one of them was Julian's, though older than she had imagined and more defined than in the other photograph—the one that stood always on the chest of drawers.

It was so much like the face of the middle-aged woman whom his arm encircled affectionately, who wore the smug, pleased smile of a mother whose son has been teasing her. She glowed with delight, her lips ready to shape fond remonstrances. She looked a pretty, silly woman and wore a flowered, full-skirted dress, too girlish for her, too tight across the bust. They were standing by the wooden fence of a little garden. Behind them, hollyhocks grew untidily and a line of washing, having flapped in the wind as the camera clicked, hung there, blurred, above their heads. Julian had stared at the photographer, grinning foolishly, almost pulling a face. 'It's all put on,' thought Edith. 'All for effect.'

When her legs stopped trembling, she went again to the drawer and fetched the letter. She could only read a little of it at a time, because the feeling of faintness and nausea came upon her in waves and she would wait, with closed eyes, till each receded. After seeing 'Dear Father' she was as still as a stone, until she could brace herself for more, for the rest of the immaturely-written, facetious letter. It contained abrupt and ungracious thanks for a watch he had received for what he referred to as his twenty-first. He seemed, Edith thought, to have expected more. A good time had been had by all, with Mum pushing the boat out to the best of her ability.

They were still living in Streatham and he was working in a car showroom, where, he implied, he spent his time envying his customers. Things weren't too easy, although Mum was wonderful, of course. When he could afford to take her out, which he only wished he were able to do more often, she enjoyed herself as if she were a young girl. It was nice of his father to have thought of him, he ended reproachfully.

Carrie Hurt pushed the bedroom door open at the same time as she rapped on it with her knuckles. 'I was to say would you come down at once, Edith. There's some people in the dining-room already.'

'I shan't be coming down,' Edith said.

'Don't you feel well?'

'Tell him I shan't be coming down.'

Edith turned her head away and remained like that until Carrie had gone. Quietly, she sat and waited for Silcox to arrive. He would do so, she knew, as soon as he could find the manageress or a maid to take his place for a moment. It would offend his pride to allow such a crisis, but he would be too seriously alarmed to prevent it.

Her hatred was now so heavy that it numbed her and she was able to sit, quite calm and patient, waiting for him, rehearsing no speeches, made quite incapable by the suddenness of the calamity and the impossibility of accepting the truth of it.

It was not so very long before she heard his hurrying footsteps. He entered the room as she had thought he would, brimming with pompous indignation. She watched this fade and another sort of anger take its place when he saw the letter in her hand, the photograph on the bed.

'No, your eyes don't deceive you,' she said.

At first, he could think of nothing better to say than 'How dare you!' He said this twice, but as it was clearly inadequate, he stepped forward and grasped her wrists, gripping them tightly, shook her back and forth until her teeth were chattering. Not for years, not since the days of his brief marriage, had he so treated a woman and he had forgotten the overwhelming sensations to be derived from doing so. He released her, but only to hit her across her face with the back of one hand then the other.

Shaken, but unfrightened, she stared at him. 'It was true all the time,' she said. 'He was really yours and you disowned him. Yet you made up that story just to have a reason for putting out the photograph and looking at it every day.'

'Why should I want to do that? He means nothing to me.' He hoped to disconcert her by a quick transition to indifference.

'And his mother—*I* was supposed to be his mother.'

He laughed theatrically at the absurdity of this idea. It was a bad performance. When he had finished being doubled-up, he wiped his eyes and said: 'Excuse me.' The words were breathed on a sigh of exquisite enjoyment.

Coming to the door for the second time, Carrie Hurt waited after knocking. She had been surprised to hear Silcox laughing so loudly as she came along the passage. She had never heard him laugh in any way before and wondered if he had gone suddenly mad. He opened the door to her, looking grave and dignified.

'Yes, I am coming now,' he said.

'They're very busy. I was told to say if you could please . . .'

'I repeat, I am coming now. Edith is unwell and we must manage for today as best we may without her. She will stay here and rest,' he added, turning and saying this directly to Edith and stressing his even tone by a steady look. He would have locked the door upon her if Carrie had not been standing by.

Edith was then alone and began to cry. She chafed her wrists that were still reddened from his grasp, and moved her head from side to side, as if trying to evade the thoughts that crowded on her.

Carrie Hurt returned presently with a glass of brandy. 'It can't do any harm,' she said. 'He told me to leave you alone, but there might be something she wants, I thought.'

She put the glass on the table beside the bed and then went over to draw the curtains. Edith sat still, with her hands clasped in her lap, and waited for her to go.

'My mother has these funny spells,' Carrie told her. Then, noticing the letter lying on the bed, she asked, 'Oh, you haven't had any bad news, have you?'

'Yes,' Edith said.

She leaned forward to take the glass, sipped from it and shuddered.

'Not your *boy*?' Carrie whispered.

Edith sighed. It seemed more than a sigh—a frightening sound, seeming to gather all the breath from her body, shuddering, expelling it.

'He isn't ill, is he?' Carrie asked, expecting worse—though Silcox, to be sure, had seemed controlled enough. And what had his dreadful laughter meant?

Edith was silent for a moment and took a little more brandy. Then she said, in a forced and rather high-pitched voice: 'He is much worse than ill. He is disgraced.'

'Oh, my God!' said Carrie eagerly.

Edith's eyes rested for a second on the photograph lying beside her on the bed and then she covered it with her hand. 'For theft,' she said, her voice strengthening, 'thieving,' she added.

'Oh dear, I'm ever so sorry,' Carrie said softly. 'I can't believe it. I always said what an open face he'd got. Don't you remember—I always said that? Who could credit it? No one could. Not that I should breathe a word about it to a single soul.'

'Mention it to whoever you like,' Edith said. 'The whole world will know, and may decide where they can lay the blame.'

She drained the glass, her eyes closed. Then, 'There's bad blood there,' she said.

When Silcox had finished his duties, he returned, but the door was locked from inside, and there was no answer when he spoke, saying her name several times in a low voice, his head bent close to the keyhole.

He went away and walked by the river in his waiter's clothes, stared at by all who passed him. When he returned to the hotel, he was stared at there, too. The kitchen porter seemed to be re-assessing him, looked at him curiously and spoke insolently. The still-room maid pressed back against the passage wall as he went by. Others seemed to avoid him.

The bedroom door was still shut, but no longer locked. He stood looking at the empty room, the hairbrush had gone from the dressing-table and only a few coat-hangers swung from the rail in the clothes' cupboard. He picked up the brandy glass and was standing there sniffing it when Carrie Hurt, who had enjoyed her afternoon, appeared in the doorway.

'I don't know if you know, she's packed and gone,' she said, 'and had the taxi take her to the train. I thought the brandy would pull her together,' she went on, looking at the glass in Silcox's hand. 'I expect the shock unhinged her and she felt she had to go. Of course, she'd want to see him, whatever happened. It must have been her first thought. I should like to say how sorry I am. You wouldn't wish such a thing on your worst enemy.'

He looked at her in bewilderment and then, seeing her glance, as it swerved from his in embarrassment, suddenly checked by something out of his sight, he walked slowly round the bed and saw there what she was staring at—the wastepaper basket heaped high with her white knitting, all cut into little shreds; even the needles had been broken in two.

Before the new couple arrived, Silcox prepared to leave. Since Edith's departure, he had spoken to no one but his customers, to whom he was as stately as ever—almost devotional he seemed in his duties, bowed over chafing-dish or bottle—almost as if his calling were sacred and he felt himself worthy of it.

On the last morning, he emptied his bedroom cupboard and then the drawers, packing with his usual care. In the bottom drawer, beneath layers of shirts, and rolled up in a damask napkin, he was horrified to discover a dozen silver-plated soup-spoons from the dining-room.

GORDON MEYER
The Circle

THE four of them were sitting on the terrace after dinner, and Brynhild (Mrs. Elizalde's father had been a devotional Wagner-goer) had just said: 'This weather: it's not right; it ought to be cold now.' It was May, winter.

A straight line produced through the Elizaldes' terrace, their golf-green lawns undulating punctiliously through the pines, to cross the coastal drive, the duned shore, the Plata's indistinguishable rendez-vous with the ocean, would first touch land 3,500 miles south, on the polar continent. The Elizaldes, retired, part-wintering on the fashionable peninsula, enjoyed it all at room temperature, from behind plate-glass; noiselessly except for the rustle of a page.

The couple sat at points distant from each other on the circle of six white wrought-iron cushioned garden chairs described to Bryn-hild's specifications; two other positions were occupied by their guests: Mr. Broadhurst, 'the chargé' as Brynhild called him; and, diametrically opposite her, beautiful Zulema Camargo, daughter of the Commander of the Armed Forces.

Brynhild's friend, Mirabel Watts, just returned to the republic from her yearly three months at home (England), had not arrived. Leonard Elizalde had gone off to his room again; he was supposed to be getting engaged to Zulema during her stay with his parents. If so, his mother thought, he was certainly leaving it to the last night.

Brynhild in any Latin American gathering, which this was not, was outstanding. She wore blue, as now, to quote the colour of her eyes. Even though her hair, too, was turning that colour, the men's gaze would focus on her to the damage of the younger women's morale. But she had, they told each other, geography on her side, being, on their continent, exotic; and forgave her with difficulty.

Zulema saw her beauty as not earthy; picturesque, safely non-voluptuous, suggesting Botticelli, except it was colder. Beauty that could be loved, she thought, only visibly. She asked herself how (knowing the men of her continent) Doctor Elizalde had let this turn into marriage.

As for herself, Zulema Camargo sat there in a striking silk yellow and black dress, in a cold fury: it was books again.

Was there anything duller than a well-informed Englishwoman? Especially when corroded by anxiety to be right. The señora de Elizalde had to make the official pronunciamento on such catechisms as the distances between various points on the earth, historical dates, what people said, and, above all, names of books and authors. She moved in fact in a realm of books.

She also excelled at crosswords and other intellectual games; and as she received regularly the best London Sunday newspapers, visitors to 'Windward' were soon shown up by those donnish little proofs of one's ignorance.

The house was so atmospheric with academic competition, Zulema suspected character to be judged according to general knowledge; and in a fortnight had learned the folly of confident utterance such as everybody in her world made.

But it wasn't only knowledge, general or particular: everything had to be right. If not, no place for it in Mrs. Elizalde's world. No right to be there, in fact. Even the weather, as she had just demonstrated.

Of course, it followed that Brynhild must herself always be right; otherwise there might be no place for her in her own world. Impossible situation.

'Creative writing,' Brynhild was saying, '*can* be taught,' and all Zulema Camargo's muscles stiffened. 'You remember that man Dominguez, Richard, who worked at your Ministry back in 1950?'

Ricardo Elizalde, Richard to his English wife except in formal matrimonial acrimony, folded his large hands; the gesture a carefully placed stress on his composure. 'Dominguez came to the Ministry of Foreign Affairs in 1952.'

'No. In 1950.'

The Doctor, in a tone now of total mildness, said:

'I remember: it was in 1952.' And Brynhild reached her flashpoint of rightness.

'Absolute nonsense! It was in 1950, the year you had the new wing added to the Ministry.'

Softly, slowly the Doctor replied: 'But my dear, I had to authorize his pension . . .'

It was almost the identical tone, and was amputated.

'We-ell my dear, all I can sa-ay (immensely long-drawn out) is that someone at your Ministry was having a little fun and games at the government's expense!'

Mrs. Elizalde looked round either side of her cigarette slanted in its black holder, and it seemed to Zulema that nothing could now follow this except the scraping of chairs.

'Roma locuta est, causa finita est!' said a voice a little too quickly, and there was the chargé looking up into the air. He had his watertight compartments: business, jolly, didactic, contrived tomfoolery; the last two had interflooded. His real credentials at Mrs. Elizalde's social occasions were preciseness and a psychasthenia for quotations.

Mrs. Elizalde, eyelids fluttering, also looked nowhere in particular, as though in silent unison with the chargé. The case was indeed finished: the Doctor did not appeal.

But that categoricalness, really it lay less in what Brynhild said, which was often just silly, than in that slow scything English drawl. Maybe she was right just now, maybe not—what did it matter?— but she wasn't always: last night at dinner she (Zulema) hadn't finished saying Sicily was the largest island in the . . . when the scythe had cut in: Oh but su-rely . . .!

'Well this Dominguez fellow decided to learn to write . . .'

When the mosquito door to the terrace squeaked, a girl in grey uniform called her mistress to the telephone, Zulema felt it was a hot day on which she had just entered an air-conditioned room.

Easy conversation broke out. Laughter escaped, although subdued. Possibly it would increase. The chargé began.

Beira, Port Said, Katmandu were the settings of the first three anecdotes. Cyprus, Jordania and Indonesia did not delay in adding themselves. And the Duke used to ring him up from the port: Broadhurst, I'm coming up for one of those curries. Hot as hell I want it!

An example of what stealth could achieve in a few minutes.

Nevertheless, the Doctor settled back more comfortably, lit a cigar, remarking on the efficacy of his country's cigars (he knew they were not good) against mosquitoes. It drew down Indonesia on him. Straight up in his chair the chargé sat, as though in a ceremonial howdah; his eyes were cold blue, the skin raw-beef Saxon red.

The Doctor didn't know where mosquitoes were worse than on a certain river running through one of his estancias. 'It's like the Jordan, just like the Jordan' came the sharp ruling; and there the Doctor's river ended. In Zulema the little interest remaining vanished altogether the next time the mosquito door squeaked.

Leonard, a boy with a reed-like physique, greeted the chargé, took the empty chair on his mother's right. Zulema watched him pour himself over it. He ended up with his left arm hanging down over the side, as if shot; his right foot, booted in suede, lay over his left knee, and owing to the body's now collapsed position, came to rest on a level with his narrow dark head. His right hand gripped his knee tightly. She understood: he was now positioned for attack or defence, and he reminded her of a crane on the dockside, the jib in the lowered position. He was as complicated as he now looked; he had just been educated in England. She supposed he would acknowledge her in his own fashion. His ears were beautiful enough to bite.

At dinner they had privately aggravated each other—about poetry. She would pick up a book of poems: Ah! Esta me *fascina*! Me en*can*ta! After reading the first verse, she would give it to him: Read that! Before he could finish three lines she would have torn it from him. On to something else.

She knew he was irritated by all this, by her 'lack of reason' as he put it, her thoughtless wordstreams, her questions which were not questions, 'because they are not properly formed, Zulema'. She knew she didn't always know what it was she wanted to know, that in two minutes she might have forgotten what it was she had asked; she knew she threw out her nets of words to catch something on which she might be able to depend. She was looking for some kind of a lead. Other people had got somewhere, she could see that, and she wanted to be there too, and all at once. But she felt instinctively that Leonardo had reached the stage only in words.

Nevertheless, she often felt with him a sense of inferiority. There were times when she didn't know what to say, and walked as if on stepping-stones. She didn't want him to feel like he did to her, and to counterbalance it, would, in argument, assume disdain. She didn't feel it, but sketched it in on her face; it was something else she was acquiring from him.

But she would learn. She would learn to joke about him, in

company too. That would break up his secret and tacit assault on
her, such as he was carrying out now.

And she knew that already she had touched his secret interior.
How would he be now? That was the current question. She was
always having to guess how he was going to react. But alone, how
different he was. . . .

Another grey-uniformed servant appeared, approached him.
Zulema watched him regard the girl with deliberate and prolonged
criticalness: if he could embarrass her, she couldn't embarrass him.

After a moment, her gaze faltered, she offered tribute in the form
of a feeble smile, as though he had at last done to her what she may
have often hoped he would.

'Usual,' he said, and turned swiftly across Zulema's line of vision
to the chargé d'affaires. 'I was just finishing reading *Pygmalion*
again.'

'Ah! *Pygmalion*,' said the chargé, and nothing more; he looked at
the Doctor, who was regarding his son. No support for *Pygmalion*
there.

'Have you read *Pygmalion*, Zulema?'

Accepting his way of saying hallo, she said, 'Yes, when I was
thirteen.'

'Oh and what possessed you to do so so early?' Leonard said, and
waited, illuminated now.

'Because I just loved it.'

She thought: He wonders how I could say I loved it before
reading it. She saw how she was beginning to think.

'You say that with the sort of enthusiasm you might have for a
meringue!'

Meant as a graceful winning shot. There was also between them
the stress of deeper things unsaid; she was accustomed to them
being uttered at a much earlier stage. She said sharply, 'And why
not?', and there was silence.

Their tension had become public, prevented conversation gathering way. The Doctor meanwhile had withdrawn into himself, to
resume for a few moments more the year-by-year plotting of the
interval widening between himself and his son, the alliance tightening with the mother.

As ambassador, he had lived in London, been well received by its
society, feeling more at home than is usually possible for a charming
foreigner to feel: after all, in England he had met Brynhild. (In

point of fact, at the Anglo-Brazilian Society's Ball at the Park Lane Hotel.) And he had moved among the English long enough to know when an ambiente is more than a hundred per cent English.

So he told himself he was not against the English educational system, only the result of it in his son, who, in spite of their enmity, did not know how to say hallo to him.

The chargé d'affaires had sensed this atmosphere; thoughtfully he devised a remark about the recent political disturbances. He addressed the Doctor and Leonard: riots couldn't interest young and pretty Latin Americans.

But Zulema said at once:

'Those are the sort of men I'd have no trouble in killing.' Sharply the chargé turned. Leonard with a smile disapproved:

'You yourself, Zulema?'

'Yes, of course. Why not?'

'But how,' he patronized, 'would you do it?' He was deliberately almost laughing.

Zulema shrugged her bare shoulders. 'Shoot them!'

The chargé wanted her to have another chance. 'Really shoot them? Come now!'

Shrewd negotiator, with the necessary lack of penetration to the human heart, he was also interested professionally; he had a report to complete.

'Yes' said Zulema.

The Doctor had not taken his eyes off her, not because he was the only one present who understood her.

Leonard remained smiling. The chargé for the moment said nothing; he was imagining it. Then:

'But tell me where?' he brightened. 'Or in the heart, or in the head? Tell me where you'd shoot them dead?'

Zulema didn't know why even with this he was pleased; she regarded him as one would a point of aim:

'In the head.'

'Make an *awful* mess!' Leonard was looking up into a ceibo tree.

'I wouldn't have to clean it.' She dismissed her questioners.

She'd do it, my god, the chargé noted. Her father, a man totally uninterested in books, had described how he would deal with agitators, slackers and revolutionaries. Of course: out here it was Haves and Have-nots in a big way. Not like those at home, but those who had never counted how much they had against those able to exist without hope. Movement from one to the other rare, or impossible. It reminded him of reading De Tocqueville. And how each side helped its members! The Have families coming to the rescue of each other, as if slight impoverishment were shipwreck. For this girl, the 'others' were animals and so to be treated: curt commands, no answering back, instant obedience, blows if necessary. She wasn't morbid, much less cruel, oh no: warm, gay, vital. . . . True product of her system, though. Yes, it was very interesting.

Zulema had read him correctly.

What could he understand with his statistics? He had no means of knowing that the majority of the people were useful for nothing, but lived by fishing, trapping, idling—as the Indians had done. Only, these had the lotería. They were also the sort that had broken into one of her family's houses, robbed, drank and ate, leaving the whisky bottles filled with their urine, the beds with their excreta. They had a sense of humour. And it was her instinct to shoot them: as one would a dog with rabies.

The mosquito door creaked again. 'To *return* . . . to the matter of creative writing . . .!' A stranger would recognize the loud order for attention. 'Ah Lennie darling, so you decided to come down and grace us with your presence. And Zulema waiting there for you, in that lovely dress. Isn't she a picture?' Brynhild's eyes, now a pair of compasses, retraced her circle. 'Now let's have Leonard's views, shall we? But first, a kiss for your mamá.'

Sitting down opposite her, Brynhild with vigorous thumps of a cigarette on a silver case, re-emphasized her chairmanship. A procedure that had to be learned: when she had lit the cigarette, the conference would resume.

But no, this time it appeared there were private agenda to be cleared up first. The heads of mother and son inclined towards each other in a renewal of ties, a bringing of each other up to date with inventories of parochial doings. Gossip. The door behind which they had retired said in bold letters: Mother and Son in conference. Zulema stared unbelievingly.

The chargé was temporarily cut off. To reach the Doctor, he would have to talk across Mrs. Elizalde, which would not do really. In any case Doctor Elizalde's attention was going another way.

Zulema had turned deliberately to the disposal of husband and father:

'Shall we go and have an ice-cream afterwards?' and Mrs. Elizalde stopped talking.

So sharply had her head turned, it appeared she had been struck in the neck.

Zulema found herself looking at two cold pale blue diamond-hard lozenges; the glacial hatred ran a diameter across the circle for no more than a second, by watch-timing. She returned her gaze to the Doctor; she would go on.

He was shifting a little in his chair. For some moments there was silent incoherence; the six of them composed a perfect model of centrifugence.

Zulema had kept her eyes on the Doctor.

'Well, yes . . . we could . . . I suppose (he consulted his wife) you wouldn't care——?'

She also had her eyes on him. '*Certainly* not! Darling must you really go to those dreadful places?'

The Doctor was now very conscious of Zulema's unwavering gaze. He looked at his wife, however, and no one could have interpreted the faint smile. With a patient equivocal submission he said:

'Well . . . I suppose that if I want an ice-cream, then I *must* go to one of those places!' He put his large head on one side. 'You don't mind, do you?'

Mrs. Elizalde looked away from him at once. She looked at something evidently familiar to her, although no one else had ever seen it. She looked to her left, and down at something as if it were lying in a corner, as it might have been a dog; and spoke to that something.

'Not at all, but if you want an ice-cream *so* badly, we can send out for one.'

First the Doctor hesitated, then rallied.

'Well, I don't know. . . . Personally I do think it would be rather ni-ice to have one, don't you think?'

Zulema caught her breath. He had drawn out the words in a slightly drawling, strained fashion: a miniature replica of his wife's manner. She was sure it wasn't intentional: no one could have ever said the Doctor was capable of gaucherie. Perhaps it was an example of how two people living together a long, long time assimilated something of each other; the way dogs and their masters were said to do.

'Well I really don't know . . .' said Mrs. Elizalde.

Her lips tightened, puckered, she looked again at the thing in the corner.

Then looked round, fastening attention. 'We were talking about creative writing . . . I say it can be taught, and should be.'

It was to be expected that her recovery should be the quickest, after the collapse of the ice-cream project. No one else was ready except perhaps the chargé, and he, Zulema had seen, liked to speak last.

The Doctor was making that sequence of little vocal sounds, prelude to one of the pondered replies he would never discharge.

'But how?' The crease in the lower part of Leonard's handsome face told Zulema he was convicting someone in advance. The either-or was his technique. Whatever the other person said placed them in one of these two categories. In either case his answer lay in ambush, and the original point discarded in favour of the demonstration that the other person had been trapped in the Leonard dichotomy.

He had told her it was logic ('not the way the people here use the word lógico'); and she supposed it all must have something to do with his English university education. Of course, a black and white world would do away with colours.

'But how?' he was saying; and then in his elegant stutter: 'I mean, I mean. . . .'

'Robert Louis Stevenson . . .' said his mother, and the Doctor sank a little deeper into his chair.

Dreadful. Things that *others* had said, expended things from expended situations. Dead unfertile world. From such people she could learn nothing unavailable in a public library. Perfect examples of 'the donkey that swallowed the books' (did that phrase exist in English?). The world in which with Leonardo she would have to live.

In her striking yellow and black dress she sat back in her white iron seat, her jewellery flashed from her ears, neck and wrists, and no one, not even Leonardo, looked at her; they were examining the question of creative writing.

It was not quite true; the Doctor was not examining the question of creative writing.

'Our daughter Holly,' said the loud voice, 'is studying creative writing. I don't mean (she added quickly) that that is her main subject: she's actually at La Seetay Oonivairsitay in Paris.'

This was for the chargé; he said:

'Really!'

'She speaks six languages. Including Russian.'

'Russian!' Now he did sit up.

'And all fluently. As a matter of fact (Brynhild fluttered her eyelids rapidly as though having a brief vision of angels), it got so expensive, that we had to stop the Russian, and then, do you know, the school wrote and told us that she was so good, they would give her the Russian lessons for nothing. Wasn't that wonderful?'

There was a ragged chorus of assent.

'Besides her B.A., she's now taken her Doctorate of Law. She paints. She plays the piano beautifully. And, well, really (her eyelids fluttered again), I don't know what she doesn't do.'

I could tell you Zulema thought.

'At the moment she's in New York on a visit; then she goes to Mexico, Peru, Colombia and Brazil on a scholarship. Everything paid.' Her mouth shut, the eyebrows lifted.

'And after that?' said the chargé, calculating the whisky left in his glass.

'After that, she returns to La Seetay Oonivairsitay. Now I wonder what's happened to Mirabel.' Brynhild's gaze went down the undulating lawns to the coastal boulevard, as though Mirabel might drop out of one of the tall palm trees.

'Is that Mirabel the wife of Robert Pratt, the oil man?' asked the chargé.

'You know her then?'

'I met them in Venezuela; you know how all the English people know each other.'

'Do I not! You know (she collected attention in a raking circular gaze), Mirabel's daughter is only 19, and she is such a beautiful daughter, really such a beautiful girl.' She looked at Zulema for just a moment. 'Mirabel took her to London to meet some nice young English boys, and what does the poor child do but throw herself into the arms of the first Latin American she meets there. She's going to marry an Argentine!'

She paused; everyone, recognizing the curtain-drop, remained silent.

'Of course, Mirabel's simply *distraught*! Can you *imagine* what it is for her! And this poor fellow, to make matters a thousand times worse, is just in England on an engineering scholarship.'

God, God, God, said Zulema under her breath savagely.

At that moment the two dogs began barking furiously; a female figure, deposited by a friend's car, was ascending the brilliantly lit lawns. Her clothes, to Zulema, identified the nationality long before the individual features became distinguishable.

It seemed certain that Brynhild was back in England, sighting a fox break from a distant covert; the warm night thrilled to the long 'Hall-o-o!'

Brynhild patted the vacant chair beside her, Mirabel seated herself with breathless dutifulness in it, the duologue commenced immediately.

The amazing, the infuriating thing was that again no one else thought of assembling their own conversation; they listened, watched, waited to be spoken to.

With her own people, she was used to brilliant, fast, superficial, instinctual and, above all, gay discussion, in which a great deal of laughter was to be heard; and after which nobody would have thought of remembering what had been said.

She looked at Doctor Elizalde, suddenly felt inconsolably sorry for him.

Yesterday, when accident had left the two of them alone at the table of a little eating place at which they had stopped on a drive through the surrounding country, he had said to her: You know, I never knew that something like this could be so enjoyable.

His wife never seemed to understand the need for an art of superficiality—why presumably she would never invite the daughter of an ex-colleague of the Doctor's known for her brilliant aimless talk. With Brynhild conversation had to be aimed. The world was ordered; one could see it in nature. She was one of those positivists who believe that when conversation stops it is because there is nothing to say.

How did Ricardo endure it all? Sitting there night after night, his mouth shut, in a membership of English guests. Didn't he ever feel the urge to resign?

Possibly. He'd given her that book by an English writer who had visited the Far East: 'I think he's a little neurotic, but it's extremely funny; let me have it back when you've finished.' Every page had a comment making the English look ridiculous; and the action of lending the book to her was the Doctor's tacit comment: everything he could not say. Perhaps such little subterfuges helped him last out the unpeopled winters on this pine-strewn peninsular Utopia.

She asked him.

He replied. At first, for Brynhild, it was like a wireless station faintly heard behind the one she wanted.

'Oh,' he said easily, 'but I don't really miss people. I just shut myself up with my books. I have my intellectual communion with myself. I reason with myself, I even . . .' he laughed a little. 'I even contradict myself!'

He thought about this for a moment, seemed to find it intriguing.

'And how do you spend your day, when the two of you are alone?'

'I get up at half-past seven, have a little breakfast in my room, then go back to bed and play patience for an hour. Then I bath and dress, by which time it's about ten-thirty. At ten-thirty I take the two spaniels for a walk, and one of them, Flotsam, always gets lost. So I return to the house, get out the station-waggon, and look for her. By the time I get back, it's lunch-time, and my wife and I meet for the first time. After lunch I take a siesta for an hour or so; then I write letters for about two hours, after which I change and join my wife for a whisky, or two, and at seven we will dine. After dinner, we play patience together, and at eleven we are in bed.' He smiled. 'You must try it sometime!'

Did he know then? She shuddered, not only at the routine, but at the expropriation of him.

The astonishing thing was how Brynhild had brought off the abduction in his own country; operating, as it were, behind the enemy lines. Her children (she always thought of them as Bryn-hild's) turned out to be agents she'd passed through the lines, for indoctrination in her own people's beliefs and subsequent recall to the campaign ground.

The Ricardo softened up by a hundred subtle blows delivered before his departure from England, was the finished product in front of her; so finished, he would never again be one hundred per cent his own nationalilty even with his compatriots. They would always say, 'He's more English than one of us', or 'He's been Englished'. Here, in his own country, he dressed in soft elegant English tweeds, a cape, suede shoes, carried gloves; even said 'My dear'. He would never retreat from this now. He'd been taken over—taken prisoner, one might say? Why not say it? The English had more than the two main methods of conquest.

He sat before her, fixed in the amber of the English situation.

The chargé was again isolated; it was possible he was growing a little sulky about it. It is true Leonard sat next to him, but his fingernails rhythmically clicking on his glass; something that looked like discontent did not invite conversation. There were four frequency bands, two double, two single sets.

'It interested me what you were saying last night about feelings,' said Zulema to the Doctor and Mrs. Elizalde began to suffer from background interference. 'I used to give into mine, but now I keep them inside me, and this upsets me mentally and physically.' She ended quite loudly.

Doctor Elizalde saw a control only half achieved; he recognized a message being relayed through him for his son. Leonard seemed not to have heard.

The Doctor began to explain his own philosophy. 'I have learned another way of dealing with the matter. In the moment I was about to explode——'

'So you did explode!'

Mirabel was looking at Brynhild who seemed to have forgotten what she was saying.

'Oh yes.' The Doctor said it quite gravely. 'And in that moment I would stop and try to find a reason for the other person's——'

'Didn't you order whisky, Zulema?' said a hard voice.

Zulema looked at her gin and tonic. 'Yes, but this is all right.' She returned to the Doctor, having missed something; he was now saying:

'Eventually I was even able to prevent——'

'No, no, no! If you ordered whisky, you must have it. That is (Brynhild tempered it a little), the girl must bring you what you ordered; then you can change it if you wish.'

'... prevent these things occurring.' Maybe he was talking experimentally, she thought.

'You did *order* whisky, didn't you?' said the voice, louder still.

You have a way of omitting my name just when it should be used, Zulema said to her mentally. 'Yes,' she said again, and shrugged in a way that seemed to infuriate the older woman; 'but I don't care, it's not important.'

Brynhild was trembling when she rose and unnecessarily shouted 'Miriam!'

She went to the terrace door, pushed the bell for long seconds; Zulema said:

'When were you able to make this change in you?'

The Doctor made a nervous movement, he unclasped his hands. 'Oh . . . about three, perhaps four years a——' and his wife swung round.

'Ricardo! Didn't you order soda? You did order soda, I distinctly heard you.'

Hearing himself called by the Spanish form, the Doctor sat back apologetically, adjusting the crease in his trousers; then, courageously jerking his head up, said in his stilted, never quite correct and charming English:

'Yes, I did pass that order, but it doesn't matter now!'

He looked away from his wife, to Zulema, smiled; uncertainly she thought.

Brynhild, standing by the door, had succeeded in holding the attention of everyone. There came a scuffling movement from the other side of the door.

'What *is* happening? Why did you bring no soda for the Doctor? And the señorita Camargo ordered whisky, not gin and tonic! One doesn't drink gin and tonic *after* dinner.'

The girl mumbled her way towards escape, Brynhild's inquisition pursuing her all the way to the frontier of all those rooms a guest would never see. Zulema, understanding, found it unbearable.

'But it doesn't matter, Brynhild.'

Brynhild turned to her, in loud triumph cried, 'That is just where you are *wrong*! It *does* matter. All these things matter.'

If you had at this moment, Zulema thought, four men round you and no women, it would certainly not matter.

The chargé was smiling the affair off to himself, curate-fashion. Leonard was prick-earedly studying the ice in his glass as his mother sat down again.

She was quivering. Suddenly Zulema knew what to do; she leaned forward, looked with a fixed sweetness at the woman nearly three times her age.

'You're furious! Aren't you?'

A ritual had been interrupted.

The intruder was laughing; she was laughing in such a way that

the older woman could not believe anything but that the girl was
on her side; which Zulema understood was what one aimed for in
order to get the best out of a child.

Brynhild's face had begun to flush with anger; all at once it
changed as if against her will. It broke up, remained an instant in a
vacuum, then took on new lineaments; Brynhild smiled. Sun after
storm.

'Yes!' She burst out laughing. 'At least I *was!*' she corrected herself.

Everything ran down gently, stopped with the quiet perfection
ending the slow movement of a Beethoven quartet. Pressures came
off; in various mouths the taste of whisky or brandy returned.

Propitious moment, thought someone, for departure. The chargé
got up, saying he thought he really ought to be going; a decree was
issued that the Doctor should drive him to his hotel, Mirabel to her
home. The Doctor, who had his mind on something else, got up
awkwardly. This was because he had got up ambiguously: for the
chargé and Mirabel, as he meant Brynhild to interpret it; for
Zulema, as he wanted Zulema to understand it. For himself, he
didn't know what he would end by doing, until his wife said, 'You
stay and talk to me, Zulema dear,' and he recognized an order.

At this, Leonard put his hands in his jacket pockets, seemed to
fail to find something, and disappeared. Brynhild, still in her chair,
lit another cigarette.

Zulema saw the light go on in Leonard's room. Presently through
the window came the portentous opening of the Linz symphony.
That was another thing: his tastes. Standard, unadventurous.
Dutiful reflection of the programmes she saw advertised in Brynhild's Sunday papers.

'He's a funny boy, Lennie; even as a child he was never
demonstrative. Especially in public.'

Brynhild was disposed to talk. Zulema did not want to talk,
certainly not with Brynhild; she wanted to think.

Who did these English think they were, with their eternal talk of
good manners? Their idea of good manners was that no one should
be late for a meal, not even for a cocktail party; that there should
be just two drinks before dinner, the second being known as 'the
other half'; that one never ate one's bread before the food was
served, nor addressed the servants direct, nor got up from the table

before the hostess, not for any emergency; that there should be no second helpings; that the conversation should be about books; and lastly, that young people should be ignored.

Even that wasn't all: they let their private tensions entwine and trice up their guests, so that one sat there all the time at full stretch.

As for that corrosive anxiety to be always right, she now suspected Brynhild desired it only in terms of other people being wrong. If everybody were to agree with her at the outset, what would she do for self-expression?

The two weeks at 'Windward' had been a school term; and Leonardo was a product of that school. Tomorrow she was going home.

'You really are *very* beautiful, my dear, you know. . . .'

Brynhild was looking straight at her.

Zulema started. It was a trick, a trap even. The last thing Brynhild should have ever said to her. She was going to collect satisfaction for the ice-cream suggestion. She looked at Brynhild cautiously. The older woman remained, cigarette-holder poised, as if above a final judgement. So coldly: as though I were a picture in a gallery.

No, but it wasn't quite like that. In Brynhild's look floated something indefinable. She realized that Brynhild was perfectly sincere—they were alone for one thing. Brynhild, for some reason, was nicer with her when they were alone together. And Leonardo was the same.

But she didn't trust Brynhild after that look over the ice-cream business, which of course had been cuttingly defeated; so she resisted the temptation to let the focus remain on her beauty.

'Will you go to the estancia before it gets too cold?' she asked, and for some moments, did not realize what was happening: Brynhild was relating everything so casually, as if discussing household shopping.

'My dear, I would always go, whenever Richard went. But since four years ago I have never been, and never will again. At that time we had received a letter from a girl friend of Holly's, in London, saying she was coming out, and would love to look us up. I wasn't well at the time, so I put her off. The next thing was a letter from Cartagena; she was apparently on a cruise, headed this way, obviously expecting to see us. She asked me to reply to the ship in Río.

'Well, I didn't.' Brynhild briefly re-examined herself on this. 'We'd had a terrific season here at the Punta, for one thing, and I just wanted to be alone with Richard. But about a week or two later we got a telephone call from Montevideo, and of course I had to tell her to come on. She did—with all her luggage.'

Brynhild leaned forward, carefully tapped ash into a tray; she had to describe the girl. 'She was what you'd call a stunner. That is to say, what we would call her. And of course, the inevitable happened.'

Zulema found herself being regarded a little closer. 'I think you must have noticed Ricardo's a susceptible man.'

Zulema said nothing; she had noticed that Brynhild had called him Ricardo.

'He also began spending money as I had never known him spend it. Every other day he would buy her something; when I remonstrated with him, he got very angry with me and said that for him she was like a daughter. The argument we had about *that* didn't improve matters.

'I knew she had only a thirty-day visa, so after about three weeks, I told her I could help her with the exit formalities. To my astonishment, she told me Ricardo was having her visa extended; which as ex-Foreign Minister he could do without any trouble.

'She then began saying how much she'd like to visit Santa Margarita, our largest estancia. But by now it wasn't only that I was feeling ill, so I put my foot firmly down and said, No, I was sorry but it would have to be another time.

'Two days later she had the impertinence to ask Ricardo at lunch; and in front of me he said, "Yes".'

It was the first time she had heard Brynhild not speaking for effect.

'You must understand that by now I was neither eating nor sleeping properly. I felt an outsider in my own home. When they kissed each other goodnight, I had to look the other way. And to make it a thousand times worse, when the girl wasn't present, Ricardo was always talking about her.

'So when he agreed to take her, something seemed to snap inside me; the fight went out of me.'

'You mean you didn't go?' This part Zulema couldn't understand.

'No. They went alone, and they stayed three weeks, during which I had the doctor sometimes twice a day. By that time, friends were asking me openly when the girl was going, and Mirabel, whom you met tonight, advised me to tell Ricardo when he came back that if the girl wasn't out in a week, I would leave.

'My dear, when they finally came back and I saw their faces, I realized I wasn't prepared to take the risk. . . . They came back as if it were all the most natural thing in the world.' Brynhild's lips drooped. 'I suppose it was. I decided to talk to her alone, and even then I knew it was a gamble. However, it came off; it was a short conversation, if that's what you call it. She went.'

Brynhild drew a breath, as if resenting the memory. Suddenly she cried:

'It lasted five whole months. *In my whole life I have never suffered so much torture.*'

Her pause, after this, created a dead silence heavy with what she could not add.

What had been dredged up subsided again inside her. 'We're together again of course, in a way of speaking, but we both know something has gone, and that we're together perhaps because there is no other distraction for him in the house. . . .

'The curious thing is that Richard is now nicer to me than at any other time in our marriage. And I am horrid to him. And even jealous!' At last she smiled.

Zulema, very still in her chair, stared at the transmuted Brynhild; it wasn't then in answer to her question that Brynhild had told her.

'I suppose she was something like me.'

Brynhild's smile was confessional. 'You are much more beautiful. And much nicer!'

She got up, remained bending over, stubbing out her cigarette; she did it with a clumsy movement. She was trembling.

Zulema got up too.

'No, don't go, I'll tell Leonard to turn off his highbrow concert, and come down. You wait here.'

She had come up close; Zulema suddenly felt an arm round her, a mouth on her cheek. It was a warm kiss. In a totally unpremeditated response her heart leaped towards the other woman.

'I know he's going to ask you tonight; I think it's always nicer if the girl knows beforehand!'

Zulema looked at her, unable to think of anything to say.

'You're just the girl for him; I'd have chosen you myself. I hope with all my heart you'll both be very happy.'

Zulema felt her thank you almost clumsy, but Brynhild didn't seem to notice, she was looking through the tall windows into the drawing room, pondering.

'You see . . . in spite of everything . . . Richard has been the only man in my life.'

Zulema waited.

'One can't stop loving a person just because of something they do to you. . . .'

A sentence fallen out of the night, connected more with the ocean invisible before them, the cosmic forces themselves; at first Zulema did not even connect it with Brynhild, who still wasn't looking at her, anyway.

'Can one?' Brynhild had turned.

Zulema realized that she, the younger woman, was being asked, as if Brynhild herself knew nothing of these things. She said: 'No,' and there was silence.

Brynhild looked into the drawing room again.

'I've never bothered to put plants in my house,' she said reflectively, and looked round in a sullen way, which Zulema recognized as the Brynhild everyone knew. 'I don't know . . . I suppose I must have a rather prosaic mind.'

Alone, Zulema realized she had sat down again in obedience to something other than herself. It was a moment to be reborn a generation later. She saw what awaited her should she remain married to Leonardo for more than eight or nine years. It would become too late; she would, like Ricardo, be expropriated, become his female counterpart: a travesty of an English lady. She would never feel completely at home there; that was probably to be expected. What was unendurable was the thought of it being made impossible for her ever to feel quite at home again among her own people—the ultimate ravage of the takeover.

From upstairs a pause in the music.

She strained her ears for noises of him. Suddenly the sounds raced out of the window as the Presto began; he would listen to the end of course. It infuriated him that she would put on a record, then perhaps forget about it. The symphony, to her, had become invested with the personality of Leonardo listening up there, so that somehow it was not Mozart she heard but Leonardo. It was not the first time this had happened.

She was in the next moment unable to think or do anything. A slow and stealthy uneasiness began to conquer her whole body. Her nerve centres tembled, and she could not control them. In this disquieting lassitude her legs weakened, her palms became moist, she swallowed less. She felt that when he came down she would scarcely be able to stand. And all the time the rumours of the outside world were receding: the shrilling grillos, cars rushing back to the capital, the heavy muffle of the waves, they were going, fading, becoming part of unreality; for reality was only this feeling of waiting for him. It enveloped her like a cocoon, insulating her from everything else she knew, so that finally, when the music cut off in the middle of a phrase, a light went out, a door slammed, something inside her loosened, broke; it was the only time she could wholeheartedly agree with Brynhild.

OLIVIA MANNING
A Spot of Leave

At five o'clock, when the afternoon was deepening into violet-scented, spring twilight, Phillips and Aphrodite met for tea at Larides'. This was the hour when the Alexandrine Greeks drank coffee. Sometimes men dropping into the café from offices and women pausing in their shopping, would stand at the counter and eat with a silver, two-pronged fork, a couple of cakes. The counter displayed immense chocolate boxes tied with ribbons. The cakes were rich and elaborate: sponge-cake, macaroon or feather-fine pastry laden with cream, strawberries, chocolate, icing, nuts, preserved fruits, rich jams, or chestnut paste. They were displayed behind glass.

'And the ladies,' thought Phillips in his captain's uniform, his young face decorated with a cavalry moustache he would have shrunk from wearing when a civilian clerk, 'the ladies are like the cakes.'

They came and went in the shop, charming in their flowered silks, their furs, their confectionery hats, their sheer silk stockings from the United States and their delicate shoes. Each whose husband was of the necessary income-level wore like a trophy on her ring finger a diamond of at least two carats. All were completed with flowers and perfumes, as though a fashionable wedding might be sprung on them at any moment. Phillips, staring at them with his slightly bulging, stone-blue eyes, nodded agreement with himself: 'Just like the cakes—and I wouldn't mind a bite.'

'It is shocking, don't you think, such a display?' said Aphrodite.

'Shocking?' Phillips turned to her and laughed. 'Far from it.'

'But in Palestine you lack sugar.'

'Well, the civilians are a bit short.'

'Here they have too much, yet they refuse to export. In this window last week there was a wedding cake—eight cakes on top of one another, white with sugar. And in Palestine children are ill for need of it.'

'Too bad,' agreed Phillips, looking back into the shop's bustle and fluffing up his moustache with his hand as dark eyes glanced towards him. He had admired Aphrodite's English every time he had been at a loss for something to say, but his ear was more intrigued by the chirruping, inaccurate French of the ladies who moved among the bows on the chocolate-boxes like flowers among butterflies. The men were as elegant. Phillips noticed one—small, elderly, plump, exquisite in silver-grey with pointed shoes—who followed a shop-girl and supervised her packing of a satin-covered box. He moved like a bright insect through the garden of sweets and women, pausing his long, quivering, forefinger over the trays of fondants, darting it like a sting when he made his choice, then rejecting and choosing again, making, un-making and re-making his mind with agitation.

'Wonder who the old boy's buying those for!' said Phillips.

'For himself.'

'Surely not.'

'Yes.' Aphrodite gave a decided shake of her head. 'He is a relative of mine. He is very rich. He always buys himself a box when he makes money on the Bourse. Every day he makes more money except when it looks as though the war might end soon, then the Bourse is frightened.'

'Really!' After some reflection Phillips said: 'You have a lot of relatives.'

'Everyone has a lot of relatives,' said Aphrodite.

Beyond the giant window-bottles filled with crystallized fruits, violets and angelica, went a stream of people: smart Greeks, rich Egyptians, some wearing the fez, servants in galabiahs, French sailors with red pom-poms on their hats and every sort of English and Allied serviceman.

Some French officers, from the pale-grey battleships that had lain motionless in Alexandria harbour since the fall of France, sat at the near-by table. They drank coffee like the Greeks. They, thought Aphrodite, had become at home here because they had adapted themselves at once. The English tried to make a place adapt itself to them. Phillips, for instance, had settled into his basket-chair and without consulting her had at once ordered tea. He had got it just as he had wanted it—hot and strong with milk and sugar. Larides' had learnt to serve it that way the day the first Englishman explained his needs. The Wrens, A.T.S., and nurses, when they arrived, had proved more exacting, for they required the old tea to be emptied out of the pots and fresh tea put in for each customer—

but, they, too, got what they wanted. They sat round the tables with the confident look of the girls she had seen in teashops when she went to stay with her husband's family at Littlehampton.

'You like the tea here?' she asked Phillips.

'Just the job,' he answered. 'Laid on as mother made it.'

'Your nurses,' said Aphrodite, watching the table opposite, 'they do not approve of us, do they? They have seen men dying and they think here are all these people who only make money out of the war.'

'They're jealous,' declared Phillips. 'They know you've got nice silk stockings and they've only got cotton ones. You have got nice silk stockings, haven't you?' he gazed humorously under the table. 'That's what we like to see when we get a spot of leave.'

'Don't women wear silk stockings in Jerusalem?'

'Well, yes, they do if they can get them—but I used to be up in the blue, you know. I can remember what a treat it was to see you girls nicely dressed. And it's still a treat. I'm glad your husband doesn't take too dim a shufti of me trotting you round a bit.'

'Why should he?' asked Aphrodite. 'He's an Englishman.'

'Even an Englishman can be jealous.'

'We are modern,' said Aphrodite, as though the suggestion of jealousy were an insult. She thought back to a few years before when, unmarried, she had the reputation of being the most 'modern' girl in Alexandria. Indeed, so 'modern' had her behaviour been that it had led to endless rows at home and her mother had said: 'You will never get a husband now. There is not a Greek of good family who would have you.' 'Then I'll marry an Englishman,' she said, and she did.

'My parents did not like me to marry James. He was only a clerk in the English bank—but I loved him. I love Englishmen. They are so intelligent, such breadth of mind, so "modern"—the Greeks are like Orientals. In England women are free.'

'Well, I suppose they are,' Phillips agreed without enthusiasm. 'But nice girls aren't too free.'

'My parents wanted me to marry a rich cotton-merchant. An old man who was always drunk. A Copt, too! Think of it. "You can reform him," my mother said, but I said: "Why should I? If he wants to be drunk all the time, it is of no interest to me." Then James was sent to work in Cairo and they were glad. I said nothing. I pretended I had forgotten him. Then one day I started to cry with a toothache. "What I suffer," I said. "Oh, what I suffer!" They were alarmed and said I must go to our dentist in Cairo. So I went and he made an X-ray of my teeth and one had twisted roots. "Look, mother," I said, "look at my insides—how terrible!" So they agreed I should go to stay with my aunt in Cairo and have my teeth mended. When I was two days in Cairo I got married to James.'

'Good Lord!' commented Phillips. 'What did the pater say?'

'You mean my father? He said much, but in the end it is all right. He is a banker. He used influence and James was brought back here to a position.'

'O.K. for James, eh?'

'We are very happy.'

'Oh, are you!' Phillips showed a twinge of annoyance that made Aphrodite smile.

She was reminded of the days before her happy marriage when she had roused endless twinges of jealousy in the young men of Alexandria. Now, after two years of contentment with James, she felt afresh the glow of the chase. In a moment the situation, which she had scarcely grasped before, fell into position and she saw herself in control. Looking upon Phillips as her natural victim, Aphrodite's eyes and colour grew brighter and her whole manner eased into an indolent charm. 'Tell me about your home in England,' she said, as she pushed back her teacup and lit a cigarette.

'Oh!' Phillips was disconcerted for a moment, but he was not unprepared. Ever since he had got through the O.C.T.U. and his office experience had led him to a job in Pal Base, he had been readjusting his background.

Aphrodite, watching him as she listened to him, saw him quite newly as rather handsome in his youthful, blue-eyed fairness. His moustache hid his worst feature, his small, prim mouth. She began to build up from what was attractive in him, the elements of romance. She knew exactly how it should continue from here and she would let it continue. She listened with all the necessary smiling interest, the glow, the flattering absorption in him that was to be his undoing. When Phillips, looking up into her fixed dark glance, blushed slightly, she thought: 'He is sweet, and only a boy.'

'What is your mother like?' she asked, keeping him talking.

'Rather handsome, the mater. Dresses awfully well, but a bit severe with the poor old pater. Plays golf, too.' He added this last touch, which he had not thought of before, and the picture came into focus.

'Have you a photograph of her?' asked Aphrodite.

'Yes—at least, I mean, no. Not with me,' Phillips blushed again.

After a smiling pause Aphrodite said: 'Tonight my husband is going out for a business meeting. Come in and have a drink and keep me company.'

''Fraid I can't. I've got a date with another fellow on leave from my office.'

She looked surprised rather than hurt, but smiled: 'I hope you're not going to Maisie's House.'

He gave her a startled stare. There was a long silence before he suggested they should meet next day for tea.

'Of course,' said Aphrodite. 'And would you like to walk with me along the Corniche?'

'I don't mind,' Phillips's manner was neither eager nor indifferent. Aphrodite could interpret his manner as she wished.

When he had seen her to a taxi, he called one for himself and started back to his hotel by the sea. Settled into his corner, watching out at the brilliance of the street in that moment before darkness and the blackout fell, he contemplated his life now lived in expensive hotels, expensive restaurants, taking tea with the daughters of wealthy bankers, jumping into taxis . . . and he murmured to himself in the almost forgotten argot of the desert: 'Bit of all right, eh, chum?'

Aphrodite's flat in the Sharia Cherif Pasha was as English as its basic Frenchness permitted. Her father had also presented her with a small house at Stanley Bay, where she and James spent the summer. She had, she realized, all she could wish. James had the characteristics she most admired in the English. He was better-looking than Phillips, he was considerate yet met her on an equal footing and showed no resentment of her intelligence. She could not had she wished have found cause for discontent, yet now she felt she was missing an excitement she must find again.

When James came home to supper, she said: 'You know Phillips, the young officer?'

'What about him?'

'You wouldn't mind, would you, if I went to bed with him?'

James did not glance up from his soup as he said: 'I'm tired and I've got to go out to that damned meeting.'

'You wouldn't mind, would you?'

'Mind what?' asked James irritably.

'What I asked—if I slept with Phillips?'

'I don't know,' James kept his glance on his plate. 'I haven't thought about it.'

'But we thought about it a long time ago. We agreed we'd be modern.'

'Then why ask me? You know you can do what you like.'

Aphrodite sighed. She wanted to get these formalities over. Almost she wished now the whole business were over and Phillips safely back in Jerusalem. Yet she was determined to go through with it and in her determination she felt a little drunk, a little lifted above the realities of her everyday life. 'I don't want to deceive you,' she said. 'I want you to be happy about it.'

'All right,' said James. 'I'm happy. Now shut up.'

When he went out, Aphrodite moved restlessly about the flat. She remained in a state of restless inactivity next day until it was time to meet Phillips. James did not speak at breakfast or at luncheon. Phillips, she knew, had only three days more leave and the knowledge filled her with a sense of urgency so that she ached with nervous strain. She ordered the house from habit and she was conscious of James with a worried impatience that was painful to her. What she felt for him was, she knew, intact, but it must remain at a standstill while she lived through this interlude that would prove to her that she was missing nothing.

After luncheon she left the house before James. 'I may not be back for dinner,' she said. He did not reply.

She met Phillips in a café near the old harbour. It was a brilliant spring day and the sea had in it the first green and purple that would deepen with summer. On the other side of the circular harbour was the castle. It stood, on the site of the ancient Pharos, cleanly edged against the sea's colour as though blown bone-white by the wind. The water within the harbour arms sprang up and down.

As they followed the Corniche road with the wind in their faces, Phillips said: 'I've been thinking of having a couple of days in Cairo.'

'You mean, after your leave?'

'No, I'd have to go tomorrow.'

'Alone?' asked Aphrodite.

'Well, the chap from my office is going. I thought of going with him.'

Aphrodite, silent, stared ahead.

'But I don't think I'll go. I like it here.'

'Ah!' Aphrodite smiled. 'Perhaps you do not want to leave me?'

Phillips cleared his throat as though he were doing a comic turn and gave her a coy glance: 'That's about it,' he said.

Conversation became easier after that. On one side of them the concrete houses and blocks of flats stretched far out of sight into the desert. On the other side splashed the mildly choppy sea, its border of rock yellow and porous like rotting cheese.

'It reminds me of Worthing,' said Phillips. 'The only thing is we don't have date palms.'

'I know. I've been to Littlehampton.'

'Good Lord, have you?' and they talked about England and English seaside towns. Aphrodite was gaily critical, while Phillips was nostalgically respectful. They passed Stanley Bay with its closed bathing huts and air of popular entertainment shut up for the winter. The houses still stretched on. In the distance, too far away to be reached, appeared among palms a white-domed palace, the only Oriental thing in sight. They came at last to a thin shelf of rock through which the ancients had cut holes. On a gusty day like this the sea came spouting through them.

'There!' said Aphrodite. 'Isn't that interesting? In the old days people used to fix musical instruments in the holes so the sea could play tunes.'

'Why on earth did they do that?'

'For amusement.'

'Rum idea.'

'But isn't it interesting? I brought you to see it.'

'Did you? Hell of a length this Corniche—as you call it. Better go back now,' and he swung round without waiting for her agreement. Now the wind was behind them, blowing their hair forward. Right at the other end of the great curve of the shore, the main part of the town, growing steely blue as the light failed, was neatly built-up on a bulge of land. A few barrage-balloons were beginning to rise like silver kidneys on threads above the harbour. The wind was growing cold.

'How about a taxi?' said Phillips at Stanley Bay. When they found one and settled inside it, Aphrodite placed herself comfortably against his shoulder. Some minutes passed before he thought to slip an arm round her.

'Now to brew up,' he said with satisfaction.

'What does that mean?'

'Tea, of course. Where shall we go?'

'The same place,' Aphrodite whispered warmly. 'The same table.'

'O.K.,' said Phillips, and: 'We're in luck,' as they entered Larides' and saw their table was free.

When the tea was poured out, when they were pressing their forks through the luscious softness of coffee-cream cakes, Aphrodite felt the moment had come to clarify and speed up the situation. Phillips might have an Englishman's shyness, but he had only three days' more leave.

'I spoke to my husband about you,' she said.

'What did you tell him? Something nice?'

'Of course. I told him I wanted to sleep with you.'

Phillips raised his eyes and fixed them on her. Even then he had little expression, but he blushed more darkly than he had done for years. 'Good Lord!' he dropped his glance. 'What made you tell him that?'

'Because I didn't want to deceive him. He must know.'

Phillips put a lump of cake into his mouth before he mumbled: 'But there isn't anything for him to know.'

Aphrodite heard because she had been listening: 'You mean you don't want to?'

Phillips swallowed down the last of his cake and pulled himself together. His manner became rather aggressive: 'You ought to know better,' he said. 'A married lady! And you said you were happy.'

'What difference does that make?'

He refused to reply. She drank some tea. There was another pause before she said with a nervous giggle: 'Why don't you want to?'

'Hell, let's drop the subject.' Phillips frowned in indignation and his voice had lost much of its gentility. A hard and edgy silence settled on them. Aphrodite tried once or twice to break it with an anecdote about this person or that passing through the café, but Phillips was unresponsive. When they parted his manner was still cold. He did not suggest their meeting again.

James, supposing Aphrodite would be out, came home late that evening. He found her sitting alone in darkness. As he switched on the light, he said: 'Home early. Did the beautiful romance fall through?'

She did not answer. She was lying back against her chair and sobbing. He stared at her for some moments, then went to her and slid his arm round her. 'What's the matter?' he asked.

She pressed her face against his middle: 'He didn't want me. Now I know I'm getting old.'

'Nonsense,' he said. 'It just showed what a fool he was.'

'No. I know. I know I'm getting old.'

V. S. NAIPAUL

A Christmas Story

THOUGH it is Christmas Eve my mind is not on Christmas. I look forward instead to the day after Boxing Day, for on that day the inspectors from the Audit Department in Port-of-Spain will be coming down to the village where the new school has been built. I await their coming with calm. There is still time, of course, to do all that is necessary. But I shall not do it, though my family, from whom the spirit of Christmas has, alas, also fled, have been begging me to lay aside my scruples, my new-found faith, and to rescue us all from disgrace and ruin. It is in my power to do so, but there comes a time in every man's life when he has to take a stand. This time, I must confess, has come very late for me.

It seems that everything has come late to me. I continued a Hindu, though of that religion I saw and knew little save meaning-less and shameful rites, until I was nearly eighteen. Why I so continued I cannot explain. Perhaps it was the inertia with which that religion deadens its devotees. It did not, after all, require much intelligence to see that Hinduism, with its animistic rites, its idolatry, its emphaisis on mango leaf, banana leaf and—the truth is the truth—cowdung, was a religion little fitted for the modern world. I had only to contrast the position of the Hindus with that of the Christians. I had only to consider the differing standards of dress, houses, food. Such differences have today more or less disappeared, and the younger generation will scarcely understand what I mean. I might even be reproached with laying too great a stress on the superficial. What can I say? Will I be believed if I say that to me the superficial has always symbolized the profound? But it is enough, I feel, to state that at eighteen my eyes were opened. I did not have to be 'converted' by the Presbyterians of the Canadian Mission. I had only to look at the work they were doing among the backward Hindus and Moslems of my district. I had only to look at their schools, to look at the houses of the converted.

My Presbyterianism, then, though late in coming, affected me deeply. I was interested in teaching—there was no other thing a man of my limited means and limited education could do—and my

Presbyterianism was a distinct advantage. It gave me a grace in the eyes of my superiors. It also enabled me to be a good teacher, for between what I taught and what I felt there was no discordance. How different the position of those who, still unconverted, attempted to teach in Presbyterian schools!

And now that the time for frankness has come I must also remark on the pleasure my new religion gave me. It was a pleasure to hear myself called Randolph, a name of rich historical associations, a name, I feel, thoroughly attuned to the times in which we live and to the society in which I found myself, and to forget that once—I still remember it with shame—I answered, with simple instinct, to the name of—Choonilal. That, however, is so much in the past. I have buried it. Yet I remember it now, not only because the time for frankness has come, but because only two weeks ago my son Winston, going through some family papers—clearly the boy had no right to be going through my private papers, but he shares his mother's curiosity—came upon the name. He teased, indeed reproached me, with it, and in a fit of anger, for which I am now grievously sorry and for which I must make time, while time there still is, to apologize to him, in a fit of anger I gave him a sound thrashing, such as I often gave in my school-teaching days, to those pupils whose persistent shortcomings were matched by the stupidity and backwardness of their parents. Backwardness has always roused me to anger.

As much as by the name Randolph, pleasure was given me by the stately and *clean*—there is no other word for it—rituals sanctioned by my new religion. How agreeable, for instance, to rise early on a Sunday morning, to bathe and breakfast and then, in the most spotless of garments, to walk along the still quiet and cool roads to our place of worship, and there to see the most respectable and respected, all dressed with a similar purity, addressing themselves to the devotions in which I myself could participate, after for long being an outsider, someone to whom the words *Christ* and *Father* meant no more than *winter* or *autumn* or *daffodil*. Such of the unconverted village folk who were energetic enough to be awake and alert at that hour gaped at us as we walked in white procession to our church. And though their admiration was sweet, I must confess that at the same time it filled me with shame to reflect that not long before I too formed part of the gaping crowd. To walk past their gaze was peculiarly painful to me, for I, more perhaps than anyone in that slow and stately procession, *knew*—and by my silence had for nearly eighteen years condoned—the practices those people indulged in in the name of religion. My attitude towards them was therefore somewhat stern, and it gave me some little consolation to know that though we were in some ways alike, we were distinguished from them not only by our names, which after all no man carries pinned to his lapel, but also by our dress. On these Sundays of which I speak the men wore trousers and jackets of white drill, quite unlike the leg-revealing dhoti which it still pleased those others to wear, a garment which I have always felt makes the wearer ridiculous. I even sported a white solar topee. The girls and ladies wore the short frocks which the others held in abhorrence; they wore hats; in every respect, I am pleased to say, they resembled their sisters who had come all the way from Canada and other countries to work among our people. I might be accused of laying too much stress on superficial things. But I ought to say in my own defence that it is my deeply held conviction that progress is not a matter of outward show, but an attitude of mind; and it was this that my religion gave me.

It might seem from what I have so far said that the embracing of Presbyterianism conferred only benefits and pleasure. I wish to make no great fuss of the trials I had to endure, but it is sufficient to state that, while at school and in other associations my fervent adherence to my new faith was viewed with favour, I had elsewhere to put up with the constant ridicule of those of my relations who continued, in spite of my example, in the ways of darkness. They spoke my name, Randolph, with accents of the purest mockery. I bore this with fortitude. It was what I expected, and I was greatly strengthened by my faith, as a miser is by the thought of his gold. In time, when they saw that their ridiculing of my name had not the slightest effect on me—on the contrary, whereas before I had in my signature suppressed my first name behind the blank initial C, now I spelt out Randolph in full—in time they desisted.

But that was not the end of my trials. I had up to that time eaten with my fingers, a manner of eating which is now so repulsive to me, so ugly, so unhygienic, that I wonder how I managed to do it until my eighteenth year. Yet I must now confess that at that time food never tasted as sweet as when eaten with the fingers, and that my first attempts to eat with the proper implements of knife and fork and spoon were almost in the nature of shameful experiments, furtively carried out; and even when I was by myself I could not get rid of the feeling of self-consciousness. It was easier to get used to the name of Randolph than to knife and fork.

Eating, then, in my determined manner one Sunday lunchtime, I heard that I had a visitor. It was a man; he didn't knock, but came straight into my room, and I knew at once that he was a relation. These people have never learned to knock or to close doors behind them.

I must confess I felt somewhat foolish to be caught with those implements in my hand.

'Hello, Randolph,' the boy Hori said, pronouncing the name in a most offensive manner.

'Good afternoon, *Hori*.'

He remained impervious to my irony. This boy, Hori, was the greatest of my tormentors. He was also the grossest. He strained charity. He was a great lump of a man and he gloried in his brutishness. He fancied himself a debater as well, and many were the discussions and arguments we had had, this lout—he strained charity, as I have said—insisting that to squat on the ground and eat off banana leaves was hygienic and proper, that knives and forks were dirty because used again and again by various persons, whereas the fingers were personal and could always be made thoroughly clean by washing. But he never had *his* fingers clean, that I knew.

'Eating, Randolph?'

'I am having my lunch, *Hori*.'

'Beef, Randolph. You are progressing, Randolph.'

'I am glad you note it, Hori.'

I cannot understand why these people should persist in this admiration for the cow, which has always seemed to me a filthy animal, far filthier than the pig, which they abhor. Yet it must be stated that this eating of beef was the most strenuous of my tests. If I persevered it was only because I was strengthened by my faith. But to be found at this juncture—I was in my Sunday suit of white drill, my prayer book was on the table, my white solar topee on the wall, and I was eating beef with knife and fork—to be found thus by Hori was a trifle embarrassing. I must have looked the picture of the over-zealous convert.

My instinct was to ask him to leave. But it occurred to me that

that would have been too easy, too cowardly a way out. Instead, I plied my knife and fork with as much skill as I could command at that time. He sat, not on a chair, but on the table, just next to my plate, the lout, and gazed at me while I ate. Ignoring his smile, I ate, as one might eat of sacrificial food. He crossed his fat legs, leaned back on his palms and examined me. I paid no attention. Then he took one of the forks that were about and began picking his teeth with it. I was angry and revolted. Tears sprang to my eyes. I rose, pushed away my plate, pushed back my chair, and asked him to leave. The violence of my reaction surprised him, and he did as I asked. As soon as he had gone I took the fork he had handled and bent it and stamped on it and then threw it out of the window.

Progress, as I have said, is an attitude of mind. And if I relate this trifling incident with such feeling, it is because it demonstrates how difficult that attitude of mind is to acquire, for there are hundreds who are ready to despise and ridicule those who they think are getting above themselves. And let people say what they will, the contempt even of the foolish is hard to bear. Let no one think, therefore, that my new religion did not bring its share of trials and tribulations. But I was sufficiently strengthened by my faith to bear them all with fortitude.

My life thereafter was a lonely one. I had cut myself off from my family, and from those large family gatherings which had hitherto given me so much pleasure and comfort, for always, I must own, at the back of my mind there had been the thought that in the event of real trouble there would be people to whom I could turn. Now I was deprived of this solace. I stuck to my vocation with a dedication which surprised even myself. To be a teacher it is necessary to be taught; and after much difficulty I managed to have myself sent to the Training College in Port-of-Spain. The competition for these places was fierce, and for many years I was passed over, because there were many others who were more fitting. Some indeed had been born of Presbyterian parents. But my zeal, which ever mounted as the failures multiplied, eventually was rewarded. I was twenty-eight when I was sent to the Training College, considerably older than most of the trainees.

It was no pleasure to me to note that during those ten years the boy Hori had been prospering. He had gone into the trucking business and he had done remarkably well. He had bought a second

truck, then a third, and it seemed that to his success there could be
no limit, while my own was always restricted to the predictable
contents of the brown-paper pay-packet at the end of the month.
The clothes in which I had taken such pride at first became less
resplendent, until I felt it as a disgrace to go to church in them. But
it became clear to me that this was yet another of the trials I was
called upon to undergo, and I endured it, until I almost took
pleasure in the darns on my sleeves and elbows.

At this time I was invited to the wedding of Hori's son, Kedar.
They marry young, these people! It was an occasion which sur-
mounted religious differences, and it was a distinct pleasure to me
to be again with the family, for their attitude had changed. They
had become reconciled to my Presbyterianism and indeed treated
me with respect for my profession, a respect which, I fear, was
sometimes missing in the attitude of my superiors and even my
pupils. The marriage rites distressed me. The makeshift though
beautiful tent, the coconut-palm arches hung with clusters of fruit,
the use of things like mango leaves and grass and saffron, the
sacrificial fire, all these things filled me with shame rather than
delight. But the rites were only a small part of the celebrations.
There was much good food, strictly vegetarian but somehow
extremely tempting; and after a period of distaste for Indian food, I
had come back to it again. The food, I say, was rich. The music
and the dancers were thrilling. The tent and the illuminations had
a charm which not even our school hall had on concert nights,
though the marriage ceremony did not of course have the grace and
dignity of those conducted, as proper marriages should be, in a
church.

Kedar received a fabulous dowry, and his bride, of whose face I
had just a glimpse when her silk veil was parted, was indeed
beautiful. But such beauty has always appeared to me skin deep.
Beauty in women is a disturbing thing. But beyond the beauty it is
always necessary to look for the greater qualities of manners and—
a thing I always remind Winston of—no one is too young or too old
to learn—manners and *ways*. She was beautiful. It was sad to think
of her joined to Kedar for life, but she was perhaps fitted for nothing
else. No need to speak of the resplendent regalia of Kedar himself:
his turban, the crown with tassels and pendant glass, his richly
embroidered silk jacket, and all those other adornments which for
that night concealed so well the truck-driver that he was.

* * *

I left the wedding profoundly saddened. I could not help reflecting on my own position and contrasting it with Hori's or even Kedar's. I was now over forty, and marriage, which in the normal way would have come to me at the age of twenty or thereabouts, was still far from me. This was my own fault. Arranged marriages like Kedar's had no part in my scheme of things. I wished to marry, as the person says in *The Vicar of Wakefield*, someone who had qualities that would wear well. My choice was severely restricted. I wished to marry a Presbyterian lady who was intelligent, well brought up and educated, and wished to marry me. This last condition, alas, I could find few willing to fulfil. And indeed I had little to offer. Among Hindus it would have been otherwise. There might have been men of substance who would have been willing to marry their daughters to a teacher, to acquire respectability and the glamour of a learned profession. Such a position has its strains, of course, for it means that the daughter remains, as it were, subject to her family; but the position is not without its charms.

You might imagine—and you would be correct—that at this time my faith was undergoing its severest strain. How often I was on the point of reneging I shudder to tell. I felt myself about to yield; I stiffened in my devotions and prayers. I reflected on the worthlessness of worldly things, but this was a reflection I found few to share. I might add here, in parentheses and without vanity, that I had had several offers from the fathers of unconverted daughters, whose only condition was the one, about my religion, which I could not accept; for my previous caste had made me acceptable to many.

In this situation of doubt, of nightly wrestling with God, an expression whose meaning I came only then fully to understand, my fortune changed. I was appointed a headmaster. Now I can speak! How many people know of the tribulations, the pettiness, the intrigue which schoolteachers have to undergo to obtain such promotion? Such jockeying, such jealousy, such ill-will comes into play. What can I say of the advances one has to make, the rebuffs one has to suffer in silence, the waiting, the undoing of the unworthy who seek to push themselves forward for positions which they are ill-qualified to fill but which, by glibness and all the outward shows of respectability and efficiency and piety, they manage to persuade our superiors that they alone can fill? I too had my adversaries. My chief rival—but let him rest in peace! I am, I trust, a Christian, and will do no man the injustice of imagining him to persist in error even after we have left this vale of tears.

In my fortune, so opportune, I saw the hand of God. I speak in all earnestness. For without this I would surely have lapsed into the ways of darkness, for who among us can so steel himself as to resist temptation for all time? In my gratitude I applied myself with renewed dedication to my task. And it was this that doubtless evoked the gratification of my superiors which was to lead to my later elevation. For at a time when most men, worn out by the struggle, are content to relax, I showed myself more eager than before. I instituted prayers four times a day. I insisted on attendance at Sunday School. I taught Sunday School myself, and with the weight of my influence persuaded the other teachers to do likewise, so that Sunday became another day for us, a day of rest which we consumed with work for the Lord.

And I did not neglect the educational side. The blackboards all now sparkled with diagrams in chalks of various colours, projects which we had in hand. Oh, the school was such a pretty sight then! I instituted a rigid system of discipline, and forbade indiscriminate flogging by pupil teachers. All flogging I did myself on Friday afternoons, sitting in impartial judgement, as it were, on the school, on pupils as well as teachers. It is surely a better system, and I am glad to say that it has now been adopted throughout the island. The most apt pupils I kept after school, and for some trifling extra fee gave them private lessons. And the school became so involved with work as an ideal that had to be joyously pursued and not as something that had to be endured, that the usefulness of these private lessons was widely appreciated, and soon larger numbers than I could cope with were staying after school for what they affectionately termed their 'private'.

And I married. It was now in my power to marry virtually anyone I pleased and there were among the Sunday School staff not a few who made their attachment to me plain. I am not such a bad-looking fellow! But I wished to marry someone who had qualities that would wear well. I was nearly fifty. I did not wish to marry someone who was much younger than myself. And it was my good fortune at this juncture to receive an offer—I hesitate to use this word, which sounds so much like the Hindu custom and reminds one of the real estate business, but here I must be frank—from no less a person than a schools inspector, who had an unmarried daughter of thirty-five, a woman neglected by the men of the island because of her attainments—yes, you read right—which were considerable, but not of the sort that proclaims itself to the world. In our attitude to women much remains to be changed! I have often, during these past days, reflected on marriage. Such a turning, a point in time whence so many consequences flow. I wonder what Winston, poor boy, will do when his time comes.

My establishment could not rival Hori's or Kedar's for splendour, but within it there was peace and culture such as I had long dreamed of. It was a plain wooooden house, but well built, built to last, unlike so many of these modern monstrosities which I see arising these days: and it was well ordered. We had simple bentwood chairs with cane bottoms. No marble-topped tables with ball-fringed lace! No glass cabinets! I hung my treasured framed teaching diploma on the wall, with my religious pictures and some scenes of the English countryside. It was also my good fortune at this time to get an old autographed photograph of one of our first missionaries. In the decoration of our humble home my wife appeared to release all the energy and experience of her thirty-five years which had so far been denied expression.

To her, as to myself, everything came late. It was our fear, confirmed by the views of many friends who behind their expressions of goodwill concealed as we presently saw much uncharitableness, that we would be unable to have children, considering our advanced years. But they, and we, underestimated the power of prayer, for within a year of our marriage Winston was born.

The birth of Winston came to us as a grace and a blessing. Yet it also filled me with anxiety, for I could not refrain from assessing the difference between our ages. It occurred to me, for instance, that he would be thirty when I was eighty. It was a disturbing thought, for the companionship of children is something which, perhaps because of my profession, I hold especially dear. My anxiety had another reason. It was that Winston, in his most formative years, would be without not only my guidance—for what guidance can a man of seventy give to a lusty youngster of twenty?—but also without my financial support.

The problem of money, strange as it might appear, considering my unexpected elevation and all its accruing benefits, was occupying the minds of both my wife and myself. For my retirement was drawing near, and my pension would scarcely be more than what I subsisted on as a simple pupil teacher. It seemed then that like those pilgrims, whose enthusiasm I admire but cannot share, I was advancing towards my goal by taking two steps forward and one step back, though in my case a likelier simile might be that I was taking one step forward and one step back. So success always turns to ashes in the mouth of those who seek it as ardently as I had! And if I had the vision and the depth of faith which I now have, I might have seen even then how completely false are the things of this world, how much they flatter only to deceive.

We were both, as I say, made restless. And now the contemplation of baby Winston was a source of much pain to both of us, for the poor innocent creature could scarcely know what anguish awaited him when we would both be withdrawn from this vale of tears. His helplessness, his dependence tortured me. I was past the age when the taking out of an insurance policy was a practicable proposition; and during my days as a simple teacher I never had the resources to do so. It seemed, then, that I was being destroyed by my own good fortune, by the fruits of all my endeavour. Yet I did not heed this sign.

I continued while I could giving private lessons. I instituted a morning session as well, in addition to the afternoon one. But I did so with a heavy heart, tormented by the thought that in a few years this privilege and its small reward would be denied me, for private lessons, it must be understood, are considered the prerogative of a headmaster: in this way he stamps his character on the school. My results in the exhibition examinations for boys under twelve continued to be heartening; they far surpassed those of many other country schools. My religious zeal continued unabated; and it was this zeal which, burning in those years when most men in my position would have relaxed—they, fortunate souls, having their children fully grown—it was this surprising zeal, I say, which also contributed, I feel, to my later elevation which, as you will see from the plain narration of these events, I did not seek.

My retirement drew nearer. I became fiercer at school. I wished all the boys under me could grow up at once. I was merciless towards the backward. My wife, poor creature, could not control her anxiety with as much success as myself. She had no occupation, no distracting vocation, in which her anxiety might have been consumed. She had only Winston, and this dear infant continually roused her to fears about his future. For his sake she would, I believe, have sacrificed her own life! It was not easy for her. And it required but the exercise of the mildest Christian charity to see that the reproaches she flung with increased acerbity and frequency at my head were but expressions of her anxiety. Sometimes, I must confess, I failed! And then my own unworthiness would torment me, as it torments me now.

We confided our problems to my wife's father, the schools inspector. Though we felt it unfair to let another partake of our troubles, it is nonetheless a recognized means of lightening any load which the individual finds too heavy to bear. But he, poor man, though as worried on his daughter's behalf as she was on Winston's, could offer only sympathy and little practical help. He reported that the authorities were unwilling to give me an extension of my tenure as headmaster. My despondency found expression in a display of temper, which he charitably forgave; for though he left the house, promising not to do another thing for us, he presently returned, and counselled patience.

So patient we were. I retired. I could hardly bear to remain at home, so used had I been to the daily round, the daily trials. I went out visiting, for no other reason than that I was afraid to be alone at home. My zeal, I believe, was remarked upon, though I took care to avoid the school, the scene of my late labours. I sought to take in for private lessons two or three pupils whose progress had deeply interested me. But my methods were no longer the methods that found favour! The parents of these children reported that the new headmaster had expressed himself strongly, and to my great disfavour, on the subject, to such a degree, in fact, that the progress of their children at school was being hampered. So I desisted; or rather, since the time has come for frankness, they left me.

The schools inspector, a regular visitor now at our humble, sad home, continued to counsel patience. I have so far refrained in this narrative from permitting my wife to speak directly; for I wish to do nothing that might increase the load she will surely have to bear, for my wife, though of considerable attainments, has not had the advantages of a formal education on which so much stress is nowadays laid. So I will refrain from chronicling the remark with which she greeted this advice of her father's. Suffice it to say that she spoke a children's rhyme without any great care for its metre or rhyme, the last of which indeed she destroyed by accidentally, in her haste, pulling down a vase from the centre-table on to the floor, where the water ran like one of the puddles which our baby Winston so lately made. After this incident relations between my wife and her father underwent a perceptible strain; and I took care to be out of the house as often as possible, and indeed it was pleasant to forget one's domestic troubles and walk abroad and be greeted as 'Headmaster' by the simple village folk.

Then, as it appears has happened so regularly throughout my life, the clouds rolled away and the sky brightened. I was appointed a School Manager. The announcement was made in the most heart-warming way possible, by the schools inspector himself, anticipating the official notification by a week or so. And the occasion became a family reunion. It was truly good to see the harassed schools inspector relaxing at last, and to see father and daughter reasonably happy with one another. My delight in this was almost as great as the delight in my new dignity.

For a school managership is a good thing to come to a man in the evening of his days. It permits an exercise of the most benign power imaginable. It permits a man at a speech day function to ask for a holiday for the pupils; and nothing is as warming as the lusty and sincere cheering that follows such a request. It gives power even over headmasters, for one can make surprise visits and it is in one's power to make reports to the authorities. It is a position of considerable responsibility as well, for a school manager manages a school as much as a managing director manages a company. It is in his power to decide whether the drains, say, need to be remade entirely or need simply be plastered over to look as new; whether one coat of paint or two are needed; whether a ceiling can be partially renovated and painted over or taken out altogether and replaced. He orders the number of desks and blackboards which he considers necessary, and the chalks and the stationery. It is, in short, a dignity ideally suited to one who has led an active life and is dismayed by the prospect of retirement. It brings honour as well as reward. It has the other advantage that school managers are like civil servants; they are seldom dismissed; and their honours tend to increase rather than diminish.

I entered on my new tasks with zeal, and once again all was well at our home. My wife's father visited us regularly, as though, poor man, anxious to share the good fortune for which he was to a large measure responsible. I looked after the school, the staff, the pupils. I visited all the parents of the pupils under my charge and spoke to them of the benefits of education, the dangers of absenteeism, and so on. I know I will be forgiven if I add that from time to time, whenever the ground appeared ripe, I sowed the seed of Presbyterianism or at any rate doubt among those who continued in the ways of darkness. Such zeal was unknown among school managers. I cannot account for it myself. It might be that my early austerity and ambition had given me something of the crusading zeal. But it was inevitable that such zeal should have been too much for some people to stomach.

For all his honour, for all the sweet cheers that greet his request for a holiday for the pupils, the school manager's position is one that sometimes attracts adverse and malicious comment. It is the fate of anyone who finds himself in a position of power and financial responsibility. The rumours persisted; and though they did not diminish the esteem in which I was so clearly held by the community—at the elections, for example, I was approached by all five candidates and asked to lend my voice to their cause, a situation of peculiar difficulty, which I resolved by promising all five to remain neutral, for which they were effusively grateful—it is no good thing for a man to walk among people who every day listen eagerly—for flesh is frail, and nothing attracts our simple villagers as much as scurrilous gossip—to slanders against himself. It was beneath my dignity, or rather, the dignity of my position, to reply to such attacks; and in this situation I turned, as I was turning with growing frequency, to my wife's father for advice. He suggested that I should relinquish one of my managerships, to indicate my disapproval of the gossip and the little esteem in which I held worldly honour. For I had so far succeeded in my new functions that I was now the manager of three schools, which was the maximum number permitted.

I followed his advice. I relinquished the managership of a school which was in a condition so derelict that not even repeated renovations could efface the original gimcrackery of its construction. This school had been the cause of most of the rumours, and my relinquishing of it attracted widespread comment and was even mentioned in the newspapers. It remained dear to me, but I was willing for it to go into other hands. This action of mine had the effect of stilling rumours and gossip. And the action proved to have its own reward, for some months later my wife's father, ever the bearer of good tidings, intimated that there was a possibility of a new school being put up in the area. I was thoroughly suited for its management; and he, the honest broker between the authorities and myself, said that my name was being mentioned in this connection. I was at that time manager of only two schools; I was entitled to a third. He warmly urged me to accept. I hesitated, and my hesitations were later proved to be justified. But the thought of a new school fashioned entirely according to my ideas and principles was too heady. I succumbed to temptation. If now I could only go back and withdraw that acceptance! The good man hurried back with the news; and within a fortnight I received the official notification.

I must confess that during the next few months I lost sight of my doubts in my zeal and enthusiasm for the new project. My two other schools suffered somewhat. For if there is a thing to delight the heart of the school manager, it is the management of a school not yet built. But, alas! We are at every step reminded of the vanity of worldly things. How often does it happen that a person, placed in the position he craves, a position which he is in every way suited to fill, suddenly loses his grip! Given the opportunity for which he longs, he is unable to make use of it. The effort goes all into the striving.

So now it happened with me. Nearly everything I touched failed to go as it should. I, so careful and correct in assessments and estimates, was now found repeatedly in error. None of my calculations were right. There were repeated shortages and stoppages. The school progressed far more slowly than I would have liked. And it was no consolation to me to find that in this moment I was alone, in this long moment of agony! Neither to my wife nor to her father could I turn for comfort. They savoured the joy of my managership of a new school without reference to me. I had my great opportunity; they had no doubt I would make use of it; and I could not bear disillusioning them or breaking into their happiness with my worries.

My errors attracted other errors. My errors multiplied, I tell you!

To cover up one error I had to commit twenty acts of concealment, and these twenty had to be concealed. I felt myself caught in a curious inefficiency that seemed entirely beyond my control, something malignant, powered by forces hostile to myself. Until at length it seemed that failure was staring me in the face, and that my entire career would be forgotten in this crowning failure. The building went up, it is true. It had a respectable appearance. It looked a building. But it was far from what I had visualized. I had miscalculated badly, and it was too late to remedy the errors. Its faults, its weaknesses would be at once apparent even to the scantily trained eye. And now night after night I was tormented by this failure of mine. With the exercise of only a little judgement it could so easily have been made right. Yet now the time for that was past! Day after day I was drawn to the building, and every day I hoped that by some miracle it would have been effaced during the night. But there it always stood, a bitter reproach.

Matters were not made easier for me by the reproaches of my wife and her father. They both rounded on me and said with justice that my failure would involve them all. And the days went by! I could not—I have never liked bickering, the answering of insult with insult—I could not reproach them with having burdened me with such an enterprise at the end of my days. I did it for their glory, for I had acquired sufficient to last me until the end of my days. I did it for my wife and her father, and for my son Winston. But who will believe me? Who will believe that a man works for the glory of others, except he work for the glory of God? They reproached me. They stood aside from me. In this moment of need they deserted me.

They were bitter days. I went for long walks through our villages in the cool of the evening. The children ran out to greet me. Mothers looked up from their cooking, fathers from their perches on the roadside culverts, and greeted me, 'Headmaster!' And soon my failure would be apparent even to the humblest among them. I had to act quickly. Failures should be destroyed. The burning down of a school is an unforgivable thing, but there are surely occasions when it can be condoned, when it is the only way out. Surely this was such an occasion! It is a drastic step. But it is one that has been taken more than once in this island. So I argued with myself. And always the answer was there; my failure had to be destroyed, not only for my own sake, but for the sake of all those, villagers included, whose fates were involved with mine.

Once I had made up my mind, I acted with decision. It was that time of year, mid-November, when people are beginning to think of Christmas to the exclusion of nearly everything else. This served my purpose well. I required—with what shame I now confess it—certain assistants, for it was necessary for me to be seen elsewhere on the day of the accident. Much money, much of what we had set aside for the future of our son Winston, had to go on this. And already it had been necessary to seal the lips of certain officials who had rejoiced in my failure and were willing to proclaim it to the world. But at last it was ready. On Boxing Day we would go to Port-of-Spain, to the races. When we returned the following day, the school would be no more. I say 'we', though my wife had not been apprised of my intentions.

With what fear, self-reproach, and self-disgust I waited for the days to pass! When I heard the Christmas carols, ever associated for me with the indefinable sweetness of Christmas Eve—which I now once more feel, thanks to my decision, though underneath there is a sense of doom and destruction, deserved, but with their own inevitable reward—when I heard carols and Christmas commercials on the radio, my heart sank; for it seemed that I had cut myself off from all about me, that once more I had become a stranger to the faith which I profess. So these days passed in sorrow, in nightly frenzies of prayer and self-castigation. Regret assailed me. Regret for what might have been, regret for what was to come. I was sinking, I felt, into a pit of defilement whence I could never emerge.

Of all this my wife knew nothing. But then she asked one day, 'What have you decided to do?' and, without waiting for my reply, at once drew up such a detailed plan, which corresponded so closely to what I had myself devised, that my heart quailed. For if, in this moment of my need, when the deepest resource was needed, I could devise a plan which might have been devised by anyone else, then discovery was certain. And to my shame, Winston, who only two or three days before had been teasing me with my previous unbaptized name, Winston took part in this discussion, with no appearance of shame on his face, only thrill and—sad am I to say it—a pride in me greater than I had ever seen the boy display.

How can one tell of the workings of the human heart? How can one speak of the urge to evil—an urge of which Christians more than anyone else are so aware—and of the countervailing urge to good? You must remember that this is the season of goodwill. And goodwill it was. For goodwill was what I was feeling towards all. At every carol my heart melted. Whenever a child rushed towards me and cried, 'Headmaster!' I was tormented by grief. For the sight of the unwashed creatures, deprived, so many of them, of schooling, which matters so much in those early years, and the absence of which ever afterwards makes itself felt, condemning a human being to an animal-like existence, the sight of these creatures, grateful towards me who had on so many evenings gone among them propagating the creed with what energy I could, unmanned me. They were proud of their new school. They were even prouder of their association with the man who had built it.

Everywhere I felt rejected. I went to church as often as I could, but even there I found rejection. And as the time drew nearer the enormity of what I proposed grew clearer to me. It was useless to tell myself that what I was proposing had been often done. The carols, the religious services, the talk of birth and life, they all unmanned me.

I walked among the children as one who had it in his power to provide or withhold blessing, and I thought of that other Walker, who said of those among whom I walked that they were blessed, and that theirs was the kingdom of heaven. And as I walked it seemed that at last I had seized the true essence of the religion I had adopted, and whose worldly success I had with such energy promoted. So that it seemed that these trials I was undergoing had been reserved to the end of my days, so that only then I could have a taste of the ecstasy about which I had so far only read. With this ecstasy I walked. It was Christmas Eve. It was Christmas Eve. My head felt drawn out of my body. I had difficulty in assessing the size and distance of objects. I felt myself tall. I felt myself part of the earth and yet removed.

And: 'No!' I said to my wife at teatime. 'No, I will not disgrace myself by this action of cowardice. Rather, I will proclaim my failure to the world and ask for my due punishment.'

She behaved as I expected. She had been busy putting up all sorts of Christmas decorations, expensive ones from the United States, which are all the rage now, so unlike the simple decorations I used to see in the homes of our early missionaries before the war.

But how changed is the house to which we moved! How far has simplicity vanished and been replaced by show! And I gloried in it!

She begged me to change my mind. She summoned Winston to her help. They both wept and implored me to go through with our plan. But I was firm. I do believe that if the schools inspector were alive, he would also have been summoned to plead with me. But he, fortunate man, passed away some three weeks ago, entrusting his daughter and grandson to my care; and this alone is my fear, that by gaining glory for myself I might be injuring them. But I was firm. And then there started another of those scenes with which I had become only too familiar, and the house which that morning was filled with the enthusiasm of Winston was changed into one of mourning. Winston sobbed, tears running down his plump cheeks and down his well-shaped nose to his firm top lip, pleading with me to burn the school down, and generally behaving as though I had deprived him of a bonfire. And then a number of things were destroyed by his mother, and she left the house with Winston, vowing never to see me again, never to be involved in the disgrace which was sure to come.

And so here I sit, waiting not for Christmas, but in this house where the autographed photograph of one of our earliest missionaries gazes down at me through his rich beard and luxuriant eyebrows, and where the walls carry so many reminders of my past life of endeavour and hardship and struggle and triumph and also, alas, final failure, I wait for the day after Boxing Day, after the races to which we were to have gone, for the visit of the inspectors of the Audit Department. The house is lonely and dark. The radios play the Christmas songs. I am very lonely. But I am strong. And here I lay down my pen. My hand tires; the beautiful letters we were taught to fashion at the mission school have begun to weaken and to straggle untidily over the ruled paper; and someone is knocking.

December 27. How can one speak of the ways of the world, how can one speak of the tribulations that come one's way? Even expiation is denied me. For even as I wrote the last sentence of the above account, there came a knocking at my door, and I went to open unto him who knocked. And lo, there was a boy, bearing tidings. And behold, towards the west the sky had reddened, the boy informed me that the school was ablaze. What could I do? My world fell about my ears. Even final expiation, final triumph, it seemed, was denied me. Certain things are not for me. In this moment of anguish and despair my first thought was for my wife. Where had she gone? I went out to seek her. When I returned, after a fruitless errand, I discovered that she and Winston had come back to seek me. Smiling through our tears, we embraced. So it was Christmas after all for us. And, with lightened heart, made heavy only by my wrestling with the Lord, we went to the races on Boxing Day, yesterday. We did not gamble. It is against our principles. The inspectors from the Audit Department sent word today that they would not, after all, come.

WILLIAM TREVOR
In at the Birth

ONCE upon a time there lived in a remote London suburb an elderly lady called Miss Efoss. Miss Efoss was a spry person, and for as long as she could control the issue she was determined to remain so. She attended the cinema and the theatre with regularity; she read at length; and she preferred the company of men and women forty years her junior. Once a year Miss Efoss still visited Athens and always on such visits she wondered why she had never settled in Greece: now, she felt, it was rather too late to make a change; in any case, she enjoyed London.

In her lifetime, nothing had passed Miss Efoss by. She had loved and been loved. She had once, even, given birth to a child. For a year or two she had known the ups and downs of early family life, although the actual legality of marriage had somehow been overlooked. Miss Efoss's baby died during a sharp attack of pneumonia; and shortly afterwards the child's father packed a suitcase one night. He said goodbye quite kindly to Miss Efoss, but she never saw him again.

In retrospect, Miss Efoss considered that she had run the gamut of human emotions. She settled down to the lively superficiality of the everyday existence she had mapped for herself. She was quite content with it. And she hardly noticed it when the Dutts entered her life.

It was Mr. Dutt who telephoned. He said: 'Ah, Miss Efoss, I wonder if you can help us. We have heard that occasionally you baby-sit. We have scoured the neighbourhood for a reliable baby-sitter. Would you be interested, Miss Efoss, in giving us a try?'

'But who are you?' said Miss Efoss. 'I don't even know you. What is your name to begin with?'

'Dutt,' said Mr. Dutt. 'We live only a couple of hundred yards from you. I think you would find it convenient.'

'Well——'

'Miss Efoss, come and see us. Come and have a drink. If you like the look of us perhaps we can arrange something. If not, we shan't be in the least offended.'

'That is very kind of you, Mr. Dutt. If you give me your address and a time I'll certainly call. In fact, I shall be delighted to do so.'

'Good, good.' And Mr. Dutt gave Miss Efoss the details, which she noted in her diary.

Mr. and Mrs. Dutt looked alike. They were small and thin with faces like greyhounds. 'We have had such difficulty in finding someone suitable to sit for us,' Mrs. Dutt said. 'All these young girls, Miss Efoss, scarcely inspire confidence.'

'We are a nervous pair, Miss Efoss,' Mr. Dutt said, laughing gently as he handed her a glass of sherry. 'We are a nervous pair and that's the truth of it.'

'There is only Mickey, you see,' explained his wife. 'I suppose we worry a bit. Though we try not to spoil him.'

Miss Efoss nodded. 'An only child is sometimes a problem.'

The Dutts agreed, staring intently at Miss Efoss, as though recognizing in her some profound quality.

'We have, as you see, the television,' Mr. Dutt remarked. 'You would not be lonely here of an evening. The radio as well. Both are simple to operate and are excellent performers.'

'And Mickey has never woken up,' said Mrs. Dutt. 'Our system is to leave our telephone behind. Thus you may easily contact us.'

'Ha, ha, ha.' Mr. Dutt was laughing. His tiny face was screwed into an unusual shape, the skin drawn tightly over his gleaming cheek-bones.

'What an amusing thing to say, Beryl! My wife is fond of a joke, Miss Efoss.'

Unaware that a joke had been made, Miss Efoss smiled.

'It would be odd if we did *not* leave our telephone behind,' Mr. Dutt went on. 'We leave the telephone *number* behind, Beryl. The telephone number of the house where we are dining. You would be surprised, Miss Efoss, to receive guests who carried with them their telephone receiver. Eh?'

'It would certainly be unusual.'

'"We have brought our own telephone, since we do not care to use another." Or: "We have brought our telephone in case anyone telephones us while we are here." Miss Efoss, will you tell me something?'

'If I can, Mr. Dutt.'

'Miss Efoss, have you ever looked up the word *joke* in the *Encyclopaedia Britannica*?'

'I don't think I have.'

'You would find it rewarding. We have the full *Encyclopaedia* here, you know. It is always at your service.'

'How kind of you.'

'I will not tell you now what the *Encyclopaedia* says on the subject. I will leave you to while away a minute or two with it. I do not think you'll find it a wasted effort.'

'I'm sure I won't.'

'My husband is a great devotee of the *Encyclopaedia*,' Mrs. Dutt said. 'He spends much of his time with it.'

'It is not always pleasure,' Mr. Dutt said. 'The accumulation of information on many subjects is part of my work.'

'Your work, Mr. Dutt?'

'Like many, nowadays, Miss Efoss, my husband works for his living.'

'You have some interesting job, Mr. Dutt?'

'Interesting, eh? Yes, I suppose it is interesting. More than that I cannot reveal. That is so, eh, Beryl?'

'My husband is on the secret list. He is forbidden to speak casually about his work. Alas, even to someone to whom we trust our child. It's a paradox, isn't it?'

'I quite understand. Naturally, Mr. Dutt's work is no affair of mine.'

'To speak lightly about it would mean marching orders for me,' Mr. Dutt said. 'No offence, I hope?'

'Of course not.'

'Sometimes people take offence. We have had some unhappy occasions, eh, Beryl?'

'People do not always understand what it means to be on the secret list, Miss Efoss. So little is taken seriously nowadays.'

Mr. Dutt hovered over Miss Efoss with his sherry decanter. He filled her glass and his wife's. He said:

'Well, Miss Efoss, what do you think of us? Can you accept the occasional evening in this room, watching our television and listening for the cry of our child?'

'Naturally, Miss Efoss, there would always be supper,' Mrs. Dutt said.

'With sherry before and brandy to finish with,' Mr. Dutt added.

'You are very generous. I can quite easily have something before I arrive.'

'No, no, no. It is out of the question. My wife is a good cook. And
I can be relied upon to keep the decanters brimming.'

'You have made it all so pleasant I am left with no option. I
should be delighted to help you out when I can manage it.'

Miss Efoss finished her sherry and rose. The Dutts rose also,
smiling benignly at their satisfactory visitor.

'Well then,' Mr. Dutt said in the hall, 'would Tuesday evening
be a time you could arrange, Miss Efoss? We are bidden to dine
with friends near by.'

'Tuesday? Yes, I think Tuesday is all right. About seven?'

Mrs. Dutt held out her hand. 'Seven would be admirable. Till
then, Miss Efoss.'

On Tuesday Mr. Dutt opened the door to Miss Efoss and led her to
the sitting-room. His wife, he explained, was still dressing. Making
conversation as he poured Miss Efoss a drink, he said:

'I married my wife when she was on the point of entering a
convent, Miss Efoss. What d'you think of that?'

'Well,' Miss Efoss said, settling herself comfortably before the
cosy-stove, 'it is hard to know what to say, Mr. Dutt. I am surprised,
I suppose.'

'Most people are surprised. I often wonder if I did the right thing.
Beryl would have made a fine nun. What d'you think?'

'I'm sure you both knew what you were doing at the time. It is
equally certain that Mrs. Dutt would have been a fine nun.'

'She had chosen a particularly severe order. That's just like Beryl,
isn't it?'

'I hardly know Mrs. Dutt. But if it is like her to have made that
choice, I can well believe it.'

'You see my wife as a serious person, Miss Efoss? Is that what
you mean?'

'In the short time I have known her, yes I think I do. Yet you
also say she relishes a joke.'

'A joke, Miss Efoss?'

'So you remarked the other evening. In relation to a slip in her
speech.'

'Ah yes. How right you are. You must forgive me if my memory
is often faulty. My work is wearing.'

Mrs. Dutt, gaily attired, entered the room. 'Here, Miss Efoss,'
she said, proffering a piece of paper, 'is the telephone number of the

house we are going to. If Mickey makes a sound please ring us up.
I will immediately return.'

'Oh but I'm sure that's not necessary. It would be a pity to spoil
your evening so. I could at least attempt to comfort him.'

'I would prefer the other arrangement. Mickey does not take
easily to strangers. His room is at the top of the house, but please
do not enter it. Were he to wake suddenly and catch sight of you he
might be extremely frightened. He is quite a nervous child. At the
slightest untoward sound do not hesitate to telephone.'

'As you wish it, Mrs. Dutt. I only suggested——'

'Experience has taught me, Miss Efoss, what is best. I have laid
you a tray in the kitchen. Everything is cold, but quite nice, I
think.'

'Thank you.'

'Then we will be away. We should be back by eleven-fifteen.'

'Do have a good evening.'

The Dutts said they intended to have a good evening, whispered
for a moment together in the hall, and were on their way. Miss
Efoss looked critically about her.

The room was of an ordinary kind. Utrillo prints on plain grey
walls. Yellowish curtains, yellowish chair-covers, a few pieces of
simple furniture on a thick grey carpet. It was warm, the sherry was
good and Miss Efoss was comfortable. It was pleasant, she reflected,
to have a change of scene without the obligation of conversation. In
a few moments, she carried her supper tray from the kitchen to the
fire. As good as his word, Mr. Dutt had left some brandy. Miss
Efoss began to think the Dutts were quite a find.

She had dropped off to sleep when they returned. Fortunately,
she heard them in the hall and had time to compose herself.

'All well?' Mrs. Dutt asked.

'Not a sound.'

'Well, I'd better change him right away. Thank you so much,
Miss Efoss.'

'Thank you. I have spent a very pleasant evening.'

'I'll drive you back,' Mr. Dutt offered. 'The car is still warm.'

In the car Mr. Dutt said: 'A child is a great comfort. Mickey is a
real joy for us. And company for Beryl. The days hang heavy when
one is alone all day.'

'Yes, a child is a comfort.'

'Perhaps you think we are too careful and fussing about Mickey?'

'Oh no, it's better than erring in the other direction.'
'It is only because we are so grateful.'
'Of course.'
'We have much to be thankful for.'
'I'm sure you deserve it all.'

Mr. Dutt had become quite maudlin by the time he delivered Miss Efoss at her flat. She wondered if he was drunk. He pressed her hand warmly and announced that he looked forward to their next meeting. 'Any time,' Miss Efoss said as she stepped from the car. 'Just ring me up. I am often free.'

After that, Miss Efoss baby-sat for the Dutts many times. They became more and more friendly towards her. They left her little bowls of chocolates and drew her attention to articles in magazines that they believed might be of interest to her. Mr. Dutt suggested further words she might care to look up in the *Encyclopaedia* and Mrs. Dutt wrote out several of her recipes.

One night, just as she was leaving, Miss Efoss said: 'You know, I think it might be a good idea for me to meet Mickey some time. Perhaps I could come in the daytime once. Then I would no longer be a stranger and could comfort him if he woke.'

'But he *doesn't* wake, Miss Efoss. He has never woken, has he? You have never had to telephone us.'

'No. That is true. But now that I have got to know you, I would like to know him as well.'

The Dutts took the compliment, smiling at one another and at Miss Efoss. Mr. Dutt said: 'It is kind of you to speak like this, Miss Efoss. But Mickey is rather scared of strangers. Just at present at any rate, if you do not mind.'

'Of course not, Mr. Dutt.'

'I fear he is a nervous child,' Mrs. Dutt said. 'Our present arrangement is carefully devised.'

'I'm sorry,' Miss Efoss said.

'No need. No need. Let us all have a final brandy,' Mr. Dutt said cheerfully.

But Miss Efoss was sorry, for she feared she had said something out of place. And then for a week or so she was worried whenever she thought of the Dutts. She felt they were mistaken in their attitude about their child; and she felt equally unable to advise them. It was not her place to speak any further on the subject, yet she was sure that to keep the child away from people just because he was nervous of them was wrong. It sounded as though there was a root to the trouble somewhere, and it sounded as though the Dutts had not attempted to discover it. She continued to baby-sit for them about once every ten days and she held her peace. Then, quite unexpectedly, something happened that puzzled Miss Efoss very much indeed.

It happened at a party given by some friends of hers. She was talking about nothing in particular to an elderly man called Summerfield. She had known him for some years but whenever they met, as on this occasion, they found themselves with little to say beyond the initial courteous greetings. Thinking that a more direct approach might yield something of interest, Miss Efoss, after the familiar lengthy silence, said: 'How are you coping with the advancing years, Mr. Summerfield? I feel I can ask you, since it is a coping I have to take in my own stride.'

'Well, well, I think I am doing well enough. My life is simple since my wife died, but there is little I complain of.'

'Loneliness is a thing that sometimes strikes at us. I find one must regard it as the toothache or similar ailment, and seek a cure.'

'Ah yes. I'm often a trifle alone.'

'I baby-sit, you know. Have you ever thought of it? Do not shy off because you are a man. A responsible person is all that is required.'

'I haven't thought of baby-sitting. Not ever I think. Though I like babies and always have done.'

'I used to do quite a lot. Now I have only the Dutts, but I go there very often. I enjoy my evenings. I like to see the TV now and again and other people's houses are interesting.'

'I know the Dutts,' said Mr. Summerfield. 'You mean the Dutts in Raeburn Road? A small weedy couple?'

'They live in Raeburn Road, certainly. They are small too, but you are unkind to call them weedy.'

'I don't particularly mean it unkindly. I have known Dutt a long time. One takes liberties, I suppose, in describing people.'

'Mr. Dutt is an interesting person. He holds some responsible position of intriguing secrecy.'

'Dutt? 25 Raeburn Road? The man is a chartered accountant.'

'I feel sure you are mistaken——'

'I cannot be mistaken. The man was once my colleague. In a very junior capacity.'

'Oh, well . . . then I must be mistaken.'

'What surprises me is that you say you baby-sit for the Dutts. I think you must be mistaken about that too.'

'Oh no, I am completely certain about that. It is for that reason that I know them at all.'

'I cannot help being surprised. Because, Miss Efoss—and of this I am certain—the Dutts have no children.'

Miss Efoss had heard of the fantasy world with which people, as they grow old, surround themselves. Yet she could not have entirely invented the Dutts in this way because Mr. Summerfield had readily agreed about their existence. Was it then for some other reason that she visited them? Did she, as soon as she entered their house, become so confused in her mind that she afterwards forgot the real purpose of her presence? Had they hired her in some other capacity altogether? A capacity she was so ashamed of that she had invented, even for herself, the euphemism of baby-sitting? Had she, she wondered, become some kind of servant to these people— imagining the warm comfortable room, the sherry, the chocolates, the brandy?

'We should be back by eleven, Miss Efoss. Here is the telephone number.' Mrs. Dutt smiled at her and a moment later the front door banged gently behind her.

It is all quite real, Miss Efoss thought. There is the sherry. There is the television set. In the kitchen on a tray I shall find my supper. It is all quite real: it is old Mr. Summerfield who is wandering in his mind. It was only when she had finished her supper that she had the idea of establishing her role beyond question. All she had to do was to go upstairs and peep at the child. She knew how to be quiet: there was no danger of waking him.

The first room she entered was full of suitcases and cardboard boxes. In the second she heard breathing and knew she was right. She snapped on the light and looked around her. It was brightly painted, with a wallpaper with elves on it. There was a rocking horse and a great pile of coloured bricks. In one of the far corners there was a large cot. It was very large and very high and it contained the sleeping figure of a very old man.

When the Dutts returned Miss Efoss said nothing. She was frightened and she didn't quite know why she was frightened. She was glad when she was back in her flat. The next day she telephoned her niece in Devon and asked if she might come down and stay for a bit.

Miss Efoss spoke to nobody about the Dutts. She gathered her strength in the country and returned to London at the end of a fortnight feeling refreshed and rational. She wrote a note to the Dutts saying she had decided to baby-sit no more. She gave no reason, but she said she hoped they would understand. Then, as best she could, she tried to forget all about them.

A year passed and then, one grey cold Sunday afternoon, Miss Efoss saw the Dutts in one of the local parks. They were sitting on a bench, huddled close together and seeming miserable. For a reason that she was afterwards unable to fathom Miss Efoss approached them.

'Good afternoon.'

The Dutts looked up at her, their thin, pale faces unsmiling and unhappy.

'Hello, Miss Efoss,' Mr. Dutt said. 'We haven't seen you for a long time, have we? How are you this nasty weather?'

'Quite well, thank you. And you? And Mrs. Dutt?'

Mr. Dutt rose and drew Miss Efoss a few yards away from his wife. 'Beryl has taken it badly,' he said. 'Mickey died. Beryl has not been herself since. You understand how it is?'

'Oh, I am sorry.'

'I try to cheer her up, but I'm afraid my efforts are all in vain. I have taken it hard myself too. Which doesn't make anything any easier.'

'I don't know what to say, Mr. Dutt. It's a great sadness for both of you.'

Mr. Dutt took Miss Efoss's arm and led her back to the seat. 'I have told Miss Efoss,' he said to his wife. Mrs. Dutt nodded.

'I'm very sorry,' Miss Efoss said again.

The Dutts looked at her, their sad, intent eyes filled with a pathetic desire for comfort. There was something almost hypnotic about them.

'I must go,' Miss Efoss said. 'Goodbye.'

'They have all died, Miss Efoss,' Mr. Dutt said. 'One by one they have all died.'

Miss Efoss paused in her retreat. She could think of nothing to say except that she was sorry.

'We are childless again,' Mr. Dutt went on. 'It is almost

unbearable to be childless again. We are so fond of them and here we are, not knowing what to do on a Sunday afternoon because we are a childless couple. The human frame, Miss Efoss, is not built to carry such misfortunes.'

'It is callous of me to say so, Mr. Dutt, but the human frame is pretty resilient. It does not seem so at times like this I know, but you will find it is so in retrospect.'

'You are a wise woman, Miss Efoss, but, as you say, it is hard to accept wisdom at a moment like this. We have lost so many over the years. They are given to us and then abruptly they are taken away. It is difficult to understand God's infinite cruelty.'

'Goodbye, Mr. Dutt. Goodbye, Mrs. Dutt.'

They did not reply, and Miss Efoss walked quickly away.

Miss Efoss began to feel older. She walked with a stick; she found the cinema tired her eyes; she read less and discovered that she was bored by the effort of sustaining long conversations. She accepted each change quite philosophically, pleased that she could do so. She found too that there were compensations; she enjoyed, more and more, thinking about the past. Quite vividly, she re-lived the parts she wished to re-live. Unlike life itself, it was pleasant to be able to pick and choose.

Again by accident, she met Mr. Dutt. She was having tea one afternoon in a quiet, old-fashioned teashop, not at all the kind of place she would have associated with Mr. Dutt. Yet there he was, standing in front of her. 'Hello, Miss Efoss,' he said.

'Why, Mr. Dutt. How are you? How is your wife? It is some time since we met.'

Mr. Dutt sat down. He ordered some tea and then he leaned forward and stared at Miss Efoss. She wondered what he was thinking about: he had the air of someone who through politeness, makes the most of a moment but whose mind is busily occupied elsewhere. As he looked at her, his face suddenly cleared. He smiled, and when he spoke he seemed to be entirely present.

'I have great news, Miss Efoss. We are both so happy about it. Miss Efoss, Beryl is expecting a child.'

Miss Efoss blinked a little. She spread some jam on her toast and said:

'Oh, I'm so glad. How delightful for you both! Mrs. Dutt will be pleased. When is it—when is it due?'

'Quite soon. Quite soon.' Mr. Dutt beamed. 'Naturally Beryl is beside herself with joy. She is busy preparing all day.'

'There is a lot to see to on these occasions.'

'Indeed there is. Beryl is knitting like a mad thing. It seems as though she can't do enough.'

'It is the biggest event in a woman's life, Mr. Dutt.'

'And often in a man's, Miss Efoss.'

'Yes, indeed.'

'We have quite recovered our good spirits.'

'I'm glad of that. You were so sadly low when last I saw you.'

'You gave us some wise words. You were more comfort than you think, you know.'

'Oh, I was inadequate. I always am with sorrow.'

'No, no. Beryl said so afterwards. It was a happy chance to have met you so.'

'Thank you, Mr. Dutt.'

'It's not easy always to accept adversity. You helped us on our way. We shall always be grateful.'

'It is kind of you to say so.'

'The longing for a child is a strange force. To attend to its needs, to give it comfort and love—I suppose there is that in all of us. There is a streak of simple generosity that we do not easily understand.'

'The older I become, Mr. Dutt, the more I realize that one understands very little. I believe one is meant not to understand. The best things are complex and mysterious. And must remain so.'

'How right you are! It is often what I say to Beryl. I shall be glad to report that you confirm my thinking.'

'On my part it is instinct rather than thinking.'

'The line between the two is less acute than many would have us believe.'

'Yes, I suppose it is.'

'Miss Efoss, may I do one thing for you?'

'What is that?'

'It is a small thing but would give me pleasure. May I pay for your tea? Beryl will be pleased if you allow me to.'

Miss Efoss laughed. 'Yes, Mr. Dutt, you may pay for my tea.' and it was as she spoke this simple sentence that it dawned upon Miss Efoss just what it was she had to do.

Miss Efoss began to sell her belongings. She sold them in many directions, keeping back only a few which she wished to give away. It took her a long time, for there was much to see to. She wrote down long lists of details, finding this method the best for arranging things in her mind. She was sorry to see the familiar objects go, yet she knew that to be sentimental about them was absurd. It was for other people now to develop a sentiment for them; and she knew that the fresh associations they would in time take on would be, in the long run, as false as hers.

Her flat became bare and cheerless. In the end there was nothing left except the property of the landlord. She wrote to him, terminating her tenancy.

The Dutts were watching the television when Miss Efoss arrived. Mr. Dutt turned down the sound and went to open the door. He smiled without speaking and brought her into the sitting-room.

'Welcome, Miss Efoss,' Mrs. Dutt said. 'We've been expecting you.'

Miss Efoss carried a small suitcase. She said: 'Your baby, Mrs. Dutt. When is your baby due? I do hope I am in time.'

'Perfect, Miss Efoss, perfect,' said Mr. Dutt. 'Beryl's child is due this very night.'

The pictures flashed silently, eerily, on the television screen. A man dressed as a pirate was stroking the head of a parrot.

Miss Efoss did not sit down. 'I am rather tired,' she said. 'Do you mind if I go straight upstairs?'

'Dear Miss Efoss, please do.' Mrs. Dutt smiled at her. 'You know your way, don't you?'

'Yes,' Miss Efoss said. 'I know my way.'

JEAN RHYS
Tigers are Better-Looking

'MEIN LIEB, Mon Cher, My Dear, Amigo,' the letter began.

I'm off. I've been wanting to go for some time, as I'm sure you know, but was waiting for the moment when I had the courage to step out into the cold world again. Didn't feel like a farewell scene.

Apart from much that it is *better* not to go into, you haven't any idea how sick I am of all the phoney talk about Communism—and the phoney talk of the other lot too, if it comes to that. You people are exactly alike, whatever you call yourselves—Untouchable. Indispensable is the motto, and you'd pine to death if you hadn't someone to look down on and insult. I got the feeling that I was surrounded by a pack of timid tigers waiting to spring the moment anybody is in trouble or hasn't any money. *But tigers are better-looking, aren't they?*

I'm taking the coach to Plymouth. I have my plans.

I came to London with high hopes, but all I got out of it was a broken leg and enough sneers to last me for the next thirty years if I live so long, which may God forbid.

Don't think I'll forget how kind you were after my accident—having me to stay with you and all that. But assez means enough.

I've drunk the milk in the refrigerator. I was thirsty after that party last night, though if you call that a party I call it a wake. Besides, I know how you dislike the stuff (Freud! Bow-wow-wow!!) So you'll have to have your tea straight, my dear.

Goodbye. I'll write you again when times are better.

HANS

There was a postscript:

Mind you write a swell article today, you tame grey mare.

Mr. Severn sighed. He had always known Hans would hop it sooner or later, so why this taste in his mouth, as if he had eaten dust?

A swell article.

The band in the Embankment Gardens played. It's the same old song once again. It's the same old tender refrain. *As the carriages came into sight some of the crowd cheered and a fat man said he couldn't see and he was going to climb a lamp-post. The figures in the carriages bowed from right to left—victims bowed to victimized. The bloodless sacrifice was being exhibited, the reminder that somewhere the sun is shining, even if it doesn't shine on everybody.*

"E looked just like a waxwork, didn't 'e?" a woman said with satisfaction. . . .

No, that would never do.

He looked out of the window at the Lunch Edition placards outside the newspaper shop opposite. 'JUBILEE PICTURES—PICTURES—PICTURES' and 'HEAT WAVE COMING'.

The flat over the shop was occupied by a raffish middle-aged woman. But today her lace-curtained windows, usually not unfriendly, added to his feeling of desolation. So did the words 'PICTURES—PICTURES—PICTURES'.

By six o'clock the floor was covered with newspapers and crumpled, discarded starts of the article which he wrote every week for an Australian paper.

He couldn't get the swing of it. The swing's the thing, as everybody knows—otherwise the cadence of the sentence. Once into it, and he could go ahead like an old horse trotting, saying anything that anybody liked.

'The tame grey mare,' he thought. Then he took up one of the newspapers and, because he had the statistical mania, began to count the advertisements. Two remedies for constipation, three for wind and stomach pains, three face creams, one skin food, one cruise to Morocco. At the end of the personal column, in small print, 'I will slay in the day of My wrath and spare not, saith the Lord God.' Who pays to put these things in anyway, who pays?

'This perpetual covert threat,' he thought. 'Everything's based on it. Disgusting. What Will They Say? And down at the bottom of the page you see what will happen to you if you don't toe the line. You will be slain and not spared. Threats and mockery, mockery and threats. . . .' And desolation, desertion, and crumpled newspapers in the room.

The only comfort allowed was the money which would buy the warm glow of drink before eating, the Jubliee laughter afterwards. Jubilant—Jubilee—Joy. . . . Words whirled round in his head, but he could not make them take shape.

'If you won't, you bloody well won't,' he said to his typewriter before he rushed down the stairs, counting the steps as he went.

After two double whiskies at his usual pub, time, which had dragged so drearily all day, began to move faster, began to gallop.

At half-past eleven Mr. Severn was walking up and down Wardour Street between two young women. The things one does on the rebound.

He knew one of them fairly well—the fatter one. She was often at the pub and he liked talking to her, and sometimes stood her drinks because she was good-natured and never made him feel nervous. That was her secret. If fair was fair, it would be her epitaph: 'I have never made anybody feel nervous—on purpose.' Doomed, of course, for that very reason. But pleasant to talk to and, usually, to look at. Her name was Maidie—Maidie Richards.

He had never seen the other girl before. She was very young and fresh, with a really glittering smile and an accent he didn't quite recognize. She was called Heather Something-or-other. In the noisy pub he thought she said Hedda. 'What an unusual name!' he had remarked. 'I said Heather, not Hedda. Hedda! I wouldn't be seen dead with a name like that.' She was sharp, bright, self-confident— nothing flabby there. It was she who had suggested this final drink.

The girls argued. They each had an arm in one of Mr. Severn's, and they argued across him. They got to Shaftesbury Avenue, turned and walked back.

'I tell you the place is in this street,' Heather said. 'The "Jim-Jam"—haven't you ever heard of it?'

'Are you sure?' Mr. Severn asked.

'Of course I'm sure. It's on the left-hand side. We've missed it somehow.'

'Well, I'm sick of walking up and down looking for it,' Maidie said. 'It's a lousy hole anyway. I don't particularly want to go, do you?'

'Not particularly,' said Mr. Severn.

'There it is,' Heather said. 'We've passed it twice. It's changed its name, that's what.'

They went up a narrow stone staircase and on the first landing a man with a yellow face appeared from behind drawn curtains and glared at them. Heather smiled. 'Good evening, Mr. Johnson. I've brought two friends along.'

'Three of you? That'll be fifteen shillings.'

'I thought it was half a crown entrance,' Maidie said so aggressively that Mr. Johnson looked at her with surprise and explained, 'This is a special night.'

'The orchestra's playing rotten, anyway,' Maidie remarked when they got into the room.

An elderly woman wearing steel-rimmed glasses was serving behind the bar. The mulatto who was playing the saxophone leaned forward and whooped.

'They play so rotten,' Maidie said, when the party was seated at a table against the wall, 'that you'd think they were doing it on purpose.'

'Oh stop grumbling,' Heather said. 'Other people don't agree with you. The place is packed every night. Besides, why should they play well. What's the difference?'

'Ah-ha,' Mr. Severn said.

'There isn't any difference if you ask me. It's all a lot of talk.'

'Quite right. All an illusion,' Mr. Severn agreed. 'A bottle of ginger ale,' he said to the waiter.

Heather said, 'We'll have to have a bottle of whisky. You don't mind, do you, dear?'

'Don't worry, child, don't worry,' Mr. Severn said. 'It was only my little joke . . . a bottle of whisky,' he told the waiter.

'Will you pay now, if you please?' the waiter asked when he brought the bottle.

'What a price!' Maidie said, frowning boldly at the waiter. 'Never mind, by the time I've had a few goes at this I ought to have forgotten my troubles.'

Heather pinched up her lips. 'Very little for me.'

'Well, it's going to be drunk,' Mr. Severn said. 'Play *Dinah*,' he shouted at the orchestra.

The saxophonist glanced at him and tittered. Nobody else took any notice.

'Sit down and have a drink, won't you?' Heather clutched at Mr. Johnson's sleeve as he passed the table, but he answered loftily, 'Sorry, I'm afraid I can't just now,' and passed on.

'People are funny about drinking,' Maidie remarked. 'They get you to buy as much as they can and then afterwards they laugh at you behind your back for buying it. But on the other hand, if you try to get out of buying it, they're damned rude. Damned rude, they

can be. I went into a place the other night where they have music—
the International Café, they call it. I had a whisky and I drank it a
bit quick because I was thirsty and feeling down and so on. Then I
thought I'd like to listen to the music—they don't play so badly
there because they say they're Hungarians—and a waiter came
along, yelling "Last drinks". "Can I have some water?" I said. "I'm
not here to serve you with water," he said. "This isn't a place to
drink water in," he said, just like that. So loud! Everybody was
staring at me.'

'Well, what do you expect?' Heather said. 'Asking for water! You
haven't got any sense. No more for me, thank you.' She put her
hand over her glass.

'Don't you trust me?' Mr. Severn asked, leering.

'I don't trust anybody. For why? Because I don't want to be let
down, that's why.'

'Sophisticated, she is,' said Maidie.

'I'd rather be sophisticated than a damned pushover like you,'
Heather retorted. 'You don't mind if I go and talk to some friends
over there, do you, dear?'

'Admirable.' Mr. Severn watched her cross the room. 'Admirable.
Disdainful debonair and with a touch of the tarbrush too, or I'm
much mistaken. Just my type. One of my types. Why is it that she
isn't quite—Now, why?' He took a yellow pencil out of his pocket
and began to draw on the tablecloth.

*Pictures, pictures, pictures. . . . Faces, faces, faces. . . . Like hyaenas, like
swine, like goats, like apes, like parrots. But not tigers, because tigers are
better-looking, aren't they? as Hans says.*

Maidie was saying, 'They've got an awfully nice "Ladies" here. I've
been having a chat with the woman; she's a friend of mine. The
window was open and the street looked so cool and peaceful. That's
why I've been so long.'

'London is getting very odd, isn't it?' Mr. Severn said in a thick
voice. 'Do you see that tall female over there, the one in the backless
evening gown? Of course, I've got my own theory about backless
evening gowns, but this isn't the moment to tell you of it. Well, that
sweetiepie's got to be at Brixton tomorrow morning at a quarter-
past nine to give a music lesson. And her greatest ambition is to get
a job as stewardess on a line running to South Africa.'

'Well, what's wrong with that?' Maidie said.

'Nothing—I just thought it was a bit mixed. Never mind. And do you see that couple over there at the bar? The lovely dark brown couple. Well, I went over to have a change of drinks and got into conversation with them. I rather palled up with the man, so I asked them to come and see me one day. When I gave them my address the girl said at once. "Is that in Mayfair?" "Good Lord, no; it's in the darkest, dingiest Bloomsbury." "I didn't come to London to go to the slums," she said with the most perfect British accent, high, sharp, clear and shattering. Then she turned her back on me and hauled the man off to the other end of the bar.'

'Girls always cotton on to things quicker,' Maidie asserted.

'The social climate of a place?' said Mr. Severn. 'Yes, I suppose they do. But some men aren't so slow either. Well, well, tigers are better-looking, aren't they?'

'You haven't been doing too badly with the whisky, dear, have you?' Maidie said rather uneasily. 'What's all this about tigers?'

Mr. Severn again addressed the orchestra in a loud voice. 'Play *Dinah*. I hate that bloody tune you keep playing. It's always the same one too. You can't fool me. Play *Dinah, is there anyone finer?* That's a good old tune.'

'I shouldn't shout so loud,' Maidie said. 'They don't like it here if you shout. Don't you see the way Johnson's looking at you?'

'Let him look.'

'Oh, do shut up. He's sending the waiter to us now.'

'Obscene drawings on the tablecloths are not allowed here,' the waiter said as he approached.

'Go to hell,' Mr. Severn said. 'What obscene drawings?'

Maidie nudged him and shook her head violently.

The waiter removed the tablecloth and brought a clean one. He pursed his lips up as he spread it and looked severely at Mr. Severn. 'No drawings of any description on tablecloths are allowed here,' he said.

'I'll draw as much as I like,' Mr. Severn said defiantly. And the next thing he knew two men had him by the collar and were pushing him towards the door.

'You let him alone,' said Maidie. 'He hasn't done anything. You are a lot of sugars.'

'Gently, gently,' said Mr. Johnson, perspiring. 'What do you want to be so rough for? I'm always telling you to do it quietly.'

As he was being hauled past the bar, Mr. Severn saw Heather,

her eyes beady with disapproval, her plump face lengthened into something twice the size of life. He made a hideous grimace at her.

'My Lawd,' she said, and averted her eyes. 'My Lawd!'

Only four men pushed them down the stairs, but when they were out in the street it looked more like fourteen, and all howling and booing. 'Now, who are all these people?' Mr. Severn thought. Then someone hit him. The man who had hit him was exactly like the waiter who had changed the tablecloth. Mr. Severn hit back as hard as he could and the waiter, if he was the waiter, staggered against the wall and toppled slowly to the ground. 'I've knocked him down,' Mr. Severn thought. 'Knocked him down!'

'Tally-ho!' he yelled in a high voice. 'What price the tame grey mare?'

The waiter got up, hesitated, thought better of it, turned round and hit Maidie instead.

'Shut up, you bloody basket,' somebody said when she began to swear, and kicked her. Three men seized Mr. Severn, ran him off the pavement and sprawled him in the middle of Wardour Street. He lay there, feeling sick, listening to Maidie. The lid was properly off there.

'Yah!' the crowd round her jeered. 'Boo!' Then it opened up, servile and respectful, to let two policemen pass.

'You big blanks,' Maidie yelled defiantly. 'You something somethings. I wasn't doing anything. That man knocked me down. How much does Johnson pay you every week for this?'

Mr. Severn got up, still feeling very sick. He heard a voice: 'That's 'em. That's the chap. That 'im what started everything.' Two policemen took him by the arms and marched him along. Maidie, also between two policemen, walked in front, weeping. As they passed through Piccadilly Circus, empty and desolate, she wailed, 'I've lost my shoe. I must stop and pick it up. I can't walk without it.'

The older policeman seemed to want to force her on, but the younger one stopped, picked the shoe up and gave it to her with a grin.

'What's she want to cry for?' Mr. Severn thought. He shouted 'Hoi, Maidie, cheer up. Cheer up, Maidie.'

'None of that,' one of his policemen said.

But when they arrived at the police station she had stopped

crying, he was glad to see. She powdered her face and began to argue with the sergeant behind the desk.

'You want to see a doctor, do you?' the sergeant said.

'I certainly do. It's a disgrace, a perfect disgrace.'

'And do you also want to see a doctor?' the sergeant asked, coldly polite, glancing at Mr. Severn.

'Why not?' Mr. Severn answered.

Maidie powdered her face again and shouted, 'God save Ireland. To hell with all dirty sneaks and Comic Cuts and what-have-yous.'

'That was my father speaking,' she said over her shoulder as she was led off.

As soon as Mr. Severn was locked into a cell he lay down on the bunk and went to sleep. When they woke him to see the doctor he was cold sober.

'What time is it?' the doctor asked. With a clock over his head, the old fool!

Mr. Severn answered coldly 'A quarter-past four.'

'Walk straight ahead. Shut your eyes and stand on one leg,' the doctor demanded, and the policeman watching this performance sneered vaguely, like schoolboys when the master baits an unpopular one.

When he got back to his cell Mr. Severn could not sleep. He lay down, stared at the lavatory seat and thought of the black eye he would have in the morning. Words and meaningless phrases still whirled tormentingly round in his head.

He read the inscriptions on the grim walls. 'Be sure your sins will find you out. B. Lewis.' 'Anne is a fine girl, one of the best, and I don't care who knows it. (Signed) Charlie S.' Somebody else had written up, 'Lord, save me; I perish,' and underneath, 'SOS, SOS, SOS (Signed) G.R.'

'Appropriate,' Mr. Severn thought, took his pencil from his pocket, wrote, 'SOS, SOS, SOS (Signed) N.S.', and dated it.

Then he lay down with his face to the wall and saw, on a level with his eyes, the words, 'I died waiting'.

Sitting in the prison van before it started, he heard somebody whistling *The Londonderry Air* and a girl talking and joking with the policemen. She had a deep, soft voice. The appropriate adjective came at once into his mind—a sexy voice.

'Sex, sexy,' he thought. 'Ridiculous word! What a giveaway!'

'What is wanted,' he decided, 'is a brand-new lot of words, words that will mean something. The only word that means anything now is death—and then it has to be my death. Your death doesn't mean much.'

The girl said, 'Ah, if I was a bird and had wings, I could fly away, couldn't I?'

'Might get shot as you went,' one of the policemen answered.

'This must be a dream,' Mr. Severn thought. He listened for Maidie's voice, but there was not a sound of her. Then the van started.

It seemed a long way to Bow Street. As soon as they got out of the van he saw Maidie, looking as if she had spent the whole night in tears. She put her hand up to her hair apologetically.

'They took my handbag away. It's awful.'

'I wish it had been Heather,' Mr. Severn thought. He tried to smile kindly.

'It'll soon be over now, we've only got to plead guilty.'

And it was over very quickly. The magistrate hardly looked at them, but for reasons of his own he fined them each thirty shillings, which entailed telephoning to a friend, getting the money sent by special messenger and an interminable wait.

It was half-past twelve when they were outside in Bow Street. Maidie stood hesitating, looking worse than ever in the yellowish, livid light. Mr. Severn hailed a taxi and offered to take her home. It was the least he could do, he told himself. Also the most.

'Oh, your poor eye!' Maidie said. 'Does it hurt?'

'Not at all now. I feel astonishingly well. It must have been good whisky.'

She stared into the cracked mirror of her handbag.

'And don't I look terrible too? But it's no use; I can't do anything with my face when it's as bad as this.'

'I'm sorry.'

'Oh, well,' she said, 'I was feeling pretty bad on account of the way that chap knocked me down and kicked me, and afterwards on account of the way the doctor asked me my age. "This woman's very drunk," he said. But I wasn't, was I? . . . Well, and when I got back into the cell, the first thing I saw was my own name written up. My Christ, it did give me a turn! Gladys Reilly—that's my real name. Maidie Richards is only what I call myself. There it was staring me in the face. "Gladys Reilly, October 15th, 1934. . . ." Besides, I hate being locked up. Whenever I think of all these people they lock up for years I shiver all over.'

'Yes,' Mr. Severn said, 'so do I.' *I died waiting.*

'I'd rather die quick, wouldn't you?'

'Yes.'

'I couldn't sleep and I kept on remembering the way the doctor said, "How old are you?" And all the policemen round were laughing, as if it was a joke. Why should it be such a joke. But they're hard up for jokes, aren't they? So when I got back I couldn't stop crying. And when I woke up I hadn't got my bag. The wardress lent me a comb. She wasn't so bad. But I do feel fed up. . . .'

'You know the room I was waiting in while you were telephoning for money?' she said. 'There was such a pretty girl there.'

'Was there?'

'Yes, a very dark girl. Rather like Dolores del Rio, only younger. But it isn't the pretty ones who get on—oh no, on the contrary. For instance, this girl. She couldn't have been prettier—lovely, she was. And she was dressed awfully nicely in a black coat and skirt and a lovely clean white blouse and a little white hat and lovely stockings and shoes. But she was frightened. She was so frightened that she was shaking all over. You saw somehow that she wasn't going to last it out. No, it isn't being pretty that does it. . . . And there was another one, with great hairy legs and no stockings, only sandals. I do think that when people have hairy legs they ought to wear stockings, don't you? Or do something about it. But no, she was just laughing and joking and saw whatever happened to her she'd come out all right. A great big, red, square face she had, and those hairy legs. But she didn't care a damn.'

'Perhaps it's being sophisticated,' Mr. Severn suggested, 'like your friend Heather.'

'Oh, her—no, she won't get on either. She's too ambitious, she wants too much. She's so sharp she cuts herself, as you might say. . . . No, it isn't being pretty and it isn't being sophisticated. It's being—adapted, that's what it is. And it isn't any good *wanting* to be adapted, you've got to be born adapted.'

'Very clear,' Mr. Severn said. Adapted to the livid sky, the ugly houses, the grinning policemen, the placards in shop windows.

'You've got to be young, too. You've got to be young to enjoy a thing like this—younger than we are,' Maidie said as the taxi drew up.

Mr. Severn stared at her, too shocked to be angry.

'Well, good-bye.'

'*Good*-bye,' said Mr. Severn, giving her a black look and ignoring her outstretched hand. 'We' indeed!

Two-hundred and ninety-six steps along Coptic Street. One-hundred and twenty round the corner. Forty stairs up to his flat. A dozen inside it. He stopped counting.

His sitting-room looked well, he thought, in spite of the crumpled papers. It was one of its good times, when the light was just right, when all the incongruous colours and shapes became a whole—the yellow-white brick wall with several of the Museum pigeons perched on it, the silvered drainpipe, the chimneys of every fantastical shape, round, square, pointed, and the odd one with the mysterious hole in the middle through which the grey, steely sky looked at you, the solitary trees—all framed in the silver oilcloth curtains (Hans's idea), and then with a turn of his head he saw the woodcuts from Amsterdam, the chintz-covered arm-chairs, the fading bowl of flowers in the long mirror.

An old gentleman wearing a felt hat and carrying a walking-stick passed the window. He stopped, took off his hat and coat and, balancing the stick on the end of his nose, walked backwards and forwards, looking up expectantly. Nothing happened. Nobody thought him worth a penny. He put his hat and coat on again and, carrying the stick in a respectable manner, vanished round the corner. And, as he did so, the tormenting phrases vanished too—'Who pays? Will you pay now, please? You don't mind if I leave you, dear? I died waiting, I died waiting. (Or was it I died hating?) That was my father speaking. Pictures, pictures, pictures. You've got to be young. But tigers are better-looking, aren't they? SOS, SOS, SOS. If I was a bird and had wings I could fly away, couldn't I? Might get shot as you went. But tigers are better-looking aren't they? You've got to be younger than we are. . . .' Other phrases, suave and slick, took their place.

The swing's the thing, the cadence of the sentence. He had got it.

He looked at his eye in the mirror, then sat down at the typewriter and with great assurance rapped out 'JUBILEE. . . .'

R. K. NARAYAN
A Horse and Two Goats

OF the seven hundred thousand villages dotting the map of India, in which the majority of India's five hundred million live, flourish, and die, Kritam was probably the tiniest, indicated on the district survey map by a microscopic dot, the map being meant more for the revenue official out to collect tax than for the guidance of the motorist, who in any case could not hope to reach it since it sprawled far from the highway at the end of a rough track furrowed up by the iron-hooped wheels of bullock carts. But its size did not prevent its giving itself the grandiose name Kritam, which meant in Tamil 'coronet' or 'crown' on the brow of this subcontinent. The village consisted of less than thirty houses, only one of them built with brick and cement. Painted a brilliant yellow and blue all over with gorgeous carvings of gods and gargoyles on its balustrade, it was known as the Big House. The other houses, distributed in four streets, were generally of bamboo thatch, straw, mud, and other unspecified material. Muni's was the last house in the fourth street, beyond which stretched the fields. In his prosperous days Muni had owned a flock of forty sheep and goats and sallied forth every morning driving the flock to the highway a couple of miles away. There he would sit on the pedestal of a clay statue of a horse while his cattle grazed around. He carried a crook at the end of a bomboo pole and snapped foliage from the avenue trees to feed his flock; he also gathered faggots and dry sticks, bundled them, and carried them home for fuel at sunset.

His wife lit the domestic fire at dawn, boiled water in a mud pot, threw into it a handful of millet flour, added salt, and gave him his first nourishment for the day. When he started out, she would put in his hand a packed lunch, once again the same millet cooked into a little ball, which he could swallow with a raw onion at midday. She was old, but he was older and needed all the attention she could give him in order to be kept alive.

His fortunes had declined gradually, unnoticed. From a flock of forty which he drove into a pen at night, his stock had now come down to two goats which were not worth the rent of a half rupee a month the Big House charged for the use of the pen in their back yard. And so the two goats were tethered to the trunk of a drumstick tree which grew in front of his hut and from which occasionally Muni could shake down drumsticks. This morning he got six. He carried them in with a sense of triumph. Although no one could say precisely who owned the tree, it was his because he lived in its shadow.

She said, 'If you were content with the drumstick leaves alone, I could boil and salt some for you.'

'Oh, I am tired of eating those leaves. I have a craving to chew the drumstick out of sauce, I tell you.'

'You have only four teeth in your jaw, but your craving is for big things. All right, get the stuff for the sauce, and I will prepare it for you. After all, next year you may not be alive to ask for anything. But first get me all the stuff, including a measure of rice or millet, and I will satisfy your unholy craving. Our store is empty today. Dhal, chili, curry leaves, mustard, coriander, gingelley oil, and one large potato. Go out and get all this.' He repeated the list after her in order not to miss any item and walked off to the shop in the third street.

He sat on an upturned packing case below the platform of the shop. The shopman paid no attention to him. Muni kept clearing his throat, coughing, and sneezing until the shopman could not stand it any more and demanded, 'What ails you? You will fly off that seat into the gutter if you sneeze so hard, young man.' Muni laughed inordinately, in order to please the shopman, at being called 'young man'. The shopman softened and said, 'You have enough of the imp inside to keep a second wife busy, but for the fact the old lady is still alive.' Muni laughed appropriately again at this joke. It completely won the shopman over; he liked his sense of humour to be appreciated. Muni engaged his attention in local gossip for a few minutes, which always ended with a reference to the postman's wife who had eloped to the city some months before.

The shopman felt most pleased to hear the worst of the postman, who had cheated him. Being an itinerant postman, he returned home to Kritam only once in ten days and every time managed to slip away again without passing the shop in the third street. By thus humouring the shopman, Muni could always ask for one or two items of food, promising repayment later. Some days the shopman was in a good mood and gave in, and sometimes he would lose his temper suddenly and bark at Muni for daring to ask for credit. This was such a day, and Muni could not progress beyond two items listed as essential components. The shopman was also displaying a remarkable memory for old facts and figures and took out an oblong ledger to support his observations. Muni felt impelled to rise and flee. But his self-respect kept him in his seat and made him listen to the worst things about himself. The shopman concluded, 'If you could find five rupees and a quarter, you would pay off an ancient debt and then could apply for admission to swarga. How much have you got now?'

'I will pay you everything on the first of the next month.'

'As always, and whom do you expect to rob by then?'

Muni felt caught and mumbled, 'My daughter has sent word that she will be sending me money.'

'Have you a daughter?' sneered the shopman. 'And she is sending you money! For what purpose, may I know?'

'Birthday, fiftieth birthday,' said Muni quietly.

'Birthday! How old are you?'

Muni repeated weakly, not being sure of it himself, 'Fifty'. He always calculated his age from the time of the great famine when he stood as high as the parapet around the village well, but who could calculate such things accurately nowadays with so many famines occurring? The shopman felt encouraged when other customers stood around to watch and comment. Muni thought helplessly, My poverty is exposed to everybody. But what can I do?

'More likely you are seventy,' said the shopman. 'You also forget that you mentioned a birthday five weeks ago when you wanted castor oil for your holy bath.'

'Bath! Who can dream of a bath when you have to scratch the tank-bed for a bowl of water? We would all be parched and dead but for the Big House, where they let us take a pot of water from their well.' After saying this Muni unobtrusively rose and moved off.

He told his wife, 'That scoundrel would not give me anything. So go out and sell the drumsticks for what they are worth.'

He flung himself down in a corner to recoup from the fatigue of his visit to the shop. His wife said, 'You are getting no sauce today, nor anything else. I can't find anything to give you to eat. Fast till the evening, it'll do you good. Take the goats and be gone now,' she cried and added, 'Don't come back before the sun is down.' He knew that if he obeyed her she would somehow conjure up some food for him in the evening. Only he must be careful not to argue and irritate her. Her temper was undependable in the morning but improved by evening time. She was sure to go out and work—grind corn in the Big House, sweep or scrub somewhere, and earn enough to buy foodstuff and keep a dinner ready for him in the evening.

Unleashing the goats from the drumstick tree, Muni started out, driving them ahead and uttering weird cries from time to time in order to urge them on. He passed through the village with his head bowed in thought. He did not want to look at anyone or be accosted. A couple of cronies lounging in the temple corridor hailed him, but he ignored their call. They had known him in the days of affluence when he lorded over a flock of fleecy sheep, not the miserable gawky goats that he had today. Of course he also used to have a few goats for those who fancied them, but real wealth lay in sheep; they bred fast and people came and bought the fleece in the shearing season; and then that famous butcher from the town came over on the weekly market days bringing him betel leaves, tobacco, and often enough some bhang, which they smoked in a hut in the coconut grove, undisturbed by wives and well-wishers. After a smoke one felt light and elated and inclined to forgive everyone including that brother-in-law of his who had once tried to set fire to his home. But all this seemed like the memoirs of a previous birth. Some pestilence afflicted his cattle (he could of course guess who had laid his animals under a curse) and even the friendly butcher would not touch one at half the price . . . and now here he was left with the two scraggy creatures. He wished someone would rid him of their company too. The shopman had said that he was seventy. At seventy, one only waited to be summoned by God. When he was dead what would his wife do? They had lived in each other's company since they were children. He was told on their day of wedding that he was ten years old and she was eight. During the wedding ceremony they had had to recite their respective ages and names. He had thrashed her only a few times in their career, and later she had the upper hand. Progeny, none. Perhaps a large progeny would have brought him the blessing of the gods. Fertility brought merit. People with fourteen sons were always so prosperous and at peace with the world and themselves. He recollected the thrill he had felt when he mentioned a daughter to that shopman; although it was not believed, what if he did not have a daughter?—his cousin in the

next village had many daughters, and any one of them was as good
as his; he was fond of them all and would buy them sweets if he
could afford it. Still, everyone in the village whispered behind their
backs that Muni and his wife were a barren couple. He avoided
looking at anyone; they all professed to be so high up, and everyone
else in the village had more money than he. 'I am the poorest fellow
in our caste and no wonder that they spurn me, but I won't look at
them either,' and so he passed on with his eyes downcast along the
edge of the street, and people left him also very much alone,
commenting only to the extent, 'Ah, there he goes with his two
great goats; if he slits their throats, he may have more peace of
mind.' 'What has he to worry about anyway? They live on nothing
and have nobody to worry about.' Thus people commented when
he passed through the village. Only on the outskirts did he lift his
head and look up. He urged and bullied the goats until they
meandered along to the foot of the horse statue on the edge of the
village. He sat on its pedestal for the rest of the day. The advantage
of this was that he could watch the highway and see the lorries and
buses pass through to the hills, and it gave him a sense of belonging
to a larger world. The pedestal of the statue was broad enough for
him to move around as the sun travelled up and westward; or he
could also crouch under the belly of the horse, for shade.

The horse was nearly life-size, moulded out of clay, baked, burnt,
and brightly coloured, and reared its head proudly, prancing its
forelegs in the air and flourishing its tail in a loop; beside the horse
stood a warrior with scythe-like mustachios, bulging eyes, and
aquiline nose. The old image-makers believed in indicating a man
of strength by bulging out his eyes and sharpening his moustache
tips, and also had decorated the man's chest with beads which
looked today like blobs of mud through the ravages of sun and wind
and rain (when it came), but Muni would insist that he had known
the beads to sparkle like the nine gems at one time in his life. The
horse itself was said to have been as white as a dhobi-washed sheet,
and had had on its back a cover of pure brocade of red and black
lace, matching the multicoloured sash around the waist of the
warrior. But none in the village remembered the splendour as no
one noticed its existence. Even Muni, who spent all his waking
hours at its foot, never bothered to look up. It was untouched by
the young vandals of the village who gashed tree trunks with knives
and tried to topple off milestones and inscribed lewd designs on all

the walls. This statue had been closer to the population of the village at one time, when this spot bordered the village; but when the highway was laid through (or perhaps when the tank and wells dried up completely here) the village moved a couple of miles inland.

Muni sat at the foot of the statue, watching his two goats graze in the arid soil among the cactus and lantana bushes. He looked at the sun; it had tilted westward no doubt, but it was not the time yet to go back home; if he went too early his wife would have no food for him. Also he must give her time to cool off her temper and feel sympathetic, and then she would scrounge and manage to get some food. He watched the mountain road for a time signal. When the green bus appeared around the bend he could leave, and his wife would feel pleased that he had let the goats feed long enough.

He noticed now a new sort of vehicle coming down at full speed. It looked both like a motor car and a bus. He used to be intrigued by the novelty of such spectacles, but of late work was going on at the source of the river on the mountain and an assortment of people and traffic went past him, and he took it all casually and described to his wife, later in the day, not everything as he once did, but only some things, only if he noticed anything special. Today, while he observed the yellow vehicle coming down, he was wondering how to describe it later when it sputtered and stopped in front of him. A red-faced foreigner who had been driving it got down and went round it, stooping, looking, and poking under the vehicle; then he straightened himself up, looked at the dashboard, stared in Muni's direction, and approached him. 'Excuse me, is there a gas station nearby, or do I have to wait until another car comes——' He suddenly looked up at the clay horse and cried, 'Marvellous!' without completing his sentence. Muni felt he should get up and run away, and cursed his age. He could not readily put his limbs into action; some years ago he could outrun a cheetah, as happened once when he went to the forest to cut fuel and it was then that two of his sheep were mauled—a sign that bad times were coming. Though he tried, he could not easily extricate himself from his seat, and then there was also the problem of the goats. He could not leave them behind.

The red-faced man wore khaki clothes—evidently a policeman or a soldier. Muni said to himself, 'He will chase or shoot if I start running. Sometimes dogs chase only those who run—O Shiva

protect me. I don't know why this man should be after me.'
Meanwhile the foreigner cried, 'Marvellous!' again, nodding his
head. He paced around the statue with his eyes fixed on it. Muni
sat frozen for a while, and then fidgeted and tried to edge away.
Now the other man suddenly pressed his palms together in a salute,
smiled, and said, 'Namaste! How do you do?'

At which Muni spoke the only English expressions he had learnt,
'Yes, no.' Having exhausted his English vocabulary, he started in
Tamil: 'My name is Muni. These two goats are mine, and no one
can gainsay it—though our village is full of slanderers these days
who will not hesitate to say that what belongs to a man doesn't
belong to him.' He rolled his eyes and shuddered at the thought of
evil-minded men and women peopling his village.

The foreigner faithfully looked in the direction indicated by
Muni's fingers, gazed for a while at the two goats and the rocks,
and with a puzzled expression took out his silver cigarette-case and
lit a cigarette. Suddenly remembering the courtesies of the season,
he asked, 'Do you smoke?' Muni answered, 'Yes, no.' Whereupon
the red-faced man took a cigarette and gave it to Muni who received
it with surprise, having had no offer of a smoke from anyone for
years now. Those days when he smoked bhang were gone with his
sheep and the large-hearted butcher. Nowadays he was not able to
find even matches, let alone bhang. (His wife went across and
borrowed a fire at dawn from a neighbour.) He had always wanted
to smoke a cigarette; only once had the shopman given him one on
credit, and he remembered how good it had tasted. The other
flicked the lighter open and offered a light to Muni. Muni felt so
confused about how to act that he blew on it and put it out. The
other, puzzled but undaunted, flourished his lighter, presented it
again, and lit Muni's cigarette. Muni drew a deep puff and started
coughing; it was racking, no doubt, but extremely pleasant. When
his cough subsided he wiped his eyes and took stock of the situation,
understanding that the other man was not an inquisitor of any kind.
Yet, in order to make sure, he remained wary. No need to run away
from a man who gave him such a potent smoke. His head was
reeling from the effect of one of those strong American cigarettes
made with roasted tobacco. The man said, 'I come from New York,'
took out a wallet from his hip pocket, and presented his card.

Muni shrank away from the card. Perhaps he was trying to
present a warrant and arrest him. Beware of khaki, one part of his

mind warned. Take all the cigarettes or bhang or whatever is offered, but don't get caught. Beware of khaki. He wished he weren't seventy as the shopman had said. At seventy one didn't run, but surrendered to whatever came. He could only ward off trouble by talk. So he went on, all in the chaste Tamil for which Kritam was famous. (Even the worst detractors could not deny that the famous poetess Avvaiyar was born in this area, although no one could say whether it was in Kritam or Kuppam, the adjoining village.) Out of this heritage the Tamil language gushed through Muni in an unimpeded flow. He said, 'Before God, sir, Bhagwan, who sees everything, I tell you, sir, that we know nothing of the case. If the murder was committed, whoever did it will not escape. Bhagwan is all-seeing. Don't ask me about it. I know nothing.' A body had been found mutilated and thrown under a tamarind tree at the border between Kritam and Kuppam a few weeks before, giving rise to much gossip and speculation. Muni added an explanation, 'Anything is possible there. People over there will stop at nothing.' The foreigner nodded his head and listened courteously though he understood nothing.

'I am sure you know when this horse was made,' said the red man and smiled ingratiatingly.

Muni reacted to the relaxed atmosphere by smiling himself, and pleaded, 'Please go away, sir, I know nothing. I promise we will hold him for you if we see any bad character around, and we will bury him up to his neck in a coconut pit if he tries to escape; but our village has always had a clean record. Must definitely be the other village.'

Now the red man implored, 'Please, please, I will speak slowly, please try to understand me. Can't you understand even a simple word of English? Everyone in this country seems to know English. I have got along with English everywhere in this country, but you don't speak it. Have you any religious or spiritual scruples for avoiding the English speech?'

Muni made some indistinct sounds in his throat and shook his head. Encouraged, the other went on to explain at length, uttering each syllable with care and deliberation. Presently he sidled over and took a seat beside the old man, explaining, 'You see, last August, we probably had the hottest summer in history, and I was working in shirt-sleeves in my office on the fortieth floor of the Empire State Building. You must have heard of the power failure,

and there I was stuck for four hours, no elevator, no air condition-
ing. All the way in the train I kept thinking, and the minute I
reached home in Connecticut, I told my wife Ruth, "We will visit
India this winter, it's time to look at other civilizations." Next day
she called the travel agent first thing and told him to fix it, and so
here I am. Ruth came with me but is staying back at Srinagar, and
I am the one doing the rounds and joining her later.'

Muni looked reflective at the end of this long peroration and said,
rather feebly, 'Yes, no,' as a concession to the other's language, and
went on in Tamil, 'When I was this high,' he indicated a foot high,
'I heard my uncle say . . .'

No one can tell what he was planning to say as the other
interrupted him at this stage to ask, 'Boy, what is the secret of your
teeth? How old are you?'

The old man forgot what he had started to say and remarked,
'Sometimes we too lose our cattle. Jackals or cheetahs may carry
them off, but sometimes it is just theft from over in the next village,
and then we will know who has done it. Our priest at the temple
can see in the camphor flame the face of the thief, and when he is
caught . . .' He gestured with his hands a perfect mincing of meat.

The American watched his hands intently and said, 'I know what
you mean. Chop something? Maybe I am holding you up and you
want to chop wood? Where is your axe? Hand it to me and show
me what to chop. I do enjoy it, you know, just a hobby. We get a
lot of driftwood along the backwater near my house, and on Sundays
I do nothing but chop wood for the fireplace. I really feel different
when I watch the fire in the fireplace, although it may take all the
sections of the Sunday *New York Times* to get a fire started,' and he
smiled at this reference.

Muni felt totally confused but decided the best thing would be to
make an attempt to get away from this place. He tried to edge out,
saying, 'Must go home,' and turned to go. The other seized his
shoulder and said desperately, 'Is there no one, absolutely no one
here, to translate for me?' He looked up and down the road, which
was deserted in this hot afternoon; a sudden gust of wind churned
up the dust and dead leaves on the roadside into a ghostly column
and propelled it towards the mountain road. The stranger almost
pinioned Muni's back to the statue and asked, 'Isn't this statue
yours? Why don't you sell it to me?'

The old man now understood the reference to the horse, thought for a second, and said in his own language, 'I was an urchin this high when I heard my grandfather explain this horse and warrior, and my grandfather himself was this high when he heard his grandfather, whose grandfather . . .'

The other man interrupted him with, 'I don't want to seem to have stopped here for nothing. I will offer you a good price for this,' he said, indicating the horse. He had concluded without the least doubt that Muni owned this mud horse. Perhaps he guessed by the way he sat at its pedestal, like other souvenir-sellers in this country presiding over their wares.

Muni followed the man's eyes and pointing fingers and dimly understood the subject matter and, feeling relieved that the theme of the mutilated body had been abandoned at least for the time being, said again, enthusiastically, 'I was this high when my grandfather told me about this horse and the warrior, and my grandfather was this high when he himself . . .' and he was getting into a deeper bog of reminiscence each time he tried to indicate the antiquity of the statue.

The Tamil that Muni spoke was stimulating even as pure sound, and the foreigner listened with fascination. 'I wish I had my tape-recorder here,' he said, assuming the pleasantest expression. 'Your language sounds wonderful. I get a kick out of every word you utter, here'—he indicated his ears—'but you don't have to waste your breath in sales talk. I appreciate the article. You don't have to explain its points.'

'I never went to a school, in those days only Brahmin went to schools, but we had to go out and work in the fields morning till night, from sowing to harvest time . . . and when Pongal came and we had cut the harvest, my father allowed me to go out and play with others at the tank, and so I don't know the Parangi language you speak, even little fellows in your country probably speak the Parangi language, but here only learned men and officers know it. We had a postman in our village who could speak to you boldly in your language, but his wife ran away with someone and he does not speak to anyone at all nowadays. Who would if a wife did what she did? Women must be watched; otherwise they will sell themselves and the home,' and he laughed at his own quip.

The foreigner laughed heartily, took out another cigarette, and offered it to Muni, who now smoked with ease, deciding to stay on if the fellow was going to be so good as to keep up his cigarette

supply. The American now stood up on the pedestal in the attitude
of a demonstrative lecturer and said, running his finger along some
of the carved decorations around the horse's neck, speaking slowly
and uttering his words syllable by syllable, 'I could give a sales talk
for this better than anyone else . . . This is a marvellous combination
of yellow and indigo, though faded now . . . How do you people of
this country achieve these flaming colours?'

Muni, now assured that the subject was still the horse and not
the dead body, said, 'This is our guardian, it means death to our
adversaries. At the end of Kali Yuga, this world and all other
worlds will be destroyed, and the Redeemer will come in the shape
of a horse called Kalki; this horse will come to life and gallop and
trample down all bad men.' As he spoke of bad men the figures of
his shopman and his brother-in-law assumed concrete forms in his
mind, and he revelled for a moment in the predicament of the fellow
under the horse's hoof: served him right for trying to set fire to his
home . . .

While he was brooding on this pleasant vision, the foreigner
utilized the pause to say, 'I assure you that this will have the best
home in the U.S.A. I'll push away the bookcase, you know I love
books and am a member of five book clubs, and the choice and
bonus volumes really mount up to a pile in our living-room, as high
as this horse itself. But they'll have to go. Ruth may disapprove,
but I will convince her. The T.V. may have to be shifted too. We
can't have everything in the living-room. Ruth will probably say
what about when we have a party? I'm going to keep him right in
the middle of the room. I don't see how that can interfere with the
party—we'll stand around him and have our drinks.'

Muni continued his description of the end of the world. 'Our
pundit discoursed at the temple once how the oceans are going to
close over the earth in a huge wave and swallow us—this horse will
grow bigger than the biggest wave and carry on its back only the
good people and kick into the floods the evil ones—plenty of them
about,' he said reflectively. 'Do you know when it is going to
happen?' he asked.

The foreigner now understood by the tone of the other that a
question was being asked and said, 'How am I transporting it? I
can push the seat back and make room in the rear. That van can
take in an elephant—waving precisely at the back of the seat.

Muni was still hovering on visions of avatars and said again, 'I never missed our pundit's discourses at the temple in those days during every bright half of the month, although he'd go on all night, and he told us that Vishnu is the highest god. Whenever evil men trouble us, he comes down to save us. He has come many times. The first time he incarnated as a great fish, and lifted the scriptures on his back when the floods and sea-waves . . .'

'I am not a millionaire, but a modest businessman. My trade is coffee.'

Amidst all this wilderness of obscure sound Muni caught the word 'coffee' and said, 'If you want to drink "kapi", drive further up, in the next town, they have Friday market, and there they open "kapi-otels"—so I learn from passers-by. Don't think I wander about. I go nowhere and look for nothing.' His thoughts went back to the avatars. 'The first avatar was in the shape of a little fish in a bowl of water, but every hour it grew bigger and bigger and became in the end a huge whale which the seas could not contain, and on the back of the whale the holy books were supported, saved, and carried.' Having launched on the first avatar it was inevitable that he should go on to the next, a wild boar on whose tusk the earth was lifted when a vicious conqueror of the earth carried it off and hid it at the bottom of the sea. After describing this avatar Muni concluded, 'God will always save us whenever we are troubled by evil beings. When we were young we staged at full moon the story of the avatars. That's how I know the stories; we played them all night until the sun rose, and sometimes the European collector would come to watch, bringing his own chair. I had a good voice and so they always taught me songs and gave me the women's roles. I was always Goddess Laxmi, and they dressed me in a brocade sari, loaned from the Big House . . .'

The foreigner said, 'I repeat I am not a millionaire. Ours is a modest business; after all, we can't afford to buy more than sixty minutes' T.V. time in a month, which works out to two minutes a day, that's all, although in the course of time we'll maybe sponsor a one-hour show regularly if our sales graph continues to go up . . .'

Muni was intoxicated by the memory of his theatrical days and was about to explain how he had painted his face and worn a wig and diamond earrings when the visitor, feeling that he had spent too much time already, said, 'Tell me, will you accept a hundred rupees or not for the horse? I'd love to take the whiskered soldier also but I've no space for him this year. I'll have to cancel my air ticket and take a boat home, I suppose. Ruth can go by air if she likes, but I will go with the horse and keep him in my cabin all the way if necessary,' and he smiled at the picture of himself voyaging across the seas hugging this horse. He added, 'I will have to pad it with straw so that it doesn't break . . .'

'When we played *Ramayana*, they dressed me as Sita,' added Muni. 'A teacher came and taught us the songs for the drama and we gave him fifty rupees. He incarnated himself as Rama, and he alone could destroy Ravana, the demon with ten heads who shook all the worlds; do you know the story of Ramayana?'

'I have my station wagon as you see. I can push the seat back and take the horse in if you will just lend me a hand with it.'

'Do you know *Mahabharata*? Krishna was the eighth avatar of Vishnu, incarnated to help the Five Brothers regain their kingdom. When Krishna was a baby he danced on the thousand-hooded giant serpent and trampled it to death; and then he suckled the breasts of the demoness and left them flat as a disc though when she came to him her bosoms were large, like mounds of earth on the banks of a dug-up canal.' He indicated two mounds with his hands. The stranger was completely mystified by the gesture. For the first time he said, 'I really wonder what you are saying because your answer is crucial. We have come to the point when we should be ready to talk business.'

'When the tenth avatar comes, do you know where you and I will be?' asked the old man.

'Lend me a hand and I can lift off the horse from its pedestal after picking out the cement at the joints. We can do anything if we have a basis of understanding.'

At this stage the mutual mystification was complete, and there was no need even to carry on a guessing game at the meaning of words. The old man chattered away in a spirit of balancing off the credits and debits of conversational exchange, and said in order to be on the credit side, 'O honourable one, I hope God has blessed you with numerous progeny. I say this because you seem to be a good man, willing to stay beside an old man and talk to him, while all day I have none to talk to except when somebody stops by to ask for a piece of tobacco. But I seldom have it, tobacco is not what it used to be at one time, and I have given up chewing. I cannot afford it nowadays.' Noting the other's interest in his speech, Muni felt encouraged to ask, 'How many children have you?' with appropriate gestures with his hands. Realizing that a question was being asked, the red man replied, 'I said a hundred,' which encouraged Muni to go into details, 'How many of your children are boys and how many girls? Where are they? Is your daughter married? Is it difficult to find a son-in-law in your country also?'

In answer to these questions the red man dashed his hand into his pocket and brought forth his wallet in order to take immediate advantage of the bearish trend in the market. He flourished a hundred-rupee currency note and asked, 'Well, this is what I meant.'

The old man now realized that some financial element was entering their talk. He peered closely at the currency note, the like of which he had never seen in his life; he knew the five and ten by their colours, although always in other people's hands, while his own earning at any time was in coppers and nickels. What was this man flourishing the note for? Perhaps asking for change. He laughed to himself at the notion of anyone coming to him for changing a thousand- or ten-thousand-rupee note. He said with a grin, 'Ask our village headman, who is also a moneylender; he can change even a lakh of rupees in gold sovereigns if you prefer it that way; he thinks nobody knows, but dig the floor of his puja room and your head will reel at the sight of the hoard. The man disguises himself in rags just to mislead the public. Talk to the headman yourself because he goes mad at the sight of me. Someone took away his pumpkins with the creeper and he, for some reason, thinks it was me and my goats ... that's why I never let my goats be seen anywhere near the farms.' His eyes travelled to his goats nosing about, attempting to wrest nutrition from minute greenery peeping out of rock and dry earth.

The foreigner followed his look and decided that it would be a sound policy to show an interest in the old man's pets. He went up casually to them and stroked their backs with every show of courteous attention. Now the truth dawned on the old man. His dream of a lifetime was about to be realized. He understood that the red man was actually making an offer for the goats. He had reared them up in the hope of selling them some day and, with the capital, opening a small shop on this very spot. Sitting here, watching the hills, he had often dreamt how he would put up a thatched roof here, spread a gunny sack out on the ground, and display on it fried nuts, coloured sweets, and green coconut for the thirsty and famished wayfarers on the highway, which was sometimes very busy. The animals were not prize ones for a cattle show, but he had spent his occasional savings to provide them some fancy diet now and then, and they did not look too bad. While he was reflecting thus, the red man shook his hand and left on his palm one hundred rupees in tens now. 'It is all for you or you may share it if you have the partner.'

The old man pointed at the station wagon and asked. 'Are you carrying them off in that?'

'Yes, of course,' said the other, understanding the transportation part of it.

The old man said, 'This will be their first ride in a motor car. Carry them off after I get out of sight, otherwise they will never follow you, but only me even if I am travelling on the path to Yama Loka.' He laughed at his own joke, brought his palms together in a salute, turned round and went off, and was soon out of sight beyond a clump of thicket.

The red man looked at the goats grazing peacefully. Perched on the pedestal of the horse, as the westerly sun touched the ancient faded colours of the statue with a fresh splendour, he ruminated, 'He must be gone to fetch some help, I suppose!' and settled down to wait. When a truck came downhill, he stopped it and got the help of a couple of men to detach the horse from its pedestal and place it in his station wagon. He gave them five rupees each, and for a further payment they siphoned off gas from the truck and helped him to start his engine.

Muni hurried homeward with the cash securely tucked away at his waist in his dhoti. He shut the street door and stole up softly to his wife as she squatted before the lit oven wondering if by a miracle food would drop from the sky. Muni displayed his fortune for the day. She snatched the notes from him, counted them by the glow of the fire, and cried, 'One hundred rupees! How did you come by it? Have you been stealing?'

'I have sold our goats to a red-faced man. He was absolutely crazy to have them, gave me all this money and carried them off in his motor car!'

Hardly had these words left his lips when they heard bleating outside. She opened the door and saw the two goats at her door. 'Here they are!' she said. 'What's the meaning of all this?'

He muttered a great curse and seized one of the goats by its ears

and shouted, 'Where is that man? Don't you know you are his?
Why did you come back?' The goat only wriggled in his grip. He
asked the same question of the other too. The goat shook itself off.
His wife glared at him and declared, 'If you have thieved, the police
will come tonight and break your bones. Don't involve me. I will go
away to my parents. . . .'

FRANK TUOHY
The Licence

AUNT Cynthia rarely made personal use of the chairs in her London drawing-room. She was kneeling now on the hearth rug, and poking at the grate from time to time with a pair of tongs. When she turned round, her face would be full of endeavour at sympathy and understanding. It is a great effort to talk to boys of Peter's age.

Awkwardly waiting for her to speak again, he looked as if he might break the chair he was sitting in.

'Does your father write to you?'

'Yes, of course.'

'Often?'

'Yes.' Adolescence still made Peter's voice thrum like a slack guitar string. 'At school we're meant to write home every week, so, as I usually do, he pretty well has to; I mean he writes something, not much though.'

His aunt struck a heated coal and it split satisfactorily, emitting branches of flame. 'What does he write about?'

Peter laughed oafishly. 'About my future mostly.'

'Surely that can wait. What about himself? Has he told you any plans?'

'We're going to Austria this summer. He wants me to learn to drive.'

'You're too young.'

'I won't be then.' He laughed again, to help things on.

She was agitated and fussed. The boy had a train to catch in half an hour's time. Though partly impelled by curiosity, her sympathy was genuine; but he deflected it at every opportunity.

'Please don't always try to shut me out, Peter.'

He looked at her with hatred and desperation.

'I suppose it isn't any use. You're just a child.'

Her husband, a barrister, came in with the evening papers.

'Hullo, Pete, old boy.'

'Hullo, Uncle Raymond.'

Raymond Pelham issued a big grin: everybody felt they had to start off cheerfully with Peter.

'Darling, Carla's been pressing your dinner jacket. Do go and see if it's all right.'

'What did she want to do that for?'

'Because we're dining at the Messiters. Darling, please.'

'I expect it's all right. Is Pete old enough to have a glass of sherry?'

'Darling, please,' Aunt Cynthia went on signalling until her husband left the room, first winking at Peter on the way.

She put a hand on Peter's knee.

'This housekeeper, Mrs. What's-her-name.'

'Mrs. Macdonnell.'

'Yes. What does your father write about her?'

'Nothing much. Why?'

His aunt turned back to the fire, armed this time with the poker.

'He got her from an agency,' Peter said, trying to help.

'Oh, God. How difficult it is!' Aunt Cynthia hit a smoking coal with some violence, but it failed to crumble. 'He's my favourite brother. I was fond of your mother too. She could be a very very sweet person.'

At this, Peter was locked in silence.

'You'd better go to your train. I'll ring the taxi rank.'

'I can go by tube.'

'With your squash racket and record-player and everything?'

'Oh, all right.'

In the hall, they listened for the taxi. When they heard it stop outside, Aunt Cynthia kissed him. He still reeked of boarding school, as men do of prison; in her arms he held himself quite still, like an animal tense and ready to leap away at the first relaxation. She let him go, with a hurt little laugh.

Afterwards she said to her husband: 'I sometimes think he hates me.'

'He probably still feels like hell, poor Pete.'

'That's no answer. It's five months now—I was counting this morning.'

She moved into his arms. Raymond knew that for her the problem was, not Peter, but her own childlessness.

Because his father had evening surgery, Peter could not be met at Shereham station. He took another taxi to the house, which lay a

mile away, among bird-haunted shrubberies. The drive spat and
crackled with new gravel.

'There he is at last! I expect you know who I am, don't you?'

The woman in the doorway spoke in a soft Edinburgh voice. She
was about forty, and wore a knitted suit and her dark hair done up
in a bun. On her bright, bird-like face, the lips were thin and
scarlet.

Peter dropped his squash racket to shake hands.

'I'm Mrs. Macdonnell. When you've got over your first shyness,
I expect you'll want to call me Helen. Come along up, then.'

Peter picked up his bags again and made off up the stairs, with
Mrs. Macdonnell following him.

'There's a big strong laddy.'

The room was small, on the sunless side of the house, a museum
of Peter's past. He put his record-player and a case of records on
the bed.

'Those'll be all the latest smash-hits.'

'No,' Peter said.

'What are they then? Dixieland?' She was showing him she knew
all the modern words.

'Bach mostly.'

'Gloomy stuff, eh? Well, I never.'

She seemed put out, and left him, shaking her head as though she
knew he'd be growing out of this phase. 'You'll be coming down
when you're ready.'

Peter's trunk would arrive later. He unpacked his suitcase quickly
and put the clothes in the drawer; if he left it, she might do it for
him. He hid under his handkerchiefs the photograph of his mother,
and the letter she had written to him before she died.

Dr. Hesketh was standing in front of the drawing-room fire with
a whisky and soda. He had reddish hair, which was growing
colourless, and a bristly moustache. He always looked ruffled and
embarrassed; everyone over the past few months had conspired to
expect too much of him.

Peter and his father shook hands. It was, nowadays, their only
way of touching, and they hardly glanced at each other.

Mrs. Macdonnell said: 'You know I think he's got quite a look of
you, Jack. Quite a look.'

At the sound of his father's Christian name, Peter flinched visibly.
His father stared at the logs in the grate.

'He's taller, though. The wee bairn's taller than his daddy.' She drained her sherry. 'Well, then, I'll be going through to get you your supper. I expect you two have lots to talk about.'

Relieved of her presence, they could talk to each other quite easily.

'Aunt Cynthia's got seats for Covent Garden next week. She wants me to go up.'

'You go then. It's no fun for you now, moping around down here.'

'Have you thought any more about my driving lessons?'

'Yes, I don't see why you shouldn't begin as soon as you can.'

'Mr. Beaman—he's the history master—let me practise stopping and starting in his mini. In the school grounds, so I didn't need a licence.'

'Well then, you know the rudiments.'

'Yes.'

Both Peter and his father knew they would over-discuss this subject: they exploited to the utmost the few topics for conversation that now remained to them.

Mrs. Macdonnell called them.

'Not much for supper, I'm afraid. Today's the day I have my hair done.'

His father ate in silence, pouring tomato ketchup onto the thawed-out fishcakes. When they had finished, he whispered to Peter: 'Give her a hand with the dishes, there's a good lad.'

He went through to the kitchen.

'That's nice of you, Peter. I see they look after your manners at that school, not like some of these places.'

Peter seized a cloth and began drying plates strenuously.

'How do you think Dad is looking?'

He did not answer.

'Lost your tongue, have you? Never mind. As I say, you'll soon get over your shyness with Helen.'

'Actually, I call him Pa.'

She laughed, 'Do you now? Old-fashioned, aren't we?'

'He's all right, I suppose.'

Mrs. Macdonnell put down the dish-mop. 'Your father's a fine good man, Peter. He wears himself out for those patients of his, but they're not grateful, not a bit of it.'

She poured bleach into the basin.

'They don't know they're lucky. I was an ill woman when I came here, Peter. You're not old enough to know about these things. Your father's been a trump to me, a real trump.'

She unbuttoned her apron. Her sentimentality was full of menace.

'There's not many like him, these days. People down here don't know they're well off. And all these foreigners that work at the big houses!—They're not healthy, you know. I wouldn't have one of them in my house. And they don't do the work, either.'

Peter ducked away as soon as he could. Upstairs he lay flat on his bed, and put a Haydn quartet on the record-player. A few minutes later she was at his door.

'D'ye like the sound o' the pipes, Peter? D'ye no like the sound of the good Scots pipes?'

'I don't know much about them,' he said politely.

'There's nothing to beat them.'

She gave no signs of going away. Soon she tried whistling and humming a bit, to help Haydn along; it was the allegretto, however, and he was too quick for her.

'What do you have, Peter?'

'What?'

'What! Did ye never learn to say "pardon"? What'll you be having for your nightcap? Will it be Horlick's or Ovaltine or cocoa or hot milk?'

'Nothing, thank you.'

'Ah, come now. Not even a nice cup of tea? Won't you join Helen in a nice cup of tea? She always has one, this time o' nights.'

'No, thank you.'

Huffed, she finally went away. Peter raised the arm of the pickup and put it back to where it had been when she first came in.

Later Peter stayed awake, listening. But the silence in the house was absolute. There was only a faint ringing sound out of the spring darkness, which might have been the blood encircling the walls of his own brain.

And then across the corridor, a small regular noise: Mrs. Macdonnell snoring. A guileless innocent murmur, it seemed to fill the whole house until Peter went to sleep.

Coming out of his bedroom, where he had been rearranging his long-playing records, Peter bumped into a small grey figure armed with a feather mop.

'They never tell me you was back! How are you then, dear?'

'I'm fine, Mrs. Parkes. How are things?'

'Oh, it's not the same.' The old woman's eyes sparkled with grief and mischief. 'It's not the same by a long chalk.'

Mrs. Macdonnell called upstairs: 'Mrs. Parkes, I've left the vacuum cleaner out, so's you can give downstairs a proper doing today.'

Mrs. Parkes made a face at Peter. 'See what I mean? Only I'm loyal, see? I won't let Doctor down. I said that to your poor mother, I won't let Doctor down.'

Relishing this, she was going to repeat it, but Mrs. Macdonnell had come half-way up the stairs, her head raised, scenting trouble.

'Your father's just off, Peter, once I've made his list out. You're going with him, aren't you?'

'Oh, all right.'

Dr. Hesketh was downstairs drinking a cup of tea. Mrs. Macdonnell stood dutifully beside him with his list. She gave Peter a little smile, which indicated the regularity and reliability of this event.

Peter's father pointed to one name. 'Who's that?'

'I can't spell the foreign names, Jack. It's that cook at Shereham Hall.'

'Right ho. Nothing going to hold us up for long there.' He pocketed his stethoscope.

'Now, boys, don't you go being late for lunch. One o'clock sharp, mind.'

Peter followed his father out to the garage.

'It's probably only corned beef, anyway,' his father said, starting the car. Peter giggled.

The houses round Shereham were bright with new paint and daffodils and pink cherry-trees were in flower in the easily run gardens. On the few remaining bits of pasture, horses and ponies which belonged to the daughters of London businessmen were frisking in the sunshine. Dr. Hesketh visited two or three council houses and a thatched cottage, in which a family waited for a grandmother to die: they had already an offer from London people. Sometimes he stopped for a moment behind the car, out of sight of the windows. He came out of the last cottage whistling, and drove to Shereham Hall.

'Got something to read, old man? I may be a bit of time here.'

'Is the cook very ill?'

'No, not really. Be a bit of time, though.'

Shereham Hall was a square Palladian mansion built of pale sandstone. In the Portico there were croquet mallets, and some hooded basket-chairs. The garden was very large and would soon be opened to the public, in aid of the District Nurses.

After half an hour, there were voices, especially his father's, which sounded louder than before. Mr. and Mrs. Tyrell Bailey, both with pale hair and long whey-coloured faces, came out with him.

Mrs. Tyrell Bailey leaned towards the car. 'So this is the boy.'

'Oh yes, the boy,' Mr. Tyrell Bailey said.

Peter was trapped, like a fish under observation in an aquarium, but before he could get out of the car, they had lost interest in him. With the slow saunter of garden-viewers, they had crossed the drive and were approaching a large magnolia-tree, which stood in full blossom near the lake. Mrs. Tyrell Bailey was telling his father about the tree, and his father was nodding a great many times.

After a few minutes Peter's father returned across the lawn, smiling to himself and mopping his hands with a handkerchief. He got into the car in silence. As a child Peter had once said to his mother: 'Pa smells like the cocktail cabinet.' This joke had not been funny a second time.

'Well, off we go.'

Gravel roared under the tyres, Shereham Hall, the basket-chairs and the magnolia-tree spun round, and the car raced towards a wall of rhododendrons. Beside the lake, the faces of the Tyrell Baileys flashed by, identically aghast. The car reached the bottom of the drive, swooped into the main road, and came to a halt.

'Get out, get out, you little fool,' Dr. Hesketh shouted. 'See what it is.'

Peter scrambled out and ran to the front of the car.

A schoolboy, several years younger than himself, was kneeling on his hands and knees in the road. The wheels of his bicycle were still spinning furiously.

'Are you all right?'

The boy got up. He wore shorts and a county school cap, and his overfed face was white with fear. His smooth knees were grazed and the palms of his hands pitted with the marks of stones.

'I think . . .' Tame, neuter-looking, he was ready to apologize. 'P'raps I should've rung my bell.'

'Are you sure you're all right? My father's a doctor, he could probably help.'

'No, I'm all right.' Nearly crying, the boy wanted to be left to himself.

Peter rummaged in his pocket and produced five shillings. 'Here, take this.'

Startled the boy said, 'Thank you, sir,' and they both blushed. He picked up his bicycle, spun the pedals once or twice, then mounted and wobbled slowly away up the hill. Peter watched him until he had disappeared round a corner.

In the car Peter's father was leaning forward with forehead resting on the top of the steering wheel.

Peter sat beside him in silence.

'Sorry, Pete. Sometimes, I can't see things—I can't——'

'Let's stay here a bit.'

His father leaned back, showing that his cheeks were wet. 'No, better get back. Helen'll be waiting lunch.' He took out a cigarette with violently trembling hands. Peter pulled out the dashboard lighter to help him.

'Now, you see, Pete, why you'd better learn to drive.'

'I want to, anyway.'

'Peter, you'd better know about this. I've been under a lot of strain lately. Very private strain.'

The expression sounded peculiar. After a moment he inquired cautiously: 'Is it about Ma?'

'No, it isn't.'

'Oh,' Peter said.

Late that night Peter heard somebody moving about the house. Without thinking, he put on his dressing-gown and crept to the end of the corridor. Mrs. Macdonnell was standing at the top of the stairs. Wearing no make-up, with her hair hanging in two long dark braids down her frilly white nightdress, she looked both archaic and sexy, like somebody out of the Brontës.

'Who is it?'

'Hesketh. I mean, Peter.'

'Must I be always after you two laddies? Somebody left the light on in the hallway.'

He shivered, clutching his shrunken fawn dressing-gown—someone at school had pinched the cord years ago. His large greyish feet were cold on the floorboards. She came closer to him.

'Off to bed with you now.'

Her eyes were an entire shock: they were hard with hatred, like little darts of steel. He turned and without dignity made his way back to his room. She was watching him the whole time, and his hair prickled and his skin crawled.

'So you're off today, are you, dear?' Mrs. Parkes said. Peter was wearing his London suit. 'Well, I can't say I blame you. That auntie of yours, Mrs. Pelham, she's a kind soul. She spoke quite nicely to me after the funeral. I told her I'd stick with Doctor, and I done it up to now. But this isn't a happy house. You're well out of it.'

Peter's provisional driving licence had arrived by the morning's post. He showed it to his father at breakfast.

'Good man. I'll fix up those driving lessons before you come back. You may as well have something to do in the last week of the holidays.'

'Do you think I'll be able to drive in Austria?'

'I don't see why not.' His father was silent, buttering a piece of toast. 'It probably won't be Austria, in fact. Helen thinks she'd prefer Switzerland.'

Their eyes failed to meet across the tablecloth.

'Oh, I see.'

When they had both finished, Peter stacked the breakfast things and carried them through to the kitchen. Mrs. Macdonnell was standing at the sink, doing the flowers.

'Well, you're off now, are you, Peter? No doubt that aunt of yours will be spoiling you again. Funny, I thought you were a nice polite boy, first of all. Well, we live and learn and that's our misfortune.'

She cut through the stalks of a bunch of jonquils; they fell stickily, one by one.

'No, don't go yet. Listen to me a momemt, Peter.' Her voice dropped. 'Now, young feller me lad, don't you be talking out of turn. No telling tales out of school, got it? Because if you do, laddie, you'll live to regret it. You'll live to regret it very much. Helen can be real nasty, when she's the mind to it. And one thing she doesn't take to is dirty little sneaking eavesdroppers. There's your daddy calling. Now remember what I said.'

Peter got into the car beside his father.

'I'll ring up about the lessons today. And you can start driving me around for practice.'

Peter did not answer. His father accepted this, and looked straight ahead, his face twitching with guilt.

Cynthia Pelham had been taking Peter out to lunch.

She had made an immense effort to stop making remarks like 'I suppose it's no use suggesting you do something about your hair?' She had refrained from straightening him up altogether, apart from insisting he got his shoes cleaned by the man on the corner of Piccadilly Circus. He bought the clothes he wanted, including two frightful ties. In the restaurant she had let him order what he liked, and allowed him, with certain afterthoughts, to drink a glass of wine. Now she pushed money under the table at him, whispering: 'The man pays.'

'It's obvious you're paying,' Peter said. 'The waiters all know.'

They returned home exhausted.

Tea was waiting and with it, by prearrangement, was Juliet, Cynthia's oldest friend.

'Washing his hands.'

'How are things?' Juliet asked.

'Worse, if anything. Of course, I scrupulously refrain from mentioning, and all that. But really, it's been half a year now. And it isn't as if everything between Jack and Elizabeth had been so absolutely marvellous, because I happen to know——'

'What on earth difference should that make to Peter?'

'No, none, I suppose.' Cynthia sighed. 'I'm sorry, darling, I'm tired. He'll be down in a minute. Try a spot of charm, will you?'

'I'm sure he's a perfectly normal boy,' Juliet said. 'It's just that——'

'It's just that he's going through a phase. I know. Jolly long phase. I wonder if a psychiatrist——'

'I'd leave him alone if I were you.'

Kneeling on the rug, Cynthia bit into a piece of bread and butter. 'Nobody helps.'

'Honestly, I'd skip it. What good bread you always have—though of course I shouldn't be eating it.'

'He's impossible.'

'I can remember when everyone said "Cynthia's impossible".'

Peter's aunt blushed a little. 'You know perfectly well that was about something quite different.'

The stairs shook overhead and the pictures began rattling.

'Peter, darling, come and have some tea.' His aunt had not called him 'darling' before, and this embarrassed both herself and him.

He shook hands with Juliet and sat down. Fair and gleaming and beautifully dressed, the two women filled the immediate view. They tried to talk about Covent Garden, but since Peter was the only one of them with any knowledge of opera, conversation did not progress. Juliet had been to Glyndebourne three or four times, but couldn't remember any of the names.

'When do you go back?' she asked him. 'I'm sorry, I don't mean school—I know everybody always asks that. I meant to Shereham.'

'The day after tomorrow.'

'So soon!'

'Peter's having driving lessons,' Aunt Cynthia said.

'Yes?'

'My father wants me to drive when we go on holiday. We're going to Austria.' He stopped, then continued: 'At least, I mean, Switzerland. Also he wants me to drive him when he visits patients.'

To Juliet, Cynthia made a tiny elbow-lifting gesture, which Peter observed.

'I think that's marvellous,' Juliet said. 'Your father will be pleased. How's he getting on with his new housekeeper?'

Peter stared at the floor between his feet. 'She does her job.'

Cynthia, collecting the teacups, muttered: 'Yes, but what job, that's what we'd all like to know.'

Peter got up and walked out of the room.

'Darling!' Juliet said.

'Have I said something awful?'

'Yes, you have.'

Cynthia went scarlet. 'Well, everything one says is awful. It's absolute hell, you don't know what I've been through.'

This evening Peter's father was waiting for him at Shereham Station.

'Hullo, old boy. Got your luggage?'

'Yes.'

'How's Aunt Cynthia?'

'She's all right,' Peter said. 'She sent you her love.'

He handed in his ticket and followed his father into the car park.

'Not too tired after all your junketings?'

'No, of course not. Why?'

'I thought of going over for a bite at the Ram at Chillington. They do quite a decent meal there. It's outside my parish, so there's no risk of meeting patients. We used to go there a lot in the old days.'

'That'd be lovely.'

'Mrs. Parkes has been leaving me something in the oven, but I told her not to bother tonight, as you were coming down.'

His father spoke excitedly and rather fast, and Peter had to wait until they got into the car before asking: 'Where's Mrs. Macdonnell?'

His father was silent a moment. 'I—I gave her the sack. We had a bit of a bust up, so I said she could leave at once. Come, now, her cooking wasn't so fancy, was it?'

Peter giggled. 'It certainly wasn't.'

His father drove very slowly through Shereham and swerved out onto the dark Chillington road.

'Pa, can I have wine at dinner?'

'Well, that's not really the object of the exercise, but I should think so. In moderation.'

A minute or two later his father drew up at the roadside.

'Got your licence on you?'

'Yes, I have.'

'Like to drive?'

'Yes, I would.'

'Good man. Hop out then, and I'll move over.'

Peter let in the clutch perfectly and the car slid off towards Chillington.

CHINUA ACHEBE
Uncle Ben's Choice

IN the year nineteen hundred and nineteen I was a young clerk in
the Niger Company at Umuru. To be a clerk in those days is like to
be a minister today. My salary was two pounds ten. You may laugh
but two pounds ten in those days is like fifty pounds today. You
could buy a big goat with four shillings. I could remember the most
senior African in the company was one Saro man on ten-thirteen-
four. He was like Governor-General in our eyes.

Like all progressive young men I joined the African Club. We
played tennis and billiards. Every year we played a tournament
with the European Club. But I was less concerned with that. What
I liked was the Saturday night dances. Women were surplus. Not
all the waw-waw women you see in townships today but beautiful
things like this.

I had a Raleigh bicycle, brand new, and everybody called me
Jolly Ben. I was selling like hot bread. But there is one thing about
me—we can laugh and joke and drink and do otherwise but I must
always keep my sense with me. My father told me that a true son of
our land must know how to sleep and keep one eye open. I never
forget it. So I played and laughed with everyone and they shouted
'Jolly Ben! Jolly Ben!' but I knew what I was doing. The women of
Umuru are very sharp; before you count A they count B. So I had
to be very careful. I never showed any of them the road to my house
and I never ate the food they cooked for fear of love medicines. I
had seen many young men kill themselves with women in those
days, so I remembered my father's word: Never let a handshake
pass the elbow.

I can say that the only exception was one tall, yellow, salt-water
girl like this called Margaret. One Sunday morning I was playing
my gramophone, a brand-new HMV Senior. (I never believe in
second-hand things. If I have no money for a new one I just keep
myself quiet; that is my motto.) I was playing this record and
standing at the window with my chewing-stick in my mouth. People
were passing in their fine-fine dresses to one church nearby. This
Margaret was going with them when she saw me. As luck would

have it I did not see her in time to hide. So that very day—she did not wait till tomorrow or next tomorrow—but as soon as church closed she returned back. According to her she wanted to convert me to Roman Catholic. Wonders will never end! Margaret Jumbo! Beautiful thing like this. But it is not Margaret I want to tell you about now. I want to tell you how I stopped all that foolishness.

It was one New Year's Eve like this. You know how New Year can pass Christmas for jollity, for we end-of-month people. By Christmas Day the month has reached twenty-hungry but on New Year your pocket is heavy. So that day I went to the Club.

When I see you young men of nowadays say you drink, I just laugh. You don't know what drink is. You drink one bottle of beer or one shot of whisky and you begin to holler like craze-man. That night I was taking it easy on White Horse. *All that are desirous to pass from Edinburgh to London or any other place on their road, let them repair to the White Horse cellar.* . . . God Almighty!

One thing with me is I never mix my drinks. The day I want to drink whisky I know that that is whisky-day; if I want to drink beer tomorrow then I know it is beer-day; I don't touch any other thing. That night I was on White Horse. I had one roasted chicken and a tin of Guinea Gold. Yes, I used to smoke in those days. I only stopped when one German doctor told me my heart was as black as a cooking-pot. Those German doctors were spirits. You know they used to give injections in the head or belly or anywhere. You just point where the thing is paining you and they give it to you right there—they don't waste time.

What was I saying? . . . Yes, I drank a bottle of White Horse and put one roasted chicken on top of it . . . Drunk? It is not in my dictionary. I have never been drunk in my life. My father used to say that the cure for drink is to say no. When I want to drink I drink, when I want to stop I stop. So about three o'clock that night I said to myself, you have had enough. So I jumped on my new Raleigh bicycle and went home quietly to sleep.

At that time our senior clerk was jailed for stealing bales of calico and I was acting in that capacity. So I lived in a small company house. You know where G. B. Olivant is today? . . . Yes, overlooking the River Niger. That is where my house was. I had two rooms on one side of it and the store-keeper had two rooms on the other side. But as luck would have it this man was on leave, so his side was vacant.

I opened the front door and went inside. Then I locked it again. I left my bicycle in the first room and went into the bedroom. I was too tired to begin to look for my lamp. So I pulled my dress and packed them on the back of the chair, and fell like a log into my big iron bed. And to God who made me, there was a woman in my bed. My mind told me at once it was Margaret. So I began to laugh and touch her here and there. She was hundred per cent naked. I continued laughing and asked her when did she come. She did not say anything and I suspected she was annoyed because she asked me to take her to the Club that day and I said no. I said to her: if you come there we will meet, I don't take anybody to the Club as such. So I suspected that is what is making her vex.

I told her not to vex but still she did not say anything. I asked her if she was asleep—just for asking sake. She said nothing. Although I told you that I did not like women to come to my house, but for every rule there must be an exception. So if I say that I was very angry to find Margaret that night I will be telling a white lie. I was still laughing when I noticed that her breasts were straight like the breasts of a girl of sixteen—or seventeen, at most. I thought that perhaps it was because of the way she was lying on her back. But when I touched the hair and it was soft like the hair of a European my laughter was quenched by force. I touched the hair on her head and it was the same. I jumped out of the bed and shouted: 'Who are you?' My head swelled up like a barrel and I was shaking. The woman sat up and stretched her hands to call me back; as she did so her fingers touched me. I jumped back at the same time and shouted again to her to call her name. Then I said to myself: How can you be afraid of a woman? Whether a white woman or a black woman, it is the same ten and ten pence. So I said: 'All right, I will soon open your mouth,' at the same time I began to look for matches on the table. The woman suspected what I was looking for. She said, 'Biko akpakwana o̱ku.'

I said: 'So you are not a white woman. Who are you? I will strike the matches now if you don't tell me.' I shook the matches to show her that I meant business. My boldness had come back and I was trying to remember the voice because it was very familiar.

'Come back to the bed and I will tell you,' was what I heard next. Whoever told me it was a familiar voice told me a lie. It was sweet like sugar but not familiar at all. So I struck the matches.

'I beg you,' was the last thing she said.

If I tell you what I did next or how I managed to come out of
that room it is pure guess-work. The next thing I remember is that
I was running like a craze-man to Matthew's house. Then I was
banging on his door with my both hands.

'Who is that?' he said from inside.

'Open,' I shouted. 'In the name of God above, open.'

I called my name but my voice was not like my voice. The door
opened very small and I saw my kinsman holding a matchet in his
right hand.

I fell down on the floor, and he said, 'God will not agree.'

It was God Himself who directed me to Matthew Obi's house
that night because I did not see where I was going. I could not say
whether I was still in this world or whether I was dead. Matthew
poured cold water on me and after some time I was able to tell him
what happened. I think I told it upside down otherwise he would
not keep asking me what was she like, what was she like.

'I told you before I did not see her,' I said.

'I see, but you heard her voice?'

'I heard her voice quite all right. And I touched her and she
touched me.'

'I don't know whether you did well or not to scare her away,' was
what Matthew said.

I don't know how to explain it but those words from Matthew
opened my eyes. I knew at once that I had been visited by Mami
Wota, the Lady of the River Niger.

Matthew said again: 'It depends what you want in life. If it is
wealth you want then you made a great mistake today, but if you
are a true son of your father then take my hand.'

We shook hands and he said: 'Our fathers never told us that a
man should prefer wealth instead of wives and children.'

Today whenever my wives make me vex I tell them: 'I don't
blame you. If I had been wise I would have taken Mami Wota.'
They laugh and ask me why did I not take her. The youngest one
says: 'Don't worry, Papa, she will come again; she will come to
morrow.' And they laugh again.

But we all know it is a joke. For where is the man who will choose
wealth instead of children? Except a crazy white man like Dr. J. M.
Stuart-Young. Oh, I didn't tell you. The same night that I drove
Mami Wota out she went to Dr. J. M. Stuart-Young, a white
merchant and became his lover. You have heard of him? . . . Oh

yes, he became the richest man in the whole country. But she did not allow him to marry. When he died, what happened? All his wealth went to outsiders. Is that good wealth? I ask you. God forbid.

KINGSLEY AMIS
The Green Man Revisited

I WANT to tell you about a very odd experience I had a few months ago—not so as to entertain you, but because I think it raises some very basic questions about, you know, what life is all about and to what extent we run our own lives. Rather worrying questions. Anyway, what happened was this . . .

My wife and I had been staying the weekend with her uncle and aunt in Westmorland, near a place called Milnethorpe. Both of us—Jane and I, that is—had things to do in London on the Monday morning, and it's a long drive from there down to Barnet, where we live, even though a good half of it is on the M6. So I said: 'Look, don't let's break our necks trying to get home in the light' (this was in August). 'Let's take it easy and stop somewhere for dinner and reckon to get home about half-past ten or eleven.' Jane said okay.

So we left Milnethorpe in the middle of the afternoon, took things fairly easily, and landed up about half-past seven or a quarter to eight at the place we'd picked out of one of the food guides before we started. I won't tell you the name of the place, because the people who run it wouldn't thank me if I did. Please don't go looking for it. I'd advise you not to.

Anyway, we parked the car in the yard and went inside. It was a nice-looking sort of place: pretty old, built a good time ago, I mean, done up in a sensible sort of way, no muzak and no bloody silly blacked-out lighting, but no olde-worlde nonsense either. I got us both a drink in the bar and went off to see about a table for dinner. I soon found the right chap, and he said: 'Table for two in half an hour—certainly, sir. Are you in the bar? I'll get someone to bring you the menu in a few minutes.' Pleasant sort of chap, a bit young for the job.

I was just going off when a sort of paunchy business-type came in and said something like 'Mr. Allington not in tonight?' and the young fellow said: 'No, sir, he's taken the evening off.' 'All right, never mind.'

Well, I'll tell you why in a minute, but I turned back to the

young fellow and said, 'Excuse me, but is your name Palmer?' and
he said: 'Yes, sir.' I said, 'Not David Palmer by any chance?' and
he said: 'No, sir. Actually, the name's George.' I said, or rather
burbled: 'A friend of mine was telling me about this place, said he'd
stayed here, liked it very much, mentioned you—anyway, I got half
the name right, and Mr. Allington is the proprietor, isn't he?'
'That's correct, sir.'

I went straight back to the bar, went up to the barman and said:
'Fred?' He said: 'Yes, sir.' I said, 'Fred Soames?' and he said: 'Fred
Browning, sir.' I just said, 'Wrong Fred'—not very polite, but it
was all I could think of. I went over to where my wife was sitting
and I'd hardly sat down before she asked: 'What's the matter?'

What was the matter calls for a bit of explanation. In 1969 I
published a novel called *The Green Man*, which was not only the title
of the book but also the name of a sort of classy pub, or inn, where
most of the action took place—very much the kind of establishment
we were in that evening. Now the landlord of The Green Man was
called Allington, and his deputy was called David Palmer, and the
barman was called Fred Soames. Allington is a very uncommon
name—I wanted that for reasons nothing to do with this story. The
other two aren't, but to have got Palmer and Fred right, so to speak,
as well as Allington was a thumping great coincidence—staggering,
in fact. But I wasn't just staggered, I was very alarmed. Because
The Green Man wasn't only the name of the pub in my book: it was
also the name of a frightening creature, a sort of solid ghost,
conjured up out of tree branches and leaves and so on, that very
nearly kills Allington and his young daughter. I didn't want to find
I was right about that too.

Jane was very sensible, as always. She said stranger coincidences
had happened and still been just coincidences, and mightn't I have
come across an innkeeper called Allington somewhere, half-forgot-
ten about it and brought it up out of my unconscious mind when I
was looking for a name for an innkeeper to put in the book, and
now the real Allington had moved from wherever I'd seen him
before to this place. And Palmer and Fred really are very common
names. And I'd got the name of the pub wrong. (I'm still not telling
you what it's called, but one of the things it isn't called is The
Green Man.) And my pub was in Hertfordshire and this place was
. . . off the M6. All very reasonable and reassuring.

Only I wasn't very reassured. I mean, I obviously couldn't just leave it there. The thing to do was get hold of this chap Palmer and see if there was, well, any more to come. Which was going to be tricky if I wasn't going to look nosey or mad or something else that would shut him up. Neither of us ate much at dinner, though there was nothing wrong with the food. We didn't say much, either. I drank a fair amount.

Then, half-way through, Palmer turned up to do his everything-all-right routine, as I'd hoped he would, and as he would have done in my book. I said yes, it was fine, thanks, and then I said we'd be very pleased if he'd join us for a brandy afterwards if he'd got time, and he said he'd be delighted. Jolly good, but I was still stuck with this problem of how to dress the thing up.

Jane had said earlier on, why didn't I just tell the truth, and I'd said that since Palmer hadn't reacted at all when I gave him my name when I was booking the table, he'd only have my word for the whole story and might think I was off my rocker. She'd said that of course she'd back me up, and I'd said he'd just think he'd got two loonies on his hands instead of one. Anyway, now she said: '*Some* people who've read *The Green Man* must have mentioned it— fancy that, Mr. Palmer, you and Mr. Allington and Fred are all in a book by somebody called Kingsley Amis.' Obvious enough when you think of it, but like a lot of obvious things, you have got to think of it.

Well, that was the line I took when Palmer rolled up for his brandy: I'm me and I wrote this book and so on. Oh really? he said, more or less. I thought we were buggered, but then he said, 'Oh yes, now you mention it, I do remember some chap saying something like that, but it must have been two or three years ago'—as if that stopped it counting for much. 'I'm not much of a reader, you see,' he said.

'What about Mr. Allington,' I said, 'doesn't he read?' 'Not what you'd call a reader,' he said. Well, that was one down to me, or one up, depending on how you look at it, because *my* Allington was a tremendous reader—French poetry and all that. Still, the approach had worked after a fashion, and Palmer very decently put up with being cross-questioned on how far this place corresponded with my place in the book. Was Mrs. Allington blonde? There wasn't a Mrs. Allington any more: she'd died of leukemia quite a long time ago. Had he got his widowed father living here? (Allington's father, that is.) No, Mr. Allington senior, and his wife, lived in Eastbourne.

Was the house, the pub, haunted at all? Not as far as Palmer knew, and he'd been there three years. In fact, the place was only about two hundred years old, which completely clobbered a good half of my novel, where the ghosts had been hard at it more than a hundred years earlier still.

Nearly all of it was like that. Of course, there were some questions I couldn't ask, for one reason or another. For instance, was Allington a boozer, like my Allington, and, even more so, had this Allington had a visit from God? In the book, God turns up in in the form of a young man to give Allington some tips on how to deal with the ghosts, who he, God, thinks are a menace to him. No point in going any further into that part.

I said nearly all the answers Palmer gave me were straight negatives. One wasn't, or rather there were two points where I scored, so to speak. One was that Allington had a fifteen-year-old daughter called Marilyn living in the house. My Allington's daughter was thirteen, and called Amy, but I'd come somewhere near the mark—too near for comfort. The other thing was a bit harder to tie down. When I'm writing a novel, I very rarely have any sort of mental picture of any of the characters, what they actually look like. I think a lot of novelists would say the same. But, I don't know why, I'd had a very clear image of what my chap David Palmer looked like, and now I'd had a really good look at George Palmer, this one here, he was nearly the same as I'd imagined: not so tall, different nose, but still nearly the same. I didn't care for that.

Palmer, George Palmer, said he had things to see to and took off. I told Jane about the resemblance. She said I could easily have imagined that, and I said I supposed I might. 'Anyway,' she said, 'what do you think of it all?' I said it could still all be coincidence. 'What could it be if it isn't coincidence?' she asked. I'd been wondering about that while we were talking to Palmer. Not an easy one. Feeling a complete bloody fool, I said I thought we could have strayed into some kind of parallel world that slightly resembles the world I had made up—like in a Science Fiction story. She didn't laugh or back away. She looked round and spotted a newspaper someone had left on one of the chairs. It was that day's *Sunday Telegraph*. She said: 'If where we are is a world that's parallel to the real world, it's bound to be different from the real world in all sorts of ways. Now you read most of the *Telegraph* this morning, the real *Telegraph*. Look at this one and see if it's any different.' Well, I did,

and it wasn't: same front page, same article on the trade unions by
Perry, that's Peregrine Worsthorne, same readers' letters, same
crossword down to the last clue. Well, that was a relief.

But I didn't stay relieved, because there was another coincidence
shaping up. It was a hot night in August when all this happened,
and Allington was out for the evening. It was on a hot night in
August, after Allington had come back from an evening out, that
the monster, the Green Man, finally takes shape and comes
pounding up the road to tear young Amy Allington to pieces. That
bit begins on page 225 in my book, if you're interested.

The other nasty little consideration was this. Unlike some novelists I could name, I invent all my characters, except for a few minor
ones here and there. What I mean is, I don't go in for just renaming
people I know and bunging them into a book. But, of course, you
can't help putting *something* of yourself into all your characters, even
if it's a surly bus-conductor who only comes in for half a page.
Obviously, this comes up most of all with your heroes. None of my
heroes, not even old Lucky Jim, are me, but they can't help having
pretty fair chunks of me in them, some more than others. And
Allington in that book was one of the some. I'm more like him than
I'm like most of the others: in particular, I'm more like my Maurice
Allington in my book than the real Allington, who, by the way,
turned out to be called John, seemed (from what I'd heard) to be
like my Maurice Allington. Sorry to be long-winded, but I want to
get that quite clear.

So, if, by some fantastic chance, the Green Man, the monster,
was going to turn up here, he, or it, seemed more likely to turn up
tonight than most nights. Furthermore, I seemed better cast for the
part of the young girl's father, who manages in the book to save her
from the monster, than this young girl's father did.

I tried to explain all this to Jane. Evidently I got it across all
right, because she said straight away: 'We'd better stay here tonight,
then.' 'If we can,' I said, meaning if there was a room. Well, there
was, and at the front of the house too—which was important,
because in the book that's the side the monster appears on.

While one of the blokes was taking our stuff out of the car and
upstairs, I said to Jane: 'I'm not going to be like a bloody fool in a
ghost story who insists on seeing things through alone, not if I can
help it—I'm going to give Bob Conquest a ring.' Bob's an old chum
of mine, and about the only one I felt I could ask to come belting

up all this way (he lives in Battersea) for such a ridiculous reason. It was just after ten by this time, and the Green Man wasn't scheduled to put in an appearance till after 1 a.m., so Bob could make it all right, if he started straight away. Fine, except his phone didn't answer: I tried twice.

Jane said: 'Get hold of Monkey. I'll speak to him.' Monkey otherwise known as Colin, is her brother: he lives with us in Barnet. Our number answered all right, but I got my son Philip, who was staying the weekend there. He said Monkey was out at a party, he didn't know where. So all I could do was the necessary but not at all helpful job of saying we wouldn't be home till the next morning. So that was that. I mean, I just couldn't start getting hold of George Palmer and asking him to sit up with us into the small hours in case a ghost came along. Could any of you? I should have said that Philip hasn't got a car.

We stayed in the bar until it closed. I said to Jane at one point: 'You don't think I'm mad, do you? Or silly or anything?' She said: 'On the contrary, I think you're being extremely practical and sensible.' Well, thank God for that. Jane believes in ghosts, you see. My own position on that is exactly that of the man who said: 'I don't believe in ghosts, but I'm afraid of them.'

Which brings me to one of the oddest things about this whole business. I'm a nervous type by nature: I never go in an aeroplane; I won't drive a car (Jane does the driving); I don't even much care for being alone in the house. But, ever since we'd decided to stay the night at this place, all the uneasiness and, let's face it, the considerable fear I'd started to feel as soon as these coincidences started coming up, it all just fell away. I felt quite confident, I felt I knew I'd be able to do whatever might be required of me.

There was one other thing to get settled. I said to Jane—we were in the bedroom by this time: 'If he turns up, what am I going to use against him?' You see, in the book, Maurice Allington has dug up a sort of magic object that sort of controls the Green Man. I hadn't. Jane saw what I was driving at. She said she'd thought of that, and took off and gave me the plain gold cross she wears round her neck, not for religious reasons: it was her grandmother's. That'll fix him, I thought, and, as before, I felt quite confident about it.

After that, we more or less sat and waited. At one point a car drove up and stopped in the car park. A man got out and went in the front door. It must have been Allington. I couldn't see much about him except that he had the wrong colour hair, but when I looked at my watch it was eight minutes to midnight, the exact time when the Allington in the book got back after his evening out the night he coped with the creature. One more bit of . . . call it confirmation.

I opened our bedroom door and listened. Soon I heard footsteps coming upstairs and going off towards the back of the house, then a door shutting, and then straight away the house seemed totally still. It can't have been much later that I said to Jane: 'Look, there's no point in me hanging round up here. He might be early, you never know. It's a warm night, I might as well go down there now.' She said: 'Are you sure you don't want me to come with you?'

'Absolutely sure,' I said, 'I'll be fine. But I do want you to watch from the window here.'

'Okay,' she said. She wished me luck and we clung to each other for a bit, and then off I went.

I was glad I'd left plenty of time, because getting out of the place turned out to be far from straightforward. Everything seemed to be locked and the key taken away. Eventually I found a scullery door with the key still in the lock. Outside it was quite bright, with a full moon, or not far off, and a couple of fairly powerful lights at the corners of the house. It was a pretty lonely spot, with only two or three other houses in sight. I remember a car went by soon after I got out there, but it was the only one. There wasn't a breath of wind. I saw Jane at our window and waved, and she waved back.

The question was, where to wait. If what was going to happen—assuming something was—went like the book, then the young girl, the daughter, was going to come out of the house because she'd thought she'd heard her father calling her (another bit of magic), and then this Green Man creature was going to come running at her from one direction or the other. I couldn't decide which was the more likely direction.

A bit of luck: near the front door there was one of those heavy wooden benches. I sat down on that and started keeping watch, first one way, then the other, half a minute at a time. Normally, ten minutes of this would have driven me off my head with boredom, but that night somehow it was all right. After some quite long time, I turned my head from right to left on schedule and there was a girl, standing a few yards away: she must have come round that side of the house. She was wearing light-green pyjamas—wrong colour again. I was going to speak to her, but there was something about the way she was standing . . .

She wasn't looking at me: in fact, I soon saw she wasn't looking at anything much. I waved my hand in front of her eyes, the way they do in films when they think someone's been hypnotized or something. I felt a perfect idiot, but her eyes didn't move. Sleepwalking, presumably: not in the book. Do people walk in their sleep? Apparently not: they only pretend to, according to what a psychiatrist chum told me afterwards, but I hadn't heard that then. All I knew, or thought I knew, was this thing everybody's heard somewhere about it being dangerous to wake a sleepwalker. So I just stayed close to the girl and went on keeping watch. A bit more time went by, and then, sure enough, I heard, faintly but clearly, the sound I'd written about: the rustling, creaking sound of the movement of something made of tree branches, twigs and clusters of leaves. And there it was, about a hundred yards away, not really much like a man, coming up at a clumsy, jolting sort of jog-trot on the grass verge, and accelerating.

I knew what I had to do. I started walking to meet it, with the cross ready in my hand. (The girl hadn't moved at all.) When the thing was about twenty yards away I saw its face, which had fungus on it, and I heard another sound I'd written about coming from what I suppose you'd have to call its mouth, like the howling of wind through trees. I stopped and steadied myself and threw the cross at it, and it vanished—immediately. That wasn't like the book, but I didn't stop to think about it. I didn't stop to look for the cross, either. When I turned back, the girl had gone. So much the better. I rushed back into the inn and up to the bedroom and knocked on the door—I'd told Jane to lock it after me.

There was a delay before she came and opened it. I could see she looked confused or something, but I didn't bother with that, because I could feel all the calm and confidence I'd had earlier, it was all just draining away from me. I sat her down on the bed and sat down myself on a chair and just rattled off what had happened as fast as I could. I must have forgotten she'd been meant to be watching.

By the time I'd finished I was shaking. So was Jane. She said: 'What made you change your mind?'

'Change my mind—what about?'

'Going out there,' she said: 'getting up again and going out.'

'But,' I said, 'I've been out there all the time.'

'Oh no you haven't,' she said. 'You came back up here after about twenty minutes, and you told me the whole thing was silly and you were going to bed, which we both did.' She seemed quite positive.

I was absolutely shattered. 'But it all really happened,' I said. 'Just the way I told you.'

'It couldn't have,' she said. 'You must have dreamed it. You certainly didn't throw the cross at anything because it's here, you gave it back to me when you came back the first time.'

And there it was, on the chain round her neck.

I broke down then. I'm not quite clear what I said or did. Jane got some sleeping-pills down me and I went off in the end. I remember thinking rather wildly that somebody or other with a funny sense of humour had got me into exactly the same predicament, the same mess, as the hero of my book had been in: seeing something that must have been supernatural and just not being believed. Because I knew I'd seen the whole thing: I knew it then and I still know it.

I woke up late, feeling terrible. Jane was sitting reading by the bed. She said: 'I've seen young Miss Allington. Your description of her fits and, she said, she used to walk in her sleep.' I asked her how she'd found out, and she said she just had: she's good at that kind of thing. Anyway, I felt better straight away. I said it looked as if we'd neither of us been dreaming, even if what I'd seen couldn't be reconciled with what she'd seen, and she agreed. After that we rather dropped the subject in a funny sort of way. We decided not to look for the cross I'd thrown at the Green Man. I said we wouldn't be able to find it. I didn't ask Jane whether she was thinking what I was thinking: that looking would be a waste of time because she was wearing it at that very moment.

We packed up, made a couple of phone-calls rearranging our appointments, paid the bill, and drove off. We still didn't talk about the main issue. But then, as we were coming off the Mill Hill roundabout—that's only about ten minutes from home—Jane said: 'What do you think happened to sort of make it all happen?' I said: 'I think someone was needed there to destroy that monster. Which means I was guided there at that time, or perhaps the time could be adjusted. I must have been, well, sent all that stuff about the Green Man and about Allington and the others.'

'To make sure you recognized the place when you got there and knew what to do,' she said. 'Who did all the guiding and the sending and so on?'

'The same chap who appeared in my book to tell Allington what he wanted done.'

'Why couldn't he have fixed the monster himself?'

'There are limitations to his power.'

'There can't be many,' she said, 'if he can make the same object be in two places at the same time.'

Yes, you see, she'd thought of that too. It's supposed to be a physical impossibility, isn't it? Anyway, I said, probably the way he'd chosen had been more fun. 'More fun,' Jane repeated. She looked very thoughtful.

As you'll have seen, there was one loose end, of a sort. Who or what was it that had taken on my shape to enter that bedroom, talk to Jane with my voice, and share her bed for at any rate a few minutes? She and I didn't discuss it for several days. Then one morning she asked me the question more or less as I've just put it.

'Interesting point,' I said. 'I don't know.'

'It's more interesting than you think,' she said. 'Because when . . . whoever it was got into bed with me, he didn't just go to sleep.'

I suppose I just looked at her.

'That's right,' she said. 'I thought I'd better go and see John before I told you.' (That's John Allison, our GP.)

'It was negative, then,' I said.

'Yes,' Jane said.

Well, that's it. A relief, of course. But in one way, rather disappointing.

DAN JACOBSON
The Zulu and the Zeide

OLD man Grossman was worse than a nuisance. He was a source
of constant anxiety and irritation; he was a menace to himself and
to the passing motorists into whose path he would step, to the
children in the street whose games he would break up, sending
them flying, to the householders who at night would approach him
with clubs in their hands, fearing him a burglar; he was a butt and
a jest to the African servants who would tease him on street corners.

It was impossible to keep him in the house. He would take any
opportunity to slip out—a door left open meant that he was on the
streets, a window unlatched was a challenge to his agility, a walk in
the park was as much a game of hide-and-seek as a walk. The old
man's health was good, physically; he was quite spry, and he could
walk far, and he could jump and duck if he had to. All his physical
activity was put to only one purpose: to running away. It was a
passion for freedom that the old man might have been said to have,
could anyone have seen what joy there could have been for him in
wandering aimlessly about the streets, in sitting footsore on pavements, in entering other people's homes, in stumbling behind
advertisement hoardings that fenced undeveloped building plots, in
toiling up the stairs of fifteen-storey blocks of flats in which he had
no business, in being brought home by large young policemen who
winked at Harry Grossman, the old man's son, as they gently
hauled his father out of their flying-squad cars.

'He's always been like this,' Harry would say, when people asked
him about his father. And when they smiled and said: 'Always?'
Harry would say, 'Always. I know what I'm talking about. He's my
father, and I know what he's like. He gave my mother enough grey
hairs before her time. All he knew was to run away.'

Harry's reward would come when the visitors would say:

'Well, at least you're being as dutiful to him as anyone can be.'

It was a reward that Harry always refused. 'Dutiful? What can
you do? There's nothing else you can do.' Harry Grossman knew
that there was nothing else he could do. Dutifulness had been his
habit of life; it had had to be, having the sort of father he had, and

the strain of duty had made him abrupt and begrudging. He even carried his thick, powerful shoulders curved inwards, to keep what he had to himself. He was a thick-set, bunch-faced man, with large bones, and short, jabbing gestures; he was in the prime of life, and he would point at the father from whom he had inherited his strength, and on whom the largeness of bone showed now only as so much extra leanness that the clothing had to cover, and say: 'You see him? Do you know what he once did? My poor mother saved enough money to send him from the old country to South Africa: she bought clothes for him, and a ticket, and she sent him to her brother, who was already here. He was going to make enough money to bring me out, and my mother and my brother, all of us. But on the boat from Bremen to London he met some other Jews who were going to South America, and they said to him: "Why are you going to South Africa? It's a wild country, the blacks there will eat you. Come to South America and you'll make a fortune." So in London he exchanges his ticket. And we don't hear from him for six months. Six months later he gets a friend to write to my mother asking her please to send him enough money to pay for his ticket back to the old country—he's dying in the Argentine, the Spaniards are killing him, he says, and he must come home. So my mother borrows from her brother to bring him back again. Instead of a fortune he brought her a new debt, and that was all.'

But Harry was dutiful, how dutiful his friends had reason to see again when they would urge him to try sending the old man to a home for the aged. 'No,' Harry would reply, his features moving heavily and reluctantly to a frown, a pout, as he showed how little the suggestion appealed to him. 'I don't like the idea. Maybe one day when he needs medical attention all the time I'll feel differently about it, but not now, not now. He wouldn't like it, he'd be unhappy. We'll look after him as long as we can. It's a job. It's something you've got to do.'

More eagerly Harry would go back to a recital of the old man's past. 'He couldn't even pay for his own passage out. I had to pay the loan back. We came out together—my mother wouldn't let him go by himself again, and I had to pay off her brother who advanced the money for us. I was a boy—what was I?—sixteen, seventeen, but I paid for his passage, and my own, and my mother's and then my brother's. It took me a long time, let me tell you. And then my troubles with him weren't over.' Harry even reproached his father for his myopia; he could clearly enough remember his chagrin when shortly after their arrival in South Africa, after it had become clear that Harry would be able to make his way in the world and be a support to the whole family, the old man—who at that time had not really been so old—had suddenly, almost dramatically, grown so short-sighted that he had been almost blind without the glasses which Harry had had to buy for him. And Harry could remember too how he had then made a practice of losing the glasses or breaking them with the greatest frequency, until it had been made clear to him that he was no longer expected to do any work. 'He doesn't do that any more. When he wants to run away now he sees to it that he's wearing his glasses. That's how he's always been. Sometimes he recognizes me, at other times, when he doesn't want to, he just doesn't know who I am.'

What Harry said was true. Sometimes the old man would call out to his son, when he would see him at the end of a passage, 'Who are you?' Or he would come upon Harry in a room and demand of him, 'What do you want in my house?'

'Your house?' Harry would say, when he felt like teasing the old man. 'Your house?'

'Out of my house!' the old man would shout back.

'Your house? Do you call this your house?' Harry would reply, smiling at the old man's fury.

Harry was the only one in the house who talked to the old man, and then he did not so much talk to him, as talk of him to others. Harry's wife was a dim and silent woman, crowded out by her husband and the large-boned sons like himself that she had borne him, and she would gladly have seen the old man in an old-age home. But her husband had said no, so she put up with the old man, though for herself she could see no possible better end for him than a period of residence in a home for aged Jews which she had once visited, and which had impressed her most favourably with its glass and yellow brick, the noiseless rubber tiles in its corridors, its secluded grassed grounds, and the uniforms worn by the attendants to the establishment. But she put up with the old man; she did not talk to him. The grandchildren had nothing to do with their grandfather—they were busy at school, playing rugby and cricket, they could hardly speak Yiddish, and they were embarrassed by him in front of their friends; when the grandfather did take notice of them it was only to call them Boers and *goyim* and *shkotzim* in sudden quavering rages which did not disturb them at all.

The house itself—a big single-storied place of brick, with a corrugated iron roof above and a wide stoep all around—Harry Grossman had bought years before. In the continual rebuilding the suburb was undergoing it was beginning to look old-fashioned. But it was solid and prosperous, and indoors curiously masculine in appearance, like the house of a widower. The furniture was of the heaviest African woods, dark, and built to last, the passages were lined with bare linoleum, and the few pictures on the walls, big brown and grey mezzotints in heavy frames, had not been looked at for years. The servants were both men, large ignored Zulus who did their work and kept up the brown gleam of the furniture.

It was from this house that old man Grossman tried to escape. He fled through the doors and the windows and into the wide sunlit streets of the town in Africa, where the blocks of flats were encroaching upon the single-storied houses behind their gardens. In these streets he wandered until he was found.

It was Johannes, one of the Zulu servants, who suggested a way of dealing with old man Grossman. He brought to the house one afternoon Paulus, whom he described as his 'brother'. Harry Grossman knew enough to know that 'brother' in this context could mean anything from the son of one's mother to a friend from a neighbouring *kraal*, but by the speech that Johannes made on Paulus' behalf he might indeed have been the latter's brother. Johannes had to speak for Paulus, for Paulus knew no English. Paulus was a 'raw boy', as raw as a boy could possibly come. He was a muscular, moustached, and bearded African, with pendulous ear-lobes showing the slits in which the tribal plugs had once hung; on his feet he wore sandals the soles of which were cut from old motor-car tyres, the thongs from red inner tubing. He wore neither hat nor socks, but he did have a pair of khaki shorts which were too small for him, and a shirt without any buttons; buttons would in any case have been of no use for the shirt could never have closed over his chest. He swelled magnificently out of his clothing, and above there was a head carried well back, so that his beard, which had been trained to grow in two sharp points from his chin, bristled ferociously forward under his melancholy and almost mandarin-like moustache. When he smiled, as he did once or twice during

Johannes' speech, he showed his white, even teeth, but for the most part he stood looking rather shyly to the side of Harry Grossman's head, with his hands behind his back and his bare knees bent a little forward, as if to show how little he was asserting himself, no matter what his 'brother' might have been saying about him.

His expression did not change when Harry said that it seemed hopeless, that Paulus was too raw, and Johannes explained what the baas had just said. He nodded agreement when Johannes explained to him that the baas said that it was a pity that he knew no English. But whenever Harry looked at him, he smiled, not ingratiatingly, but simply smiling above his beard, as though saying: 'Try me.' Then he looked grave again as Johannes expatiated on his virtues. Johannes pleaded for his 'brother'. He said that the baas knew that he, Johannes, was a good boy. Would he, then, recommend to the baas a boy who was not a good boy too? The baas could see for himself, Johannes said, that Paulus was not one of these town boys, these street loafers: he was a good boy, come straight from the *kraal*. He was not a thief or a drinker. He was strong, he was a hard worker, he was clean, and he could be as gentle as a woman. If he, Johannes, were not telling the truth about all these things, then he deserved to be chased away. If Paulus failed in any single respect, then he, Johannes, would voluntarily leave the service of the baas, because he had said untrue things to the baas. But if the baas believed him, and gave Paulus his chance, then he, Johannes, would teach Paulus all the things of the house and the garden, so that Paulus would be useful to the baas in ways other than the particular task for which he was asking the baas to hire him. And, rather daringly, Johannes said that it did not matter so much if Paulus knew no English, because the old baas, the *oubaas*, knew no English either.

It was as something in the nature of a joke—almost a joke against his father—that Harry Grossman gave Paulus his chance. He was given a room in the servants' quarters in the backyard, into which he brought a tin trunk painted red and black, a roll of blankets, and a guitar with a picture of a cowboy on the back. He was given a houseboy's outfit of blue denim blouse and shorts, with red piping round the edges, into which he fitted, with his beard and his physique, like a king in exile in some pantomime. He was given his food three times a day, after the white people had eaten, a bar of soap every week, cast-off clothing at odd intervals, and the sum of one pound five shillings per week, five shillings of which he took, the rest being left at his request, with the baas, as savings. He had a free afternoon once a week, and he was allowed to entertain not more than two friends at any one time in his room. In all the particulars that Johannes had enumerated, Johannes was proved reliable. Paulus was not one of these town boys, these street loafers. He did not steal or drink, he was clean and he was honest and hard-working. And he could be as gentle as a woman.

It took Paulus some time to settle down to his job; he had to conquer not only his own shyness and strangeness in the new house filled with strange people—let alone the city, which, since taking occupation of his room, he had hardly dared to enter—but also the hostility of old man Grossman, who took immediate fright at Paulus and redoubled his efforts to get away from the house upon Paulus' entry into it. As it happened, the first result of this persistence on the part of the old man was that Paulus was able to get the measure of the job, for he came to it with a willingness of spirit that the old man could not vanquish, but could only teach. Paulus had been given no instructions, he had merely been told to see that the old man did not get himself into trouble, and after a few days of bewilderment Paulus found his way. He simply went along with the old man.

At first he did so cautiously, following the old man at a distance, for he knew the other did not trust him. But later he was able to follow the old man openly; still later he was able to walk side by side with him, and the old man did not try to escape from him. When old man Grossman went out, Paulus went too, and there was no longer any need for the doors and windows to be watched, or the police to be telephoned. The young bearded Zulu and the old bearded Jew from Lithuania walked together in the streets of the town that was strange to them both; together they looked over the fences of the large gardens and into the shining foyers of the blocks of flats; together they stood on the pavements of the main arterial roads and watched the cars and trucks rush between the tall buildings; together they walked in the small, sandy parks, and when the old man was tired Paulus saw to it that he sat on a bench and rested. They could not sit on the bench together, for only whites were allowed to sit on the benches, but Paulus would squat on the ground at the old man's feet and wait until he judged the old man had rested long enough, before moving on again. Together they stared into the windows of the suburban shops, and though neither of them could read the signs outside the shops, the advertisements on billboards, the traffic signs at the side of the road, Paulus learned to wait for the traffic lights to change from red to green before crossing a street, and together they stared at the Coca-Cola girls and the advertisements for beer and the cinema posters. On a piece of cardboard which Paulus carried in the pocket of his blouse Harry had had one of his sons print the old man's name and address, and whenever Paulus was uncertain of the way home, he would approach an African or a friendly-looking white man and show him the card, and try his best to follow the instructions, or at least the gesticulations which were all of the answers of the white men that meant anything to him. But there were enough Africans to be found, usually, who were more sophisticated than himself, and though they teased him for his 'rawness' and for holding the sort of job he had, they helped him too. Neither Paulus nor old man Grossman were aware that when they crossed a street hand-in-hand, as they sometimes did when the traffic was particularly heavy, there were people who averted their eyes from the sight of this degradation, which could come upon a man when he was senile and dependent.

Paulus knew only Zulu, the old man knew only Yiddish, so there was no language in which they could talk to one another. But they talked all the same: they both commented on or complained to each other of the things they saw around them, and often they agreed with one another, smiling and nodding their heads and explaining again with their hands what each happened to be talking about. They both seemed to believe that they were talking about the same things, and often they undoubtedly were, when they lifted their heads sharply to see an aeroplane cross the blue sky between two buildings, or when they reached the top of a steep road and turned to look back the way they had come, and saw below them the clean impervious towers of the city thrust nakedly against the sky in brand-new piles of concrete and glass and facebrick. Then down they would go again, among the houses and the gardens where the beneficent climate encouraged both palms and oak trees to grow indiscriminately among each other—as they did in the garden of the house to which, in the evenings, Paulus and old man Grossman would eventually return.

In and about the house Paulus soon became as indispensable to

the old man as he was on their expeditions out of it. Paulus dressed
him and bathed him and trimmed his beard, and when the old man
woke distressed in the middle of the night it would be for Paulus
that he would call—'*Der schwarzer*,' he would shout (for he never
learned Paulus' name), '*vo's der schwarzer*'—and Paulus would
change his sheets and pyjamas and put him back to bed again.
'Baas *Zeide*,' Paulus called the old man, picking up the Yiddish
word for grandfather from the children of the house.

That was something that Harry Grossman told everyone of. For
Harry persisted in regarding the arrangement as a kind of joke, and
the more the arrangement succeeded the more determinedly did he
try to turn it into a joke not only against his father but against
Paulus too. It had been a joke that his father should be looked after
by a raw Zulu: it was going to be a joke that the Zulu was successful
at it. 'Baas *Zeide*! That's what *der schwarzer* calls him—have you
ever heard the like of it? And you should see the two of them,
walking about in the streets hand-in-hand like two schoolgirls. Two
clever ones, *der schwarzer* and my father going for a promenade, and
between them I tell you you wouldn't be able to find out what day
of the week or what time of day it is.'

And when people said, 'Still that Paulus seems a very good boy,'
Harry would reply:

'Why shouldn't he be? With all his knowledge, are there so many
better jobs that he'd be able to find? He keeps the old man happy—
very good, very nice, but don't forget that that's what he's paid to
do. What does he know any better to do, a simple kaffir from the
kraal? He knows he's got a good job, and he'd be a fool if he threw
it away. Do you think,' Harry would say, and this too would
insistently be part of the joke, 'if I had nothing else to do with my
time I wouldn't be able to make the old man happy?' Harry would
look about his sitting-room, where the floorboards bore the weight
of his furniture, or when they sat on the stoep he would measure
with his glance the spacious garden aloof from the street beyond the
hedge. 'I've got other things to do. And I had other things to do,
plenty of them, all my life, and not only for myself.' The thought of
them would send him back to his joke. 'No, I think the old man has
just about found his level in *der schwarzer*—and I don't think *der
schwarzer* could cope with anything else.'

Harry teased the old man to his face too, about his 'black friend',
and he would ask him what he would do if Paulus went away; once

he jokingly threatened to send the Zulu away. But the old man didn't believe the threat, for Paulus was in his room at the time, and the old man simply left Harry and went straight to Paulus, and sat in the room with him. Harry did not follow him: he would never have gone into any of his servants' rooms, least of all that of Paulus. For though he made a joke of him to others, to Paulus himself he always spoke gruffly, unjokingly, with no patience. On that day he had merely shouted after the old man, 'Another time he won't be there.'

Yet it was strange to see how Harry Grossman would always be drawn to the room in which he knew his father and Paulus to be. Night after night he came into the old man's bedroom when Paulus was dressing or undressing the old man; almost as often Harry stood in the steamy, untidy bathroom when the old man was being bathed. At these times he hardly spoke, he offered no explanation of his presence. He stood dourly and silently in the room, in his customary powerful, begrudging stance, with one hand clasping the wrist of the other and both supporting his waist, and he watched Paulus at work. The backs of Paulus' hands were smooth and hairless, they were paler on the palms and at the finger-nails, and they worked deftly about the body of the old man, who was submissive under their ministrations. At first Paulus had sometimes smiled at Harry while he worked, with his straightforward, even smile in which there was no invitation to a complicity in patronage, but rather an encouragement to Harry to draw forward. After the first few evenings Paulus no longer smiled at his master, but he could not restrain himself, even under Harry's stare, from talking in a soft, continuous flow of Zulu, to encourage the old man and to exhort him to be helpful and to express his pleasure in how well the work was going. When Paulus at last wiped the gleaming soapsuds from his hands he would occasionally, when the old man was tired, stoop low and with a laugh pick him up and carry him easily down the passage to his bedroom. Harry would follow; he would stand in the passage and watch the burdened, bare-footed Zulu until the door of his father's room closed behind them both.

Only once did Harry wait on such an evening for Paulus to re-appear from his father's room. Paulus had already come out, had passed him in the narrow passage, and had already subduedly said: 'Good night, baas,' before Harry called suddenly:

'Hey! Wait!'

'Baas,' Paulus said, turning his head. Then he came quickly to Harry. 'Baas,' he said again, puzzled to know why his baas, who so rarely spoke to him, should suddenly have called him like this, when his work was over.

Harry waited again before speaking, waited long enough for Paulus to say: 'Baas?' once more, to move a little closer, and to lift his head for a moment before lowering it respectfully.

'The *oubaas* was tired tonight,' Harry said. 'Where did you take him? What did you do with him?'

'Baas?'

'You heard what I said. What did you do with him that he looked so tired?'

'Baas—I—' Paulus was flustered, and his hands beat in the air, but with care, so that he would not touch his baas. 'Please baas.' He brought both hands to his mouth, closing it forcibly. He flung his hands away. 'Johannes,' he said with relief, and he had already taken the first step down the passage to call his interpreter.

'No!' Harry called. 'You mean you don't understand what I say? I know you don't,' Harry shouted, though in fact he had forgotten until Paulus had reminded him. The sight of Paulus' puzzled and guilty face before him filled him with a lust to see this man, this nurse with the face and the figure of a warrior, look more puzzled and guilty yet; and Harry knew that it could so easily be done, it could be done simply by talking to him in the language he could not understand. 'You're a fool,' Harry said. 'You're like a child. You understand nothing, and it's just as well for you that you need nothing. You'll always be where you are, running to do what the white baas tells you to do. Look how you stand! Do you think I understood English when I came here?' Then with contempt, using one of the few Zulu words he knew: '*Hamba!* Go! Do you think I want to see you?'

'*Au* baas!' Paulus exclaimed in distress. He could not remonstrate; he could only open his hands in a gesture to show that he understood neither the words Harry used, nor in what he had been remiss that Harry should have spoken in such angry tones to him. But Harry gestured him away, and had the satisfaction of seeing Paulus shuffle off like a schoolboy.

Harry was the only person who knew that he and his father had quarrelled shortly before the accident that ended the old man's life. That was one story about his father he was never to repeat.

Late in the afternoon they quarrelled, after Harry had come back from the shop in which he made his living. He came back to find his father wandering about the house, shouting for *der schwarzer*, and his wife complaining that she had already told the old man at least five times that *der schwarzer* was not in the house: it was Paulus' afternoon off.

Harry went to his father, and he too told him, '*Der schwarzer*'s not here.' The old man turned away and continued going from room to room, peering in through the doors. '*Der schwarzer*'s not here,' Harry repeated. 'What do you want him for?'

Still the old man ignored him. He went down the passage towards the bedrooms. 'What do you want?' Harry called after him.

The old man went into every bedroom, still shouting for *der schwarzer*. Only when he was in his own bare bedroom did he look at Harry. 'Where's *der schwarzer*?'

'I've told you ten times I don't know where he is. What do you want him for?'

'I want *der schwarzer*.'

'I know you want him. But he isn't here.'

'I want *der schwarzer*.'

'Do you think I haven't heard you? He isn't here.'

'Bring him to me,' the old man said.

'I can't bring him to you. I don't know where he is.' Harry steadied himself against his own anger. He said quietly: 'Tell me what you want. I'll do it for you. I'm here, I can do what *der schwarzer* can do for you.'

'Where's *der schwarzer*?'

'I've told you he isn't here,' Harry shouted. 'Why don't you tell me what you want? What's the matter with me—can't you tell me what you want?'

'I want *der schwarzer*.'

'Please,' Harry said. He threw out his arms towards his father, but the gesture was abrupt, almost as though he were thrusting him away. 'Why can't you ask me? You can ask me—haven't I done enough for you already? Do you want to go for a walk?—I'll take you for a walk. What do you want? Do you want—do you want—?' Harry could not think what his father might want. 'I'll do it,' he said. 'You don't need *der schwarzer*.'

Then Harry saw that his father was weeping. His eyes were hidden behind the thick glasses that he had to wear: his glasses and beard made of his face a mask of age. But Harry knew when the old man was weeping—he had seen him crying too often before, when they had found him at the end of a street after he had wandered away, or even, years earlier, when he had lost another of the miserable jobs that seemed to be the only ones he could find in a country in which his son had, later, prospered.

'Father,' Harry asked, 'what have I done? Do you think I've sent *der schwarzer* away?' His father turned away, between the narrow bed and the narrow wardrobe. 'He's coming—' Harry said, but he could not look at his father's back, at his hollowed neck, on which the hairs that Paulus had clipped glistened above the pale brown discolorations of age—Harry could not look at the neck turned stiffly away from him while he had to try to promise the return of the Zulu. He dropped his hands and walked out of the room.

No one knew how the old man managed to get out of the house and through the front gate without having been seen. But he did manage it, and in the road he was struck down by a man on a bicycle. It was enough. He died a few days later in the hospital.

Harry's wife wept, even the grandsons wept; Paulus wept. Harry himself was stony, and his bunched, protuberant features were immovable; they seemed locked upon the bones of his face. A few days after the funeral he called Paulus and Johannes into the kitchen and said to Johannes: 'Tell him he must go. His work is finished.'

Johannes translated for Paulus, and then, after Paulus had spoken, he turned to Harry. 'He says, yes baas.' Paulus kept his eyes on the ground; he did not look up even when Harry looked directly at him. Harry knew that this was not out of fear or shyness, but out of courtesy for his master's grief—which was what they could not but be talking of, when they talked of his work.

'Here's his pay.' Harry thrust a few notes towards Paulus, who took them in his cupped hands, and retreated.

Harry waited for them to go, but Paulus stayed in the room, and consulted with Johannes in a low voice. Johannes turned to his master. 'He says, baas, that the baas still has his savings.'

Harry had forgotten about Paulus' saving. He told Johannes that he had forgotten, and that he did not have enough money at the moment, but would bring the money the next day. Johannes translated and Paulus nodded gratefully. Both he and Johannes were subdued by the death there had been in the house.

Harry's dealings with Paulus were over. He took what was to have been his last look at Paulus, but this look stirred him once more against the Zulu. As harshly as he told Paulus that he had to go, so now, implacably, seeing Paulus in the mockery and simplicity of his houseboy's clothing, feeding his anger to the very end, Harry said: 'Ask him what he's been saving for. What's he going to do with the fortune he's made?'

Johannes spoke to Paulus and came back with a reply. 'He says, baas, that he is saving to bring his wife and children from Zululand to Johannesburg. He is saving, baas,' Johannes said, for Harry had not seemed to understand, 'to bring his family to this town also.'

The two Zulus were bewildered to know why it was then that Harry Grossman's clenched, fist-like features should have fallen from one another, or why he stared with such guilt and despair at Paulus, while he cried, 'What else could I have done? I did my best!' before the first tears came.

BENEDICT KIELY
God's Own Country

THE plump girl from Cork City who was the editor's secretary
came into the newsroom where the four of us huddled together, and
said, so rapidly that we had to ask her to say it all over again:
Goodness gracious, Mr. Slattery, you are, you really are,
smouldering.

She was plump and very pretty and enticingly perfumed and
everyone of the four of us, that is everyone of us except Jeremiah,
would have been overjoyed to make advances to her except that,
being from Cork City, she talked so rapidly that we never had time
to get a word in edgeways. She said: Goodness gracious, Mr.
Slattery, you are, you really are, smouldering.

Now that our attention had been drawn to it, he really was
smouldering. He sat, crouched as close as he could get to the paltry
coal fire: the old ramshackle building, all rooms of no definable
geometrical shape, would have collapsed with Merulius Lacrymans,
the most noxious form of dry rot, the tertiary syphilis of ageing
buildings, if central heating had ever been installed. Jeremiah
nursed the fire between his bony knees. He toasted, or tried to toast,
his chapped chilblained hands above the pitiful glow. The management of that small weekly newspaper were too mean to spend much
money on fuel; and in that bitter spring Jeremiah was the coldest
man in the city. He tried, it seemed, to suck what little heat there
was into his bloodless body. He certainly allowed none of it to pass
him by so as to mollify the three of us who sat, while he crouched,
working doggedly with our overcoats and woollen scarves on. The
big poet who wrote the cinema reviews, and who hadn't been inside
a cinema since he left for a drink at the intermission in *Gone With
The Wind* and never went back, was typing, with woollen gloves on,
with one finger; and for panache more than for actual necessity he
wore a motor-cycling helmet with fleece-lined flaps over his ears.
The big poet had already told Jeremiah that Jeremiah was a raven,
a scrawny starved raven, quothing and croaking nevermore, crumpled up there in his black greatcoat over a fire that wouldn't boil an
egg. Jeremiah only crouched closer to the fire and, since we knew

how cold he always was, we left him be and forgot all about him, and he might well have gone on fire, nobody, not even himself, noticing, if the plump pretty secretary, a golden perfumed ball hopping from the parlour into the hall, hadn't bounced, warming the world, being the true honey of delight, into the room.

It was the turned-up fold of the right leg of his shiny black trousers. He extinguished himself wearily, putting on, to protect the fingers of his right hand, a leather motoring-gauntlet. He had lost, or had never possessed, the left-hand gauntlet. He moved a little back from the fire, he even tried to sit up straight. She picked up the telephone on the table before me. Her rounded left haunch, packed tightly in a sort of golden cloth, was within eating distance, if I'd had a knife and fork. She said to the switch that she would take that call now from where she was in the newsroom. She was silent for a while. The golden haunch moved ever so slightly, rose and fell, in fact, as if it breathed. She said: Certainly, your Grace.

—No, your Grace.

—To the island, your Grace.

—A reporter, your Grace.

—Of course, your Grace.

—And photographer, your Grace.

—An American bishop, your Grace.

—How interesting, your Grace.

—Confirmation, your Grace.

—All the way from Georgia, your Grace.

—Goodness gracious, your Grace.

—Lifeboat, your Grace.

—Yes, your Grace.

—No, your Grace.

—Next Thursday, your Grace.

—I'll make a note of it, your Grace.

—And tell the editor when he comes in from the nunciature, your Grace.

The nunciature was the place where the editor, promoting the Pope's wishes by promoting the Catholic press, did most of his drinking. He had a great tongue for the Italian wine.

—Lifeboat, your Grace.

—Absolutely, your Grace.

—Goodbye, your Grace.

The big poet said: That wouldn't have been His Grace you were talking to?

—That man, she said, thinks he's three rungs of the ladder above the Pope of Rome and with right of succession to the Lord Himself.

She made for the door. The gold blinded me. She turned at the door, said to us all, or to three of us: Watch him. Don't let him make a holocaust of himself. Clean him up and feed him. He's for the Islands of the West, Hy-Breasil, the Isle of the Blest, next Thursday with the Greatest Grace of all the Graces, and a Yankee bishop who thinks it would do something for him to bestow the holy sacrament of confirmation on the young savages out there. Not that it will do much for them. It would take more than two bishops and the Holy Ghost. . . .

She was still talking as she vanished. The door crashed shut behind her and the room was dark again, and colder than ever. Jeremiah was visibly shuddering, audibly chattering, because to his bloodlessness and to the chill of the room and of the harsh day of east wind, had been added the worst cold of all: terror.

—Take him out, the big poet said, before he freezes us to death. Buy him a hot whiskey. You can buy me one when I finish my column.

As he tapped with one gloved finger and, with a free and open mind and no prejudice, critically evaluated what he had not seen, he also lifted up his voice and sang: When the roses bloom again down by yon river, and the robin redbreast sings his sweet refrain, in the days of auld lang syne, I'll be with you sweetheart mine, I'll be with you when the roses bloom again.

In Mulligan's in Poolbeg Street, established 1782, the year of the great Convention of the heroic patriotic Volunteers at Dungannon when the leaders of the nation, sort of, were inspired by the example of American Independence, I said to Jeremiah: Be a blood. Come alive. Break out. Face them. Show them. Fuck the begrudgers. Die, if die you must, on your feet and fighting.

He said: It's very well for you to talk. You can eat.

—Everybody, for God's sake, can eat.

—I can't eat. I can only nibble.

—You can drink, though. You have no trouble at all with the drink.

His first hot whiskey was gone, but hadn't done him any good that you'd notice.

—Only whiskey, he said, and sometimes on good days, stout. But even milk makes me ill, unless it's hot and with pepper sprinkled on it.

I pretended to laugh at him, to jolly him out of it, yet he really had me worried. For he was a good helpless intelligent chap, and his nerves had gone to hell in the seminary that he had had to leave, and the oddest rumours about his eating or non-eating habits were going around the town. That, for instance, he had been seen in a certain hotel, nibbling at biscuits left behind by another customer, and when the waiter, who was a friend of mine, asked him in all kindness did he need lunch, he had slunk away, the waiter said, like a shadow that had neither substance nor sunshine to account for its being there in the first place. He was no man, I had to agree, to face on an empty stomach a spring gale, or even a half or a hatful of a gale, on the wild western Altantic coast.

—And the thought of that bishop, he said, puts the heart across me. He's a boor and a bully of the most violent description. He's a hierarchical Genghis Khan.

—Not half as bad as he's painted.

—Half's bad enough.

So I told some story, once told to me by a Belfast man, about some charitable act performed by the same bishop. It didn't sound at all convincing. Nor was Jeremiah convinced.

—If he ever was charitable, he said, be sure that it wasn't his own money he gave away.

—You won't have to see much of him, Jeremiah. Keep out of his path. Don't encounter him.

—But I'll encounter the uncandid cameraman who'll be my constant companion. With his good tweeds and his cameras that all the gold in the mint wouldn't buy. How do the mean crowd that run that paper ever manage to pay him enough to satisfy him? He invited me to his home to dinner. Once. To patronise me. To show me what he had and I hadn't. He ran out six times during dinner to ring the doorbell, and we had to stop eating and listen to the chimes. A different chime in every room. Like living in the bloody belfry. Searchlights he has on the lawn to illuminate the house on feast-days. Like they do in America, I'm told. Letting his light shine in the uncomprehending darkness. Some men in this town can't pay the electricity bill, but he suffers from a surplus. And this bishop is a friend of his. Stops with him when he comes to town. His wife's uncle is a monsignor in His Grace's diocese. Practically inlaws. They call each other by their Christian names. I was permitted and privileged to see the room the bishop sleeps in, with its own special bathroom, toilet seat reserved for the episcopal arse, a layman would have to have his arse specially anointed to sit on it. Let me tell you that it filled me with awe. When they have clerical visitors, he told me, they couldn't have them shaving in the ordinary bathroom. I hadn't the courage to ask him was there anything forbidding that in Canon Law, Pastoral Theology, or the Maynooth Statutes. God look down on me between the two of them, and an American bishop thrown in for good luck. They say that in the United States the bishops are just bigger and more brutal.

—Jeremiah, I said severely, you're lucky to be out with that cameraman. He'll teach you to be a newsman. Just study how he works. He can smell news like, like . . .

The struggle for words went on until he helped me out. He was quick-witted; and even on him the third hot whiskey was bound to have some effect: to send what blood there was in his veins toe-dancing merrily to his brain.

—Like a buzzard smells dead meat, he said.

Then the poet joined us. Having an inherited gift for cobbling he had recently cobbled for himself a pair of shoes but, since measure-ment was not his might, they turned out to be too big even for him, thus, for any mortal man. But he had not given up hope of encountering in a public bar some Cyclopean for whose benefit he had, in his subconscious, been working, and of finding him able and willing to purchase those shoes. He carried them, unwrapped, under his arm. They always excited comment; and many were the men who tried and failed to fill them. That night we toured the town with them, adding to our company, en route, an Irish professor from Rathfarnham, a French professor from Marseilles, a lady novelist, a uniformed American soldier with an Irish name, who came from Boston and General Patch's army which had passed by Marseilles and wrecked it in the process. Outside Saint Vincent's hospital in Saint Stephen's Green a total stranger, walking past us, collapsed. He was a very big man, with enormous feet. But when the men from Boston and Marseilles, and the poet and myself, carried him into the hospital he was dead.

All that, as you are about to observe, is another story.

We failed, as it so happened, to sell the shoes.

* * *

On that corner of the western coast of Ireland the difference between a gale and a half-gale is that in a half-gale you take a chance and go out, in a gale you stay ashore.

The night before the voyage they rested in a hotel in Galway City. The wind rattled the casements and now and again blew open the door of the bar in which Jeremiah sat alone, until well after midnight, over one miserable whiskey. Nobody bothered to talk to him, not even in Galway where the very lobsters will welcome the stranger. The bar was draughty. He wore his black greatcoat, a relic of his clerical ambitions. It enlarged his body to the point of monstrosity, and minimized his head. Dripping customers came and drank and steamed and went again. When the door blew open he could see the downpours of rain hopping like hailstones on the street. The spluttering radio talked of floods, and trees blown down, and crops destroyed, and an oil-tanker in peril off the Tuskar Rock. The cameraman had eaten a horse of a dinner, washed it down with the best wine, said his prayers, and gone to bed, to be, he said, fresh and fit for the morning. Jeremiah was hungry, but less than ever could he eat: with fear of the storm and of the western sea as yet unseen and of the bull of a bishop and, perhaps too, he thought, that visiting American would be no better. At midnight he drained his glass dry and afterwards tilted it several times to his lips, drinking, or inhaling, only wind. He would have ordered another whiskey but the bar was crowded by that time, and the barman was surrounded by his privileged friends who were drinking after hours. The wind no longer blew the door open for the door was double-bolted against the night. But the booming, buffeting, and rattling of the storm could still be heard, at times bellowing like a brazen bishop, threatening Jeremiah. The customers kept coming and crowding through a dark passage that joined the bar and the kitchen. They acted as if they had spent all day in the kitchen and had every intention of spending all night in the bar. Each one of them favoured Jeremiah with a startled look where he sat, black, deformed by that greatcoat, hunched-up in his black cold corner. Nobody joined him. He went to bed, to a narrow, hard, excessively-white bed with a ridge up the middle and a downward slope on each side. The rubber hot-water bottle had already gone cold. The rain threatened to smash the window-panes. He spread his greatcoat over his feet, wearing his socks in bed, and, cursing the day he was born, fell asleep from sheer misery.

Early next morning he had his baptism of salt water, not sea-spray but rain blown sideways and so salty that it made a crust around the lips.

—That out there, said the cameraman in the security of his car, is what they call the poteen cross.

The seats in the car were covered with a red plush, in its turn covered by a protective and easily-washable, transparent plastic that Jeremiah knew had been put there to prevent himself or his greatcoat or his greasy, shiny pants from making direct contact with the red plush.

—Did you never hear of the poteen cross?

—No, said Jeremiah.

They had stopped in a pelting village on the westward road. The doors were shut, the windows still blinded. It was no morning for early rising. The sea was audible, but not visible. The rain came bellying inshore on gusts of wind. On a gravelled space down a slope towards the sound of the sea stood a huge bare black cross: well, not completely bare for it carried, criss-crossed, the spear that pierced, that other spear that bore aloft the sponge soaked in vinegar; and it was topped by a gigantic crown of thorns. The cameraman said: 'When the Redemptorist Fathers preached hellfire against the men who made the poteen, they ordered the moon-shiners, under pain of mortal sin, to come here and leave their stills at the foot of the cross. The last sinner to hold out against them came in the end with his still but, there before him, he saw a better model that somebody else had left, so he took it away with him. There's a London magazine wants a picture of that cross.

—It wouldn't, said Jeremiah, make much of a picture.

—With somebody beside it pointing up at it, it wouldn't be so bad. The light's not good. But I think we could manage.

—We, said Jeremiah.

—You wouldn't like me, he said, to get up on the cross? Have you brought the nails?

He posed, nevertheless, and pointed up at the cross. What else could he do? We saw the picture afterwards in that London magazine. Jeremiah looked like a sable bloated demon trying to prove to benighted sinners that Christ was gone and dead and never would rise again. But it was undeniably an effective picture. Jeremiah posed and pointed. He was salted and sodden while the cameraman, secure in yellow oilskins and sou'wester, darted out,

took three shots, darted in again, doffed the oil-skins, and was as
dry as snuff. They drove on westwards.

—That coat of yours, said the cameraman. You should have
fitted yourself out with oilskins. That coat of yours will soak up all
the water from here to Long Island.

—Stinks a bit too, he said on reflection. The Beeoh is flying.

That was meant to be some sort of a joke and, for the sake of
civility, Jeremiah tried to laugh. They crossed a stone bridge over a
brown-and-white, foaming, flooded river, turned left down a byroad,
followed the course of the river, sometimes so close to it that the
floodwater lapped the edge of the road, sometimes swinging a little
away from it through a misted landscape of small fields, thatched
cabins dour and withdrawn in the storm, shapeless expanses of rock
and heather, until they came to where the brown-and-white water
tumbled into the peace of a little land-locked harbour. The lifeboat
that, by special arrangement, was to carry the party to the island
was there, but no lifeboatmen, no party. A few small craft lay on a
sandy slope in the shelter of a breakwater. Jeremiah and the
cameraman could have been the only people alive in a swamped
world. They waited: the cameraman in the car with the heat on;
Jeremiah, to get away from him for a while, prowling around empty
cold sheds that were, at least, dry, but that stank of dead fish and
were floored with peat-mould terrazzoed, it would seem, by fragments broken from many previous generations of lobsters. Beyond
the breakwater and a rocky headland the sea boomed, but the water
in the sheltered harbour was smooth and black as ink. He was
hungry again but knew that if he had food, any food other than dry
biscuits, he wouldn't be able to eat it. All food now would smell of
stale fish. He was cold, as always. When he was out of sight of the
cameraman he pranced, to warm himself, on peat-mould and
lobsters. He was only moderately successful. But his greatcoat, at
least, steamed.

The rain eased off, the sky brightened, but the wind seemed to
grow in fury, surf and spray went up straight and shining into the
air beyond the breakwater, leaped it and came down with a flat slap
on the sandy slope and the sleeping small craft. Then, like Apache
on an Arizona skyline, the people began to appear: a group of three,
suddenly, from behind a standing rock; a group of seven or eight
rising sharply into sight on a hilltop on the switchback riverside
road, dropping out of sight into a hollow, surfacing again, followed

by other groups that appeared and disappeared in the same disconcerting manner. As the sky cleared, the uniform darkness breaking up into bullocks of black wind-goaded clouds, the landscape of rock and heather, patchwork fields divided by grey, high, drystone walls, came out into the light; and from every small farmhouse thus revealed, people came, following footpaths, crossing stiles, calling to each other across patches of light-green oats and dark-green potatoes. It was a sudden miracle of growth, of human life appearing where there had been nothing but wind and rain and mist. Within three-quarters of an hour there were a hundred or more people around the harbour, lean hard-faced fishermen and small farmers, dark-haired laughing girls, old women in coloured shawls, talking Irish, talking English, posing in groups for the cameraman who in his yellow oilskins moved among them like a gigantic canary. They waved and called to Jeremiah where he stood, withdrawn, and on the defensive, in the sheltered doorway of a fish-stinking shed.

A black Volkswagen came down the road followed by a red Volkswagen. From the black car a stout priest stepped forth, surveyed the crowd like a general estimating the strength of his mustered troops, shook hands with the cameraman as if he were meeting an old friend. From the red car a young man stepped out, then held the door for a gaunt middle-aged lady who emerged with an effort, head first: the local schoolteachers, by the cut of them. They picked out from the crowd a group of twelve to twenty, lined them up, backs to the wall, in the shelter of the breakwater. The tall lady waved her arms and the groups began to sing.

—Ecce sacerdos magnus, they sang.

A black limousine, with the traction power of two thousand Jerusalem asses on the first Holy Thursday, came, appearing and disappearing, down the switchback road. This was it, Jeremiah knew, and shuddered. On the back of an open truck behind the limousine came the lifeboatmen, all like the cameraman, in bright yellow oilskins.

—This is God's own country, said the American bishop, and ye are God's own people.

Jeremiah was still at a safe distance, yet near enough to hear the booming clerical-American voice. The sea boomed beyond the wall.

The spray soared, then slapped down on the sand, sparing the sheltered singers.

—Faith of our fathers, they sang, living still, in spite of dungeon, fire, and sword.

Circling the crowd the great canary, camera now at ease, approached Jeremiah.

—Get with it, Dracula, he said.

He didn't much bother to lower his voice.

—Come out of your corner fighting. Get in and get a story. That Yank is news. He was run out of Rumania by the Communists.

—He also comes, said Jeremiah, from Savannah, Georgia.

—So what?

—He doesn't exactly qualify as a Yankee.

—Oh Jesus, geography, said the cameraman. We'll give you full marks for geography. They'll look lovely in the paper where your story should be. If he came from bloody Patagonia, he's here now. Go get him.

Then he was gone, waving his camera. The American bishop, a tall and stately man, was advancing, blessing as he went, to the stone steps that went down the harbour wall to the moored lifeboat. He was in God's own country and God's own people, well-marshalled by the stout parish priest, were all around him. The Irish bishop, a tall and stately man, stood still, thoughtfully watching the approaching cameraman and Jeremiah most reluctantly plodding in the rear, his progress, to his relief, made more difficult by the mush of wet peat-mould underfoot, growing deeper and deeper as he approached the wall where sailing hookers were loaded with fuel for the peatless island. Yet, slowly as he moved, he was still close enough to see clearly what happened and to hear clearly what was said.

The bishop, tall and stately and monarch even over the parish priest, looked with a cold eye at the advancing cameraman. There was no ring kissing. The bishop did not reach out his hand to have his ring saluted. That was odd, to begin with. Then he said loudly: What do you want?

—Your Grace, said the great canary.

He made a sort of a curtsey, clumsily, because he was hobbled in creaking oilskins.

—Your Grace, he said, out on the island there's a nonagenarian,

the oldest inhabitant, and when we get there I'd like to get a picture
of you giving him your blessing.

His Grace said nothing. His Grace turned very red in the face. In
increased terror, Jeremiah remembered that inlaws could have their
tiffs and that clerical inlaws were well known to be hell incarnate.
His Grace right-about-wheeled, showed to the mainland and all on
it a black broad back, right-quick-marched towards the lifeboat,
sinking to the ankles as he thundered on in the soft wet mould, but
by no means abating his speed which could have been a fair five
miles an hour. His long coat-tails flapped in the wind. The wet
mould fountained up like snow from a snow-plough. The sea
boomed. The spray splattered. The great canary had shrunk as if
plucked. Jeremiah's coat steamed worse then ever in the frenzy of
his fear. If he treats his own like that, he thought, what in God's
holy name will he do to me? Yet he couldn't resist saying: That
man could pose like Nelson on his pillar watching his world collapse.

The canary cameraman hadn't a word to say.

Once aboard the lugger the bishops had swathed themselves in
oilskins provided by the lifeboat's captain, and the cameraman
mustered enough of his ancient gall to mutter to Jeremiah that that
was the first time that he or anybody else had seen canary-coloured
bishops.

—Snap them, said Jeremiah. You could sell it to the magazines
in Bucharest. Episcopal American agent turns yellow.

But the cameraman was still too crestfallen, and made no move,
and clearly looked relieved when the Irish bishop, tall and stately
even if a little grotesque in oilskins, descended carefully into the
for'ard foxhole, sat close into the corner, took out his rosary beads
and began to pray silently: he knew the tricks of his western sea.
Lulled by the security of the landlocked sheltered harbour, the
American bishop, tall and stately even if a little grotesque in
oilskins, stood like Nelson on the foredeck. He surveyed the shore of
rock, small fields, drystone walls, small thatched farmhouses, oats,
potatoes, grazing black cattle, all misting over for more rain. Then
he turned his back on the mainland and looked at the people, now
marshalled all together by the parish priest and the two teachers in
the lee of the harbour wall. The choir sang: Holy God, we praise
thy name. Lord of all, we bow before thee.

An outrider of the squall of rain that the wind was driving inshore

cornered cunningly around harbour wall and headland, and disre-
spectfully spattered the American bishop. Secure in oilskins and the
Grace of state he ignored it. The cameraman dived into the stern
foxhole. Jeremiah by now was so sodden that the squall had no
effect on him. An uncle of his, a farmer in the County Longford,
had worn the same heavy woollen underwear winter and summer
and argued eloquently that what kept the heat in kept it out. That
soaking salty steaming greatcoat could, likewise, stand upright on
its own against the fury of the Bay of Biscay. It was a fortress for
Jeremiah; and with his right hand, reaching out through the
loophole of the sleeve, he touched the tough stubby oaken mast, a
talismanic touch, a prayer to the rooted essence of the earth to
protect him from the capricious fury of the sea. Then with the
bishop, a yellow figurehead, at the prow, and Jeremiah, a sable
figureheard, at the stern, they moved smoothly towards the open
ocean; and, having withdrawn a little from the land, the bishop
raised his hand, as Lord Nelson would not have done, and said:
This is God's own country. Ye are God's own people.

The choir sang: Hail Glorious Saint Patrick, dear Saint of our
isle.

From the conscripted and marshalled people came a cheer loud
enough to drown the hymn; and then the sea, with as little regard
for the cloth as had the Rumanian Reds, struck like an angry bull
and the boat, Jeremiah says, stood on its nose, and only a miracle
of the highest order kept the American bishop out of the drink.
Jeremiah could see him, down, far down at the bottom of a dizzy
slope, then up, far up, shining like the sun between sea and sky, as
the boat reared back on its haunches and Jeremiah felt on the back
of his head the blow of a gigantic fist. It was simply salt seawater in
a solid block, striking and bursting like a bomb. By the time he had
wiped his eyes and the boat was again, for a few brief moments, on
an even keel, there were two bishops sheltering in the for'ard
foxhole: the two most quiet and prayerful men he had ever seen.

—On the ocean that hollows the rocks where ye dwell, Jeremiah
recited out as loudly as he could because no ears could hear even a
bull bellowing above the roar and movement and torment of the
sea.

—A shadowy land, he went on, has appeared as they tell. Men
thought it a region of sunshine and rest, and they called it Hy-
Breasil the Isle of the Blest.

To make matters easier, if not tolerable, he composed his mind and said to himself: Lifeboats can't sink.

On this harshly-ocean-bitten coast there was the poetic legend of the visionary who sailed west, ever west, to find the island where the souls of the blest are forever happy.

—Rash dreamer return, Jeremiah shouted, oh ye winds of the main, bear him back to his own native Ara again.

For his defiance the sea repaid him in three thundering salty buffets and a sudden angled attack that sent the boat hissing along on its side and placed Jeremiah with both arms around the mast. In the brief following lull he said more quietly, pacifying the sea, acknowledging its power: Night fell on the deep amid tempest and spray, and he died on the ocean, away far away.

He was far too frightened to be seasick, which was just as well, considering the windy vacuum he had for a stomach. The boat pranced and rolled. He held on to the mast, but now almost nonchalantly and only with one arm. The sea buffeted him into dreams of that luckless searcher for Hy-Breasil, or dreams of Brendan the Navigator, long before Columbus, sailing bravely on and on and making landfall on Miami Beach. Secure in those dreams he found to his amazement that he could contemn the snubbed cameraman and the praying bishops hiding in their foxholes. He, Jeremiah, belonged with the nonchalant lifeboatmen studying the sea as a man through the smoke of a good pipe might look at the face of a friend. One of them, indeed, was so nonchalant that he sat on the hatchroof above the bishops, his feet on the gunwale chain so that, when the boat dipped his way, his feet a few times went well out of sight in the water. Those lifeboatmen were less men than great yellow seabirds and Jeremiah, although a landlubber and as black as a raven, willed to be with them as far as he could, for the moment, go. He studied on the crazy pattern of tossing waters the ironic glint of sunshine on steel-blue hills racing to collide and crash and burst into blinding silver. He recalled sunshine on quiet, stable, green fields that he was half-reconciled never to see again. He was on the way to the Isle of the Blest.

Yet it was no island that first appeared to remind him, after two hours of trance, that men, other than the lifeboat's crew and cargo, did exist: no island, but the high bird-flight of a dozen black currachs, appearing and disappearing, forming into single file, six to either side of the lifeboat, forming a guard of honour as if they had been cavalry on display in a London park, to escort the sacerdotes magni safely into the island harbour. Afterwards Jeremiah was to learn that lifeboats could sink and had done so, yet he says that even had he known through the wildest heart of that voyage it would have made no difference. Stunned, but salted, by the sea he arose a new man.

The parish church was a plain granite cross high on a windy, shelterless hilltop. It grew up from the rock it was cut from. No gale nor half-gale, nor the gates of hell, could prevail against it.

To west and south-west the land sank, then swept up dizzily again to a high bare horizon and, beyond that there could be nothing but monstrous seacliffs and the ocean. To east and northeast small patchwork fields, bright green, dark green, golden, netted by greystone walls, dotted by white and golden cabins all newly limewashed and thatched for the coming of the great priests, sloped down to a sea in the lee of the island and incredibly calm. The half-gale was still strong. But the island was steady underfoot. Far away the mainland, now a bit here, now a bit there, showed itself, glistening, out of the wandering squalls.

—Rock of ages cleft for me, he hummed with a reckless merriment that would have frightened him if he had stopped to reason about it, let me hide myself in thee. He was safe in the arms of Jesus, he was deep in the heart of Texas. The granite cruciform church was his shelter from the gale, providing him, by the protection of its apse and right arm, with a sunny corner to hide in and smoke in. He was still giddy from the swing of the sea. He was also, being, alas, human and subject to frailty, tempted to rejoice at the downfall and humiliation of another. He hath put down the mighty, he began to chant but stopped to consider that as yet there was little sign of the lowly being exalted.

This corner of the cross was quiet. One narrow yellow grained door was securely shut. All the bustle, all the traffic was out around the front porch: white-jacketed white jerseyed islanders sitting on stone walls, women in coloured shawls crowding and pushing, children hymn-singing in English, Irish, and Latin, real Tower of Babel stuff, the cameraman photographing groups of people, and photographing the bishops from a safe distance, and the church from every angle short of the one the angels saw it from. He was no longer a great clumsy canary. He was splendid in his most expensive tweeds. He was, nevertheless, a cowed and broken man.

For back at the harbour, at the moment of disembarkation, it had happened again.

The two bishops, divested of oilskins, tall and black but not stately, are clambering up a ladder on to the high slippy quayside, and they are anything but acrobatic. Jeremiah, a few yards away, is struggling to tear from his body his sodden greatcoat, to hang it to dry under the direction of an islandman, in the lee of a boathouse where nets are laid to dry. The cameraman has jocosely snapped him. Then he directs the camera on the clambering bishops only to be vetoed by a voice, iron and Irish and clanging.

—Put away that camera, the Irish voice says, until the opportune time.

—Why Peter, says the American voice, that would make a fun picture.

—In Ireland we don't want or need fun pictures of the hierarchy. We're not clowns.

It is arguable, Jeremiah thinks. He recalls that archbishops, on their own territory and when in full regimentals, are entitled to wear red boots. But he keeps his back turned on the passing parade in sudden terror that his eyes might reveal his thoughts. He hears the cameraman say: Your Grace, there is on the island the oldest inhabitant, a nonagenerian. I'd like to . . .

But there is no response. The procession has passed on. Fickle, Jeremiah knows, is the favour of princes, particularly when, like the Grand Turk, they are related to you. But whatever or how grievous the cause of offence had been that led to these repeated snubs, Jeremiah feels for the first time, burning through empty belly and meagre body, the corps-spirit of the pressman. Who in hell, anyway, is a bishop that he won't stand and pose like any other mortal man? All men are subject to the camera. Face up to it, grin, watch the little birdie. Only murderers are allowed to creep past, faces covered. If he won't be photographed, then to hell with him. He will be scantily written about, even if he is Twenty Times His Grace. And to hell also with all American bishops and Rumanian Reds, and with all colour stories of confirmations and of simple island people who, more than likely, spend the long winter nights making love to their own domestic animals which, as far as Jeremiah is concerned, they have a perfect right to do.

So here in the corner of the granite cross he had found peace. He didn't need to see the nonsense going on out there. When the time came to type, as no doubt it would, the Holy Ghost would guide his fingertips. The moment on the quayside mingled with the moment in the shelter of the church and he realized, for the first time since anger had possessed him, that he had left his greatcoat still drying with the nets. He had been distracted by a call to coffee and sandwiches intended to keep them from collapsing until the show was over. But to hell, too, he decided with all greatcoats; a man could stand on his own legs. He smoked, and was content, and heard far away the voices of children, angels singing. Then the narrow, yellow, grained door opened, a great venerable head, a portion of surpliced body, appeared, a voice louder than the choirs of angels said: Come here, pressman.

Jeremiah went there.

—On the alert I'm glad to see, His Grace said. Waiting to see me. What can I do for you?

Jeremiah, to begin with, bent one knee and kissed his ring. That little bit of ballet enabled him to avoid saying whether he had or had not been on the alert, waiting for an interview.

—You must be starved, His Grace said. That was a rough journey.

They were in the outer room of the sacristy. The walls were mostly presses all painted the same pale yellow, with graining, as the narrow door. In an inner room the American bishop, head bowed, was talking to two tiny nuns. From one of the presses His Grace took a bottle and a half-pint tumbler and half-filled the tumbler with Jameson neat.

—Throw that back, he ordered. 'Twill keep the wind out of your stomach.

He watched benevolently while Jeremiah gasped and drank. The whiskey struck like a hammer. How was His Grace to know that Jeremiah's stomach had in it nothing at all, but wind? Jeremiah's head spun. This, he now knew, was what people meant when they talked about the bishop's bottle. His Grace restored bottle and glass to the press.

—We mustn't, he said, shock the good sisters.

He handed Jeremiah a sheaf of typescript. He said: 'It's all there. Names. History. Local lore. All the blah-blah, as you fellows say. Here, have a cigar. It belongs to our American Mightyship. They

never travel without them. God bless you now. Is there anything
else I can do for you?

Jeremiah's head had ceased to spin. His eyes had misted for a
while with the warmth of the malt on an empty stomach, but now
the mist cleared and he could see, he felt, to a great distance. The
malt, too, had set the island rocking but with a gentle soothing
motion.

—There's a man here, he said, the oldest inhabitant, a nonagenarian. The cameraman who's with me would like a picture.

—No sooner said than done, oh gentleman of the press. That
should make a most edifying picture. I'll call himself away from the
nuns. We'll just have time before the ceremony.

But, for reasons never known to me or Jeremiah, he laughed all
the time as he led the way around the right arm of the cross to the
front of the church; and brought with him another cigar for the
cameraman, and shook hands with him, and offered him his ring to
be kissed.

Apart from Jeremiah and the cameraman and the island doctor it
was a clerical dinner, the island parish priest as host, a dozen well-
conditioned men sitting down to good food, and wines that had
crossed from Spain on the trawlers without paying a penny to the
revenue.

—One of the best men in the business, said His Grace, although
he'd sell us all body and soul to the *News of the World*.

He was talking about the cameraman, and at table, and in his
presence. But he was laughing, and inciting the gathering to
laughter. Whatever cloud there had been between the relatives had
blown away with the storm, or with Jeremiah's diplomacy. So
Jeremiah felt like Tallyrand. He was more than a little drunk. He
was confirmed and made strong by the sea and the bishop's whiskey.
He was hungry as hell.

—And Spanish ale, he muttered, shall give you hope, my dark
Rosaleen.

His mutter was overheard, relayed around the table, and accepted
as unquestionable wit. He was triumphant. He ate. He fell to, like a
savage. He drank, he said afterwards—although we suspected that
he had conned the names from a wine merchant's list, red and white
Poblet, and red Rioja, and red Valdapenas, and another wine that
came from the plain to the west of Tarragona where the Cistercians

had a monastery: the lot washed down with Fundadór brandy
which the American bishop told him had been the brandy specially
set aside for the Conclave of Pope John the Twenty-third.

—Thou art Peter, said Jeremiah, and upon this rock.

Once again the remark was relayed around the table. Awash on
the smuggled products of Spain, Jeremiah was in grave danger of
becoming the life and soul of the party.

A boy-child had that day been born on the island. The American
bishop had asked the parents could he baptize the child and name
it after himself.

—Episcopus Americanus O'Flaherty, said Jeremiah.

Pope John's Fundadór circled the board. The merriment knew no
bounds. His Grace told how the great traveller, O'Donovan, had
dwelt among the Turkomans of ancient Merv, whom he finally grew
to detest because they wouldn't let him go home, but who liked him
so much they called all their male children after him: O'Donovan
Beg, O'Donovan Khan, O'Donovan Bahadur, and so on.

It was the custom in ancient Merv, said His Grace, to call the
newborn babes after any distinguished visitor who happened to be
in the oasis at the time.

—It was not the custom in Rumania, said Jeremiah.

Renewed merriment. When the uproar died down, the American
bishop, with tears in his eyes, said: But this is God's Own Country.
Ye are God's Own People.

Jeremiah got drunk, but nobody minded. Later, outside a bar
close by the harbour, he was photographed feeding whiskey out of a
basin to a horse. The horse was delighted. The picture appeared in
a London magazine, side-by-side with a picture of the nonagenarian
flanked by bishops.

—You got him to pose, said the cameraman, when he rusted on
me.

He meant, not the horse, but the bishop.

—Jer, he said, you'll make a newsman yet.

So, as Jer, a new man, eater of meat and vegetables, acknowledged gentleman of the press, he came back from the Isle of the
Blest, sitting on the hatch above the bishops, feet on the gunwale
chain. He was not beyond hoping that the swing of the sea and the
tilt of the boat might salt his feet. It didn't. The easy evening sway
would have lulled a child in the cradle.

—Episcopus Americanus O'Flaherty, he said to the lifeboatman
who sat beside him and who had enough Latin to clerk Mass.

—True for you, said the lifeboatman. Small good that christening
will do the poor boy. As long as he lives on that island he'll never
be known as anything but An Teasbog Beag—the Little Bishop. If
he goes to the States itself, the name could follow him there. His
sons and even his daughters will be known as the Little Bishops. Or
his eldest son may be called Mac an Easboig, the Son of the Bishop.
They'll lose O'Flaherty and be called Macanespie. That's how
names were invented since the time of King Brian Boru who bate
the Danes.

Behind them the island stepped away into the mist: the wanderer,
crazed for Hy-Breasil, would never find it. The rain would slant for
ever on rocks and small fields, on ancient forts and cliffs with
seabirds crying around them, on currachs riding the waves as the
gulls do. Visitors would be enthralled by ancient ways, and basking
sharks captured. But as long as winds rage and tides run, that male
child, growing up to be a lean tanned young man in white jacket
and soft pampooties, leaning into the wind as he walks as his
forebears have always done, courteous as a prince but also ready to
fight at the drop of a half-glass of whiskey, sailing with the trawlers
as far away as the Faroes, will continue, because of this day, to be
known as the Little Bishop.

In the foxhole underneath Jeremiah, the American bishop was
telling the Irish bishop and the cameraman that in the neighbourhood of the Okeefenokee Swamp, out of which the Suwannee River
drags its corpse, and generally in the state of Georgia, there were
many Southern Baptists with Irish Catholic names.

The water in the land-locked harbour was deadly still, and deep
purple in the dusk. Sleepy gulls foraged on the edge of the tide, or
called from inland over the small fields. Jer's greatcoat was still on
the island, dry by now, and stiff with salt. He never wanted to see it
again.

Shadowy people gathered on the harbour wall. The choir sang:
Sweet Sacrament Divine, dear home of every heart.

—Ye are God's own people, said the American bishop. This is
God's own country.

—Fuck, said the cameraman and in a painfully audible voice.

He had sunk over the ankles in soggy peat-mould, losing one
shoe. But while he stood on one leg and Jer groped for the missing

shoe, the bishops and the people and the parish priest and the choir, and the cameraman himself, all joked and laughed. When the shoe was retrieved they went on their way rejoicing.

In Galway City Jer ate a dinner of parsnips and rare roast meat and sauté potatoes that would have stunned an ox; and washed it down with red wine.

Far away the island gulls nested on his discarded greatcoat.

BERNARD MALAMUD
The Silver Crown

GANS, the father, lay dying in a hospital bed. Different doctors said different things, held different theories. There was talk of an exploratory operation but they thought it might kill him. One doctor said cancer.

'Of the heart,' the old man said bitterly.

'It wouldn't be impossible.'

The young Gans, Albert, a high school biology teacher, in the afternoons walked the streets in sorrow. What can anybody do about cancer? His soles wore thin with walking. He was easily irritated; angered by the war, atom bomb, pollution, death, obviously the strain of worrying about his father's illness. To be able to do nothing for him made him frantic. He had done nothing for him all his life.

A female colleague, an English teacher he had slept with once, a girl who was visibly aging, advised, 'If the doctors don't know, Albert, try a faith healer. Different people know different things; nobody knows everything. You can't tell about the human body.'

Albert laughed mirthlessly but listened. If specialists disagree who do you agree with? If you've tried everything what else can you try?

One afternoon after a long walk alone, as he was about to descend the subway stairs somewhere in the Bronx, still burdened by his worries, uneasy that nothing had changed, he was accosted by a fat girl with bare meaty arms who thrust a soiled card at him that he tried to avoid. She was a stupefying sight, retarded at the very least. Fifteen, he'd say, though she looks thirty and probably has the mentality of age ten. Her skin glowed, face wet, fleshy, the small mouth open and would be forever; eyes set wide apart on the broad unfocused face, either washed-out green or brown, or one of each— he wasn't sure. She seemed not to mind his appraisal, gurgled faintly. Her thick hair was braided in two ropelike strands; she wore bulging cloth slippers, bursting at seams and soles; a faded red skirt down to massive ankles; and a heavy brown sweater vest, buttoned over blown breasts, though the weather was still hot September.

The teacher's impulse was to pass by her outthrust plump baby hand. Instead he took the card from her. Simple curiosity—once you had learned to read you read anything? Charitable impulse?

Albert recognized Yiddish and Hebrew but read in English: 'Heal The Sick. Save The Dying. Make A Silver Crown.'

'What kind of silver crown would that be?'

She uttered impossible noises. Depressed, he looked away.

When his eyes turned to hers she ran off.

He studied the card. 'Make A Silver Crown.' It gave a rabbi's name and address no less: Jonas Lifschitz, close by in the neighborhood. The silver crown mystified him. He had no idea what it had to do with saving the dying but felt he ought to know. Although at first repelled by the thought, he made up his mind to visit the rabbi and felt, in a way, relieved.

The teacher hastened along the street a few blocks until he came to the address on the card, a battered synagogue in a store, Congregation Theodor Herzl, painted in large uneven white letters on the plate-glass window. The rabbi's name, in smaller, gold letters, was A. Marcus. In the doorway to the left of the store the number of the house was repeated in tin numerals, and on a card under the vacant name plate under the mezuzah, appeared in pencil, 'Rabbi J. Lifschitz. Retired. Consultations. Ring The Bell.' The bell, when he decided to chance it, did not work—seemed dead to the touch—so Albert, his heartbeat erratic, turned the knob. The door gave easily enough and he hesitantly walked up a dark flight of narrow wooden stairs. Ascending, assailed by doubts, peering up through the gloom, he thought of turning back but at the first-floor landing compelled himself to knock loudly on the door.

'Anybody home here?'

He rapped harder, annoyed with himself for being there, engaging in the act of entrance—who would have predicted it an hour ago? The door opened a crack and that broad, badly formed face appeared. The retarded girl, squinting one bulbous eye, made noises like two eggs frying, and ducked back, slamming the door. The teacher, after momentary reflection, thrust it open in time to see her, bulky as she was, running swiftly along the long tight corridor, her body bumping the walls before she disappeared into a room at the rear.

Albert entered cautiously, with a sense of embarrassment, if not danger, warning himself to depart at once; yet stayed to peek curiously into a front room off the hallway, darkened by lowered green shades through which thread-like rivulets of light streamed. The shades resembled faded maps of ancient lands. An old gray-bearded man with thickened left eyelid, wearing a yarmulke, sat heavily asleep, a book in his lap, on a sagging armchair. Someone in the room gave off a stale odor, unless it was the armchair. As Albert stared, the old man awoke in a hurry. The small thick book on his lap fell with a thump to the floor, but instead of picking it up, he shoved it with a kick of his heel under the chair.

'So where were we?' he inquired pleasantly, a bit breathless.

The teacher removed his hat, remembered whose house he was in, and put it back on his head.

He introduced himself. 'I was looking for Rabbi J. Lifschitz. Your—ah—girl let me in.'

'Rabbi Lifschitz; this was my daughter Rifkele. She's not perfect, though God who made her in His image is Himself perfection. What this means I don't have to tell you.'

His heavy eyelid went down in a wink, apparently involuntarily.

'What does it mean?' Albert asked.

'In her way she is also perfect.'

'Anyway she let me in and here I am.'

'So what did you decide?'

'Concerning what if I may ask?'

'What did you decide about what we were talking about—the silver crown?'

His eyes roved as he spoke; he rubbed a nervous thumb and forefinger. Crafty type, the teacher decided. Him I have to watch myself with.

'I came here to find out about this crown you advertised,' he said, 'but actually we haven't talked about it or anything else. When I entered here you were sound asleep.'

'At my age—' the rabbi explained with a little laugh.

'I don't mean any criticism. All I'm saying is I am a stranger to you.'

'How can we be strangers if we both believe in God.'

Albert made no argument of it.

The rabbi raised the two shades and the last of daylight fell into the spacious high-ceilinged room, crowded with at least a dozen stiff-back and folding chairs, plus a broken sofa. What kind of operation is he running here? Group consultations? He dispensed rabbinic therapy? The teacher felt renewed distaste for himself for having come. On the wall hung a single oval mirror, framed in gold-plated groupings of joined metal circles, large and small; but no pictures. Despite the empty chairs, or perhaps because of them, the room seemed barren.

The teacher observed that the rabbi's trousers were a week from ragged. He was wearing an unpressed worn black suit-coat and a yellowed white shirt without a tie. His wet grayish-blue eyes were restless. Rabbi Lifschitz was a dark-faced man with brown eye pouches and smelled of old age. This was the odor. It was hard to say whether he resembled his daughter; Rifkele resembled her species.

'So sit,' said the old rabbi with a light sigh. 'Not on the couch, sit on a chair.'

'Which in particular?'

'You have a first-class humour.' Smiling absently he pointed to two kitchen chairs and seated himself in one.

He offered a thin cigarette.

'I'm off them,' the teacher explained.

'I also.' The old man put the pack away. 'So who is sick?' he inquired.

Albert tightened at the question as he recalled the card he had taken from the girl: 'Heal The Sick. Save The Dying.'

'To come to the point, my father's in the hospital with a serious ailment. In fact he's dying.'

The rabbi, nodding gravely, dug into his pants pocket for a pair of glasses, wiped them with a large soiled handkerchief and put them on, lifting the wire earpieces over each fleshy ear.

'So we will make then a crown for him?'

'That depends. The crown is what I came here to find out about.'

'What do you wish to find out?'

'I'll be frank with you.' The teacher blew his nose and slowly wiped it. 'My cast of mind is naturally empiric and objective—you might say non-mystical. I'm suspicious of faith healing but I've come here, frankly, because I want to do anything possible to help my father recover his former health. To put it otherwise, I don't want anything to go untried.'

'You love your father?' the rabbi clucked, a glaze of sentiment veiling his eyes.

'What I feel is obvious. My real concern right now mainly is how does the crown work. Could you be explicit about the mechanism of it all? Who wears it, for instance? Does he? Do you? Or do I have to? In other words, how does it function? And if you wouldn't mind saying, what's the principle, or rationale, behind it? This is terra incognita for me, but I think I might be willing to take a chance if I could justify it to myself. Could I see a sample of the crown, for instance, if you have one on hand?'

The rabbi, with an absent-minded start, seemed to interrupt himself about to pick his nose.

'What is the crown?' he asked, at first haughtily, then again, gently. 'It's a crown, nothing else. There are crowns in Mishna, Proverbs, Kabbalah; the holy scrolls of the Torah are often protected by crowns. But this one is different, this you will understand when it does the work. It's a miracle. A sample doesn't exist. The crown has to be made individual for your father. Then his health will be restored. There are two prices——'

'Kindly explain what's supposed to cure the sickness,' Albert said. 'Does it work like sympathetic magic? I'm not nay-saying, you understand. I just happen to be interested in all kinds of phenomena. Is the crown supposed to draw off the illness like some kind of poultice, or what?'

'The crown is not a medicine, it is the health of your father. We offer the crown to God and God returns to your father his health. But first we got to make it the way it must be made—this I will do with my assistant, a retired jeweler. He has helped me to make a thousand crowns. Believe me, he knows silver—the right amount to the ounce according to the size you wish. Then I will say the blessings. Without the right blessings, exact to each word, the crown don't work. I don't have to tell you why. When the crown is finished your father will get better. This I will guarantee you. Let me read you some words from the mystic book.'

'The Kabbalah?' the teacher asked respectfully.

'Like the Kabbalah.'

The rabbi rose, went to his armchair, got slowly down on his hands and knees and withdrew the book he had shoved under the misshapen chair, a thick small volume with faded purple covers, not a word imprinted on it. The rabbi kissed the book and murmured a prayer.

'I hid it for a minute,' he explained, 'when you came in the room. It's a terrible thing nowadays, goyim come in your house in the middle of the day and take away that which belongs to you, if not your life itself.'

'I told you right away that your daughter had let me in,' Albert said in embarrassment.

'Once you mentioned I knew.'

The teacher then asked: 'Suppose I am a non-believer? Will the crown work if it's ordered by a person who has his doubts?'

'Doubts we all got. We doubt God and God doubts us. This is natural on account of the nature of existence. Of this kind doubts I am not afraid so long as you love your father.'

'You're putting it as sort of a paradox.'

'So what's so bad about a paradox?'

'My father wasn't the easiest man in the world to get along with, and neither am I for that matter, but he has been generous to me and I'd like to repay him in some way.'

'God respects a grateful son. If you love your father this will go in the crown and help him to recover his health. Do you understand Hebrew?'

'Unfortunately not.'

The rabbi flipped a few pages of his thick tome, peered at one closely and read aloud in Hebrew which he then translated into English. '"The crown is the fruit of God's grace. His grace is love of creation." These words I will read seven times over the silver crown. This is the most important blessing.'

'Fine. But what about those two prices you mentioned a minute ago?'

'This depends how quick you wish the cure.'

'I want the cure to be immediate, otherwise there's no sense to the whole deal,' Albert said, controlling anger. 'If you're questioning my sincerity, I've already told you I'm considering this recourse even though it goes against the grain of some of my strongest convictions. I've gone out of my way to make my pros and cons absolutely clear.'

'Who says no?'

The teacher became aware of Rifkele standing at the door, eating a slice of bread with lumps of butter on it. She beheld him in mild stupefaction, as though seeing him for the first time.

'Shpeter, Rifkele,' the rabbi said patiently.

The girl shoved the bread into her mouth and ran ponderously down the passageway.

'Anyway, what about those two prices?' Albert asked, annoyed by the interruption. Every time Rifkele appeared his doubts of the enterprise rose before him like warriors with spears.

'We got two kinds crowns,' said the rabbi. 'One is for 401 and the other is 986.'

'Dollars, you mean, for God's sake?—that's fantastic.'

'The crown is pure silver. The client pays in silver dollars. So the silver dollars we melt—more for the large-size crown, less for the medium.'

'What about the small?'

'There is no small. What good is a small crown?'

'I wouldn't know, but the assumption seems to be the bigger the better. Tell me, please, what can a 986 crown do that a 401 can't? Does the patient get better faster with the larger one? It hastens the reaction?'

The rabbi, five fingers hidden in his limp beard, assented.

'Are there any other costs?'

'Costs?'

'Over and above the quoted prices?'

'The price is the price, there is no extra. The price is for the silver and for the work and for the blessings.'

'Now would you kindly tell me, assuming I decide to get involved in this, where am I supposed to lay my hands on 401 silver dollars? Or if I should opt for the 986 job, where can I get a pile of cartwheels of that amount? I don't suppose that any bank in the whole Bronx would keep that many silver dollars on hand nowadays. The Bronx is no longer the Wild West, Rabbi Lifschitz. But what's more to the point, isn't it true the mint isn't making silver dollars all silver any more?'

'So if they are not making we will get wholesale. If you will leave with me the cash I will order the silver from a wholesaler, and we will save you the trouble to go to the bank. It will be the same amount of silver, only in small bars, I will weigh them on a scale in front of your eyes.'

'One other question. Would you take my personal check in payment? I could give it to you right away once I've made my final decision.'

'I wish I could, Mr. Gans,' said the rabbi, his veined hand still nervously exploring his beard, 'but it's better cash when the patient is so sick, so I can start to work right away. A check sometimes comes back, or gets lost in the bank, and this interferes with the crown.'

Albert did not ask how, suspecting that a bounced check, or a lost one, wasn't the problem. No doubt some customers for crowns had stopped their checks on afterthought.

As the teacher reflected concerning his next move—should he, shouldn't he?—weighing a rational thought against a sentimental, the old rabbi sat in his chair, reading quickly in his small mystic book, his lips hastening along silently.

Albert at last got up.

'I'll decide the question once and for all tonight. If I go ahead and commit myself on the crown I'll bring you the cash after work tomorrow.'

'Go in good health,' said the rabbi. Removing his glasses he wiped both eyes with his handkerchief.

Wet or dry? thought the teacher.

As he let himself out of the downstairs door, more inclined than not toward trying the crown, he felt relieved, almost euphoric.

But by the next morning, after a difficult night, Albert's mood had about-faced. He fought gloom, irritation, felt flashes of hot and cold anger. It's throwing money away, pure and simple. I'm dealing with a clever confidence man, that's plain to me, but for some reason I am not resisting strongly. Maybe my subconscious is telling me to go along with a blowing wind and have the crown made. After that we'll see what happens—whether it rains, snows, or spring comes. Not much will happen, I suppose, but whatever does, my conscience will be in the clear.

But when he visited Rabbi Lifschitz that afternoon in the same roomful of empty chairs, though the teacher carried the required cash in his wallet, he was still uncomfortable about parting with it.

'Where do the crowns go after they are used and the patient recovers his health?' he cleverly asked the rabbi.

'I'm glad you asked me this question,' said the rabbi alertly, his thick lid drooping. 'They are melted and the silver we give to the poor. A mitzvah for one makes a mitzvah for another.'

'To the poor you say?'

'There are plenty poor people, Mr. Gans. Sometimes they need a crown for a sick wife or a sick child. Where will they get the silver?'

'I see what you mean—recycled, sort of, but can't a crown be re-used as it is? I mean do you permit a period of time to go by before you melt them down? Suppose a dying man who recovers gets seriously ill again at a future date?'

'For a new sickness you will need a new crown. Tomorrow the world is not the same as today, though God listens with the same ear.'

'Look, Rabbi Lifschitz,' Albert said impatiently, 'I'll tell you frankly that I am inching toward ordering the crown, but it would make my decision a whole lot easier all around if you would let me have a quick look at one of them—it wouldn't have to be for more than five seconds—at a crown-in-progress for some other client.'

'What will you see in five seconds?'

'Enough—whether the object is believable, worth the fuss and not inconsequential investment.'

'Mr. Gans,' replied the rabbi, 'this is not a showcase business. You are not buying from me a new Chevrolet automobile. Your father lays now dying in the hospital. Do you love him? Do you wish me to make a crown that will cure him?'

The teacher's anger flared. 'Don't be stupid, rabbi, I've answered that. Please don't sidetrack the real issue. You're working on my guilt so I'll suspend my perfectly reasonable doubts of the whole freaking business. I won't fall for that.'

They glared at each other. The rabbi's beard quivered. Albert ground his teeth.

Rifkele, in a nearby room, moaned.

The rabbi, breathing emotionally, after a moment relented.

'I will show you the crown,' he sighed.

'Accept my apologies for losing my temper.'

The rabbi accepted. 'Now tell me please what kind of sickness your father has got.'

'Ah,' said Albert, 'nobody is certain for sure. One day he got into bed, turned to the wall and said, "I'm sick." They suspected leukemia at first but the lab tests didn't confirm it.'

'You talked to the doctors?'

'In droves. Till I was blue in the face. A bunch of ignoramuses,' said the teacher hoarsely. 'Anyway, nobody knows exactly what he has wrong with him. The theories include rare blood diseases, also a possible carcinoma of certain endocrine glands. You name it, I've heard it, with complications suggested, like Parkinson's or Addison's disease, multiple sclerosis, or something similar, alone or in combination with other sicknesses. It's a mysterious case, all in all.'

'This means you will need a special crown,' said the rabbi.

The teacher bridled. 'What do you mean special? What will it cost?'

'The cost will be the same,' the rabbi answered dryly, 'but the design and the kind of blessings will be different. When you are dealing with such a mystery you got to make another one but it must be bigger.'

'How would that work?'

'Like two winds that they meet in the sky. A white and a blue. The blue says, "Not only I am blue but inside I am also purple and orange." So the white goes away.'

'If you can work it up for the same price, that's up to you.'

Rabbi Lifschitz then drew down the two green window shades and shut the door, darkening the room.

'Sit,' he said in the heavy dark, 'I will show you the crown.'

'I'm sitting.'

'So sit where you are, but turn your head to the wall where is the mirror.'

'But why so dark?'

'You will see light.'

He heard the rabbi strike a match and it flared momentarily, casting shadows of candles and chairs amid the empty chairs in the room.

'Look now in the mirror.'

'I'm looking.'

'What do you see?'

'Nothing.'

'Look with your eyes.'

A silver candelabrum, first with three, then five, then seven burning bony candlesticks appeared like ghostly hands with flaming fingertips in the oval mirror. The heat of it hit Albert in the face and for a moment he was stunned.

But recalling the games of his childhood, he thought, who's kidding who? It's one of those illusion things I remember from when I was a kid. In that case I'm getting the hell out of here. I can stand maybe mystery but not magic tricks or dealing with a rabbinical magician.

The candelabrum had vanished, although not its light, and he now saw the rabbi's somber face in the glass, his gaze addressing him. Albert glanced quickly around to see if anyone was standing at his shoulder, but nobody was. Where the rabbi was hiding at the moment the teacher did not know; but in the lit glass appeared his old man's lined and shrunken face, his sad eyes, compelling, inquisitive, weary, perhaps even frightened, as though they had seen more than they had cared to but were still looking.

What's this, slides or home movies? Albert sought some source of projection but saw no ray of light from wall or ceiling, nor object or image that might be reflected by the mirror.

The rabbi's eyes glowed like sun-filled clouds. A moon rose in the blue sky. The teacher dared not move, afraid to discover he was unable to. He then beheld a shining crown on the rabbi's head.

It had appeared at first like a braided mother-of-pearl turban, then had luminously become—like an intricate star in the night sky—a silver crown, constructed of bars, triangles, half-moons, and crescents, spires, turrets, trees, points of spears; as though a wild storm had swept them up from the earth and flung them together in its vortex, twisted into a single glowing interlocked sculpture, a forest of disparate objects.

The sight in the ghostly mirror, a crown of rare beauty—very impressive, Albert thought—lasted no longer than five short seconds, then the reflecting glass by degrees turned dark and empty.

The shades were up. The single bulb in a frosted lily fixture on the ceiling shone harshly in the room. It was night.

The old rabbi sat, exhausted, on the broken sofa.

'So you saw it?'

'I saw something.'

'You believe what you saw—the crown?'

'I believe I saw. Anyway, I'll take it.'

The rabbi gazed at him blankly.

'I mean I agree to have the crown made,' Albert said, having to clear his throat.

'Which size?'

'Which size was the one I saw?'

'Both sizes. This is the same design for both sizes, but there is more silver and also more blessings for the $986 size.'

'But didn't you say that the design for my father's crown, because of the special nature of his illness, would have a different style, plus some special blessings?'

The rabbi nodded. 'This comes also in two sizes—the $401 and $986.'

The teacher hesitated a split second. 'Make it the big one,' he said decisively.

He had his wallet in his hand and counted out fifteen new bills— nine one hundreds, four twenties, a five and a single—adding to $986.

Putting on his glasses, the rabbi hastily counted the money, snapping with thumb and forefinger each crisp bill as though to be sure none had stuck together. He folded the stiff paper and thrust the wad into his pants pocket.

'Could I have a receipt?'

'I would like to give you a receipt,' said Rabbi Lifschitz earnestly, 'but for the crowns there are no receipts. Some things are not a business.'

'If money is exchanged, why not?'

'God will not allow. My father did not give receipts and also my grandfather.'

'How can I prove I paid you if something goes wrong?'

'You have my word, nothing will go wrong.'

'Yes, but suppose something unforeseen did,' Albert insisted, 'would you return the cash?'

'Here is your cash,' said the rabbi, handing the teacher the packet of folded bills.

'Never mind,' said Albert hastily. 'Could you tell me when the crown will be ready?'

'Tomorrow night before Shabbos, the latest.'

'So soon?'

'Your father is dying.'

'That's right, but the crown looks like a pretty intricate piece of work to put together out of all those odd pieces.'

'We will hurry.'

'I wouldn't want you to rush the job in any way that would— let's say—prejudice the potency of the crown, or for that matter, in any way impair the quality of it as I saw it in the mirror—or however I saw it.'

Down came the rabbi's eyelid, quickly raised without a sign of self-consciousness.

'Mr. Gans, all my crowns are first-class jobs. About this you got nothing to worry about.'

They then shook hands. Albert, still assailed by doubts, stepped into the corridor. He felt he did not, in essence, trust the rabbi; and suspected that Rabbi Lifschitz knew it and did not, in essence, trust him.

Rifkele, panting like a cow for a bull, let him out the front door, perfectly.

In the subway, Albert figured he would call it an investment in experience and see what came of it. Education costs money but how else can you get it? He pictured the crown as he had seen it established on the rabbi's head, and then seemed to remember that as he had stared at the man's shifty face in the mirror the thickened lid of his right eye had slowly dropped into a full wink. Did he recall this in truth, or was he seeing in his mind's eye and transposing into the past something that had happened just before he left the house? What does he mean by his wink?—not only is he a fake but he kids you? Uneasy once more, the teacher clearly remembered, when he was staring into the rabbi's fish eyes in the glass, after which they had lit in visionary light, that he had fought a hunger to sleep; and the next thing there's the sight of the old boy, as though on the television screen, wearing this high-hat magic crown.

Albert, rising, cried, 'Hypnosis! The bastard magician hypnotized me! He never did produce a silver crown, it's out of my inagina-tion—I've been suckered!'

He was outraged by the knavery, hypocrisy, fat nerve of Rabbi Jonas Lifschitz. The concept of a curative crown, if he had ever for a moment believed in it, crumbled in his brain and all he could think of were 986 blackbirds flying in the sky. As three curious passengers watched, Albert bolted out of the car at the next stop, rushed up the stairs, hurried across the street, then cooled his impatient heels for twenty-two minutes till the next train clattered into the station, and he rode back to the stop near the rabbi's house. Though he banged with both fists on the door, kicked at it, 'rang' the useless bell until his thumb was blistered, the boxlike wooden house, including dilapidated synagogue store, was dark, monumen-tally starkly still, like a gigantic, slightly tilted tombstone in a vast graveyard; and in the end unable to arouse a soul, the teacher, long past midnight, had to head home.

He awoke next morning cursing the rabbi and his own stupidity for having got involved with a faith healer. This is what happens when a man—even for a minute—surrenders his true beliefs. There are less punishing ways to help the dying. Albert considered calling the cops but had no receipt and did not want to appear that much a fool. He was tempted, for the first time in six years of teaching, to phone in sick; then take a cab to the rabbi's house and demand the return of his cash. The thought agitated him. On the other hand, suppose Rabbi Lifschitz was seriously at work assembling the crown with his helper; on which, let's say, after he had bought the silver and paid the retired jeweler for his work, he made, let's say, a hundred bucks clear profit—not so very much; and there really *was* a silver crown, and the rabbi sincerely and religiously believed it would reverse the course of his father's illness? Although nervously disturbed by his suspicions, Albert felt he had better not get the police into the act too soon because the crown wasn't promised—didn't the old gent say—until before the Sabbath, which gave him till sunset tonight.

If he produces the thing by then, I have no case against him even if it's a piece of junk. So I better wait. But what a dope I was to order the $986 job instead of the $401. On that decision alone I lost $585.

After a distracted day's work Albert taxied to the rabbi's house and tried to rouse him, even hallooing at the blank windows facing the street; but either nobody was home or they were both hiding, the rabbi under the broken sofa, Rifkele trying to shove her bulk under a bathtub. Albert decided to wait them out. Soon the old boy would have to leave the house to step into the shul on Friday night. He would speak to him, warn him to come clean. But the sun set; dusk settled on the earth; and though the autumn stars and a sliver of moon gleamed in the sky, the house was dark, shades drawn; and no Rabbi Lifschitz emerged. Lights had gone on in the little shul, candles were lit. It occurred to Albert, with chagrin, that the rabbi might be already worshipping; he might all this time have been in the synagogue.

The teacher entered the long, brightly lit store. On yellow folding chairs scattered around the room sat a dozen men holding worn prayer books, praying. The Rabbi A. Marcus, a middle-aged man with a high voice and a short reddish beard, was dovening at the Ark, his back to the congregation.

As Albert entered and embarrassedly searched from face to face, the congregants stared at him. The old rabbi was not among them. Disappointed, the teacher withdrew.

A man sitting by the door touched his sleeve.

'Stay awhile and read with us.'

'Excuse me, I'd like to but I'm looking for a friend.'

'Look,' said the man, 'maybe you'll find him.'

Albert waited across the street under a chestnut tree losing its leaves. He waited patiently—till tomorrow if he had to.

Shortly after nine the lights went out in the synagogue and the last of the worshippers left for home. The red-bearded rabbi then emerged with his key in his hand to lock the store door.

'Excuse me, rabbi,' said Albert, approaching. 'Are you acquainted with Rabbi Jonas Lifschitz, who lives upstairs with his daughter Rifkele—if she is his daughter?'

'He used to come here,' said the rabbi with a small smile, 'but since he retired he prefers a big synagogue on Mosholu Parkway, a palace.'

'Will he be home soon, do you think?'

'Maybe in an hour. It's Shabbat, he must walk.'

'Do you—ah—happen to know anything about his work on silver crowns?'

'What kind of silver crowns?'

'To assist the sick, the dying?'

'No,' said the rabbi, locking the shul door, pocketing the key, and hurrying away.

The teacher, eating his heart, waited under the chestnut tree till past midnight, all the while urging himself to give up and go home but unable to unstick the glue of his frustration and rage. Then shortly before 1 a.m. he saw some shadows moving and two people drifting up the shadow-encrusted street. One was the old rabbi, in a new caftan and snappy black Homburg, walking tiredly. Rifkele, in sexy yellow mini, exposing to above the big-bone knees her legs like poles, walked lightly behind him, stopping to strike her ears with her hands. A long white shawl, pulled short on the right shoulder, hung down to her left shoe.

'On my income their glad rags.'

Rifkele chanted a long 'boooo' and slapped both ears with her pudgy hands to keep from hearing it.

They toiled up the ill-lit narrow staircase, the teacher trailing them.

'I came to see my crown,' he told the pale, astonished rabbi, in the front room.

'The crown,' the rabbi said haughtily, 'is already finished. Go home and wait, your father will soon get better.'

'I called the hospital before leaving my apartment, there's been no improvement.'

'How can you expect so soon improvement if the doctors themselves don't know what is the sickness? You must give the crown a little more time. God Himself has trouble to understand human sickness.'

'I came to see the thing I paid for.'

'I showed you already, you saw before you ordered.'

'That was an image of a facsimile, maybe, or something of the sort. I insist on seeing the real thing, for which I paid close to one thousand smackers.'

'Listen, Mr. Gans,' said the rabbi patiently, 'there are some things we are allowed to see which He let us see them. Sometimes I wish He didn't let us. There are other things we are not allowed to see—Moses knew this—and one is God's face, and another is the real crown that He makes and blesses it. A miracle is a miracle, this is God's business.'

'Don't you see it?'

'Not with my eyes.'

'I don't believe a word of it, you faker, two-bit magician.'

'The crown is a real crown. If you think there is magic, it is on account those people that they insist to see it—we try to give them an idea. For those who believe, there is no magic.'

'Rifkele,' the rabbi said hurriedly, 'bring to Papa my book of letters.'

She left the room, after a while, a little in fright, her eyes evasive; and returned in ten minutes, after flushing the toilet, in a shapeless long flannel nightgown, carrying a large yellowed notebook whose loose pages were thickly interleaved with old correspondence.

'Testimonials,' said the rabbi.

Turning several loose pages, with trembling hand he extracted a letter and read it aloud, his voice husky with emotion.

'"Dear Rabbi Lifschitz: Since the miraculous recovery of my mother, Mrs. Max Cohen, from her recent illness, my impulse is to cover your bare feet with kisses. Your crown worked wonders and I am recommending it to all my friends. Yours truly and sincerely, (Mrs.) Esther Polatnik."'

'This is a college teacher.'

He read another. '"Dear Rabbi Lifschitz, Your $986 crown totally and completely cured my father of cancer of the pancreas, with serious complications of the lungs, after nothing else had worked. Never before have I believed in miraculous occurrences, but from now on I will have less doubts. My thanks to you and God. Most sincerely, Daniel Schwartz.'''

'A lawyer,' said the rabbi.

He offered the book to Albert. 'Look yourself. Mr. Gans, hundreds of letters.'

Albert wouldn't touch it.

'There's only one thing I want to look at, Rabbi Lifschitz, and it's not a book of useless testimonials. I want to see my father's silver crown.'

'This is impossible. I already explained to you why I can't do this. God's word is God's law.'

'So if it's the law you're citing, either I see the crown in the next five minutes, or the first thing tomorrow morning I'm reporting you and your activities to the Bronx County District Attorney.'

'Booo-ooo,' sang Rifkele, banging her ears.

'Shut up!' Albert said.

'Have respect,' cried the rabbi. 'Grubber yung!'

'I will swear out a complaint and the D.A. will shut you down, the whole freaking plant, if you don't at once return the $986 you swindled me out of.'

The rabbi wavered in his tracks. 'Is this the way to talk to a rabbi of God?'

'A thief is a thief.'

Rifkele blubbered, squealed.

'Sha,' the rabbi thickly whispered to Albert, 'clasping and unclasping his gray hands. 'You'll frighten the neighbors. Listen to me, Mr. Gans, you saw with your eyes what it looks like the real crown. I give you my word that nobody of my whole clientele ever saw this before. I showed you for your father's sake so you would tell me to make the crown which will save him. Don't spoil now the miracle.'

'Miracle,' Albert bellowed, 'it's a freaking fake magic, with an idiot girl for a come-on and hypnotic mirrors. I was mesmerized, suckered by you.'

'Be kind,' begged the rabbi, tottering as he wandered amid empty chairs. 'Be merciful to an old man. Think of my poor child. Think of your father who loves you.'

'He hates me, the son-of-a-bitch, I hope he croaks.'

In an explosion of silence the girl slobbered in fright.

'Aha,' cried the wild-eyed rabbi, pointing a finger at God in heaven.

'Murderer,' he cried, aghast.

Moaning, father and daughter rushed into each other's arms, as Albert, wearing a massive, spike-laden headache, rushed down the booming stairs.

An hour later the elder Gans shut his eyes and expired.

SUSAN HILL
Cockles and Mussels

BOTH the lounge and dining-room of the Delacourt Guest House commanded a view of the sea.

'There is nothing at all gloomy *here*, nobody has to suffer some dark, poky bedroom with outlook on to a wall,' said Mrs. Muriel Hennessy, the proprietress. Though she did not count the cook, Mrs. Rourke.

There had been, until five years ago, a Mr. Hennessy, dealer in fine wines and spirits. In the early days of their marriage, they had gone around the Châteaux of France together every spring, tasting, buying. But Mr. Hennessy had begun to drink, two, and later three, bottles of sherry a day, the relationship had soured, his wife had put money aside, secretly, in a building society account.

After his death, she had waited six, decent months before leaving their bungalow in the home counties and travelling to the sea, to make her fresh start with the Delacourt Guest House.

'It has always been a little, private longing of mine,' she had told her friends, giving a small sherry party to say goodbye, 'to be of some service to others, give a few, retired people a very comfortable and happy home.' Though, in fairness she was forced to admit to prospective clients that her charges were somewhat higher for the larger, front bedrooms.

A year ago, Miss Avis Parson had come into money from a deceased aunt, and then she had been able to take one of these, to move from a pink room overlooking the garden, into a blue room, overlooking the sea.

Mrs. Hennessy was fond of saying laughingly that Miss Parson had 'served her time', she deserved to come into her inheritance. For she did not like to think of any of her residents pinching and scraping, anxious about where the next month's rent was coming from.

It was not the quietness, not the gentle slope of the Guest House garden, down towards the promenade, not the different moods of the sea, for which Miss Parson was grateful. They pleased her well enough, but nothing happened, it was all a little dull.

'I am sixty-nine,' she said, brushing her white hair, which was as long as it had ever been when she was a young girl, 'I am not like old Mr. Brotherton, who is fit only to doze and dream and remember little incidents of his naval past. I have my eyes open to modern life and what goes on about me.' For, from the side window of the blue bedroom, she could see towards the Lower Bay, and it was to the Lower Bay that the day trippers came. Mrs. Muriel Hennessy, and, indeed, all the property owners and shopkeepers and residents of the upper town, held day trippers in the lowest possible esteem. 'They are not *real* visitors,' she would say, bringing the tea trolley with their late, hot drinks around the lounge, 'they come in charabancs and throw away their litter, they do nothing for the image of the town.'

And, along the foreshore and up and down the narrow streets of the Lower Bay were all the most common attractions, the souvenir gift shops full of rose-painted pottery and highly varnished shells, the ice cream and fish and chip parlours with tall stools set against eau de nil marble counters, the rifle ranges and the five shilling photographers and the sellers of novelty balloons.

At the far end of the foreshore was the Fun Fair, and, opposite the Fun Fair, beside the lifeboat house, the shellfish booths, where cockles and mussels and winkles and shrimps were shovelled into little paper cones and sprinkled with malt vinegar.

'Everything is so vulgar on the Lower Bay,' said Mrs. Hennessy, 'everything is so cheap and nasty, it smells so, I wonder anyone at all can bear it.'

But, in her heart Miss Avis Parson felt that life as it should be lived was lived along the foreshore of the Lower Bay. At night, she drew the curtains of her side window and sat, watching the flickering lights of the amusement arcade and the Fun Fair, saw the big wheel turn round in an arc of gold and mauve and the water chute cascade electric blue. If she opened her window, and the breeze was in the right direction, she could hear the shrieks and cries of girls as their skirts went above their heads on the swing-boats, the crack and pop of bullets on the rifle range. The hours between ten and midnight, when everything was abruptly doused and darkened, filled Miss Parson with excitement and little, sudden spurts of longing. I have lived too sheltered a life, she thought, I have never known enough about the truth of things, about what really goes on. For she had been companion to her father in his Rectory—Miss Parson the

Parson's daughter, said the village children, though she did not mind—and later, to her unmarried brother in Wales, the years in which she had meant to do this and that had slipped too quickly by.

That summer, when she moved into her more expensive, blue front room at the Delacourt Guest House, the weather was almost always good, the days long and hot and the beaches bright and noisy with dry trippers.

Mrs. Hennessy turned away importunate families, evening after evening, at the door. 'I am not a hotel for passing visitors, I am entirely devoted to the care of the elderly, of my permanent residents,' she told them, smoothing down the skirts of her pastel linen dresses, watching them go off in their laden cars, hot and tired and disappointed down the drive.

In the afternoons, tea was served on the terrace and the deck-chairs were occupied by old Mr. Brotherton and Mrs. de Vere and the Misses Phoebe and Ethel Haynes, sleeping under striped umbrellas to shade them from the glare of the sun.

Miss Parson took little solitary walks up Cliff Terrace, behind the Guest House, and the desire to venture along into the streets and shops and arcades of the Lower Bay became an obsession with her. Though she would have said nothing about it, and she was not, in any case, anxious to chat a great deal with any of her fellow guests, she saw herself as both younger than they were and somehow less permanent, for was she not entirely free, might she not suddenly choose to move on? She had money, she had her health, one day she might buy a flat in some quiet place abroad, might go on a cruise or pay an extended visit to her old school friend in Edinburgh. She reviewed her situation daily. And, meanwhile, she longed to mingle with the crowds who came in charabancs and private cars, to unmask the noisy secrets of the ghost train and eat shrimps and winkles with her fingers, sitting beside the sea.

It was only her sudden discovery of the drinking habits of Mrs. Rourke which, for a short while, diverted her attention.

When the lights of the Fun Fair were switched out, Miss Parson left her chair by the window, after drawing the curtains again, and prepared herself for bed. As long as there had been something to watch and listen to, the attraction of roundabout music and the lights flickering in the sky, she was never tired, her mind was filled with pictures of the scene, couples arm-in-arm together and the mothers of grown-up families, ridiculous in cardboard hats, middle-aged romances brought to a point of decision among the dodgems. But later, in the abrupt darkness, she remembered that she was sixty-nine years old and knew nothing, was ready to climb a little stiffly into her divan bed. But before doing so, she went quietly along the corridor to the bathroom, and it was just outside the bathroom that Miss Parson first found the cook, Mrs. Rourke, her eyes curiously glazed, unable to focus on Miss Parson's face, and her hand clutching at the bare wall. Mrs. Rourke had been cook for seven months, at the Delacourt Guest House.

The following day, old Mr. Brotherton complained again, loudly, about the quality of the mashed potato. 'There are lumps,' he said querulously, paddling them about in the serving dish with a spoon, 'there are more lumps at every meal, every day there are more.'

Rita, the day-time waitress, shot him an evil look, but in the kitchen she exaggerated the nature and number of the complaints to Mrs. Hennessy.

'You needn't think the staff have never noticed,' she added, balancing four vegetable dishes along her outstretched arm, 'it isn't as if any of *us* are exactly satisfied.'

Mrs. Hennessy lifted a fork out of the remaining potatoes, and peered into them. She could not see any lump, and had she not had trouble and worry enough over cooks, in years past? Was this not always the season for groundless complaints? The heat was proving too much for them. She decided to say nothing.

Some nights later, Miss Parson heard the uncertain footsteps of the cook fumbling along her corridor, the slight brushing of her guiding hand, along the wall. When she opened the door, a few moments later, the faint, sour smell of Mrs. Rourke's whisky hung about on the air.

In her narrow back bedroom, at the far end of the landing, Mrs. Ruby Rourke lay with her coat still on, feet propped up on her pillow, and looked down at her own ankles. A fine pair of legs, for a woman your age, she thought, the finest pair of legs for miles. And her eyes filled with sudden tears of pride, that years of standing beside sinks and ovens had not thickened the muscles or spread the veins. Only her feet were bad now, the bunions sticking out like red noses on their side, under the fine stockings.

A year ago, she had been cooking for thirty-five secretarials in a London hostel, and when they had passed her by on the stairs,

SUSAN HILL

going out to dinners and parties with a stream of young men, she had looked at their legs and not had any cause to envy them, had seen over-fleshed knees and thick calves, lack of any shapeliness or finesse. And they've other lessons to learn, she had thought, looking at herself in the wardrobe mirror, it takes a woman in her fifties to know how to enjoy herself. *I* wouldn't be in their shoes, wouldn't be eighteen or twenty again, thank you very much.

But in the nights she had woken and heard them clattering up the stairs, laughing inconsiderately, and had not been able to get to sleep again for hours, had been obliged to get up and search about in her wardrobe for a bottle of gin. In the mornings, the skin around her eyes looked puffed and swollen.

When she had been asked to leave the hostel, there had not been another job in London, in the end she had had to travel up here and apply to the Delacourt Guest House.

'Oh, I like old people, I like to see they get nourishing meals,' she had told Mrs. Hennessy, crossing her legs to reveal their elegant shape, under the short black skirt. 'I couldn't get along with those young girls, oh, no, couldn't take to their noisy, selfish little ways. It was something like living in a zoo, Mrs. Hennessy, and half the food picked and poked at in a *very* dissatisfied way.'

'I daresay they were dieting, Mrs. Rourke, that is what young girls all do, nowadays.' Mrs Hennessy was looking at the careful make-up and wondering what age the woman might really be, and if there were not something a little unsuitable about vanity, in an institutional cook.

'I am fifty,' said Mrs. Rourke, who was fifty-seven, 'and I am thankful that I have never had to diet, my figure is all that it should be.'

Mrs Hennessy had inclined her head and begun to wonder about the lack of any recent references. But in the end the problem was solved for her, by the absence of any other applicant.

On the last Friday in July the temperature reached 84 degrees and the season for day trippers was at its height.

Sitting in the garden of the Delacourt Guest House, Miss Parson felt restless, felt the summer again passing her by, and was irritated with those around her, by the talk of the Misses Haynes, who were spiritualists, and the snores of old Mr. Brotherton. I have no place here, she thought, it is a house for old and dying people and I shall begin to grow like them, and trivialities of everyday life here will assume a greater and greater importance, the times of meals will be all I have to look forward to. And it will be my own fault.

For she had been both startled and aroused by her discovery that Mrs. Rourke came home the worse for drink. *She* has some kind of experience and pleasure, Miss Parson thought, some merrymaking and delight in life, she is a woman unafraid of the world, she has the courage of her convictions and laughs in the face of propriety. For the drunkenness of the cook seemed to her entirely romantic, it had no weak or pathetic aspect.

The hard, straight sunlight lay across the Victorian house, and the terrace and garden, it was too hot, now, for any of the residents except Miss Parson herself, and old Mr. Brotherton, snoring under a panama hat. From the beaches came the high, sharp cries of children, the sea glittered in ridges for miles out.

I have no courage, I am too concerned about the opinions of others, too afraid of their displeasure. I am anxious to walk down on to the Lower Bay and see the sights, observe the people, anxious to eat cockles and mussels and go along into the Fun Fair, and is that not a very slight, harmless ambition? Yet I have sat here for week after week and only ventured out into the respectable, upper part of the town, only walked the streets and bought from the shops approved of by women like Mrs. Hennessy. It is a very poor thing, I do not deserve to have any excitement out of life, any new experiences, I am made of flimsier stuff than a cook!

In her agitation, Miss Parson got up quickly from the striped deckchair and began to walk round and round the garden, rubbing her fingers about in the palms of her hands, wanting to make a decision.

On the hot, Saturday evening, Miss Parson ate very little supper, and did not go into the lounge afterwards, to take coffee.

'I have some business in the town—a friend to see,' she said hastily, in reply to the inquisitive expression of Mrs. Hennessy, for none of the guests ever went far, in the evenings. But then, she was annoyed with herself, for she paid good money to live here, she was her own mistress, why was it at all necessary to explain her doings in that flustered way?

'On Saturday night, Miss Parson? Oh, are you quite sure that you are wise? The town is so full of rowdy strangers, I am a little concerned as to whether you will be quite safe.'

Miss Parson would have said, and that is why I am all the more eager to go, but little Mrs. Pardue, with the pink bald patch showing through her grey hair, said, 'Rowdy people do not come up to *this* end of the town, I am thankful to say,' and in the subsequent murmur of relief and agreement, Miss Parson slipped out.

She felt not merely excited but guilty. The Lower Bay was, in a sense, quite forbidden territory, in the tacit agreement of the residents of the Delacourt, and she could only guess at what they might say of her visit, were they to find out. One or two of them did not entirely like her. 'There is just *something* about Miss Parson,' Miss Phoebe Haynes had said, 'she is not really altogether one of us.'

On leaving Cliff Terrace, Miss Parson made a detour, up to the top of the hill and around the avenue, for someone might be watching her, unseen, from a bedroom window, and then a report would be made at once to the lounge, and to Mrs. Hennessy. The ghost of Miss Parson's father warned her, as she altered course and made for the Harbour road, that she was acting a lie. The road dipped and the Guest House was out of sight. And I do not care, Miss Parson said, gripping her pouched black handbag, I have done nothing with my freedom, nothing at all, it is quite time I grasped at my opportunities and enjoyed some small, innocent adventure.

She wore well-fitting leather shoes, and a lightweight coat, in case the evening should turn chilly, for she did not intend to return early to the Delacourt Guest House.

From her back bedroom window, Mrs. Rourke saw Miss Parson set out up Cliff Terrace, and then, glancing up again from powdering carefully around her eyes, saw her turn, and go off towards the Lower Bay.

'Well!' she said to her own image in the mirror, and was taken once again by the elegance of her own figure, the shapeliness of leg and ankle. She had always insisted, at every place of employment, upon Saturday as one of her regular nights off, everything happened on a Saturday, you never knew your luck.

For a long time Miss Parson simply walked slowly along the pavements, looking at people's faces. These are the old and the modern young, mingling together, she thought, these are the day trippers, this is life. Middle-aged men in shirts, open over sun-reddened chests, wore pressed-paper hats in imitation of cowboys or undertakers or policemen, and Miss Parson stared into their eyes, anxious to learn the secrets of enjoyment. It was very crowded, very warm in among the booths and cafés, the night air flashed with multi-coloured lights, and along the pier they bobbed, orange and green and red, reflected in the dark sea.

I am very happy, I am watching the world go by, discovering things I never knew, Miss Parson told herself, sitting down on a foreshore bench while she emptied sand out of her shoes, there is nothing to be ashamed of or snobbish about it, that I can see. Loudspeakers sent the metallic beat of popular music out across the street.

Somewhere, far down beyond the green railings and the piled-up deckchairs, the long, pale shelf of sand, the edge of the sea, creaming and stirring a little in the darkness. I would like to walk there, too, thought Miss Parson, it is many years since I have been on a beach at night. Though as children they had spent their holidays at Bexhill, and she had walked the dog Beaver out, after dark, smelling the salt and the green smell of seaweed and imagining her own future, filled with rich, nameless excitements.

A car began to hoot on the roadway, nosing into the back of jaywalkers. Miss Parson got up and went across to the Seagull Milk Bar, to perch uncertainly on a high stool with tubular steel legs and drink a cup of expensive tea. All around her, everyone moved, laughed and chatted across the tables, over plates of waffles and haddock, peas and chips and every movement reflected brightly in the mirrors above the counter, so that Miss Parson, watching, felt uncertain of which was real and which the image. Under a table, a small child in green bathing trunks dribbled lemonade gently on to its bare legs from the end of a straw.

'There you go, my duck,' a man said, helping her down from the precarious stool, and she noticed the reddish hairs, matted all the way up his arms.

But it was going through the glittering golden archway of the Fun Fair, and standing just a little way inside, which brought home to her where she had come, alone on a Saturday evening, how many unwritten rules of proper conduct she had disobeyed. For a moment, she held her breath and was doubtful, would have gone quickly away, the noise and the clamour of people and machines and lights

around her was more than she felt able to take. The smell of the
place came out towards her. But then, she went ahead, fumbling in
her purse for money, and joined the queue leading to the switchback
railway.

On the fourth, reckless plunge over the crest of the metal track
and down, down, slicing into the darkness, Miss Parson opened her
eyes and saw that the woman next to her was clutching on to her
sleeve, eyes huge in her melon-shaped face.

'Oh!' she said, 'Oh!' and the hand gripped tighter, though no
sound coming out of the woman's mouth could be heard above the
noise, there was only the purse of her lips, purple-looking under the
artificial lights. She is laughing, Miss Parson realized suddenly,
there is nothing wrong with her whatsoever, she is simply laughing,
and she felt friendly, warmed by the careless grasping of the
stranger's hand, the gesture of conviviality on the switchback.

As they climbed and plunged again, Miss Parson thought of old
Mr. Brotherton, and of Mrs. Hennessy, stout and managerial in a
linen dress, and began to laugh, to feel superior to all of them, as
one who has outwitted everyone else in the battle of life, discovered
some amazing secret.

Returning to the ground again, she was obliged to lean for some
moments against the ticket booth, unable quite to recover her
breath. Overhead, the big wheel spun in a flashing circle, as if
gathering speed to take off like a top into the sky.

The cockles were hard to eat, she was uncertain which way to
prise them out of their hard, little shells, and in her mouth they
tasted as they smelled, strong as brine and heavily vinegared. But
there was something rich and coarse and satisfying about eating
such things, and about queuing up to buy more, to hover in her
choice between the brown-pink whiskered shrimps and mussels,
rubber-smooth and yet curiously gritty in the mouth.

The foreshore was now more crowded than ever, the voices more
raucous, shrieking and cat-calling and squabbling, now and then.
Miss Parson got up from her bench when the man next to her began
to slip sideways heavily and to snore like old Mr. Brotherton, huge
hands upturned and loose on his trousers. But, after all, it is only
another human being, she told herself, only another aspect of life,
and she felt herself expanding and blossoming with new insights
and knowledge, open to a stream of experience.

A trickle of juice was left in the paper cone after she had eaten the last mussel, so that, in screwing it up, she stained her coat sleeve. The smell was blotted at once into the cloth, and came up sharply into her nostrils. It would stay there, now, certain proof, in all the months to come, of her evening in the Lower Bay, her new-found courage.

A gang of men and girls came stepping out in a row, arms linked, breasting the whole width of the road, and singing, and for a second Miss Parson was caught up among them, she could see the white teeth and peacock-painted eyes of the girls, smell the men's sweat, and then they parted and went on like the tide, leaving her behind.

In the orange-painted Bingo Booth, opening out on to the street, a game finished and, looking up from her unsuccessful card, the cook, Mrs. Rourke, saw Miss Avis Parson. Earlier, she had found one or two people to talk to, someone had bought her a drink, but it had come to nothing, the bar had emptied and filled up again and she was left to apply fresh lipstick and do something herself about the empty glass.

'Well, now!' she said, therefore, touching Miss Parson lightly on the arm, for familiar company was suddenly better than none, better than the old routine of trying to strike up a new acquaintance. 'Well, here's a thing!'

Though a thought crossed her mind, to wonder if the old girl might not be a bit unwell, a bit wandering all of a sudden, standing down here and smelling of shellfish and vinegar on a July Saturday night. She had always had a peculiar fear of madness.

'It has all been a splendid treat, Mrs. Rourke, this is a whole new world to me. I have been telling myself for so long, promising myself, you know, that I would be as bold as could be and venture down among the holidaymakers, and now here I am! But I am really just a little bit tired, I do confess to you, my feet are feeling rather swollen.'

It did not surprise her, for nothing was surprising now, when Mrs. Rourke, too, took hold of her arm.

'It's the sand,' she said, confidentially, nodding into Miss Parson's face, 'the sand gets into them, plays them up. You can't tell me.'

'Yes? Well then, that is very likely the case and perhaps I have had enough for one day, perhaps I should be getting home. . . .'

Miss Parson thought that the cook might be older than she looked, though she admired her care for her own appearance, the brightness of rouge and lipstick and the height of her heels. They were walking uphill now, between the last of the gift shops, and away from the sea, and Miss Parson saw that everyone, here, was arm-in-arm with everyone else, it must be the way of things, the air was close with bonhomie.

'My treat, dear,' said Mrs. Rourke, making her way firmly between backs and elbows to the lounge bar. 'What's it to be?'

But, sitting at the little, low table and surreptitiously easing a shoe from off one of her feet, Miss Parson felt depressed, thought perhaps it is all a little aimless, all too trivial to count as life, perhaps I have been wrong to come riding on switchbacks and eating strange food and drinking sweet sherry in the Lower Bay.

Mrs. Rourke was telling her some story, her eyes protuberant in a flushed face, and Miss Parson thought of the nights when she had found her leaning unsteadily against the Guest House wall, wondered in a moment of panic where it would all end.

Mrs. Rourke had forgotten exactly who she was with, was launched, now, into the full tale of her bad treatment at the hands of her previous employers, the London secetarial school.

'Take no nonsense, good cooks are in short supply, my hubbie would have said.' She wiped lipstick carefully off her glass with the corner of a handkerchief. 'He was a chauffeur,' she told the dazed Miss Parson. 'There wasn't anything you could tell Rourke about the tricks of employers.'

'I think I really should like to be getting back now,' said Miss Avis Parson. But when she stood, the lounge tipped and spun round, there was a curious, high-pitched echo inside her head.

In the Delacourt Guest House, Mrs. Hennessy switched off the parchment-shaded lamps in the lounge, and closed the top windows, wondering if she had been wise to let Miss Parson have a key.

The whole street seemed to be singing, now, everyone came pouring out on to the pavements as the stalls and cafés began to close, and the smell of beer and human bodies mingled with the faint ozone of the sea.

'Steady she goes,' said Mrs. Rourke, stepping off the kerb and on to it again sharply. 'Take it gently.'

'Oh, the nice fresh air, the nice, *nice*, fresh air.'

Can't hold a drink, thought Mrs. Rourke with disgust, doesn't know the first thing about it. Aloud she said: 'We're two merry lonely old ladies,' as they came up the Harbour road, leaving the trippers behind them, facing the stars, 'two lonely old souls.'

There is something wrong, thought Miss Parson, something very wrong indeed, I do not wish to be here, led along the streets by a drunken cook, and called an old woman and lonely, there is nothing at all like that about me, and she can know nothing. I would prefer to forget this incident. But, climbing Cliff Terrace, her legs felt weak under her and she was obliged to hold on to Mrs. Rourke's arm again for a little support.

'It's a bit of a hole, Miss Parson, a bit of a one-eyed hole. I'm used to a good deal better than this, I deserve it, you know, this is not the sort of carry-on I'm accustomed to.'

I do not trust you, Miss Parson thought, I have learned a very great deal tonight, about the ways of the world, and I do not feel able to trust you, you will not get away with anything with me. But she could not altogether follow what the other woman was saying.

'Come along, old girl.'

But Miss Parson had stopped and bent over to examine her shoes. Behind them, the lights of the Fun Fair were gutted, the whole of the bay was given over once more to the incoming sea.

At four, Miss Parson woke in severe abdominal pain, so that, after staggering to the bathroom and back again, she collapsed at the side of her bed and was forced to crawl up, hand-over-hand, and ring the service bell.

Towards morning, the doctor was called, for the pain and sickness had worsened, she became delirious and then semi-conscious.

At breakfast in the dining-room there was an air of alarm and expectancy, questions were asked and speculations aroused, and old Mr. Brotherton refused to eat more than a triangle of toast. 'It is the cook,' he muttered, leaning forward and speaking up so that he should be heard quite clearly at all the tables, 'the food is bad, it is not surprising that Miss Parson has been taken ill. Something should be said to the cook, I have said so before, I hope you will all bear me out.'

So that, throughout the next few days, when Miss Parson's condition worsened and, in the end she was taken to the hospital, the cry grew louder of 'the cook, the cook' as a crowd might mutter, 'Guilty! Guilty! Off with her head!' And Mrs. Hennessy, who had discovered the gin and whisky bottles in Mrs. Rourke's wardrobe, felt that more than goodwill was now at stake, something public would have to be done.

'It is acute food poisoning,' she told Mrs. Rourke, sitting at the desk in her tidy office, 'the doctor is extremely worried, Miss Parson is quite dangerously sick.'

Nor was she pleased when the lies came out so glibly, the long, garbled tale about Miss Parson's eating cockles and mussels and drinking alcohol in the Lower Bay. For surely they *were* lies, she thought, when the cook had been formally dismissed, surely the aloof, prim little Miss Parson would never have been so foolish? Though Mrs. Hennessy recalled that there had so often been a strange look on her face, a furtive, secretive expression, and perhaps she had been growing a little senile, perhaps there was a hardening of the arteries and she had begun to act in that way common among the old, as though a new, alien personality had been suddenly assumed.

Well then, it will not do for her to come back *here*, for this is only a Guest House, not a nursing or a geriatric home, I am neither trained nor equipped nor willing to cater for the senile and unreliable, the responsibility would be altogether too great. She thought that there were no relatives of Miss Parson, but somewhere, an old school friend—in Edinburgh? Or perhaps, simply, the doctor could fill out a form and the whole thing be done locally, some suitable home would be quickly found.

In the event, that was not necessary, Miss Avis Parson died in her bed at the General Hospital of a heart attack, following the ravages of food poisoning. The doctor, bringing the news to Mrs. Hennessy, warned against any future use of shellfish, cockles or mussels, shrimps or crab, in the cooking at the Delacourt Guest House.

'Old people,' he said, almost apologetically, standing on the doorstep beside his car, 'nothing indigestible, nothing, really, in the seafood line, Mrs. Hennessy, take my advice upon it.'

It was only out of respect for the memory of the recently deceased Miss Parson that she did not speak of her own, long-existing ban on all crustacea from the menus of the Delacourt.

On the train, Mrs. Rourke lifted her coat up on to the rack, tidied up her face in the tiny, rectangular mirror, and then walked along to the buffet car for a drink. She had found, only the day after her dismissal from the Guest House, an appointment as cook to a boys' approved school in rural Norfolk. They had not asked for an interview or anything more than verbal references simply because they were, they said, desperate, they would take her on a month's probation.

Like one of the bloody inmates, Mrs. Rourke thought bitterly, imagining the remoteness of the countryside, the absence of any Gaiety and Life, like a bloody prisoner myself. But then she rebuked herself, for she did not like to swear, it was a sign of weakness, a loosening of her grip. Instead, she looked down into her glass for a moment, and then drank, quickly, to the memory of the seaside, and of Miss Avis Parson.

GEORGE MACKAY BROWN
Tithonus

FRAGMENTS FROM THE DIARY OF A LAIRD

THEY are all, especially the women, excited in Torsay today. There is a new child in the village, a little girl. The birth has happened in a house where—so Traill the postman assured me—no one for the past ten years has expected it. The door of Maurice Garth the fisherman and his wife Armingert had seemed to be marked with the sign of barrenness. They were married twenty-one years ago, when Maurice was thirty and Armingert nineteen. One might have expected a large family, five or six at least, from such a healthy devoted pair. (They had both come from tumultuous households to the cold empty cottage at the end of the village.) But the years passed and no young voice broke the quiet dialogue of Maurice and Armingert. To all the islanders it seemed a pity: nothing but beautiful children could have come from their loins.

I was hauling my dinghy up the loch shore this afternoon—it was too bright a day, the trout saw through every gesture and feint— when I saw the woman on the road above. It seemed to me then that she had been waiting to speak to me for some time. I knew who she must be as soon as she opened her mouth. The butterings of her tongue, and the sudden knife flashes, had been described to me often enough. She was Maggie Swintoun. I had been well warned about her by the factor and the minister and the postman. Her idle and wayward tongue, they told me, had done harm to the reputation of more than one person in Torsay; so I'm sure that when I turned my loch-dazzled face to her it did not wear a welcoming expression.

'O sir, you'll never guess,' she said, in the rapt secret voice of all news bearers. 'A bairn was born in the village this morning, and at the Garth cottage of all places—a girl. I think it's right that you should know. Dr. Wayne from Hamnavoe took it into the world. I was there helping. I could hardly believe it when they sent for me.'

The face was withdrawn from the loch side. A rare morning was in front of her, telling the news in shop, smithy, manse, and at the doors of all the crofts round about.

I mounted my horse that, patient beast, had been cropping the thin loch-side grass all morning and cantered back to The Hall over the stony dusty road.

Now I knew why a light had been burning at two o'clock in the cottage at the end of the village. I had got up at that time to let Tobias the cat in.

This is the first child to be born in the island since I came to be laird here. I feel that in some way she belongs to me. I stood at the high window of The Hall looking down at the Garth cottage till the light began to fade.

The generations have been renewed. The island is greatly enriched since yesterday.

I suppose that emotionally I am a kind of neutral person, in the sense that I attract neither very much love nor very much dislike. It is eight years since I arrived from London to live in the island that my grand-uncle, the laird of Torsay, a man I had never seen in my life, left to me. On the slope behind the village with its pier and shop and church is The Hall—the laird's residence—that was built in the late seventeenth century, a large elegant house with eighteen rooms, and a garden, and a stable. I am on speaking terms with everyone in the village and with most of the farmers and crofters in the hinterland. Certain people—William Copinsay the shopkeeper, Maggie Swintoun, Grossiter from the farm of Wear—I pass with as curt a nod as I can manage. If I do have a friend, I suppose he must be James MacIntosh who came to be the schoolmaster in the village two summers ago. We play chess in the school-house every Friday night, summer and winter. Occasionally, when he is out walking with his dog, he calls at my place and we drink whatever is in the whisky decanter. (But I insist that his dog, a furtive collie called Joe who occasionally bares his teeth at passers-by, is not let further than the kitchen—Tobias must not be annoyed.) MacIntosh comes from Perth. He is a pleasant enough man. I think his chief interest is politics, but I do nothing to encourage him when he starts about the Irish question, or the Liberal schism, or the suffragettes, or what the Japanese can be expected to do in such and such an eventuality. I am sure, if I let him go on, that some fine evening he will declare himself to be a socialist. I set the decanter squarely between us whenever I hear the first opinionated murmurings; in those malty depths, and there alone, will any argument be.

I think MacIntosh is quite happy living in this island. He is too lazy and too good-natured to be hustled about in a big city school. It is almost certain that he has no real vocation for his job. He has gone to the university, and taken an arts degree, and then enrolled in teaching for want of anything better. But perhaps I do him wrong; perhaps he is dedicated after all to make 'clever de'ils' of the Torsay children. At any rate, the parents and the minister—our education committee representative—seem to have no objection to him. My reason for thinking that he is without taste or talent for the classoom is that he never mentions his work to me; but there again it could simply be, as with politics, that he receives no encouragement.

There is a curious shifting relationship between us, sometimes cordial, sometimes veiled and hostile. He becomes aware from time to time of the social gulf between us, and it is on these occasions that he says and does things to humble me—I must learn that we are living now in the age of equality. But under it all he is such a good-natured chap; after ten minutes or so of unbated tongues we are at peace again over chess-board or decanter.

Last night MacIntosh said, between two bouts of chess in the school-house, 'It's a very strange thing, I did not think I could ever be so intrigued by a child. Most of them are formed of the common clay after all. O, you know what I mean—from time to time a beautiful child, or a clever child, comes to the school, and you teach him or her for a year or two, then away they go to the big school in the town, or back to work on the farm, and you never think more about them. But this pupil is just that wee bit different.'

'What on earth are you talking about?' I said.

'The Garth girl who lives at the end of the village—Thora—you know, her father has the fishing boat *Rain Goose*.'

'Is that her name, Thora?' I said. (For I had seen the quiet face among a drift of school-children in the playground, at four o'clock, going home then alone to Maurice and Armingert's door. I had seen bright hair at the end of the small stone pier, waiting for a boat to come in from the west. I had seen the solemn clasped hands, bearing the small bible, outside the kirk door on a Sunday morning. But beyond that the girl and I had never exchanged a single word. As I say, I did not even know her name till last night.)

'She is a very strange girl, that one,' said MacIntosh. 'There is a *something* about her. Would you please not drop your ash on the mat?

(There's an ash tray.) I'm not like some folk. I can't afford to buy a new mat every month. Mrs. Baillie asked me to mention it to you.'

My pipe and his dog cancel each other out. Mrs. Baillie is his housekeeper.

'To me she looks an ordinary enough child,' I said. 'In what way is she different?'

MacIntosh could not say how this girl was different. She was made of the common clay—'like all of us, like all of us,' he hastened to assure me, thereby putting all the islanders, including the laird and Halcro the beachcomber, on the same footing. Still, there was something special about the girl, he insisted, goodness knows what. . . .

MacIntosh won the third hard-fought game. He exulted. Victory always makes him reckless and generous. 'Smoke, man, smoke in here any time you like. To hell with Mrs. Baillie. Get your pipe out. I'll sweep any ash up myself.'

I met Thora Garth on the brae outside the kirk as I was going home from the school-house. She put on me a brief pellucid unsmiling look as we passed. She was carrying a pail of milk from the farm of Gardyke.

Fifteen years ago, in my grand-uncle's day, the island women stopped and curtsied whenever the laird went past. A century ago a single glance from the great man of The Hall turned them to stone in their fields.

All that is changed.

Traill the postman had put a letter through my window while I was at the school-house. The familiar official writing was on the envelope. I lit the lamp. I was secure in my island for another six months. The usual hundred pounds was enclosed, in a mixture of tens and fives and singles. There was no message; there was usually no need for the Edinburgh lawyer to have anything special to say. He had simply to disburse in two instalments the two hundred pounds a year that my grand-uncle left me, so that I can live out my life as a gentleman in the great Hall of Torsay.

Thora Garth returned this morning from the senior school in Hamnavoe, at the end of her first session there. I happened to be down at the pier when the weekly mail steamer drew alongside. Several islanders were there, as always on that important occasion. The rope came snaking ashore. A seaman shouted banter to the fishermen and Robbie Tenston the farmer of Dale (who had just come out of the hotel bar). The minister turned away, pretending not to have heard the swear-words. I found Maurice Garth standing beside me. 'What's wrong with the creels today?' I said to him. . . . 'I'm expecting Thora,' Maurice said in that mild shy murmur that many of the islanders have. 'She should be on the boat. It's the summer holidays—she'll be home for seven weeks.'

Sure enough, there was the tilted serious freckled face above the rail. She acknowledged her father with a slight sideways movement of her hand. At that moment I was distracted by an argument that had broken out on the pier. Robbie Tenston of Dale was claiming possession of a large square plywood box that had just been swung ashore from the *Pomona*.

'Nonsense,' cried William Copinsay the general merchant. 'Don't be foolish. It's loaves. It's the bread I always get from the baker in the town on a Friday.'

And indeed—though I hated to agree with Copinsay—there was no doubt that the box contained bread; the incense of new baking drifted across the pier.

'Don't you call me a fool,' said Robbie Tenston in his dark dangerous drinking voice. 'This is a box of plants, if you want to know. It's for my wife's greenhouse. The market gardener wrote to say that it was coming on the boat today. That's why I'm here, man. Let go of it now.'

Copinsay and Robbie Tenston had each laid hands on the rope that was round the box. A circle of onlookers gathered raggedly about them.

The trouble was, the label had somehow got scraped off in transit. (But Robbie must have been stupid to have missed that delicious smell of new rolls and loaves. Besides, roots and greenery would never have weighed so much.)

They wrestled for the box, both of them red in the face. It had all the makings of a disgraceful scene. Four of the crew had stopped working. They watched from the derrick, delighted. The skipper leaned out of his cabin, grinning eagerly. They could have told who owned the box by rights, but they wanted the entertainment to go on for some time yet.

Mr. Evelyn the minister attempted to settle the affair. 'Now now,' he said, 'now now—it is simply a matter of undoing the rope— please, Mr. Copinsay—Robert, I beg you—and looking inside.'

They paid no attention to him. The farmer dragged the box from the weaker hands of the merchant. Copinsay's face was twisted with rage and spite. 'You old miserly bastard!' shouted Robbie.

The skipper leaned further out of his cabin. He put his pipe carefully on the ledge and clapped his hands. Maggie Swintoun and a few other women came down the pier from their houses, attracted by the hullabaloo.

At that point Copinsay flung himself on Robbie Tenston and began to scratch at his face like a woman. He screamed a few falsetto incoherences.

The dispute had reached a dangerous stage. (I felt that, as the chief man in the island, I should be doing something about it, but I am morbidly afraid of making a fool of myself in front of these people.) Robbie could have taken the merchant in his great earth-red hands and broken him. He could have picked him up and flung him into the sea. He tried first of all to shake himself free from the hysterical clutchings of William Copinsay. He struck Copinsay an awkward blow on the shoulder. They whirled each other round like mad dancers between the horsebox and the gangway. Then—still grappling—they achieved some kind of a stillness; through it they glared at each other.

God knows what might have happened then.

It was Thora Garth who restored peace to the island. It was extraordinary, the way the focus shifted from the two buffoons to the girl. But suddenly everyone on the pier, including the skipper and the fighters and myself, was looking at her alone. She had left the steamer and was standing on the pier beside the disputed box. She had one hand on it, laid flat. With the other she pointed to William Copinsay.

'The box belongs to him,' she said quietly. 'Robbie, the box belongs to Mr. Copinsay.'

That was the end of the fracas. Robbie Tenston seemed to accept her verdict at once. He pushed Mr. Copinsay away. He muttered a grudging 'Well, don't let him or anybody ever call me a fool again.' He walked up the pier, his face encrimsoned, past Maggie Swintoun and the other women who were flocking to the scene, too late, with their false chorus of commiseration and accusation. 'That Robbie Tenston should be reported to the police,' said Maggie Swintoun flatly. 'It's that pub to blame. It should be closed down. Drink is the cause of all the trouble in Torsay. Them in authority should be doing something about it.' . . . . She kept looking at me out of the corner of her eye.

Mr. Copinsay sat on his box of bread and began to weep silently. I could not bear any more of it.

The seamen had returned to their work, swinging ashore mail-bags, crates of beer, saddlery, a bicycle, newspapers. Steve Mack the skipper was lighting his pipe and looking inland to the island hills as if nothing untoward had happened.

I left the women cluck-clucking with sympathy around Copinsay Agonistes. I took my box of books that was sent each month from the library in the town—there was never likely to be any fighting about that piece of cargo—and walked up the pier.

From the gate of The Hall I looked back at the village. Thora Garth was greeting her mother in the open door of their cottage. Maurice carried his daughter's case. The woman and the girl—the one was as tall as the other now—leaned towards each other and kissed briefly. The dog barked and danced around them.

On the top of the island, where the road cuts into the shoulder of the hill, a small dark figure throbbed for a minute against the sky. It was Robbie Tenston bearing his resentment and shame home to Dale.

This evening I called in at the hotel bar for a glass of beer—a thing I rarely do; but it has been, for Orkney, a warm day, and also I must confess I am missing James MacIntosh already—he went home to Perth for the summer vacation two days ago. Seven weeks without chess and argument is a long time.

Maurice Garth was sitting in the window seat drinking stout. I took my glass of beer across to his table.

'Well,' I said, 'and how is Thora liking the big school in Hamnavoe?'

'She isn't clever,' he said, smiling. 'I doubt she won't go very far as a scholar. But what is there for a lass to do in Torsay nowadays? Everybody's leaving the island. I suppose in the end she might get some kind of job in the town.'

'It was remarkable,' I said, 'the way Thora put a stop to that fight on the pier this morning.'

'Oh, I don't know,' said Maurice. 'That pair of idiots! Any fool could have seen that it was a bread box. I hope we'll hear no more about it. I hope there isn't going to be any trouble about it with the police.'

'They might have done each other an injury,' I said. 'It was your Thora who brought them to their senses. I never saw anything quite so astonishing.'

'No, no,' said Maurice, raising his hand. 'Don't say that. Thora's just an ordinary lass. There's nothing so very strange about it. Thora just pointed out what was what to that pair of fools. Say no more about it.'

Maurice Garth is a placid man. Such vehemence is strange, coming from him. But perhaps it was that he had drunk too many glasses of stout.

There has been a fine morsel of scandal in the village this morning. The Swintoun woman has been going about the doors at all hours, her cheeks aflame with excitement. It seems that the younger son of Wear, the main farm in the island, has been jilted. Everything has been set fair for a wedding for three months past. Consignments of new furniture, carpets, curtains, crockery have been arriving in the steamer from Hamnavoe; to be fetched later the same afternoon by a farm servant in a cart. They do things in style at Wear. The first friends have gone with their gifts, even. I myself wandered about the empty caverns of this house all one morning last week, considering whether this oil painting or that antique vase might be acceptable. The truth is, I can hardly afford any more to give them a present of money. In the end I thought they might be happy with an old silk sampler framed in mahogany that one of my grand-aunts made in the middle of Queen Victoria's reign. It is a beautiful piece of work. At Wear they would expect something new and glittery from the laird. I hoped, however, that the bride might be pleased with my present.

The Rev. Mr. Evelyn was going to have made the first proclamation from the pulpit next Sunday morning. (I never attend the church services here myself, being nominally an Episcopalian, like most of the other Orkney lairds.)

Well, the island won't have to worry any more about this particular ceremony, for—so Traill the postman told me over the garden wall this morning—the prospective bride has gone to live in a wooden shack at the other end of the island—a hut left over from the Kaiser's war—with Shaun Midhouse, a deck hand on the *Pomona*, a man of no particular comeliness or gifts—in fact, a rather unprepossessing character—certainly not what the women of Torsay would call 'a good catch', by any means.

I am sorry for Jack Grossiter of Wear. He seems a decent enough young chap, not at all like some others in the household. His father of all men I dislike in Torsay. He is arrogant and overbearing towards those whom he considers his inferiors; but you never saw such cap-raisings and foot-scrapings as when he chances to meet the minister or the schoolmaster or myself on the road. He is also the wealthiest man in the island, yet the good tilth that he works belongs to me, and I am forbidden by law to charge more than a derisory rent for it. I try not to let this curious situation influence me, but of course it does nothing to sweeten my regard for the man. In addition to everything else he is an upstart and an ignoramus. How delighted he was when his only daughter Sophie married that custom house officer two years ago—that was a feather in his cap, for according to the curious snobbery of folk like Grossiter a man who has a pen-and-paper job is a superior animal altogether to a crofter who labours all his life among earth and blood and dung. The eldest son Andrew will follow him in Wear, no doubt, for since that piece of socialism was enacted in parliament in 1882 even death does not break the secure chain of a family's tenure.... For Andrew, in his turn, a good match was likewise negotiated, no less than Mr. Copinsay the merchant's daughter. Wear will be none the poorer for that alliance. Only Jack Grossiter remained unmarried. Whom he took to wife was of comparatively small importance—a hill croft would be found for him when the time came. I could imagine well enough the brutish reasonings of the man of Wear, once his second son began to be shaken with the ruddiness and restlessness of virility. There was now, for instance, that bonny respectable well-handed lass in the village—Thora Garth—what objection could there be to her? She would make a good wife to any man, though of course her father was only a fisherman and not over-burdened with wealth. One afternoon—I can picture it all— the man of Wear would have said a few words to Maurice Garth in the pub, and bought him a dram. One evening soon after that Jack Grossiter and Thora would have been left alone together in the sea-bright room above the shore; a first few cold words passed between them. It gradually became known in the village that they were engaged. I have seen them, once or twice this summer, walking along the shore together into the sunset.

Now, suddenly, this has shaken the island.

The first unusual thing to happen was that Thora went missing, one morning last week. She simply walked out of the house with never a word to her parents. There had been no quarrel, so Armingert assured the neighbours. For the first hour or two she didn't worry about Thora; she might have walked up to Wear, or called on Minnie Farquharson who was working on the bridal dress. But she did not come home for her dinner, and that was unusual, that was a bit worrying. Armingert called at this door and that in the afternoon. No-one had seen Thora since morning. Eventually it was Benny Smith the ferryman who let out the truth, casually, to Maurice Garth, at the end of the pier, when he got back from Hamnavoe in the early evening. He had taken Thora across in his boat the *Lintie* about ten o'clock that morning. She hadn't said a word to him all the way across. It wasn't any concern of his, and anyway she wasn't the kind of young woman who likes her affairs to be known.

Well, that was a bit of a relief to Maurice and Armingert. They reasoned that Thora must suddenly have thought of some necessary wedding purchase; she would be staying overnight with one of her Hamnavoe friends (one of the girls she had been to school with); she would be back on the *Pomona* the next morning.

And in fact she did come back on Friday on board the *Pomona*. She walked at once from the boat to her parents' door. Who was trailing two paces behind her but Shaun Midhouse, one of the crew of the *Pomona*? Thora opened the cottage door and went inside (Shaun lingered at the gate). She told her mother—Maurice was at the lobsters—that she could not marry Jack Grossiter of Wear after all, because she had discovered that she liked somebody else much better. There was a long silence in the kitchen. Then her mother asked who this other man was. Thora pointed through the window. The deck-hand was shuffling about on the road outside with that hangdog look that he has when he isn't working or drinking. 'That's my man,' Thora said—'I'm going to live with him.' Armingert said that she would give much pain and grief to those near to her if she did what she said she was going to do. Thora said she realized that. 'I'm sorry,' she said. Then she left the cottage and walked up the brae to the farm of Wear. Shaun went a few paces with her through the village, but left her outside the hotel and went back on board the *Pomona*; the boat was due to sail again in ten minutes.

Thora wouldn't go into the farmhouse. She said what she had to say standing in the door, and it only lasted a minute. Then she turned and walked slowly across the yard to the road. The old man went a few steps after her, shouting and shaking his fists. His elder son Andrew called him back, coldly—his father mustn't make a fool of himself before the whole district. Let the slut go. His father must remember that he was the most important farmer in Torsay.

Jack had already taken his white face from the door—it hasn't been seen anywhere in the island since. I am deeply sorry for him.

I ought to go along and see these people. God knows what I can say to them. I am hopeless in such situations. I was not created to be a bringer of salves and oils.

I saw the minister coming out of the farmhouse two days ago. . . .

The eastern part of the island is very desolate, scarred with peat-bogs and Pictish burial places. During the war the army built an artillery battery on the links there. (They commandeered the site— my subsequent granting of permission was an empty token.) All that is left of the camp now, among concrete foundations, is a single wooden hut that had been the officers' mess. No-one has lived there since 1919—inside it must be all dampness and mildew. Tom Christianson the shepherd saw, two days after the breaking of the engagement, smoke coming from the chimney of the hut. He kept an eye on the place; later that afternoon a van drove up; Shaun Midhouse carried from van to hut a mattress, a sack of coal, a box of groceries. He reported the facts to me. That night, late, I walked between the hills and saw a single lamp burning in the window.

Thora Garth and Shaun Midhouse have been living there for a full week now—as Mr. Copinsay the merchant says, 'in sin'; managing to look, as he says it, both pained and pleased.

Two nights ago Armingert and Maurice came to see me.

'Shaun Midhouse is such a poor weed of a creature,' said Armingert in my cold library. 'What ever could any girl see in the likes of *that*?'

Maurice shook his head. They are, both these dear folk, very troubled.

'Jack Grossiter is ill,' said Armingert. 'I never saw a boy so upset. I am very very sorry for him.'

'I will go and see him tomorrow,' I said.

'What trouble she has caused,' said Armingert. 'I did not think such a thing was possible. If she had suddenly attacked us with a knife it would have been easier to bear. She is a bad cruel deceptive girl.'

'She is our daughter,' said Maurice gently.

'We have no business to inflict our troubles on you,' said Armingert. 'What we have come about is this, all the same. We understand that you own that war-time site. They are sitting unbidden in your property, Thora and that creature. That is what it amounts to. You could evict them.'

I shook my head.

'You could have the law on them,' she insisted. 'You could force them out. She would have to come home then, if you did that. That would bring her to her senses.'

'I'm sorry,' I said. 'There is something at work here that none of us understands, some kind of an elemental force. It is terrible and it is delicate at the same time. It must work itself out in Thora and Shaun Midhouse. I am not wise enough to interfere.'

There was silence in the library for a long time after that.

Armingert looked hurt and lost. No doubt but she is offended with me.

'He is right,' said Maurice at last. 'She is our daughter. We must just try to be patient.'

Then they both got to their feet. They looked tired and sad. They who had been childless for so long in their youth are now childless again; and they are growing old; and an area of their life where there was nothingness twenty years ago is now all vivid pain.

I knew it would happen some day: that old school-house dog has savaged one of the islanders, and a child at that. I was in the garden, filling a bowl with gooseberries, when I heard the terrible outcry from the village, a mingling of snarls and screams. 'Joe, you brute!' came James MacIntosh's voice (it was a still summer evening; every sound carried for miles)—'Bad dog! Get into the house this minute!' . . . And then in a soothing voice, 'Let's see your leg then. It's only a graze, Mansie. You got a fright, that's all. . . . That bad Joe. . . . Shush now, no need to kick up such a row. You'll deafen the whole village.' . . . This Mansie, whoever he was, refused to be comforted. The lamentation came nearer. I heard the school-house door being banged shut (my garden wall is too high to see the village): James MacIntosh had gone indoors, possibly to chastise his cur. Presently a boy, sobbing and snivelling in spasms, appeared on the road. He leaned against a pillar to get his breath. 'Hello,' I said, 'would you like some gooseberries?'

Greed and self-pity contended in Mansie's face. He unlatched the gate and came in, limping. There was a livid crescent mark below his knee. He picked a fat gooseberry from my bowl. He looked at it wonderingly. His lips were still shivering with shock.

'That damn fool of a dog,' I said. 'Did he seize you then? You'd better come into the kitchen. I'll put some disinfectant on it. I have bandages.'

The cupped palm of his hand brimmed with gooseberries. He bit into several, one after the other, with a half-reluctant lingering relish. Then he crammed six or seven into his mouth till his cheek bulged. His brown eyes dissolved in rapture; he closed them; there was a runnel of juice from one corner of his mouth to his chin.

The day was ending in a riot of colour westward. Crimson and saffron and jet the sea blazed, like stained glass.

'The disinfectant,' I said. 'It's in the kitchen.'

He balanced the last of the gooseberries on the tip of his tongue, rolled it round inside his mouth, and bit on it. 'It's nothing,' he said. 'I was in the village visiting my grand-da. It was me to blame really. I kicked Joe's bone at the school gate. I must be getting home now. Thora'll be wondering about me.' . . .

So, he was one of the Midhouse boys. He looked like neither of his parents. He had the shy swift gentle eyes of Maurice his grandfather. He relished gooseberries the way that old Maurice sipped his stout in the hotel bar.

'And anyway,' he said, 'I wouldn't come into your house to save my life.'

'What's wrong with my house?' I said.

'It's the laird's house,' he said. 'It's The Hall. I'm against all that kind of thing. I'm a communist.' (He was maybe ten years old.)

'There isn't anything very grand about this great ruckle of stones,' I said. 'It's falling to pieces. You should see the inside of it. Just look at this wilderness of a garden. I'll tell you the truth, Mansie— I'm nearly as poor as Ezra the tinker. So come in till I fix your leg.'

He shook his head. 'It's the principle of it,' said Mansie. 'You oppressed my ancestors. You taxed them to death. You drove them to Canada and New Zealand. You made them work in your fields for nothing. They built this house for you, yes, and their hands were red carrying up stones from the shore. I wouldn't go through your door for a pension. What does one man want with a big house like this anyway? Thora and me and my brothers live in two small rooms up at Solsetter.

'I'm sorry, Mansie,' I said. 'I promise I won't ever be wicked like that again. But I am worried about that bite on your leg.'

'It's the same with the kirk,' said Mansie. 'Do you think I could have just one more gooseberry? I would never enter that kirk door. All that talk about sin and hell and angels. Do you know what I think about the Bible? It's one long fairy-tale from beginning to end. I'm an atheist, too. You can tell the minister what I said if you like. I don't care. I don't care for any of you.'

The rich evening light smote the west gable of The Hall. The great house took, briefly, a splendour. The wall flushed and darkened. Then with all its withered stonework and ramshackle rooms it began to enter the night.

The gooseberry bush twanged. The young anarchist was plucking another fruit.

'I don't believe in anything,' he said. 'Nothing at all. You are born. You live for a while. Then you die. My grandma died last year. Do you know what she is now? Dust in the kirkyard. They could have put her in a ditch, it would have been all the same. When you're dead you're dead.'

'You'd better be getting home then, comrade, before it's dark,' I said.

'Do you know this,' he said, 'I have no father. At least, I do have a father but he doesn't live with us any more. He went away one day, suddenly. Oh, a while ago now, last winter. Jock Ritch saw him once in Falmouth. He was on a trawler. We don't know where he is. I'm glad he's gone. I didn't like him. And I'll tell you another thing.'

'Tomorrow,' I said. 'You must go home now. You must get that bite seen to. If you don't, some day there'll be an old man hobbling round this village with a wooden leg. And it'll be you, if you don't show that wound to your mother right away.'

'Rob and Willie and me,' he said, 'we're bastards. I bet I've shocked you. I bet you think I said a bad word. You see, Thora was never married. Thora, she's my mother. I suppose you would say "illegitimate" but it's just the same thing. The gooseberries were good. They're not your gooseberries though. They belong to the whole island by rights. I was only taking my share.'

The darkness had come down so suddenly that I could not say when the boy left my door. I was aware only that one smell had been subtracted from the enchanting cluster of smells that gather about an island on a late summer evening. A shadow was gone from the garden. I turned and went inside, carrying the bowl of gooseberries. (There would be one pot of jam less next winter.) I traversed, going to the kitchen, a corridor with an ancient ineradicable sweetness of rot in it.

I have been ill, it seems. I still feel like a ghost in a prison of bone. I have been very ill, James MacIntosh says. 'I thought you were for the kirkyard,' he told me last night. 'That's the truth. I thought an ancient proud island family was guttering out at last.' . . . He said after a time, 'There's something tough about you, man. I think you'll see the boots off us all.' He put the kettle on my fire to make a pot of tea. 'I don't suppose now,' he said, 'that you'll be up to a game of chess just yet. Quite so.' He is a sweet considerate man. 'I'll fill your hot-water bottle before I go,' he said, 'it's very cold up in that bedroom.'

The whole house is like a winter labyrinth in the heart of this summer-time island. It is all this dampness and rot, I'm sure, that made me so ill last month. The Hall is withering slowly about me. I cannot afford now to re-slate the roof. There is warping and woodworm and patches of damp everywhere. The three long corridors empty their overplus of draught into every mildewed bedroom. Even last October, when the men from the fishing boat broke the billiard-room window, going between the hotel and the barn dance at Dale, I had to go without tobacco for a fortnight or so until the joiner was paid. Not much can be done these days on two hundred pounds a year.

'James,' I said, 'I'm going to shift out of that bedroom. Another winter there and I'd be a gonner. I wonder if I could get a small bed fitted into some corner of the kitchen—over there, for example, out of the draught. I don't mind eating and sleeping in the same room.'

This morning (Saturday) MacIntosh came up from the schoolhouse with a small iron folding bed. 'It's been in the outhouse since I came to Torsay,' he said. 'The last teacher must have had it for one of his kids. It's a bit rusty, man, but it's sound, perfectly sound.

Look for yourself. If you'll just shift that heap of books out of the
corner I'll get it fixed up in no time.' . . .

We drank some tea while blankets and pillows were airing at the
kitchen fire. I tried to smoke my pipe but the thing tasted foul—the
room plunged; there was a blackness before my eyes; I began to
sweat. 'You're not entirely well yet by any means,' said the
schoolmaster. 'Put that pipe away. It'll be a week or two before you
can get over the door, far less down to the hotel for a pint. I'm
telling you, you've been very ill. You don't seem to realize how
desperate it was with you. But for one thing only you'd be in the
family vault.'

People who have been in the darkness for a while long to know
how it was with them when they were no longer there to observe
and evaluate. They resent their absence from the dear ecstatic flesh:
they suspect too that they may have been caught out by their
attendants in some weakness or shame that they themselves make
light of, or even indulge, in the ordinary round. At the same time
there is a kind of vanity in sickness. It sets a person apart from the
folk who only eat and sleep and sorrow and work. Those dullards
become the servants of the hero who has ventured into the shadowy
border-land next to the kingdom of death—the sickness bestows a
special quality on him, a seal of gentility almost. There are people
who wear their scars and pock-marks like decorations. The biog-
raphy of such a one is a pattern of small sicknesses, until at last the
kingdom he has fought against and been fascinated with for so long
besets him with irresistible steel and fire. There is one last trumpet
call under a dark tower. . . .

This afternoon, by means of subtle insistent questions, I got from
James MacIntosh the story of my trouble. He would much rather
have been sitting with me in amiable silence over a chess-board. I
knew of course the beginning of the story; how I had had to drag
myself about the house for some days at the end of May with a gray
quake on me. To get potatoes from the garden—a simple job like
that—was a burdensome penance. The road to the village and the
tobacco jar on Mr. Copinsay's shelf was a wearisome 'via crucis',
but at last I could not even get that far. My pipe lay cold on the
window-sill for two days. Sometime during the third day the sun
became a blackness.

'Pneumonia,' said James MacIntosh. 'That's what it was. Dr.
Wayne stood in the school-house door and barked at me. *The laird*

up yonder, your friend, he has double pneumonia. By rights he should be in the hospital in Kirkwall. That's out of the question, he's too ill. He'll have to bide where he is . . . Now then (says he) *there's not a hell of a lot I can do for him. That's the truth. It's a dicey thing, pneumonia. It comes to a crisis. The sick man reaches a crossroads, if you understand what I mean. He lingers there for an hour or two. Then he simply goes one way or the other. There's no telling. What is essential though* (says the old quack) *is good nursing. There must be somebody with him night and day—two, if possible, one to relieve the other. Now then, you must know some woman or other in the island who has experience of this kind of thing. Get her.* . . . And out of the house he stumps with his black bag, down the road, back to the ferryboat at the pier.

'So there you lay, in that great carved mahogany bed upstairs, sweating and raving. Old Wayne had laid the responsibility fairly and squarely on me. I had to get a nurse. But what nurse? And where? The only person who does any kind of nursing in the island is that Maggie Swintoun—at least, she brings most of the island bairns into the world, and it's her they generally send for when anybody dies. But nursing—I never actually heard of her attending sick folk. And besides, I knew you disliked the woman. If you were to open your eyes and see that face at the foot of the bed it would most likely, I thought, be the end of you. But that didn't prevent Mistress Swintoun from offering her services that same day. There she stood, keening and whispering at the foot of the stair—she had had the impudence to come in without knocking. *I hear the laird isn't well, the poor man* (says she). *Well now, if there's anything I can do. I don't mind sitting up all night.* . . . And the eyes of her going here and there over the portraits in the staircase and over all the silver plate in the hall-stand. *Thank you all the same,* said I, *but other arrangements have been made.* . . . Off she went then, like a cat leaving a fish on a doorstep. I was worried all the same, I can tell you. I went down to the village to have a consultation with Minnie Farquharson the seamstress. She knows everybody in Torsay, what they can do and what they can't do. She demurred. In the old days there would have been no difficulty: the island was teeming with kindly capable women who would have been ideal for the job. But things are different now, Minnie pointed out. Torsay is half empty. Most of the houses are in ruin. The young women are away in the town, working in shops and offices. All that's left in the way of women-folk are school bairns and "puir auld bodies". She honestly couldn't think of a single suitable person. *"Now* (says she) *I doubt you'll have to put an advertisement in* The Orcadian.

'I knew, as I walked back up the brae, that by the time the advertisement—"Wanted, experienced private nurse to attend gentleman"—had appeared, and been answered, and the nurse interviewed and approved and brought over to Torsay, there would have been no patient for her to attend to. The marble jaws would have swallowed you up. . . .

'When I turned in at the gate of The Hall, I saw washed sheets and pillow-cases hanging in the garden, between the potato patch and the gooseberry bushes, where no washing has ever flapped in the wind for ten years and more. (You hang your shirts and socks, I know, in front of the stove.) I went into the house. The fire was lit in the kitchen. The windows along the corridor were open, and there was a clean sweet air everywhere instead of those gray draughts. I'm not a superstitious man, but I swear my hand was shaking when I opened the door of your bedroom. And there she was, bent over you and putting cold linen to the beaded agony on your face.'

'Who?' I said.

'And there she stayed for ten days, feeding you, washing you, comforting you, keeping the glim of life in you night and day. Nobody ever relieved her. God knows when she slept. She was never, as far as I could make out, a minute away from your room. But of course she must have been, to cook, wash, prepare the medicines, things like that. She had even set jars of flowers in odd niches and corners. The house began to smell fragrant.'

I said, 'Yes, but who?'

'She told me, standing there in your bedroom that first day, that I didn't need to worry any longer. She thought she could manage. What could I do anyway, she said, with the school bairns to teach from ten in the morning till four in the afternoon? And she smiled at me, as though there was some kind of conspiracy between us. And she nodded, half in dismissal and half in affirmation. I went down that road to the schoolhouse with a burden lifted from me, I can tell you. *Well, if he doesn't get better,* I thought, *it won't be for want of a good nurse.'*

'You haven't told me her name,' I said.

'On the Thursday old Wayne came out of The Hall shaking his head. I saw him from the school window. He was still shaking his

head when he stepped on board the *Lintie* at the pier. That was the
day of the crisis. I ran up to your house as soon as the school was
let out at half past three (for I couldn't bear to wait till four o'clock).
The flame was gulping in the lamp all right. Your pulse had no
cohesion or rhythm. There were great gaps in your breathing. I
stood there, expecting darkness and silence pretty soon. What is it
above all that a woman gives to a man? God knows. Some strong
pure dark essence of the earth that seems not to be a part of the
sun-loving clay of men at all. The woman was never away from
your bedside that night. I slept, on and off, between two chairs in
the kitchen. At sunrise next morning you spoke for the first time for,
I think, twelve days. You asked for—of all things—a cup of tea.
But the nurse, she was no longer there.'

'For God's sake,' I said, 'tell me who she is.'

'You'll have to be doing with my crude services,' said James
MacIntosh, till you're able to do for yourself. You should be out
and about in a week, if this good weather holds. I thought I told
you who she was.'

'You didn't,' I said.

'Well now,' he said, 'I thought I did. It was Thora Garth, of
course.'

This morning I had a visit from a young man I have never seen
before. It turns out that he is a missionary, a kind of lay Presbyterian
preacher. There has been no minister in Torsay since the Rev. Mr.
Evelyn retired three years ago; the spiritual needs of the few people
remaining have been attended to, now and then, by ministers from
other islands.

This missionary is an earnest young bachelor. He has a sense of
vocation but no humour. Someone in the village must have told him
about me. 'Mister, you'd better call on the old man up at The Hall.
You'll likely be able to understand the posh way he speaks. He only
manages down to the village once a week nowadays for his tobacco
and his margarine and his loaf. He has nothing to live on but an
annuity—nowadays, with the price of things, it would hardly keep
a cat. The likes of him is too grand of course to apply for Social
Security. God knows what way he manages to live at all. He's never
been a church man, but I'm sure he'd be pleased to see an educated
person like you.' . . . I can just imagine Andrew Grossiter, or one of
the elders, saying that to the newcomer some Sunday morning after

the service, pointing up the brae to the big house with the fallen slates and the broken sundial.

So, here he was, this young preacher, come to visit me out of Christian duty. He put on me a bright kind smile from time to time.

'I like it here, in Torsay,' he said. 'Indeed I do. It's a great change from the city. I expect it'll take me a wee while to get used to country ways. I come from Glasgow myself. For example, I'm as certain as can be that someone had died in the village this morning. I saw a man carrying trestles into one of the houses. There was a coffin in the back of his van. By rights I should have been told about it at once. It's my duty to visit the bereaved relatives. I'll be wanted of course for the funeral. Ah well, I'll make enquiries this afternoon sometime.'

He eyed with a kind of innocent distaste the sole habitable room left in my house, the kitchen. If I had known he was coming I might have tidied the place up a bit. But for the sake of truth it's best when visitors come unexpectedly on the loaf and cracked mug on the table, the unmade bed, the webbed windows, and all the mingled smells of aged bachelordom.

'Death is a common thing in Torsay nowadays,' I said. 'Nearly everybody left in the village is old. There's hardly a young person in the whole island except yourself.'

'I hope you don't mind my visiting you,' said the missionary. 'I understand you're an Episcopalian. These days we must try to be as ecumenical as we can. Now sir, please don't be offended at what I'm going to say. It could be that, what with old age and the fact that you're not so able as you used to be, you find yourself with less money than you could be doing with—for example, to buy a bag of coal or a bit of butcher-meat.'

'I manage quite well,' I said. 'I have an annuity from my grand-uncle. I own this house. I don't eat a great deal.'

'Quite so,' he said. 'But the cost of everything keeps going up. Your income hardly covers the little luxuries that make life a bit more bearable. Now, I've been looking through the local church accounts and I've discovered that there are one or two small bequests that I have the disposal of. I don't see why you shouldn't be a beneficiary. They're for every poor person in the island, whatever church he belongs to, or indeed if he belongs to no church at all.'

'I don't need a thing,' I said.

'Well,' he said, 'if ever you feel like speaking to me about it. The money is there. It's for everybody in Torsay who needs it.'

'Torsay will soon require nothing,' I said.

'I must go down to the village now and see about this death,' he said. 'I noticed three young men in dark suits coming off the *Pomona* this morning. They must be relatives of some kind. . . . I'll find my own way out. Don't bother. This is a fascinating old house right enough. These stones, if only they could speak. God bless you, now.'

He left me then, that earnest innocent young man. I was glad in a way to see the back of him—though I liked him well enough—for I was longing for a pipeful of tobacco, and I'm as certain as can be that he is one of those evangelicals who disapprove of smoking and drinking.

So, there is another death in the island. Month by month Torsay is re-entering the eternal loneliness and silence. The old ones die. The young ones go away to farm in other places, or to car factories in Coventry or Bathgate. The fertile end of the island is littered with roofless windowless crofts. Sometimes, on a fine afternoon, I take my stick and walk for an hour about my domain. Last week I passed Dale, which Robbie Tenston used to farm. (He has been in Australia for fifteen years.) I pushed open the warped door of the dwelling-house. A great gray ewe lurched past me out of the darkness and nearly knocked me over. Birds whirred up through the bare rafters. There were bits of furniture here and there—a table, a couple of chairs, a wooden shut-bed. A framed photograph of the Channel Fleet still hung at the damp wall. There were empty bottles and jam jars all over the floor among sheep-turds and bird-splashes. . . . Most of the farm houses in Torsay are like that now.

It is an island dedicated to extinction. I can never imagine young people coming back to these uncultivated fields and eyeless ruins. Soon now, I know, the place will be finally abandoned to gulls and crows and rabbits. When first I came to Torsay fifty years ago, summoned from London by my grand-uncle's executor, I could still read the heraldry and the Latin motto over the great Hall door. There is a vague shape on the sandstone lintel now; otherwise it is indecipherable. All that style and history and romance have melted back into the stone.

Life in a flourishing island is a kind of fruitful interweaving music of birth and marriage and death: a trio. The old pass mildly into the darkness to make way for their bright grandchildren. There is

only one dancer in the island now and he carries the hour-glass and
the spade and the scythe.

How many have died in the past few years? I cannot remember
all the names. The severest loss, as far as I am concerned, is James
MacIntosh. The school above the village closed ten years ago, when
the dominie retired. There were not enough pupils to justify a new
teacher. He did not want to leave Torsay—his whole life was
entirely rooted here. He loved the trout fishing, and our chess and
few drams twice a week; he liked to follow the careers of his former
pupils in every part of the world—he had given so much of his life
to them. What did he know of his few remaining relatives in
Perthshire? 'Here I am and here I'll bide,' he said to me the day the
school closed. I offered him a croft a mile away—Unibreck—that
had just been vacated: the young crofter had got a job in an
Edinburgh brewery. James MacIntosh lived there for two winters,
reading his 'Forward' and working out chess moves from the manual
he kept beside his bed. . . . One morning Maggie Swintoun put her
head in at my kitchen door when I was setting the fire. 'O sir,' she
wailed, 'a terrible thing has happened!' Every broken window, every
winter cough, every sparrow-fall was stuff of tragedy to Maggie
Swintoun. I didn't bother even to look round at the woman—I
went on laying a careful stratum of sticks on the crumpled paper.
'Up at Unibreck,' she cried, 'your friend, poor Mr. MacIntosh the
teacher. I expected it. He hasn't been looking well this past month
and more.' . . . She must have been put out by the coal-blackened
face I turned on her, for she went away without rounding off her
knell. I gathered later that the postman, going with a couple of
letters to the cottage, had found James MacIntosh cold and silent
in his armchair. . . . I know he would have liked to be buried in
Torsay. Those same relatives that he had had no communication
with for a quarter of a century ordered his body to be taken down
to Dundee. There he was burned in a crematorium and his dust
thrown among alien winds.

Maggie Swintoun herself is a silence about the doors of the
village. Her ghost is there, a shivering silence, between the sea and
the hill. In no long time now that frail remembered keen will be lost
in the greater silence of Torsay.

The shutters have been up for two years in the general store.
William Copinsay was summoned by a stroke one winter evening
from his money bags. They left him in the kirkyard, with pennies

for eyes, to grope his way towards that unbearable treasure that is laid up (some say) for all who have performed decent acts of charity in their lives; the acts themselves, subtleties and shadows and gleams in time being (they say again) but fore-reflections of that hoarded perdurable reality. (I do not believe this myself. I believe in the 'twelve winds' of Housman that assemble the stuff of life for a year or two and then disperse it again.) Anyway, William Copinsay is dead.

Grossiter died at the auction mart in Hamnavoe, among the beasts and the whisky-smelling farmers, one Wednesday afternoon last spring.

Of course I know who has died in Torsay today. I knew hours before that young missionary opened his mouth. I had seen the lamp burning in a window at the end of the village at two o'clock in the morning.

It is not the old man who had died, either. His death could not have given me this unutterable grief that I felt then, and still feel. The heart of the island has stopped beating. I am the laird of a place that has no substance or meaning any more.

I will go down to the cottage sometime today. I will knock at the door. I will ask for permission to look into that still face.

The only child I have had has been taken from me; the only woman I could ever have loved; the only dust that I wished my own dust to be mingled with.

But in the fifty years that Thora Garth and I have lived in this island together we have never exchanged one word.

PATRICK WHITE
Five-Twenty

MOST evenings, weather permitting, the Natwicks sat on the front veranda to watch the traffic. During the day the stream flowed, but towards five it began to thicken, it sometimes jammed solid like: the semi-trailers and refrigeration units, the decent old-style sedans, the mini-cars, the bombs, the Holdens and the Holdens. She didn't know most of the names. Royal did, he was a man, though never ever mechanical himself. She liked him to tell her about the vehicles, or listen to him take part in conversation with anyone who stopped at the fence. He could hold his own, on account of he was more educated, and an invalid has time to think.

They used to sit side by side on the tiled veranda, him in his wheelchair she had got him after the artheritis took over, her in the old cane. The old cane chair wasn't hardly presentable any more; she had torn her winter cardy on a nail and laddered several pairs of stockings. You hadn't the heart to get rid of it, though. They brought it with them from Sarsaparilla after they sold the business. And now they could sit in comfort to watch the traffic, the big steel insects of nowadays, which put the wind up her at times.

Royal said, 'I reckon we're a shingle short to'uv ended up on the Parramatta Road.'

'You said we'd still see life,' she reminded, 'even if we lost the use of our legs.'

'But look at the traffic! Worse every year. And air. Rot a man's lungs quicker than the cigarettes. You should'uv headed me off. You who's supposed to be practical!'

'I thought it was what you wanted,' she said, keeping it soft; she had never been one to crow.

'Anyway, I already lost the use of me legs.'

As if she was to blame for that too. She was so shocked the chair sort of jumped. It made her blood run cold to hear the metal feet screak against the little draught-board tiles.

'Well, I 'aven't!' she protested. 'I got me legs, and will be able to get from 'ere to anywhere and bring 'ome the shopping. While I got me strength.'

She tried never to upset him by any show of emotion, but now she was so upset herself.

They watched the traffic in the evenings, as the orange light was stacked up in thick slabs, and the neon signs were coming on.

'See that bloke down there in the parti-coloured Holden?'

'Which?' she asked.

'The one level with our own gate.'

'The pink and brown?' She couldn't take all that interest tonight, only you must never stop humouring a sick man.

'Yairs. Pink. Fancy a man in a pink car!'

'Dusty pink is fashionable.' She knew that for sure.

'But a man!'

'Perhaps his wife chose it. Perhaps he's got a domineering wife.'

Royal laughed low. 'Looks the sort of coot who might like to be domineered, and if that's what he wants, it's none of our business, is it?'

She laughed to keep him company. They were such mates, everybody said. And it was true. She didn't know what she would do if Royal passed on first.

That evening the traffic had jammed. Some of the drivers began tooting. Some of them stuck their heads out, and yarned to one another. But the man in the pink-and-brown Holden just sat. He didn't look to either side.

Come to think of it, she had noticed him pass before. Yes. Though he wasn't in no way a noticeable man. Yes. She looked at her watch.

'Five-twenty,' she said. 'I seen that man in the pink-and-brown before. He's pretty regular. Looks like a business executive.'

Royal cleared his throat and spat. It didn't make the edge of the veranda. Better not to notice it, because he'd only create it she did. She'd get out the watering-can after she had pushed him inside.

'Business executives!' she heard. 'They're afraid people are gunner think they're poor class without they *execute*. In our day nobody was ashamed to *do*. Isn't that about right, eh?' She didn't answer because she knew she wasn't meant to. 'Funny sort of head that cove's got. Like it was half squashed. Silly-lookun bloody head!'

'Could have been born with it,' she suggested. 'Can't help what you're born with. Like your religion.'

There was the evening the Chev got crushed, only a young fellow too. Ahhh, it had stuck in her throat, thinking of the wife and kiddies. She ran in, and out again as quick as she could, with a couple of blankets, and the rug that was a present from Hazel. She had grabbed a pillow off their own bed.

She only faintly heard Royal shouting from the wheel-chair.

She arranged the blankets and the pillow on the pavement, under the orange sky. The young fellow was looking pretty sick, kept on turning his head as though he recognized and wanted to tell her something. Then the photographer from the *Mirror* took his picture, said she ought to be in it to add a touch of human interest, but she wouldn't. A priest came, the *Mirror* took his picture, administering what Mrs. Dolan said they call Extreme Unkshun. Well, you couldn't poke fun at a person's religion any more than the shape of their head, and Mrs. Dolan was a decent neighbour, the whole family, and clean.

When she got back to the veranda, Royal, a big man, had slipped down in his wheel-chair.

He said, or gasped, 'Wotcher wanter do that for, Ella? How are we gunner get the blood off?'

She hadn't thought about the blood, when of course she was all smeared with it, and the blankets, and Hazel's good Onkaparinka. Anyway, it was her who would get the blood off.

'You soak it in milk or something,' she said. 'I'll ask. Don't you worry.'

Then she did something. She bent down and kissed Royal on the forehead in front of the whole Parramatta Road. She regretted it at once, because he looked that powerless in his invalid chair, and his forehead felt cold and sweaty.

But you can't undo things that are done.

It was a blessing they could sit on the front veranda. Royal suffered a lot by now. He had his long-standing hernia, which they couldn't have operated on, on account of he was afraid of his heart. And then the artheritis.

'Arthritis.'

'All right,' she accepted the correction. 'Arth-er-itis.'

It was all very well for men, they could manage more of the hard words.

'What have we got for tea?' he asked.

'Well, she said, fanning out her hands on the points of her elbows, and smiling, 'it's a surprise.'

She looked at her watch. It was five-twenty.

'It's a coupler nice little bits of fillet Mr. Ballard let me have.'

'Wotcher mean let you have? Didn't you pay for them?'
She had to laugh. 'Anything I have I pay for!'
'Well? Think we're in the fillet-eating class?'
'It's only a treat, Royal,' she said. 'I got a chump chop for myself.
I like a nice chop.'
He stopped complaining, and she was relieved.
'There's that gentleman,' she said, 'in the Holden.'
They watched him pass, as sober as their own habits.

Royal—he had been his mother's little king. Most of his mates called
him 'Roy'. Perhaps only her and Mrs. Natwick had stuck to the
christened name, they felt it suited.

She often wondered how Royal had ever fancied her: such a big
man, with glossy hair, black, and a nose like on someone historical.
She would never have said it, but she was proud of Royal's nose.
She was proud of the photo he had of the old family home in Kent,
the thatch so lovely, and Grannie Natwick sitting in her apron on a
rush-bottom chair in front, looking certainly not all that different
from Mum, with the aunts gathered round in leggermutton sleeves,
all big nosey women like Royal.

She had heard Mum telling Royal's mother, 'Ella's a plain little
thing, but what's better than cheerful and willing?' She had always
been on the mousey side, she supposed, which didn't mean she
couldn't chatter with the right person. She heard Mum telling Mrs.
Natwick, 'My Ella can wash and bake against any comers. Clever
with her needle too.' She had never entered any of the competitions,
like they told her she ought to, it would have made her nervous.

It was all the stranger that Royal had ever fancied her.

Once as they sat on the veranda watching the evening traffic, she
said, 'Remember how you used to ride out in the old days from
"Bugilbar" to Cootramundra?'

'Cootamundra.'

'Yes,' she said. 'Cootramundra.' (That's why they'd called the
house 'Coota' when they moved to the Parramatta Road.)

She had been so dazzled on one occasion by his parti-coloured
forehead and his black hair, after he had got down from the saddle,
after he had taken off his hat, she had run and fetched a duster, and
dusted Royal Natwick's boots. The pair of new elastic-sides was
white with dust from the long ride. It only occurred to her as she
polished she might be doing something shameful, but when she

looked up, it seemed as though Royal Natwick saw nothing peculiar in Ella McWhirter dusting his boots. He might even have expected it. She was so glad she could have cried.

Old Mr. Natwick had come out from Kent when a youth, and after working at several uncongenial jobs, and studying at night, had been taken on as book-keeper at 'Bugilbar'. He was much valued in the end by the owners, and always made use of. The father would have liked his son to follow in his footsteps, and taught him how to keep the books, but Royal wasn't going to hang around any family of purse-proud squatters, telling them the things they wanted to hear. He had ideas of his own for becoming rich and important.

So when he married Ella McWhirter, which nobody could ever understand, not even Ella herself, perhaps only Royal, who never bothered to explain (why should he?) they moved to Juggerawa, and took over the general store. It was in a bad way, and soon was in a worse, because Royal's ideas were above those of his customers.

Fulbrook was the next stage. He found employment as book-keeper on a grazing property outside. She felt so humiliated on account of his humiliation. It didn't matter about herself because she always expected less. She took a job in Fulbrook from the start, at the 'Dixie Cafe' in High Street. She worked there several years as waitress, helping out with the scrubbing for the sake of the extra money. She had never hated anything, but got to hate the flies trampling in the sugar and on the necks of the tomato sauce bottles.

At weekends her husband usually came in, and when she wasn't needed in the shop, they lay on the bed in her upstairs room, listening to the corrugated iron and the warping white-washed weatherboard. She would have loved to do something for him, but in his distress he complained about 'wet kisses'. It surprised her. She had always been afraid he might find her a bit too dry in her show of affection.

Those years at the 'Dixie Cafe' certainly dried her up. She got those freckly patches and seams in her skin in spite of the lotions used as directed. Not that it matters so much in anyone born plain. Perhaps her plainness helped her save. There was never a day when she didn't study her savings-book, it became her favourite recreation.

Royal, on the other hand, wasn't the type that dried up, being fleshier, and dark. He even put on weight out at the grazing property, where they soon thought the world of him. When the young ladies were short of a man for tennis the book-keeper was often invited, and to a ball once at the homestead. He was earning good money, and he too saved a bit, though his instincts weren't as mean as hers. For instance, he fancied a choice cigar. In his youth Royal was a natty dresser.

Sometimes the young ladies, if they decided to inspect the latest at Ryan's Emporium, or Mr. Philup, if he felt like grogging up with the locals, would drive him in, and as he got out they would look funny at the book-keeper's wife they had heard about, they must have, serving out the plates of frizzled steak and limp chips. Royal always waited to see his employers drive off before coming in.

In spite of the savings, this might have gone on much longer than it did if old Mr. Natwick hadn't died. It appeared he had been a very prudent man. He left them a nice little legacy. The evening of the news, Royal was driven in by Mr. Philup and they had a few at the Imperial. Afterwards the book-keeper was dropped off, because he proposed to spend the night with his wife and catch the early train to attend his father's funeral.

They lay in the hot little room and discussed the future. She had never felt so hectic. Royal got the idea he would like to develop a grocery business in one of the posh outer suburbs of Sydney. 'Interest the monied residents in some of the luxury lines. Appeal to the imagination as well as the stomach.'

She was impressed, of course, but not as much as she should have been. She wasn't sure, but perhaps she was short on imagination. Certainly their prospects had made her downright feverish, but for no distinct, sufficient reason.

'And have a baby.' She heard her own unnatural voice.

'Eh?'

'We could start a baby.' Her voice grew word by word drier.

'There's no reason why we couldn't have a baby. Or two.' He laughed. 'But starting a new life isn't the time to start a baby.' He dug her in the ribs. 'And you the practical one!'

She agreed it would be foolish, and presently Royal fell asleep.

What could she do for him? As he lay there breathing she would have loved to stroke his nose she could see faintly in the light from the window. Again unpractical, she would have liked to kiss it. Or bite it suddenly off.

She was so disgusted with herself she got creaking off the bed and walked flat across the boards to the washstand and swallowed a couple of Aspros to put her solidly to sleep.

All their life together she had to try in some way to make amends to Royal, not only for her foolishness, but for some of the thoughts that got into her head. Because she hadn't the imagination, the thoughts couldn't have been her own. They must have been put into her.

It was easier of course in later life, after he had cracked up, what with his hernia, and heart, and the artheritis taking over. Fortunately she was given the strength to help him into the wheel-chair, and later still, to lift, or drag him up on the pillows and over, to rub the bed-sores, and stick the pan under him. But even during the years at Sarsaparilla she could make amends in many little ways, though with him still in his prime, naturally he mustn't know of them. So all her acts were mostly for her own self-gratification.

The store at Sarsaparilla, if it didn't exactly flourish, gave them a decent living. She had her problems, though. Some of the locals just couldn't accept that Royal was a superior man. Perhaps she had been partly to blame, she hardly dared admit it, for showing one or two 'friends' the photo of the family home in Kent. She couldn't resist telling the story of one of the aunts, Miss Ethel Natwick, who followed her brother to New South Wales. Ethel was persuaded to accept a situation at Government House, but didn't like it and went back, in spite of the Governor's lady insisting she valued Ethel as a close personal friend. When people began to laugh at Royal on account of his auntie and the family home, as you couldn't help finding out in a place like Sarsaparilla, it was her, she knew, it was her to blame. It hurt her deeply.

Of course Royal could be difficult. Said stockbrokers had no palate and less imagination. Royal said no Australian grocer could make a go of it if it wasn't for flour, granulated sugar, and tomato sauce. Some of the customers turned nasty in retaliation. This was where she could help, and did, because Royal was out on delivery more often than not. It embarrassed her only when some of them took it for granted she was on their side. As if he wasn't her husband. Once or twice she had gone out crying afterwards, amongst the wormy wattles and hens' droppings. Anyone across the gully could have heard her blowing her nose behind the store, but she didn't care. Poor Royal.

There was that Mr. Ogburn said, 'A selfish, swollen-headed slob who'll chew you up and swallow you down.' She wouldn't let herself hear any more of what he had to say. Mr. Ogburn had a hare-lip, badly sewn, opening and closing. There was nothing frightened her so much as even a well-disguised hare-lip. She got the palpitations after the scene with Mr. Ogburn.

Not that there was anything wrong with her.

She only hadn't had the baby. It was her secret grief on black evenings as she walked slowly looking for the eggs a flighty hen might have hid in the bracken.

Dr. Bamforth said, looking at the nib of his fountain pen, 'You know, don't you, it's sometimes the man?'

She didn't even want to hear, let alone think about it. In any case she wouldn't tell Royal, because a man's pride could be so easily hurt.

After they had sold out at Sarsaparilla and come to live at what they called 'Coota' on the Parramatta Road, it was both easier and more difficult, because if they were not exactly elderly they were getting on. Royal used to potter about in the beginning, while taking care, on account of the hernia and his heart. There was the business of the lawn-mowing, not that you could call it lawn, but it was what she had. She loved her garden. In front certainly there was only the two squares of rather sooty grass which she would keep in order with the pushmower. The lawn seemed to get on Royal's nerves until the artheritis took hold of him. He had never liked mowing. He would lean against the veranda post, and shout, 'Don't know why we don't do what they've done down the street. Root the stuff out. Put down a green concrete lawn.'

'That would be copying,' she answered back.

She hoped it didn't sound stubborn. As she pushed the mower she bent her head, and smiled, waiting for him to cool off. The scent of grass and a few clippings flew up through the traffic fumes reminding you of summer.

While Royal shuffled along the veranda and leaned against another post. 'Or pebbles. You can buy clean, river pebbles. A few plastic shrubs, and there's the answer.'

He only gave up when his trouble forced him into the chair. You couldn't drive yourself up and down a veranda shouting at someone from a wheel-chair without the passers-by thinking you was a nut. So he quietened.

He watched her, though. From under the peak of his cap. Because she felt he might still resent her mowing the lawn, she would try to reassure him as she pushed. 'What's wrong, *eh*? While I still have me health, me *strength*—I was always what they call *wiry*—why shouldn't I cut the *grass*?'

She would come and sit beside him, to keep him company in watching the traffic, and invent games to amuse her invalid husband.

'Isn't that the feller we expect?' she might ask. 'The one that passes at five-twenty,' looking at her watch, 'in the old pink-and-brown Holden?'

They enjoyed their snort of amusement all the better because no one else knew the reason for it.

Once when the traffic was particularly dense, and that sort of chemical smell from one of the factories was thickening in the evening air, Royal drew her attention. 'Looks like he's got something on his mind.'

Could have too. Or it might have been the traffic block. The way he held his hands curved listlessly around the inactive wheel reminded her of possums and monkeys she had seen in cages. She shifted a bit. Her squeaky old chair. She felt uneasy for ever having found the man, not a joke, but half of one.

Royal's chair moved so smoothly on its rubber-tyred wheels it was easy to push him, specially after her practice with the mower. There were ramps where necessary now, to cover steps, and she would sometimes wheel him out to the back, where she grew hollyhock and sunflower against the palings, and a vegetable or two on raised beds.

Royal would sit not looking at the garden from under the peak of his cap.

She never attempted to take him down the shady side, between them and Dolans, because the path was narrow from plants spilling over, and the shade might have lowered his spirits.

She loved her garden.

The shady side was where she kept her staghorn ferns, and fishbones, and the pots of maidenhair. The water lay sparkling on the maidenhair even in the middle of the day. In the blaze of summer the light at either end of the tunnel was like you were looking through a sheet of yellow cellophane, but as the days

shortened, the light deepened to a cold, tingling green, which might
have made a person nervous who didn't know the tunnel by heart.

Take Mrs. Dolan the evening she came in to ask for the loan of a
cupful of sugar. 'You gave me a shock, Mrs. Natwick. What ever
are you up to?'

'Looking at the plants,' Mrs. Natwick answered, whether Mrs.
Dolan would think it peculiar or not.

It was the season of cinerarias, which she always planted on that
side, it was sheltered and cold-green. The wind couldn't bash the
big spires and umbrellas of blue and purple. Visiting cats were the
only danger, messing and pouncing. She disliked cats for the smell
they left, but didn't have the heart to disturb their elastic forms
curled at the cineraria roots, exposing their colourless pads, and
sometimes pink, swollen teats. Blushing only slightly for it, she
would stand and examine the details of the sleeping cats.

If Royal called she could hear his voice through the window.
'Where'uv you got to, Ella?'

After he was forced to take to his bed, his voice began to sort of
dry up like his body. There were times when it sounded less like a
voice than a breath of drowsiness or pain.

'Ella,' he was calling. 'I dropped the paper. Where are yer all this
time? You know I can't pick up the paper.'

She knew. Guilt sent her scuttling to him, deliberately composing
her eyes and mouth so as to arrive looking cheerful.

'I was in the garden,' she confessed, 'looking at the cinerarias.'

'The what?' It was a name Royal could never learn.

The room was smelling of sickness and the bottles standing on
odd plates.

'It fell,' he complained.

She picked up the paper as quick as she could.

'Want to go la-la first?' she asked, because by now he depended
on her to raise him and stick the pan under.

But she couldn't distract him from her shortcomings; he was
shaking the paper at her. 'Haven't you lived with me long enough
to know how to treat a newspaper?'

He hit it with his set hand, and certainly the paper looked a mess,
like an old white battered brolly.

'Mucked up! You gotter keep the pages *aligned*. A paper's not
readable otherwise. Of course you wouldn't understand because
you don't read it, without it's to see who's died.' He began to cough.

'Like me to bring you some Bovril?' she asked him as tenderly as she knew.

'Bovril's the morning,' he coughed.

She knew that, but wanted to do something for him.

After she had rearranged the paper she walked out so carefully it made her go lopsided, out to the front veranda. Nothing would halt the traffic, not sickness, not death even.

She sat with her arms folded, realizing at last how they were aching.

'He hasn't been,' she had to call after looking at her watch.

'Who?' she heard the voice rustling back.

'The gentleman in the pink Holden.'

She listened to the silence, wondering whether she had done right.

When Royal called back, 'Could'uv had a blow-out.' Then he laughed. 'Could'uv stopped to get grogged up.' She heard the frail rustling of the paper. 'Or taken an axe to somebody like they do nowadays.'

She closed her eyes, whether for Royal, or what she remembered of the man sitting in the Holden.

Although it was cold she continued watching after dark. Might have caught a chill, when she couldn't afford to. She only went inside to make the bread-and-milk Royal fancied of an evening.

She watched most attentively, always at the time, but he didn't pass, and didn't pass.

'Who?'

'The gentleman in the Holden.'

'Gone on holiday.' Royal sighed, and she knew it was the point where a normal person would have turned over, so she went to turn him.

One morning she said on going in, 'Fancy, I had a dream, it was about that man! He was standing on the side path alongside the cinerarias. I know it was him because of his funny-shaped head.'

'What happened in the dream?' Royal hadn't opened his eyes yet; she hadn't helped him in with his teeth.

'I dunno,' she said, 'it was just a dream.'

That wasn't strictly truthful, because the Holden gentleman had looked at her, she had seen his eyes. Nothing was spoken, though.

'It was a sort of red and purple dream. That was the cinerarias,' she said.

'I don't dream. You don't when you don't sleep. Pills aren't sleep.'

She was horrified at her reverberating dream. 'Would you like a nice soft-boiled egg?'

'Eggs all have a taste.'

'But you gotter eat *something*!'

On another morning she told him—she could have bitten off her tongue—she *was* stupid, *stupid*, 'I had a dream.'

'What sort of dream?'

'Oh,' she said, 'a silly one. Not worth telling. I dreamed I dropped an egg on the side path, and it turned into two. Not two. A double-yolker.'

She never realized Royal was so much like Mrs. Natwick. It was as she raised him on his pillows. Or he had got like that in his sickness. Old men and old women were not unlike.

'Wasn't that a silly one?' she coaxed.

Every evening she sat on the front veranda and watched the traffic as though Royal had been beside her. Looked at her watch. And turned her face away from the steady-flowing stream. The way she bunched her small chest she could have had a sour breath mounting in her throat. Sometimes she had, it was nervousness.

When she went inside she announced. 'He didn't pass.'

Royal said—he had taken to speaking from behind his eyelids. 'Something muster happened to 'im. He didn't go on holiday. He went and died.'

'Oh, no! He wasn't of an age!'

At once she saw how stupid she was, and went out to get the bread-and-milk.

She would sit at the bedside, almost crouching against the edge of the mattress, because she wanted Royal to feel she was close, and he seemed to realize, though he mostly kept his eyelids down.

Then one evening she came running, she felt silly, her calves felt silly, her voice, 'He's come! At five-twenty! In a new cream Holden!'

Royal said without opening his eyes, 'See? I said 'e'd gone on holiday.'

More than ever she saw the look of Mrs. Natwick.'

Now every evening Royal asked, 'Has he been, Ella?'

Trying not to make it sound irritable or superior, she would answer, 'Not yet. It's only five.'

Every evening she sat watching, and sometimes would turn

proud, arching her back, as she looked down from the veranda. The man was so small and ordinary.

She went in on one occasion, into the more than electric light, lowering her eyelids against the dazzle. 'You know, Royal, you could feel prouder of men when they rode horses. As they looked down at yer from under the brim of their hats. Remember that hat you used to wear? Riding in to Cootramundra?'

Royal died quietly that same year before the cinerarias had folded, while the cold westerlies were still blowing; the back page of the *Herald* was full of those who had been carried off. She was left with his hand, already set, in her own. They hadn't spoken, except about whether she had put out the garbage.

Everybody was very kind. She wouldn't have liked to admit it was enjoyable being a widow. She sat around for longer than she had ever sat, and let the dust gather. In the beginning acquaintances and neighbours brought her little presents of food: a billy-can of giblet soup, moulded veal with hard-boiled egg making a pattern in the jelly, cakes so dainty you couldn't taste them. But when she was no longer a novelty they left off coming. She didn't care any more than she cared about the dust. Sometimes she would catch sight of her face in the glass, and was surprised to see herself looking so calm and white.

Of course she was calm. The feeling part of her had been removed. What remained was a slack, discardable eiderdown. Must have been the pills Doctor gave.

Well-meaning people would call to her over the front fence, 'Don't you feel lonely, Mrs. Natwick.' They spoke with a restrained horror, as though she had been suffering from an incurable disease.

But she called back proud and slow, 'I'm under sedation.'

'Arrr!' They nodded thoughtfully. 'What's 'e given yer?'

She shook her head. 'Pills,' she called back. 'They say they're the ones the actress died of.'

The people walked on, impressed.

As the evenings grew longer and heavier she sat later on the front veranda watching the traffic of the Parramatta Road, its flow becoming syrupy and almost benign: big bulbous sedate buses, chrysalis cars still without a life of their own, clinging in line to the back of their host-articulator, trucks loaded for distances, empty loose-sounding jolly lorries. Sometimes women, looking out from

the cabins of trucks from beside their men, shared her lack of
curiosity. The light was so fluid nobody lasted long enough. You
would never have thought boys could kick a person to death, seeing
their long soft hair floating behind their sports models.

Every evening she watched the cream Holden pass. And looked
at her watch. It was like Royal was sitting beside her. Once she
heard herself, 'Thought he was gunner look round tonight, in our
direction.' How could a person feel lonely?

She was, though. She came face to face with it walking through
the wreckage of her garden in the long slow steamy late summer.
The Holden didn't pass of course of a Saturday or Sunday.
Something, something had tricked her, not the pills, before the pills.
She couldn't blame anybody, probably only herself. Everything
depended on yourself. Take the garden. It was a shambles. She
would have liked to protest, but began to cough from running her
head against some powdery mildew. She could only blunder at first,
like a cow, or runty starved heifer, on breaking into a garden. She
had lost her old wiriness. She shambled, snapping dead stems,
uprooting. Along the bleached palings there was a fretwork of
hollyhock, the brown fur of rotting sunflower. She rushed at a
praying mantis, a big pale one, and deliberately broke its back, and
was sorry afterwards for what was done so easy and thoughtless.

As she stood panting in her black, finally yawning, she saw all
she had to repair. The thought of the seasons piling up ahead made
her feel tired but necessary, and she went in to bathe her face.
Royal's denture in a tumbler on top of the medicine cabinet, she
ought to move, or give to the Sallies. In the meantime she changed
the water. She never forgot it. The teeth looked amazingly alive.

All that autumn, winter, she was continually amazed, at the dust
she had let gather in the house, at old photographs, books, clothes.
There was a feather she couldn't remember wearing, a scarlet
feather, she *can't* have worn, and gloves with little fussy ruffles at
the wrists, silver piping, like a snail had laid its trail round the
edges. There was, she knew, funny things she had bought at times,
and never worn, but she couldn't remember the gloves or the
feather. And books. She had collected a few, though never a reader
herself. Old people liked to give old books, and you took them so as
not to hurt anybody's feelings. *Hubert's Crusade* for instance. Lovely
golden curls. Could have been Royal's father's book. Everybody
was a child once. And almost everybody had one. At least if she had

had a child she would have known it wasn't a white turnip, more of a praying mantis, which snaps too easy.

In the same box she had put away a coloured picture, *Cities of the Plain*, she couldn't remember seeing it before. The people escaping from the burning cities had committed some sin or other nobody ever thought, let alone talked, about. As they hurried between rocks, through what must have been the 'desert places', their faces looked long and wooden. All they had recently experienced could have shocked the expression out of them. She was fascinated by what made her shiver. And the couples with their arms still around one another. Well, if you were damned, better hang on to your sin. She didn't blame them.

She put the box away. Its inlay as well as its contents made it something secret and precious.

The autumn was still and golden, the winter vicious only in fits. It was what you could call a good winter. The cold floods of air and more concentrated streams of dark-green light poured along the shady side of the house where her cinerarias had massed. She had never seen such cinerarias: some of the spired ones reached almost as high as her chin, the solid heads of others waited in the tunnel of dark light to club you with their colours, of purple and drenching blue, and what they called 'wine'. She couldn't believe wine would have made her drunker.

Just as she would sit every evening watching the traffic, evening was the time she liked best to visit the cinerarias, when the icy cold seemed to make the flowers burn their deepest, purest. So it was again evening when her two objects converged: for some blissfully confident reason she hadn't bothered to ask herself whether she had seen the car pass, till here was this figure coming towards her along the tunnel. She knew at once who it was, although she had never seen him on his feet; she had never seen him full-face, but knew from the funny shape of his head as Royal had been the first to notice. He was not at all an impressive man, not much taller than herself, but broad. His footsteps on the brickwork sounded purposeful.

'Will you let me use your phone, please, madam?' he asked in a prepared voice. 'I'm having trouble with the Holden.'

This was the situation she had always been expecting: somebody asking to use the phone as a way to afterwards murdering you. Now that it might be about to happen she couldn't care.

She said yes. She thought her voice sounded muzzy. Perhaps he would think she was drunk.

She went on looking at him, at his eyes. His nose, like the shape of his head, wasn't up to much, but his eyes, his eyes, she dared to think, were filled with kindness.

'Cold, eh? but clean cold!' He laughed friendly, shuffling on the brick paving because she was keeping him waiting.

Only then she noticed his mouth. He had a hare-lip, there was no mistaking, although it was well sewn. She felt so calm in the circumstances. She would have even liked to touch it.

But said, 'Why, yes—the telephone,' she said, 'it's this way,' she said, 'it's just off the kitchen—because that's where you spend most of your life. Or in bed,' she ended.

She wished she hadn't added that. For the first time since they had been together she felt upset, thinking he might suspect her of wrong intentions.

But he laughed and said, 'That's correct! You got something there!' It sounded manly rather than educated.

She realized he was still waiting, and took him to the telephone.

While he was phoning she didn't listen. She never listened when other people were talking on the phone. The sight of her own kitchen surprised her. While his familiar voice went on. It was the voice she had held conversations with.

But he was ugly, real ugly, *deformed*. It if wasn't for the voice, the eyes. She couldn't remember the eyes, but seemed to know about them.

Then she heard him laying the coins beside the phone, extra loud, to show.

He came back into the kitchen smiling and looking. She could smell him now, and he had the smell of a clean man.

She became embarrassed at herself, and took him quickly out.

'Fair bit of garden you got.' He stood with his calves curved through his trousers. A cocky little chap, but nice.

'Oh,' she said, 'this', she said, angrily almost, 'is nothing. You oughter see it. There's sunflower and hollyhock all along the palings. I'm famous for me hollyhocks!' She had never boasted in her life. 'But not now—it isn't the season. And I let it go. Mr. Natwick passed on. You should'uv seen the cassia this autumn. Now it's only sticks, of course. And hibiscus. There's cream, gold, cerise, scarlet—double and single.'

She was dressing in them for him, revolving on high heels and changing frilly skirts.

He said, 'Gardening's not in my line,' turning his head to hide something, perhaps he was ashamed of his hare-lip.

'No,' she agreed. 'Not everybody's a gardener.'

'But like a garden.'

'My husband didn't even like it. He didn't have to tell me,' she added.

As they moved across the wintry grass, past the empty clothes line, the man looked at his watch, and said, 'I was reckoning on visiting somebody in hospital tonight. Looks like I shan't make it if the N.R.M.A. takes as long as usual.'

'Do they?' she said, clearing her throat. 'It isn't somebody close, I hope? The sick person?'

Yes he said they was close.

'Nothing serious?' she almost bellowed.

He said it was serious.

Oh she nearly burst out laughing at the bandaged figure they were sitting beside particularly at the bandaged face. She would have laughed at a brain tumour.

'I'm sorry,' she said. 'I understand. Mr. Natwick was for many years an invalid.'

Those teeth in the tumbler on top of the medicine cabinet. Looking at her. Teeth can look, worse than eyes. But she couldn't help it, she meant everything she said, and thought.

At this moment they were pressing inside the dark-green tunnel, her sleeve rubbing his, as the crimson-to-purple light was dying.

'These are the cinerarias,' she said.

'The what?' He didn't know, any more than Royal.

As she was about to explain she got switched to another language. Her throat became a long palpitating funnel through which the words she expected to use were poured out in a stream of almost formless agonized sound.

'What is it?' he asked, touching her.

If it had happened to herself she would have felt frightened, it occurred to her, but he didn't seem to be.

'What is it?' he kept repeating in his familiar voice, touching, even holding her.

And for answer, in the new language, she was holding him. They were holding each other, his hard body against her eiderdowny one. As the silence closed round them again, inside the tunnel of light, his face, to which she was very close, seemed to be unlocking, the wound of his mouth, which should have been more horrible, struggling to open. She could see he had recognized her.

She kissed above his mouth. She kissed as though she might never succeed in healing all the wounds they had ever suffered.

How long they stood together she wasn't interested in knowing. Outside them the river of traffic continued to flow between its brick and concrete banks. Even if it overflowed it couldn't have drowned them.

When the man said in his gentlest voice, 'Better go out in front. The N.R.M.A. might have come.'

'Yes,' she agreed. 'The N.R.M.A.'

So they shuffled, still holding each other, along the narrow path. She imagined how long and wooden their faces must look. She wouldn't look at him now, though, just as she wouldn't look back at the still faintly smouldering joys they had experienced together in the past.

When they came out, apart, and into the night, there was the N.R.M.A., his pointed ruby of a light burning on top of the cabin.

'When will you come?' she asked.

'Tomorrow.'

'Tomorrow. You'll stay to tea.'

He couldn't stay.

'I'll make you a *pot* of tea?'

But he didn't drink it.

'Coffee, then?'

He said, 'I like a nice cup of coffee.'

Going down the path he didn't look back, or opening the gate. She would not let herself think of reasons or possibilities, she would not think, but stood planted in the path, swayed slightly by the motion of the night.

Mrs. Dolan said, 'You bring the saucepan to the boil. You got that?'

'Yeeehs.' Mrs. Natwick had never been a dab at coffee.

'Then you throw in some cold water. That's what sends the gravel to the bottom.' This morning Mrs. Dolan had to laugh at her own jokes.

'That's the part that frightens me,' Mrs. Natwick admitted.

'Well, you just do it, and see,' said Mrs. Dolan; she was too busy.

After she had bought the coffee Mrs. Natwick stayed in the city to muck around. If she had stayed at home her nerves might have wound themselves tighter, waiting for evening to come. Though mucking around only irritated in the end. She had never been an idle woman. So she stopped at the cosmetics as though she didn't have to decide, this was her purpose, and said to the young lady lounging behind one of the counters, 'I'm thinking of investing in a lipstick, dear. Can you please advise me?'

As a concession to the girl she tried to make it a laughing matter, but the young person was bored, she didn't bat a silver eyelid. 'Elderly ladies,' she said, 'go for the brighter stuff.'

Mrs. Natwick ('my little Ella') had never felt so meek. Mum must be turning in her grave.

'This is a favourite.' With a flick of her long fingers, the girl exposed the weapon. It looked too slippery-pointed, crimson-purple, out of its golden sheath.

Mrs. Natwick's knees were shaking. 'Isn't it a bit noticeable?' she asked, again trying to make it a joke.

But the white-haired girl gave a serious laugh. 'What's wrong with noticeable?'

As Mrs. Natwick tried it out on the back of her hand the way she had seen others do, the girl was jogging from foot to foot behind the counter. She was humming between her teeth, behind her white-smeared lips, probably thinking about a lover. Mrs. Natwick blushed. What if she couldn't learn to get the tip of her lipstick back inside its sheath?

She might have gone quickly away without another word if the young lady hadn't been so professional and bored. Still humming, she brought out a little pack of rouge.

'Never saw myself with mauve cheeks!' It was at least dry, and easy to handle.

'It's what they wear.'

Mrs. Natwick didn't dare refuse. She watched the long fingers with their silver nails doing up the parcel. The fingers looked as though they might resent touching anything but cosmetics; a lover was probably beneath contempt.

The girl gave her the change, and she went away without counting it.

* * *

She wasn't quiet, though, not a bit, booming and clanging in front of the toilet mirror. She tried to make a thin line, but her mouth exploded into a purple flower. She dabbed the dry-feeling pad on either cheek, and thick, mauve-scented shadows fell. She could hear and feel her heart behaving like a squeezed, rubber ball as she stood looking. Then she got at the lipstick again, still unsheathed. Her mouth was becoming enormous, so thick with grease she could hardly close her own lips underneath. A visible dew was gathering round the purple shadows on her cheeks.

She began to retch like, but dry, and rub, over the basin, scrubbing with the nailbrush. More than likely some would stay behind in the pores and be seen. Though you didn't have to see, to see.

There were Royal's teeth in the tumbler on top of the medicine cabinet. Ought to hide the teeth. What if somebody wanted to use the toilet? She must move the teeth. But didn't. In the present circumstances she couldn't have raised her arms that high.

Around five she made the coffee, throwing in the cold water at the end with a gesture copied from Mrs. Dolan. If the gravel hadn't sunk to the bottom he wouldn't notice the first time, provided the coffee was hot. She could warm up the made coffee in a jiffy.

As she sat on the veranda waiting, the cane chair shifted and squealed under her. If it hadn't been for her weight it might have run away across the tiles, like one of those old planchette boards, writing the answers to questions.

There was an accident this evening down at the intersection. A head-on collision. Bodies were carried out of the crumpled cars, and she remembered a past occasion when she had run with blankets, and Hazel's Onkaparinka, and a pillow from their own bed. She had been so grateful to the victim. She could not give him enough, or receive enough of the warm blood. She had come back, she remembered, sprinkled.

This evening she had to save herself up. Kept on looking at her watch. The old cane chair squealing, ready to write the answers if she let it. Was he hurt? Was he killed, then? Was he—what?

Mrs. Dolan it was, sticking her head over the palings. 'Don't like the accidents, Mrs. Natwick. It's the blood. The blood turns me up.'

Mrs. Natwick averted her face. Though unmoved by present blood. If only the squealing chair would stop trying to buck her off.

'Did your friend enjoy the coffee?' Mrs. Dolan shouted; nothing nasty in her: Mrs. Dolan was sincere.

'Hasn't been yet,' Mrs. Natwick mumbled from glancing at her watch. 'Got held up.'

'It's the traffic. The traffic at this time of evenun.'

'Always on the dot before.'

'Working back. Or made a mistake over the day.'

Could you make a mistake? Mrs. Natwick contemplated. Tomorrow had always meant tomorrow.

'Or he could'uv,' Mrs. Dolan shouted, but didn't say it. 'I better go inside,' she said instead. 'They'll be wonderun where I am.'

Down at the intersection the bodies were lying wrapped in someone else's blankets, looking like the grey parcels of mice cats sometimes vomit up.

It was long past five-twenty, not all that long really, but drawing in. The sky was heaped with cold fire. Her city was burning.

She got up finally, and the chair escaped with a last squeal, writing its answer on the tiles.

No, it wasn't lust, not if the Royal God Almighty with bared teeth should strike her down. Or yes, though, it was. She was lusting after the expression of eyes she could hardly remember for seeing so briefly.

In the effort to see, she drove her memory wildly, while her body stumbled around and around the paths of the burning city there was now no point in escaping. You would shrivel up in time along with the polyanthers and out-of-season hibiscus. All the randy mouths would be stopped sooner or later with black.

The cinerarias seemed to have grown so luxuriant she had to force her way past them, down the narrow brick path. When she heard the latch click, and saw him coming towards her.

'Why,' she screamed laughing though it sounded angry, she *was*, 'I'd given you up, you know! It's long after five-twenty!'

As she pushed fiercely towards him, past the cinerarias, snapping one or two of those which were most heavily loaded, she realized he couldn't have known that she set her watch, her life, by his constant behaviour. He wouldn't have dawdled so.

'What is it?' she called at last, in exasperation at the distance which continued separating them.

He was far too slow, treading the slippery moss of her too shaded path. While she floundered on. She couldn't reach the expression of his eyes.

He said, and she could hardly recognize the faded voice, 'There's something—I been feeling off colour most of the day.' His misshapen head was certainly lolling as he advanced.

'Tell me!' She heard her voice commanding, like that of a man, or a mother, when she had practised to be a lover; she could still smell the smell of rouge. 'Won't you tell me—*dearest*?' It was thin and unconvincing now. (As a girl she had once got a letter from her cousin Kath Salter, who she hardly knew: *Dearest Ella* . . .)

Oh dear. She had reached him. And was given all strength—that of the lover she had aimed at being.

Straddling the path, unequally matched—he couldn't compete against her strength—she spoke with an acquired, a deafening softness, as the inclining cinerarias snapped.

'You will tell me what is wrong—dear, dear.' She breathed with trumpets.

He hung his head. 'It's all right. It's the pain—here—in my arm—no, the shoulder.'

'Ohhhhh!' She ground her face into his shoulder forgetting it wasn't *her* pain.

Then she remembered, and looked into his eyes and said, 'We'll save you. You'll see.'

It was she who needed saving. She knew she was trying to enter by his eyes. To drown in them rather than be left.

Because, in spite of her will to hold him, he was slipping from her, down amongst the cinerarias, which were snapping off one by one around them.

A cat shot out. At one time she had been so poor in spirit she had wished she was a cat.

'It's all right,' either voice was saying.

Lying amongst the smashed plants, he was smiling at her dreadfully, not his mouth, she no longer bothered about that lip, but with his eyes.

'More air!' she cried. 'What you need is air!' hacking at one or two cinerarias which remained erect.

Their sap was stifling, their bristling columns callous.

'Oh! Oh!' she panted. 'Oh God! Dear love!' comforting with hands and hair and words.

Words.

While all he could say was, 'It's all right.'

Or not that at last. He folded his lips into a white seam. His eyes were swimming out of reach.

'Eh? Dear—dearest—darl—darlig—darling love—*love*—LOVE?' All the new words still stiff in her mouth, that she had heard so far only from the mouths of actors.

The words were too strong she could see. She was losing him. The traffic was hanging together only by charred silences.

She flung herself and covered his body, trying to force kisses— no, breath, into his mouth, she had heard about it.

She had seen turkeys, feathers sawing against each other's feathers, rising afterwards like new noisy silk.

She knelt up, and the wing-tips of her hair still dabbled limply in his cheeks. 'Eh? Ohh luff!' She could hardly breathe it.

She hadn't had time to ask his name, before she must have killed him by loving too deep, and too adulterously.

ELSPETH DAVIE
Concerto

About halfway through the concerto some of those sitting in the organ gallery, facing the rest of the audience and overlooking the orchestra, become aware of a disturbance in the body of the hall. The seats in this gallery face the conductor who for the last minutes has been leaning out over the rostrum whacking down a thicket of cellos with one hand and with the other cunningly lifting the uncertain horns higher and still higher up into a perilous place above the other instruments. Behind him the whole auditorium opens out, shell-shaped, its steep and shallow shelves, boxes, and ledges neatly packed with people. The sloping ground floor and overhanging gallery have few empty seats and the place has a smooth appearance—a sober mosaic of browns and greys flicked here and there with scarlet.

At last the horns make it. But there is a quavering on the long-drawn-out top note which bring a momentary grimace to the conductor's mouth as though he had bitten through something sour. The horn-players lower their instruments and stare in front of them with expressionless faces. At any other time some eyes in this audience might have studied the faces closely to discover which man had produced the wavering note—whether there was a corresponding wavering in the eyes of one of them or a slight wryness about the lips. But not tonight. Tonight all eyes have been directed to another spot.

The disturbance comes from the middle stalls. Down there a man has got to his feet and is leaning over the row in front. He appears to be conducting on his own account. He too entreats, he exhorts. He too encourages something to rise. Now a small group of people are up on their feet, and just as the horns extricate themselves, this man who is conducting operations down in the stalls manages to persuade the group to lift something up out of the darkness between the narrow seats. It is a tricky business, but at last a man is pulled clear and comes into view in a horizontal position, his long legs and his shoulders supported by several persons who have started to shuffle sideways with their burden along the row. Everyone now seems anxious to support this thin figure. Each leg is held by at least three people and the arms are carried on either side by two men and two women. Someone cups his head. Another handles the feet. Even those who are too far away to be actually supporting any part of his body feel it their duty to stretch out a finger simply to touch him, as a sacred object might be touched in a procession. He moves, propelled by these reverent touches, bouncing a little in the anxious arms. It is almost as though he were bouncing in time to a great pounding of drums. For since the horn players lowered their instruments the music has grown violent in tempo and volume.

But suddenly without warning the violent music stops. There is a second of stunning silence. Then the solo violinist who has stood patiently for some time letting the waves of sound crash over his bowed head, begins a series of scales which climb very quietly, one after the other, up onto a note so high that the silence can also be heard like a slight hiss directly above his head. This silence and the icy note of the single violin come as a shock to those whose eyes are riveted on the scene going on down below. For it is no longer merely a mimed scene floating in the middle distance. The silence has shifted it nearer as though a protective membrane which sealed it off had been abruptly ripped. Now there are sounds coming up—ordinary sounds which in the circumstances sound horrible. There is a dull bumping and dragging of feet, a rustling and breathing, low voices arguing. Obviously the thing is beginning to get the upper hand. It is attracting more and more interest. Heads are turning and the people in the organ gallery can see the round, blank, listening faces on either side change suddenly to keen, watchful profiles. There are even heads peering from the plush-covered front rows of the dress circle—the silver heads and craning necks of elderly ladies, long-trained never to peer or crane.

But there is one head which, shockingly, has not turned at all after the first quick glance behind. It is the man who is seated at the end of the row immediately in front of that from which the invalid has been lifted. Everyone else in his row is up ready to help. The man must have skin of leather and iron nerves. Eyes which might have scrutinized the horn-players now study his face to see whether he is going to relent, to find out if there is about him the slightest flicker of an uneasy conscience. But no. What kind of man is this? Is he the sort of man who might see his own mother carried past on a stretcher without shifting his legs out of the way? He does not turn his head even when the horizontal figure is moving directly behind his seat. At that moment, however, the man and woman who are holding an arm, suddenly let it go—the better to support the fainting man's back while manoeuvring the awkward turn into the middle aisle of the hall. The arm swings down heavily and deals the man still seated in front a clout over the ear. It is an admonitory blow, as though from his deepest unconscious or perhaps from death itself, the invalid is aware there is still someone around who is not giving him the same tender attention all the others have shown.

There is now a fervent longing for the music to gather its forces again and crush the disturbance before it gets out of hand. But there is no hint of this happening. The violinist is still playing his icy scales, accompanied as though from remotest space by the strings and woodwinds. A man of fifty, he is tall and exceedingly thin with a bony hatchet face and fairish-grey hair brushed back from his brow. This brow gives the impression of being unnaturally exposed, as though his skull, and particularly the bone of his temples, had resisted a continual pressure of music which would have caused most other skulls to cave in. His eyes are deepset and give him a sightless look while he is playing. Strangely enough he is not unlike the man who is being carried out up the aisle. One is narrow and vertical with huge hands like an elongated Gothic cathedral figure—grotesque or splendid, depending on how the light might fall from a stained glass window. The other is stiff, horizontal and grey like the stretched-out figure on a tomb. The prostrate man has his own look of dedication, though in his case it is not to music, for by his collapse he has destroyed any possibility of listening.

These two figures, the vertical and the horizontal, in their terrifying absorption, their absolute disregard for everything else, seem somehow related. Both have their supporters, though now it seems that the horizontal has the greater following. The devoted inner circle round him have made sure of that. Great, ever-widening rings of curiosity ripple out towards him, interlinking with the rings still concentrating on the violinist and causing even there a shimmer of awareness. The conductor of the devotees in the stalls is now walking backwards up the aisle on his tiptoes, well in front of the others. With his right hand he beckons reassuringly to the group coming up after him and with his powerful left he attempts to quell any sign of interference from those siting on either side of the aisle. But those nearest the door, paralysed till now, suddenly spring to their feet and fight for first place to heave their weight against it. The doors crash outward and the heaped figures pitch through.

This crash has coincided to a split second with the quietest bars of the concerto—that point where not only the soloist but all other players have lowered their instruments—all, that is to say, except the flute. This flute has started up as though playing solely for the benefit of the group just outside the door, visible in the brilliant light of the vestibule. As though involved in a ritual dance they crouch, rise, bend, and kneel beneath the hands of their leader who is now signalling to invisible figures further out. Someone carrying a jug and tumbler appears and kneels, and a chinking of glass comes from the centre of the group. It is a light sound but clear as a bell, and it combines with the flute in a duet which can be heard to the furthest corners of the hall.

At this point several people turn their eyes, in desperation, and stare at the unmoving man sitting now quite isolated at the end of his row. No one could say why it is imperative to turn to him. Isn't he a brute, after all—a stubborn, fat man with a crimson face, conspicuous only in being a figure of monumental unhelpfulness? Yet something about the man suggests that, like some squat, purple-cheeked Atlas, he is supporting the whole weight of the hall on his shoulders. The short, bulging neck holds up the overhanging gallery. The legs are planted like pillars to the floor, and over his paunch the fingers come together in a massive lock. His bottom is sunk into the plush of his seat like a bulbous root into the deep earth. Nothing can budge him now. He is dedicated to absolute immobility, and the whole house knows it.

This man has never taken his eyes off the violinist. He stares ahead, unblinking—his blue, slightly protuberant eyes fixed. It is as though on him rather than on the conductor has now fallen the responsibility of holding audience and orchestra together—of pushing back the white heads in the dress circle, checking the obstreperous group outside the door, and by a superhuman effort of will turning the curious eye of the audience back into a listening ear. The soloist lifts his violin and for the first time throws a piercing glance down into the body of the hall. He exchanges one look with the immobile man sitting there. There is no recognizable emotion in this look, nothing that would ordinarily be called human warmth.

Yet the man below glows and shines for an instant as though caught in a flare of brilliant light. The violinist raises his bow and begins to play.

In the meantime one of the group outside in the vestibule has at last remembered about the open doors. He pulls them to violently and the drama outside is shut away, at any rate from the ears—for figures can still be seen moving about behind the obscure glass. All the same there is a feeling of uneasiness—a feeling that the fellow lying behind that door will not allow himself to be shut away and forgotten after swaying the entire audience. This unease is justified. Scarcely have those around the door drawn their first breath of relief before it swings open again and the leader of the group strides in. His air is even more commanding than before. Now he looks like an ambassador from an important state. He walks along the empty row looking for something, before starting to tip up the seats and feel about on the floor. By this time the music has again gathered volume and nobody can hear the sound of the seats, though he is as skilful and rhythmical in the way he raps them back as the man behind the kettledrums. And now he is finished with that row and goes into the one in front where the stout man is sitting. He works his way along the seats, tipping, patting, and groping till he reaches him. Now he is actually feeling around the other's feet. But the man—this rapt buddha of non-helpfulness—shifts neither his legs nor his eyes. He allows the other to squeeze past him, to glare at him, and even to push his foot aside.

At first there is mounting curiosity as to what the searcher will come up with. Yet the seated man has manged to concentrate most of this curiosity upon himself and then, by not moving a hair or allowing his attention to swerve for an instant, has redirected it up towards the orchestra. This is something which almost amounts to an athletic feat. The sheer effort of lifting the crowd on his eyeballs alone is appalling.

The swing doors again open and a woman appears and moves diffidently, apologetically, down the gangway, all the time looking towards the searcher and waiting for a sign. But the man is now working along a row further back and keeps shaking his head. Suddenly he disappears. He has pounced on something down there. It is a long handbag in imitation plum-coloured leather with a zip pocket at the back—useful but not elegant. An advertisement would describe it as a bag which could go anywhere. And it has been kicked around a lot. Already it has travelled back a couple of rows and sideways ten feet or so. The man and woman join up enthusiastically and are soon on their way out again, the woman peering meantime into the bag to assure herself that, in spite of the hideous confusion of the last ten minutes, everything is intact inside, right down to the fragile mirror in the lid of her compact.

Now some of those in the audience had imagined it might be a pair of spectacles the man was hunting for—spectacles belonging to the fainting man who, added to the horrors of coming to in a strange place, would find himself unable to focus on the strange faces looming over him. A few have never been able to shake off a suspicion that all this time these spectacles have been lying, ground to powder, under the stubborn heels of the man sitting at the end of the row. At sight of the handbag, however, some tie linking them to the group outside the door snaps for ever. As the man and woman finally push their way out there is a glimpse of a deserted vestibule. The group, as though sensing a defeat, have disappeared.

The music is sweeping to its climax. One by one each section of the orchestra is gathered up and whirled higher and higher in a struggle to reach the four, slow, separate chords which end the concerto. On this level plateau they at last emerge into safety, and the end is in sight. The fourth and final chord crashes down, submerging all doubts, and a great burst of clapping and stamping follows it. For a while the stout man refuses to join in the applause. One might even imagine he was receiving some of it for himself, along with the soloist, the conductor, and the rest of the orchestra. But now for the first time he lowers the heavy lids of his eyes towards the ground and allows himself a discreet smile. Then he lifts his hands and begins to clap. His applauding heels shuffle the floor.

BIOGRAPHICAL NOTES

CHINUA ACHEBE was born in 1930. He was educated at the University of Ibadan and worked for the Nigerian Broadcasting Corporation after a period as Senior Research Fellow at the Institute of African Studies, Nsukka. After teaching in the United States he returned to his country as Professor of English, University of Nigeria, Nsukka. His books include the novels *Things Fall Apart* (1958) and *The Anthills of the Savannah* (1987) and the collection of short stories *Girls at War* (1972).

KINGSLEY AMIS was born in Norbury in 1922 and educated at the City of London School and St. John's College, Oxford. From *Lucky Jim* (1954) onwards he has been the author of numerous novels. He has edited stories by G. K. Chesterton (1972) and written a book on Kipling and his background. His earlier short stories are collected as *My Enemy's Enemy* (1962). His novel *The Old Devils* won the Booker Prize in 1986.

BATES, HERBERT ERNEST (1905–1974). Educated the Grammar School, Kettering. Worked as a provincial journalist and clerk before publishing first novel at the age of twenty; subsequently established an international reputation as a novelist and short-story writer. His stories are widely anthologized; his novels have been translated into sixteen languages. He has also written plays and many essays on country life. His publications include more than twenty collections of short stories. *The Watercress Girl*, from which the selected story is taken, appeared in 1959.

GEORGE MACKAY BROWN was born in 1921 and educated at the University of Edinburgh. He lives in his native Orkney and writes about the life of its people. As well as poems and a play he has published the novels *Greenvoe* and *Magnus*, and several volumes of short stories, including *Hawkfall* (1974).

MORLEY CALLAGHAN, Canadian novelist, was born in Toronto in 1903. He attended the University of Toronto, followed by law school, and lives in the city. His books include *Native Argosy* (1929), *They Shall Inherit the Earth* (1935), *The Loved and the Lost* (1951), *The Man with the Coat* (1955, McLean's Prize), *A Passion in Rome* (1961), and a collection of short stories, *Stories* (1964). Later volumes are *A Fine and Private Place* (1976), *Close to the Sun Again* (1977), and *No Man's Meat* (1978).

ELSPETH DAVIE is an Edinburgh writer and former art-school student married to a philosopher. She is represented in the anthology of experimental writing edited by Giles Gordon, *Beyond the Words* (1975) and has published two collections of her stories, *The High Tide Talkers* (1976) and *The Night of the Funny Hats* (1980) as well as a novel, *Climate on a Stair* (1978). She was awarded the Katherine Mansfield Prize in 1978.

DAVIES, RHYS, O.B.E. (1903–1978). Educated Porth County School. Published a great many books, including several volumes of short stories. The selected story comes from *The Darling of Her Heart and Other Stories* (1958).

GORDIMER, NADINE (1923). Born in South Africa, educated at Witwatersrand. Won the W. H. Smith Literary Award, 1961; the James Tait Black Memorial Prize, 1971; and the Booker Prize (co-winner), 1974. She continues to be a prolific and successful novelist with a world-wide reputation. The selected story is taken from *Six Feet of the Country* (1956).

HARTLEY, LESLIE POLES, C.B.E. (1895–1972). Educated Harrow and Balliol College, Oxford. Has written literary criticism for a number of weekly reviews since 1923, but is renowned chiefly as one of the leading novelists of our day. He has also published seven collections of short stories, including *Two for the River* (1961), from which the selected story is taken.

SUSAN HILL was born in 1942 and after grammar schools in Scarborough and Coventry read English at King's College, London. Married to the Shakespearian scholar Stanley Wells, she lives with her family in a village near Oxford. Her books include *Do Me a Favour* (1963), *A Change for the Better* (1969), *The Albatross* (1971, stories), *Strange Meeting* (1971), *In the Springtime of the Year* (1974), and many other stories and radio plays.

DAN JACOBSON was born in Johannesberg in 1929 and educated at the University of Witwatersrand. After working in South Africa as a journalist and in commerce he came to London to write in 1954. His books include *The Trap* (1955) and *A Dance in the Sun* (1956), these two novellas reissued together by OUP in 1988, *A Long Way from London* (1958), *The Evidence of Love* (1960), *Inklings* (1972, stories), *Through the Wilderness: Selected Stories* (1973; Penguin, 1977), and *Her Story* (1987).

JENKINS, MAY C. Born in Morayshire, educated High School for Girls, Aberdeen, and Aberdeen University. Has taught English and Speech-Training; now a features writer on a newspaper. Has had poems (including a collection, *Flitting*, 1966), short stories, and articles published, and short stories and talks broadcast.

JHABVALA, R. PRAWER (1927). Born of Polish parents in Gemany; came to England in 1939, and was educated here; has a University of London M. A. in English. Married an Indian architect and lived in India for many years before moving to New York in 1975. In the same year she won the Booker Prize for her novel *Heat and Dust*. The selected story is taken from her collection *Like Birds, Like Fishes* (1962).

JONES, SIR LAWRENCE EVELYN, Bt., M.C., T.D., F.R.S.L. (1885–1969). Educated Eton and Balliol College, Oxford. Barrister, Inner Temple. Has published many works, including three autobiographical volumes. The short story by which he is represented here is taken from *The Bishop's Aunt* (1961).

BENEDICT KIELY was born at Dromore in County Tyrone in 1919 and is a graduate of the National University of Ireland. He has been a journalist, a visiting professor at American universities, and now lectures in Dublin. His books include *Land Without Stars* (1946), *Modern Irish Fiction* (1948), *Honey Seems Bitter* (1954), *The Captain with the Whiskers* (1960), *Dogs Enjoy the Morning* (1968), and *A Ball of Malt* (1970, stories).

LAMMING, GEORGE (1927). Born in Barbados, where he was educated at Harrison College. Taught in Trinidad. Emigrated to England in 1950; worked as a free-lance broadcaster in the B.B.C. Caribbean Service for about six years. Has published several novels. 'A Wedding in Spring' is taken from *West Indian Stories*, edited by Andrew Salkey (1960).

LAVIN, MARY (Mrs. William Walsh) (1912). Born in East Walpole, Mass., U.S.A., and educated National University of Ireland, Dublin (Graduate, M.A.). Member of Irish Academy of Letters.

Guggenheim Fellow, 1959, 1961, 1962. Her published works include several volumes of short stories, among them *Tales from Bective Bridge* (1942) for which she received the James Tait Black Memorial Prize, and *The Great Wave* (1961), from which the selected story is taken.

LOFTS, NORAH (Mrs. Robert Jorisch) (1904). Educated West Suffolk County School. As Norah Lofts and as Peter Curtis she has published more than twenty books, including *Heaven in Your Hand* (1959), from which the selected story it taken.

BERNARD MALAMUD was born in 1914 and teaches at Bennington College, Vermont. He was born in New York City and educated at City College and Columbia University. In 1979 he became President of the American PEN Center. Among his books are *The Natural* (1952), *The Assistant* (1957), *The Magic Barrel* (1958, stories; National Book Award), *The Fixer* (1966, Pulitzer Prize), *Rembrandt's Hat* (1973, stories) *Dubin's Lives* (1979).

OLIVIA MANNING was born in Portsmouth and married to Professor R. D. Smith. She died in 1980. During the 1939–45 war she was with her husband in Romania and Greece and her best-known series of novels, *Balkan Trilogy*, is based on this period (*The Great Fortune* (1960); *The Spoilt City* (1962); *Friends and Heroes* (1965)). *A Romantic Hero* (1967) is a volume of short stories.

GORDON MEYER was educated at Oxford and worked for an import-export firm in Buenos Aires before his early death in 1968. He wrote travel books on his experiences in Bolivia and Paraguay. Many of his stories about South America were collected in the volume *Exiles* (1967).

MEYNELL, VIOLA (Mrs. John Dallyn) (died 1956). Author of many novels, of biographical works, and of poems and short stories. The story by which she is represented here is taken from her *Collected Stories* (1957).

V. S. NAIPAUL was born in 1932 and brought up in Trinidad. He was educated at Queen's Royal College there and at University College, Oxford. His books include *A House for Mr. Biswas* (1961), *Mr. Stone and the Knights Companion* (1963), *The Mimic Men* (1967), *A Flag on the Island* (1967, short stories), *In a Free State* (1971, a novel which won the Booker Prize), *A Bend in the River* (1979), and *The Enigma of Arrival* (1987).

R. K. NARAYAN was born in Madras in 1907 and educated at Maharaja's College, Mysore. His books published in England include *The Man-Eaters of Malgudi* (1961), *Gods, Demons and Others* (1964), *The Sweet Vendor* (1967), *A Horse and Two Goats* (1970, short stories), and *The Painter of Signs* (1977). Autobiography: *Reminiscences* (1973). He has translated the *Ramayana* (1973) and the *Maha bharata* (1978).

NAUGHTON, BILL (1910). Born in County Mayo, and brought up in Bolton. Left school at fourteen to become a weaver and then a dyer. Married at nineteen, became unemployed, and got casual work as labourer, barman, salesman, and coal-heaver. For some years was a heavy-lorry driver. Has been a full-time writer since 1945; has published several novels and over a hundred stories, and has written radio and television plays. The selected story is taken from *Late Night on Watling Street* (1959).

OWOYELE, DAVID OLABODE (1934). Born in Nigeria. 'Trained to be a teacher but didn't do much of teaching. Did about two years in the drawing office of a town planning department (neither of us ever discovered why). Has published only short stories; written for radio and television in Nigeria. Tireless collector of rejection slips and proud possessor of unpublished and unpublishable novels.'

JEAN RHYS was born in Dominica in 1894. After a period at the RADA she lived and wrote in Paris between the wars. Her earlier novels *After Leaving Mr. Mackenzie* (1930), *Voyage in the Dark* (1934), and *Good Morning Midnight* (1939), which had enjoyed a coterie reputation, were reissued in the Sixties as a result of a revival of interest in her work. Collections of short stories are *The Left Bank* (1927) and *Tigers Are Better-Looking* (1967).

SANSOM, WILLIAM, F.R.S.L. (1912–1976). Educated Uppingham School, and variously in Europe. Has written regularly for literary periodicals in England; books translated into many foreign languages; awarded Travel Scholarships in 1946, literary bursary in 1947, by the Society of Authors. His published works include several novels and some volumes of short stories. *Among the Dahlias*, from which the selected tale is taken, appeared in 1957.

FRANK SARGESON, born in 1903, is the most distinguished New Zealand short-story writer and has been described as the founding father of the literature of his country. He was born in Hamilton and educated at Auckland University. His books include *That Summer* (1946, a long story which first made him known to British readers), *I Saw in My Dream* (1949), *Collected Stories 1935–63* (1965), *The Stories of Frank Sargeson* (Auckland, 1973; New York, 1974).

SHADBOLT, MAURICE FRANCIS RICHARD (1932). Born in Auckland, N.Z., and educated Te Kuiti High School, Avondale College, and Auckland University. For a time, documentary film director; now a free-lance journalist and writer. His published works include *The New Zealanders* (a volume of stories), *An Ear of the Dragon*, and *Summer Fires and Winter Country* (1963), from which the selected story is taken.

STIVENS, DAL (1911). A fifth-generation Australian who lives in Sydney. Spent the years 1949–57 in London. Awarded Commonwealth Literary Fellowships by the Australian Government in 1951 and 1962. His stories have been frequently broadcast by the B.B.C., and included in many anthologies, including collections in German, French, Yugoslav, and Czech. Author of four novels and five volumes of short stories. The selected story appeared in *The Scholarly Mouse* (1958), which is now out of print.

ELIZABETH TAYLOR was born in Reading in 1912 and died in 1975. Her first novel, *At Mrs. Lippincote's*, was published in 1945. As well as other novels she published several collections of short stories. These books include *Hester Lilly and Other Stories* (1958), *A Dedicated Man* (1965) and *Mrs. Palfrey at the Claremont* (1972).

WILLIAM TREVOR was born in 1928 in Mitchellstown, County Cork. He lives and works in London. His novel *The Old Boys* was published in 1964 and he has published many short stories. Other books include *The Children of Dynmouth* (1976), *Lovers of their Time* (1978), *Other People's Worlds* (1980), and *Fools of Fortune* (1983), which won the Whitbread Award.

FRANK TUOHY was born in 1925 and educated at Stowe and King's College, Cambridge. He lectured abroad for the British Council in Finland, Sweden, Poland, and Brazil. Among his books are a collection of short stories, *The Admiral and the Nuns* (1962), and *The Ice Saints* (1964), one of several novels. His *Live Bait* (1978) won the Heinemann Award.

JOHN UPDIKE was born in 1932 in Shillington, Pennsylvania, and educated at Harvard and the Ruskin School of Art, Oxford. For two years he was a staff contributor to the *New Yorker* magazine. Among his numerous books are the following collections of short stories: *Pigeon Feathers, The Same Door, Too Far to Go: The Maples Stories, Problems and Other Stories*. His novels include *The Poorhouse Fair, Rabbit Run, Couples, Rabbit Redux, Bech: A Book, Bech is Back*, and *Roger's Version*.

USTINOV, PETER ALEXANDER, F.R.S.A. (1921). Actor, dramatist, film director. Joint Director, Nottingham Playhouse, since 1963. Educated Westminster School. Has published many plays, a novel, and a collection of short stories, *Add a Dash of Pity* (1959), from which the selected story is taken.

WAIN, JOHN BARRINGTON (1925). Educated Newcastle under Lyme and St. John's College, Oxford. Fereday Fellow of St. John's College, Oxford, 1946–49; Lecturer in English Literature, University of Reading, 1947–55. Since 1955 has been a free-lance author and critic, Director of Poetry Book Society's festival, 'Poetry at The Mermaid', London, 1961. His publications include several novels, some volumes of criticism, and an autobiography. The selected story comes from his collection of short stories, *Nuncle and Other Stories* (1960).

PATRICK WHITE is the son of an Australian sheep-grazing family but was born in England in 1912 and educated at Cheltenham and King's College, Cambridge. During the war he served in the RAF. His novels include *The Tree of Man* (1955), *Voss* (1957), *The Solid Mandala* (1966), *The Vivisector* (1970), *A Fringe of Leaves* (1976), *The Twyborn Affair* (1979). His two collections of short stories are *The Burnt Ones* (1964) and *The Cockatoos* (1974). He published his autobiography in 1981. In 1972 he was awarded the Nobel Prize for Literature.

WILSON, ANGUS FRANK JOHNSTONE, C.B.E., C.Lit., F.R.S.L. (1913). Educated Westminster School and Merton College, Oxford. He worked for some time in the Foreign Office (1949–55), then as deputy superintendent at the Reading Room at the British Museum. Novels such as *Anglo-Saxon Attitudes* (1956), *The Old Men at the Zoo* (1961), and *Late Call* (1964) have made him one of our leading novelists.

ACKNOWLEDGEMENTS

We are grateful for permission to include the following copyright stories.

Chinua Achebe: 'Uncle Ben's Choice' from *Girls at War and Other Stories*. Copyright © 1972, 1973 by Chinua Achebe. Reprinted by permission of David Bolt Associates, and of Doubleday, A Division of Bantam, Doubleday, Dell Publishing, Inc.

Kingsley Amis: 'The Green Man Revisited'. © 1973 Kingsley Amis. Reprinted by permission of Jonathan Clowes on behalf of Kingsley Amis.

George Mackay Brown: 'Tithonus' from *Hawkfall*. Reprinted by permission of the Hogarth Press on behalf of the author.

H. E. Bates: 'Great Uncle Crow' from *The Watercress Girl and Other Stories* (Michael Joseph Ltd., 1959). Reprinted by permission of Laurence Pollinger Ltd., on behalf of the Estate of H. E. Bates.

Morley Callaghan: 'Last Spring They Came Over' from *Stories* (Macmillan & Co. of Canada, 1959). Reprinted by permission of the author. 'The Runaway' from *Stories*. Reprinted by permission of the author.

Elspeth Davie: 'Concerto' from *Beyond the Words*, ed. Giles Gordon (Hutchinson). Reprinted by permission of Anthony Sheil Associates Ltd.

Rhys Davies: 'Afternoon of a Faun' from *The Darling of Her Heart and Other Stories* (Heinemann, 1958). Copyright © Rhys Davies 1958. Reprinted by permission of Curtis Brown Group Ltd.

Nadine Gordimer: 'Charmed Lives' from *Six Feet of The Country: Short Stories*. Copyright © 1956, renewed 1984 by Nadine Gordimer. Reprinted by permission of A. P. Watt Ltd., and Russel & Volkening, Inc., as agents for the author.

L. P. Hartley: 'A High Dive' from *Two for the River* in *The Complete Short Stories of L. P. Hartley*. Copyright © the Executors of the Estate of the late L. P. Hartley. Reprinted by permission of Hamish Hamilton Ltd.

Susan Hill: 'Cockles and Mussels' from *The Albatross and Other Stories* (Hamish Hamilton). Reprinted by permission of Richard Scott Simon Ltd.

Dan Jacobson: 'The Zulu and the Zeide' from *Inklings*. Reprinted by permission of A. M. Heath & Co. Ltd., for the author.

May C. Jenkins: 'I Can Play "Schools"' reprinted by permission of the author.

Ruth Prawer Jhabvala: 'The Interview' from *Like Birds, Like Fishes and Other Stories*. Reprinted by permission of A. M. Heath.

L. E. Jones: 'The Bishop's Aunt' from *The Bishop's Aunt and Other Stories*. Reprinted by permission of Grafton Books.

Benedict Kiely: 'God's Own Country' reprinted from *A Ball of Malt and Madame Butterfly* by permission of A. P. Watt Ltd., and from *The State of Ireland*, copyright © 1963, 1973, 1978, 1979, 1980 by Benedict Kiely, by permission of David R. Godine, Publisher.

George Lamming: 'A Wedding in Spring'. Reprinted by permission of the author.

Mary Lavin: 'The Great Wave' from *The Stories of Mary Lavin*, Volume One. Reprinted by permission of Constable Publishers and the author.

Nora Lofts: 'Forty Years On'. Copyright © 1958 by Norah Lofts. Reprinted by permission of Curtis Brown on behalf of the Estate of Norah Lofts.

Bernard Malamud: 'The Silver Crown' from *Rembrandt's Hat*. Copyright © 1972, 1973 by Bernard Malamud. Reprinted by permission of Chatto & Windus on behalf of the Estate of Bernard Malamud, and Farrar, Straus & Giroux, Inc.

Olivia Manning: 'A Spot of Leave' from *A Romantic Hero*. Reprinted by permission of William Heinemann Ltd.

Gordon Meyer: 'The Circle' from *Exiles*. Reprinted by permission of Alan Ross, London Magazine Editions.

V. S. Naipaul: 'A Christmas Story' from *A Flag on the Island*. Reprinted by permission of Aitken & Stone Ltd.

R. K. Narayan: 'A Horse and Two Goats' from *A Horse and Two Goats*. Reprinted by permission of David Higham Associates Ltd.

Bill Naughton: 'Late Night on Watling Street' from *Late Night on Watling Street*. Reprinted by permission of the author.

David Owoyele: 'The Will of Allah' from *Reflections* (African Universities Press, Ibadan). Reprinted by permission of the publisher.

Jean Rhys: 'Tigers are Better-Looking', Copyright © 1974, 1987 by the Estate of Jean Rhys. Reprinted from *Tigers are Better-Looking* by permission of André Deutsch, and from *Jean Rhys: The Collected Short Stories*, published by W. W. Norton & Company, Inc., by permission of Wallace & Sheil Agency, Inc.

William Sansom: 'Cat up a Tree' from *Among the Dahlias*. Copyright © William Sansom 1957. Reprinted by permission of Elaine Greene Ltd.

Frank Sargeson: 'A Hen and Some Eggs' from *Collected Stories* (Longman Paul Ltd).

Maurice Shadbolt: 'The People Before' from *Summer Fires and Winter Country* (Eyre & Spottiswoode, 1963). Copyright © 1962, 1963 by Maurice Shadbolt. Reprinted by permission of Curtis Brown Ltd.

Dal Stivens: 'The Pepper-Tree' from *The Scholarly Mouse and Other Tales* (Angus & Robertson, 1958). Reprinted by permission of the author.

Elizabeth Taylor: 'A Dedicated Man' from *A Dedicated Man*. Reprinted by permission of A. M. Heath on behalf of the Estate of the Late Elizabeth Taylor.

William Trevor: 'In at the Birth' from *The Day We Got Drunk on Cake*. Reprinted by permission of John Johnson (Authors' Agent) Ltd.

Frank Tuohy: 'The Licence' from *The Collected Stories of Frank Tuohy*. Reprinted by permission of A. D. Peters & Co. Ltd.

John Updike: 'Should Wizard Hit Mommy?' from *Pigeon Feathers and Other Stories*. Copyright © 1960 by John Updike. Reprinted by permission of André Deutsch, and Alfred A. Knopf, Inc.

Peter Ustinov: 'The Man in the Moon' from *Add a Dash of Pity* (Heinemann, 1959: Panther Books 1976, reprinted 1977, 1979, 1984. Reprinted by permission of the author and Pavor S. A.

John Wain: 'A Message from the Pig-Man' from *Nuncle and Other Stories*. Copyright © John Wain 1960. Reprinted by permission of Curtis Brown Ltd., London.

Patrick White: 'Five-Twenty' from *The Cockatoos*. Reprinted by permission of Barbara Mobbs, Literary Agent.

Sir Angus Wilson: 'Ten Minutes to Twelve' from *A Bit Off the Map and Other Stories*. Copyright © Angus Wilson 1957. Reprinted by permission of Secker & Warburg Ltd., and Curtis Brown Ltd., London.

We have been unable to trace the copyright holders for the following:

Viola Meynell: 'The Size of a Pocket Handkerchief' from *Collected Stories* (Max Reinhardt, 1957).

If contacted the publishers will be pleased to make correct acknowledgement in any future reprints and/or new editions.